William John Conybeare, J. S. Howson

The Life and Epistles of St. Paul

Vol. 1

SALZWASSER
VERLAG

William John Conybeare, J. S. Howson

The Life and Epistles of St. Paul

Vol. 1

Reprint of the original, first published in 1864.

1st Edition 2022 | ISBN: 978-3-75259-153-8

Verlag (Publisher): Salzwasser Verlag GmbH, Zeilweg 44, 60439 Frankfurt, Deutschland
Vertretungsberechtigt (Authorized to represent): E. Roepke, Zeilweg 44, 60439 Frankfurt, Deutschland
Druck (Print): Books on Demand GmbH, In de Tarpen 42, 22848 Norderstedt, Deutschland

THE

LIFE AND EPISTLES

OF

ST. PAUL.

BY

THE REV. W. J. CONYBEARE, M.A.
LATE FELLOW OF TRINITY COLLEGE, CAMBRIDGE,

AND

THE REV. J. S. HOWSON, M.A.
PRINCIPAL OF THE COLLEGIATE INSTITUTION, LIVERPOOL.

It is very meet, right, and our bounden duty that we should at all times and in all places give thanks unto Thee, O Lord, Holy Father, Almighty, Everlasting God, through Jesus Christ our Lord, according to whose most true promise the Holy Ghost came down from heaven, lighting upon the Apostles, to teach them, and to lead them to all truth; giving them boldness with fervent zeal constantly to preach the Gospel to all nations; whereby we have been brought out of darkness and error, into the clear light and true knowledge of thee, and of thy Son Jesus Christ."—*Proper Preface to the Trisagium for Whitsunday.*

"Ἀφέντες τοὺς ἄλλους ἅπαντας, Παῦλον προστησώμεθα μόνον τοῦ λόγου συνίστορα, κἂν τούτῳ θεωρήσωμεν οἷόν ἐστι ψυχῶν ἐπιμέλεια. Ὡς ἂν δὲ ῥᾷστα τοῦτο γνοίημεν, τὶ Παῦλος αὐτὸς περὶ Παύλου φησὶν ἀκούσωμεν. . . . Νομοθετεῖ δούλοις καὶ δεσπόταις, ἄρχουσι καὶ ἀρχομένοις, ἀνδράσι καὶ γυναιξὶν, σοφίᾳ καὶ ἀμαθίᾳ· πάντων ὑπερμαχεῖ· πάντων ὑπερεύχεται . . . κῆρυξ ἐθνῶν, Ἰουδαίων προστάτης."—GREG. NAZ. *Oratio Apologetica.*

IN TWO VOLUMES.

VOL. I.

SEVENTH EDITION.

NEW YORK

1864.

LIST OF MAPS

IN

THE FIRST VOLUME.

LIST OF ENGRAVINGS ON WOOD.

IN

THE FIRST VOLUME.

CONTENTS

OF

THE FIRST VOLUME.

CHAPTER III.

CHAPTER IV.

CHAPTER V.

CHAPTER VI.

CHAPTER VII.

PAGE

CHAPTER VIII.

CHAPTER IX.

CHAPTER X.

CHAPTER XI.

CHAPTER XII.

CHAPTER XIII.

INTRODUCTION.

The purpose of this work is to give a living picture of St. Paul himself, and of the circumstances by which he was surrounded.

The biography of the Apostle must be compiled from two sources; first, his own letters, and secondly, the narrative in the Acts of the Apostles. The latter, after a slight sketch of his early history, supplies us with fuller details of his middle life; and his Epistles afford much subsidiary information concerning his missionary labours during the same period. The light concentrated upon this portion of his course, makes darker by contrast the obscurity which rests upon the remainder; for we are left to gain what knowledge we can of his later years, from scattered hints in a few short letters of his own, and from a single sentence of his disciple Clement.

But in order to present anything like a living picture of St. Paul's career, much more is necessary than a mere transcript of the Scriptural narrative, even where it is fullest. Every step of his course brings us into contact with some new phase of ancient life, unfamiliar to our modern experience, and upon which we must throw light from other sources, if we wish it to form a distinct image in the mind. For example, to comprehend the influences under which he grew to manhood, we must realise the position of a Jewish family in Tarsus, "the chief city of Cilicia;" we must understand the kind of education which the son of such a family would receive as a boy in his Hebrew home, or in the schools of his native city, and in his riper youth "at the feet of Gamaliel" in Jerusalem; we must be acquainted with the profession for which he was to be prepared by this training, and appreciate the station and duties of an expounder of the Law. And that we may be fully qualified to do all this, we should have a clear view of the state of the Roman empire at the same time, and especially of its system in the provinces; we should also understand the political position of the Jews of the "dispersion;" we should be (so to speak) hearers in their synagogues; we should be students of their Rabbinical theology. And in like manner, as we follow the Apostle in the different stages of his varied and adventurous career, we must strive continually to bring out in their true brightness the half effaced forms and colouring of the scene in which he acts; and while he "becomes all things to all men, that he might by all means save some," we must form to ourselves a living likeness of the *things* and of the *men* among which he moved, if we would rightly estimate his work. Thus we must study Christianity rising in the midst of Judaism, we must realize the position of its early churches with their mixed society, to which Jews, Proselytes, and Heathens had each contributed a characteristic element; we must qualify ourselves to be umpires (if we may so speak) in their violent internal divisions; we must listen to the strife of their schismatic parties, when one said "I am of Paul, and another, I am of Apollos;" we must study the true character of those early heresies which even denied the resurrection, and advocated impurity and lawlessness, claiming the right "to sin that grace might abound,"[1] "defiling the mind and conscience"[2] of their followers, and making them abominable and disobedient, and "to every good work reprobate;[3] we must trace the extent to which Greek philosophy, Judaizing formalism, and Eastern superstition blended their tainting influence with the pure fermentation of that new leaven which was at last to leaven the whole mass of civilized society.

Again, to understand St. Paul's personal history as a missionary to the heathen, we must know the state of the different populations which he visited; the character of the Greek and Roman civilization at the epoch; the points of intersection between the political history of the world and the scriptural narrative; the social organization and gradation of ranks, for which he enjoins respect; the position of women, to which he especially refers in many of his letters; the relations between parents and children,

[1] Rom vi. 1. [2] Tit. i. 15. [3] Tit. i. 16.

slaves and masters, which he not vainly sought to imbue with the loving spirit of the Gospel; the quality and influence, under the early empire, of the Greek and Roman religions, whose effete corruptness he denounces with such indignant scorn; the public amusements of the people, whence he draws topics of warning or illustration; the operation of the Roman law, under which he was so frequently arraigned; the courts in which he was tried, and the magistrates by whose sentence he suffered; the legionary soldiers who acted as his guards; the roads by which he travelled, whether through the mountains of Lycaonia or the marshes of Latium; the course of commerce by which his journeys were so often regulated; and the character of that imperfect navigation by which his life was so many times[1] endangered.

While thus trying to live in the life of a bygone age, and to call up the figure of the past from its tomb, duly robed in all its former raiment, every help is welcome which enables us to fill up the dim outline in any part of its reality. Especially we delight to look upon the only one of the manifold features of that past existence, which still is living. We remember with pleasure that the earth, the sea, and the sky still combine for us in the same landscapes which passed before the eyes of the wayfaring Apostle. The plain of Cilicia, the snowy distances of Taurus, the cold and rapid stream of the Cydnus, the broad Orontes under the shadow of its steep banks with their thickets of jasmine and oleander; the hills which "stand about Jerusalem,"[2] the "arched fountains cold" in the ravines below, and those "flowery brooks beneath, that wash their hallowed feet;" the capes and islands of the Grecian Sea, the craggy summit of Areopagus, the landlocked harbour of Syracuse, the towering cone of Etna, the voluptuous loveliness of the Campanian shore; all these remain to us, the imperishable handiwork of nature. We can still look upon the same trees and flowers which he saw clothing the mountains, giving color to the plains, or reflected in the rivers; we may think of him among the palms of Syria, the cedars of Lebanon, the olives of Attica, the green Isthmian pines of Corinth, whose leaves wove those "fading garlands," which he contrasts[3]

[1] 2 Cor. xi. 25, "thrice have I suffered shipwreck;" and this was before he was wrecked upon Melita.

[2] "The hills stand about Jerusalem; even so standeth the Lord round about his people." Ps. cxxv. 2.

[3] 1 Cor. ix. 25.

with the "incorruptible crown," the prize for which he fought. Nay we can even still look upon some of the works of man which filled him with wonder, or moved him to indignation. The temples "made with hands"[1] which rose before him—the very apotheosis of idolatry—on the Acropolis, still stand in almost undiminished majesty and beauty. The mole on which he landed at Puteoli still stretches its ruins into the blue waters of the bay. The remains of the Baian Villas whose marble porticoes he then beheld glittering in the sunset—his first specimen of Italian luxury—still are seen along the shore. We may still enter Rome as he did by the same Appian Road, through the same Capenian Gate, and wander among the ruins of "Cæsar's palace"[2] on the Palatine, while our eye rests upon the same aqueducts radiating over the Campagna to the unchanging hills. Those who have visited these spots must often have felt a thrill of recollection as they trod in the footsteps of the Apostle; they must have been conscious how much the identity of the outward scene brought them into communion with him, while they tried to image to themselves the feelings with which he must have looked upon the objects before them. They who have experienced this will feel how imperfect a biography of St. Paul must be, without faithful representations of the places which he visited. It is hoped that the views which are contained in the present work, and which have been drawn for this special object, will supply this desideratum. And it is evident that, for the purposes of such a biography, nothing but true and faithful representations of the real scenes will be valuable; these are what is wanted, and not ideal representations, even though copied from the works of the greatest masters; for, as it has been well said, "nature and reality painted at the time, and on the spot, a nobler cartoon of St. Paul's preaching at Athens than the immortal Rafaelle afterwards has done."[3]

For a similar reason Maps have been added, exhibiting with as much accuracy as can at present be attained the physical features of the countries visited, and some of the ancient routes through them, together with plans of the most important cities, and maritime charts of the coasts where they were required.

While thus endeavouring to represent faithfully the natural

[1] Acts xvii. 24. [2] Phil. i. 13.
[3] Wordsworth's "Athens and Attica," p. 76.

objects and architectural remains connected with the narrative, it has likewise been attempted to give such illustrations as were needful of the minor productions of human art as they existed in the first century. For this purpose engravings of Coins have been given in all cases where they seemed to throw light on the circumstances mentioned in the history; and recourse has been had to the stores of Pompeii and Herculaneum, as well as to the collection of the Vatican, and the columns of Trajan and Antoninus.

But after all this is done—after we have endeavoured, with every help we can command, to reproduce the picture of St. Paul's deeds and times—how small would our knowledge of himself remain, if we had no other record of him left us but the story of his adventures. If his letters had never come down to us, we should have known indeed what he did and suffered, but we should have had very little idea of what he was.[1] Even if we could perfectly succeed in restoring the image of the scenes and circumstances in which he moved,—even if we could, as in a magic mirror, behold him speaking in the school of Tyrannus, with his Ephesian hearers in their national costume around him,—we should still see very little of Paul of Tarsus. We must listen to his words, if we would learn to know him. If fancy did her utmost, she could give us only his outward not his inward life. "His bodily presence" (so his enemies declared) "was weak and contemptible;" but "his letters" (even they allowed) "were weighty and powerful."[2] Moreover an effort of imagination and memory is needed to recal the past, but in his Epistles St. Paul is present with us. "His words are not dead words, they are living creatures with hands and feet,"[3] touching in a thousand hearts at this very hour the same chord of feeling which vibrated to their first utterance. We, the Christians of the nineteenth century, can bear witness now, as fully as could a Byzantine audience fourteen hundred years ago, to the saying of Chrysostom, that "Paul by his letters still lives in the mouths of men throughout the whole world; by them not only his own converts, but all the

[1] For his speeches recorded in the Acts, characteristic as they are, would by themselves have been too few and too short to add much to our knowledge of St. Paul; but illustrated as they now are by his Epistles, they become an important part of his personal biography.

[2] 2 Cor. x. 10.

[3] Luther, as quoted in Archdeacon Hare's "Mission of the Comforter," p. 449.

faithful even unto this day, yea and all the saints who are yet to be born, until Christ's coming again, both have been and shall be blessed."[1] His Epistles are to his inward life, what the mountains and rivers of Asia and Greece and Italy are to his outward life,—the imperishable part which still remains to us, when all that time can ruin has passed away.

It is in these letters then that we must study the true life of St. Paul, from its inmost depths and springs of action, which were "hidden with Christ in God," down to its most minute developements, and peculiar individual manifestations. In them we learn (to use the language of Gregory Nazianzene) "what is told of Paul by Paul himself."[2] Their most sacred contents indeed rise above all that is peculiar to the individual writer; for they are the communications of God to man concerning the faith and life of Christians; which St. Paul declared (as he often asserts) by the immediate revelation of Christ himself. But his manner of teaching these eternal truths is coloured by his human character, and peculiar to himself. And such individual features are naturally impressed much more upon epistles than upon any other kind of composition. For here we have not treatises, or sermons, which may dwell in the general and abstract, but real letters, written to meet the actual wants of living men; giving immediate answers to real questions, and warnings against pressing dangers; full of the interests of the passing hour. And this, which must be more or less the case with all epistles addressed to particular Churches, is especially so with those of St. Paul. In his case it is not too much to say that his letters are himself—a portrait painted by his own hand, of which every feature may be "known and read of all men."

It is not merely that in them we see the proof of his powerful

[1] De Sacerdotio, IV. 7. The whole passage is well worth quoting:

Πόθεν ανὰ τὴν οἰκουμένην ἅπασαν πολὺς ἐν τοῖς ἀπάντων ἐςὶ ςόμασιν; Πόθεν οὐ παρ' ἡμῖν μόνον, ἀλλά ϗ παρὰ Ιουδαίοις, καὶ Ἕλλησι μάλιςα πάντων θαυμάζεται; οὐκ ἀπὸ τῆς τῶν Ἐπιςολῶν αρετῆς; Δι' ἧς οὐ τοὺς τότε μόνον πιςοὺς, αλλά ϗ τοὺς ἐξ ἐκείνων μέχρι τῆς σήμερον γινομένους, ϗ τοὺς μέλλοντας δὲ ἔσεσθαι μέχρι τῆς εσχάτης τοῦ Χρίςου παρουσίας ὠφέλησέ τε ϗ ὠφελήσει· ϗ οὐ παύσεται τοῦτο ποιῶν, ἕως ἂν τὸ τῶν ἀνθρώπων διαμένῃ γένος. Ὥσπερ γὰρ τεῖχος ἐξ ἀδάμαντος κατασκευασθὲν, οὕτω τὰς πανταχοῦ τῆς οἰκουμένης Εκκλησίας τὰ τούτου τειχίζει γράμματα. Καὶ καθάπερ τὶς ἀριςεὺς γενναιότατος ἕςηκε ϗ νῦν μέσος, αἰχμαλωτίζων πᾶν νόημα εἰς τὴν ὑπακοὴν τοῦ Χριςου, καὶ καθαιρῶν λογισμοὺς καὶ πᾶν ὕψωμα ἐπαιρόμενον κατὰ τῆς γνώσεως τοῦ Θεοῦ. Ταῦτα δὲ πάντα ἐργάζεται, δι' ὧν ἡμῖν κατέλιπεν Επιςολῶν τῶν θαυμασίων ἐκείνων, ϗ τῆς θείας πεπληρωμένων σοφίας.

[2] Τί Παῦλος αὐτὸς περὶ Παύλου φησί. *Greg. Naz. Oratio Apologetica.*

intellect, his insight into the foundations of natural theology,[1] and of moral philosophy;[2] for in such points, though the philosophical expression might belong to himself, the truths expressed were taught him of God. It is not only that we there find models of the sublimest eloquence, when he is kindled by the vision of the glories to come, the perfect triumph of good over evil, the manifestation of the sons of God, and their transformation into God's likeness, when they shall see Him no longer[3] "in a glass darkly, but face to face,"—for in such strains as these it was not so much he that spake, as the Spirit of God speaking in him;[4]—but in his letters, besides all this which is divine, we trace every shade, even to the faintest, of his human character also. Here we see that fearless independence with which he "withstood Peter to the face, because he was to be blamed;"[5]—that impetuosity which breaks out in his apostrophe to the "foolish Galatians;"[6]—that earnest indignation which bids his converts "beware of dogs, beware of the concision,"[7] and pours itself forth in the emphatic "God forbid,"[8] which meets every Antinomian suggestion;—that fervid patriotism which makes him "wish that he were himself accursed from Christ for his brethren, his kinsmen according to the flesh, who are Israelites;"[9]—that generosity which looked for no other reward than "to preach the glad tidings of Christ without charge,"[10] and made him feel that he would rather "die, than that any man should make this glorying void;"—that dread of officious interference which led him to shrink from "building on another man's foundation;"[11]—that delicacy which shows itself in his appeal to Philemon, whom he might have commanded, "yet for love's sake rather beseeching him, being such an one as Paul the aged, and now also a prisoner of Jesus Christ,"[12] and which is even more striking in some of his farewell greetings, as (for instance) when he bids the Romans "salute Rufus, and *her who is both his mother and mine;*"[13]—that scrupulous fear of evil appearance which "would not eat any man's bread for nought, but wrought with labour and travail night and day, that he might not be chargeable to any of

[1] Rom. i. 20. [2] Rom. ii. 14, 15.
[3] 1 Cor. xiii. 12. [4] Mat. x. 20. [5] Gal. ii. 11.
[6] Gal. iii. 1. [7] Phil. iii. 2.
[8] Rom. vi. 2. 1 Cor. vi. 15, &c. It is difficult to express the force of μὴ γένοιτο by any other English phrase.
[9] Rom. ix. 3. [10] 1 Cor. ix. 18 and 15. [11] Rom. xv. 20.
[12] Philemon 9. [13] Rom. xvi. 13.

them;"[1] that refined courtesy which cannot bring itself to blame till it has first praised,[2] and which makes him deem it needful almost to apologize for the freedom of giving advice to those who were not personally known to him;[3]—that self-denying love which "will eat no flesh while the world standeth, lest he make his brother to offend;"[4]—that impatience of exclusive formalism with which he overwhelms the Judaizers of Galatia, joined with a forbearance so gentle for the innocent weakness of scrupulous consciences;[5]—that grief for the sins of others, which moved him to tears when he spoke of the enemies of the cross of Christ, "of whom I tell you even weeping;"[6]—that noble freedom from jealousy with which he speaks of those who out of rivalry to himself, preach Christ even of envy and strife, supposing to add affliction to his bonds, "What then? notwithstanding every way, whether in pretence or in truth, Christ is preached; and I therein do rejoice, yea and will rejoice;"[7]—that tender friendship which watches over the health of Timothy, even with a mother's care;[8]—that intense sympathy in the joys and sorrows of his converts, which could say, even to the rebellious Corinthians, "ye are in our hearts, to die and live with you;"[9]—that longing desire for the intercourse of affection, and that sense of loneliness when it was withheld, which perhaps is the most touching feature of all, because it approaches most nearly to a weakness, "When I came to Troas to preach Christ's gospel, and a door was opened to me of the Lord, I had no rest in my spirit, because I found not Titus my brother; but taking my leave of them, I went from thence into Macedonia." And "when I was come into Macedonia, my flesh had no rest, but I was troubled on every side; without were fightings, within were fears. Nevertheless God, who comforteth those that are cast down, comforted me by the coming of Titus."[10] "Do thy diligence to come shortly unto me; for Demas hath forsaken me, having loved this present world, and is departed

[1] 1 Thess. ii. 9.

[2] Compare the laudatory expressions in 1 Cor. i. 5–7, and 2 Cor. i. 6–7, with the heavy and unmingled censure conveyed in the whole subsequent part of these Epistles.

[3] Rom. xv. 14, 15. "And I myself also am persuaded of you, my brethren, that ye also are full of goodness, filled with all knowledge, able also to admonish one another Nevertheless, brethren, I have written the more boldly unto you in some sort, as putting you in mind."

[4] 1 Cor. viii. 13. [5] 1 Cor. viii. 12, and Rom. xiv. 21. [6] Phil. iii. 18.

[7] Phil. i. 15. [8] 1 Tim. v. 23. [9] 2 Cor. vii. 3.

[10] 2 Cor. ii. 13, and vii. 5

unto Thessalonica; Crescens to Galatia, Titus unto Dalmatia; only Luke is with me."[1]

Nor is it only in the substance, but even in the style of these writings that we recognize the man Paul of Tarsus. In the parenthetical constructions and broken sentences, we see the rapidity with which the thoughts crowded upon him, almost too fast for utterance; we see him animated rather than weighed down by "that which cometh upon him daily, the care of all the churches,"[2] as he pours forth his warnings or his arguments in a stream of eager and impetuous dictation, with which the pen of the faithful Tertius can hardly keep pace.[3] And above all, we trace his presence in the postscript to every letter, which he adds as an authentication in his own characteristic handwriting,[4] "which is the token in every epistle; so I write."[5] Sometimes as he takes up the pen he is moved with indignation when he thinks of the false brethren among those whom he addresses; "the salutation of me Paul with my own hand,—if any man love not the Lord Jesus Christ, let him be Anathema."[6] Sometimes, as he raises his hand to write, he feels it cramped by the fetters which bind him to the soldier who guards him,[7] "I Paul salute you with my own hand,—remember my chains." Yet he always ends with the same blessing, "The grace of our Lord Jesus Christ be with you," to which he sometimes adds still further a few last words of affectionate remembrance, "My love be with you all in Christ Jesus."[8]

But although the letters of St. Paul are so essential a part of his personal biography, it is a difficult question to decide upon the form in which they should be given in a work like this. The object to be sought is, that they may really represent in English what they were to their Greek readers when first written. Now this object would not be attained if the authorized version were adhered to, and yet a departure from that whereof so much is interwoven with the memory and deepest feelings of every religious mind should be grounded on strong and sufficient cause. It is hoped that the following reasons may be held such.

[1] 2 Tim. iv. 9. [2] 2 Cor. xi. 28.

[3] Rom. xvi. 22. "I, Tertius, who wrote this Epistle, salute you in the Lord."

[4] Gal. vi. 11. "Ye see the size of the characters (πηλίκοις γράμμασιν) in which I write to you with my own hand."

[5] 2 Thess. iii. 17. [6] 1 Cor. xvi. 22. [7] Coloss. iv. 18.

[8] 1 Cor. xvi. 24.

1st. The authorized version was meant to be a standard of authority and ultimate appeal in controversy; hence it could not venture to depart, as an ordinary translation would do, from the exact words of the original, even where some amplification was absolutely required to complete the sense. It was to be the version unanimously accepted by all parties, and therefore must simply represent the Greek text word for word. This it does most faithfully so far as the critical knowledge of the sixteenth[1] century permitted. But the result of this method is sometimes to produce a translation unintelligible to the English reader.[2] Also if the text admit of two interpretations, our version endeavours, if possible, to preserve the same ambiguity, and effects this often with admirable skill; but such indecision, although a merit in an authoritative version, would be a fault in a translation which had a different object.

2d. The imperfect knowledge existing at the time when our Bible was translated, made it inevitable that the translators should occasionally render the original incorrectly; and the same cause has made their version of many of the argumentative portions of the Epistles perplexed and obscure.

3d. Such passages as are affected by the above-mentioned objections might, it is true, have been recast, and the authorized translation retained in all cases where it is correct and clear; but if this had been done, a patchwork effect would have been produced like that of new cloth upon old garments; moreover the devotional associations of the reader would have been offended, and it would have been a rash experiment to provoke such a contrast between the matchless style of the authorized version and that of the modern translator, thus placed side by side.

4th. The style adopted for the present purpose should not be antiquated; for St. Paul was writing in the language used by his Hellenistic readers in every day life.

5th. In order to give the true meaning of the original, something of paraphrase is often absolutely required. St. Paul's style is extremely elliptical, and the gaps must be filled up. And moreover the great difficulty in understanding his argument is to trace clearly the transitions[3] by which he passes from one step to an-

[1] Being executed at the very beginning of the seventeenth.

[2] Yet had any other course been adopted, every sect would have had its own Bible; as it is, this one translation has been all but unanimously received for three centuries.

[3] In the translation of the Epistles given in the present work it has been the especial

other. For this purpose something must be supplied beyond the mere literal rendering of the words.

For these reasons the translation of the Epistles adopted in this work is to a certain degree paraphrastic. At the same time nothing has been added by way of paraphrase which was not virtually expressed in the original.

It has not been thought necessary to interrupt the reader by a note, in every instance where the translation varies from the Authorised Version. It has been assumed that the readers of the notes will have sufficient knowledge to understand the reason of such variations in the more obvious cases. But it is hoped that no passage of real difficulty has been passed over without explanation.

The authorities consulted upon the chronology of St. Paul's life, the reasons for the views taken of disputed points in it, and for the dates of the Epistles, are stated (so far as seems needful) in the body of the work or in the Appendix, and need not be further referred to here.

In conclusion, the authors would express their hope that this biography may, in its measure, be useful in strengthening the hearts of some against the peculiar form of unbelief most current at the present day. The more faithfully we can represent to ourselves the life, outward and inward, of St. Paul, in all its fulness, the more unreasonable must appear the theory that Christianity had a mythical origin; and the stronger must be our ground for believing his testimony to the divine nature and miraculous history of our Redeemer. No reasonable man can learn to know and love the Apostle of the Gentiles without asking himself the question "What was the principle by which through such a life he was animated? What was the strength in which he laboured with such immense results?" Nor can the most sceptical inquirer doubt for one moment the full sincerity of St. Paul's belief that "the life which he lived in the flesh he lived by the faith of the Son of God, who died and gave Himself for him."[1] "To believe in Christ crucified and risen, to serve Him

aim of the translator to represent these transitions correctly. They very often depend upon a word, which suggests a new thought, and are quite lost by a want of attention to the verbal coincidence. Thus, for instance, in Rom. x. 16, 17. Τίς ἐπίςευσε τῇ ἀκοῇ ἡμῶν; Ἄρα ἡ πίςις ἐξ ἀκοῆς. "*Who hath given faith to our telling? So then faith cometh by telling;*" how completely is the connection destroyed by such inattention in the authorized version: "*Who hath believed our report? So then faith cometh by hearing.*"

[1] Gal. ii. 20.

on earth, to be with Him hereafter;—these, if we may trust the account of his own motives by any human writer whatever, were the chief if not the only thoughts which sustained Paul of Tarsus through all the troubles and sorrows of his twenty years' conflict. His sagacity, his cheerfulness, his forethought, his im partial and clear-judging reason, all the natural elements of his strong character are not indeed to be overlooked: but the more highly we exalt these in our estimate of his work, the larger share we attribute to them in the performance of his mission, the more are we compelled to believe that he spoke the words of truth and soberness when he told the Corinthians that 'last of all Christ was seen of him also,'[1] that 'by the grace of God he was what he was,' that 'whilst he laboured more abundantly than all, it was not he, but the grace of God that was in him.'"[2]

P. S.—It may be well to add, that while Mr. Conybeare and Mr. Howson have undertaken the joint revision of the whole work, the translation of the Epistles and Speeches of St. Paul is contributed by the former, and the Historical and Geographical portion of the work principally by the latter; Mr. Howson having written Chapters I., II., III., IV., V., VI., VII., VIII., IX., X., XI., XII., XIV., XVI., XX., XXI., XXII., XXIII., XXIV., *with the exception of the Epistles and Speeches therein contained; and Mr. Conybeare having written the Introduction and Appendix, and Chapters* XIII., XV., XVII., XVIII., XIX., XXV., XXVI., XXVII., XXVIII.

[1] 1 Cor. xv. 10. [2] Stanley's Sermons, p. 186.

PREFACE TO THE AMERICAN EDITION.

THE Publisher, in presenting "THE LIFE AND EPISTLES OF ST PAUL," by the Rev. W. J. CONYBEARE and Rev. J. S. HOWSON, needs no apology. During the short interval since its publication in England it has commanded the admiration of scholars and intelligent readers of the Bible both in this country and Europe, and has passed through the ordeal of criticism in the leading Quarterlies and Journals of both countries and received the highest commendation. The expense of the English edition, however, is such as necessarily to limit its circulation in this country, and the desire has been repeatedly expressed that the work should be published in a form and at a price which would bring it within the reach of ministers, students, and intelligent readers generally. The present edition, it is believed, will meet the existing want. Though offered at one half of the cost of the London copy, the work has in no way suffered from abridgment, but has been preserved complete in every respect. The notes, coins, maps, plans, and wood engravings generally have been retained, and yet the size of the work has been reduced from the unwieldy quarto to a convenient octavo form.

The steel engravings, which appear in the English edition simply as embellishments, which are familiar to most readers, and which are in no way essential to the text or to the value of the work, have been omitted—since the expense of reproducing them here would be such as greatly to increase the cost of the work, and yet add nothing to its usefulness.

The North British Review for February, 1854, after a highly commendatory criticism of this work, makes the following remarks:

"We commend the book to that numerous class, increasing every day, whose early culture has necessarily been defective, but whose intelligence and thirst for knowledge is continually sharpened by the general diffusion of thought and education. Such persons, if they are already Christians by conviction, are naturally more and more dissatisfied with the popular commentaries on the Bible; and if they are sceptical and irreligious, this great evil is probably caused by the undeniable existence of difficulties which such commentaries shrink from fairly meeting. They will find in the work before us a valuable help towards understanding the New Testament. The Greek and Latin quotations are almost entirely confined to the notes: any unlearned reader may study the text with ease and profit. And it is from a sense of the great value of the book in this respect, that we would earnestly entreat the publishers to supply it in a cheaper and more convenient form. In these days a quarto book, except for reference, is a monster *feræ naturæ*."

THE

LIFE AND EPISTLES

OF

ST. PAUL.

CHAPTER I.

"And the title was written in Hebrew, and Greek and Latin."—Joh. xix. 20.

GREAT MEN OF GREAT PERIODS.—PERIOD OF CHRIST'S APOSTLES.—JEWS, GREEKS, AND ROMANS.—RELIGIOUS CIVILISATION OF THE JEWS.—THEIR HISTORY AND ITS RELATION TO THAT OF THE WORLD.—HEATHEN PREPARATION FOR THE GOSPEL.—CHARACTER AND LANGUAGE OF THE GREEKS.—ALEXANDRIA.—ANTIOCH AND ALEXANDRIA.—GROWTH AND GOVERNMENT OF THE ROMAN EMPIRE.—MISERY OF ITALY AND THE PROVINCES.—PREPARATION IN THE EMPIRE FOR CHRISTIANITY.—DISPERSION OF THE JEWS IN ASIA, AFRICA, AND EUROPE.—PROSELYTES.—PROVINCES OF CILICIA AND JUDÆA.—THEIR GEOGRAPHY AND HISTORY.—CILICIA UNDER THE ROMANS.—TARSUS.—CICERO.—POLITICAL CHANGES IN JUDÆA.—HEROD AND HIS FAMILY.—THE ROMAN GOVERNORS.—CONCLUSION.

THE life of a great man, in a great period of the world's history, is a subject to command the attention of every thoughtful mind. Alexander on his Eastern expedition, spreading the civilisation of Greece over the Asiatic and African shores of the Mediterranean Sea,—Julius Cæsar contending against the Gauls, and subduing the barbarism of Western Europe to the order and discipline of Roman Government,—Charlemagne compressing the separating atoms of the feudal world, and reviving for a time the image of imperial unity,—Columbus sailing westward over the Atlantic to discover a new world which might receive the arts and religion of the old,—Napoleon on his rapid campaigns, shattering the ancient system of European states, and leaving a chasm between our present and the past:—these are the colossal figures of history, which stamp with the impress of their personal greatness the centuries in which they lived.

The interest with which we look upon such men is natural and inevitable, even when we are deeply conscious that, in their character and their work, evil was mixed up in large proportions with the good, and when we find it difficult to discover the providential design which drew the features of their respective epochs. But this natural feeling rises into something higher, if we can be assured that the period we contemplate was designedly prepared for great results, that the work we admire was a work of unmixed good, and the man whose actions we follow was an instrument specially prepared by the hands of God. Such a period was that in which the civilised world was united under the first Roman emperors: such a work was the first preaching of the Gospel: and such a man was Paul of Tarsus.

Before we enter upon the particulars of his life and the history of his work, it is desirable to say something, in this introductory chapter, concerning the general features of the age which was prepared for him. We shall not attempt any minute delineation of the institutions and social habits of the period. Many of these will be brought before us in detail in the course of the present work. We shall only notice here those circumstances in the state of the world, which seem to bear the traces of a providential pre-arrangement.

Casting this general view on the age of the first Roman emperors, which was also the age of Jesus Christ and His Apostles, we find our attention arrested by three great varieties of national life. The Jew, the Greek, and the Roman appear to divide the world between them. The outward condition of Jerusalem itself, at this epoch, might be taken as a type of the civilised world. Herod the Great, who rebuilt the Temple, had erected, for Greek and Roman entertainments, a theatre within the same walls, and an amphitheatre in the neighbouring plain.[1] His coins, and those of his grandson Agrippa, bore Greek inscriptions:[2] that piece of money, which was brought to our Saviour (Matt. xxii. Mark xii. Luke

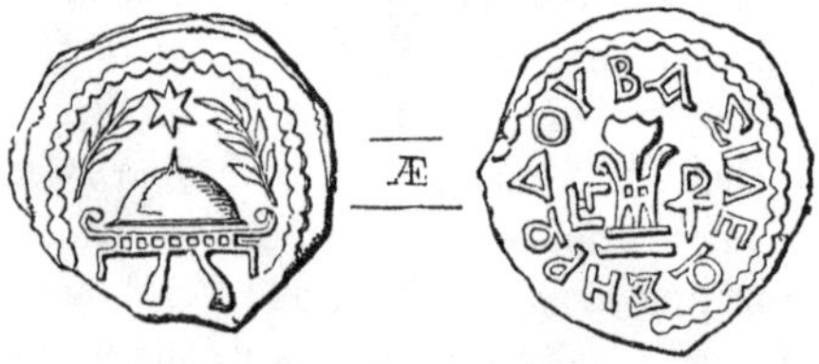

COIN OF HEROD THE GREAT.

[1] Joseph. *Ant.* xv. 8, 1. B. J. i. 21, 8.

[2] These two coins of Herod the Great and his grandson Agrippa I., with the Denarius of Tiberius, are taken, by Mr. Akerman's kind permission, from his excellent little work, "Numismatic Illustrations of the New Testament."

COIN OF HEROD AGRIPPA I.

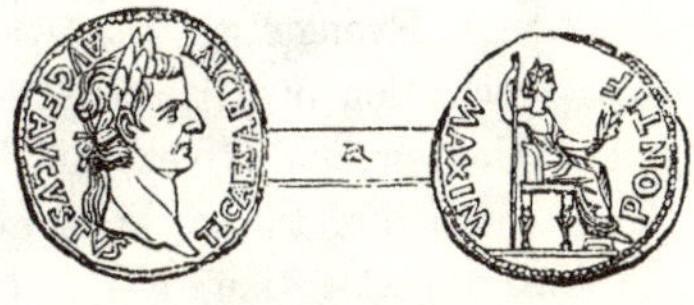

DENARIUS OF TIBERIUS.

xx.), was the silver *Denarius*, the "image" was that of the emperor, the "superscription" was in Latin: and at the same time when the common currency consisted of such pieces as these,—since coins with the images of men or with heathen symbols would have been a profanation to the "Treasury,"—there might be found on the tables of the money-changers in the Temple, shekels and half-shekels with Samaritan letters, minted under the Maccabees. Greek and Roman names were borne by multitudes of those Jews who came up to worship at the festivals. Greek and Latin words were current in the popular "Hebrew" of the day: and while this Syro-Chaldaic dialect was spoken by the mass of the people with the tenacious affection of old custom, Greek had long been well-known among the upper classes in the larger towns, and Latin was used in the courts of law, and in the official correspondence of magistrates.[1] On a critical occasion of St. Paul's life,[2] when he was standing on the stair between the Temple and the fortress, he first spoke to the commander of the garrison in Greek, and then turned round and addressed his countrymen in Hebrew; while the letter[3] of Claudius Lysias was written, and the oration[4] of Tertullus spoken, in Latin. We are told by the historian Josephus,[5] that on a parapet of stone in the Temple area, where a flight of fourteen steps led up from the outer to the inner court, pillars were placed at equal distances, with notices, some in Greek and some in Latin, that no alien should enter the sacred enclosure of the Hebrews. And we are told

[1] Val. Max. ii. 2. Magistratus vero prisci quantopere suam populique Romani majestatem retinentes se gesserint, hinc cognosci potest, quod inter cætera obtinendæ gravitatis indicia, illud quoque magna cum perseverantia custodiebant, ne Græcis unquam, nisi Latinè responsa darent. Quinetiam ipsa linguæ volubilitate, quâ plurimum valent, excussâ, per interpretem loqui cogebant; non in urbe tantum nostra, sed etiam in Græcia et Asia: quo scilicet Latinæ vocis honos per omnes gentes venerabilior diffunderetur. Nec illis deerant studia doctrinæ, sed nulla non in re pallium togæ subjici debere arbitrabantur: indignum esse existimantes, illecebris et suavitate literarum imperii pondus et auctoritatem domari.

[2] Acts xxi. xxii.

[3] Acts xxiii. The letter was what was technically called an *Elogium*, or certificate, and there is hardly any doubt that it was in Latin. See De Wette and Olshausen, *in loc.*

[4] Acts xxiv. Mr. Milman (Bampton Lectures, p. 185) has remarked on the peculiarly Latin character of Tertullus's address: and the preceding quotation from Valerius Maximus seems to imply that its language was Latin.

[5] B. J. v. 5, 2. Compare vi. 2, 4.

by two of the Evangelists,[1] that when our blessed Saviour was crucified, "the superscription of His accusation" was written above His cross "in letters of Hebrew, and Greek, and Latin."

The condition of the world in general at that period wears a similar appearance to a Christian's eye. He sees the Greek and Roman elements brought into remarkable union with the older and more sacred elements of Judaism. He sees in the Hebrew nation a divinely-laid foundation for the superstructure of the Church, and in the dispersion of the Jews a soil made ready in fitting places for the seed of the Gospel. He sees in the spread of the language and commerce of the Greeks, and in the high perfection of their poetry and philosophy, appropriate means for the rapid communication of Christian ideas, and for bringing them into close connection with the best thoughts of unassisted humanity. And he sees in the union of so many incoherent provinces under the law and government of Rome, a strong framework which might keep together for a sufficient period those masses of social life which the Gospel was intended to pervade. The City of God is built at the confluence of three civilisations. We recognise with gratitude the hand of God in the history of His world: and we turn with devout feelings to trace the course of these three streams of civilised life, from their early source to the time of their meeting in the Apostolic age.

We need not linger about the fountains of the national life of the Jews. We know that they gushed forth at first, and flowed in their appointed channels, at the command of God. The call of Abraham, when one family was chosen to keep and hand down the deposit of divine truth,—the series of providences which brought the ancestors of the Jews into Egypt,—the long captivity on the banks of the Nile,—the work of Moses, whereby the bondsmen were made into a nation,—all these things are represented in the Old Testament as occurring under the immediate direction of Almighty power. The people of Israel were taken out of the midst of an idolatrous world, to become the depositaries of a purer knowledge of the one true God than was given to any other people. At a time when (humanly speaking) the world could hardly have preserved a spiritual religion in its highest purity, they received a divine revelation enshrined in symbols and ceremonies, whereby it might be safely kept till the time of its development in a purer and more heavenly form.

The peculiarity of the Hebrew civilisation did not consist in the culture of the imagination and intellect, like that of the Greeks, nor in the organisation of government, like that of Rome,—but its distinguishing feature was *Religion.* To say nothing of the Scriptures, the prophets, the miracles of the Jews,—their frequent festivals, their constant sacrifices,—

[1] Luke xxiii. 38. John xix. 20.

everything in their collective and private life was connected with a revealed religion: their wars, their heroes, their poetry, had a sacred character,—their national code was full of the details of public worship,—their ordinary employments were touched at every point by divinely-appointed and significant ceremonies. Nor was this religion, as were the religions of the heathen world, a creed which could not be the common property of the instructed and the ignorant. It was neither a recondite philosophy which might not be communicated to the masses of the people, nor a weak superstition, controlling the conduct of the lower classes, and ridiculed by the higher. The religion of Moses was for the use of all and the benefit of all.[1] The poorest peasant of Galilee had the same part in it as the wisest Rabbi of Jerusalem. The children of all families were taught to claim their share in the privileges of the chosen people.

And how different was the nature of this religion from that of the contemporary Gentiles! The pious feelings of the Jew were not dissipated and distracted by a fantastic mythology, where a thousand different objects of worship, with contradictory attributes, might claim the attention of the devout mind. "One God," the Creator and Judge of the world, and the Author of all good, was the only object of adoration And there was nothing of that wide separation between religion and morality, which among other nations was the road to all impurity. The will and approbation of Jehovah was the motive and support of all holiness: faith in His word was the power which raised men above their natural weakness: while even the divinities of Greece and Rome were often the personifications of human passions, and the example and sanction of vice. And still farther:—the devotional scriptures of the Jews express that heartfelt sense of infirmity and sin, that peculiar spirit of prayer, that real communion with God, with which the Christian, in his best moments, has the truest sympathy.[2] So that, while the best hymns of Greece[3] are ouly mythological pictures, and the literature of heathen Rome hardly produces anything which can be called a prayer, the Hebrew psalms

[1] *ὅπερ ἐκ φιλοσοφίας τῆς δοκιμωτάτης περιγίνεται τοῖς ὁμιληταῖς ἀυτῆς, τοῦτο διὰ νόμων καὶ ἐθῶν Ἰουδαίοις, ἐπιστήμη τοῦ ἀνωτάτου καὶ πρεσβυτάτου πάντων, τὸν ἐπὶ τοῖς γενητοῖς θεοῖς πλάνον ἀπωσαμένοις.* Quoted with other passages from Philo by Neander, General Church History, vol. i. pp. 70, 71. (Torrey's translation, Edinburgh, 1847.)

[2] Neander observes that it has been justly remarked that the distinctive peculiarity (die auszeichnende Eigenthumlichkeit) of the Hebrew nation from the very first, was, that *conscience* was more alive among them than any other people. Pflanzung und Leitung, p. 91, ed. 1847. See also the Eng. Trans. of the former edition, vol. i. p. 61.

[3] There are some exceptions, as in the hymn of the Stoic Cleanthes. who was born at Assos 350 years before St. Paul was there; yet it breathes the sentiment rather of acquiescence in the determinations of Fate, than of resignation to the goodness of Providence. See Mr. Cotton's notice of Cleanthes in Smith's Dictionary of Biography and Mythology.

have passed into the devotions of the Christian church. There is a light on all the mountains of Judæa which never shone on Olympus or Parnassus: and the "Hill of Zion," in which "it pleased God to dwell," is the type of "the joy of the whole earth,"[1] while the seven hills of Rome are the symbol of tyranny and idolatry. "He showed His word unto Jacob, His statutes and ordinances unto Israel. He dealt not so with any nation; neither had the heathen knowledge of His laws."[2]

But not only was a holy religion the characteristic of the civilisation of the Jews, but their religious feelings were directed to something in the future, and all the circumstances of their national life tended to fix their thoughts on One that was to come. By types and by promises, their eyes were continually turned towards a Messiah. Their history was a continued prophecy. All the great stages of their national existence were accompanied by effusions of prophetic light.[3] Abraham was called from his father's house, and it was revealed that in him "all families of the earth should be blessed." Moses formed Abraham's descendants into a people, by giving them a law and national institutions; but while so doing he spake before of Him who was hereafter to be raised up "a Prophet like unto himself." David reigned, and during that reign, which made so deep and lasting an impression on the Jewish mind, psalms were written which spoke of the future King. And with the approach of that captivity, the pathetic recollection of which became perpetual, the prophecies took a bolder range, and embraced within their widening circle the redemption both of Jews and Gentiles. Thus the pious Hebrew was always, as it were, in the attitude of *expectation*. And it has been well remarked that, while the golden age of the Greeks and Romans was the past, that of the Jews was the future. While other nations were growing weary of their gods,—without anything in their mythology or philosophy to satisfy the deep cravings of their nature,—with religion operating rather as a barrier than a link between the educated and the ignorant,—with morality divorced from theology,—the whole Jewish people were united in a feeling of attachment to their sacred institutions, and found in the facts of their past history a sure pledge of the fulfilment of their national hopes.

It is true that the Jewish nation, again and again, during several centuries, fell into idolatry. It is true that their superiority to other nations consisted in the light which they possessed, and not in the use which they made of it; and that a carnal life continually dragged them down from the spiritual eminence on which they might have stood. But the divine purposes were not frustrated. The chosen people was subjected to

[1] Ps. xlviii. 2. lxviii. 16.
[2] Ps. cxlvii. 19, 20.
[3] Davison, Warburtonian Lectures on Prophecy, pp. 98, 107, 147, 201, &c.

the chastisement and discipline of severe sufferings: and they were fitted by a long training for the accomplishment of that work, to the conscious performance of which they did not willingly rise. They were hard pressed in their own country by the incursions of their idolatrous neighbours, and in the end they were carried into a distant captivity. From the time of their return from Babylon they were no longer idolaters. They presented to the world the example of a pure Monotheism. And in the active times which preceded and followed the birth of Christ, those Greeks or Romans who visited the Jews in their own land where they still lingered at the portals of the East, and those vast numbers of proselytes whom the dispersed Jews had gathered round them in various countries, were made familiar with the worship of one God and Father of all.[1]

The influence of the Jews upon the heathen world was exercised mainly through their *dispersion:* but this subject must be deferred for a few pages, till we have examined some of the developments of the Greek and Roman nationalities. A few words, however, may be allowed in passing, upon the consequences of the *geographical position* of Judæa.

The situation of this little but eventful country is such, that its inhabitants were brought into contact successively with all the civilized nations of antiquity. Not to dwell upon its proximity to Egypt on the one hand, and to Assyria on the other, and the influences which those ancient kingdoms may thereby have exercised or received, Palestine lay in the road of Alexander's Eastern expedition. The Greek conqueror was there before he founded his mercantile metropolis in Egypt, and then went to India, to return and die at Babylon. And again, when his empire was divided, and Greek kingdoms were erected in Europe, Asia, and Africa, Palestine lay between the rival monarchies of the Ptolemies at Alexandria and the Seleucidæ at Antioch,—too near to both to be safe from the invasion of their arms or the influence of their customs and their language. And finally, when the time came for the Romans to embrace the whole of the Mediterranean within the circle of their power, the coast-line of Judæa was the last remote portion which was needed to complete the fated circumference.

The full effect of this geographical position of Judæa can only be seen by following the course of Greek and Roman life, till they were brought so remarkably into contact with each other, and with that of the Jews: and we turn to those other two nations of antiquity, the steps of whose progress were successive stages in what is called in the Epistle to the Ephesians (i 10) "the dispensation of the fulness of time."

[1] Humboldt has remarked, in the chapter on Poetic Descriptions of Nature (Kosmos, Sabine's Eng. Trans., vol. ii. p. 44), that the descriptive poetry of the Hebrews is a reflex of Monotheism, and pourtrays nature, not as self-subsisting, but ever in relation to a Higher Power

If we think of the civilisation of the Greeks, we have no difficulty in fixing on its chief characteristics. High perfection of the intellect and imagination, displaying itself in all the various forms of art, poetry, literature, and philosophy—restless activity of mind and body, finding its exercise in athletic games or in subtle disputations—love of the beautiful—quick perception—indefatigable inquiry—all these enter into the very idea of the Greek race. This is not the place to inquire how far these qualities were due to an innate peculiarity, or how far they grew up, by gradual development, amidst the natural influences of their native country,—the variety of their hills and plains, the clear lights and warm shadows of their climate, the mingled land and water of their coasts. We have only to do with this national character so far as, under divine Providence, it was made subservient to the spread of the Gospel.

We shall see how remarkably it subserved this purpose, if we consider the tendency of the Greeks to trade and colonisation. Their mental activity was accompanied with great physical restlessness. This clever people always exhibited a disposition to spread themselves. Without aiming at universal conquest, they displayed (if we may use the word) a remarkable catholicity of character, and a singular power of adaptation to those whom they called Barbarians. In this respect they were strongly contrasted with the Egyptians, whose immemorial civilisation was confined to the long valley which extends from the cataracts to the mouths of the Nile. The Hellenic tribes, on the other hand, though they despised foreigners, were never unwilling to visit them and to cultivate their acquaintance. At the earliest period at which history enables us to discover them, we see them moving about in their ships on the shores and among the islands of their native seas; and, three or four centuries before the Christian era, Asia Minor, beyond which the Persians had not been permitted to advance, was bordered by a fringe of Greek colonies; and Lower Italy, when the Roman republic was just beginning to be conscious of its strength, had received the name of Greece itself. To all these places they carried their arts and literature, their philosophy, their mythology, and their amusements. They carried also their arms and their trade. The heroic age had passed away, and fabulous voyages had given place to real expeditions against Sicily and constant traffic with the Black Sea. They were gradually taking the place of the Phœnicians in the empire of the Mediterranean. They were, indeed, less exclusively mercantile than those old discoverers. Their voyages were not so long. But their influence on general civilisation was greater and more permanent. The earliest ideas of scientific navigation and geography are due to the Greeks. The later Greek travellers, Pausanias and Strabo, will be our best sources of information on the topography of St. Paul's journeys.

With this view of the Hellenic character before us, we are prepared to appreciate the vast results of Alexander's conquests.[1] He took up the meshes of the net of Greek civilisation, which were lying in disorder on the edges of the Asiatic shore, and spread them over all the countries which he traversed in his wonderful campaigns. The East and the West were suddenly brought together. Separated tribes were united under a common government. New cities were built, as the centres of political life. New lines of communication were opened, as the channels of commercial activity. The new culture penetrated the mountain ranges of Pisidia and Lycaonia. The Tigris and Euphrates became Greek rivers. The language of Athens was heard among the Jewish colonies of Babylonia; and a Grecian Babylon was built by the conqueror in Egypt, and called by his name.

The empire of Alexander was divided, but the effects of his campaigns and policy did not cease. The influence of the fresh elements of social life was rather increased by being brought into independent action within the spheres of distinct kingdoms. Our attention is particularly called to two of the monarchical lines, which descended from Alexander's generals,—

COIN OF ANTIOCHUS EPIPHANES, WITH PORTRAIT.

the Ptolemies, or the Greek kings of Egypt,—and the Seleucidæ, or the Greek kings of Syria.[2] Their respective capitals, *Alexandria* and *Antioch*, became the metropolitan centres of commercial and civilised life in the East. They rose suddenly; and their very appearance marked them as the cities of a new epoch. Like Berlin and St. Petersburg, they were modern cities built by great kings at a definite time and for a definite purpose.[3] Their

[1] Plutarch, paraphrasing Alexander's saying to Diogenes, remarks that his mission was—*τὰ βαρβαρικὰ τοῖς Ἑλληνικοῖς κεράσαι, καὶ τὴν Ἑλλάδα σπεῖραι*: Orat. i.. de Alex. Virtute *s.* fortuna, § 11.

[2] This coin, with the portrait of Antiochus (IV.) Epiphanes, is from the British Museum (whence much other assistance has been obtained for this work, chiefly through the kindness of C. Newton, Esq., student of Ch. Ch.). Portraits on coins began with Alexander. For their historical importance, see K. O. Müller's Handbuch der Archäologie der Alten Kunst, § 162, p. 169, Welcker's edition, 1848. For the series of the Seleucidæ, see Vaillant, "Seleucidarum Imperium, sive Historia Regum Syriæ ad fidem Numismatum accommodata:" Paris, 1681. (2nd Ed. Hag. 1732.)

[3] An account of the building of Antioch will be given hereafter. For that of Alex

histories are no unimportant chapters in the history of the world. Both of them were connected with St Paul: one indirectly, as the birthplace of Apollos; the other directly, as the scene of some of the most important passages of the Apostle's own life. Both abounded in Jews from their first foundation. Both became the residences of Roman governors, and both were patriarchates of the primitive Church. But before they had received either the Roman discipline or the Christian doctrine, they had served their appointed purpose of spreading the Greek language and habits, of creating new lines of commercial intercourse by land and sea, and of centralising in themselves the mercantile life of the Levant. Even the Acts of the Apostles remind us of the traffic of Antioch with Cyprus and the neighbouring coasts, and of the sailing of Alexandrian corn-ships to the more distant harbours of Malta and Puteoli.

Of all the Greek elements which the cities of Antioch and Alexandria were the means of circulating, the spread of the language is the most important. Its connection with the whole system of Christian doctrine—with many of the controversies and divisions of the Church—is very momentous. That language, which is the richest and most delicate that the world has seen, became the language of theology. The Greek tongue became to the Christian more than it had been to the Roman or the Jew. The mother-tongue of Ignatius at Antioch, was that in which Philo composed his treatises at Alexandria, and which Cicero spoke at Athens. It is difficult to state in a few words the important relation which *Alexandria* more especially was destined to bear to the whole Christian Church. In that city, the representative of the Greeks of the East, where the most remarkable fusion took place of the peculiarities of Greek, Jewish, and Oriental life, and at the time when all these had been brought in contact with the mind of educated Romans,—a *theological language* was formed, rich in the phrases of various schools, and suited to convey Christian ideas to all the world. It was not an accident that the New Testament was written in Greek, the language which can best express the highest thoughts and worthiest feelings of the intellect and heart, and which is adapted to be the instrument of education for all nations: nor was it an accident that the composition of these books and the promulgation of the Gospel were delayed, till the instruction of our Lord, and the writings of His Apostles, could be expressed in the dialect of Alexandria. This, also, must be ascribed to the foreknowledge of Him, who "winked at the times of ignorance," but who "made of one blood all nations of men for to dwell on all the face of the earth, and determined the times before appointed and the bounds of their habitation."[1]

andria, see Müller, § 149, pp. 153, 154. Ammianus calls it *vertex omnium civitatum*. The architect was Dinocrates, who renewed the temple at Ephesus (Acts xix.).

[1] Acts xvii. 30, 26.

We do not forget that the social condition of the Greeks had been falling, during this period, into the lowest corruption. The disastrous quarrels of Alexander's generals had been continued among their successors. Political integrity was lost. The Greeks spent their life in worthless and frivolous amusements. Their religion, though beautiful beyond expression as giving subjects for art and poetry, was utterly powerless, and worse than powerless, in checking their bad propensities. Their philosophers were sophists; their women might be briefly divided into two classes,—those who were highly educated and openly profligate on the one side, and those who lived in domestic and ignorant seclusion on the other. And it cannot be denied that all these causes of degradation spread with the diffusion of the race and the language; like Sybaris and Syracuse, Antioch and Alexandria became almost worse than Athens and Corinth. But the very diffusion and development of this corruption was preparing the way, because it showed the necessity, for the interposition of a Gospel. The disease itself seemed to call for a *Healer*. And if the prevailing evils of the Greek population presented obstacles, on a large scale, to the progress of Christianity,—yet they showed to all future time the weakness of man's highest powers, if unassisted from above; and there must have been many who groaned under the burden of a corruption which they could not shake off, and who were ready to welcome the voice of Him, who "took our infirmities, and bare our sicknesses." The "Greeks,"[1] who are mentioned by St. John as coming to see JESUS at the feast, were, we trust, the types of a large class; and we may conceive His answer to Andrew and Philip as expressing the fulfilment of the appointed times in the widest sense—"The hour is come, that the Son of Man should be glorified."

Such was the civilisation and corruption connected with the spread of the Greek language when the Roman power approached to the eastern parts of the Mediterranean Sea. For some centuries this irresistible force had been gathering strength on the western side of the Apennines. Gradually, but surely, and with ever-increasing rapidity, it made to itself a wider space—northward into Etruria, southward into Campania. It passed beyond its Italian boundaries. And six hundred years after the building of the city, the Roman eagle had seized on Africa at the point of Carthage, and Greece at the Isthmus of Corinth, and had turned its eye

[1] Ἕλληνες, xii. 20. It ought to be observed here, that the word "*Grecian*" in the English translation of the New Testament is used for a Hellenist, or Grecising Jew (Ἑλληνιστὴς)—as Acts vi. 1. ix. 29—while the word "*Greek*" is used for one who was by birth a Gentile (Ἕλλην), and who might, or might not, be a proselyte to Judaism, or a convert to Christianity. It is agreed by the modern critics (Griesbach, Scholz, Lachmann, De Wette) that in Acts xi. 20, the true reading is Ἕλληνας not Ἑλληνιστὰς, "Greeks" not "Grecians."

towards the East. The defenceless prey was made secure, by craft or by war; and before the birth of our Saviour, all those coasts, from Ephesus to Tarsus and Antioch, and round by the Holy Land to Alexandria and Cyrene, were tributary to the city of the Tiber. We have to describe in a few words the characteristics of this new dominion, and to point out its providential connection with the spread and consolidation of the Church.

In the first place, this dominion was not a pervading influence exerted by a restless and intellectual people, but it was the grasping power of an external government. The idea of law had grown up with the growth of the Romans; and wherever they went they carried it with them. Wherever their armies were marching or encamping, there always attended them, like a mysterious presence, the spirit of the City of Rome. Universal conquest and permanent occupation were the ends at which they aimed. Strength and organisation were the characteristics of their sway. We have seen how the Greek science and commerce were wafted, by irregular winds, from coast to coast: and now we follow the advance of legions, governors, and judges along the Roman Roads, which pursued their undeviating course over plains and mountains, and bound the City to the furthest extremities of the provinces.

There is no better way of obtaining a clear view of the features and a correct idea of the spirit of the Roman age, than by considering the material works which still remain as its imperishable monuments. Whether undertaken by the hands of the government, or for the ostentation of private luxury, they were marked by vast extent and accomplished at an enormous expenditure. The gigantic roads of the empire have been unrivalled till the present century. Solid structures of all kinds, for utility, amusement and worship, were erected in Italy and the provinces,—amphitheatres of stone, magnificent harbours, bridges sepulchres, and temples. The decoration of wealthy houses was celebrated by the poets of the day. The pomp of buildings in the cities was rivalled by astonishing villas in the country. The enormous baths, by which travellers are surprised, belong to a period somewhat later than that of St. Paul; but the aqueducts, which still remain in the Campagna, were some of them new when he visited Rome. Of the metropolis itself it may be enough to say, that his life is exactly embraced between its two great times of renovation, that of Augustus on the one hand, who (to use his own expression) having found it a city of brick left it a city of marble, and that of Nero on the other, when the great conflagration afforded an opportunity for a new arrangement of its streets and buildings.

These great works may be safely taken as emblems of the magnitude, strength, grandeur, and solidity of the empire; but they are emblems, no less, of the tyranny and cruelty which had presided over its formation, and of the general suffering which pervaded it. The statues, with which the metropolis and the Roman houses were profusely decorated, had been brought from plundered provinces, and many of them had swelled the triumphs of conquerors on the Capitol. The amphitheatres were built for shows of gladiators, and were the scenes of a bloody cruelty, which had been quite unknown in the licentious exhibitions of the Greek theatre The roads, baths, harbours, aqueducts, had been constructed by slave-labour. And the country-villas, which the Italian traveller lingered to admire, were themselves vast establishments of slaves.

It is easy to see how much misery followed in the train of Rome's advancing greatness. Cruel suffering was a characteristic feature of the close of the republic. Slave wars, civil wars, wars of conquest, had left their disastrous results behind them. No country recovers rapidly from the effects of a war which has been conducted within its frontier; and there was no district of the empire which had not been the scene of some recent campaign. None had suffered more than Italy itself. Its old stock of freemen, who had cultivated its fair plains and terraced vineyards, was utterly worn out. The general depopulation was badly compensated by the establishment of military colonies. Inordinate wealth and slave factories were the prominent features of the desolate prospect. The words of the great historian may fill up the picture. "As regards the manners and mode of life of the Romans, their great object at this time was the acquisition and possession of money. Their moral conduct, which had been corrupt enough before the social war, became still more so by their systematic plunder and rapine. Immense riches were accumulated and squandered upon brutal pleasures. The simplicity of the old manners and mode of living had been abandoned for Greek luxuries and frivolities, and the whole household arrangements had become altered. The Roman houses had formerly been quite simple, and were built either of brick or peperino, but in most cases of the former material; now, on the other hand, every one would live in a splendid house and be surrounded by luxuries. The condition of Italy after the Social and Civil wars was indescribably wretched. Samnium had become almost a desert; and as

[1] Plena domus tunc omnis, et ingens stabat acervus
Numorum, Spartana chlamys, conchylia Coa,
Et cum Parrhasii tabulis signisque Myronis
Phidiacum vivebat ebur, nec non Polycleti
Multus ubique labor: raræ sine Mentore mensæ.
Inde *Dolabellæ* atque hinc *Antonius*, inde
Sacrilegus *Verres* referebant navibus altis
Occulta spolia et *plures de pace triumphos*.—Juv. viii. 100.

For a multitude of details, see the 164th and 165th sections of K. O. Müller's Handbuch der Archäologie.

late as the time of Strabo (vi. p. 253), there was scarcely any town in that country which was not in ruins. But worse things were yet to come."[1]

This disastrous condition was not confined to Italy. In some respects the provinces had their own peculiar sufferings. To take the case of Asia Minor. It had been plundered and ravaged by successive generals,—by Scipio in the war against Antiochus of Syria,—by Manlius in his Galatian campaign,—by Pompey in the struggle with Mithridates.[2] The rapacity of governors and their officials followed that of generals and their armies. We know what Cilicia suffered under Dolabella and his agent Verres; and Cicero reveals to us the oppression of his predecessor Appius in the same province, contrasted with his own boasted clemency. Some portions of this beautiful and inexhaustible country revived under the emperors.[3] But it was only an outward prosperity. Whatever may have been the improvement in the external details of provincial government, we cannot believe that governors were gentle and forbearing, when Caligula was on the throne, and when Nero was seeking statues for his golden house. The contempt in which the Greek provincials themselves were held by the Romans may be learnt from the later correspondence of the Emperor Trajan with Pliny the governor of Bithynia. We need not hesitate to take it for granted, that those who were sent from Rome to dispense justice at Ephesus or Tarsus, were more frequently like Appius and Verres, than Cicero[4] and Flaccus,—more like Pilate and Felix, than Gallio or Sergius Paulus.

It would be a delusion to imagine, that when the world was reduced under one sceptre, any real principle of unity held its different parts together. The emperor was deified, because men were enslaved. There was no true peace when Augustus closed the Temple of Janus. The empire was only the order of external government, with a chaos both of opinions and morals within. The writings of Tacitus and Juvenal remain to attest the corruption which festered in all ranks, alike in the senate and the family. The old severity of manners, and the old faith in the better part of the Roman religion, were gone. The licentious creeds and prac-

[1] Niebuhr's Lectures on the History of Rome, vol. i. pp. 421, 422.

[2] Pliny points out the connection of these conquests with the development of Roman luxury: "Victoria illa *Pompeii* primum ad margaritas gemmasque mores inclinavit." H. N. xxxvii. 6. See what he says on the spoils of *Scipio Asiaticus* and *Cn. Manlius*, xxxiii. 53. xxxiv. 8. cf. Liv. xxxix. 6.

[3] See Niebuhr's Lectures, vol. i. p. 406, and the note.

[4] Much of our best information concerning the state of the provinces is derived from Cicero's celebrated "Speeches against Verres," and his own "Cilician Correspondence," to which we shall again have occasion to refer. His "Speech in Defence of Flaccus" throws much light on the condition of the Jews under the Romans. We must not place too much confidence in the picture there given of this Ephesian governor.

vices of Greece and the East had inundated Italy and the West: and the Pantheon was only the monument of a compromise among a multitude of effete superstitions. It is true that a remarkable religious toleration was produced by this state of things: and it is probable that for some short time Christianity itself shared the advantage of it. But still the temper of the times was essentially both cruel and profane; and the Apostles were soon exposed to its bitter persecution. The Roman empire was destitute of that unity which the Gospel gives to mankind. It was a kingdom of this world; and the human race were groaning for the better peace of "a kingdom not of this world."

Thus, in the very condition of the Roman empire, and the miserable state of its mixed population, we can recognise a negative preparation for the Gospel of Christ. This tyranny and oppression called for a *Consoler*, as much as the moral sickness of the Greeks called for a Healer; a Messiah was needed by the whole empire as much as by the Jews, though not looked for with the same conscious expectation. But we have no difficulty in going much further than this, and we cannot hesitate to discover in the circumstances of the world at this period, significant traces of a positive preparation for the Gospel.

It should be remembered, in the first place, that the Romans had already become Greek to some considerable extent, before they were the political masters of those eastern countries, where the language, mythology, and literature of Greece had become more or less familiar. How early, how widely, and how permanently this Greek influence prevailed, and how deeply it entered into the mind of educated Romans, we know from their surviving writings, and from the biography of eminent men. Cicero, who was governor of Cilicia about half a century before the birth of St. Paul, speaks in strong terms of the universal spread of the Greek tongue among the instructed classes;[1] and about the time of the Apostle's martyrdom, Agricola, the conqueror of Britain, was receiving a Greek education at Marseilles.[2] Is it too much to say, that the general Latin conquest was providentially delayed till the Romans had been sufficiently imbued with the language and ideas of their predecessors, and had incorporated many parts of that civilisation with their own?

And if the mysterious wisdom of the divine pre-arrangements is illustrated by the period of the spread of the Greek language, it is illus-

[1] Cicero, in his speech for Archias (who was born at *Antioch*, "celebri urbe et copiosa, atque eruditissimis hominibus liberalissimisque studiis affluente"), says, in reference to this spread of the Greek literature and language,—"Erat Italia tunc plena Græcarum artium ac disciplinarum:" and again, "Græca leguntur in omnibus fere gentibus: Latina suis finibus, exiguis sane, continentur."

[2] Tac. Agr.: "Sedem ac magistram studiorum Massiliam habuit, locum Græca comitate et provinciali parsimonia mistum ac bene compositum"

trated no less by that of the completion and maturity of the Roman government. When all parts of the civilised world were bound together in one empire,—when one common organisation pervaded the whole,—when channels of communication were everywhere opened—when new facilities of travelling were provided,—then was "the fulness of times" (Gal. iv. 4), then the Messiah came. The Greek language had already been prepared as a medium for preserving and transmitting the doctrine: the Roman government was now prepared to help the progress even of that religion which it persecuted. The manner in which it spread through the provinces is well exemplified in the life of St. Paul: his right of citizenship rescued him in Judæa and in Macedonia; he converted one governor in Cyprus, was protected by another in Achaia, and was sent from Jerusalem to Rome by a third. The time was indeed approaching, when all the complicated weight of the central tyranny, and of the provincial governments, was to fall on the new and irresistible religion. But before this took place, it had begun to grow up in close connection with all departments of the empire. When the supreme government itself became Christian, the ecclesiastical polity was permanently regulated in conformity with the actual constitution of the state. Nor was the empire broken up, till the separate fragments, which have become the nations of modern Europe, were themselves portions of the Catholic Church.

But in all that we have said of the condition of the Roman world, one important and widely diffused element of its population has not been mentioned. We have lost sight for some time of the Jews, and we must return to the subject of their dispersion, which was purposely deferred till we had shown how the intellectual civilisation of the Greeks, and the organising civilisation of the Romans, had, through a long series of remarkable events, been brought in contact with the religious civilisation of the Hebrews; it remains that we point out that one peculiarity of the Jewish people, which made this contact almost universal in every part of the empire.

Their dispersion began early; though, early and late, their attachment to Judæa has always been the same. Like the Highlanders of Switzerland and Scotland, they seem to have combined a tendency to foreign settlements with the most passionate love of their native land. The first scattering of the Jews was compulsory, and began with the Assyrian exile, when, about the time of the building of Rome, natives of Galilee and Samaria were carried away by the Eastern monarchs; and this was followed by the Babylonian exile, when the tribes of Judah and Benjamin were removed at different epochs,—when Daniel was brought to Babylon, and Ezekiel to the river Chebar. That this earliest dispersion was not without influential results may be inferred from these facts:—that, about the time of the battles of Salamis and Marathon, a Jew was the minister, another Jew the cupbearer, and a Jewess the consort, of a Persian monarch. That they enjoyed many privileges in this foreign country, and that their condition was not always oppressive, may be gathered from this,—that when Cyrus gave them permission to return, the majority remained in their new home, in preference to their native land Thus that great Jewish colony began in Babylonia, the existence of which may be traced in Apostolic times,[1] and which retained its influence long after in the Talmudical schools. These Hebrew settlements may be followed through various parts of the continental East, to the borders of the Caspian, and even to China.[2] We however are more concerned with the coasts and islands of Western Asia. Jews had settled in Syria and Phœnicia before the time of Alexander the Great. But in treating of this subject, the great stress is to be laid on the policy of Seleucus, who, in founding Antioch, raised them to the same political position with the other citizens. One of his successors on the throne, Antiochus the Great, established two thousand Jewish families in Lydia and Phrygia. From hence they would spread into Pamphylia and Galatia, and along the western coasts from Ephesus to Troas. And the ordinary channels of communication, in conjunction with that tendency to trade which already began to characterise this wonderful people, would easily bring them to the islands, such as Cyprus[3] and Rhodes.

Their oldest settlement in Africa was that which took place after the murder of the Babylonian governor of Judæa, and which is connected with the name of the prophet Jeremiah.[4] But, as in the case of Antioch, our chief attention is called to the great metropolis of the period of the Greek kings. The Jewish quarter of Alexandria is well known in history; and the colony of Hellenistic Jews in Lower Egypt is of greater importance than that of their Aramaic brethren in Babylonia. Alexander himself brought Jews and Samaritans to his famous city; Ptolemy Lagus brought many more; and many betook themselves hither of their free will, that they might escape from the incessant troubles which disturbed the peace of their fatherland. Nor was their influence confined to Egypt, but they became known on one side in Ethiopia, the country of Queen Candace,[5] and spread on the other in great numbers to the "parts of Libya about Cyrene."[6]

[1] See 1 Pet. v. 13.

[2] See "Ritter's Erdkunde," Thl. 4 (*Asien.*) 598.

[3] The farming of the copper mines in Cyprus by Herod (Jos. A. xvi. 4, 5) may have attracted many Jews. M. Salvador, in his last work (Histoire de la Domination Romaine en Judée, &c., 1847), says it actually did; but this is not proved. There is a Cyprian inscription in "Böckh" (No. 2628), which seems to refer to one of the Herods.

[4] See 2 Kings xxv. 22–26. Jer. xliii. xliv.

[5] Acts viii. 27.

[6] Acts ii. 10. The second book of Maccabees is the abridgment of a work written

Under what circumstances the Jews made their first appearance in Europe is unknown; but it is natural to suppose that those islands of the Archipelago which, as Humboldt[1] has said, were like a bridge for the passage of civilisation, became the means of the advance of Judaism. The journey of the proselyte Lydia from Thyatira to Philippi (A. xvi. 14), and the voyage of Aquila and Priscilla from Corinth to Ephesus (A. xviii. 18), are only specimens of mercantile excursions which must have begun at a far earlier period. Philo mentions Jews in Thessaly, Bœotia, Macedonia, Ætolia, and Attica, in Argos and Corinth, in the other parts of Peloponnesus, and in the islands of Eubœa and Crete: and St. Luke, in the Acts of the Apostles, speaks of them in Philippi, Thessalonica, and Berœa, in Athens, in Corinth, and in Rome. The first Jews came to Rome to decorate a triumph; but they were soon set free from captivity, and gave the name to the "Synagogue of the Libertines"[2] in Jerusalem. They owed to Julius Cæsar those privileges in the Western Capital which they had obtained from Alexander in the Eastern. They became influential, and made proselytes. They spread into other towns of Italy; and in the time of St. Paul's boyhood we find them in large numbers in the island of Sardinia, just as we have previously seen them established in that of Cyprus.[3] With regard to Gaul, we know at least that two sons of Herod were banished, about this same period, to the banks of the Rhone; and if St. Paul ever accomplished that journey to Spain, of which he speaks in his letters, it is probable that he found there some of the scattered children of his own people. We do not seek to pursue them further; but, after a few words on the proselytes, we must return to the earliest scenes of the Apostle's career.[4]

The subject of the proselytes is sufficiently important to demand a separate notice. Under this term we include at present all those who were attracted in various degrees of intensity towards Judaism,—from those who by circumcision had obtained full access to all the privileges of the temple-worship, to those who only professed a general respect for the Mosaic religion, and attended as hearers in the synagogues. Many pros-

by a Hellenistic Jew of Cyrene. A Jew or proselyte of Cyrene bore our Saviour's cross. And the mention of this city occurs more than once in the Acts of the Apostles.

[1] Kosmos, Sabine's English Translation, vol. ii. p. 120.

[2] This body doubtless consisted of manumitted Jewish slaves. See Wolf and the later commentators on Acts vi. 9.

[3] In this case, however, they were forcibly sent to the island, to die of the bad climate See Tac. Ann. ii. 85. Suet. Tib. 36. Jos. An. xviii. 3, 5.

[4] The history of the Jewish dispersions will be found in an excellent little essay devoted to the subject, Joh. Remond's "Versuch einer Geschichte der Ausbreitung des Judenthums von Cyrus bis auf den gänzlichen Untergang des Jüdischen Staats:" Leipzig, 1789; in the introductory chapter of "Wiltsch's Handbuch der Kirchlichen Geographie," Gotha, 1843, which has been principally used here; and in a chapter in the second volume of Jost's larger work, -the "Geschichte der Israeliten," 1820–28.

elytes were attached to the Jewish communities wherever they were dispersed.[1] Even in their own country and its vicinity, the number, both in early and later times, was not inconsiderable. The Queen of Sheba, in the Old Testament; Candace, Queen of Ethiopia, in the New; and King Izates, with his mother Helena, mentioned by Josephus, are only royal representatives of a large class. During the time of the Maccabees, some alien tribes were forcibly incorporated with the Jews. This was the case with the Ituræans, and probably with the Moabites, and, above all, with the Edomites, with whose name that of the Herodian family is historically connected.[2] How far Judaism extended among the vague collection of tribes called Arabians, we can only conjecture from the curious history of the Homerites,[3] and from the actions of such chieftains as Aretas (2 Cor. xi. 32). But as we travel towards the West and North, into countries better known, we find no lack of evidence of the moral effect of the synagogues, with their worship of JEHOVAH, and their prophecies of the Messiah. "Nicolas of Antioch" (Acts vi. 5) is only one of that "vast multitude of Greeks" who were attracted in that city to the Jewish doctrine and ritual.[4] In Damascus, we are even told by the same authority that the great majority of the women were proselytes; a fact which receives a remarkable illustration from what happened to Paul at Iconium (Acts xiii. 50). But all further details may be postponed till we follow him into the synagogues, where he so often addressed a mingled audience of "Jews of the dispersion" and "devout" strangers.

This chapter may be suitably concluded by some notice of the provinces of *Cilicia* and *Judæa.* This will serve as an illustration of what has been said above, concerning the state of the Roman provinces generally; it will exemplify the mixture of Jews, Greeks, and Romans in the east of the Mediterranean, and it will be a fit introduction to what must immediately succeed. For these are the two provinces which require our attention in the early life of the Apostle Paul.

Both these provinces were once under the sceptre of the line of the Seleucidæ, or Greek kings of Syria; and both of them, though originally

[1] The following are the testimonies of prejudiced Heathens:

Ἡ χώρα Ἰουδαία καὶ αὐτοὶ Ἰουδαῖοι ὠνομάδαται . . . ἡ δὲ ἐπίκλησις αὕτῃ . . . φέρει . . . . καὶ ἐπὶ τοὺς ἄλλους ἀνθρώπους, ὅσοι τὰ νόμιμα ἀυτῶν, καίπερ ἀλλοεθνεῖς ὄντες, ζηλοῦσι.—*Dio. Cas.* xxxvii. 16, 17.

Transgressi in morem eorum (Judæorum) idem usurpant. Nec quicquam prius imbuunter quam contemnere Deos, exuere patriam, parentes, liberos, fratres vilia habere -*Tac. H. V.* 5.

> Romanas autem soliti contemnere leges,
> Judaicum ediscunt et servant ac metuunt jus,
> Tradidit arcano quodcunque volumine Moses.—*Juv.* xiv. 100.

[2] See Wiltsch as above, and the passages quoted from Josephus.

[3] See it in Basnage, Histoire des Juifs, book vi. ch. 20.

[4] Joseph. B. J. vii. 3. 3.

inhabited by a "barbarous" population, received more or less of the influence of Greek civilisation. If the map is consulted, it will be seen that Antioch, the capital of the Greco-Syrian kings, is situated nearly in the angle where the coast-line of Cilicia, running eastwards, and that of Judæa, extended northwards, are brought to an abrupt meeting. It will be seen also, that, more or less parallel to each of these coasts, there is a line of mountains, not far from the sea, which are brought into contact with each other in heavy and confused forms, near the same angle; the principal break in the continuity of either of them being the valley of the Orontes, which passes by Antioch. One of these mountain lines is the range of *Mount Taurus,* which is so often mentioned as a great geographical boundary by the writers of Greece and Rome; and *Cilicia* extends partly over Taurus itself, and partly between it and the sea. The other range is that of *Lebanon*—a name made sacred by the scriptures and poetry of the Jews; and where its towering eminences subside towards the south into a land of hills and vallies and level plains, there is *Judæa,* once the country of promise and possession to the chosen people, but a Roman province in the time of the Apostles.

Cilicia, in the sense in which the word was used under the early Roman emperors, comprehended two districts, of nearly equal extent,[1] but of very different character. The Western portion, or *Rough Cilicia,* as it was called, was a collection of the branches of Mount Taurus, which come down in large masses to the sea, and form that projection of the coast which divides the Bay of Issus from that of Pamphylia. The inhabitants of the whole of this district were notorious for their robberies:[2] the northern portion, under the name of Isauria, providing innumerable strongholds for marauders by land; and the southern, with its excellent timber, its cliffs, and small harbours, being a natural home for pirates. The Isaurians maintained their independence with such determined obstinacy, that in a later period of the Empire, the Romans were willing to resign all appearance of subduing them, and were content to surround them with a *cordon* of forts. The natives of the coast of Rough Cilicia began to extend their piracies as the strength of the kings of Syria and Egypt declined. They found in the progress of the Roman power, for some time, an encouragement rather than a hindrance; for they were actively engaged in an extensive and abominable slave trade, of which the island of Delos was the great market; and the opulent families of Rome were in need of slaves, and were not more scrupulous than some Christian nations of modern times about the means of obtaining them. But the expeditions of these buc-

[1] Mannert says (Geographie der Griechen und Römer, "Kleinasien," 1801) that the eastern division is about 15 German geographical miles in breadth by 20 in length, the western 10 by 30. Cilicia, p. 33.

[2] See a very descriptive passage in Ammian. Marc. xiv. 2

caneers of the Mediterranean became at last quite intolerable; their fleets seemed innumerable; their connexions were extended far beyond their own coasts; all commerce was paralysed; and they began to arouse that attention at Rome which the more distant pirates of the Eastern Archipelago are beginning to excite in England. A vast expedition was fitted out under the command of Pompey the Great; thousands of piratic vessels were burnt on the coast of Cilicia, and the inhabitants dispersed. A perpetual service was thus done to the cause of civilisation, and the Mediterranean was made safe for the voyages of merchants and Apostles. The town of Soli, on the borders of the two divisions of Cilicia, received the name of Pompeiopolis,[1] in honour of the great conqueror, and the splendid remains of a colonnade which led from the harbour to the city may be considered a monument of this signal destruction of the enemies of order and peace.

The Eastern, or *Flat Cilicia*, was a rich and extensive plain. Its prolific vegetation is praised both by the earlier and later classical writers,[2] and even under the neglectful government of the Turks, is still noticed by modern travellers.[3] From this circumstance, and still more from its peculiar physical configuration, it was a possession of great political importance. Walled off from the neighbouring countries by a high barrier of mountains,[4] which sweep irregularly round it from Pompeiopolis and Rough Cilicia to the Syrian coast on the North of Antioch,—with one pass leading up into the interior of Asia Minor, and another giving access to the valley of the Orontes,—it was naturally the high road both of trading caravans and of military expeditions. Through this country Cyrus marched, to depose his brother from the Persian throne. It was here that the decisive victory was obtained by Alexander over Darius. This

1 A similar case, on a small scale, is that of Philippeville in Algeria; and the progress of the French power, since the accession of Louis Philippe, in Northern Africa, is perhaps the nearest parallel in modern times to the history of a Roman province. As far as regards the pirates, Lord Exmouth, in 1816, really did the work of Pompey the Great. It may be doubted whether Marshal Bugeaud was more lenient to the Arabs, than Cicero to the Eleuthero-Cilicians.

Chrysippus the Stoic, whose father was a native of Tarsus, and Aratus, whom St. Paul quotes, lived at Soli. Cf. Mannert, p. 69.

2 For instance, Xen. Anab. i. 2. Ammian. Marc. xiv. 7.

3 Laborde's illustrated work on Syria and Asia Minor contains some luxuriant specimens of the modern vegetation of Tarsus; but the banana and the prickly pear were introduced into the Mediterranean long after St. Paul's day.

4 This mountain-wall is described by no one more accurately and vividly than by Quintus Curtius:—"Perpetuo jugo montis asperi et prærupti Cilicia includitur: quod quum a mari surgat, velut sinu quodam flexuque curvatum, rursus altero cornu in diversum litus excurrit. Per hoc dorsum, quà maximè introrsum mari cedit, asperi tres aditus, et perangusti sunt, quorum uno Cilicia intranda est, Campestris eadem, quà vergit ad mare, planitiem ejus crebris distinguentibus rivis. Pyramus et Cydnus inclyti amnes fluunt." De Rebus Gestis Alex. iii. 4.

plain has since seen the hosts of Western Crusaders; and, in our own day, has been the field of operations of hostile Mahommedan armies, Turkish and Egyptian. The Greek kings of Egypt endeavoured, long ago, to tear it from the Greek kings of Syria. The Romans left it at first in the possession of Antiochus: but the line of Mount Taurus could not permanently arrest them: and the letters of Cicero are among the earliest and most interesting monuments of Roman Cilicia.

Situated near the western border of the Cilician plain, where the river Cydnus flows in a cold and rapid stream[1] from the snows of Taurus to the sea, was the city of Tarsus, the capital of the whole province, and "no mean city" (A. xxi. 39) in the history of the ancient world. Its coins

COIN OF TARSUS. HADRIAN.

reveal to us its greatness through a long series of years:—alike in the period which intervened between Xerxes and Alexander,—and under the Roman sway, when it exulted in the name of *Metropolis*,—and long after Hadrian had rebuilt it, and issued his new coinage with the old mythological types.[2] In the intermediate period, which is that of St. Paul, we have the testimony of a native of this part of Asia Minor, from which we may infer that Tarsus was in the Eastern basin of the Mediterranean, almost what Marseilles was in the Western. Strabo says[3] that, in all that relates to philosophy and general education, it was even more illustrious than Athens and Alexandria. From his description it is evident that its main character was that of a Greek city, where the Greek language was spoken, and Greek literature studiously cultivated. But we should be wrong in supposing that the general population of the province was of Greek origin, or spoke the Greek tongue. When Cyrus came with his

[1] Διαῤῥεῖ ἀυτὴν μέσην ὁ Κύδνος ..... ψυχρόν τε καὶ ταχὺ τὸ ῥεῦμά ἐστιν. Strabo, xiv. 5.

[2] This coin was struck under Hadrian, and is preserved in the British Museum. *Anazarbus* on the Pyramus was a rival city, and from the time of Caracalla is found assuming the title of Metropolis; but it was only an empty honour. Eckhel says of it (p. 42): "Hoc titulo constanter deinceps gloriabatur, etsi is præter honorem illi nihil addidit; nam quod ad juris contentionem attinebat, id omne ad Tarsum veram Ciliciæ metropolim pertinuit, ut existimat Belleyus." The same figures of the Lion and the Bull appear in a fine series of silver coins assigned by the Duc de Luynes (Numismatique des Satrapies) to the period between Xerxes and Alexander.

[3] Bk. xiv. ch. 5. The passage will be quoted at length hereafter.

army from the Western Coast, and still later, when Alexander penetrated into Cilicia, they found the inhabitants "Barbarians." Nor is it likely that the old race would be destroyed, or the old language obliterated, especially in the mountain districts, during the reign of the Seleucid kings. We must rather conceive of Tarsus as like Brest in Brittany, or like Toulon, in Provence,—a city where the language of refinement is spoken and written, in the midst of a ruder population, who use a different language, and possess no literature of their own.

If we turn now to consider the position of this province and city under the Romans, we are led to notice two different systems of policy which they adopted in their subject dominions. The purpose of Rome was to make the world subservient to herself: but this might be accomplished directly or indirectly. A governor might be sent from Rome to take the absolute command of a province: or some native chief might have a kingdom, an ethnarchy, or a tetrarchy assigned to him, in which he was nominally independent, but really subservient, and often tributary. Some provinces were rich and productive, or essentially important in the military sense, and these were committed to Romans under the Senate or the Emperor. Others might be worthless or troublesome, and fit only to reward the services of an useful instrument, or to occupy the energies of a dangerous ally. Both these systems were adopted in the East and in the West. We have examples of both—in Spain and in Gaul—in Cilicia and in Judæa. In Asia Minor they were so irregularly combined, and the territories of the independent sovereigns were so capriciously granted or removed, extended or curtailed, that it is often difficult to ascertain what the actual boundaries of the provinces were at a given epoch. Not to enter into any minute history in the case of Cilicia, it will be enough to say, that its rich and level plain in the East was made a Roman province by Pompey, and so remained, while certain districts in the Western portion were assigned, at different periods, to various native chieftains.[1] Thus the territories of Amyntas, King of Galatia, were extended in this direction by Antony, when he was preparing for his great struggle with Augustus:[2]—just as a modern Rajah may be strengthened on the banks

[1] To Ariobarzanes of Cappadocia by the influence of Pompey; to Tarkondimotus, whose sons espoused the cause of Antony; and finally to Archelaus by Augustus. Some part of the coast also was at one time assigned to Cleopatra, for the sake of the timber for shipbuilding. See Mannert's Geographie, "Kleinasien," pp. 45, 46.

[2] The territories of Amyntas were brought down to the coast of Pamphylia, so as to include the important harbour of Side. There is no better way of studying the history of Asia Minor than by means of coins, with the assistance of Eckhel, Mionnet, Sestini, &c. The writer of this is desirous to acknowledge his obligations to many conversations with the gentlemen who are occupied in the Medal Room of the British Museum, Mr. Burgon, Mr. Newton, &c.

of the Indus, in connection with our wars against Scinde and the Sikhs.[1] For some time the whole of Cilicia was a consolidated province under the first emperors: but again, in the reign of Claudius, we find a portion of the same Western district assigned to a king called Polemo II. It is needless to pursue the history further. In St. Paul's early life the political state of the inhabitants of Cilicia would be that of subjects of a Roman governor: and Roman officials, if not Roman soldiers, would be a familiar sight to the Jews who were settled in Tarsus.[2]

We shall have many opportunities of describing the condition of provinces under the dominion of Rome; but it may be interesting here to allude to the information which may be gathered from the writings of that distinguished man, who was governor of Cilicia a few years after its first reduction by Pompey. He was entrusted with the civil and military superintendence of a large district in this corner of the Mediterranean, comprehending not only Cilicia, but Pamphylia, Pisidia, Lycaonia, and the island of Cyprus; and he has left a record of all the details of his policy in a long series of letters, which are a curious monument of the Roman procedure in the management of conquered provinces, and which possess a double interest to us, from their frequent allusions to the same places which St. Paul refers to in his Epistles. This correspondence represents to us the governor as surrounded by the adulation of obsequious Asiatic Greeks. He travels with an interpreter, for Latin is the official language; he puts down banditti, and is saluted by the title of Imperator; letters are written on various, subjects, to the governors of neighbouring provinces,—for instance, Syria, Asia, and Bithynia; ceremonious communications take place with the independent chieftains. The friendly relations of Cicero with Deiotarus, King of Galatia, and his son, remind us of the interview of Pilate and Herod in the Gospel, or of Festus and Agrippa in the Acts. Cicero's letters are rather too full of a boastful commendation of his own integrity; but from what he says that he did, we may infer by contrast what was done by others who were less scrupulous in the discharge of the same responsibilities. He allowed free access to his person: he refused expensive monuments in his honour; he declined the proffered present of the pauper King of Cappadocia;[3] he abstained from exacting the customary expenses from the states which he traversed on his march; he remitted to the treasury the monies which were not expended on his province; he would not place in official situations those who

[1] This has been the case with the Rajah of Bahawalpoor. See the articles on Indian news in the newspapers of 1848.

[2] Tarsus, as an *Urbs Libera*, would have the privilege of being garrisoned by its own soldiers. See next Chapter.

[3] See Hor. 1. Ep. vi. 39:

Mancipiis locuples eget æris Cappadocum Rex.

were engaged in trade; he treated the local Greek magistrates with due consideration, and contrived at the same time to give satisfaction to the Publicans. From all this it may be easily inferred with how much corruption, cruelty, and pride, the Romans usually governed; and how miserable must have been the condition of a province under a Verres or an Appius, a Pilate or a Felix. So far as we remember, the Jews are not mentioned in any of Cicero's Cilician letters: but if we may draw conclusions from a speech which he made at Rome in defence of a contemporary governor of Asia,[1] he regarded them with much contempt, and would be likely to treat them with harshness and injustice.[2]

That Polemo II., who has lately been mentioned as a king in Cilicia, was one of those curious links which the history of those times exhibits between Heathenism, Judaism, and Christianity. He became a Jew to marry Berenice,[3] who afterwards forsook him, and whose name, after once appearing in Sacred History (Acts xxv. xxvi.), is lastly associated with that of Titus, the destroyer of Jerusalem. The name of Berenice will at once suggest the family of the Herods, and transport our thoughts to Judæa.

The same general features may be traced in this province as in that which we have been attempting to describe. In some respects, indeed, the details of its history are different. When Cilicia was a province, it formed a separate jurisdiction, with a governor of its own, immediately responsible to Rome: but Judæa, in its provincial period, was only an appendage to Syria. It has been said[4] that the position of the ruler resident at Cæsarea in connection with the supreme authority at Antioch may be best understood by comparing it with that of the governor of Madras or Bombay under the governor-general who resides at Calcutta. The comparison is very just: and British India might supply a further parallel. We might say that when Judæa was not strictly a province, but a monarchy under the protectorate of Rome, it bore the same relation to the contiguous province of Syria, which the territories of the king of Oude[5] bear to the presidency of Bengal. Judæa was twice a monarchy: and thus its history furnishes illustrations of the two systems pursued by the Romans, of direct and indirect government.

[1] This was L. Valerius Flaccus, who had served in Cilicia, and was afterwards made Governor of *Asia*,—that district with which, and its capital Ephesus, we are so familiar in the Acts of the Apostles.

[2] See especially Cic. Flac. 28, and for the opinion which educated Romans had of the Jews, see Hor. 1 Sat. iv. 143. v. 100. ix. 69.

[3] "Ut erat vir stolidi ingenii, &c." says Eckhel. He was the last King of Pontus. By Caligula he was made King of Bosphorus; but Claudius gave him part of Cilicia instead of it. See Joseph. A. xx. 7, 3. Dio. Cass. lx. 8. Suet. Nero. 18.

[4] See the introduction to Dr. Traill's Josephus, a work which has been unfortunately interrupted by the death of the translator during the Irish famine.

[5] Another coincidence is, that we made the Nabob of Oude a king. He had previously been hereditary Vizier of the Mogul.

Another important contrast must be noticed in the histories of these two provinces. In the Greek period of Judæa, there was a time of noble and vigorous independence. Antiochus Epiphanes, the eighth of the line of the Seleucidæ, in pursuance of a general system of policy, by which he sought to unite all his different territories through the Greek religion, endeavoured to introduce the worship of Jupiter into Jerusalem. Such an attempt might have been very successful in Syria or Cilicia: but in Judæa it kindled a flame of religious indignation, which did not cease to burn till the yoke of the Seleucidæ was entirely thrown off: the name of Antiochus Epiphanes was ever afterwards held in abhorrence by the Jews, and a special fast was kept up in memory of the time when the "abomination of desolation" stood in the holy place. The champions of the independence of the Jewish nation and the purity of the Jewish religion were the family of the Maccabees or Asmonæans: and a hundred years before the birth of Christ the first Hyrcanus was reigning over a prosperous and independent kingdom. But in the time of the second Hyrcanus and his brother, the family of the Maccabees was not what it had been, and Judæa was ripening for the dominion of Rome. Pompey the Great, the same conqueror who had already subjected Cilicia, appeared in Damascus, and there judged the cause of the two brothers. All the country was full of his fame.[1] In the spring of the year 63 he came down by the valley of the Jordan, his Roman soldiers occupied the ford where Joshua had crossed over, and from the Mount of Olives he looked down upon Jerusalem. From that day Judæa was virtually under the government

COIN OF ANTIOCHUS EPIPHANES, WITH HEAD OF JUPITER.[2]

[1] See Jost's "Allgemeine Geschichte des Israelitischen Volks," vol. ii. p. 18–21, where a good and rapid sketch of the events is given.

[2] This beautiful coin, preserved in the British Museum, is given here, in consequence of the head of Jupiter which appears on the obverse, in place of the portrait usual in the Alexandrian, Seleucid, and Macedonian series. Since such emblems on ancient coins have always sacred meanings, it is very probable that this arose from the religious movement alluded to in the text. For the religious symbolism of Greek and Roman coins, see Mr. Burgon's "Inquiry into the Motive which influenced the Ancients in the Choice of the Various Representations which we find stamped on their Money," in the Numismatic Journal for Sept. 1836.

REMAINS OF THE ANCIENT BRIDGE AT JERUSALEM.

of Rome.[1] It is true, that, after a brief support given to the reigning family, a new native dynasty was raised to the throne. Antipater, a man of Idumean birth, had been minister of the Maccabæan kings: but they were the *Rois Fainéants* of Palestine, and he was the *Maire du Palais.* In the midst of the confusion of the great civil wars, the Herodian family succeeded to the Asmonæan, as the Carlovingian line in France succeeded that of Clovis. As Pepin was followed by Charlemagne, so Antipater prepared a crown for his son Herod.

At first Herod the Great espoused the cause of Antony; but he contrived to remedy his mistake by paying a prompt visit after the battle of Actium, to Augustus in the island of Rhodes. This singular interview of the Jewish prince with the Roman conqueror in a Greek island was the beginning of an important period for the Hebrew nation. An exotic civilisation was systematically introduced and extended. Those Greek influences, which had been begun under the Seleucidæ, and not discontinued under the Asmonæans, were now more widely diffused: and the Roman customs,[2] which had hitherto been comparatively unknown, were now made familiar. Herod was indeed too wise, and knew the Jews too well, to attempt, like Antiochus, to introduce foreign institutions, without any regard to their religious feelings. He endeavoured to ingratiate himself with them by rebuilding and decorating their national temple; and a part of that magnificent bridge which was connected with the great southern colonnade is still believed to exist,—remaining, in its vast proportions and Roman form, an appropriate monument of the Herodian period of Judæa.[3] The period when Herod was reigning at Jerusalem under the protectorate of Augustus was chiefly remarkable for great architectural works, for the promotion of commerce, the influx of strangers, and the increased diffusion of the two great languages of the heathen world. The names of places are themselves a monument of the spirit of the times. As Tarsus was called Juliopolis from Julius Cæsar, and Soli Pompeiopolis from his great rival, so Samaria was called Sebaste after the Greek name of Augustus, and the new metropolis, which was built by Herod on the sea-shore, was called Cæsarea in honour of the same Latin emperor: while Antipatris,

1 Pompey heard of the death of Mithridates at Jericho. His army crossed at Scythopolis, by the ford immediately below the lake of Tiberias. (See Herod. i. 105.)

2 Antiochus Epiphanes (who was called Epimanes from his mad conduct) is said to have made himself ridiculous by adopting Roman fashions, and walking about the streets of Antioch in a toga.

3 It is right to say that there is much controversy about the real origin of these remains. Dr. Robinson believes that they were part of a bridge connected with the Temple, but strangely refers them to the time of Solomon: Mr. Williams holds them to be a fragment of the great Christian works constructed in this southern part of the Temple-area in the age of Justinian: Mr. Fergusson conceives them to be part of the bridge which joined Mount Zion to the Temple, but assigns them to Herod.

on the road (A. xxiii. 31) between the old capital and the new, still commemorated the name of the king's Idumæan father. We must not suppose that the internal change in the minds of the people was proportional to the magnitude of these outward improvements. They suffered much, and their hatred grew towards Rome and towards the Herods. A parallel might be drawn between the state of Judæa under Herod the Great, and that of Egypt under Mahomet Ali,[1] where great works have been successfully accomplished, where the spread of ideas has been promoted, traffic made busy and prosperous, and communication with the civilised world wonderfully increased,—but where the mass of the people has continued to be miserable and degraded.

After Herod's death, the same influences still continued to operate in Judæa. Archelaus persevered in his father's policy, though destitute of his father's energy. The same may be said of the other sons, Antipas and Philip, in their contiguous principalities. All the Herods were great builders, and eager partizans of the Roman emperors: and we are familiar in the Gospels with that *Cæsarea* (Cæsarea Philippi), which one of them built in the upper part of the valley of the Jordan, and named in honour of Augustus,—and with that *Tiberias* on the banks of the lake of Gennesareth, which bore the name of his wicked successor. But while Antipas and Philip still retained their dominions under the protectorate of the emperor, Archelaus had been banished, and the weight of the Roman power had descended still more heavily on Judæa. It was placed under the direct jurisdiction of a governor, residing at Cæsarea by the Sea, and depending, as we have seen above, on the governor of Syria at Antioch. And now we are made familiar with those features which might be adduced as characterising any other province of the same epoch,—the prætorium (Joh. xviii. 28),—the publicans (Luke iii. 12. xix. 2),—the tribute-money (Mat. xxii. 19),—soldiers and centurions recruited in Italy (Acts x. 1),[2]—Cæsar the only king (Joh. xix. 15)—and the ultimate appeal against the injustice of the governor (Acts xxv. 11). In this period the ministry, death, and resurrection of Jesus Christ took place, the first preaching of his Apostles, and the conversion of St. Paul. But once more a change came over the political fortunes of Judæa. Herod Agrippa was the friend of Caligula, as Herod the Great had been the friend of Augustus; and when Tiberius died, he received the grant of an independent principality

[1] There are many points of resemblance between the character and fortunes of Herod and those of Mahomet Ali: the chief differences are those of the times. Herod secured his position by the influence of Augustus; Mahomet Ali secured his by the agreement of the European powers.

[2] There is little doubt that this is the meaning of the "*Italian Band.*" Most of the soldiers quartered in Syria were recruited in the province. See a full discussion of this subject in Biscoe's "History of the Acts confirmed," chap. ix. The "Augustan Band" (xxvii. 1) seems to have a different meaning. See Vol. II. chap. xxii.

in the north of Palestine.[1] He was able to ingratiate himself with Claudius, the succeeding emperor. Judæa was added to his dominion, which now embraced the whole circle of the territory ruled by his grandfather. By this time St. Paul was actively pursuing his apostolic career. We need not, therefore, advance beyond this point, in a chapter which is only intended to be a general introduction to the Apostle's history.

Our desire has been to give a picture of the condition of the world at this particular epoch: and we have thought that no grouping would be so successful as that which should consist of Jews, Greeks, and Romans. Nor is this an artificial or unnatural arrangement: for these three nations were the divisions of the civilised world. And in the view of a religious mind they were more than this. They were "the three peoples of God's election; two for things temporal, and one for things eternal. Yet even in the things eternal they were allowed to minister. Greek cultivation and Roman polity prepared men for Christianity."[2] These three peoples stand in the closest relation to the whole human race. The Christian, when he imagines himself among those spectators who stood round the cross, and gazes in spirit upon that "superscription," which the Jewish scribe, the Greek proselyte, and the Roman soldier could read, each in his own tongue, feels that he is among those who are the representatives of all humanity.[3] In the ages which precede the crucifixion, these three languages were like threads which guided us through the labyrinth of history. And they are still among the best guides of our thought, as we travel through the ages which succeed it. How great has been the honour of the Greek and Latin tongues! They followed the fortunes of a triumphant church. Instead of heathen languages, they gradually became Christian. As before they had been employed to express the best thoughts of unassisted humanity, so afterwards they became the exponents of Christian doctrine and the channels of Christian devotion. The words of Plato and Cicero fell from the lips and pen of Chrysostom and Augustine. And still those two languages are associated together in the work of Christian education, and made the instruments for training the minds

[1] He obtained under Caligula, first, the tetrarchy of his uncle Philip, who died; and then that of his uncle Antipas, who followed his brother Archelaus into banishment.

[2] Dr. Arnold, in the journal of his tour in 1840 (Life, ii. 413, 2d edit.). The passage continues thus:—"As Mahometanism can bear witness; for the East, when it abandoned Greece and Rome, could only reproduce Judaism. Mahometanism, six hundred years after Christ, proving that the Eastern man could bear nothing perfect, justifies the wisdom of God in Judaism."

[3] This is true in another, and perhaps a higher sense. The *Roman*, powerful but not happy—the *Greek*, distracted with the enquiries of an unsatisfying philosophy—the *Jew*, bound hand and foot with the chain of a ceremonial law, all are together round the cross. CHRIST is crucified in the midst of them—crucified for all. The "superscription of His accusation" speaks to all the same language of peace, pardon, and love.

of the young in the greatest nations of the earth. And how deep and pathetic is the interest which attaches to the Hebrew! Here the thread seems to be broken. "JESUS, King of the Jews," in Hebrew characters. It is like the last word of the Jewish Scriptures,—the last warning of the chosen people. A cloud henceforth is upon the people and the language of Israel. "Blindness in part is happened unto Israel, till the fulness of the Gentiles be come in." Once again Jesus, after His ascension, spake openly from Heaven "in the Hebrew tongue" (Acts xxvi. 14): but the words were addressed to that Apostle who was called to preach the Gospel to the philosophers of Greece, and in the emperor's palace at Rome.

Here lies Faustina. In peace.[1]

[1] A Christian tomb with the three languages, from Maitland's "Church in the Catacombs," p. 77. The name is *Latin*, the inscription *Greek*, and the word Shalom or "Peace" is in *Hebrew*.

·CHAPTER II.

"Die Juden waren daselbst für die Heiden dasselbe, was Johannes der Täufer für die Juden in ihrem Lande war."—(*Wiltsch, Handbuch der Kirchlichen Geographie.*)

JEWISH ORIGIN OF THE CHURCH.—SECTS AND PARTIES OF THE JEWS.—PHARISEES AND SADDUCEES.—ST. PAUL A PHARISEE.—HELLENISTS AND ARAMÆANS.—ST. PAUL'S FAMILY HELLENISTIC BUT NOT HELLENISING.—HIS INFANCY AT TARSUS.—THE TRIBE OF BENJAMIN.—HIS FATHER'S CITIZENSHIP.—SCENERY OF THE PLACE.—HIS CHILDHOOD.—HE IS SENT TO JERUSALEM.—STATE OF JUDÆA AND JERUSALEM.—RABBINICAL SCHOOLS.—GAMALIEL.—MODE OF TEACHING.—SYNAGOGUES.—STUDENT-LIFE OF ST. PAUL.—HIS EARLY MANHOOD.—FIRST ASPECT OF THE CHURCH.—ST. STEPHEN.—THE SANHEDRIN.—ST. STEPHEN THE FORERUNNER OF ST. PAUL.—HIS MARTYRDOM AND PRAYER.

Christianity has been represented by some of the modern Jews as a mere school of Judaism. Instead of opposing it as a system antagonistic and subversive of the Mosaic religion, they speak of it as a phase or development of that religion itself,—as simply one of the rich outgrowths from the fertile Jewish soil. They point out the causes which combined in the first century to produce this Christian development of Judaism. It has even been hinted that Christianity has done a good work in preparing the world for receiving the pure Mosaic principles which will, at length, be universal.[1] We are not unwilling to accept some of these phrases as expressing a great and important truth. Christianity *is* a school of Judaism: but it is the school which absorbs and interprets the teaching of all others. It is a development; but it is that development which was divinely foreknown and predetermined. It is the grain of which mere Judaism is now the worthless husk. It is the image of Truth in its full proportions; and the Jewish remnants are now as the shapeless fragments which remain of the block of marble when the statue is completed. When we look back at the Apostolic age, we see that growth proceeding which separated the husk from the grain. We see the image of Truth coming out in clear

1 Some of these works have furnished us with useful suggestions, and in some cases the very words have been adopted. There is much in such Jewish writings which no ordinary Christian can read without deep pain; but the pain is not so deep as when the same things are suggested, or borrowed, by those who call themselves Christians

expressiveness, and the useless fragments falling off like scales, under the careful work of divinely-guided hands. If we are to realise the earliest appearance of the Church, such as it was when Paul first saw it, we must view it as arising in the midst of Judaism: and if we are to comprehend all the feelings and principles of this Apostle, we must consider first the Jewish preparation of his own younger days. To these two subjects the present chapter will be devoted.

We are very familiar with one division which ran through the Jewish nation in the first century. The Sadducees and Pharisees are frequently mentioned in the New Testament, and we are there informed of the tenets of these two prevailing parties. The belief in a future state may be said to have been an open question among the Jews, when our Lord appeared and "brought life and immortality to light." We find the Sadducees established im the highest office of the priesthood, and possessed of the greatest powers in the Sanhedrin: and yet they did not believe in any future state, nor in any spiritual existence independent of the body. The Sadducees said that there was "no resurrection, neither Angel nor Spirit."[1] They do not appear to have held doctrines which are commonly called licentious or immoral. On the contrary, they adhered strictly to the moral tenets of the Law, as opposed to its mere formal technicalities. They did not overload the Sacred Books with traditions, or encumber the duties of life with a multitude of minute observances. They were the disciples of reason without enthusiasm,—they made few proselytes,—their numbers were not great, and they were confined principally to the richer members of the nation.[2] The Pharisees, on the other hand, were the enthusiasts of the later Judaism. They "compassed sea and land to make one proselyte." Their power and influence with the mass of the people was immense. The loss of the national independence of the Jews,—the gradual extinction of their political life, directly by the Romans, and indirectly by the family of Herod,—caused their feelings to rally round their Law and their Religion, as the only centre of unity which now remained to them. Those, therefore, who gave their energies to the interpretation and exposition of the Law, not curtailing any of the doctrines which were virtually contained in it, and which had been revealed with more or less clearness, but rather accumulating articles of faith, and multiplying the requirements of devotion:—who themselves practiced a severe

[1] Acts xxiii. 8. See Matt. xxii. 23–34.

[2] Josephus says of the Sadducees: Εἰς ὀλίγους τε ἄνδρας οὗτος ὁ λόγος ἀφίκετο, τοὺς μέντοι πρώτους τοῖς ἀξιώμασι. Πράσσεταί τε ἀπ' αὐτῶν οὐδὲν ὡς εἰπεῖν· ὁπότε γὰρ ἐπ' ἀρχὰς παρέλθοιεν, ἀκουσίως μὲν καὶ κατ' ἀνάγκας, προσχωροῦσι δ' οὖν οἷς ὁ Φαρισαῖος λέγει, διὰ τὸ μὴ ἄλλως ἀνεκτοὺς γένεσθαι τοῖς πλήθεσιν. Ant. xviii. 1, 4. And again: Τῶν μὲν Σαδδουκαίων τοὺς εὐπόρους μόνον πειθόντων, τὸ δὲ δημοτικὸν οὐχ ἑπόμενον αὐτοῖς ἐχόντων, τῶν δὲ Φαρισαίων τὸ πλῆθος σύμμαχον ἐχόντων, xiii. 10, 6. See the question asked. John vii. 48.

and ostentatious religion, being liberal in almsgiving, fasting frequently, making long prayers, and carrying casuistical distinctions into the smallest details of conduct;—who consecrated, moreover, their best zeal and exertions to the spread of the fame of Judaism, and to the increase of the nation's power in the only way which now was practicable,—could not fail to command the reverence of great numbers of the people. It was no longer possible to fortify Jerusalem against the heathen: but the Law could be fortified like an impregnable city. The place of the brave is on the walls and in the front of the battle: and the hopes of the nation rested on those who defended the sacred outworks, and made successful inroads on the territories of the Gentiles.

Such were the Pharisees. And now, before proceeding to other features of Judaism and their relation to the Church, we can hardly help glancing at St. Paul. He was "a Pharisee, the son of a Pharisee."[1] and he was educated by Gamaliel,[2] "a Pharisee."[3] Both his father and his teacher belonged to this sect. And on three distinct occasions he tells us that he himself was a member of it. Once when at his trial, before a mixed assembly of Pharisees and Sadducees, the words just quoted were spoken, and his connection with the Pharisees asserted with such effect, that the feelings of this popular party were immediately enlisted on his side. "And when he had so said, there arose a dissension between the Pharisees and the Sadducees; and the multitude was divided. . . . And there arose a great cry; and the Scribes that were of the Pharisees' part arose, and strove, saying, We find no evil in this man."[4] The second time was, when, on a calmer occasion, he was pleading before Agrippa, and said to the king, in the presence of Festus: "The Jews knew me from the beginning, if they would testify, that after the most straitest sect of our religion I lived a Pharisee."[5] And once more, when writing from Rome to the Philippians, he gives force to his argument against the Judaizers, by telling them that if any other man thought he had whereof he might trust in the flesh, he had more:—"circumcised the eighth day, of the stock of Israel, of the tribe of Benjamin, a Hebrew of the Hebrews; as touching the Law, a Pharisee."[6] And not only was he himself a Pharisee, but his father also. He was "a Pharisee, the son of a Pharisee." This short sentence sums up nearly all we know of St. Paul's parents. If we think of his earliest life, we are to conceive of him as born in a Pharisaic family, and as brought up from his infancy in the "straitest sect of the Jews' religion." His childhood was nurtured in the strictest belief. The stories of the Old Testament,—the angelic appearances,—the prophetic visions,—to him were literally true. They needed no Sadducean explanation. The world of

[1] Acts xxiii. 6. [2] Acts xxii. 3. [3] Acts v. 34.
[4] Acts xxiii. [5] Acts xxvi. [6] Philip. iii. 4, 5

spirits was a reality to him. The resurrection of the dead was an article of his faith. And to exhort him to the practice of religion, he had before him the example of his father, praying and walking with broad phylacteries, scrupulous and exact in his legal observances. And he had, moreover, as it seems, the memory and tradition of ancestral piety: for he tells us in one of his latest letters,[1] that he served God "from his forefathers." All influences combined to make him "more exceedingly zealous of the traditions of his fathers,"[2] and "touching the righteousness which is in the Law, blameless."[3] Every thing tended to prepare him to be an eminent member of that theological party, to which so many of the Jews were looking for the preservation of their national life, and the extension of their national creed.

But in this mention of the Pharisees and Sadducees, we are far from exhausting the subject of Jewish divisions, and far from enumerating all those phases of opinion which must have had some connection with the growth of rising Christianity, and those elements which may have contributed to form the character of the Apostle to the Heathens. There was a sect in Judæa which is not mentioned in the Scriptures, but which must have acquired considerable influence in the time of the Apostles, as may be inferred from the space devoted to it by Josephus and Philo.[4] These were the *Essenes*, who retired from the theological and political distractions of Jerusalem and the larger towns, and founded peaceful communities in the desert or in villages, where their life was spent in contemplation, and in the practices of ascetic piety. It has been suggested that John the Baptist was one of them. There is no proof that this was the case: but we need not doubt that they did represent religious cravings which Christianity satisfied. Another party was that of the *Zealots*,[5] who were as politically fanatical as the Essenes were religiously contemplative, and whose zeal was kindled with the burning desire to throw off the Roman yoke from the neck of Israel. Very different from them were the *Herodians*, twice mentioned in the Gospels,[6] who held that the hopes of Judaism rested on the Herods, and who almost looked to that family for the fulfil-

[1] 2 Tim. i. 3. [2] Gal. i. 14. [3] Phil. iii. 6.

[4] See the long details given by the former writer in book ii. ch. 8 of the "Jewish Wars;" and by the latter in the treatise "Quod omnis probus liber;" and in the fragment from Eusebius, in Mangey's Philo, ii. p. 632. The Essenes lived chiefly in the neighbourhood of the Dead Sea. Pliny says of them: "Ab occidente litora Esseni fugiunt, usque qua nocent: gens sola, et in toto orbe præter cæteras mira, sine ulla fœmina, sine pecunia, socia palmarum. In diem ex æquo convenarum turba renascitur, large frequentantibus, quos vita fessos ad mores eorum fortunæ fluctus agitat. Ita per seculorum millia (incredibile dictu) gens æterna est, in qua nemo nascitur. Tam fœcunda illis aliorum vitæ pœnitentia est." N. H. v. 15.

[5] See Basnage's Histoire des Juifs. Liv. i. ch. 17.

[6] Mark iii. 6. Matt. xxii. 16. See Mark xii. 13

ment of the prophecies of the Messiah. And if we were simply enumerating the divisions, and describing the sects of the Jews, it would be necessary to mention the *Therapeutæ*,[1] a widely-spread community in Egypt, who lived even in greater seclusion than the Essenes in Judæa. The *Samaritans* also would require our attention. But we must turn from these sects and parties to a wider division, which arose from that dispersion of the Hebrew people, to which some space has been devoted in the preceding chapter.

We have seen that early colonies of the Jews were settled in Babylonia and Mesopotamia. Their connection with their brethren in Judæa was continually maintained: and they were bound to them by the link of a common language. The Jews of Palestine and Syria, with those who lived on the Tigris and Euphrates, interpreted the Scriptures through the Targums[2] or Chaldee paraphrases, and spoke kindred dialects of the language of Aram:[3] and hence they were called *Aramæan* Jews. We have also had occasion to notice that other dispersion of the nation through those countries where Greek was spoken. Their settlements began with Alexander's conquests, and were continued under the successors of those who partitioned his empire. Alexandria was their capital. They used the Septuagint translation of the Bible; and they were commonly called *Hellenists*, or Jews of the Grecian speech.

The mere difference of language would account in some degree for the mutual dislike with which we know that these two sections of the Jewish race regarded one another. We are all aware how closely the use of a hereditary dialect is bound up with the warmest feelings of the heart. And in this case the Aramæan language was the sacred tongue of Palestine. It is true that the tradition of the language of the Jews had been broken, as the continuity of their political life had been rudely interrupted. The Hebrew of the time of Christ was not the oldest Hebrew of the Israelites; but it was a kindred dialect; and old enough to command a reverent affection. Though not the language of Moses and David, it was that of Ezra and Nehemiah. And it is not unnatural that the Ara-

1 Described in great detail by Philo in his treatise De Vita Contemplativa.

2 It is uncertain when the written Targums came into use, but the practice of paraphrasing orally in Chaldee must have begun soon after the Captivity.

3 Aram—the "Highlands" of the Semitic tribes—comprehended the tract of country which extended from Taurus and Lebanon to Mesopotamia and Arabia: for references, see Winer's Realwörterbuch. There were two main dialects of the Aramæan stock, the eastern or Babylonian, commonly called *Chaldee* (the "Syrian tongue" of 2 Kings xviii. 26. Isai. xxxvi. 11. Ezr. iv. 7. Dan. ii. 4); and the western, which is the parent of the *Syriac*, now, like the former, almost a dead language. The first of these dialects began to supplant the older *Hebrew* of Judæa from the time of the captivity, and was the "Hebrew" of the New Testament, Luke xxiii. 38. John xix. 20. Acts xxi. 40. xxii. 2. xxvi. 14. *Arabic*, the most perfect of the Semitic languages, has now generally overspread those regions.

mæans should have revolted from the speech of the Greek idolaters and the tyrant Antiochus,—a speech which they associated moreover with innovating doctrines and dangerous speculations.

For the division went deeper than a mere superficial diversity of speech. It was not only a division, like the modern one of German and Spanish Jews, where those who hold substantially the same doctrines have accidentally been led to speak different languages. But there was a diversity of religious views and opinions. This is not the place for examining that system of mystic interpretation called the Cabbala,[1] and for determining how far its origin might be due to Alexandria or to Babylon. It is enough to say, generally, that in the Aramæan theology, Oriental elements prevailed rather than Greek, and that the subject of the Babylonian influences has more connection with the life of St. Peter than that of St. Paul. The Hellenists, on the other hand, or Jews who spoke Greek, who lived in Greek countries, and were influenced by Greek civilisation, are associated in the closest manner with the Apostle of the Gentiles. They are more than once mentioned in the Acts, where our English translation names them "Grecians," to distinguish them from the Heathen or Proselyte "Greeks."[2] Alexandria was the metropolis of their theology. Philo was their great representative. He was an old man when St. Paul was in his maturity: his writings were probably known to the Apostle; and they have descended with the inspired Epistles to our own day. The work of the learned Hellenists may be briefly described as this,—to accommodate Jewish doctrines to the mind of the Greeks, and to make the Greek language express the mind of the Jews. The Hebrew principles were "disengaged as much as possible from local and national conditions, and presented in a form adapted to the Hellenic world."[3] All this was hateful to the zealous Aramæans. The men of the East rose up against those of the West. The Greek learning was not more repugnant to the Roman Cato, than it was to the strict Hebrews. They had a saying, "Cursed be he who teacheth his son the learning of the Greeks."[4] We could imagine

[1] Basnage devotes many chapters to this subject: see his third book.

[2] See Chap. I. p. 12, note.

[3] "L'objet principal des Juifs hellénistes ou Alexandrins, consistait à initier les hommes instruits des populations étrangères à la sagesse des livres sacrés. Ils se dirigaient d'après la conviction antique manifestée en ces termes par Moïse : 'Ma doctrine se répandra comme la rosée ; ma parole découlera comme une fine pluie sur l'herbe tendre, comme la grosse pluie sur la plante avancée.' (Deut. xxxii. 1, 2.) De là vient que les écrivains de cette école s'appliquaient à dégager les principes hébraïques de la plupart des conditions nationales et locales ; à les présenter dans la langue et sous les formes appropriées au monde grec : ils établissaient des rapprochements plus ou moins spécieux avec les doctrines des autres peuples, et ils mettaient en opposition la moralité profonde de leurs lois constitutives avec les tendances vraiment immorales qui régnaient alors en tous lieux." Salvador, J. C. &c., vol. i. pp. 131, 132.

[4] This repugnance is illustrated by many passages in the Talmudic writings. Rabbi

them using the words of the prophet Joel (iii. 6), "The children of Judah and the children of Jerusalem have ye sold unto the Grecians, that ye might remove them from their border:" and we cannot be surprised that, even in the deep peace and charity of the Church's earliest days, this inveterate division re-appeared, and that, "when the number of the disciples was multiplied, there arose a murmuring of the Grecians against the Hebrews."[1]

It would be an interesting subject of enquiry to ascertain in what proportions these two parties were distributed in the different countries where the Jews were dispersed, in what places they came into the strongest collision, and how far they were fused and united together. In the city of Alexandria, the emporium of Greek commerce from the time of its foundation, where since the earliest Ptolemies, literature, philosophy, and criticism had never ceased to excite the utmost intellectual activity, where the Septuagint translation of the Scripture had been made, and where a Jewish temple and ceremonial worship had been established in rivalry to that in Jerusalem,[2]—there is no doubt that the Hellenistic element largely prevailed. But although (strictly speaking) the Alexandrian Jews were nearly all Hellenists, it does not follow that they were all Hellenizers. In other words, although their speech and their Scriptures were Greek, the theological views of many among them undoubtedly remained Hebrew. There must have been many who were attached to the traditions of Palestine, and who looked suspiciously on their more speculative brethren: and we have no difficulty in recognising the picture presented in a pleasing German fiction,[3] which describes the debates and struggles of the two tendencies in this city, to be very correct. In Palestine itself, we have every reason to believe that the native population was entirely Aramæan,

Levi Ben Chajathah, going down to Cæsarea, heard them reciting their phylacteries in Greek, and would have forbidden them; which when Rabbi Jose heard, he was very angry, and said, "If a man doth not know how to recite in the holy tongue, must he not recite them at all? Let him perform his duty in what language he can." The following saying is attributed to Rabban Simeon, the son of Gamaliel: "There were a thousand boys in my father's school, of whom five hundred learned the law, and five hundred the wisdom of the Greeks; and there is not one of the latter now alive, excepting myself here, and my uncle's son in Asia." See Lightfoot, Heb. & Talm. Ex. on Acts (vi. 1). Biscoe quotes from Lightfoot in his History of the Acts confirmed, ch. iv. § 2. Josephus implies in the passage quoted below (Ant. xx. 11, 2), that a knowledge of Greek was lightly regarded by the Jews of Palestine.

[1] Acts vi. 1.

[2] This temple was not in the city of Alexandria, but at Leontopolis. It was built (or rather it was an old heathen temple repaired) by Onias, from whose family the high-priesthood had been transferred to the family of the Maccabees, and who had fled into Egypt in the time of Ptolemy Philopator. It remained in existence till destroyed by Vespasian. See Josephus, B. J. i. 1, 1. vii. 10, 3. Ant. xiii. 3.

[3] "Helon's Pilgrimage to Jerusalem," published in German in 1820, translated into English in 1824.

though there was no lack of Hellenistic synagogues[1] at Jerusalem, which at the seasons of the festivals would be crowded with foreign pilgrims, and become the scene of animated discussions. Syria was connected by the link of language with Palestine and Babylonia: but Antioch, its metropolis, commercially and politically resembled Alexandria: and it is probable that, when Barnabas and Saul were establishing the great Christian community in that city,[2] the majority of the Jews were "Grecians" rather than "Hebrews." In Asia Minor we should at first sight be tempted to imagine that the Grecian tendency would predominate: but when we find that Antiochus brought Babylonian Jews into Lydia and Phrygia, we must not make too confident a conclusion in this direction; and we have grounds for imagining that many Israelitish families in the remote districts (possibly that of Timotheus at Lystra)[3] may have cherished the forms of the traditionary faith of the Eastern Jews, and lived uninfluenced by Hellenistic novelties. The residents in maritime and commercial towns would not be strangers to the Western developments of religious doctrines; and when Apollos came from Alexandria to Ephesus,[4] he would find himself in a theological atmosphere not very different from that of his native city. Tarsus in Cilicia will naturally be included under the same class of cities of the West, by those who remember Strabo's assertion that, in literature and philosophy, its fame exceeded that of Athens and Alexandria. At the same time, we cannot be sure that the very celebrity of its heathen schools might not induce the families of Jewish residents to retire all the more strictly into a religious Hebrew seclusion.

That such a seclusion of their family from Gentile influences was maintained by the parents of St. Paul, is highly probable. We have no means of knowing how long they themselves, or their ancestors, had been Jews of the dispersion. A tradition is mentioned by Jerome[5] that they came

[1] See Acts vi. 9.
[2] Acts xi. 25, &c.
[3] Acts xvi. 1. 2 Tim. i. 5.
[4] Acts. xviii. 24.

[5] He begins his notice of Paul in the Catalogue of Ecclesiastical Writers thus: "Paulus Apostolus, qui ante Saulus, extra numerum duodecim Apostolorum, de tribu Benjamin et oppido Judææ Gischalis fuit, quo a Romanis capto cum parentibus suis Tarsum Ciliciæ commigravit; a quibus ob studia legis missus Hierosolyman, a Gamaliele viro doctissimo, cujus Lucas meminit, eruditus est." And again he alludes to it with more doubt in the Commentary on the Epistle to Philemon, in reference to the passage where Epaphras is called his "fellow-prisoner." "Quis sit Epaphras concaptivus Pauli, talem fabulam accepimus. Aiunt parentes Apostoli Pauli de Gischalis regione fuisse Judææ: et eos, cum tota provincia Romana vastaretur manu, et dispergerentur in orbe Judæi, in Tarsum urbem Ciliciæ fuisse translatos: parentum conditionem adolescentulum Paulum secutum: et sic posse stare illud quod de se ipse testatur: Hebræi sunt? et ego: Israelitæ sunt? et ego: Semen Abrahæ sunt? et ego (2 Cor. xi.): et rursus alibi: Hebræus ex Hebræis (Phil. iii.): et cætera quæ illum Judæum magis indicunt quam Tarsensem. Quod si ita est, possumus et Epaphram illo tempore captum suspicari, quo captus est Paulus: et cum parentibus suis in Colossis urbe Asiæ colloca-

originally from Giscala, a town in Galilee, when it was stormed by the Romans. The story involves an anachronism, and contradicts the Acts of the Apostles. Yet it need not be entirely disregarded; especially when we find St. Paul speaking of himself as "a Hebrew of the Hebrews,"[1] and when we remember that the word "Hebrew" is used for an Aramaic Jew, as opposed to a "Grecian" or Hellenist.[2] Nor is it unlikely in itself that before they settled in Tarsus, the family had belonged to the Eastern dispersion, or to the Jews of Palestine. But, however this may be, St. Paul himself must be called a Hellenist; because the language of his infancy was that idiom of the Grecian Jews in which all his letters were written. Though, in conformity with the strong feeling of the Jews of all times, he might learn his earliest sentences from the Scripture in Hebrew, yet he was familiar with the Septuagint translation at an early age. For it is observed that, when he quotes from the Old Testament, his quotations are from that version; and that, not only when he cites its very words, but when (as is often the case) he quotes it from memory.[3] Considering the accurate knowledge of the original Hebrew which he must have acquired under Gamaliel at Jerusalem, it has been inferred that this can only arise from his having been thoroughly imbued at an earlier period with the Hellenistic Scriptures. The readiness, too, with which he expressed himself in Greek, even before such an audience as that upon the Areopagus at Athens, shows a command of the language which a Jew would not, in all probability, have attained, had not Greek been the language of his childhood.

But still the vernacular Hebrew of Palestine would not have been a

tum, Christi postea recepisse sermonem." It is unnecessary to dwell on the anachronism, or on the absolute contradiction to Acts xxii. 3.

1 Phil. iii. 5. Cave sees nothing more in this phrase than that "his parents were Jews, and that of the ancient stock, not entering in by the gate of proselytism, but originally descended from the nation."—Life of St. Paul, i. 2. Benson, on the other hand, argues, from this passage and from 2 Cor. xi. 22, that there was a difference between a "Hebrew" and an "Israelite."—"A person might be descended from Israel, and yet not be a Hebrew but a Hellenist. . . . St. Paul appeareth to me to have plainly intimated, that a man might be of the stock of Israel and of the tribe of Benjamin, and yet not be a Hebrew of the Hebrews; but that, as to himself, he was, both by father and mother, a Hebrew; or of the race of that sort of Jews which were generally most esteemed by their nation."—History of the First Planting of the Christian Religion, vol. i. p. 117.

2 Acts vi. 1. For the absurd Ebionite story that St. Paul was by birth not a Jew at all, but a Greek, see the next Chapter.

3 See Tholuck's Essay (mentioned below, p. 50, note), Eng. Trans. p. 9. Out of eighty-eight quotations from the Old Testament, Koppe gives grounds for thinking that forty-nine were cited from memory. And Bleek thinks that every one of his citations without exception is from memory. He adds, however, that the Apostle's memory reverts occasionally to the Hebrew text, as well as to that of the Septuagint. See an article in the Christian Remembrancer for April, 1848, on Grinfield's Hellenistic Ed. of the N. T.

foreign tongue to the infant Saul; on the contrary, he may have heard it spoken almost as often as the Greek. For no doubt his parents, proud of their Jewish origin, and living comparatively near to Palestine, would retain the power of conversing with their friends from thence in the ancient speech. Mercantile connections from the Syrian coast would be frequently arriving, whose conversation would be in Aramaic; in all probability there were kinsfolk still settled in Judæa, as we afterwards find the nephew of St. Paul in Jerusalem.[1] We may compare the situation of such a family (so far as concerns their language) to that of the French Huguenots who settled in London after the revocation of the Edict of Nantes. These French families, though they soon learned to use the English as the medium of their common intercourse and the language of their household, yet, for several generations, spoke French with equal familiarity and greater affection.[2]

Moreover, it may be considered as certain that the family of St. Paul, though Hellenistic in speech, were no *Hellenizers* in theology; they were not at all inclined to adopt Greek habits or Greek opinions. The manner in which St. Paul speaks of himself, his father, and his ancestors, implies the most uncontaminated hereditary Judaism. "Are they Hebrews? so am I. Are they Israelites? so am I. Are they the seed of Abraham? so am I."[3]—"A Pharisee" and "the son of a Pharisee."[4]—"Circumcised the eighth day, of the stock of Israel, of the tribe of Benjamin, *a Hebrew of the Hebrews*."[5]

There is therefore little doubt that, though the native of a city filled with a Greek population and incorporated with the Roman Empire, yet Saul was born and spent his earliest days in the shelter of a home which was Hebrew, not in name only but in spirit. The Roman power did not press upon his infancy: the Greek ideas did not haunt his childhood: but he grew up an Israelitish boy, nurtured in those histories of the chosen people which he was destined so often to repeat in the synagogues,[6] with the new and wonderful commentary supplied by the life and resurrection of a crucified Messiah. "From a child he knew the Scriptures," which ultimately made him "wise unto salvation through faith which is in Christ Jesus," as he says of Timothy in the second Epistle (iii. 15). And the groups around his childhood were such as that which he beautifully de-

[1] Acts xxiii. 16.

[2] St. Paul's ready use of the spoken Aramaic appears in his speech upon the stairs of the Castle of Antonia at Jerusalem, "in the Hebrew tongue." This familiarity, however, he would necessarily have acquired during his student-life at Jerusalem, if he had not possessed it before. The difficult question of the "Gift of Tongues" will be discussed hereafter.

[3] 2 Cor. xi. 22. [4] Acts xxiii. 6. [5] Phil. iii. 5

[6] Acts xiii. 16–41. See xvii. 2, 3, 10, 11. xxviii. 23.

scribes in another part of the same letter to that disciple, where he speaks of "his grandmother Lois, and his mother Eunice." (i. 5.)

We should be glad to know something of the mother of St. Paul. But though he alludes to his father, he does not mention her. He speaks of himself as set apart by God "from his mother's womb," that the Son of God should in due time be revealed in him, and by him preached to the Heathen.[1] But this is all. We find notices of his sister and his sister's son,[2] and of some more distant relatives:[3] but we know nothing of her who was nearer to him than all of them. He tells us of his instructor Gamaliel; but of her, who, if she lived, was his earliest and best teacher, he tells us nothing. Did she die like Rachel, the mother of Benjamin, the great ancestor of his tribe; leaving his father to mourn and set a monument on her grave, like Jacob, by the way of Bethlehem?[4] Or did she live to grieve over her son's apostacy from the faith of the Pharisees, and die herself unreconciled to the obedience of Christ? Or did she believe and obey the Saviour of her son? These are questions which we cannot answer. If we wish to realise the earliest infancy of the Apostle, we must be content with a simple picture of a Jewish mother and her child. Such a picture is presented to us in the short history of Elizabeth and John the Baptist, and what is wanting in one of the inspired Books of St. Luke may be supplied, in some degree, by the other.

The same feelings which welcomed the birth and celebrated the naming of a son in the "hill country" of Judæa,[5] prevailed also among the Jews of the dispersion. As the "neighbours and cousins" of Elizabeth "heard how the Lord had showed great mercy upon her, and rejoiced with her," —so it would be in the household at Tarsus, when Saul was born. In a nation to which the birth of a Messiah was promised, and at a period when the aspirations after the fulfilment of the promise were continually becoming more conscious and more urgent, the birth of a son was the fulfilment of a mother's highest happiness: and to the father also (if we may thus invert the words of Jeremiah) "blessed was the man who brought tidings, saying, A man child is born unto thee; making him glad."[6] On the eighth day the child was circumcised and named. In the case of John the Baptist, "they sought to call him Zacharias, after the name of his father. But his mother answered, and said, Not so; but he shall be called John." And when the appeal was made to his father, he signified his assent, in obedience to the vision. It was not unusual, on the one hand, to call a Jewish child after the name of his father; and, on the other hand, it was a common practice, in all ages of Jewish history, even without a prophetic intimation, to adopt a name expressive of religious

[1] Gal. i. 15. [2] Acts xxiii. 16. [3] Rom. xvi. 7, 11, 21
[4] Gen xxxv. 16-20. xlviii. 7. [5] Luke i. 39. [6] Jer. xx. 15.

feelings. When the infant at Tarsus received the name of Saul, it might be "after the name of his father;" and it was a name of traditional celebrity in the tribe of Benjamin, for it was that of the first king anointed by Samuel.[1] Or, when his father said "his name is Saul," it may have been intended to denote (in conformity with the Hebrew derivation of the word) that he was a son who had long been desired, the first born of his parents, the child of prayer, who was thenceforth, like Samuel, to be consecrated to God.[2] "For this child I prayed," said the wife of Elkanah; "and the Lord hath given me my petition which I asked of Him: therefore also I have lent him to the Lord; as long as he liveth he shall be lent unto the Lord."[3]

Admitted into covenant with God by circumcision, the Jewish child had thenceforward a full claim to all the privileges of the chosen people. His was the benediction of the 128th Psalm:—"The Lord shall bless thee out of Zion: thou shalt see the good of Jerusalem all the days of thy life." From that time, whoever it might be who watched over Saul's infancy, whether, like king Lemuel,[4] he learnt "the prophecy that his mother taught him," or whether he was under the care of others, like those who were with the sons of king David and king Ahab,[5]—we are at no loss to learn what the first ideas were, with which his early thought was made familiar. The rules respecting the diligent education of children, which were laid down by Moses in the 6th and 11th chapters of Deuteronomy, were doubtless carefully observed: and he was trained in that peculiarly *historical* instruction, spoken of in the 78th Psalm, which implies the continuance of a chosen people, with glorious recollections of the past, and great anticipations for the future: "The Lord made a covenant with Jacob, and gave Israel a law, which He commanded our forefathers to teach their children; that their posterity might know it, and the children which were yet unborn; to the intent that when they came up, they might shew their children the same: that they might put their trust in God, and not to forget the works of the Lord, but to keep His commandments." (ver. 5–7.) The histories of Abraham and Isaac, of Jacob and his twelve sons, of Moses among the bulrushes, of Joshua and Samuel, Elijah, Daniel, and the Maccabees, were the stories of his childhood. The destruction of Pharaoh in the Red Sea, the thunders of Mount Sinai, the dreary journeys in the wilderness, the land that flowed with milk and honey,—this was the

[1] "A name frequent and common in the tribe of Benjamin ever since the first King of Israel, who was of that name, was chosen out of that tribe; in memory whereof they were wont to give their children this name at their circumcision." Cave, i. 3; but he gives no proof.

[2] This is suggested by Neander, Pfl. und Leit. 138.

[3] 1 Sam. i. 27, 28.

[4] Prov. xxxi. 1. Cf. Susanna, 3. 2 Tim. iii. 15, with 1 Tim. i. 5.

[5] 1 Chron xxvii. 32. 2 Kings x. 1. 5. Cf. Joseph. vit. 76. Ant. xvi. 8, 3.

earliest imagery presented to his opening mind. The triumphant songs of Zion, the lamentations by the waters of Babylon, the prophetic praises of the Messiah, were the songs around his cradle.

Above all, he would be familiar with the destinies of his own illustrious tribe.[1] The life of the timid Patriarch, the father of the twelve; the sad death of Rachel near the city where the Messiah was to be born; the loneliness of Jacob, who sought to comfort himself in Benoni "the son of her sorrow," by calling him Benjamin[2] "the son of his right hand;" and then the youthful days of this youngest of the twelve brethren, the famine, and the journeys into Egypt, the severity of Joseph, and the wonderful story of the silver cup in the mouth of the sack;—these are the narratives to which he listened with intense and eager interest. How little was it imagined that, as Benjamin was the youngest and most honoured of the Patriarchs, so this listening child of Benjamin should be associated with the twelve servants of the Messiah of God, the last and most illustrious of the Apostles! But many years of ignorance were yet to pass away, before that mysterious Providence, which brought Benjamin to Joseph in Egypt, should bring his descendant to the knowledge and love of JESUS, the Son of Mary. Some of the early Christian writers see in the dying benediction of Jacob, when he said that "Benjamin should ravin as a wolf, in the morning devour the prey, and at night divide the spoil,"[3] a prophetic intimation of him who, in the morning of his life, should tear the sheep of God, and in its evening feed them, as the teacher of the nations.[4] When St. Paul was a child and learnt the words of this saying, no Christian thoughts were associated with it, or with that other more peaceful prophecy of Moses, when he said of Benjamin, "The beloved of the Lord shall dwell in safety by Him: and the Lord shall cover him all the day

[1] It may be thought that here, and below, p. 53, too much prominence has been given to the attachment of a Jew in the Apostolic age to his own particular tribe. It is difficult to ascertain how far the tribe-feeling of early times lingered on in combination with the national feeling, which grew up after the Captivity. But when we consider the care with which the genealogies were kept, and when we find the tribe of Barnabas specified (Acts iv. 36), and of Anna the prophetess (Luke ii. 36), and when we find St. Paul alluding in a pointed manner to his tribe (see Rom. xi. 1, Phil. iii. 5, and compare Acts xiii. 21), it does not seem unnatural to believe that pious families of so famous a stock as that of Benjamin should retain the hereditary enthusiasm of their sacred clanship. See, moreover, Matt. xix. 28. Rev. v. 5. vii. 4–8.

[2] Gen. xxxv. 18.

[3] Gen. xlix. 27.

[4] Nam mihi Paulum etiam Genesis olim repromisit. Inter illas enim figuras et propheticas super filios suos benedictiones Jacob, cum ad Benjamin dixisset: Benjamin, inquit, lupus rapax ad matutinum comedet adhuc, et ad vesperam dabit escam. Ex tribu enim Benjamin oriturum Paulum providebat, lupum rapacem ad matutinum comedentem, id est, prima ætate vastaturum pecora Domini ut persecutorem, ecclesiarum, dehinc ad vesperam escam daturum, id est, devergente jam ætate oves Christi educaturum ut doctorem nationum.—Tertull. adv. Marcionem, v. 1.

long, and he shall dwell between His shoulders."[1] But he was familiar with the prophetical words, and could follow in imagination the fortunes of the sons of Benjamin, and knew how they went through the wilderness with Rachel's other children, the tribes of Ephraim and Manasseh, forming with them the third of the four companies on the march, and reposing with them at night on the west of the encampment.[2] He heard how their lands were assigned to them in the promised country along the borders of Judah:[3] and how Saul, whose name he bore, was chosen from the tribe which was the smallest,[4] when "little Benjamin"[5] became the "ruler" of Israel. He knew that when the ten tribes revolted, Benjamin was faithful:[6] and he learnt to follow its honourable history even in the dismal years of the Babylonian Captivity, when Mordecai, "a Benjamite who had been carried away,"[7] saved the nation: and when, instead of destruction, "The Jews," through him, "had light, and gladness, and joy, and honour; and in every province, and in every city, whithersoever the king's commandment and his decree came, the Jews had joy and gladness, a feast and a good day. And many of the people of the land became Jews; for the fear of the Jews fell upon them."[8]

Such were the influences which cradled the infancy of St. Paul; and such was the early teaching under which his mind gradually rose to the realisation of his position as a Hebrew child in a city of Gentiles. Of the exact period of his birth we possess no authentic information. From a passage in a sermon attributed to St. Chrysostom, it has been inferred[9] that he was born in the year 2 of our era. The date is not improbable; but the genuineness of the sermon is suspected; and if it was the undoubted work of the eloquent Father, we have no reason to believe that he possessed any certain means of ascertaining the fact. Nor need we be anxious to possess the information. We have a better chronology than that which reckons by years and months. We know that he was a young man at the time of St. Stephen's martyrdom,[10] and therefore we know what were the features of the period, and what the circumstances of the world, at the beginning of his eventful life. He must have been born in the later years of Herod, or the earlier of his son Archelaus. It was the strongest and most flourishing time of the reign of Augustus. The world was at peace: the pirates of the Levant were dispersed; and Cilicia was

[1] Deut. xxxiii. 12. [2] Numb. ii. 18–24. x. 22–24.
[3] Joshua xviii. 11. [4] 1 Sam. ix. 21. [5] Ps. lxviii. 27.
[6] 2 Chron. xi. See 1 Kings xii. [7] Esther ii. 5, 6. [8] Esther viii. 16, 17.
[9] This is on the supposition that he died A. D. 66, at the age of 68. The sermon is one on SS. Peter and Paul, printed by Savile at the end of the fifth volume of his edition, but considered by him not genuine. See Tillemont. Schrader endeavours to prove that he was born about 14 A. D. See his arguments in vol. i. sect. 2, of his work, "Der Apostel Paulus," 1830.
[10] Acts vii. 58.

lying at rest, or in stupor, with other provinces, under the wide shadow of the Roman power. Many governors had ruled there since the days of Cicero. Athenodorus, the emperor's tutor, had been one of them. It was about the time when Horace and Mæcenas died, with others whose names will never be forgotten; and it was about the time when Caligula was born, with others who were destined to make the world miserable. Thus is the epoch fixed in the manner in which the imagination most easily apprehends it. During this pause in the world's history St. Paul was born.

It was a pause, too, in the history of the sufferings of the Jews. That lenient treatment which had been begun by Julius Cæsar was continued by Augustus;[1] and the days of severity were not yet come, when Tiberius and Claudius[2] drove them into banishment, and Caligula oppressed them with every mark of contumely and scorn. We have good reason to believe that at the period of the Apostle's birth the Jews were unmolested at Tarsus, where his father lived and enjoyed the rights of a Roman citizen. It is a mistake to suppose that this citizenship was a privilege which belonged to the members of the family, as being natives of this city.[3] Tarsus was not a *municipium*, nor was it a *colonia*, like Philippi in Macedonia,[4] or Antioch in Pisidia: but it was a "free city"[5] (*urbs libera*), like the Syrian Antioch and its neighbour-city, Seleucia on the sea. Such a city had the privilege of being governed by its own magistrates, and was exempted from the occupation of a Roman garrison, but its citizens did not necessarily possess the *civitas* of Rome. Tarsus had received great benefits both from Julius Cæsar and Augustus, but the father of St. Paul was not on that account a Roman citizen. This privilege had been granted to him, or had descended to him, as an individual right; he might have pur-

1 Cæsar, like Alexander, treated the Jews with much consideration. Suetonius speaks in strong terms of their grief at his death, Cæs. 84. Augustus permitted the largess, when it fell on a Sabbath, to be put off till the next day. Mangey's Philo. ii. 568, 569: compare Hor. Sat. i. 9, 69.

2 For some notices of the condition of the Jews under the Romans at this time, see Ganz. Vermischte Schriften, i. 13. "Die Gesetzgebung über die Juden in Rom, und die kirchliche Würde derselben in Römischen Reich." Berlin, 1834.

3 Some of the older biographers of St. Paul assume this without any hesitation. Thus Tillemont says that Augustus gave to Tarsus, among other privileges, "le droit de colonie libre et de bourgeoisie Romaine:" and Cave says that this city was a municipium, and that therefore Paul was a Roman citizen. The Tribune (Acts xxi. 39. xxii 24), as Dr. Bloomfield remarks (on xvi. 37), knew that St. Paul was a Tarsian, without being aware that he was a citizen.

4 Acts xvi. 12.

5 See Plin. N. H. v. 22. Appian, B. C. v. 7. Compare iv. 64. From Appian it appears that Antony gave Tarsus the privileges of an *Urbs libera*, though it had previously taken the side of Augustus, and been named Juliopolis. See Dio Chrys. Tarsic. post. ii. 36 ed. Reiske

chased it for a "large sum" of money;[1] but it is more probable that it came to him as the reward of services rendered, during the civil wars, to some influential Roman. That Jews were not unfrequently Roman citizens, we learn from Josephus, who mentions in the "Antiquities"[2] some even of the equestrian order who were illegally scourged and crucified by Florus at Jerusalem; and (what is more to our present point) enumerates certain of his countrymen who possessed the Roman franchise at Ephesus, in that important series of decrees relating to the Jews, which were issued in the time of Julius Cæsar, and are preserved in the second book of the "Jewish War."[3] The family of St. Paul were in the same position at Tarsus as those who were Jews of Asia Minor and yet citizens of Rome at Ephesus; and thus it came to pass, that, while many of his contemporaries were willing to expend "a large sum" in the purchase of "this freedom," the Apostle himself was "free-born."

The question of the double name of "Saul" and "Paul" will require our attention hereafter, when we come in the course of our narrative to that interview with Sergius Paulus in Cyprus, coincidently with which, the appellation in the Acts of the Apostles is suddenly changed. Many opinions have been held on this subject, both by ancient and modern theologians.[4] At present it will be enough to say, that though we cannot overlook the coincidence, or believe it accidental, yet it is most probable that both names were borne by him in his childhood, that "Saul" was the name of his Hebrew home, and "Paul" that by which he was known among the Gentiles. It will be observed that "*Paulus*," the name by which he is always mentioned after his departure from Cyprus, and by which he always designates himself in his Epistles, is a Roman, not a Greek, word. And it will be remembered, that, among those whom he calls his "kinsmen" in the Epistle to the Romans, two of the number, *Junia* and *Lucius*, have Roman names, while the others are Greek.[5] All this may point to a strong Roman connection. These names may have something to do with that honourable citizenship which was an heirloom in the household; and the appellation "Paulus" may be due to some such feelings as those which induced the historian Josephus to call himself "Flavius," in honour of Vespasian and the Flavian family.

If we turn now to consider the social position of the Apostle's father

[1] See Acts xxii. 28. [2] xiv. 10, 3. [3] ii. 14, 9.

[4] Some of the opinions of the ancient writers may be seen in Tillemont. Origen says that he had both names from the first; that he used one among the Jews, and the other afterwards. Augustine, that he took the name when he began to preach. Chrysostom, that he received a new title, like Peter, at his ordination in Antioch. Bede, that he did not receive it till the Proconsul was converted; and Jerome, that it was meant to commemorate that victory. Tillemont, note 3 on St. Paul

[5] Rom. xvi. 7, 11, 21.

and family, we cannot on the one hand confidently argue, from the possession of the citizenship, that they were in the enjoyment of affluence and outward distinction. The *civitas* of Rome, though at that time it could not be purchased without heavy expense, did not depend upon any conditions of wealth, where it was bestowed by authority. On the other hand, it is certain that the manual trade, which we know that St. Paul exercised, cannot be adduced as an argument to prove that his circumstances were narrow and mean ; still less, as some have imagined, that he lived in absolute poverty. It was a custom among the Jews that all boys should learn a trade. "What is commanded of a father towards his son?" asks a Talmudic writer. "To circumcise him, to teach him the law, to teach him a trade." Rabbi Judah saith, "He that teacheth not his son a trade, does the same as if he taught him to be a thief;" and Rabban Gamaliel saith, "He that hath a trade in his hand, to what is he like? he is like a vineyard that is fenced." And if in compliance with this good and useful custom of the Jews, the father of the young Cilician sought to make choice of a trade, which might fortify his son against idleness or against adversity, none would occur to him more naturally than the profitable occupation of the making of tents, the material of which was hair-cloth, supplied by the goats of his native province, and sold in the markets of the Levant by the well-known name of *cilicium*.[1] The most reasonable conjecture is that his father's business was concerned with these markets, and that, like many of his dispersed countrymen, he was actively occupied in the traffic of the Mediterranean coasts: and the remote dispersion of those relations, whom he mentions in his letter from Corinth to Rome, is favourable to this opinion. But whatever might be the station and employment of his father or his kinsmen, whether they were elevated by wealth above, or depressed by poverty below, the average of the Jews of Asia Minor and Italy, we are disposed to believe that this family were possessed of that highest respectability which is worthy of deliberate esteem. The words of Scripture seem to claim for them the tradition of a good and religious reputation. The strict piety of St. Paul's ancestors

[1] Tondentur capræ quod magnis villis sunt in magna parte Phrygiæ; unde cilicia et cætera ejus generis ferri solent. Sed quod primum ea tonsura in Cilicia sit instituta, nomen id Cilicas adjecisse dicunt. Varro, de Re Rustica, lib. ii. ch. xi.: compare Virg. Georg. iii. 311–313. See the extract in Ducange: *Κιλίκια· τράγοι ἀπὸ Κιλικίας οἱ δασεῖς· πάνυ γὰρ ἐκεῖσε ὑπερέχουσι οἱ τοιοῦτοι τράγοι, ὅθεν καὶ τὰ ἐκ τριχῶν συντιθέμενα Κιλίκια λέγονται.* It is still manufactured in Asia Minor. Hair-cloth of this kind is often mentioned as used for penitential discipline, in the Lives of the Saints. The word is still retained in French, Spanish, and Italian ("Di vil cilicio mi parean coperti." Dante, Purg. xiii. 58). See the Dictionnaire de l'Académie, the Diccionario de la Academia, and the Vocabulario degli Academici della Crusca; and further references under the word "Cilicium" in Smith's Dictionary of Antiquities, and Rich's Illustrated Companion to the Dictionary.

has already been remarked; some of his kinsmen embraced Christianity before the Apostle himself,[1] and the excellent discretion of his nephew will be the subject of our admiration, when we come to consider the dangerous circumstances which led to the nocturnal journey from Jerusalem to Cæsarea.[2]

But though a cloud rests on the actual year of St. Paul's birth, and the circumstances of his father's household must be left to imagination, we have the great satisfaction of knowing the exact features of the scenery in the midst of which his childhood was spent. The plain, the mountain, the river, and the sea still remain to us. The rich harvests of corn still grow luxuriantly after the rains in spring. The same tents of goat's hair are still seen covering the plains in the busy harvest.[3] There is the same solitude and silence in the intolerable heat and dust of the summer. Then, as now, the mothers and children of Tarsus went out in the cool evenings, and looked from the gardens round the city, or from their terraced roofs upon the heights of Taurus. The same sunset lingered on the pointed summits. The same shadows gathered in the deep ravines. The river Cydnus has suffered some changes in the course of 1800 years. Instead of rushing, as in the time of Xenophon, like the Rhone at Geneva, in a stream of two hundred feet broad through the city, it now flows idly past it on the east. The Channel, which floated the ships of Antony and Cleopatra, is now filled up; and wide unhealthy lagoons occupy the place of the ancient docks.[4] But its upper waters still flow, as formerly, cold and clear from the snows of Taurus: and its waterfalls still break over

[1] "Salute Andronicus and Junia, my kinsmen, and my fellow-prisoners, who are of note among the Apostles, who also were in Christ before me." Rom. xvi. 7. It is proper to remark that the word *συγγενεῖς* in this chapter (verses 7, 11, 21) has been thought by some to mean only that the persons alluded to were of Jewish extraction. See Lardner's Works, vol. v. p. 473, and the Appendix to the English translation of Tholuck's tract on the early life of St. Paul. Origen thinks that the Apostle speaks spiritually of the baptized; Estius supposes he means that they were members of the tribe of Benjamin. See Tillemont, note 2.

[2] Acts xxiii.

[3] "The plain presented the appearance of an immense sheet of corn-stubble, dotted with small camps of tents: these tents are made of hair-cloth, and the peasantry reside in them at this season, while the harvest is reaping and the corn treading out."—Beaufort's Karamania, p. 273.

[4] This is the Ῥῆγμα, or "bar," at the mouth of the river (*αἱ τοῦ Κύδνου ἐκβολαὶ κατὰ τὸ Ῥῆγμα καλούμενον*), of which Strabo speaks thus: *Ἔστι δὲ λιμνάζων τόπος, ἔχων καὶ παλαιὰ νεώρια, εἰς ὃν ἐμπίπτει ὁ Κύδνος, ὁ διαῤῥέων τὴν Ταρσὸν, τὰς ἀρχὰς ἔχων ἀπὸ τοῦ ὑπερκειμένου τῆς πόλεως Ταύρου· καὶ ἔστιν ἐπίνειον ἡ λίμνη τῆς Ταρσοῦ.* xiv. 5. The land at the mouth of the Cydnus (as in the case of the Pyramus and other rivers on that coast) has since that time encroached on the sea. The unhealthiness of the sea-coast near the Gulf of Scanderoon is notorious, as can be testified by two of those who have contributed drawings to this book. To one of them, the Rev. C. P. Wilbraham, Vicar of Audley, Staffordshire, the editors and publishers take this opportunity of expressing their thanks.

the same rocks, when the snows are melting, like the Rhine at Schaffhausen. We find a pleasure in thinking that the footsteps of the young Apostle often wandered by the side of this stream, and that his eyes often looked on these falls. We can hardly believe that he who spoke to the Lystrians of the "rain from heaven," and the "fruitful seasons," and of the "living God who made heaven and earth and the sea,"[1] could have looked with indifference on beautiful and impressive scenery. Gamaliel was celebrated for his love of nature: and the young Jew, who was destined to be his most famous pupil, spent his early days in the close neighbourhood of much that was well adapted to foster such a taste. Or if it be thought that in attributing such feelings to him we are writing in the spirit of modern times; and if it be contended that he would be more influenced by the realities of human life than by the impressions of nature,—then let the youthful Saul be imagined on the banks of the Cydnus, where it flowed through the city in a stream less clear and fresh, where the wharves were covered with merchandize, in the midst of groups of men in various costumes, speaking various dialects. St. Basil says, that in his day Tarsus was a point of union for Syrians, Cilicians, Isaurians, and Cappadocians.[2] To these we must add the Greek merchant, and the agent of Roman luxury. And one more must be added—the Jew,—even then the pilgrim of Commerce, trading with every nation, and blending with none. In this mixed company Saul, at an early age, might become familiar with the activities of life and the diversities of human character, and even in his childhood make some acquaintance with those various races, which in his manhood he was destined to influence.

We have seen what his infancy was: we must now glance at his boyhood. It is usually the case that the features of a strong character display themselves early. His impetuous fiery disposition would sometimes need control. Flashes of indignation would reveal his impatience and his honesty.[3] The affectionate tenderness of his nature would not be without an object of attachment, if that sister, who was afterwards married,[4] was his playmate at Tarsus. The work of tent-making, rather an amusement than a trade, might sometimes occupy those young hands, which were marked with the toil of years when he held them to the view of the Elders at Miletus.[5] His education was conducted at home rather than at school:

[1] Acts xiv. 17, 15.

[2] Πόλιν τοσαύτην ἔχουσαν εὐκληρίας, ὥστε Ἰσαύρους καὶ Κίλικας, Καπποδόκας τε καὶ Σύρους δι' ἑαυτῆς συνάπτειν.—Ep. v., Eusebio Samosatorum Episcopo.

[3] See Acts ix. 1, 2, xxiii. 1-5; and compare Acts xiii. 13, xv. 38, with 2 Tim. iv. 11,

[4] Acts xxiii. 16.

[5] Acts xx. 34. "Ye yourselves know that *these hands* have ministered to my necessities, and to them that were with me." Compare xviii. 3. 1 Cor. iv. 12. 1 Thess. ii. 9. 2 Thess. iii. 8.

for, though Tarsus was celebrated for its learning, the Hebrew boy would not lightly be exposed to the influence of Gentile teaching. Or, if he went to a school, it was not a Greek school, but rather to some room connected with the synagogue, where a noisy class of Jewish children received the rudiments of instruction, seated on the ground with their teacher, after the manner of Mahomedan children in the East, who may be seen or heard at their lessons near the mosque.[1] At such a school, it may be, he learnt to read and to write, going and returning under the care of some attendant, according to that custom, which he afterwards used as an illustration in the Epistle to the Galatians[2] (and perhaps he remembered his own early days while he wrote the passage) when he spoke of the Law as the Slave who conducts us to the School of Christ. His religious knowledge, as his years advanced, was obtained from hearing the law read in the synagogue, from listening to the arguments and discussions of learned doctors, and from that habit of questioning and answering, which was permitted even to the children among the Jews. Familiar with the pathetic history of the Jewish sufferings, he would feel his heart filled with that love to his own people which breaks out in the Epistle to the Romans (ix. 4, 6)—to that people "whose were the adoption and the glory and the covenants, and of whom, as concerning the flesh, Christ was to come,"—a love not then, as it was afterwards, blended with love towards all mankind, "to the Jew first, and also to the Gentile,"—but rather united with a bitter hatred to the Gentile children whom he saw around him. His idea of the Messiah, so far as it was distinct, would be the carnal notion of a temporal prince—a "Christ known after the flesh,"[3]—and he looked forward with the hope of a Hebrew to the restoration of "the kingdom to Israel."[4] He would be known at Tarsus as a child of promise, and as

[1] This is written from the recollection of a Mahomedan school at Blidah in Algeria, where the mosques can now be entered with impunity. The children, with the teacher, were on a kind of upper story like a shelf, within the mosque. All were seated on this floor, in the way described by Maimonides below. The children wrote on boards, and recited what they wrote; the master addressed them in rapid succession; and the confused sound of voices was unceasing. For pictures of an Egyptian and a Turkish school, see the Bible Cyclopedia, 1841; and the Cyclopedia of Biblical Literature, 1847.

[2] Ὁ νόμος παιδαγωγὸς ἡμῶν γέγονεν εἰς Χριστόν. Gal. iii. 24, incorrectly rendered in the English translation. As a Jewish illustration of a custom well known among the Greeks and Romans, see the quotation in Buxtorf's Synagoga Judaica, ch. vii. "Quando quis filium suum studio Legis consecrat, pingebant ipsi super pergameno vel tabella aliqua elementa literarum, quibus etiam mel illinebant, deinde eum bene lotum, mundis vestibus indutum, placentis ex melle et lacte confectis, ut et fructibus ac tragematis instructum, tradebant alicui Rabbino, qui eum deducat in scholam: hic eum ora pallii sui opertum ad Præceptorem ducebat, a quo literas cognoscere discebat, illectus suavitate deliciarum illarum, et sic reducebatur ad matrem suam." The Rabbi's cloak was spread over the child to teach him modesty. The honey and honey-cakes symbolized such passages as Deut. xxxii. 13. Cant. iv. 11. Ps. xix. 10.

[3] 2 Cor. v. 16.

[4] Acts i. 6.

one likely to uphold the honour of the law against the half-infidel teaching of the day. But the time was drawing near, when his training was to become more exact and systematic. He was destined for the school of Jerusalem. The educational maxim of the Jews, at a later period, was as follows :—"At five years of age, let children begin the Scripture ; at ten, the Mischna ; at thirteen, let them be subjects of the law."[1] There is no reason to suppose that the general practice was very different before the floating maxims of the great doctors were brought together in the Mischna. It may therefore be concluded, with a strong degree of probability, that Saul was sent to the Holy City[2] between the ages of ten and thirteen. Had it been later than the age of thirteen, he could hardly have said that he had been "brought up"[3] in Jerusalem.

The first time any one leaves the land of his birth to visit a foreign and distant country, is an important epoch in his life. In the case of one who has taken this first journey at an early age, and whose character is enthusiastic and susceptible of lively impressions from without, this epoch is usually remembered with peculiar distinctness. But when the country which is thus visited has furnished the imagery for the dreams of childhood, and is felt to be more truly the young traveller's home than the land he is leaving, then the journey assumes the sacred character of a pilgrimage. The nearest parallel which can be found to the visits of the scattered Jews to Jerusalem, is in the periodical expedition of the Mahomedan pilgrims to the sanctuary at Mecca. Nor is there anything which ought to shock the mind in such a comparison ; for that localising spirit was the same thing to the Jews under the highest sanction, which it is to the Mahomedans through the memory of a prophet who was the enemy and not

1 Quoted by Tholuck from the Mischna, Pirke Avoth, ch. v. § 21. We learn from Buxtorf that at 13 there was a ceremony something like Christian confirmation. The boy was then called בר מצוה—"Filius Præcepti :" and the father declared in the presence of the Jews that his son fully understood the Law, and was fully responsible for his sins. Syn. Jud. ibid.

2 See Tholuck's excellent remarks on the early life of the Apostle, in the *Studien und Kritiken*, vol. viii. pp. 364–393, or in the English translation in Clark's Biblical Cabinet, No. 28 ; and separately in his series of Tracts, No. 38. As Olshausen remarks, Acts xxvi. 4.—"My manner of life *from my youth*, which was *at the first* (ἀπ' ἀρχῆς) among mine own nation at Jerusalem, know all the Jews, which knew me from the beginning (ἄνωθεν,"—implies that he came from Tarsus at an early age.

3 Ἀνατεθραμμένος. Acts xxii. 3. Cave assumes that "in his youth he was brought up in the schools of Tarsus, fully instructed in all the liberal arts and sciences, whereby he became admirably acquainted with foreign and external authors" (i. 4) ; and that it was after having "run through the whole circle of the sciences, and laid the sure foundations of human learning at Tarsus" (i. 5), that he was sent to study the Law under Gamaliel. So Lardner seems to think. Hist. of the Ap. and Ev. ch. xi. Hemsen is of opinion that, though as a Jew and a Pharisee he would not be educated in the heathen schools of Tarsus, he did not go to Jerusalem to be trained under Gamaliel till about the age of thirty, and after the ascension of Christ. Der Apostel Paulus, p 4–8.

the forerunner of Christ. As the disciples of Islam may be seen, at stated seasons, flocking towards Cairo or Damascus, the meeting-places of the African and Asiatic caravans,—so Saul had often seen the Hebrew pilgrims from the interior of Asia Minor come down through the passes of the mountains, and join others at Tarsus who were bound for Jerusalem. They returned when the festivals were over; and he heard them talk of the Holy City, of Herod and the New Temple, and of the great teachers and doctors of the law. And at length Saul himself was to go,—to see the land of promise and the city of David, and grow up a learned Rabbi "at the feet of Gamaliel."

COIN OF TARSUS.[1]

With his father, or under the care of some other friend older than himself, he left Tarsus and went to Jerusalem. It is not probable that they travelled by the long and laborious land-journey which leads from the Cilician plain through the defiles of Mount Amanus to Antioch, and thence along the rugged Phœnician shore through Tyre and Sidon to Judæa. The Jews, when they went to the festivals, or to carry contributions, like the Mahomedans of modern days, would follow the lines of natural traffic:[2] and now that the Eastern Sea had been cleared of its pirates, the obvious course would be to travel by water. The Jews, though merchants, were not seamen. We may imagine Saul, therefore, setting sail from the Cydnus on his first voyage, in some Phœnician trader, under the patronage of the gods of Tyre; or in company with Greek mariners, in a vessel adorned with some mythological emblem, like that Alexandrian corn-ship which subsequently brought him to Italy, "whose sign was Castor and Pollux."[3] Gradually they lost sight of Taurus, and the heights of Lebanon came into view. The one had sheltered his early home, but the other had been a familiar form to his Jewish forefathers.

[1] From the British Museum. It may be observed that this coin illustrates the mode of strengthening sails by rope-bands, mentioned in Mr. Smith's important work on the "Voyage and Shipwreck of St. Paul. 1848." p. 163.

[2] In 1820, Abd-el-Kader went with his father on board a French brig to Alexandria, on their way to Mecca. See M. Bareste's Memoir of the ex-Emir; Paris, 1848.

[3] Acts xxviii. 11.

How histories would crowd into his mind as the vessel moved on over the waves, and he gazed upon the furrowed flanks of the great Hebrew mountain! Had the voyage been taken fifty years earlier, the vessel would probably have been bound for Ptolemais, which still bore the name of the Greek kings of Egypt;[1] but in the reign of Augustus or Tiberius, it is more likely that she sailed round the headland of Carmel, and came to anchor in the new harbour of Cæsarea,—the handsome city which Herod had rebuilt, and named in honour of the Emperor.

To imagine incidents when none are recorded, and confidently lay down a route without any authority, would be inexcusable in writing on this subject. But to imagine the feelings of a Hebrew boy on his first visit to the Holy Land, is neither difficult nor blamable. During this journey Saul had around him a different scenery and different cultivation from what he had been accustomed to,—not a river, and a wide plain covered with harvests of corn, but a succession of hills and vallies, with terraced vineyards watered by artificial irrigation. If it was the time of a festival, many pilgrims were moving in the same direction, with music and songs of Zion. The ordinary road would probably be that mentioned in the Acts, which led from Cæsarea through the town of Antipatris (xxiii. 31). But neither of these places would possess much interest for a "Hebrew of the Hebrews." The one was associated with the thoughts of the Romans and of modern times; the other had been built by Herod in memory of Antipater, his Idumean father. But objects were not wanting of the deepest interest to a child of Benjamin. Those far hill-tops on the left were close upon Mount Gilboa, even if the very place could not be seen where "the Philistines fought against Israel . . . and the battle went sore against Saul . . . and he fell on his sword . . . and died, and his three sons, and his armour-bearer, and all his men, that same day together."[2] After passing through the lots of the tribes of Manasseh and Ephraim, the traveller from Cæsarea came to the borders of Benjamin. The children of Rachel were together in Canaan as they had been in the desert. The lot of Benjamin was entered near Bethel, memorable for the piety of Jacob, the songs of Deborah, the sin of Jeroboam, and the zeal of Josiah.[3] Onward a short distance was Gibeah, the home of Saul when he was anointed King,[4] and the scene of the crime and desolation of the tribe, which made it the smallest of the tribes of Israel.[5] Might it not be too truly said concerning the Israelites even of that period: "They have deeply corrupted themselves, as in the days of Gibeah: therefore the Lord will remember their iniquity, He will visit their sins"?[6] At a later stage of his life, such thoughts of the unbelief and iniquity of Israel accompanied St. Paul

[1] See, for instance, 1 Mac. v. 15. x. 1.
[2] 1 Sam. xxxi. 1–6.
[3] Gen. xxviii. Judg. iv. 5. 1 Kings xii. 29. 2 Kings xxiii. 15.
[4] 1 Sam. x. 26 xv. 34.
[5] Judges xx. 43, &c.
[6] Hosea ix. 9

wherever he went. At the early age of twelve years, all his enthusiasm could find an adequate object in the earthly Jerusalem ; the first view of which would be descried about this part of the journey. From the time when the line of the city wall was seen, all else was forgotten. The further border of Benjamin was almost reached. The Rabbis said that the boundary line of Benjamin and Judah, the two faithful tribes, passed through the Temple.[1] And this City and Temple was the common sanctuary of all Israelites. "Thither the tribes go up, even the tribes of the Lord : to testify unto Israel, to give thanks unto the name of the Lord. There is little Benjamin their ruler, and the princes of Judah their council, the princes of Zebulon and the princes of Nephthali : for there is the seat of judgment, even the seat of the house of David." And now the Temple's glittering roof was seen, with the buildings of Zion crowning the eminence above it, and the ridge of the Mount of Olives rising high over all. And now the city gate was passed, with that thrill of the heart which none but a Jew could know. "Our feet stand within thy gates, O Jerusalem. O pray for the peace of Jerusalem : they shall prosper that love thee. Peace be within thy walls : and plenteousness within thy palaces. O God, wonderful art thou in thy holy places : even the God of Israel. He will give strength and power unto His people. Blessed be God."[2]

And now that this young enthusiastic Jew is come into the land of his forefathers, and is about to receive his education in the schools of the Holy City, we may pause to give some description of the state of Judæa and Jerusalem. We have seen that it is impossible to fix the exact date of his arrival, but we know the general features of the period ; and we can easily form to ourselves some idea of the political and religious condition of Palestine.

Herod was now dead. The tyrant had been called to his last account : and that eventful reign, which had destroyed the nationality of the Jews, while it maintained their apparent independence, was over. It is most likely that Archelaus also had ceased to govern, and was already in exile. His accession to power had been attended with dreadful fighting in the streets, with bloodshed at sacred festivals, and with wholesale crucifixions : his reign of ten years was one continued season of disorder and discontent ; and, at last, he was banished to Vienna on the Rhone, that Judæa might be formally constituted into a Roman province.[3] We suppose Saul to

[1] "Sanedrin (ad plagam templi australem) in parte seu portione Judæ, et divina præsentia (seu occidentalis templi pars) in portione Benjamin."—Gemara Babylonia ad tit. Zebachim, cap. 5. fol. 54. b. See Selden de Synedriis Hebræorum, II. xv. 4 (Seldeni Opera, 1726, vol. i. f. 1545).

[2] See Ps. lxviii. and cxxii.

[3] While the question of succession was pending, the Roman soldiers under Sabinus had a desperate conflict with the Jews ; fighting and sacrificing went on together. Varus, the governor of Syria, marched from Antioch to Jerusalem, and 2000 Jews were

have come from Tarsus to Jerusalem when one of the four governors, who preceded Pontius Pilate, was in power,—either Coponius, or Marcus Ambivius, or Annius Rufus, or Valerius Gratus. The governor resided in the town of Cæsarea. Soldiers were quartered there and at Jerusalem, and throughout Judæa, wherever the turbulence of the people made garrisons necessary. Centurions were in the country towns;[1] soldiers on the banks of the Jordan.[2] There was no longer the semblance of independence. The revolution, of which Herod had sown the seeds, now came to maturity. The only change since his death in the appearance of the country was that everything became more Roman than before. Roman money was current in the markets. Roman words were incorporated in the popular language. Roman buildings were conspicuous in all the towns. Even those two independent principalities which two sons of Herod governed, between the provinces of Judæa and Syria, exhibited all the general character of the epoch. Philip the tetrarch of Gaulonitis, called Bethsaida, on the north of the lake of Gennesareth, by the name of Julias, in honour of the family who reigned at Rome. Antipas, the tetrarch of Galilee, built Tiberias on the south of the same lake, in honour of the emperor who about this time (A. D. 14) succeeded his illustrious step-father.

TIBERIUS WITH TOGA.[3]

These political changes had been attended with a gradual alteration in the national feelings of the Jews with regard to their religion. That the sentiment of political nationality was not extinguished was proved too well by all the horrors of Vespasian's and Hadrian's reigns; but there was a growing tendency to cling rather to their law and religion as the centre of their unity. The great conquests of the heathen powers may have been

crucified. The Herodian family, after their father's death, had gone to Rome, where Augustus received them in the Temple of Apollo. Archelaus had never the title of king, though his father had desired it.

1 Luke vii. 1-10.

2 Luke iii. 14.

3 Statue of Tiberius, from the "Musée des Antiques," vol. ii. (Bouillon, Paris.) The statue is in the Louvre. We cannot look upon the portrait of Tiberius without deep interest, when we remember how it must have been engraven on the mind of St. Paul, who would see it before him wherever he went, till it was replaced by those of Caligula

intended by Divine Providence to prepare this change in the Jewish mind. Even under the Maccabees, the idea of the state began to give place, in some degree, to the idea of religious life.[1] Under Herod, the old unity was utterly broken to pieces. The high priests were set up and put down at his caprice; and the jurisdiction of the Sanhedrin was still more abridged; and high priests were raised and deposed, as the Christian patriarchs of Constantinople have for some ages been raised and deposed by the Sultan: so that it is often a matter of great difficulty to ascertain who was high priest at Jerusalem in any given year at this period.[2] Thus the hearts of the Jews turned more and more towards the fulfilment of Prophecy,—to the practice of Religion,—to the interpretation of the Law. All else was now hopeless. The Pharisees, the Scribes, and the Lawyers were growing into a more important body even than the Priests and the Levites;[3] and that system of "Rabbinism" was beginning, "which, supplanting the original religion of the Jews, became, after the ruin of the Temple and the extinction of the public worship, a new bond of national union, the great distinctive feature in the character of modern Judaism."[4]

The Apostolic age was remarkable for the growth of learned Rabbinical schools; but of these the most eminent were the rival schools of Hillel and Schammai. These sages of the law were spoken of by the Jews, and their proverbs quoted, as the seven wise men were quoted by the Greeks. Their traditional systems run through all the Talmudical writings, as the doctrines of the Scotists and Thomists run through the Middle Ages.[5] Both were Pharisaic schools: but the former upheld the honour of tradition as even superior to the law; the latter despised the traditionists when they clashed with Moses. The antagonism between them was so great, that it was said that "Elijah the Tishbite would never be able to reconcile the disciples of Hillel and Schammai."

Of these two schools, that of Hillel was by far the most influential in

and Claudius. The image of the emperor was at that time the object of religious reverence: the emperor was a deity on earth (Dîs æqua potestas. Juv. iv. 71); and the worship paid to him was a real worship (see Merivale's Life of Augustus, p. 159). It is a striking thought, that in those times (setting aside effete forms of religion), the only two genuine worships in the civilised world were the worship of a Tiberius or a Claudius on the one hand, and the worship of Christ on the other.

[1] The Jewish writer, Jost, seems to speak too strongly of this change See the early part of the second volume of his Allg. Gesch. des Isr. Volks.

[2] See Acts xxiii. 5.

[3] In earlier periods of Jewish history, the prophets seem often to have been a more influential body than the priests. It is remarkable that we do not read of "Schools of the Prophets" in any of the Levitical cities. In these schools, some were Levites, as Samuel; some belonged to the other tribes, as Saul and David.

[4] Milman's History of the Jews, vol. iii. p. 100.

[5] See Prideaux's Connection, part II. pref. p. 12, and the beginning of book viii.

its own day, and its decisions have been held authoritative by the greater number of later Rabbis. The most eminent ornament of this school was Gamaliel,[1] whose fame is celebrated in the Talmud. Hillel was the father of Simeon, and Simeon the father of Gamaliel. It has been imagined by some that Simeon was the same old man who took the infant Saviour in his arms, and pronounced the *Nunc Dimittis.*[2] It is difficult to give a conclusive proof of this; but there is no doubt that this Gamaliel was the same who wisely pleaded the cause of St. Peter and the other Apostles,[3] and who had previously educated the future Apostle, St. Paul.[4] His learning was so eminent, and his character so revered, that he is one of the seven who alone among Jewish doctors have been honoured with the title of "Rabban."[5] As Aquinas, among the schoolmen, was called *Doctor Angelicus*, and Bonaventura *Doctor Seraphicus*, so Gamaliel was called the "Beauty of the Law;" and it is a saying of the Talmud, that "since Rabban Gamaliel died, the glory of the law has ceased." He was a Pharisee; but anecdotes[6] are told of him, which show that he was not trammelled by the narrow bigotry of the sect. He had no antipathy to the Greek learning. He rose above the prejudices of his party. Our impulse is to class him with the best of the Pharisees, like Nicodemus and Joseph of Arimathæa. Candour and wisdom seem to have been the features of his character; and this agrees with what we read of him in the Acts of the Apostles,[7] that he was "had in reputation of all the people," and with his honest and intelligent argument when Peter was brought before the Council. It has been imagined by some that he became a Christian:[8] and why he did not become so is known only to Him who understands the secrets of the human heart. But he lived and died a Jew; and a well-known prayer against Christian heretics was composed or

[1] For Gamaliel, see Lightfoot on Acts v. 34 (both in the *Commentary* and the *Hebrew and Talmudical Exercitations*); also on Matt. xiii. 2.

[2] Luke ii. 25–35. [3] Acts v. 34–40. [4] Acts xxii. 3.

[5] This title is the same as "Rabboni" addressed to our Lord by Mary Magdalene.

[6] He bathed once at Ptolemais in an apartment where a statue was erected to a heathen goddess; and being asked how he could reconcile this with the Jewish law, he replied, that the bath was there before the statue; that the bath was not made for the goddess, but the statue for the bath. Tholuck, Eng. Transl. p. 17.

[7] Acts v. 34. Yet Nicodemus and Joseph declared themselves the friends of Christ, which Gamaliel never did. And we should hardly expect to find a violent persecutor among the pupils of a really candid and unprejudiced man. Schrader has an indignant chapter against Gamaliel, and especially against the "unchristian" sentiment that the truth of a religion is to be tested by its success. Der Apostel Paulus, vol. ii. ch. 5.

[8] In the Clementine Recognitions (i. 65), Clement is made to say,—"Latenter frater noster erat in fide, sed consilio nostro inter eos erat:" and the plan is more fully stated in the next section (66). Cotelerius says in a note: "Vulpinum hoc consilium Apostolis indignum est. Decepit tamen Bedam Pseudo-Clemens Rufini. At non ego credulus illis." See Bede on Acts v. 34, and Retract. ibid.; and compare Lightfoot's Comm. The story is adopted by Baronius: see the notes to next Chapter.

sanctioned by him.[1] He died eighteen years before the destruction of Jerusalem,[2] about the time of St. Paul's shipwreck at Malta, and was buried with great honour. Another of his pupils, Onkelos, the author of the celebrated Targum, raised to him such a funeral-pile of rich materials as had never been known, except at the burial of a king.

If we were briefly to specify the three effects which the teaching and example of Gamaliel may be supposed to have produced on the mind of St. Paul, they would be as follows:—candour and honesty of judgment,—a willingness to study and make use of Greek authors,—and a keen and watchful enthusiasm for the Jewish law. We shall see these traits of character soon exemplified in his life. But it is time that we should inquire into the manner of communicating instruction, and learn something concerning the places where instruction was communicated, in the schools of Jerusalem.

Until the formation of the later Rabbinical colleges, which flourished after the Jews were driven from Jerusalem, the instruction in the divinity schools seems to have been chiefly oral. There was a prejudice against the use of any book except the Sacred Writings. The system was one of Scriptural Exegesis.[3] Josephus remarks, at the close of his Antiquities,[4] that the one thing most prized by his countrymen was power in the exposition of Scripture. "They give to that man," he says, "the testimony of being a wise man, who is fully acquainted with our laws, and is able to interpret their meaning." So far as we are able to learn from our sources of information, the method of instruction was something of this kind.[5] At the meetings of learned men, some passage of the Old Testament was taken as a text, or some topic for discussion propounded in Hebrew, translated into the vernacular tongue by means of a Chaldee paraphrase, and made the subject of commentary: various interpretations were given: aphorisms were propounded: allegories suggested: and the opinions of ancient doc-

[1] Lightfoot's Exercitations on Acts v. 34. Otho's Lexicon Rabbinicum, sub voc. Gamaliel. The prayer is given in Mr. Horne's Introduction to the Scriptures, 8th ed. vol. iii. p. 261, as follows: "Let there be no hope to them who apostatise from the true religion; and let heretics, how many soever they be, all perish as in a moment. And let the kingdom of pride be speedily rooted out and broken in our days. Blessed art thou, O Lord our God, who destroyest the wicked, and bringest down the proud." This prayer is attributed by some to "Samuel the Little," who lived in the time of Gamaliel. There is a story that this Samuel the Little was the Apostle Paul himself, "Paulus" meaning "little," and "Samuel" being contracted into "Saul." See Basnage, bk. iii. ch. i. §§ 12, 13.

[2] His son Simeon, who succeeded him as president of the Council, perished in the ruins of the city. Lightf. Exerc. as above.

[3] See the remarks on this subject in the early part of the second volume of Jost's Allg. Gesch. des Isr. Volks.

[4] xx. 11. 2.

[5] See Jost as above; and Dr. Kitto's Cyclopedia of Biblical Literature, art. "Schools" and "Synagogues."

tors quoted and discussed. At these discussions the younger students were present, to listen or to enquire,—or, in the sacred words of St. Luke, "both hearing them and asking them questions:" for it was a peculiarity of the Jewish schools, that the pupil was encouraged to catechize the teacher. Contradictory opinions were expressed with the utmost freedom. This is evident from a cursory examination of the Talmud, which gives us the best notions of the scholastic disputes of the Jews. This remarkable body of Rabbinical jurisprudence has been compared to the Roman body of civil law: but in one respect it might suggest a better comparison with our own English common law, in that it is a vast accumulation of various and often inconsistent precedents: the arguments and opinions which it contains, shew very plainly that the Jewish doctors must often have been occupied with the most frivolous questions; that the "mint, anise, and cummin" were eagerly discussed, while the "weightier matters of the law" were neglected:—but we should not be justified in passing a hasty judgment on ancient volumes, which are full of acknowledged difficulties What we read of the system of the Cabbala has often the appearance of unintelligible jargon: but in all ages it has been true that "the words of the wise are as goads, and as nails fastened by the masters of assemblies."[1] If we could look back on the assemblies of the Rabbis of Jerusalem, with Gamaliel in the midst, and Saul among the younger speakers, it is possible that the scene would be as strange and as different from a place of modern education, as the schools now seen by travellers in the East differ from contemporary schools in England. But the same might be said of the walks of Plato in the Academy, or the lectures of Aristotle in the Lyceum. It is certain that these free and public discussions of the Jews tended to create a high degree of general intelligence among the people; that the students were trained there in a system of excellent dialectics; that they learnt to express themselves in a rapid and sententious style, often with much poetical feeling; and acquired an admirable acquaintance with the words of the ancient Scriptures.[2]

These "Assemblies of the Wise" were possibly a continuation of the "Schools of the Prophets," which are mentioned in the historical books of the Old Testament. Wherever the earlier meetings were held, whether at the gate of the city, or in some more secluded place, we read of no buildings for purposes of worship or instruction before the Captivity. During that melancholy period, when they mourned over their separation from the

[1] Eccles. xii. 11.

[2] Many details are brought together by Meuchen, De Scholis Hebræorum, in his "Novum Testamentum ex Talmude illustratum." It seems that half-yearly examinations were held on four sabbaths of the months Adar and Elul (February and August), when the scholars made recitations and were promoted: the punishments were, confinement, flogging, and excommunication.

COIN OF CYRENE.[1]

Temple, the necessity of assemblies must have been deeply felt, for united prayer and mutual exhortation, for the singing of the "Songs of Zion," and for remembering the "Word of the Lord." When they returned, the public reading of the law became a practice of universal interest: and from this period we must date the erection of *Synagogues*[2] in the different towns of Palestine. So that St. James could say, in the council at Jerusalem: "Moses of old time hath in every city them that preach him, being read in the synagogues every Sabbath day."[3] To this later period the 74th Psalm may be referred,[4] which laments over "the burning of all the synagogues of God in the land."[5] These buildings are not mentioned by Josephus in any of the earlier passages of his history. But in the time of the Apostles we have the fullest evidence that they existed in all the small towns in Judæa, and in all the principal cities where the Jews were dispersed abroad. It seems that the synagogues often consisted of two apartments, one for prayer, preaching, and the offices of public worship; the other for the meetings of learned men, for discussion concerning questions of religion and discipline, and for purposes of education.[6] Thus the *Synagogues* and the *Schools* cannot be considered as two separate subjects. No doubt a distinction must be drawn between the smaller schools of the country villages, and the great divinity schools of Jerusalem. The synagogue which was built by the Centurion at Capernaum[7] was no doubt a far less important place than those synagogues in the Holy City, where "the Libertines, and Cyrenians, and Alexandrians, with those of Asia and

[1] From the British Museum. The beautiful coins of Cyrene shew how entirely it was a Greek city, and therefore imply that its Jews were Hellenistic, like those of Alexandria. See above, p. 18, note.

[2] See Vitringa de Synagoga Vetere, especially bk. i. pt. 2, ch. 12. Basnage assigns the erection of *synagogues* to the time of the Maccabees. Meuschen says that *schools* were established by Ezra; but he gives no proof. It is probable that they were nearly contemporaneous.

[3] Acts xv. 21.

[4] See Ewald's Poetische Bücher des Alten Bundes, and Tholuck's Psalmen für Geistliche und Laien. Mr. Phillips considers this psalm to be simply prophetic of the destruction in the Roman war: Psalms in Heb. and Comm. 1846.

[5] Ps. lxxiv. 8.

[6] The place where the Jews met for worship was called בית הכנסת, as opposed to the בית מדרש, where lectures were given. The term Beth-Midrash is still said to be used in Poland and Germany for the place where Jewish lectures are given on the law.

[7] Luke vii. 5

Cilicia," rose up as one man, and disputed against St. Stephen.[1] We have here five groups of foreign Jews,—two from Africa, two from Western Asia, and one from Europe: and there is no doubt that the Israelites of Syria, Babylonia, and the East were similarly represented. The Rabbinical writers say that there were 480 synagogues in Jerusalem; and though this must be an exaggeration, yet no doubt all shades of Hellenistic and Aramaic opinions found a home in the common metropolis. It is easy to see that an eager and enthusiastic student could have had no lack of excitements to stimulate his religious and intellectual activity, if he spent the years of his youth in that city "at the feet of Gamaliel."

It has been contended, that when St. Paul said he was "brought up" in Jerusalem, "at the feet of Gamaliel," he meant that he had lived at the Rabban's house, and eaten at his table.[2] But the words evidently point to the customary posture of Jewish students at a school. There is a curious passage in the Talmud, where it is said, that "from the days of Moses to Rabban Gamaliel, they stood up to learn the Law; but when Rabban Gamaliel died, sickness came into the world, and they sat down to learn the Law."[3] We need not stop to criticise this sentence, and it is not easy to reconcile it with other authorities on the same subject. "To sit at the feet of a teacher" was a proverbial expression; as when Mary is said to have "sat at Jesus' feet and heard His word."[4] But the proverbial expression must have arisen from a well-known custom. The teacher was seated on an elevated platform, or on the ground, and the pupils around him on low seats or on the floor. Maimonides says:—"How do the masters teach? The doctor sits at the head, and the disciples around him like a crown, that they may all see the doctor and hear his words. Nor is the doctor seated on a seat, and the disciples on the ground; but all are on seats, or all on the floor."[5] St. Ambrose says, in his Commentary on the 1st Epistle to the Corinthians (xiv.), that "it is the tradition of the syna-

[1] Acts vi. 9. It is difficult to classify the synagogues mentioned in this passage. An "Alexandrian Synagogue," built by Alexandrian artisans who were employed about the Temple, is mentioned in the Talmud. See Otho's Lexicon Rabbinicum, sub voc. Synagoga. We have ventured below to use the phrase "Cilician Synagogue," which cannot involve any serious inaccuracy.

[2] Petitus, as quoted by Vitringa, p. 168.

[3] Tradunt magistri nostri; a diebus Mosis usque ad Rabban Gamalielem non didicerunt Legem, nisi stantes; verum a quo mortuus est Rabban Gamaliel, descendit morbus in mundum, et didicerunt Legem sedentes; atque hoc illud est, quod aiunt: a quo tempore Rabban Gamaliel mortuus est, cessavit Gloria Legis. Quoted by Vitringa. p. 167. See Lightfoot on Luke ii. 46; and on Matt. xiii. 2.

[4] Luke x. 39. See viii. 35.

[5] Quomodo docere solent Magistri? Doctor sedet ad summum, et discipuli illum circumcingunt instar coronæ, ut omnes Doctorem intueri et ipsius verba audire possint. Neque sedet Doctor in sedili et discipuli ejus in solo, sed vel omnes sedent in terrâ vel omnes in sedilibus. Quoted by Vitringa, p 166

gogue that they sit while they dispute; the elders in dignity on high chairs, those beneath them on low seats, and the last of all on mats upon the pavement."[1] And again Philo says, that the children of the Essenes sat at the feet of the masters, who interpreted the law, and explained its figurative sense.[2] And the same thing is expressed in that maxim of the Jews—"Place thyself in the dust at the feet of the wise."[3]

In this posture the Apostle of the Gentiles spent his schoolboy days, an eager and indefatigable student. "He that giveth his mind to the law of the Most High, and is occupied in the meditation thereof, will seek out the wisdom of all the ancient, and be occupied in prophecies. He will keep the sayings of the renowned men; and where subtle parables are, he will be there also. He will seek out the secrets of grave sentences, and be conversant in dark parables. He shall serve among great men, and appear among princes: he will travel through strange countries; for he hath tried the good and the evil among men."[4] Such was the pattern proposed to himself by an ardent follower of the Rabbis; and we cannot wonder that Saul, with such a standard before him, and with so ardent a temperament, "made progress in the Jews' religion above many of his contemporaries in his own nation, being more exceedingly zealous of the traditions of his Fathers."[5] Intellectually, his mind was trained to logical acuteness, his memory became well stored with "hard sentences of old," and he acquired the facility of quick and apt quotation of Scripture Morally, he was a strict observer of the requirements of the Law; and, while he led a careful conscientious life, after the example of his ancestors[6] he gradually imbibed the spirit of a fervent persecuting zeal. Among his fellow students, who flocked to Jerusalem from Egypt and Babylonia, from the coasts of Greece and his native Cilicia, he was known and held in high estimation as a rising light in Israel. And if we may draw a natural inference from another sentence of the letter which has just been quoted, he was far from indifferent to the praise of men.[7] Students of the law were called "the holy people;" and we know one occasion when it was said, "This people who knoweth not the Law are cursed."[8] And we can im-

[1] Hæc traditio synagogæ est, ut sedentes disputent, seniores dignitate in cathedris, sequentes in subselliis, novissimi in pavimento super mattas. Amb. Com. in 1 Cor. xiv. (Basle. 1567, p. 284.)

[2] *Ἱερὰ ἡ ἑβδόμη νενόμισται, καθ' ἣν τῶν ἄλλων ἀνέχοντες ἔργων, καὶ εἰς ἱεροὺς ἀφικνούμενοι τόπους, οἳ καλοῦνται συναγωγαὶ, καθ' ἡλικίας ἐν τάξεσιν ὑπὸ πρεσβυτέροις νέοι καθέζονται, μετὰ κόσμου τοῦ προσήκοντος ἔχοντες ἀκροατικῶς.* Mangey's Philo. ii. p. 458.

[3] Sit domus tua conventus sapientum et *pulveriza te in pulvere pedum eorum*, et bibe cum siti verba eorum. Pirke Avoth. cap. 1, § 4, quoted by Vitringa, p. 168.

[4] Eccles. xxxix. 1–4. [5] Gal. i. 14. [6] 2 Tim. i. 3.

[7] Gal. i. 10. *Ἄρτι γὰρ ἀνθρώπους πείθω . . . εἰ γὰρ ἔτι ἀνθρώποις ἤρεσκον, Χριστοῦ δοῦλος οὐκ ἂν ἤμην.* "Am I *now* seeking to conciliate men? . . . Nay, if I still strove (as once I did) to please men, I should not be the servant of Christ."

[8] John vii. 49.

agine him saying to himself, with all the rising pride of a successful Pharisee, in the language of the Book of Wisdom: "I shall have estimation among the multitude, and honour with the elders, though I be young. I shall be found of a quick conceit in judgment, and shall be admired in the sight of great men. When I hold my tongue, they shall bide my leisure; and when I speak, they shall give good ear unto me." [1]

While thus he was passing through the busy years of his student-life, nursing his religious enthusiasm and growing in self-righteousness, others were advancing towards their manhood, not far from Jerusalem, of whom then he knew nothing, but for whose cause he was destined to count that loss which now was his highest gain.[2] There was one at Hebron, the son of a priest "of the course of Abia," who was soon to make his voice heard throughout Israel as the preacher of repentance; there were boys by the Lake of Galilee, mending their fathers' nets, who were hereafter to be the teachers of the World; and there was ONE, at Nazareth, for the sake of whose love—they, and Saul himself, and thousands of faithful hearts throughout all future ages, should unite in saying:—"He must increase, but I must decrease." It is possible that Gamaliel may have been one of those doctors with whom JESUS was found conversing in the Temple. It is probable that Saul may have been within the precincts of the Temple at some festival, when Mary and Joseph came up from Galilee. It is certain that the eyes of the Saviour and of His future disciple must often have rested on the same objects,—the same crowd of pilgrims and worshippers,—the same walls of the Holy City,—the same olives on the other side of the valley of Jehoshaphat. But at present they were strangers. The mysterious human life of JESUS was silently advancing towards its great consummation. Saul was growing more and more familiar with the outward observances of the Law, and gaining that experience of the "spirit of bondage" which should enable him to understand himself, and to teach to others, the blessings of the "spirit of adoption." He was feeling the pressure of that yoke, which in the words of St. Peter, "neither his fathers nor he were able to bear." He was learning (in proportion as his conscientiousness increased) to tremble at the slightest deviation from the Law as jeopardising salvation: "whence arose that tormenting scrupulosity which invented a number of limitations, in order (by such self-imposed restraint) to guard against every possible transgression of the Law."[3] The struggles of this period of his life he has himself described in the seventh chapter of Romans. Meanwhile, year after year passed away. John the Baptist appeared by the waters of the Jordan. The greatest event of the world's history was finished on Calvary. The sacrifice for sin was offered at a time when sin appeared to be most triumphant. At

[1] Wisdom viii. 10–12.
[2] See Phil. iii. 5–7.
[3] Neander Pfl. und L. (Eng Trans. p. 137.)

the period of the Crucifixion, three of the principal persons who demand the historian's attention are—the Emperor Tiberius, spending his life of shameless lust on the island of Capreæ,—his vile minister, Sejanus, revelling in cruelty at Rome,—and Pontius Pilate at Jerusalem, mingling with the sacrifices the blood of the Galileans.[1] How refreshing is it to turn from these characters to such scenes as that where St. John receives his Lord's dying words from the cross, or where St. Thomas meets Him after the resurrection, to have his doubts turned into faith, or where St. Stephen sheds the first blood of martyrdom, praying for his murderers!

This first martyrdom has the deepest interest for us; since it is the first occasion when Saul comes before us in his early manhood. Where had he been during these years which we have rapidly passed over in a few lines,—the years in which the foundations of Christianity were laid? We cannot assume that he had remained continuously in Jerusalem. Many years had elapsed since he came, a boy, from his home at Tarsus. He must have attained the age of twenty-five or thirty years when our Lord's public ministry began. His education was completed; and we may conjecture, with much probability, that he returned to Tarsus. When he says, in the first letter to the Corinthians (ix. 1),—"Have I not seen the Lord?" and when he speaks in the second (v. 16) of having "known Christ after the flesh," he seems only to allude, in the first case, to his vision on the road to Damascus; and, in the second, to his carnal opinions concerning the Messiah. It is hardly conceivable, that if he had been at Jerusalem during our Lord's public ministration there, he should never allude to the fact.[2] In this case, he would surely have been among the persecutors of Jesus, and have referred to this as the ground of his remorse, instead of expressing his repentance for his opposition merely to the Saviour's followers.[3]

If he returned to the banks of the Cydnus, he would find that many changes had taken place among his friends in the interval which had brought him from boyhood to manhood. But the only change in himself was that he brought back with him, to gratify the pride of his parents, if they still were living, a mature knowledge of the Law, a stricter life, a more fervent zeal. And here, in the schools of Tarsus, he had abundant opportunity for becoming acquainted with that Greek literature, the taste for which he had caught from Gamaliel, and for studying the writings of

[1] Luke xiii. 1.

[2] In the absense of more information, it is difficult to write with confidence concerning this part of St. Paul's life. Benson thinks he was a young student during our Lord's ministry, and places a considerable interval between the Ascension of Christ and the persecution of Stephen. Lardner thinks that the restraint and retirement of a student might have kept him in ignorance of what was going on in the world. Hemsen's opinion has been given above.

[3] 1 Cor. xv. 9. Acts xxii. 20.

Philo and the Hellenistic Jews. Supposing him to be thus employed, we will describe in a few words the first beginnings of the Apostolic Church, and the appearance presented by it to that Judaism in the midst of which it rose, and follow its short history to the point where the "young man, whose name was Saul," reappears at Jerusalem, in connection with his friends of the Cilician Synagogue, "disputing with Stephen."

Before our Saviour ascended into heaven, He said to His disciples: "Ye shall be witnesses unto me both in Jerusalem, and in all Judæa, and in Samaria, and unto the uttermost part of the earth."[1] And when Matthias had been chosen, and the promised blessing had been received on the day of Pentecost, this order was strictly followed. First the Gospel was proclaimed in the City of Jerusalem, and the numbers of those who believed gradually rose from 120 to 5000.[2] Until the disciples were "scattered,"[3] "upon the persecution that arose about Stephen,"[4] Jerusalem was the scene of all that took place in the Church of Christ. We read as yet of no communication of the truth to the Gentiles, nor to the Samaritans; no hint even of any Apostolic preaching in the country parts of Judæa. It providentially happened, indeed, that the first outburst of the new doctrine, with all its miraculous evidence, was witnessed by "Jews and proselytes" from all parts of the world.[5] They had come up to the Festival of Pentecost from the banks of the Tigris and Euphrates, of the Nile and of the Tiber, from the provinces of Asia Minor, from the desert of Arabia, and from the islands of the Greek Sea; aad when they returned to their homes, they carried with them news which prepared the way for the Glad Tidings about to issue from Mount Zion to "the uttermost parts of the earth." But as yet the Gospel lingered on the Holy Hill. The first acts of the Apostles were "prayer and supplication" in the "upper room;" breaking of bread "from house to house;"[6] miracles in the Temple; gatherings of the people in Solomon's cloister, and the bearing of testimony in the council chamber of the Sanhedrin.

One of the chief characteristics of the Apostolic Church, considered in itself, was the bountiful charity of its members one towards another. Many of the Jews of Palestine, and therefore many of the earliest Christian converts, were extremely poor. The odium incurred by adopting the new doctrine might undermine the livelihood of some who depended on their trade for support, and this would make alms-giving necessary. But the Jews of Palestine were relatively poor, compared with those of the dispersion. We see this exemplified on later occasions, in the contributions

[1] Acts i. 8. [2] Acts i. 15. ii. 41. iv. 4.
[3] Acts viii. 1. [4] Acts xi. 19. [5] Acts ii. 9–11.
[6] Or rather "at home" (κατ' οἶκον. Acts ii. 46)—i. e. in their meetings at the private houses of Christians, as opposed to the public devotions in the Temple.

which St. Paul more than once anxiously promoted.[1] And in the very first days of the Church, we find its wealthier members placing their entire possessions at the disposal of the Apostles. Not that there was any abolition of the rights of property, as the words of St. Peter to Ananias very well show.[2] But those who were rich gave up what God had given them, in the spirit of generous self-sacrifice, and according to the true principle of Christian communism, which regards property as entrusted to the possessor, not for himself, but for the good of the whole community,—to be distributed according to such methods as his charitable feeling and conscientious judgment may approve. The Apostolic Church was, in this respect, in a healthier condition than the Church of modern days. But even then we find ungenerous and suspicious sentiments growing up in the midst of the general benevolence. That old jealousy between the Aramaic and Hellenistic Jews reappeared. Their party feeling was excited by some real or apparent unfairness in the distribution of the fund set apart for the poor. "A murmuring of the Grecians against the Hebrews,"[3] or of the Hebrews against the Grecians, had been a common occurrence for at least two centuries; and, notwithstanding the power of the Divine Spirit, none will wonder that it broke out again even among those who had become obedient to the doctrine of Christ. That the widows' fund might be carefully distributed, seven almoners or deacons were appointed, of whom the most eminent was St. Stephen, described as a man "full of faith, and of the Holy Ghost," and as one who, "full of faith and power, did great wonders and miracles among the people." It will be observed that these seven men have Greek names, and that one was a proselyte from the Greco-Syrian city of Antioch. It was natural, from the peculiar character of the quarrel, that Hellenistic Jews should have been appointed to this office. And this circumstance must be looked on as divinely arranged. For the introduction of that party, which was most free from local and national prejudices, into the very ministry of the Church, must have had an important influence in preparing the way for the admission of the Gentiles.

Looking back, from our point of view, upon the community at Jerusalem, we see in it the beginning of that great society, the Church, which has continued to our own time, distinct both from Jews and Heathen, and which will continue till it absorbs both the Heathen and the Jews. But to the contemporary Jews themselves it wore a very different appearance. From the Hebrew point of view, the disciples of Christ would be regarded as a Jewish sect or synagogue. The synagogues, as we have seen, were very numerous at Jerusalem. There were already the Cilician Synagogue, the Alexandrian Synagogue, the Synagogue of the Libertines,—and to

[1] Acts xi. 29, 30; and again Rom. xv. 25, 26, compared with Acts xxiv. 17 1 Cor. xvi. 1-4. 2 Cor. viii. 1-4.

[2] Acts v. 4.

[3] Acts vi. 1

these was now added (if we may use so bold an expression) the Nazarene Synagogue, or the Synagogue of the Galilæans. Not that any separate building was erected for the devotions of the Christians; for they met from house to house for prayer and the breaking of bread. But they were by no means separated from the nation;[1] they attended the festivals; they worshipped in the Temple. They were a new and singular party in the nation, holding peculiar opinions, and interpreting the Scriptures in a peculiar way. This is the aspect under which the Church would first present itself to the Jews, and among others to Saul himself. Many different opinions were expressed in the synagogues concerning the nature and office of the Messiah. These Galilæans would be distinguished as holding the strange opinion that the true Messiah was that notorious "malefactor," who had been crucified at the last Passover. All parties in the nation united to oppose, and if possible to crush, the monstrous heresy.

The first attempts to put down the new faith came from the Sadducees. The high priest and his immediate adherents[2] belonged to this party. They hated the doctrine of the resurrection; and the resurrection of Jesus Christ was the corner-stone of all St. Peter's teaching. He and the other Apostles were brought before the Sanhedrin, who in the first instance were content to enjoin silence on them. The order was disobeyed, and they were summoned again. The consequences might have been fatal: but that the jealousy between the Sadducees and Pharisees was overruled, and the instrumentality of one man's wisdom was used, by Almighty God, for the protection of His servants. Gamaliel, the eminent Pharisee, argued, that if this cause were not of God, it would come to nothing, like the work of other impostors; but, if it were of God, they could not safely resist what must certainly prevail: and the Apostles of Jesus Christ were scourged, and allowed to "depart from the presence of the council, rejoicing that they were counted worthy to suffer shame for His name."[3] But it was impossible that those Pharisees, whom Christ had always rebuked, should long continue to be protectors of the Christians. On this occasion we find the teacher, Gamaliel, taking St. Peter's part: at the next persecution, Saul, the pupil, is actively concerned in the murder of St. Stephen. It was the same alternation of the two prevailing parties, first opposing each other, and then uniting to oppose the Gospel, of which Saul himself had such intimate experience when he became St. Paul.[4]

[1] "The worship of the temple and the synagogue still went side by side with the prayers, and the breaking of bread from house to house. . . . The Jewish family life was the highest expression of Christian unity. . . . The fulfilment of the ancient law was the aspect of Christianity to which the attention of the Church was most directed." Mr. Stanley's Sermon on St. Peter, p. 92; see James ii. 2, where the word "synagogue" is applied to Christian assemblies.

[2] Acts iv. 1. v. 17. [3] Acts v. 41. [4] See Acts xxiii. 6, 9, 14, 20.

In many particulars St. Stephen was the forerunner of St. Paul. Up to this time the conflict had been chiefly maintained with the Aramaic Jews; but Stephen carried the war of the Gospel into the territory of the Hellenists. The learned members of the foreign synagogues endeavoured to refute him by argument or by clamour. The *Cilician* Synagogue is particularly mentioned (Acts vi. 9, 10) as having furnished some conspicuous opponents to Stephen, who "were not able to resist the wisdom and the spirit with which he spake." We cannot doubt, from what follows, that Saul of Tarsus, already distinguished by his zeal and talents among the younger champions of Pharisaism, bore a leading part in the discussions which here took place. He was now, though still "a young man" (Acts vii. 58), yet no longer in the first opening of youth. This is evident from the fact that he was appointed to an important ecclesiastical and political office immediately afterwards. Such an appointment he could hardly have received from the Sanhedrin before the age of thirty, and probably not so early; for we must remember that a peculiar respect for seniority distinguished the Rabbinical authorities. We can imagine Saul, then, the foremost in the Cilician Synagogue, "disputing" against the new doctrines of the Hellenistic Deacon, in all the energy of vigorous manhood, and with all the vehement logic of the Rabbis. How often must these scenes have been recalled to his mind, when he himself took the place of Stephen in many a Synagogue, and bore the brunt of the like furious assault; surrounded by "Jews filled with envy, who spake against those things which were spoken by Paul, contradicting and blaspheming."[1] But this clamour and these arguments were not sufficient to convince or intimidate St. Stephen. False witnesses were then suborned to accuse him of blasphemy against Moses and against God,—who asserted, when he was dragged before the Sanhedrin, that they had heard him say that Jesus of Nazareth should destroy the temple, and change the Mosaic customs. It is evident, from the nature of this accusation, how remarkably his doctrine was an anticipation of St. Paul's. As an Hellenistic Jew, he was less entangled in the prejudices of Hebrew nationality than his Aramaic brethren; and he seems to have a fuller understanding of the final intention of the Gospel than St. Peter and the Apostles had yet attained to. Not doubting the divinity of the Mosaic economy, and not faithless to the God of Abraham, Isaac, and Jacob, he yet saw that the time was coming, yea, then was, when the "true worshippers" should worship Him, not in the Temple only or in any one sacred spot, but everywhere throughout the earth, "in spirit and in truth;" and for this doctrine he was doomed to die.

When we speak of the *Sanhedrin*, we are brought into contact with an important controversy. It is much disputed whether it had at this period

[1] Acts xiii. 45.

the power of inflicting death.[1] On the one hand, we apparently find the existence of this power denied by the Jews themselves at the trial of our Lord;[2] and, on the other, we apparently find it assumed and acted on in the case of St. Stephen. The Sanhedrin at Jerusalem, like the Areopagus at Athens, was the highest and most awful court of judicature, especially in matters that pertained to religion; but like that Athenian tribunal, its real power gradually shrunk, though the reverence attached to its decisions remained. It probably assumed its systematic form under the second Hyrcanus; and it became a fixed institution in the Commonwealth under his sons, who would be glad to have their authority nominally limited, but really supported, by such a Council.[3] Under the Herods, and under the Romans, its jurisdiction was curtailed;[4] and we are informed, on Talmudical authority,[5] that, forty years before the destruction of Jerusalem, it was formally deprived of the power of inflicting death. If this is true, we must consider the proceedings at the death of St. Stephen as tumultuous and irregular. And nothing is more probable than that Pontius Pilate (if indeed he was not absent at the time) would willingly connive, in the spirit of Gallio at Corinth, at an act of unauthorised cruelty in "a question of words and names and of the Jewish law,"[6] and that the Jews would willingly assume as much power as they dared, when the honour of Moses and the Temple was in jeopardy.

The council assembled in solemn and formal state to try the blasphemer. There was great and general excitement in Jerusalem. "The people, the scribes, and the elders" had been "stirred up" by the members of the Hellenistic Synagogue.[7] It is evident, from that vivid expression which is

1 Most of the modern German critics (Neander, De Wette, Olshausen, &c.) are of opinion that they had not at this time the power of life and death. A very careful and elaborate argument for the opposite view will be found in Biscoe's History of the Acts confirmed, ch. vi. See also Krebs, Obs. in N. T. e Flavio Josepho, pp. 64 and 155. Mr. Milman says that in his "opinion, formed upon the study of the cotemporary Jewish history, the power of the Sanhedrin, at this period of political change and confusion, on this, as well as on other points, was altogether undefined."—History of Christianity, vol. i. p. 340. Compare the narrative of the death of St. James. Joseph. A. xx. 9.

2 John xviii. 31, xix. 6. See the Commentaries of Tittman and Lücke.

3 Jost's Allg. Gesch., vol. ii. p. 6, &c. The Greek term συνέδριον, from which 'Sanhedrin" (סנהדרין) is derived, makes it probable that its systematic organization dates from the Greco-Macedonian period.

4 We see the beginning of this in the first passage where the council is mentioned by Josephus, Antiq. xiv. 9. See Selden de Synedriis Hebræorum, II. xv. 15. "Principes Synedrii . . . . summotos interdum fuisse perinde ac Pontifices, idque imprimis seculis illis recentioribus, quibus reipublicæ, imperii, jurisdictionis facies pro dominantium victorumque arbitratu crebro mutabat, non est cur omnino dubitemus: etiam et constitutos subinde a Romanis, prout gubernandi ratio exigebat." Opera I. f. 1572.

5 Otho, Lexicon Rabbinicum, sub voc. Synedrium.

6 Acts xviii. 15.

7 vi. 12.

quoted from the accusers' mouths,—"*this place*"—"*this holy place*,"—that the meeting of the Sanhedrin took place in the close neighbourhood of the Temple. Their ancient and solemn room of assembly was the hall Gazith,[1] or the "Stone-Chamber," partly within the Temple Court and partly without it. The president sat in the less sacred portion, and around him, in a semi-circle, were the rest of the seventy judges.[2]

Before these judges Stephen was made to stand, confronted by his accusers. The eyes of all were fixed upon his countenance, which grew bright as they gazed on it, with a supernatural radiance and serenity. In the beautiful Jewish expression of the Scripture, "They saw his face as it had been that of an angel." The judges, when they saw his glorified countenance, might have remembered the shining on the face of Moses,[3] and trembled lest Stephen's voice should be about to speak the will of Jehovah, like that of the great lawgiver. Instead of being occupied with the faded glories of the Second Temple, they might have recognised in the spectacle before them the Shechinah of the Christian soul, which is the living Sanctuary of God. But the trial proceeded. The judicial question, to which the accused was required to plead, was put by the president: "Are these things so?" And then Stephen answered, and his clear voice was heard in the silent council-hall, as he went through the history of the chosen people, proving his own deep faith in the sacredness of the Jewish economy, but suggesting, here and there, that spiritual interpretation of it which had always been the true one, and the truth of which was now to be made manifest to all.[4] He began, with a wise discretion, from the call of Abraham, and travelled historically in his argument through all the great stages of their national existence,—from Abraham to Joseph,—from Joseph to Moses,—from Moses to David and Solomon. And as he went on he selected and glanced at those points which made for his own cause. He showed that God's blessing rested on the faith of Abraham, though he had "not so much as to set his foot on" in the land of promise (v. 5), on the piety of Joseph, though he was an exile in Egypt (v. 9), and on the holiness of the Burning Bush, though in the desert of Sinai (v. 30). He

[1] Otho, Lexicon Rabbinicum, sub voc. Conclave; and Selden de Synedriis Hebræorum, II. x. 2, II. xv. 4. (ff. 1431 & 1544.) See above p. 54, n. 1. It appears that the Talmudical authorities differ as to whether it was on the south or north side of the Temple. But they agree in placing it to the east of the Most Holy Place.

[2] Selden describes the form in which the Sanhedrin sat, and gives a diagram with the "President of the Council" in the middle, the "Father of the Council" by his side, and "Scribes" at the extremities of the semicircle: II. vi. 1. ff. 1318, 1319.

[3] Exodus xxxiv. 29–35: see 2 Cor. iii. 7, 13. Chrysostom imagines (Hom. xv.) that the angelic brightness on Stephen's face might be intended to alarm the judges; for as he says, it is possible for a countenance full of spiritual grace to be awful and terrible to those who are full of hate.

[4] For an analysis of this speech, see Schöttgen's Horæ Hebraicæ; Kuinoel's Commentary; and also Neander in the Pfl. und Leit.

dwelt in detail on the Lawgiver, in such a way as to show his own unquestionable orthodoxy; but he quoted the promise concerning "the prophet like unto Moses" (v. 37), and reminded his hearers that the law, in which they trusted, had not kept their forefathers from idolatry (v. 39, &c.). And so he passed on to the Temple, which had so prominent a reference to the charge against him: and while he spoke of it, he alluded to the words of Solomon himself,[1] and of the prophet Isaiah,[2] who denied that any temple "made with hands" could be the place of God's highest worship. And thus far they listened to him. It was the story of the chosen people, to which every Jew listened with interest and pride.

It is remarkable, as we have said before, how completely St. Stephen is the forerunner of St. Paul, both in the form and the matter of this defence. His securing the attention of the Jews by adopting the historical method, is exactly what the Apostle did in the synagogue at Antioch in Pisidia.[3] His assertion of his attachment to the true principles of the Mosaic religion is exactly what was said to Agrippa: "I continue unto this day, witnessing both to small and great, saying none other things than those which the prophets and Moses did say should come."[4] It is deeply interesting to think of Saul as listening to the martyr's voice, as he antedated those very arguments which he himself was destined to reiterate in synagogues and before kings. There is no reason to doubt that he was present,[5] although he may not have been qualified to vote[6] in the Sanhedrin. And it is evident, from the thoughts which occurred to him in his subsequent vision within the precincts of the Temple,[7] how deep an impression St. Stephen's death had left on his memory. And there are even verbal coincidences which may be traced between this address and St.

[1] 1 Kings viii. 27. 2 Chron. ii. 6. vi. 18.

[2] Is. lxvi. 1, 2. [3] Acts xiii. 16–22. [4] Acts xxvi. 22.

[5] Mr. Humphry remarks (Comm. on Acts, 1847, p. 48), that it is not improbable we owe to him the defence of St. Stephen as given in the Acts. Besides the resemblance mentioned in the text, he points out the similarity between Acts vii. 44, and Heb. viii. 5, between Acts vii. 5-8, and Rom. iv. 10–19, and between Acts vii. 60, and 2 Tim. iv. 16. And if the Epistle to the Hebrews was written by St. Paul, may we not suppose that this scene was present to his mind when he wrote, "Jesus suffered without the gate: let us go forth therefore unto Him without the camp, bearing His reproach"? (xiii. 12, 13.)

[6] One of the necessary qualifications of members of the Sanhedrin was, that they should be the fathers of children, because such were supposed more likely to lean towards mercy. See Selden, quoting from Maimonides: "In nullo Synedriorum cooptabant quempiam cui proles deesset, unde fieret misericors:" and again from the Jerusalem Gemara, "Is qui non vidit sibi liberos, judiciis pecuniariis idoneus est, at vero non capitalibus," II. ix. 4, f. 1422. If this was the rule when Stephen was tried, and if Saul was one of the judges, he must have been married at the time.

[7] He said in his trance, "Lord, they know that I imprisoned and beat in every synagogue them that believed on thee; and when the blood of thy martyr Stephen was shed, I also was standing by, and consenting unto his death, and kept the raiment of them that slew him." Acts xxii. 19, 20.

Paul's speeches or writings. The words used by Stephen of the Temple call to mind those which were used at Athens.[1] When he speaks of the law as received "by the disposition of angels," he anticipates a phrase in the Epistle to the Galatians (iii. 19). His exclamation at the end, "Ye stiffnecked and uncircumcised in heart . . . who have received the law . . . and have not kept it," is only an indignant condensation of the argument in the Epistle to the Romans: "Behold thou art called a Jew, and restest in the law, and makest thy boast of God, and knowest His will . . . Thou, therefore, that makest thy boast of the law, through breaking the law dishonourest thou God? . . . He is not a Jew which is one outwardly; neither is that circumcision which is outward in the flesh; but he is a Jew which is one inwardly: and circumcision is that of the heart, in the spirit, and not in the letter; whose praise is not of man, but of God." (ii. 17–29).

The rebuke which Stephen, full of the Divine Spirit, suddenly broke away from the course of his narrative to pronounce, was the signal for a general outburst of furious rage on the part of his judges.[2] They "gnashed on him with their teeth" in the same spirit in which they had said, not long before, to the blind man who was healed—"Thou wast altogether born in sins, and dost thou teach us?"[3] But, in contrast with the malignant hatred which had blinded their eyes, Stephen's serene faith was supernaturally exalted into a direct vision of the blessedness of the Redeemed. He, whose face had been like that of an angel on earth, was made like one of those angels themselves, "who do always behold the face of our Father which is in Heaven."[4] "He being full of the Holy Ghost, looked up steadfastly into Heaven, and saw the glory of God, and Jesus standing on the right hand of God." The scene before his eyes was no longer the council-hall at Jerusalem and the circle of his infuriated judges; but he gazed up into the endless courts of the celestial Jerusalem, with its "innumerable company of angels," and saw Jesus, in whose righteous cause he was about to die. In other places, where our Saviour is spoken of in His glorified state, He is said to be, not standing, but seated, at the right hand of the Father.[5] Here alone He is said to be standing. It is as if (according to Chrysostom's[6] beautiful thought) He had risen from His throne, to

[1] Acts xvii. 24.

[2] It is evident that the speech was interrupted. We may infer what the conclusion would have been from the analogy of St. Paul's speech at Antioch in Pisidia, Acts xiii.

[3] John ix. 34.

[4] Matt. xviii. 10.

[5] As in Eph. i. 20. Col. iii. 1. Heb. i. 3. viii. 1. x. 12. xii. 2: compare Rom. viii. 34, and 1 Pet. iii. 22.

[6] Τί οὖν ἑστῶτα καὶ οὐχὶ καθήμενον; ἵνα δείξῃ τὴν ἀντίληψιν τὴν εἰς τὸν μάρτυρα· καὶ γὰρ περὶ τοῦ Πατρὸς λέγεται· "ἀνάστα ὁ Θεός." καὶ πάλιν, "νῦν ἀναστήσομαι, λέγει Κύριος· θήσομαι ἐν σωτηρίῳ·" ἵνα οὖν πολλὴν τῷ ἀθλητῇ τὴν προθυμίαν παράσχῃ, καὶ πείσῃ τοὺς μαινομένους ἐκείνους καθυφεῖναι τῆς κάτ' αὐτοῦ λύττης, τὸ τοῦ βοηθοῦντος

succour His persecuted servant, and to receive him to Himself. And when Stephen saw his Lord—perhaps with the memories of what he had seen on earth crowding into his mind,—he suddenly exclaimed, in the ecstacy of his vision: "Behold! I see the Heavens opened and the Son of Man standing on the right hand of God!"

This was too much for the Jews to bear. The blasphemy of Jesus had been repeated. The follower of Jesus was hurried to destruction. "They cried out with a loud voice, and stopped their ears, and ran upon him with one accord." It is evident that it was a savage and disorderly condemnation.[1] They dragged him out of the council-hall, and, making a sudden rush and tumult through the streets, hurried him to one of the gates of the city,—and somewhere about the rocky edges of the ravine of Jehoshaphat, where the Mount of Olives looks down upon Gethsemane and Siloam, or on the open ground to the north, which travellers cross when they go towards Samaria or Damascus,—with stones that lay without the walls of the Holy City, this heavenly-minded martyr was murdered. The exact place of his death is not known. There are two traditions,[2]—an ancient

ἐπιδείκνυται σχῆμα. Ἐκ τοῦ εἰς τὴν ἀνάληψ. λογ. ς. The passage is given at length in Cramer's Catena on the Acts. A similar passage is quoted by Mr. Humphry from Gregory the Great: "Scitis, fratres, quia sedere judicantis est, stare vero pugnantis vel adjuvantis. Stephanus autem vidit, quem adjutorem habuit." Hom. xxix. in Fest. Ascens.

1. As to whether it was a judicial sentence at all, see above, p. 69, note 1.

2 It is well known that the tradition which identifies St. Stephen's gate with the Damascus gate, and places the scene of martyrdom on the north, can be traced from an early period to the fifteenth century; and that the modern tradition, which places both the gate and the martyrdom on the east, can be traced back to the same century. See Dr. Robinson's Researches, i. pp. 475, 476; and Williams' Holy City, p. 364. It is probable that the popular opinion regarding these sacred sites was suddenly changed by some monks from interested motives. The writer of this believes that he is the first to notice a curious turning-point in the history of the traditional belief. In a journal of the fifteenth century ("*Fabri Evagatorium,*" unknown till published in 1843 in the "Bibliothek des Literarischen Vereins in Stuttgart," though a German abridgment is in Dr. Robinson's List) the *gate* of St. Stephen is on the north, but the place of *martyrdom* on the east. He goes out of the gate on the north, "quæ olim dicebatur porta Ephraim, quia per eam via est ad montem Ephraim, nunc vero dicitur porta S. Stephani, quia per eam fuit eductus et extra in valle lapidatus: per hanc portam est via in Sichem, Samariam et Galilæam provinciam." Then turning to the right, and round the N. E. angle of the wall, he descends to the stone where the clothes of the murderers were laid, not far from the *Golden Gate.* "Super hanc petram posuerunt vestimenta sua carnifices . . . et Saulus adolescens huic aderat spectaculo, et zelo pro Judaismo accensus omnium vestimenta custodiebat, ut sine sollicitudine lapidarent. Sedebat autem Saulus supra vestimenta et petram, fremens in Stephanum et blasphemans Christum. Hunc ergo locum deosculati sumus, et indulgentias recepimus." A little further on—"Ad locum venimus, in quo Stephanus fuit lapidatus . . . in hoc ergo loco ipsos lapides deosculati sumus, et indulgentias suscepimus." Vol. iii. pp. 367, 368, 370. We cannot be sure of the exact position of the Gate of Ephraim or of Stephen mentioned in the Evagatorium. There are at present two gates in the northern wall of Jerusalem; the *Damascus Gate,*—and one to the east of it, now closed up, com

one, which places it on the north, beyond the Damascus gate; and a modern one, which leads travellers through what is now called the gate of St. Stephen, to a spot near the brook Kedron, over against the garden of Gethsemane. But those who look upon Jerusalem from an elevated point on the north-east, have both these positions in view; and any one who stood there on that day[1] might have seen the crowd rush forth from the gate, and the witnesses (who according to the law were required to throw the first stones[2]) cast off their outer garments, and lay them down at the feet of Saul.

The contrast is striking between the indignant zeal which the martyr[3] had just expressed against the sin of his judges, and the forgiving love which he shewed to themselves, when they became his murderers. He first uttered a prayer for himself in the words of Jesus Christ, which he knew were spoken from the cross, and which he may himself have heard from those holy lips. And then, deliberately kneeling down, in that posture of humility in which the body most naturally expresses the supplication of the mind, and which has been consecrated as the attitude of Christian devotion by Stephen and by Paul himself,[4]—he gave the last few moments of his consciousness to a prayer for the forgiveness of his enemies: and the words were scarcely spoken when death seized upon him, or rather, in the words of Scripture, "he fell asleep."

"And Saul was consenting to his death." A Spanish painter,[5] in a

monly called *Herod's Gate.* Dr. Robinson (i. 473) seems to think that the Gate of Ephraim (Neh. xii. 39) and the Gate of Benjamin (Jer. xxxvii. 13) are identical with the former; and (i. 476) he identifies the Porta Sancti Stephani of the Middle Ages with the former, but the Porta Benjamin with the latter. Schulz ("Jerusalem, 1845," p. 51) believes the Porta Sancti Stephani to be the modern Herod's Gate, while he considers the Damascus Gate to be the old Gate of Ephraim, and transfers the Porta Benjamin to the east side of the city. He suggests that the Arabic name of Herod's Gate, "Babez-Zahari"—"the Gate of Flowers" may be a translation of the Greek Στέφανος. See Kiepert's map, which accompanies his Memoir.

[1] There is a legend that St. Mary was standing on a rock on the other side of the valley. An old traveller says, describing the descent of the Mount of Olives, "In ye way they shew'd us ye rock whereon o^r Lady stood when she saw St. Steven ston'd to death." Below is the Garden of Gethsemane. He adds, "A little beyond they shew'd us ye rock where St. Steven was ston'd to death; proceeding towards Damascus gate on ye right hand of ye way, is Jeremiah's grotto, where he compos'd his Lamentations, &c."—E. Chaloner's Travels in 1688,—a MS. in the possession of the Duke of Sutherland.

[2] See Deut. xvii. 5-7. The stoning was always outside the city, Levit. xxiv. 14. 1 Kings xxi. 10, 13. For the forms and regulations at the execution, as enumerated by the Talmudists, see Otho, Lexicon Rabbinicum, sub voc. Lapidatio.

[3] The Christian use of the word μάρτυρ begins with St. Stephen. See Mr. Humphry's note on Acts xxii. 20. "Thy martyr Stephen," &c.

[4] At Miletus (Acts xx. 36), and at Tyre (Acts xxi. 5). See Acts ix. 40.

[5] Vicente Joannes, the founder of the Valencian school, one of the most austere of the grave and serious painters of Spain. The picture is one of a series on St. Stephen;

picture of Stephen conducted to the place of execution, has represented Saul as walking by the martyr's side with melancholy calmness. He consents to his death from a sincere, though mistaken, conviction of duty; and the expression of his countenance is strongly contrasted with the rage of the baffled Jewish doctors and the ferocity of the crowd who flock to the scene of bloodshed. Literally considered, such a representation is scarcely consistent either with Saul's conduct immediately afterwards, or with his own expressions concerning himself at the later periods of his life.[1] But the picture, though historically incorrect, is poetically true. The painter has worked according to the true idea of his art in throwing upon the persecutor's countenance the shadow of his coming repentance. We cannot dissociate the martyrdom of Stephen from the conversion of Paul. The spectacle of so much constancy, so much faith, so much love, could not be lost. It is hardly too much to say with Augustine,[2] that "the Church owes Paul to the prayer of Stephen."

SI STEPHANUS NON ORASSET
ECCLESIA PAULUM NON HABERET

Note on the "Libertines" and the "Citizenship of St. Paul."

Since this chapter was sent to press, the writer has seen Wieseler's Chronologie des Apostolischen Zeitalters (Göttingen, 1848); a work of which both the text and the notes are of great importance. Dr. Wieseler argues (note, pp. 61–63) that St. Paul was probably a *Cilician Libertinus.* Great numbers of Jews had been made slaves in the civil wars, and then manumitted. A slave manumitted with due formalities became a Roman citizen. Now we find St. Paul taking an active part in the persecution of Stephen; and the verse which describes Stephen's great opponents,[3] may be so translated as to mean "Libertines" from "Cyrene, Alexandria, Cilicia, and Asia." Thus it is natural to conclude that the Apostle, with other Cilician Jews, may have been, like Horace, "libertino patre natus."[4] The two passages from Tacitus and Philo, which prove how numerous the Jewish Libertini were in the empire, will come under notice hereafter, in connection with Rome.

it was once in the church of St. Stephen at Valencia, and is now in the Royal Gallery at Madrid. See Stirling's Annals of the Artists of Spain, i. 363.

[1] See Acts xxii. 4. xxvi. 10. Phil. iii. 6. 1 Tim. i. 13.

[2] Sermo I & IV. in festo sancti Stephani.

[3] Acts vi. 9

[4] Sat. i. 6, 45.

CHAPTER III

Ἐνόμισαν ἀπηλλάχθαι της ἐν τοῖς τοιούτοις διαλέξεως ἀπαλλαγεντες Στέφανιυ, κα. Στέφανου σφοδρότερον εὗρον ἕτερον.—S. Chrysost. Hom. xx. in Act. App.

FUNERAL OF ST. STEPHEN.—SAUL'S CONTINUED PERSECUTION.—FLIGHT OF THE CHRISTIANS.—PHILIP AND THE SAMARITANS.—SAUL'S JOURNEY TO DAMASCUS.—ARETAS, KING OF PETRA.—ROADS FROM JERUSALEM TO DAMASCUS.—NEAPOLIS.—HISTORY AND DESCRIPTION OF DAMASCUS.—THE NARRATIVES OF THE MIRACLE.—IT WAS A REAL VISION OF JESUS CHRIST.—THREE DAYS IN DAMASCUS.—ANANIAS.—BAPTISM AND FIRST PREACHING OF SAUL.—HE RETIRES INTO ARABIA.—MEANING OF THE TERM ARABIA.—PETRA AND THE DESERT.—CONSPIRACY AT DAMASCUS.—ESCAPE TO JERUSALEM.—BARNABAS.—FORTNIGHT WITH ST. PETER.—CONSPIRACY.—VISION IN THE TEMPLE.—SAUL WITHDRAWS TO SYRIA AND CILICIA.

THE death of St. Stephen is a bright passage in the earliest history of the Church. Where, in the annals of the world, can we find so perfect an image of a pure and blessed saint as that which is drawn in the concluding verses of the seventh chapter of the Acts of the Apostles? And the brightness which invests the scene of the martyr's last moments is the more impressive from its contrast with all that has preceded it since the Crucifixion of Christ. The first Apostle who died was a traitor. The first disciples of the Christian Apostles whose deaths are recorded were liars and hypocrites. The kingdom of the Son of Man was founded in darkness and gloom. But a heavenly light reappeared with the martyrdom of St. Stephen. The revelation of such a character at the moment of death was the strongest of all evidences, and the highest of all encouragements. Nothing could more confidently assert the divine power of the new religion; nothing could prophesy more surely the certainty of its final victory.

To us who have the experience of many centuries of Christian history, and who can look back, through a long series of martyrdoms, to this, which was the beginning and example of the rest, these thoughts are easy and obvious; but to the friends and associates of the murdered Saint, such feelings of cheerful and confident assurance were perhaps more difficult. Though Christ was indeed risen from the dead, His disciples could hardly yet be able to realize the full triumph of the Cross over death

Even many years afterwards, Paul the Apostle wrote to the Thessalonians, concerning those who had "fallen asleep"[1] more peaceably than Stephen, that they ought not to sorrow for them as those without hope; and now, at the very beginning of the Gospel, the grief of the Christians must have been great indeed, when the corpse of their champion and their brother lay at the feet of Saul the murderer.[2] Yet, amidst the consternation of some and the fury of others, friends of the martyr were found,[3] who gave him all the melancholy honours of a Jewish funeral, and carefully buried him,[4] as Joseph buried his father, "with great and sore lamentation."[5]

After the death and burial of Stephen the persecution still raged in Jerusalem. That temporary protection which had been extended to the rising sect by such men as Gamaliel was now at an end. Pharisees and Sadducees—priests and people—alike indulged the most violent and ungovernable fury. It does not seem that any check was laid upon them by the Roman authorities. Either the procurator was absent from the

[1] 1 Thess. iv. 13. See Acts vii. 60.

[2] Maundrell says, after visiting the spot assigned by tradition to the death of Stephen: "not far from it is a grot, into which they tell you the outrageous Jewish zealots cast his body when they had satiated their fury upon him."—Travels, p. 103.

[3] Ἄνδρες εὐλαβεῖς. (Acts viii. 2.)—"Rabidos Judæos nihil veriti." Beza; probably Hellenistic Jews, and possibly Christians. (See Luke ii. 25. Acts ii. 5.) Hammond (on x. 2) thinks they were proselytes.

[4] Συνεκόμισαν. viii. 2. We are told by Baronius, on the authority of Lucian, a presbyter of Jerusalem, that Gamaliel, as a secret Christian, sent a number of Christians to remove the body of Stephen, and to bury it at his villa, twenty miles from Jerusalem, and that he made lamentation over him seventy days. Not to dwell on the untrustworthiness of Lucian's letter, known only in the Latin translation of Avitus (and Baronius says,—"quinam fuerit Avitus iste haud penitus dixerim"), it should be observed that such a funeral is very inconsistent with all the other occurrences at the time. The whole story is very curious, and will be found in vol. vii., under the year 415,—a year remarkable as the time when "magnus ille protomartyr Stephanus rursus in miraculis redivivus apparuit." Gamaliel appeared to Lucian in a vision by night; and, besides recounting the funeral of Stephen, told how he had protected Nicodemus at the same villa till his death, when he was buried in the same tomb, as also ultimately Gamaliel himself, with his son Abibus,—his wife and his eldest son being buried elsewhere, for they were not Christians. The relics were duly found and authenticated by miracles, in the presence of John, Bishop of Jerusalem, who came from that Synod of Diospolis (Lydda) where Pelagius retracted his errors. The day which commemorates this in the Martyrologium Romanum is August 3; see the notes under that day. The story will be found also in Photius, clxxi. col. 383–6 (Rouen, 1653), and in Bede, Retract. in Acts v. 34.

[5] Ἐποιήσαντο κοπετὸν μέγαν ἐπ' αὐτῷ; see Gen. l. 10. Chrysostom remarks that his own beautiful words are his best epitaph—Ἱκανὸν αὐτῷ ἐπιτάφιον διεξῆλθεν ὁ εὐαγγελιστής, καὶ θεὶς τὰ γόνατα εἰπών, κ. τ. λ. Hom. xviii. in Act. Baronius, under the year 34 (vol. i.), where the same story is told more briefly, argues from it in favour of the opinion that sumptuous and prolonged honours ought to be paid to the remains of martyrs. See Jerome as there quoted.

city, or he was willing to connive at what seemed to him an ordinary religious quarrel.

The eminent and active agent in this persecution was Saul. There are strong grounds for believing that, if he was not a member of the Sanhedrin at the time of St. Stephen's death, he was elected into that powerful senate soon after; possibly as a reward for the zeal he had shown against the heretic. He himself says that in Jerusalem he not only exercised the power of imprisonment by commission from the High Priests, but also, when the Christians were put to death, *gave his vote* against them.[1] From this expression it is natural to infer that he was a member of that supreme court of judicature. However this might be, his zeal in conducting the persecution was unbounded. We cannot help observing how frequently strong expressions concerning his share in the injustice and cruelty now perpetrated are multiplied in the Scriptures. In St. Luke's narrative, in St. Paul's own speeches, in his earlier and later epistles, the subject recurs again and again. He "made havoc of the Church," invading the sanctuaries of domestic life, "entering into every house:"[2] and those whom he thus tore from their homes he "committed to prison;" or, in his own words at a later period, when he had recognised as God's people those whom he now imagined to be His enemies, "thinking that he ought to do many things contrary to the name of Jesus of Nazareth . . . in Jerusalem . . . he shut up many of the saints in prison."[3] And not only did men thus suffer at his hands, but women also,—a fact three times repeated as a great aggravation of his cruelty.[4] These persecuted people were scourged—"often" scourged, "—in many synagogues."[5] Nor was Stephen the only one who suffered death, as we may infer from the Apostle's own confession.[6] And, what was worse than scourging or than death itself, he used every effort to make them "blaspheme" that Holy Name whereby they were called.[7] His fame as an inquisitor was notorious far

[1] Κατήνεγκα ψῆφον. (Acts xxvi. 10.) If this inference is well founded, and if the qualification for a member of the Sanhedrin mentioned in the last chapter (page 71) was a necessary qualification, Saul must have been a married man, and the father of a family. If so, it is probable that his wife and children did not long survive; for otherwise, some notice of them would have occurred in the subsequent narrative, or some allusion to them in the Epistles. And we know that, if ever he had a wife, she was not living when he wrote his first letter to the Corinthians. (1 Cor. vii.) It was customary among the Jews to marry at a very early age. See Buxt. Syn. Jud. ch. vi.

[2] Acts viii. 3. See ix. 2.

[3] xxvi. 9, 10. See xxii. 3.

[4] viii. 3. ix. 2. xxii. 4.

[5] xxvi. 10.

[6] "I persecuted this way unto the death, binding and delivering into prison both men and women" (xxii. 4); "and when they were put to death, I gave my vote against them." (xxvi. 10.)

[7] Ἠνάγκαζον βλασφημεῖν. (Acts xxvi. 11.) It is not said that he succeeded in causing any to blaspheme. It may be necessary to explain to some readers that the Greek imperfect merely denotes that the attempt was made; so in Gal. i. 23, alluded to at the end of this chapter.

and wide. Even at Damascus Ananias had heard[1] "how much evil he had done to Christ's saints at Jerusalem." He was known there[2] as "he that destroyed them which call on this Name in Jerusalem." It was not without reason that, in the deep repentance of his later years, he remembered how he had "persecuted the Church of God and wasted it,"[3]—how he had been "a blasphemer, a persecutor and injurious;"[4]—and that he felt he was "not meet to be called an Apostle," because he "had persecuted the Church of God."[5]

From such cruelty, and such efforts to make them deny that Name which they honoured above all names, the disciples naturally fled. In consequence of "the persecution against the Church at Jerusalem, they were all scattered abroad throughout the regions of Judæa and Samaria." The Apostles only remained.[6] But this dispersion led to great results. The moment of lowest depression was the very time of the Church's first missionary triumph. "They that were scattered abroad went everywhere preaching the Word."[7] First the Samaritans, and then the Gentiles, received that Gospel, which the Jews attempted to destroy. Thus did the providence of God begin to accomplish, by unconscious instruments, the prophecy and command which had been given:—"Ye shall be witnesses unto Me, both in Jerusalem, and in all Judæa, and in Samaria, and unto the uttermost part of the earth."[8]

The Jew looked upon the Samaritan as he looked upon the Gentile. His hostility to the Samaritan was probably the greater, in proportion as he was nearer. In conformity with the economy which was observed before the resurrection, Jesus Christ had said to His disciples, "Go not into the way of the Gentiles, and into any city of the Samaritans enter ye not: but go rather to the lost sheep of the house of Israel."[9] Yet did the Saviour give anticipative hints of His favour to Gentiles and Samaritans, in His mercy to the Syrophenician woman, and His interview with the woman at the well of Sychar. And now the time was come for both the "middle walls of partition" to be destroyed. The dispersion brought Philip, the companion of Stephen, the second of the seven, to a city of Samaria.[10] He came with the power of miracles and with the news of salvation. The Samaritans were convinced by what they saw; they listened to what he said; "and there was great joy in that city." When the news

[1] ix. 13.

[2] ix. 21.

[3] Gal. i. 13; see also Phil. iii. 6.

[4] 1 Tim. i. 13.

[5] 1 Cor. xv. 9. It should be observed that in all these passages from the Epistles the same word (διώκω, διώκτης) is used.

[6] Acts viii. 1.

[7] viii. 4. See xi. 19–21.

[8] i. 8.

[9] Matt. x. 5, 6.

[10] Πόλιν τῆς Σαμαρείας. (Acts viii. 5.) This was probably the ancient capital, at that time called "Sebaste." The city of Sychar (John iv. 5) had also received a Greek name. It was then "Neapolis," and is still "Nablous."

came to Jerusalem, Peter and John were sent by the Apostles, and the same miraculous testimony attended their presence, which had been given on the day of Pentecost. The Divine Power in Peter rebuked the powers of evil, which were working[1] among the Samaritans in the person of Simon Magus, as Paul afterwards, on his first preaching to the Gentiles, rebuked in Cyprus Elymas the sorcerer. The two Apostles returned to Jerusalem, preaching as they went "in many villages of the Samaritans" the Gospel which had been welcomed in the city.

Once more we are permitted to see Philip on his labour of love. We obtain a glimpse of him on the road which leads down by Gaza[2] to Egypt. The chamberlain of Queen Candace[3] is passing southwards on his return from Jerusalem, and reading in his chariot the prophecies of Isaiah. Æthiopia is "stretching out her hands unto God,"[4] and the suppliant is not unheard. A teacher is provided at the moment of anxious inquiry. The stranger goes "on his way rejoicing;" a proselyte who had found the Messiah; a Christian baptized "with water and the Holy Ghost." The Evangelist, having finished the work for which he had been sent, is called elsewhere by the Spirit of God. He proceeds to Cæsarea, and we hear of him no more, till, after the lapse of more than twenty years, he received under his roof in that city one who, like himself, had travelled in obedience to the Divine command "preaching in all the cities."[5]

Our attention is now called to that other traveller. We turn from the "desert road" on the south of Palestine to the desert road on the north; from the border of Arabia near Gaza, to its border near Damascus. "From Dan to Beersheba" the Gospel is rapidly spreading. The dispersion of the Christians had not been confined to Judæa and Samaria. "On the persecution that arose about Stephen" they had "travelled as far as Phœnicia and Syria."[6] "Saul, yet breathing out threatenings and slaugh-

[1] Προϋπῆρχεν. (Acts viii. 9.) Simon was in Samaria before Philip came, as Elymas was with Sergius Paulus before the arrival of St. Paul. Compare viii. 9–24, with xiii. 6–12. There is good reason for believing that Simon Magus is the same person mentioned by Josephus (Ant. xx. 7, 2), as connected with Felix and Drusilla. See Acts xxiv. 24.

[2] See some remarks on the words αὕτη ἐστὶν ἔρημος in Greswell's Dissertations, vol. i. pp. 177–180.

[3] Candace is the name, not of an individual, but of a dynasty,—like Aretas in Arabia, or like Pharaoh and Ptolemy. By Æthiopia is meant Meroë on the Upper Nile. Queens of Meroë with the title of Candace are mentioned by Dio Cass. liv. 5. Strabo, xviii. Plin. H. N. vi. 29, 35. See also Euseb. H. E. ii. 1. Probably this chamberlain was a Jew. See Olshausen.

[4] Ps. lxviii. 31.

[5] "But Philip was found at Azotus; and, passing through, he preached in all the cities, till he came to Cæsarea." (Acts viii. 40.) "And the next day we that were of Paul's company departed, and came to Cæsarea; and we entered into the house of Philip the Evangelist, which was one of the seven, and abode with him." (xxi. 8.)

[6] Acts xi. 19.

ter against the disciples of the Lord,"[1] determined to follow them. "Being exceedingly mad against them, he persecuted them even to strange cities."[2] He went of his own accord to the high priest, and desired of him letters to the synagogues in Damascus, where he had reason to believe that Christians were to be found. And armed with this "authority and commission,"[3] intending "if he found any of this way, whether they were men or women,"[4] to bring them bound unto Jerusalem to be punished,"[5] he journeyed to Damascus.

The great Sanhedrin claimed over the Jews in foreign cities the same power, in religious questions, which they exercised at Jerusalem. The Jews in Damascus were very numerous; and there were peculiar circumstances in the political condition of Damascus at this time, which may have given facilities to conspiracies or deeds of violence conducted by the Jews. There was war between Aretas, who reigned at Petra, the desert-metropolis of Stony Arabia,[6] and Herod Antipas, his son-in-law, the Tetrarch of Galilee. A misunderstanding concerning the boundaries of the two principalities had been aggravated into an inveterate quarrel by Herod's unfaithfulness to the daughter of the Arabian king, and his shameful attachment to "his brother Philip's wife." The Jews generally sympathised with the cause of Aretas, rejoiced when Herod's army was cut off, and declared that this disaster was a judgment for the murder of John the Baptist. Herod wrote to Rome and obtained an order for assistance from Vitellius, the Governor of Syria. But when Vitellius was on his march through Judæa, from Antioch towards Petra, he suddenly heard of the death of Tiberius (A. D. 37); and the Roman army was withdrawn, before the war was brought to a conclusion. It is evident that the relations of the neighbouring powers must have been for some years in a very unsettled

1 Acts ix. 1. 2 xxvi. 11. 3 xxvi. 12. 4 ix. 2. 5 xxii. 5.

6 In this mountainous district of Arabia, which had been the scene of the wanderings of the Israelites, and which contained the graves both of Moses and Aaron, the Nabathæan Arabs after the time of the Babylonian captivity (or, possibly, the Edomites before them. See Robinson, Bib. Res. vol. ii. pp. 557, 573) grew into a civilised nation, built a great mercantile city at Petra, and were ruled by a line of kings, who bore the title of "Aretas." The Aretas dynasty ceased in the second century, when Arabia Petræa became a Roman province under Trajan. In the Roman period, a great road united Ailah on the Red Sea with Petra, and thence diverged to the left towards Jerusalem and the ports of the Mediterranean; and to the right towards Damascus, in a direction not very different from that of the modern caravan-road from Damascus to Mecca. This state of things did not last very long. (Compare, for instance, the Peutingerian Table with the Antonine Itinerary.) The Arabs of this district fell back into their old nomadic state. Petra was long undiscovered. Burckhardt was the first to see it, and Laborde the first to visit it. Now it is well known to Oriental travellers. Its Rock-theatre and other remains still exist, to show its ancient character of a city of the Roman Empire. See Mannert's Geographie der G. und R. pt. vi. vol. i. pp. 133–138. For notices of the different kings who bore the name of "Aretas," see Winer's Realwörterbuch.

condition along the frontiers of Arabia, Judæa, and Syria; and the falling of a rich border-town like Damascus from the hands of the Romans into those of Aretas would be a natural occurrence of the war. If it could be proved that the city was placed in the power of the Arabian Ethnarch[1] under these particular circumstances, and at the time of St. Paul's journey, good reason would be assigned for believing it probable that the ends for which he went were assisted by the political relations of Damascus. And it would indeed be a singular coincidence, if his zeal in persecuting the Christians were promoted by the sympathy of the Jews for the fate of John the Baptist.

But there are grave objections to this view of the occupation of Damascus by Aretas. Such a liberty taken by a petty chieftain with the Roman power would have been an act of great audacity; and it is difficult to believe that Vitellius would have closed the campaign, if such a city was in the hands of an enemy. It is more likely that Caligula,—who in many ways contradicted the policy of his predecessor,—who banished Herod Antipas and patronised Herod Agrippa,—assigned the city of Damascus as a free gift to Aretas.[2] This supposition, as well as the former, will perfectly explain the remarkable passage in St. Paul's letters, where he distinctly says that it was garrisoned by the Ethnarch of Aretas, at the time of his escape. Many such changes of territorial occupation took place under the Emperors,[3] which would have been lost to history, were it not for the information derived from[4] a coin, an inscription, or the incidental remark of a writer who had different ends in view. Any attempt to make this escape from Damascus a fixed point of absolute chronology will be unsuccessful; but, from what has been said, it may fairly be collected,

[1] 2 Cor. xi. 32.

[2] This is argued with great force by Wieseler, who, so far as we know, is the first to suggest this explanation. His argument is not quite conclusive; because it is seldom easy to give a confident opinion on the details of a campaign, unless its history is minutely recorded. The strength of Wieseler's argument consists in this, that his different lines of reasoning converge to the same result. See his "Chronologie des Apostolischen Zeitalters," pp. 161–175; and compare pp. 142–3, and the note.

[3] See, for instance, what is said by Josephus (Ant. xviii. 5, 4) of various arrangements in the East at this very crisis. Similar changes in Asia Minor have been alluded to before, Ch. I. p. 23.

[4] Wieseler justly lays some stress on the circumstance that there are coins of Augustus and Tiberius, and, again, of Nero and his successors, but none of Caligula and Claudius, which imply that Damascus was Roman. But we cannot acquiesce in the conclusion which he draws from the coin of Mionnet, with the inscription ΒΑΣΙΛΕΩΣ · ΑΡΕΤΟΥ · ΦΙΛΕΛΛΗΝΟΣ. It seems to be one of those coins with this inscription (two of which are in the British Museum, and one is represented at the end of this chapter), assigned by Eckhel to an earlier Aretas, who was contemporary with the last of the Seleucidæ, and in whose power we know that Damascus once was. (See Joseph. Ant. xiii. 13, 3. B. J. i. 6, 2, and Wieseler, p. 169.) The general appearance and character of these coins justifies Eckhel's opinion, and it is difficult to explain the word φιλέλληνος on the other supposition

that Saul's journey from Jerusalem to Damascus took place not far from that year which saw the death of Tiberius and the accession of Caligula.

No journey was ever taken, on which so much interest is concentrated, as this of St. Paul from Jerusalem to Damascus.[1] It is so critical a passage in the history of God's dealings with man, and we feel it to be so closely bound up with all our best knowledge and best happiness in this life, and with all our hopes for the world to come, that the mind is delighted to dwell upon it, and we are eager to learn or imagine all its details. The conversion of Saul was like the call of a second Abraham. But we know almost more of the Patriarch's journey through this same district, from the north to the south, than we do of the Apostle's in an opposite direction. It is easy to conceive of Abraham travelling with his flocks and herds and camels. The primitive features of the East continue still unaltered in the desert; and the Arabian Sheikh still remains to us a living picture of the Patriarch of Genesis. But before the first century of the Christian era, the patriarchal life of Palestine had been modified, not only by the invasions and settlements of Babylonia and Persia, but by large influxes of Greek and Roman civilisation. It is difficult to guess what was the appearance of Saul's company on that memorable occasion.[2] We neither know how he travelled, nor who his associates were, nor where he rested on his way, nor what road he followed from the Judæan to the Syrian capital.

His journey must have brought him somewhere into the vicinity of the Sea of Tiberias. But where he approached the nearest to the shores of this sacred lake,—whether he crossed the Jordan where, in its lower course, it flows southwards to the Dead Sea, or where its upper windings enrich the valley at the base of Mount Hermon,—we do not know. And there is one thought which makes us glad that it should be so. It is remarkable that Galilee, where Jesus worked so many of His miracles, is the scene of none of those transactions which are related in the Acts. The blue waters of Tiberias, with their fishing-boats and towns on the brink of the shore, are consecrated to the Gospels. A greater than Paul was here. When we come to the travels of the Apostles, the scenery is no longer limited and Jewish, but Catholic and widely-extended, like the Gospel

[1] For descriptions of Damascus, see Lamartine's Voyage en Orient; Addison's Damascus and Palmyra; Fisher's Syria; The Modern Traveller; The Crescent and the Cross; Lord Castlereagh's Journey to Damascus; Eōthen; and Miss Martineau's Eastern Life. The two last, in other respects the most unsatisfactory, give the best idea of a journey from Jerusalem to Damascus.

[2] In pictures, St. Paul is represented as on horseback on this journey. Probably this is the reason why Lord Lyttelton, in his observations on St. Paul's conversion, uses the phrase—"Those in company with him *fell down from their horses*, together with Saul." p. 318. (Works, 1774.) There is no proof that this was the case, though it is very probable.

which they preached: and the Sea, which will be so often spread before us in the life of St. Paul, will not be the little Lake of Galilee, but the great Mediterranean, which washed the shores and carried the ships of the historical nations of antiquity.[1]

Two principal roads can be mentioned, one of which probably conducted the travellers from Jerusalem to Damascus. The track of the caravans, in ancient and modern times, from Egypt to the Syrian capital, has always led through Gaza and Ramleh, and then turning eastwards about the borders of Galilee and Samaria, has descended near Mount Tabor towards the Sea of Tiberias; and so, crossing the Jordan a little to the north of the Lake by Jacob's Bridge, proceeds through the desert country which stretches to the base of Antilibanus.[2] A similar track from Jerusalem falls into this Egyptian road in the neighbourhood of Djenin, at the entrance of Galilee; and Saul and his company may have travelled by this route, performing the journey of one hundred and thirty-six miles, like the modern caravans, in about six days.[3] But at this period, that great work of Roman road-making, which was actively going on in all parts of the empire, must have extended, in some degree, to Syria and Judæa; and, if the Roman roads were already constructed here, there is no doubt that they followed the direction indicated by the later Itineraries.[4] This direction is from Jerusalem to Neapolis (the ancient Sychar), and thence over the Jordan to the south of the Lake, near Scythopolis, where the soldiers of Pompey crossed the river, and where the Galilean pilgrims used to cross it at the time of the festivals, to avoid Samaria. From Scythopolis it led to Gadara, a Roman city, the ruins of which are still remaining, and so to Damascus.[5]

Whatever road was followed in Saul's journey to Damascus, it is almost certain that the earlier portion of it brought him to Neapolis, the Sychar of the Old Testament, and the Nablous of the modern Samaritans. This city was one of the stages in the Itineraries. Dr. Robinson followed a

[1] The next historical notice of the sea of Tiberius or Gennesareth, after that which occurs in the Gospels, is in Josephus.

[2] See the following passages in Dr. Robinson's Researches, vol. iii., pp. 181, 236, 276, 316.

[3] See Fisher's Syria, i. 7.

[4] See Wesseling's Itineraries, and two later editions; one by Fortia d'Urban at Paris, and the other by Parthy and Pinder at Berlin.

[5] It is very conceivable that he travelled by Cæsarea Philippi, the city which Herod Philip had built at the fountains of the Jordan, on the natural line of communication between Tyre and Damascus, and likely to have been one of the "foreign cities" (Acts xxvi. 12) which harboured Christian fugitives. Here, too, he would be in the footsteps of St. Peter; for here the great confession (Mat. xvi.) seems to have been made; and this road also would probably have brought him past Neapolis. It is hardly likely that he would have taken the Petra road (above, p. 81, n. 6), for both the modern caravans and the ancient itineraries cross the Jordan more to the north.

BRIDGE OVER THE JORDAN, SOUTH OF LAKE OF TIBERIAS.

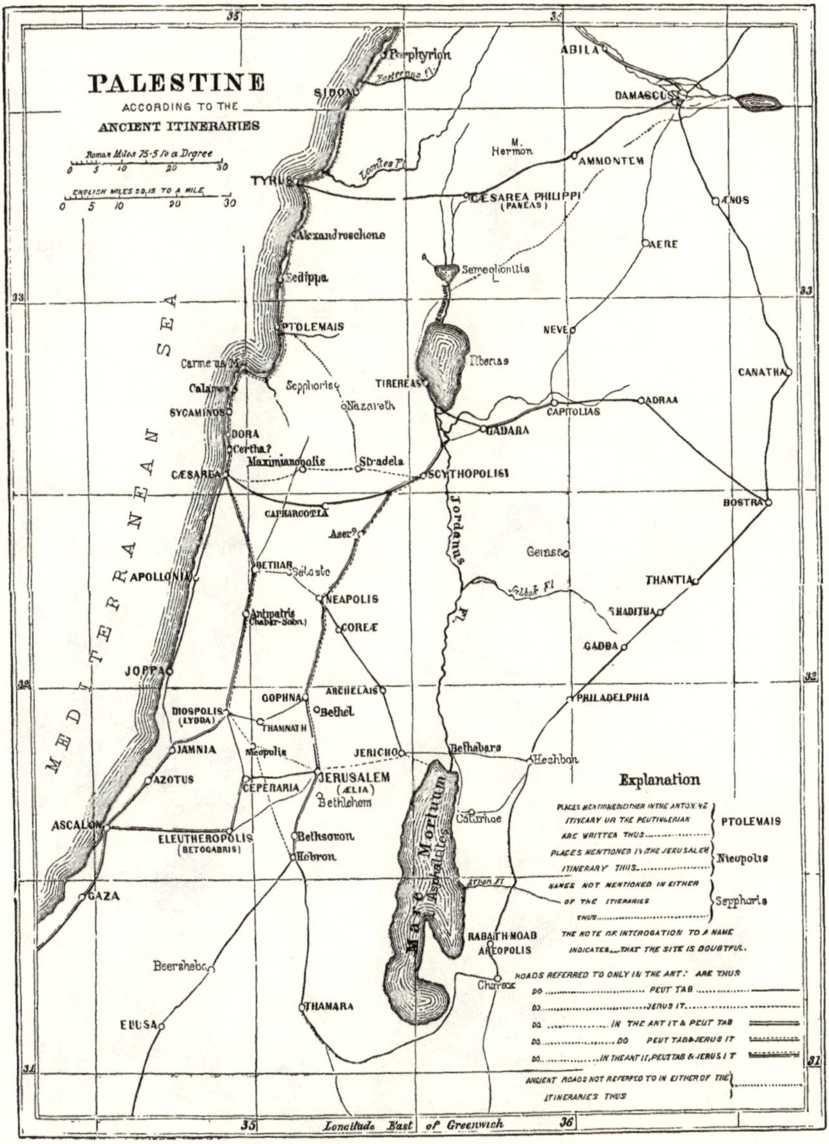

PALESTINE
ACCORDING TO THE
ANCIENT ITINERARIES
Roman Miles 75·5 to a Degree
English Miles 20,15 to a mile
MEDITERRANEAN SEA
Porphyrion
SIDON
ABILA
DAMASCUS
M. Hermon
AMMONTEM
Leontes Fl.
TYRUS
CÆSAREA PHILIPPI (PANEAS)
ÆNOS
Alexandroschene
AERE
Semechonitis L.
Ecdippa
PTOLEMAIS
NEVE
Tiberias
Carmelus M.
Calamon
Sepphoris
TIBERIAS
CANATHA
SYCAMINOS
Nazareth
ADRAA
CAPITOLIAS
GADARA
DORA
Certha?
Maximianopolis
Stradela
CÆSAREA
SCYTHOPOLIS
CAPHARCOTIA
BOSTRA
Aser?
Jordanus Fl.
Gerasa
BETHAR
Sebaste
THANTIA
APOLLONIA
NEAPOLIS
Antipatris (Chabar-Saba)
Jabok Fl.
SHADITHA
COREÆ
GADDA
JOPPA
ARCHELAIS
GOPHNA
PHILADELPHIA
DIOSPOLIS (LYDDA)
Bethel
THAMNATH
JAMNIA
Neopolis
JERICHO
Bethabara
Heshbon
AZOTUS
CEPERARIA
JERUSALEM (ÆLIA)
Bethlehem
Mare Mortuum
Asphaltites
Callirhoe
ASCALON
ELEUTHEROPOLIS (BETOGABRIS)
Bethsoron
Hebron
GAZA
Arnon Fl.
RABATH-MOAB
AREOPOLIS
Beersheba
Charax
THAMARA
ELUSA
Longitude East of Greenwich
Explanation
PLACES MENTIONED EITHER IN THE ANTONINE ITINERARY OR THE PEUTINGERIAN ARE WRITTEN THUS
PTOLEMAIS
PLACES MENTIONED IN THE JERUSALEM ITINERARY THUS
Neopolis
NAMES NOT MENTIONED IN EITHER OF THE ITINERARIES THUS
Sepphoris
THE NOTE OF INTERROGATION TO A NAME INDICATES THAT THE SITE IS DOUBTFUL.
ROADS REFERRED TO ONLY IN THE ANT: ARE THUS
DO PEUT TAB
DO JERUS IT
DO IN THE ANT IT & PEUT TAB
DO DO PEUT TAB & JERUS IT
DO IN THE ANT IT, PEUT TAB & JERUS IT
ANCIENT ROADS NOT REFERRED TO IN EITHER OF THE ITINERARIES THUS

Roman pavement for some considerable distance in the neighbourhood of Bethel.[1] This northern road went over the elevated ridges which intervene between the valley of the Jordan and the plain on the Mediterranean coast. As the travellers gained the high ground, the young Pharisee may have looked back,—and, when he saw the city in the midst of its hills, with the mountains of Moab in the distance,—confident in the righteousness of his cause,—he may have thought proudly of the 125th Psalm: "The hills stand about Jerusalem: even so standeth the Lord round about his people, from this time forth for evermore." His present enterprise was undertaken for the honour of Zion. He was blindly fulfilling the words of One who said: "Whosoever killeth you, will think that he doeth God service."[2] Passing through the hills of Samaria, from which he might occasionally obtain a glimpse of the Mediterranean on the left, he would come to Jacob's Well, at the opening of that beautiful valley which lies between Ebal and Gerizim. This, too, is the scene of a Gospel history. The same woman, with whom JESUS spoke, might be again at the well as the Inquisitor passed. But as yet he knew nothing of the breaking down of the "middle wall of partition."[3] He could, indeed, have said to the Samaritans: "Ye worship ye know not what: we know what we worship: for salvation is of the Jews."[4] But he could not have understood the meaning of those other words: "The hour cometh when ye shall neither in Jerusalem, nor yet in this mountain, worship the Father: the true worshippers shall worship Him in spirit and in truth."[5] His was not yet the spirit of CHRIST. The zeal which burnt in him was that of James and John, before their illumination, when they wished to call down fire from heaven, even as Elias did, on the inhospitable Samaritan village.[6] Philip had already been preaching to the poor Samaritans, and John had revisited them, in company with Peter, with feelings wonderfully changed.[7] But Saul knew nothing of the little Church of Samaritan Christians; or, if he heard of them and lingered among them, he lingered only to injure and oppress. The Syrian city was still the great object before him. And now, when he had passed through Samaria and was entering Galilee, the snowy peak of Mount Hermon, the highest point of Antilibanus, almost as far to the north as Damascus, would come into view. This is that tower of "Lebanon which looketh towards Damascus."[8] It is already the great landmark of his journey, as he passes through Galilee towards the Lake of Tiberias, and the valley of the Jordan.

Leaving now the "sea of Galilee," deep among its hills, as a sanctuary of the holiest thoughts, and imagining the Jordan to be passed, we follow the company of travellers over the barren uplands, which stretch in dreary

[1] Researches, iii. 77.
[2] John xvi. 2.
[3] Eph. ii. 14.
[4] John iv. 22.
[5] Ibid. 21, 23.
[6] Luke ix. 51-56.
[7] See above, p. 80.
[8] Song of Sol vii 4.

succession along the base of Antilibanus. All around are stony hills and thirsty plains, through which the withered stems of the scanty vegetation hardly penetrate. Over this desert, under the burning sky, the impetuous Saul holds his course, full of the fiery zeal with which Elijah travelled of yore, on his mysterious errand, through the same "wilderness of Damascus."[1] "The earth in its length and its breadth, and all the deep universe of sky, is steeped in light and heat." When some eminence is gained, the vast horizon is seen stretching on all sides, like the ocean, without a boundary; except where the steep sides of Lebanon interrupt it, as the promontories of a mountainous coast stretch out into a motionless sea. The fiery sun is overhead; and that refreshing view is anxiously looked for,—Damascus seen from afar, within the desert circumference, resting like an island of Paradise, in the green enclosure of its beautiful gardens

COIN OF DAMASCUS.[2]

This view is so celebrated, and the history of the place is so illustrious, that we may well be excused if we linger a moment, that we may describe them both. Damascus is the oldest city in the world.[3] Its fame begins with the earliest patriarchs, and continues to modern times. While other cities of the East have risen and decayed, Damascus is still what it was. It was founded before Baalbec and Palmyra, and it has outlived them both. While Babylon is a heap in the desert, and Tyre a ruin on the shore, it remains what it is called in the prophecies of Isaiah, "the head of Syria."[4] Abraham's steward was "Eliezer of Damascus,"[5] and the limit of his warlike expedition in the rescue of Lot was "Hobah, which is on the left hand of Damascus."[6] How important a place it was in the flourishing period of the Jewish monarchy, we know from the garrisons which David placed there,[7] and from the opposition it presented to Solomon.[8]

[1] 1 Kings xix. 15.

[2] The word ΠΗΓΑΙ, "fountains," on this coin should be particularly noticed. The cast was obtained from Paris by the kindness of Mr. Akerman.

[3] Josephus makes it even older than Abraham. (Ant. i. 6, 3.) For the traditions of the events in the infancy of the human race, which are supposed to have happened in its vicinity, see Pococke, ii. 115, 116. The story that the murder of Abel took place here is alluded to by Shakspere, 1 K. Hen. VI. i. 3.

[4] Isai. vii. 8. [5] Gen. xv. 2. [6] Gen. xiv. 15.

[7] 2 Sam. viii. 6. 1 Chron. xviii. 6. [8] 1 Kings xi. 24

The history of Naaman and the Hebrew captive, Elisha and Gehazi, and of the proud preference of its fresh rivers to the thirsty waters of Israel, are familiar to every one. And how close its relations continued to be with the Jews, we know from the chronicles of Jeroboam and Ahaz, and the prophecies of Isaiah and Amos.[1] Its mercantile greatness is indicated by Ezekiel in the remarkable words addressed to Tyre,[2]—"Syria was thy merchant by reason of the multitude of the wares of thy making: they occupied in thy fairs with emeralds, purple, and broidered work, and fine linen, and coral, and agate. Damascus was thy merchant in the multitude of the wares of thy making, for the multitude of all riches; in the wine of Helbon, and white wool."[3] Leaving the Jewish annals, we might follow its history through continuous centuries, from the time when Alexander sent Parmenio to take it, while the conqueror himself was marching from Tarsus to Tyre,[4]—to its occupation by Pompey,[5]—to the letters of Julian the Apostate, who describes it as "the eye of the East,"[6]—and onward through its golden days, when it was the residence of the Ommiad Caliphs, and the metropolis of the Mahomedan world,—and through the period when its fame was mingled with that of Saladin and Tamerlane,—to our own days, when the praise of its beauty is celebrated by every traveller from Europe. It is evident, to use the words of Lamartine, that, like Constantinople, it was a "predestinated capital." Nor is it difficult to explain why its freshness has never faded through all this series of vicissitudes and wars.

Among the rocks and brushwood at the base of Antilibanus are the fountains of a copious and perennial stream, which, after running a course of no great distance to the south-east, loses itself in a desert lake. But before it reaches this dreary boundary, it has distributed its channels over the intermediate space, and left a wide area behind it, rich with prolific vegetation. These are the "streams from Lebanon," which are known to us in the imagery of Scripture;[7]—the "rivers of Damascus," which Naaman not unnaturally preferred to all the "waters of Israel."[8] By

[1] See 2 Kings xiv. 28, xvi. 9, 10. 2 Chr. xxiv. 23, xxviii. 5, 23. Isai. vii. 8. Amos i. 3, 5.

[2] The port of Beyroot is now to Damascus what Tyre was of old.

[3] Ezek. xxvii. 16, 18.

[4] Quintus Curtius, iii. 13, iv. 1. Arrian, ii. 11.

[5] See above, Ch. I. p. 26. Its relative importance was not so great when it was under a Western power like that of the Seleucidæ or the Romans: hence we find it less frequently mentioned than we might expect in Greek and Roman writers. This arose from the building of Antioch and other cities in Northern Syria.

[6] Julian, Ep. xxiv. *Τὴν Δίος πόλιν ἀληθῶς, καὶ τὸν τῆς Ἑώας ἁπάσης ὀφθαλμόν τὴν ἱερὰν καὶ μεγίστην Δάμασκον λέγω.* There is some reason to believe that this letter is not genuine. See the 54th note in Gibbon's Decline and Fall, ch. li.

[7] Song of Sol. iv. 15.

[8] 2 Kings v. 12.

Greek writers the stream is called Chrysorrhoas,[1] or "the river of gold." And this stream is the inestimable unexhausted treasure of Damascus. The habitations of men must always have been gathered around it, as the Nile has inevitably attracted an immemorial population to its banks. The desert is a fortification round Damascus. The river is its life. It is drawn out into watercourses, and spread in all directions. For miles around it is a wilderness of gardens,—gardens with roses among the tangled shrubberies, and with fruit on the branches overhead. Every where among the trees the murmur of unseen rivulets is heard. Even in the city, which is in the midst of the garden, the clear rushing of the current is a perpetual refreshment. Every dwelling has its fountain : and at night, when the sun has set behind Mount Lebanon, the lights of the city are seen flashing on the waters.

It is not to be wondered at that the view of Damascus, when the dim outline of the gardens has become distinct, and the city is seen gleaming white in the midst of them, should be universally famous. All travellers in all ages have paused to feast their eyes with the prospect ; and the prospect has been always the same. It is true that in the Apostle's day there were no cupolas and no minarets : Justinian had not built St. Sophia, and the caliphs had erected no mosques. But the white buildings of the city gleamed then, as they do now, in the centre of a verdant inexhaustible paradise. The Syrian gardens, with their low walls and waterwheels, and careless mixture of fruits and flowers, were the same then as they are now. The same figures would be seen in the green approaches to the town, camels and mules, horses and asses, with Syrian peasants, and Arabs from beyond Palmyra. We know the very time of the day when Saul was entering these shady avenues. It was at mid-day,[2] the birds were silent in the trees. The hush of noon was in the city. The sun was burning fiercely in the sky. The persecutor's companions were enjoying the cool refreshment of the shade after their journey : and his eyes rested with satisfaction on those walls which were the end of his mission, and contained the victims of his righteous zeal.

We have been tempted into some prolixity in describing Damascus. But, in describing the solemn and miraculous event which took place in its neighbourhood, we hesitate to enlarge upon the words of Scripture. And Scripture relates its circumstances in minute detail. If the importance we are intended to attach to particular events in early Christianity is to be

[1] Strabo, xvi. 2. Ptolem. v. 15, 9. See Plin. H. N. v. 16.

[2] Acts xxii. 6, xxvi. 13. Notices of the traditionary place where the vision was seen are to be found both in the older and later travellers. Irby and Mangles say it is "outside the eastern gate :" and in the Boat and Caravan it is described as "about a mile from the town, and near the Christian burying-ground which belongs to the Armenians."

measured by the prominence assigned to them in the Sacred Records, we must confess that, next after the Passion of our blessed Lord, the event to which our serious attention is especially called is the Conversion of St. Paul. Besides various allusions to it in his own epistles, three detailed narratives of the occurrence are found in the Acts. Once it is related by St. Luke (ix.),—twice by the Apostle himself,—in his address to his countrymen at Jerusalem (xxii.),—in his defence before Agrippa at Cæsarea (xxvi.). And as, when the same thing is told in more than one of the Holy Gospels, the accounts do not verbally agree, so it is here. St. Luke is more brief than St. Paul. And each of St. Paul's statements supplies something not found in the other. The peculiar difference of these two statements, in their relation to the circumstances under which they were given, and as they illustrate the Apostle's wisdom in pleading the cause of the Gospel and reasoning with his opponents, will be made the subject of some remarks in the later chapters of this book. At present it is our natural course simply to gather the facts from the Apostle's own words, with a careful reference to the shorter narrative given by St. Luke.

In the twenty-second and twenty-sixth chapters of the Acts we are told that it was "about noon"—"at mid-day"—when the "great light" shone "suddenly" from heaven (xxii. 6, xxvi. 13). And those who have had experience of the glare of a mid-day sun in the East, will best understand the description of that light, which is said to have been "a light above the brightness of the sun, shining round about Paul and them that journeyed with him." All fell to the ground in terror (xxvi. 14), or stood dumb with amazement (ix. 7). Suddenly surrounded by a light so terrible and incomprehensible, "they were afraid." "They heard not the voice of Him that spake to Paul" (xxii. 9), or, if they heard a voice, "they saw no man" (ix. 7).[1] The whole scene was evidently one of the utmost confusion: and the accounts are such as to express, in the most striking manner, the bewilderment and alarm of the travellers.

But while the others were stunned, stupified and confused, a clear light broke terribly on the soul of one of those who were prostrated on the ground.[2] A voice spoke articulately to him, which to the rest was a sound mysterious and indistinct. He heard what they did not hear. He

[1] It has been thought both more prudent and more honest to leave these well-known discrepancies exactly as they are found in the Bible. They will be differently explained by different readers, according to their views of the inspiration of Scripture. Those who do not receive the doctrine of Verbal Inspiration will find in these discrepancies a confirmation of the general truth of the narrative. Those who lay stress on this doctrine may fairly be permitted to suppose that the stupified companions of Saul fell to the ground and then rose, and that they heard the voice but did not understand it. Much has been written on this subject by the various commentators.

[2] It is evident from Acts ix. 6, 8, xxvi. 16, that Saul was prostrate on the ground when Jesus Christ spoke to him.

saw what they did not see. To them the awful sound was without a meaning: he heard the voice of the Son of God. To them it was a bright light which suddenly surrounded them: he saw Jesus, whom he was persecuting. The awful dialogue can only be given in the language of Scripture Yet we may reverentially observe that the words which Jesus spoke were "in the Hebrew tongue." The same language,[1] in which, during His earthly life, He spoke to Peter and John, to the blind man by the walls of Jericho, to the woman who washed His feet with her tears—the same sacred language was used when He spoke from heaven to His persecutor on earth. And as on earth He had always spoken in parables, so it was now. That voice which had drawn lessons from the lilies that grew in Galilee, and from the birds that flew over the mountain slopes near the sea of Tiberias, was now pleased to call His last Apostle with a figure of the like significance: "Saul, Saul, why persecutest thou me? It is hard for thee to kick against the goad." As the ox rebels in vain against the goad[2] of its master, and as all its struggles do nought but increase its distress—so is thy rebellion vain against the power of my grace. I have admonished thee by the word of my truth, by the death of my saints, by the voice of thy conscience.[3] Struggle no more against conviction, "lest a worse thing come unto thee."

It is evident that this revelation was not merely an inward impression made on the mind of Saul during a trance or ecstacy. It was the direct perception of the visible presence of Jesus Christ. This is asserted in various passages, both positively and incidentally. In his first letter to the Corinthians, when he contends for the validity of his own apostleship, his argument is, "Am I not an Apostle? Have I not seen Jesus Christ, the Lord?" And when he adduces the evidence for the truth of the Resurrection, his argument is again, "He was seen .... by Cephas .... by James .... by all the Apostles .... last of all by me .... as one born out of due time" (xv. 8). By Cephas and by James at Jerusalem the reality of Saul's conversion was doubted;[5] but "Barnabas brought him to the

[1] It is only said in one account (xxvi. 14) that Jesus Christ spoke in Hebrew. But this appears incidentally in the other accounts from the Hebrew form Σαοὺλ being used (ix. 4, xxii. 8). In ix. 1, 8, &c., it is the Greek Σαῦλος, a difference which is not noticed in the English translation. So Ananias (whose name is Aramaic) seems to have addressed Saul in Hebrew, not Greek. (ix. 17, xxii. 13.)

[2] The *κέντρον*, or *stimulus*, is the goad or sharp-pointed pole, which in southern Europe and in the Levant is seen in the hands of those who are ploughing or driving cattle. The words *σκληρόν σοι πρὸς κέντρα λακτίζειν*, in ix. 5, are an interpolation from xxvi. 14. They are in the Vulgate, but not in the Greek MSS. For instances of this proverb, which is very frequent both in Greek and Latin writers, see Wetstein.

[3] "Pupugi te stimulis miraculorum, prædicationis Stephani aliorumque, remorsibus conscientiæ et inspirationibus internis. Alios adhibebo stimulos sed acriores et majori damno tuo." Tirinus in Poole's Synopsis.

[4] 1 Cor. ix. 1.

[5] Acts ix. 27.

Apostles, and related to them how he had seen the Lord in the way, and had spoken with him." And similarly Ananias had said to him at their first meeting in Damascus; "The Lord hath sent me, even Jesus who appeared to thee in the way as thou camest" (ix. 17). "The God of our fathers hath chosen thee that thou shouldest see that just one, and shouldest hear the voice of his mouth" (xxii. 14). The very words which were spoken by the Saviour, imply the same important truth. He does not say,[1] "I am the Son of God—the Eternal Word—the Lord of men and of angels:"—but, "I am Jesus" (ix. 5, xxvi. 15), "Jesus of Nazareth" (xxii. 8). "I am that man, whom not having seen thou hatest, the despised prophet of Nazareth, who was mocked and crucified at Jerusalem, who died and was buried. But now I appear to thee, that thou mayest know the truth of my Resurrection, that I may convince thee of thy sin, and call thee to be my Apostle."

The direct and immediate character of this call, without the intervention of any human agency, is another point on which St. Paul himself, in the course of his apostolic life, laid the utmost stress; and one, therefore, which it is incumbent on us to notice here. "A called Apostle," "an Apostle by the will of God,"[2] "an Apostle sent not from men, nor by man, but by Jesus Christ, and God the Father, who raised Him from the dead;"[3] these are the phrases under which he describes himself, in the cases where his authority was in danger of being questioned. No human instrumentality intervened, to throw the slightest doubt upon the reality of the communication between Christ Himself and the Apostle of the Heathen. And, as he was directly and miraculously called, so was the work

[1] *Διατί μὴ εἶπεν, ἐγώ εἰμι ὁ Υἱὸς τοῦ Θεοῦ; ἐγώ εἰμι ὁ ἐν ἀρχῇ Λόγος· ἐγώ εἰμι ὁ ἐν δεξιᾷ καθήμενος τοῦ Πατρός· ὁ ἐν μορφῇ Θεοῦ ὑπάρχων· ὁ τὸν οὐρανὸν τείνας· ὁ τὴν γῆν ἐργασάμενος· ὁ τὴν θάλατταν ἁπλώσας· ὁ τοὺς Ἀγγέλους ποίησας· ὁ πανταχοῦ παρὼν καὶ τὰ πάντα πληρῶν· ὁ προὼν καὶ γεννηθείς; διατί μὴ εἶπε τὰ σεμνὰ ἐκεῖνα καὶ μέγαλα καὶ ὑψηλά;—ἀλλ' "ἐγώ εἰμι Ἰησοῦς ὁ Ναζωραῖος, ὃν σὺ διώκεις·" ἀπὸ τῆς κάτω πόλεως, ἀπὸ τοῦ κάτω χωρίου καὶ τοῦ τόπου; διότι ἠγνόει αὐτὸν ὁ διώκων· εἰ γὰρ ᾔδει αὐτὸν, οὐκ ἂν ἐδίωξεν· ἠγνόει ὅτι ἐκ τοῦ Πατρὸς ἦν γεννηθείς· ὅτι δὲ ἀπὸ Ναζαρὲτ ἦν, ᾔδει· εἰ οὖν εἶπεν αὐτῷ, Ἐγώ εἰμι ὁ Υἱὸς τοῦ Θεοῦ· ὁ ἐν ἀρχῇ Λόγος· ὁ τὸν οὐρανὸν ποιήσας, εἶχεν εἰπεῖν, ἄλλος τε ἐκεῖνος, καὶ ἄλλον ἐγὼ διώκω· εἰ εἶπεν αὐτῷ ἐκεῖνα τὰ μεγάλα καὶ λαμπρὰ καὶ ὑψηλὰ, εἶχεν εἰπεῖν, οὐκ ἔστιν οὗτος ὁ σταυρωθείς· ἀλλ' ἵνα μάθῃ ὅτι ἐκεῖνον διώκει τὸν σαρκωθέντα, τὸν μορφὴν δούλου λαβόντα, τὸν μετ' αὐτοῦ συναναστραφέντα, τὸν ἀποθανόντα, τὸν ταφέντα, ἀπὸ τοῦ κάτω χωρίου, λέγει· "ἐγώ εἰμι Ἰησοῦς ὁ Ναζωραῖος, ὃν σὺ διώκεις·" ὃν οἶδας, ὃν γνωρίζεις, τὸν μετὰ σοῦ ἀναστρεφόμενον.* Chrysostom in Cramer's Catena, p. 152.

[2] *Κλητὸς ἀπόστολος.* Rom. i. 1. 1 Cor. i. 1.) *Ἀπόστολος διὰ θελήματος Θεοῦ.* (2 Cor. i. 1. Eph. i. 1. Col. i. 1.) These expressions are not used by St. Peter, St. James, St. Jude, or St. John. And it is remarkable that they are not used by St. Paul himself in the Epistles addressed to those who were most firmly attached to him. They are found in the letters to the Christians of Achaia, but not in those to the Christians of Macedonia. (See 1 Thess. i. 1. 2 Thess. i. 1. Phil. i. 1.) And though in the letters to the Ephesians and Colossians, not in that to Philemon, which is believed to have been sent at the same time. See Philemon, 1.

[3] *Οὐκ ἀπ' ἀνθρώπων, οὐδὲ δι' ἀνθρώπου.* Gal. i. 1.

immediately indicated, to which he was set apart, and in which in after years he always gloried,—the work of "preaching among the Gentiles the unsearchable riches of Christ."[1] Unless indeed we are to consider the words which he used before Agrippa[2] as a condensed statement[3] of all that was revealed to him, both in his vision on the way, and afterwards by Ananias in the city: "I am Jesus, whom thou persecutest: but rise, and stand upon thy feet; for I have appeared unto thee for this purpose, to make thee a minister and a witness both of these things which thou hast seen, and of those things in which I will appear unto thee, delivering thee from the people, and from the Gentiles, unto whom now I send thee, to open their eyes, and to turn them from darkness to light, and from the power of Satan unto God, that they may receive forgiveness of sins, and inheritance among them which are sanctified by faith that is in Me."

But the full intimation of all the labours and sufferings that were before him was still reserved. He was told to arise and go into the city, and there it should be told him what it had been ordained[4] that he should do. He arose humbled and subdued, and ready to obey whatever might be the will of Him who had spoken to him from heaven. But when he opened his eyes, all was dark around him. The brilliancy of the vision had made him blind. Those who were with him saw, as before, the trees and the sky, and the road leading into Damascus. But he was in darkness, and they led him by the hand into the city. Thus entered Saul into Damascus;—not, as he had expected, to triumph in an enterprize on which his soul was set, to brave all difficulties and dangers, to enter into houses and carry off prisoners to Jerusalem;—but he passed himself like a prisoner beneath the gateway and through the street called "Straight," where he saw not the crowd of those who gazed on him, he was led by the hands of others, trembling and helpless to the house of Judas,[5] his dark and solitary lodging.

Three days the blindness continued. Only one other space of three days' duration can be mentioned of equal importance in the history of the world. The conflict of Saul's feelings was so great, and his remorse so piercing and so deep, that during this time he neither ate nor drank.[6] He could have no communion with the Christians, for they had been terrified by the news of his approach. And the unconverted Jews could have no true sympathy with his present state of mind. He fasted and prayed in

[1] Eph. iii. 8. See Rom. xi. 13. xv. 16. Gal. ii. 8. 1 Tim. ii. 7. 2 Tim. i. 11, &c

[2] Acts xxvi. 15–18.

[3] It did not fall in with Paul's plan in his speech before Agrippa (xxvi.) to mention Ananias, as, in his speech to the Jews at Jerusalem (xxii.) he avoided any explicit mention of the Gentiles, while giving the narrative of his conversion.

[4] Κἀκεῖ σοι λαληθήσεται περὶ πάντων ὧν τέτακταί σοι ποιῆσαι· is the expression in his own speech. (xxii. 10.) See ix. 6, and compare xxvi. 16.

[5] Acts ix. 11. [6] ix. 9.

silence. The recollections of his early years,—the passages of the ancient Scriptures which he had never understood,—the thought of his own cruelty and violence,—the memory of the last looks of Stephen,—all these crowded into his mind, and made the three days equal to long years of repentance. And if we may imagine one feeling above all others to have kept possession of his heart, it would be the feeling suggested by Christ's expostulation: "Why persecutest thou ME?"[1] This feeling would be attended with thoughts of peace, with hope, and with faith. He waited on God: and in his blindness a vision was granted to him. He seemed to behold one who came in to him,—and he knew by revelation that his name was Ananias,—and it appeared to him that the stranger laid his hand on him, that he might receive his sight.[2]

The economy of visions, by which God revealed and accomplished His will, is remarkably similar in the case of Ananias and Saul at Damascus, and in that of Peter and Cornelius at Joppa and Cæsarea. The simultaneous preparation of the hearts of Ananias and Saul, and the simultaneous preparation of those of Peter and Cornelius,—the questioning and hesitation of Peter, and the questioning and hesitation of Ananias,—the one doubting whether he might make friendship with the Gentiles, the other doubting whether he might approach the enemy of the Church,—the unhesitating obedience of each, when the Divine will was made clearly known,—the state of mind in which both the Pharisee and the Centurion were found,—each waiting to see what the Lord would say unto them,—this close analogy will not be forgotten by those who reverently read the two consecutive chapters, in which the baptism of Saul and the baptism of Cornelius are narrated in the Acts of the Apostles.[3]

And in another respect there is a close parallelism between the two histories. The same exact topography characterizes them both. In the one case we have the lodging with "Simon the Tanner," and the house "by the sea-side" (x. 6),—in the other we have "the house of Judas," and "the street called Straight" (ix. 11). And as the shore, where "the saint beside the ocean prayed," is an unchanging feature of Joppa, which will ever be dear to the Christian heart;[4] so are we allowed to bear in mind that the thoroughfares of Eastern cities do not change,[5] and to believe that the "Straight Street," which still extends through Damascus in long perspective from the Eastern Gate, is the street where Ananias spoke to Saul. More than this we do not venture to say. In the first days of the Church, and for some time afterwards, the local knowledge of the

[1] See Mat. xxv. 40, 45. [2] Acts ix. 12.

[3] Acts ix. and x. Compare also xi. 5–18, with xxii. 12–16.

[4] See "The Christian Year;" Monday in Easter Week.

[5] See Lord Nugent's remarks on the Jerusalem Bazaar, in his "Sacred and Classical Lands," vol. ii. pp. 40, 41.

Christians at Damascus might be cherished and vividly retained. But now that through long ages Christianity in the East has been weak and degraded, and Mahommedanism strong and tyrannical, we can only say that the spots still shown to travellers as the sites of the house of Ananias, and the house of Judas, and the place of baptism, may possibly be true.[1]

We know nothing concerning Ananias, except what we learn from St. Luke or from St. Paul. He was a Jew who had become a "disciple" of Christ (ix. 10), and he was well reputed and held to be "devout according to the law," among "all the Jews who dwelt there" (xxii. 12). He is never mentioned by St. Paul in his Epistles; and the later stories respecting his history are unsupported by proof.[2] Though he was not ignorant of the new convert's previous character, it seems evident that he had no personal acquaintance with him; or he would hardly have been described as "one called Saul, of Tarsus," lodging in the house of Judas. He was not an Apostle, nor one of the conspicuous members of the Church. And it was not without a deep significance,[3] that he, who was called to be an Apostle, should be baptized by one of whom the Church knows nothing, but that he was a Christian "disciple," and had been a "devout" Jew.

Ananias came into the house where Saul, faint and exhausted[4] with three days' abstinence, still remained in darkness. When he laid his hands on his head, as the vision had foretold, immediately he would be recognised as the messenger of God, even before the words were spoken, "Brother Saul, the Lord, even Jesus, that appeared unto thee in the way as thou camest, hath sent me, that thou mightest receive thy sight, and be filled with the Holy Ghost." These words were followed, as were the words of Jesus Himself when He spoke to the blind, with an instantaneous

[1] See, for instance, some of the older travellers, as Thevenot, parts i. and ii. Maundrell (1714), p. 36. Pococke, ii. 119.

[2] Tradition says that he was one of the seventy disciples, that he was afterwards Bishop of Damascus, and stoned after many tortures under Licinius (or Lucianus) the Governor. Augustine says he was a priest at the time of St. Paul's baptism. Œcumenius calls him a deacon. His day is kept on Oct. 1, by the Greeks, on Jan. 25, by the Latins. See the Acta Sanctorum under that day. Baronius (sub anno 35) says that he had fled from Jerusalem in the persecution of Stephen, and formed a Christian community at Damascus. The Acta ex MS. Græco in the Acta Sanctorum make him go from Antioch to Damascus.

[3] Ananias, as Chrysostom says, was not one τῶν κορυφαίων ἀποστόλων, because Paul was not to be taught of men. On the other hand, this very circumstance shows the importance attached by God to baptism. Olshausen remarks very justly:—"Höchst wichtig ist hier der Umstand, dass der Apostel Paulus keineswegs bloss vermittelst dieser wunderbaren Berufung durch den Herrn selbst Glied der Kirche wird, sondern dass er sich noch taufen lassen muss." He adds that this baptism of Paul by Ananias did not imply any inferiority or dependence, more than in the case of our Lord and John the Baptist.

[4] See Acts ix. 19

dissipation of darkness: "There fell from his eyes as it had been scales:[1] and he received sight forthwith" (ix. 18): or, in his own more vivid expression, "the same hour he looked up on the face of Ananias" (xxii. 13). It was a face he had never seen before. But the expression of Christian love assured him of reconciliation with God. He learnt that "the God of his fathers" had chosen him "to know His will,"—"to see that Just One,"—"to hear the voice of His mouth,"—to be "His witness unto all men."[2] He was baptized, and "the rivers of Damascus" became more to him than "all the waters of Judah"[3] had been. His body was strengthened with food; and his soul was made strong to "suffer great things" for the name of Jesus, and to bear that Name "before the Gentiles, and kings, and the children of Israel."[4]

He began by proclaiming the honour of that Name to the children of Israel in Damascus. He was "not disobedient to the heavenly vision" (xxvi. 19), but "straightway preached in the synagogues" that Jesus was "the Son of God,"[5]—and "showed unto them that they should repent and turn to God, and do works meet for repentance." His Rabbinical and Pharisaic learning was now used to uphold the cause which he came to destroy. The Jews were astounded. They knew what he had been at Jerusalem. They knew why he had come to Damascus. And now they saw him contradicting the whole previous course of his life, and utterly discarding that "commission of the high-priests," which had been the authority of his journey. Yet it was evident that his conduct was not the result of a wayward and irregular impulse. His convictions never hesitated; his energy grew continually stronger,[6] as he strove in the synagogues, maintaining the truth against the Jews, and "arguing and proving that Jesus was indeed the Messiah."[7]

The period of his first teaching at Damascus does not seem to have lasted long. Indeed it is evident that his life could not have been safe, had he remained. The fury of the Jews when they had recovered from their first surprise must have been excited to the utmost pitch; and they would soon have received a new commissioner from Jerusalem armed with full powers to supersede and punish one whom they must have regarded as the most faithless of apostates. Saul left the city, but not to return to

[1] It is difficult to see why the words *ἀπέπεσον ἀπὸ τῶν ὀφθαλμῶν αὐτοῦ ὡσεὶ λεπίδες* should be considered merely descriptive by Olshausen and others. One of the arguments for taking them literally is the peculiar exactness of St. Luke in speaking on such subjects. See a paper on the medical style of St. Luke in the Gentleman's Magazine for June 1841.

[2] xxii. 14, 15. [3] See 2 Kings v. 12. [4] See Acts ix. 15, 16.

[5] ix. 20. Where Ἰησοῦν, and not Χριστὸν, is the true reading. Verse 22 (*ὅτι οὗτός ἐστιν ὁ Χριστὸς*) would make this probable, if the authority of the MSS. were not decisive.

[6] *Σαῦλος δὲ μᾶλλον ἐνεδυναμοῦτο.* (ix. 22.)

συμβιβάζων ὅτι οὗτός ἐστιν ὁ Χριστός. (Ibid.)

Jerusalem. Conscious of his divine mission, he never felt that it was necessary to consult "those who were Apostles before him, but he went into Arabia, and returned again into Damascus." [1]

Many questions have been raised concerning this journey into Arabia. The first question relates to the meaning of the word. From the time when the word "Arabia" was first used by any of the writers of Greece or Rome,[2] it has always been a term of vague and uncertain import. Sometimes it includes Damascus;[3] sometimes it ranges over the Lebanon itself, and extends even to the borders of Cilicia.[4] The native geographers usually reckon that stony district, of which Petra was the capital, as belonging to Egypt,—and that wide desert towards the Euphrates, where the Bedouins of all ages have lived in tents, as belonging to Syria,—and have limited the name to the Peninsula between the Red Sea and the Persian Gulf, where Jemen, or "Araby the Blest," is secluded on the south.[5] In the three-fold division of Ptolemy, which remains in our popular language when we speak of this still untravelled region, both the first and second of these districts were included under the name of the third. And we must suppose St. Paul to have gone into one of the former, either that which touched Syria and Mesopotamia, or that which touched Palestine and Egypt. If he went into the first, we need not suppose him to have travelled far from Damascus. For though the strong powers of Syria and Mesopotamia might check the Arabian tribes, and retrench the Arabian name in this direction, yet the Gardens of Damascus were on the verge of the desert, and Damascus was almost as much an Arabian as a Syrian town.

And if he went into Petræan Arabia, there still remains the question of his motive for the journey, and his employment when there. Either retiring before the opposition at Damascus, he went to preach the Gospel, and then, in the synagogues of that singular capital, which was built amidst the rocks of Edom,[6] whence "Arabians" came to the festivals at

[1] Gal. i. 17.

[2] Herodotus speaks of Syria as the coast of Arabia. *Τῆς Ἀραβίας τὰ παρὰ θαλάσσαν Σύριοι νέμονται.* (ii. 12.) Xenophon, in the Anabasis (i. 5) calls a district in Mesopotamia, to the north of Babylonia, by the name of Arabia; and *Σκηνῖται Ἄραβες* are placed by Strabo (xvi. 1, and xvi. 3) in the same district.

[3] *Ὅτι δὲ Δαμασκὸς τῆς Ἀραβικῆς γῆς ἦν καὶ ἔστιν, εἰ καὶ νῦν προσνενέμηται τῇ Συροφοινίκῃ λεγομένῃ οὐδ' ὑμῶν τινὲς ἀρνήσασθαι δύνανται.* Justin Mart. c. Tryph. Jebb's ed. 1719, p. 239. "Damascus Arabiæ retro deputabatur, antequam transcripta erat in Syrophœnicem ex distinctione Syriarum." Tertull. adv. Marc. iii. 13, and adv. Jud. § 9.

[4] "Arabia . . . amplitudine longissima a monte Amano, a regione Ciliciæ Commagenesque descendit . . . nec non in media Syriæ ad Libanum montem penetrantibus Nubeis." (Plin. H. N. vi. 32.) And so Plutarch, in the Life of Pompey (§ 56), speaks of Arabs in Mount Amanus.

[5] See Mannert's Geographie der Griechen und Römer, and Winer's Realwörterbuch.

[6] Strabo, in his description of Petra, says that his friend Athenodorus found great

Jerusalem, he testified of Jesus; or he went for the purpose of contemplation and solitary communion with God, to deepen his repentance and fortify his soul with prayer; and then perhaps his steps were turned to those mountain heights by the Red Sea, which Moses and Elijah had trodden before him. We cannot attempt to decide the question. The views which different inquirers take of it will probably depend on their own tendency to the practical or the ascetic life. On the one hand, it may be argued that such zeal could not be restrained, that Saul could not be silent, but that he would rejoice in carrying into the metropolis of King Aretas the Gospel which his Ethnarch could afterwards hinder at Damascus.[2] On the other hand, it may be said that, with such convictions recently worked in his mind, he would yearn for solitude,—that a time of austere meditation before the beginning of a great work is in conformity with the economy of God,—that we find it quite natural, if Paul followed the example of the Great Lawgiver and the Great Prophet, and of ONE greater than Moses and Elijah, who, after His baptism and before His ministry, "returned from Jordan and was led by the Spirit into the wilderness."[3]

While Saul is in Arabia, preaching the Gospel in obscurity, or preparing for his varied work by the intuition of Sacred Truth,—it seems the natural place for some reflections on the reality and the momentous significance of his conversion. It has already been remarked, in what we have drawn from the statements of Scripture, that he was called directly by Christ without the intervention of any other Apostle, and that the purpose of his call was clearly indicated, when Ananias baptized him. He was an Apostle "not of men, neither by man,"[4] and the Divine will was "to work among the Gentiles by his ministry."[5] But the unbeliever may still say that there are other questions of primary importance. He may suggest that this apparent change in the current of Saul's thoughts, and this actual revolution in the manner of his life, was either the contrivance of deep and deliberate imposture, or the result of wild and extravagant fanaticism. Both in ancient and modern times, some have been found who have resolved this great occurrence in the promptings of self-interest, or have ventured to call it the offspring of delusion. There is an old story mentioned by Epiphanius, from which it appears that the Ebionites were content to find a motive for the change, in an idle story that he first became a Jew that he might marry the High Priest's daughter, and then became the antagonist of Judaism because the High Priest deceived him.[6]

numbers of strangers there. 'Αθηνόδωρος, ἀνὴρ φιλόσοφος καὶ ἡμῖν ἑταῖρος .... εὑρεῖν ἐπιδημοῦντας ἔφη πολλοὺς μὲν 'Ρωμαίων, πολλοὺς δὲ καὶ τῶν ἄλλων ξένων. (xvi. 4.) In the same paragraph, after describing its cliffs and peculiar situation, he says that it was distant three or four days' journey from Jericho. See above, p. 81, n. 6.

[1] Acts ii. 11.
[2] See 2 Cor. xi. 32.
[3] Luke iv. 1.
[4] Gal. i. 1.
[5] Acts xxi. 19.
[6] Τοῦ Παύλου κατηγοροῦντες οὐκ αἰσχύνονται ἐπιπλάστοις τισὶ τοῖς τῶν ψευδαπο-

And there are modern Jews, who are satisfied with saying that he changed rapidly from one passion to another, like those impetuous souls who cannot hate or love by halves.[1] Can we then say that St. Paul was simply an *enthusiast* or an *impostor*? The question has been so well answered in a celebrated English book,[2] that we are content to refer to it. It will never be possible for any to believe St. Paul to have been a mere enthusiast, who duly considers his calmness, his wisdom, his prudence, and, above all, his humility, a virtue which is not less inconsistent with fanaticism than with imposture. And how can we suppose that he was an impostor who changed his religion for selfish purposes? Was he influenced by the ostentation of learning? He suddenly cast aside all that he had been taught by Gamaliel, or acquired through long years of study, and took up the opinions of the fishermen of Galilee, whom he had scarcely ever seen, and who had never been educated in the schools. Was it the love of power which prompted the change? He abdicated in a moment the authority which he possessed, for power "over a flock of sheep driven to the slaughter, whose Shepherd himself had been murdered a little before;" and "all he could hope from that power was to be marked out in a particular manner for the same knife, which he had seen so bloodily drawn against them." Was it the love of wealth? Whatever might be his own worldly possessions at the time, he joined himself to those who were certainly poor, and the prospect before him was that which was actually realised, of ministering to his necessities with the labour of his hands.[3] Was it the love of fame? His prophetic power must have been miraculous, if he could look beyond the shame and scorn which then rested on the servants of a crucified master, to that glory with which Christendom now surrounds the memory of St. Paul.

And if the conversion of St. Paul was not the act of an enthusiast or an impostor, then it ought to be considered how much this wonderful oc-

τόλων αὐτῶν κακούργοις καὶ πλάνης λόγοις πεποιημένοις. Ταρσέα *μὲν αὐτὸν, ὡς αὐτὸς ὁμολογεῖ καὶ οὐκ ἀρνεῖται, λέγοντες.* 'Εξ 'Ελλήνων *δὲ αὐτὸν ὑποτίθενται, λαβόντες τὴν πρόφασιν ἐκ τοῦ τόπου διὰ τὸ φιλάληθες ὑπ' αὐτοῦ ῥηθὲν, ὅτι* Ταρσεύς *εἰμι, οὐκ ἀσήμου πόλεως πολίτης·* (Acts xxi.) *εἶτα φάσκουσιν αὐτὸν εἶναι* Ἕλληνα, *καὶ* 'Ελληνίδος *μητρὸς καὶ* Ἕλληνος *πατρὸς παῖδα· ἀναβεβηκέναι δὲ εἰς* Ιεροσόλυμα, *καὶ χρόνον ἐκεῖ μεμενηκέναι, ἐπιτεθυμηκέναι δὲ θυγατέρα τοῦ ἱερέως πρὸς γάμον ἀγαγέσθαι, καὶ τούτου ἕνεκα προσήλυτον γενέσθαι καὶ περιτμηθῆναι· εἶτα μὴ λαβόντα τὴν κόρην ὠργίσθαι καὶ κατὰ περιτομῆς γεγραφέναι, καὶ κατὰ* Σαββάτου *καὶ νομοθεσίας.* Epiph. ad Hær. i. 2, § 16. Below in § 25, he argues the impossibility of this story from its contradiction to Phil. iii. and 2 Cor. xi. Barnabas, though a Cyprian, was a Levite, and why not Paul a Jew, though a Tarsian? And are we to believe, he adds, what Ebion says of Paul, or what Peter says of him. (2 Pet. iii.)?

[1] Such is M. Salvador's explanation. Jésus Christ et sa Doctrine, liv. iii. § 2. Paul et l'Eglise.

[2] Lyttelton's Observations on the Conversion and Apostleship of St. Paul.

[3] Acts xx. 33, 44. 1 Cor. xv. 8. 1 Thess. ii. 4, 5, 6, 9, &c.

currence involves. As Lord Lyttelton observes, "the conversion and apostleship of St. Paul alone, duly considered, is of itself a demonstration sufficient to prove Christianity to be a divine revelation." Saul was arrested at the height of his zeal, and in the midst of his fury. In the words of Chrysostom, "Christ, like a skilful physician, healed him when his fever was at the worst:"[1] and he proceeds to remark, in the same eloquent sermon, that the truth of Christ's resurrection, and the present power of Him who had been crucified, were shown far more forcibly, than they could have been if Paul had been otherwise called. Nor ought we to forget the great religious lessons we are taught to gather from this event. We see the value set by God upon honesty and integrity, when we find that he, "who was before a blasphemer and a persecutor and injurious, obtained mercy because he did it ignorantly in unbelief."[2] And we learn the encouragement given to all sinners who repent, when we are told that "for this cause he obtained mercy that in him first Jesus Christ might shew forth all long suffering, for a pattern to them which should hereafter believe on Him to life everlasting."

We return to the narrative. Saul's time of retirement in Arabia was not of long continuance. He was not destined to be the Evangelist of the East. In the Epistle to the Galatians,[3] the time, from his conversion to his final departure from Damascus, is said to have been "three years," which, according to the Jewish way of reckoning, may have been three entire years, or only one year with parts of two others. Meantime Saul had "returned to Damascus, preaching boldly in the name of Jesus." (ix. 27.) The Jews, being no longer able to meet him in controversy, resorted

[1] *Καθάπερ ἰατρὸς ἄριστος, ἀκμάζοντος ἔτι τοῦ πυρετοῦ, τὸ βοήθημα αὐτῷ ἐπήγαγεν ὁ Χρίστος.* (Hom. xix. in Act.) See the same homily below.

[2] 1 Tim. i. 13. See Luke xii. 48. xxiii. 34. Acts iii. 17. 1 Cor. ii. 8. On the other hand, "unbelieving ignorance" is often mentioned in Scripture, as an aggravation of sin: *e. g.* Eph. iv. 18, 19. 2 Thess. i. 7, 8. We should bear in mind Aristotle's distinction (Eth. Nic. iii. 1.) of *ἀγνοῶν* and *δι' ἀγνοίαν*,—thus stated by Aquinas on this very passage,—"Aliud est ignoranter agere, aliud par ignorantiam: *ignoranter* facit aliquid qui nescit quod facit, tamen si sciret etiam faceret illud: *per ignorantiam* facit qui facit aliquid quod non faceret si nosset." Div. Thom. Comm. in Paul. Ep. p. 391. See the note of Estius, and especially the following remark: "Objectum seu materia misericordiæ, miseria est; unde quando miseria major, tanto magis nata est misericordiam commovere." A man is deeply wretched who sins through ignorance; and, as Augustine says, Paul in his unconverted state was like a sick man who through madness tries to kill his physician.

[3] In Acts ix. 23, the time is said to have been "many days." Dr. Paley has observed in a note on the Horæ Paulinæ (p. 82) a similar instance in the Old Testament (1 Kings ii. 38, 39.), where "many days" is used to denote a space of "three years:"—"And Shimei dwelt at Jerusalem *many days*; and it came to pass, at the end of *three years*, that two of the servants of Shimei ran away." The edition of the Horæ Paulinæ referred to in this work is that of Mr. Tate, entitled "The Continuous History of St. Paul," 1840.

to that which is the last argument of a desperate cause:[1] they resolved to assassinate him. Saul became acquainted with the conspiracy; and all due precautions were taken to evade the danger. But the political circumstances of Damascus at the time made escape very difficult. Either in the course of the hostilities which prevailed along the Syrian frontiers between Herod Antipas and the Romans, on one side, and Aretas, King of Petra, on the other,—and possibly in consequence of that absence of Vitellius,[2] which was caused by the emperor's death,—the Arabian monarch had made himself master of Damascus, and the Jews, who sympathised with Aretas, were high in the favour of his officer, the Ethnarch.[3] Or Tiberius had ceased to reign, and his successor had assigned Damascus to the King of Petra, and the Jews had gained over his officer and his soldiers, as Pilate's soldiers had once been gained over at Jerusalem. St. Paul at least expressly informs us,[4] that "the Ethnarch kept watch over the city, with a garrison, purposing to apprehend him." St. Luke says,[5] that the Jews "watched the city-gates day and night, with the intention of killing him." The Jews furnished the motive, the Ethnarch the military force. The anxiety of the "disciples" was doubtless great, as when Peter was imprisoned by Herod, "and prayer was made without ceasing of the Church unto God for him."[6] Their anxiety became the instrument of his safety. From an unguarded part of the wall, in the darkness of the night, probably where some overhanging houses, as is usual in Eastern cities, opened upon the outer country, they let him down from a window[7] in a basket.[8] There was something of humiliation in this mode of escape; and this, perhaps, is the reason why, in a letter written "fourteen years" after-

[1] 'Επὶ τον ἰσχυρόν συλλόγισμὸν ἔρχονται οἱ Ιουδαῖοι. κ. τ. λ. S. Chrys. Hom. xx.

[2] See above, p. 81.

[3] Some have supposed that this Ethnarch was merely an officer who regulated the affairs of the Jews themselves, such as we know to have existed under this title in cities with many Jewish residents. See Joseph. Ant. xiv. 7, 2, and 8, 5. B. J. ii. 6, 3. Anger imagines that he was an officer of Aretas accidentally residing in Damascus, who induced the Roman government to aid the conspiracy of the Jews. Neither hypothesis seems very probable. Schrader suggests (p. 153) that the Ethnarch's wife might, perhaps, be a Jewish proselyte, as we know was the case with a vast number of the women of Damascus.

[4] 2 Cor. xi. 32, ἐφρούρει. [5] Acts ix. 24. [6] Acts xii. 5.

[7] Διὰ θυρίδος. (2 Cor. xi. 32.) So Rahab let down the spies; and so David escaped from Saul. The word θυρίς is used in the LXX. in both instances. Καὶ κατεχάλασεν αὐτοὺς διὰ τῆς θυρίδος. (Josh. ii. 15.) Καὶ κατάγει ἡ Μελχολ τὸν Δαβὶδ διὰ τῆς θυρίδος, καὶ ἀπῆλθε καὶ ἔφυγε καὶ σώζεται. (1 Sam. xix. 12.)

[8] The word in 2 Cor. xi. 32, is σαργάνη; in Acts ix. 25, it is σπυρίς, the word used in the Gospels, in the narrative of the miracle of feeding the "four thousand," as opposed to that of feeding the "five thousand," when κόφινος is used. Compare Mat. xiv. 20. Mark vi. 43. Luke ix. 17. John vi. 13, with Mat. xv. 37. Mark viii. 8, and both with Mat. xvi. 9, 10. See Prof. Blunt's Scriptural Coincidences, pt iv. § xi. 1847. In Rich's Companion to the Dictionary, contrast the illustration under Sporta (σπυρίς) with that under Cophinus (κόφινος

WALL OF DAMASCUS.

wards, he specifies the details, "glorying in his infirmities," when he is about to speak of "his visions and revelations of the Lord."[1]

Thus already the Apostle had experience of "perils by his own countrymen, and perils in the city." Already "in journeyings often, in weariness and painfulness"[2] he began to learn "how great things he was to suffer" for the name of Christ.[3] Preserved from destruction at Damascus, he turned his steps towards Jerusalem. His motive for the journey, as he tells us in the Epistle to the Galatians, was a desire to become acquainted with Peter.[4] Not that he was ignorant of the true principles of the Gospel. He expressly tells us that he neither needed nor received any instruction in Christianity from those who were "apostles before him." But he must have heard much from the Christians at Damascus of the Galilean fisherman. Can we wonder that he should desire to see the Chief of the Twelve,—the brother with whom now he was consciously united in the bonds of a common apostleship,—and who had long on earth been the constant companion of his LORD?

How changed was everything since he had last travelled this road between Damascus and Jerusalem. If, when the day broke, he looked back upon that city from which he had escaped under the shelter of night, as his eye ranged over the fresh gardens and the wide desert, how the remembrance of that first terrible vision would call forth a deep thanksgiving to Him, who had called him to be a "partaker of His sufferings."[5] And what feelings must have attended his approach to Jerusalem. "He was returning to it from a spiritual, as Ezra had from a bodily, captivity, and to his renewed mind all things appeared new. What an emotion smote his heart at the first distant view of the Temple, that house of sacrifice, that edifice of prophecy. Its sacrifices had been realised, the Lamb of God had been offered: its prophecies had been fulfilled, the Lord had

[1] 2 Cor. xi. 30. xii. 1–5. Both Schrader and Wieseler are of opinion that the vision mentioned here is that which he saw at Jerusalem, on his return from Damascus (Acts xxii. 17. See below, p. 103), and which was naturally associated in his mind with the recollection of his escape. Schrader's remarks on the train of ideas are worth quoting. "Wie genau er hier die Flucht von Damaskus und die Entzückung mit einander verbindet, zeigt sein ganzer Gedankengang. Er hat vorher eine Menge seiner Leiden als Christ aufgezählt. Nun nimmt sein Geist plötzlich einen höhern Aufschwung; ein Theil der Vergangenheit schwebt ihm auf einmal lebendig vor der Seele; seine Rede wird abgebrochener, wie ein gehemmter Strom, der auf einmal wieder durchbricht: Gott weiss, dass ich nicht lüge—ich floh von Damaskus—doch nein, es ist nicht gut, dass ich mich rühme—ich kenne einen Christen—er kam in Entzückung, Gott weiss es wie —er wurde in das Paradies versetzt, Gott weiss, wie es zuging—ja ich könnte mich wohl rühmen, ohne zu lügen, aber ich will es nicht. Wer fühlt es nicht, dass hier vom Anfang bis zu Ende alles Eins ist und nicht auseinander gerissen werden darf?" pp. 157, 158.

[2] 2 Cor. xi. 26, 27.

[3] Acts ix. 16.

[4] Ἱστορῆσαι Πέτρον. i. 18. See the remarks of Jerome and Chrysostom on this passage.

[5] 1 Pet. iv. 5.

come unto it. As he approached the gates, he might have trodden the very spot where he had so exultingly assisted in the death of Stephen, and he entered them perfectly content, were it God's will, to be dragged out through them to the same fate. He would feel a peculiar tie of brotherhood to that martyr, for he could not be now ignorant that the same Jesus who in such glory had called him, had but a little while before appeared in the same glory to assure the expiring Stephen. The ecstatic look and words of the dying saint now came fresh upon his memory with their real meaning. When he entered into the city, what deep thoughts were suggested by the haunts of his youth, and by the sight of the spots where he had so eagerly sought that knowledge which he had now so eagerly abandoned. What an intolerable burden had he cast off. He felt as a glorified spirit may be supposed to feel on revisiting the scenes of its fleshly sojourn." [1]

Yet not without grief and awe could he look upon that city of his forefathers, over which he now knew that the judgment of God was impending. And not without sad emotions could one of so tender a nature think of the alienation of those who had once been his warmest associates. The grief of Gamaliel, the indignation of the Pharisees, the fury of the Hellenistic Synagogues, all this, he knew, was before him. The sanguine hopes, however, springing from his own honest convictions, and his fervent zeal to communicate the truth to others, predominated in his mind. He thought that they would believe as he had believed. He argued thus with himself, —that they well knew that he had "imprisoned and beaten in every synagogue them that believed in Jesus Christ,"—and that "when the blood of His martyr Stephen was shed, he also was standing by and consenting unto his death, and kept the raiment of them that slew him,"[2]—and that when they saw the change which had been produced in him, and heard the miraculous history he could tell them, they would not refuse to "receive his testimony."

Thus, with fervent zeal, and sanguine expectations, "he attempted to join himself to the disciples" of Christ.[3] But, as the Jews hated him, so the Christians suspected him. His escape had been too hurried to allow of his bringing "letters of commendation." Whatever distant rumour might have reached them of an apparition on his journey, of his conduct at Damascus, of his retirement in Arabia, they could not believe that he was really a disciple. And then it was that Barnabas, already known to us as a generous contributor of his wealth to the poor,[4] came forward again as the "Son of Consolation,"—"took him by the hand," and brought

[1] Scripture Biography, by Rev. R. W. Evans, second series, p. 337

[2] The argument used in his ecstacy in the Temple (Acts xxii. 17–21), when it was revealed to him that those in Jerusalem would not receive his testimony.

[3] Acts ix. 26.

[4] See Acts iv. 36

him to the Apostles.[1] It is probable that Barnabas and Saul were acquainted with each other before. Cyprus is within a few hours' sail from Cilicia. The schools of Tarsus may naturally have attracted one, who, though a Levite, was a Hellenist: and there the friendship may have begun, which lasted through many vicissitudes, till it was rudely interrupted in the dispute at Antioch.[2] When Barnabas related how "the Lord" Jesus Christ had personally appeared to Saul, and had even spoken to him, and how he had boldly maintained the Christian cause in the synagogues of Damascus, then the Apostles laid aside their hesitation. Peter's argument must have been what it was on another occasion; "Forasmuch as God hath given unto him the like gift as He did unto me, who am I that I should withstand God?"[3] He and James, the Lord's brother, the only other Apostle[4] who was in Jerusalem at the time, gave to him "the right hands of fellowship." And he was with them, "coming in and going out," more than forgiven for Christ's sake, welcomed and beloved as a friend and a brother.

This first meeting of the fisherman of Galilee and the tentmaker of Tarsus, the chosen companion of Jesus on earth, and the chosen Pharisee who saw Jesus in the heavens, the Apostle of the circumcision and the Apostle of the Gentiles, is passed over in Scripture in a few words. The Divine record does not linger in dramatic description on those passages which a mere human writing would labour to embellish. What took place in the intercourse of these two Saints,—what was said of Jesus of Nazareth who suffered, died, and was buried,—and of Jesus, the glorified Lord, who had risen and ascended, and become "head over all things to the Church,"—what was felt of Christian love and devotion,—what was learnt, under the Spirit's teaching, of Christian truth, has not been revealed, and cannot be known. The intercourse was full of present comfort, and full of great consequences. But it did not last long. Fifteen days passed away, and the Apostles were compelled to part. The same zeal which had caused his voice to be heard in the Hellenistic synagogues in the persecution against Stephen, now led Saul in the same synagogues to declare fearlessly his adherence to Stephen's cause. The same fury which had caused the murder of Stephen, now brought the murderer of Stephen to the verge of assassination. Once more, as at Damascus, the Jews made a conspiracy to put Saul to death: and once more he was rescued by the anxiety of the brethren.[5]

[1] Acts ix. 27 [2] Acts xv. 39. [3] See Acts xi. 17.

[4] "When Saul was come to Jerusalem . . . Barnabas took him and brought him to the Apostles . . . and he was with them coming in and going out at Jerusalem." (Acts ix. 26–28.) "After three years I went up to Jerusalem to see Peter, and abode with him fifteen days. But other of the Apostles saw I none, save James the Lord's brother." (Gal. i. 18, 19.)

[5] Acts ix. 29, 30.

Reluctantly, and not without a direct intimation from on high, he retired from the work of preaching the Gospel in Jerusalem. As he was praying one day in the Temple, it came to pass that he fell into a trance,[1] and in his ecstacy he saw Jesus, who spoke to him and said, "Make haste and get thee quickly out of Jerusalem: for they will not receive thy testimony concerning me." He hesitated to obey the command, his desire to do God's will leading him to struggle against the hindrances of God's providence—and the memory of Stephen, which haunted him even in his trance, furnishing him with an argument.[2] But the command was more peremptory than before: "Depart; for I will send thee far hence unto the Gentiles." The scene of his apostolic victories was not to be Jerusalem. For the third time it was declared to him that the field of his labours was among the Gentiles. This secret revelation to his soul conspired with the outward difficulties of his situation. The care of God gave the highest sanction to the anxiety of the brethren. And he suffered himself to be withdrawn from the Holy City.

They brought him down to Cæsarea by the sea,[3] and from Cæsarea they sent him to Tarsus.[4] His own expression in the Epistle to the Galatians (i. 21) is that he went "into the regions of Syria and Cilicia." From this it has been inferred that he went first from Cæsarea to Antioch, and then from Antioch to Tarsus. And such a course would have been perfectly natural: for the communication of the city of Cæsar and the Herods with the metropolis of Syria, either by sea and the harbour of Seleucia, or by the great coast-road through Tyre and Sidon, was easy and frequent. But the supposition is unnecessary. In consequence of the range of Mount Taurus, Cilicia has a greater geographical affinity with Syria than with Asia Minor. Hence it has existed in frequent political combination with it from the time of the old Persian satrapies to the mod-

[1] See Acts xxii. 17–21. Though Schrader is sometimes laboriously unsuccessful in explaining the miraculous, yet we need not entirely disregard what he says (p. 160) concerning the oppression of spirit, under the sense of being mistrusted and opposed, with which Saul came to pray in the Temple. And we may compare the preparation for St. Peter's vision, before the conversion of Cornelius.

[2] Compare the similar expostulations of Ananias, ix. 13, and of Peter, x. 14.

[3] Olshausen is certainly mistaken in supposing that Cæsarea Philippi is meant. Whenever "Cæsarea" is spoken of absolutely, it always means Cæsarea Stratonis. And even if it is assumed that Saul travelled by land through Syria to Tarsus, this would not have been the natural course. His words are "Um zu Lande nach Tarsus von Jerusalem auszugehen, würde Paulus nicht den weitern Weg über Cæsarea Stratonis gewählt haben." But though it may be true that this Cæsarea is nearer the Syrian frontier than the other, the physical character of the country is such that he would naturally go by the other Cæsarea, unless indeed he travelled by Damascus to Antioch, which is highly improbable. See also a good note by Mr. Tate in the "Continuous History," &c., p. 106.

[4] Acts ix. 30.

ern pachalics of the Sultan: and "*Syria and Cilicia*" appears in history almost as a generic geographical term, the more important district being mentioned first.[1] Within the limits of this region Saul's activities were now exercised in studying and in teaching at Tarsus,—or in founding those Churches[2] which were afterwards greeted in the Apostolic letter from Jerusalem, as the brethren "in Antioch, and Syria, and Cilicia," and which Paul himself confirmed after his separation from Barnabas, travelling through "Syria and Cilicia."

Whatever might be the extent of his journeys within these limits, we know at least that he was at Tarsus. Once more we find him in the home of his childhood. It is the last time we are distinctly told that he was there. Now at least, if not before, we may be sure that he would come into active intercourse with the heathen philosophers of the place.[3] In his last residence at Tarsus, a few years before, he was a Jew, and not only a Jew but a Pharisee, and he looked on the Gentiles around him as outcasts from the favour of God. Now he was a Christian, and not only a Christian, but conscious of his mission as the Apostle of the Gentiles. Therefore, he would surely meet the philosophers, and prepare to argue with them on their own ground, as afterwards in the "market" at Athens with "the Epicureans and the Stoics."[4] Many Stoics of Tarsus were men of celebrity in the Roman Empire. Athenodorus, the tutor of Augustus, has been already mentioned.[5] He was probably by this time deceased, and receiving those divine honours, which, as Lucian informs us, were paid to him after his death. The tutor of Tiberius also was a Tarsian and a Stoic. His name was Nestor. He was probably at this time alive: for he lingered to the age of ninety-two,[6] and, in all likelihood, survived his

[1] This is well illustrated by the hopeless feeling of the Greek soldiers in the Anabasis, when Cyrus had drawn them into Cilicia; by various passages in the history of the Seleucidæ; by the arrangements of the Romans with Antiochus; by the division of provinces in the Notitia; and by the course of the Mahommedan conquests.

[2] Acts xv. 23, 41. When we find the existence of Cilician Churches mentioned, the obvious inference is that St. Paul founded them during this period.

[3] The passage in Strabo, referred to above, Ch. I. p. 22, is so important that we give a free translation of it here. "The men of this place are so zealous in the study of philosophy and the whole circle of education, that they surpass both Athens and Alexandria, and every place that could be mentioned, where schools of philosophers are found. And the difference amounts to this. Here, those who are fond of learning are all natives, and strangers do not willingly reside here: and they themselves do not remain, but finish their education abroad, and gladly take up their residence elsewhere, and few return. Whereas, in the other cities which I have just mentioned, except Alexandria, the contrary takes place: for many come to them and live there willingly; but you will see few of the natives either going abroad for the sake of philosophy, or caring to study it at home. The Alexandrians have both characters; for they receive many strangers, and send out of their own people not a few."

[4] Acts xvii. 17, 18. [5] See p. 45.

[6] See the Treatise called "Macrobii," ascribed to Lucian, where Athenodorus and

wicked pupil, whose death we have recently noticed. Now among these eminent sages and instructors of heathen emperors was one whose teaching was destined to survive, when the Stoic philosophy should have perished, and whose words still instruct the rulers of every civilised nation How far Saul's arguments had any success in this quarter we cannot even guess; and we must not anticipate the conversion of Cornelius. At least, he was preparing for the future. In the synagogue we cannot believe that he was silent or unsuccessful. In his own family, we may well imagine that some of those Christian "kinsmen,"[1] whose names are handed down to us,—possibly his sister, the playmate of his childhood, and his sister's son,[2] who afterwards saved his life,—were, at this time, by his exertions gathered into the fold of Christ.

Here this Chapter must close; while Saul is in exile from the earthly Jerusalem, but diligently occupied in building up the walls of the "Jerusalem which is above." And it was not without one great and important consequence that that short fortnight had been spent in Jerusalem. He was now known to Peter and to James. His vocation was fully ascertained and recognised by the heads of the Judæan Christians. It is true that he was yet "unknown by face" to the scattered Churches of Judæa.[3] But they honoured him of whom they had heard so much. And when the news came to them at intervals of all that he was doing for the cause of Christ, they praised God and said, "Behold! he who was once our persecutor is now bearing the glad tidings of that faith which formerly he laboured to root out;" "and they glorified God in him."

Nestor are enumerated among those philosophers who have lived to a great age. Ἀθηνόδωρος, Σάνδωνος, Ταρσεὺς, Στωικὸς, ὅς καὶ διδάσκαλος ἐγένετο Καίσαρος Σεβαστοῦ Θεοῦ, ὑφ' οὗ ἡ Ταρσέων πόλις καὶ φόρων ἐκουφίσθη, δύο καὶ ὀγδοήκοντα ἔτη βιοὺς, ἐτελεύτησεν ἐν τῇ πατρίδι, καὶ τιμὰς ὁ Ταρσέων δῆμος ἀυτῷ κατ' ἔτος ἕκαστον ἀπονέμει ὡς ἥρωϊ. Νέστωρ δὲ Στωικὸς ἀπὸ Ταρσοῦ, διδασκαλος Καίσαρος Τιβερίου, ἔτη δυὸ καὶ ἐνενήκοντα, § 21. Strabo mentions another Tarsian called Nestor, an Academician, who was the tutor of Marcellus, xiv. 5.

[1] Rom. xvi. See p. 46.

[2] About twenty years after this time (Acts xxiii. 17, 23) he is called *νεανίας*, the very word which is used of Saul himself (Acts vii. 58) at the stoning of Stephen. It is justly remarked by Hemsen (p. 39), that the young man's anxiety for his uncle (xxiii. 16–23) seems to imply a closer affection than that resulting from relationship alone.

[3] See Gal. i. 21–24. The Greek words *ἀκούοντες ἦσαν . . . . νῦν εὐαγγελίζεται*, seem to imply a continued preaching of the Gospel, the intelligence of which came now and then to Judæa. From the following words, however (*ἔπειτα διὰ δεκατεσσάρων ἐτῶν*), St. Paul appears to describe in i. 23, 24 the effect produced by the tidings not only of his labors in Tarsus, but of his subsequent and more extensive labours as a missionary to the Heathen. It should be added, that Wieseler thinks he staid only half a year at Tarsus.

COIN OF ARETAS, KING OF DAMASCUS.[1]

[1] From the British Museum. The inscription is given above, p. 82, n. 4. Since that note was written, some important confirmation has been received of the opinion there expressed. Mr. Burgon, of the British Museum, says in a letter: "I have carefully looked at our two coins of Aretas, and compared them with those described by Mionnet, p. 284. I feel convinced that they are much earlier than the reigns of Caligula or Claudius, and rank with the coins of the later Seleucidæ or Tigranes. These coins of Aretas do not appear to have dates: and, even granting that the coin of Mionnet, No. 20 p. 284, bears Α Ρ, which I doubt, he himself (no mean judge in such a matter) does not cite Α Ρ *as a date*,—and I should not admit it as such, till other coins be produced with unquestionable dates. Nothing is more common than for the most careful and learned men to draw false inferences from books on coins, if they have not practical knowledge enough on the subject to guide them in matters which may be regarded as *technical*. Sestini (Classes Generales, Florence, 1821, p, 141) does cite Α Ρ as a date, and he is an authority as good as Mionnet; but in this case I think him wrong. As to the word ΦΙΛΕΛΛΗΝ, it is worth observing that the later kings of Cappadocia (fearing the Roman Power) call themselves ΦΙΛΟΡΩΜΑΙΟΣ."

It should be added, that there are certain consular denarii of the Plautian family, where King Aretas is represented as kneeling in submission by the side of a camel. An engraving of one of these coins is to be found in the "Thesaurus Morellianus, &c.," 1734, Pl. I. fig. 1. This is doubtless the same Arabian monarch who is commemorated on the former coin,—not the earlier Aretas of the Maccabees, nor the later Aretas of St. Paul,—but the king who submitted to Scaurus. The Roman general's name is in the exergue with that of Aretas: and it is interesting to contrast the coin in which the Arabian king calls himself the friend of the Greeks, with that in which he acknowledges himself the subject of the Romans.

CHAPTER IV.

"Attendat unusquisque vestrum, fratres mei, quit habeat Christianus. Quod homo est, commune cum multis: quod Christianus est, secernitur a multis; et plus ad illum pertinet quod Christianus, quam quod homo."—Aug. in Joh. Ev. cap. i. tract. v.

WIDER DIFFUSION OF CHRISTIANITY.—ANTIOCH.—CHRONOLOGY OF THE ACTS. —REIGN OF CALIGULA.—CLAUDIUS AND HEROD AGRIPPA I.—THE YEAR 44. —CONVERSION OF THE GENTILES.—ST. PETER AND CORNELIUS.—JOPPA AND CÆSAREA.—ST. PETER'S VISION.—BAPTISM OF CORNELIUS.—INTELLIGENCE FROM ANTIOCH.—MISSION OF BARNABAS.—SAUL WITH BARNABAS AT ANTIOCH.—THE NAME "CHRISTIAN."—DESCRIPTION AND HISTORY OF ANTIOCH. —CHARACTER OF ITS INHABITANTS.—EARTHQUAKES.—FAMINE.—BARNABAS AND SAUL AT JERUSALEM.—DEATH OF ST. JAMES AND OF HEROD AGRIPPA —RETURN WITH MARK TO ANTIOCH.—PROVIDENTIAL PREPARATION OF ST. PAUL.—RESULTS OF HIS MISSION TO JERUSALEM.

HITHERTO the history of the Christian Church has been confined within Jewish limits. We have followed its progress beyond the walls of Jerusalem, but hardly yet beyond the boundaries of Palestine. If any traveller from a distant country has been admitted into the community of believers, the place of his baptism has not been more remote than the "desert" of Gaza. If any "aliens from the commonwealth of Israel" have been admitted to the citizenship of the spiritual Israelites, they have been "strangers" who dwell among the hills of Samaria. But the time is rapidly approaching when the knowledge of Christ must spread more rapidly,—when those who possessed not that Book, which caused perplexity on the road to Ethiopia, will hear and adore His name,—and greater strangers than those who drew water from the well of Sychar will come nigh to the Fountain of Life. The same dispersion which gathered in the Samaritans, will gather in the Gentiles also. The "middle wall of partition" being utterly broken down, all will be called by the new and glorious name of "Christian."

And as we follow the progress of events, and find that all movements in the Church begin to have more and more reference to the Heathen, we observe that these movements begin to circulate more and more round a new centre of activity. Not Jerusalem, but Antioch, not the Holy City of God's ancient people, but the profane city of the Greeks and Romans, is the place to which the student of sacred history is now directed. During the remainder of the Acts of the Apostles our attention is at least divided between Jerusalem and Antioch, until at last, after following St Paul's many journeys, we come with him to Rome. For some time Constantinople must remain a city of the future; but we are more than once reminded of the greatness of Alexandria:[1] and thus even in the life of the Apostle we find prophetic intimations of four of the five great centres of the early Catholic Church.

At present we are occupied with Antioch, and the point before us is that particular moment in the Church's history, when it was first called Christian. Both the *place* and the *event* are remarkable: and the *time*, if we are able to determine it, is worthy of our attention. Though we are following the course of an individual biography, it is necessary to pause, on critical occasions, to look around on what is passing in the empire at large. And, happily, we are now arrived at a point where we are able distinctly to see the path of the Apostle's life intersecting the general history of the period. This, therefore, is the right place for a few chronological remarks.[2] A few such remarks, made once for all, may justify what has gone before, and prepare the way for subsequent chapters.

Some readers may be surprised that up to this point we have made no attempts to ascertain or to state exact chronological details. But theologians are well aware of the difficulties with which such enquiries are attended, in the beginnings of St. Paul's biography. The early chapters in the Acts are like the narratives in the Gospels. It is often hardly possible to learn how far the events related were contemporary or consecutive. It is impossible to determine the relations of time, which subsist between Paul's retirement into Arabia and Peter's visit to the converted Samaritans,[3] or between the journey of one apostle from Joppa to Cæsarea and the journey of the other from Jerusalem to Tarsus.[4] Still less have we sufficient data for pronouncing upon the absolute chronology of the earliest transactions in the Church. No one can tell what particular folly or crime was engaging Caligula's attention, when Paul was first made a Christian at Damascus. No one can tell on what work of love the Chris-

[1] See Acts vi. 9, (with ii. 10) xxvii. 6, xxviii. 11; and compare Acts xviii. 24, xix. 1, with 1 Cor. i. 12, iii. 4–6, and Tit. iii. 13.

[2] The chronological authorities principally referred to in this work have been the following English books:—1. Bp. Pearson's *Annales Paulini*, in the Enchiridion Theologicum; 2. The late Professor Burton's *Attempt to ascertain the Chronology of the Acts, &c.*, 1830; 3. Greswell's *Dissertations, &c.*; 4. Mr. Browne's *Ordo Sæclorum:* and the following German books:—1. The first volume of Schrader's *Apostel Paulus;* 2. Anger's Treatise *De temporum in Actis Apostolorum ratione*, Leipsig. 1833; 3. Wieseler's *Chronologie des Apostolischen Zeitalters*.

[3] Acts viii. and Acts ix. (with Gal. i.)

[4] Acts ix. and Acts x.

tians were occupied when the emperor was inaugurating his bridge at Puteoli,[1] or exhibiting his fantastic pride on the shores of the British Sea.[2] In a work of this kind it is better to place the events of the Apostle's life in the broad light cast by the leading features of the period, than to attempt to illustrate them by the help of dates, which, after all, can be only conjectural. Thus we have been content to say, that he was born in the strongest and most flourishing period of the reign of Augustus; and that he was converted from the religion of the Pharisees about the time when Caligula succeeded Tiberius. But soon after we enter on the reign of Claudius we encounter a coincidence which arrests our attention. We must first take a rapid glance at the reign of his predecessor. Though the cruelty of that reign stung the Jews in every part of the empire, and produced an indignation which never subsided, one short paragraph will be enough for all that need be said concerning the abominable tyrant.[3]

CALIGULA.[5]

In the early part of the year 37 Tiberius died, and at the close of the same year Nero was born. Between the reigns of these two emperors are those of Caligula and Claudius. The four years during which Caligula sat on the throne of the world were miserable for all the provinces, both in the west and in the east.[4] In Gaul, his insults were aggravated by his personal presence. In Syria his caprices were felt more remotely but not less keenly. The changes of administration were rapid and various. In the year 36, the two great actors in the crime of the crucifixion had disappeared from the public places of Judæa. Pontius Pilate[6] had been dis-

[1] Where St. Paul afterwards landed, Acts xxviii. 13.

[2] Herod was with Caligula in this progress. This emperor's triumph had no more meaning than Napoleon's column at Boulogne; but in the next reign Britain was really conquered. See below.

[3] The reader is here requested to refer to pp. 29, 44, 45, 55, 64, 69, and the notes.

[4] It is much to be regretted that the books of Tacitus, which contained the life of Caligula, are lost. Our information must be derived from Dio Cassius, Suetonius, and Josephus.

[5] From the Musée Royal (Laurent, Paris), vol. ii.

[6] He did not arrive at Rome till after the death of Tiberius. Like his predecessor

missed by Vitellius to Rome, and Marcellus sent to govern in his stead. Caiaphas had been deposed by the same secular authority, and succeeded by Jonathan. Now, in the year 37, Vitellius was recalled from Syria, and Petronius came to occupy the governor's residence at Antioch. Marcellus at Cæsarea made way for Marullus: and Theophilus was made high-priest at Jerusalem in the place of his brother Jonathan. Agrippa, the grandson of Herod the Great, was brought out of the prison where Tiberius had confined him, and Caligula gave a royal crown,[1] with the tetrarchies of two of his uncles, to the frivolous friend of his youth. And as this reign began with restless change, so it ended in cruelty and impiety. The emperor, in the career of his blasphemous arrogance, attempted to force the Jews to worship him as God.[2] One universal feeling of horror pervaded the scattered Israelites, who, though they had scorned the Messiah promised to their fathers, were unable to degrade themselves by a return to idolatry. Petronius, who foresaw what the struggle must be, wrote letters of expostulation to his master: Agrippa, who was then in Italy, implored his patron to pause in what he did: an embassy was sent from Alexandria, and the venerable and learned Philo[3] was himself commissioned to state the inexorable requirements of the Jewish religion. Everything appeared to be hopeless, when the murder of Caligula, on the 24th of January, in the year 41, gave a sudden relief to the persecuted people.

With the accession of Claudius (A. D. 41) the Holy Land had a king once more. Judæa was added to the tetrarchies of Philip and Antipas, and Herod Agrippa I. ruled over the wide territory which had been governed by his grandfather. With the alleviation of the distress of the Jews, proportionate suffering came upon the Christians. The "rest" which, in the distractions of Caligula's reign, the churches had enjoyed "throughout all Judæa, and Galilee, and Samaria," was now at an end. "About this time Herod the king stretched forth his hands to vex certain of the church." He slew one Apostle, and "because he saw it pleased the Jews," he proceeded to imprison another. But he was not long spared to seek popularity among the Jews, or to murder and oppress the Chris-

he had governed Judæa during ten or eleven years, the emperor having a great dislike to frequent changes in the provinces.

1 Tiberius had imprisoned him, because of a conversation overheard by a slave, when Caligula and Herod Agrippa were together in a carriage. Agrippa was much at Rome both at the beginning and end of Caligula's reign. See p. 29, n. 1.

2 It appears from Dio Cassius and Suetonius that this was part of a general system for extending the worship of himself through the empire.

3 See above, pp. 36, 37, and 65. The "Legatio ad Caium" in Philo is, next after Josephus, the most important writing of the period for throwing light on the condition of the Jews in Caligula's reign. The Jewish envoys had their interview with the emperor at Puteoli, in the autumn of the same year (40 A. D.) in which he had made his progress through Gaul to the shore of the ocean.

tians. In the year 44 he perished by that sudden and dreadful death which is recorded in detail by Josephus and St. Luke.[1] In close coincidence with this event we have the mention of a certain journey of St. Paul to Jerusalem. Here then we have one of those lines of intersection between the sacred history and the general history of the world, on which the attention of intelligent Christians ought to be fixed. This year, 44 A. D., and another year, the year 60 A. D. (in which Felix ceased to be governor of Judæa, and, leaving St. Paul bound at Cæsarea, was succeeded by Festus), are the two chronological pivots of the apostolic history.[2] By help of them we find its exact place in the general history of the world. Between these two limits the greater part of what we are told of St. Paul is situated and included.

Using the year 44 as a starting-point for the future, we gain a new light for tracing the Apostle's steps. It is evident that we have only to ascertain the successive intervals of his life, in order to see him at every point, in his connection with the transactions of the empire. We shall observe this often as we proceed. At present it is more important to remark that the same date throws some light on that earlier part of the Apostle's path which is confessedly obscure. Reckoning backwards, we remember that "three years" intervened between his conversion and return to Jerusalem.[3] Those who assign the former event to 39 or 40, and those who fix on 37 or some earlier year, differ as to the length of time he spent at Tarsus, or in "Syria and Cilicia."[4] All that we can say with certainty is, that St. Paul was converted more than three years before the year 44.[5]

[1] Ant. xix. 8. Acts xii. The proof that his death took place in 44 may be seen in Anger and Wieseler; and, indeed, it is hardly doubted by any. A coincident and corroborative proof of the time of St. Paul's journey to Jerusalem, is afforded by the mention of the *Famine*, which is doubtless that recorded by Josephus (see below, p. 126, note). Anger has shown (pp. 41–45) that this famine must be assigned to the interval between 44 and 47; and Wieseler (pp. 157–161) has fixed it more closely to the year 45.

[2] It ought to be stated, that the latter date cannot be established by the same exact proof as the former; but, as a *political fact*, it must always be a cardinal point of reference in any system of Scripture chronology. Anger and Wieseler, by a careful induction of particulars, have made it highly probable that Festus succeeded Felix in the year 60. Burton places this event in the year 55, and there are many other opinions. More will be said on this subject when we come to Acts xxiv. 27.

[3] Gal. i. 18.

[4] Acts ix. 30. Gal. i. 21. Wieseler (pp. 147, 148), with Schrader (p. 59), thinks that he stayed at Tarsus only half a year or a year; Anger (pp. 171, 172), that he was there two years, between 41 and 43; Hemsen (p. 40), that he spent there the years 40, 41, and 42. Among the English writers, Bp. Pearson (p. 359) imagines that great part of the interval after 39 was passed in Syria; Burton (pp. 18, and 43), who places the conversion very early, is forced to allow nine or ten years for the time spent in Syria and Cilicia.

[5] Wieseler places the Conversion in the year 39 or 40. As we have said before the

The date thus important for all students of Bible chronology is worthy of special regard by the Christians of Britain. For in that year the Emperor Claudius returned from the shores of this island to the metropolis of his empire. He came here in command of a military expedition, to complete the work which the landing of Cæsar a century before, had begun, or at least predicted.[1] When Claudius came to Britain, its inhabitants were not Christian. They could hardly in any sense be said to have been civilised. He came, as he thought, to add a barbarous province to his already gigantic empire: but he really came to prepare the way for the silent progress of the Christian Church. His troops were the instruments of bringing among our barbarous ancestors those charities which were just then beginning to display themselves[2] in Antioch and Jerusalem. A "*new name*" was faintly rising on the Syrian shore, which was destined to spread like the cloud seen by the Prophet's servant from the brow of Mount Carmel. A better civilisation, a better citizenship, than that of the Roman empire, was preparing for us and for many. One Apostle at Tarsus was waiting for his call to proclaim the Gospel of Christ to the Gentiles. Another Apostle at Joppa was receiving a divine intimation that "God is no respecter of persons, but that in every nation he that feareth Him and worketh righteousness, is accepted with Him."[3]

If we could ascertain the exact chronological arrangement of these passages of Apostolical history, great light would be thrown on the circumstantial details of the admission of Gentiles to the Church, and on the growth of the Church's conviction on this momentous subject. We should then be able to form some idea of the meaning and results of the fortnight spent by Paul and Peter together at Jerusalem. But it is not permitted to us to know the manner and degree in which the different Apostles were illuminated. We have not been informed whether Paul ever felt the difficulty of Peter,—whether he knew from the first the full significance of his call,—whether he learnt the truth by visions, or by the gradual workings of his mind under the teaching of the Holy Spirit. All we can confidently assert is, that he did not learn from St. Peter the mystery "which in other ages was not made known unto the sons of men, as it was now revealed unto God's holy apostles by the Spirit; that the Gentiles should be fellow-heirs, and of the same body, and partakers of His promise in Christ by the Gospel."[4]

force of his reasoning consists in the convergence of his different lines of argument to one point. The following passages should be especially observed as bearing on this particular question, pp. 162–167, and 176–208.

[1] It may be gathered from Dio Cassius, lx. 21, 23, 24 (with Suet. Claud. 17), that the emperor left Rome in July, 43, and returned in January, 45. See Anger, p. 40, n. *h*.

[2] See Acts xi. 22–24, and 27–30.

[3] Acts x. 34, 35.

[4] Eph. iii. 4–6. See Col. i. 26, 27.

If St. Paul was converted in 39 or 40, and if the above-mentioned rest of the churches was in the last years of Caligula (A. D. 39–41), and if this rest was the occasion of that journey to Lydda and Joppa which ultimately brought St. Peter to Cæsarea, then it is evident that St. Paul was at Damascus or in Arabia when Cornelius was baptized.[1] Paul was summoned to evangelize the Heathen, and Peter began the work, almost simultaneously. The great transaction of admitting the Gentiles to the Church was already accomplished when the two Apostles met at Jerusalem. St. Paul would thus learn that the door had been opened to him by the hand of another; and when he went to Tarsus, the later agreement[2] might then have been partially adopted, that he should "go to the Heathen," while Peter remained as the Apostle of "the Circumcision."

If we are to bring down the conversion of Cornelius nearer to the year 44, and to place it in that interval of time which St. Paul spent at Tarsus,[3] then it is natural to suppose that his conversations prepared Peter's mind for the change which was at hand, and sowed the seeds of that revolution of opinion of which the vision at Joppa was the crisis and completion. Paul might learn from Peter (as possibly also from Barnabas) many of the details of our blessed Saviour's life. And Peter, meanwhile, might gather from him some of those higher views concerning the Gospel which prepared him for the miracles which he afterwards saw in the household of the Roman centurion. Whatever might be the obscurity of St. Paul's early knowledge, whether it was revealed to him or not that the Gentile converts would be called to overleap the ceremonies of Judaism on their entrance into the Church of Christ,—he could not fail to have a clear understanding that his own work was to lie among the Gentiles. This had been announced to him at his first conversion (Acts xxvi. 17, 18), in the words of Ananias (Acts ix. 15): and in the vision preceding his retirement to Tarsus (Acts xxii. 21), the words which commanded him to go were, "Depart, for I will send thee far hence to the Gentiles."

In considering, then, the conversion of Cornelius to have happened after this journey from Jerusalem to Tarsus, and before the mission of Barnabas to Antioch, we are adopting the opinion most in accordance with the independent standing-point occupied by St. Paul. And this, moreover, is the view which harmonises best with the narrative of Scripture, where the *order* ought to be reverently regarded as well as the *words*. In the order of Scripture narration, if it cannot be proved that the preach-

[1] This is Wieseler's view; but his arguments are not conclusive. By some (as by Schrader) it is hastily taken for granted that St Paul preached the Gospel to Gentiles at Damascus.

[2] Gal. ii. 9.

[3] On the duration of this interval, see above, p. 112, note 4.

ing of Peter at Cæsarea was chronologically earlier than the preaching of Paul at Antioch, it is at least brought before us theologically, as the beginning of the Gospel made known to the Heathen. When an important change is at hand, God usually causes a silent preparation in the minds of men, and some great fact occurs, which may be taken as a type and symbol of the general movement. Such a fact was the conversion of Cornelius, and so we must consider it.

The whole transaction is related and reiterated with so much minuteness,[1] that if we were writing a history of the Church, we should be required to dwell on it at length. But here, we have only to do with it, as the point of union between Jews and Gentiles, and as the bright starting-point of St. Paul's career. A few words may be allowed, which are suggested by this view of the transaction as a typical fact in the progress of God's dispensations. The two men to whom the revelations were made, and even the places where the divine interferences occurred, were characteristic of the event. Cornelius was in Cæsarea and St. Peter in Joppa;—the Roman soldier in the modern city, which was built and named in the Emperor's honour,—the Jewish Apostle in the ancient sea-port which associates its name with the early passages of Hebrew history,—with the voyage of Jonah, the building of the Temple, the wars of the Maccabees.[2] All the splendour of Cæsarea, its buildings and its ships, and the Temple of Rome and the Emperor, which the sailors saw far out at sea,[3] all has long since vanished. Herod's magnificent city is a wreck on the shore. A few ruins are all that remain of the harbour. Joppa lingers on, like the Jewish people, dejected but not destroyed. Cæsarea has perished, like the Roman Empire which called it into existence.

And no men could well be more contrasted with each other than those two men, in whom the Heathen and Jewish worlds met and were reconciled. We know what Peter was—a Galilean fisherman, brought up in the rudest district of an obscure province, with no learning but such as he might have gathered in the synagogue of his native town. All his early days he had dragged his nets in the lake of Gennesareth. And now he was at Joppa, lodging in the house of Simon the tanner, the apostle of a religion that was to change the world. Cornelius was an officer in the Roman army. No name was more honourable at Rome than that of the *Cornelian House.* It was the name borne by the Scipios, and by Sulla, and the mother of the Gracchi. In the Roman army, as in the army of modern Austria, the soldiers were drawn from different countries and spoke different languages. Along the coast of which we are speaking,

[1] See the whole narrative, Acts x. 1—xi. 19.

[2] Jonah i. 3. 2 Chr. ii. 16. See Josh. xix. 46. Ezra iii. 7, and various passages in the Apocrypha. 1 Esd. v. 55. 1 Mac. x. 75. xiv. 5. 2 Mac. xii. 3, &c.

[3] A full account of Cæsarea will be given hereafter.

many of them were recruited from Syria and Judæa.[1] But the corps to which Cornelius belonged seems to have been a cohort of Italians separate from the legionary soldiers,[2] and hence called the "Italian cohort." He was no doubt a true-born Italian. Educated in Rome, or some provincial town, he had entered upon a soldier's life, dreaming perhaps of military glory, but dreaming as little of that better glory which now surrounds the Cornelian name,—as Peter dreamt at the lake of Gennesareth of becoming the chosen companion of the Messiah of Israel, and of throwing open the doors of the Catholic Church to the dwellers in Asia and Africa, to the barbarians on the remote and unvisited shores of Europe, and to the undiscovered countries of the West.

But to return to our proper narrative. When intelligence came to Jerusalem that Peter had broken through the restraints of the Jewish law, and had even "eaten" at the table of the Gentiles,[3] there was general surprise and displeasure among "those of the circumcision." But when he explained to them all the transaction, they approved his conduct, and praised God for His mercy to the heathen.[4] And soon news came from a greater distance, which showed that the same unexpected change was operating more widely. We have seen that the persecution, in which Stephen was killed, resulted in a general dispersion of the Christians. Wherever they went, they spoke to their Jewish brethren of their faith that the promises had been fulfilled in the life and resurrection of Jesus Christ. This dispersion and preaching of the Gospel extended even to the island of Cyprus, and along the Phœnician coast as far as Antioch. For some time the glad tidings were made known only to the scattered children of Israel.[5] But at length some of the Hellenistic Jews, natives of Cyprus and Cyrene, spoke to the Greeks[6] themselves at Antioch, and the Divine

[1] Joseph. A. xiv. 15, 10. B. J. i. 17, 1.

[2] Not a cohort of the "*Legio Italica*," of which we read at a later period (Tacit. H. i. 59, 64. ii. 41, 100. iii. 14). This legion was raised by Nero (Dio. Cass. lv. 24. Suet. Nero, 19). See Biscoe, p. 304, note *s.*, and the whole of his elaborate discussion, pp. 300–314. Wieseler (Chronol. p. 145, note 2) thinks they were Italian volunteers. There is an inscription in Gruter, in which the following words occur: "Cohors militum Italicorum voluntaria, quæ est in Syria." See it in Akerman's Numismatic Illustrations, p. 34.

[3] *Συνέφαγες αὐτοῖς.* Acts xi. 3. See x. 48. No such freedom of intercourse took place in his own reception of his Gentile guests, x. 23. (*αὐτοὺς ἐξένισε.*)

[4] xi. 18.

[5] See xi. 19–20.

[6] xi. 20. There seems no doubt that Ἕλληνας is the right reading (see Griesbach, Lachmann, Olshausen, and De Wette; and Mr. Tate's note, p. 133), probably in the sense of Greek proselytes of the Gate. Thus they were in the same position as Cornelius. It has been doubted which case was prior in point of time. Some are of opinion that the events at Antioch took place first. Others believe that those who spoke to the Greeks at Antioch had previously heard of the conversion of Cornelius

Spirit gave such power to the Word, that a vast number "believed and turned to the Lord." The news was not long in travelling to Jerusalem. Perhaps some message was sent in haste to the Apostles of the Church. The Jewish Christians in Antioch might be perplexed how to deal with their new Gentile converts: and it is not unnatural to suppose that the presence of Barnabas might be anxiously desired by the fellow-missionaries of his native island.

We ought to observe the honourable place which the island of Cyprus was permitted to occupy in the first work of Christianity. We shall soon trace the footsteps of the Apostle of the heathen in the beginning of his travels over the length of this island; and see here the first earthly potentate converted and linking his name for ever with that of St. Paul.[1] Now, while Saul is yet at Tarsus, men of Cyprus are made the instruments of awakening the Gentiles; one of them might be that "Mnason of Cyprus," who afterwards (then "a disciple of old standing") was his host at Jerusalem;[2] and Joses the Levite of Cyprus,[3] whom the Apostles had long ago called "the Son of Consolation," and who had removed all the prejudice which looked suspiciously on Saul's conversion,[4] is the first teacher sent by the Mother-Church to the new disciples at Antioch. "He was a good man, and full of the Holy Ghost and of faith." He rejoiced when he saw what God's grace was doing; he exhorted[5] all to cling fast to the Saviour whom they had found, and he laboured himself with abundant success. But feeling the greatness of the work, and remembering the zeal and strong character of his friend, whose vocation to this particular task of instructing the heathen was doubtless well known to him, "he departed to Tarsus to seek Saul."

Whatever length of time had elapsed since Saul came from Jerusalem to Tarsus, and however that time had been employed by him,—whether he had already founded any of those churches in his native Cilicia, which we read of soon after (Acts xv. 41),—whether he had there undergone any of those manifold labours and sufferings recorded by himself (2 Cor. xi.) but omitted by St. Luke,—whether by active intercourse with the Gentiles, by study of their literature, by travelling, by discoursing with the philosophers, he had been making himself acquainted with their opinions and their prejudices, and so preparing his mind for the work that was before him,—or whether he had been waiting in silence for the call of

There seems no objection to supposing the two cases nearly simultaneous, that of Cornelius being the great typical transaction on which our attention is to be fixed.

[1] *Διελθόντες τὴν νῆσον . . . τῷ ἀνθυπάτῳ Σεργίῳ Παύλῳ . . . . Σαῦλος, ὁ καὶ Παῦλος* Acts xiii. 6–9.

[2] *Ἀρχαίῳ μαθητῇ*, Acts xxi. 16. [3] Acts iv. 36. [4] Acts ix. 27.

[5] *Παρεκάλει*, xi. 23. Compare *υἱὸς παρακλήσεως* (iv. 36), which ought rather to be translated "Son of Exhortation" or "Son of Prophecy" (בר נבואה). See xiii. 1.

God's providence, praying for guidance from above, reflecting on the condition of the Gentiles, and gazing more and more closely on the plan of the world's redemption,—however this may be, it must have been an eventful day when Barnabas, having come across the sea from Seleucia, or round by the defiles of Mount Amanus, suddenly appeared in the streets of Tarsus. The last time the two friends met was in Jerusalem. All that they then hoped, and probably more than they then thought possible, had occurred. "God had granted to the Gentiles repentance unto life" (xi. 18). Barnabas had "seen the grace of God" (xi. 23) with his own eyes at Antioch, and under his own teaching "a great multitude" (xi. 24) had been "added to the Lord." But he needed assistance. He needed the presence of one whose wisdom was higher than his own, whose zeal was an example to all, and whose peculiar mission had been miraculously declared. Saul recognized the voice of God in the words of Barnabas: and the two friends travelled in all haste to the Syrian metropolis.[1]

There they continued "a whole year," actively prosecuting the sacred work, teaching and confirming those who joined themselves to the assemblies[2] of the ever-increasing Church. As new converts, in vast numbers, came in from the ranks of the Gentiles, the Church began to lose its ancient appearance of a Jewish sect,[3] and to stand out in relief, as a great self-existent community, in the face both of Jews and Gentiles. Hitherto it had been possible, and even natural, that the Christians should be considered, by the Jews themselves, and by the Gentiles whose notice they attracted, as only one among the many theological parties which prevailed in Jerusalem, and in the Dispersion. But when Gentiles began to listen to what was preached concerning Christ,—when they were united as brethren on equal terms, and admitted to baptism without the necessity of previous circumcision,—when the Mosaic features of this society were lost in the wider character of the New Covenant,—then it became evident that these men were something more than the Pharisees or Sadducees, the Essenes[4] or Herodians, or any sect or party among the Jews. Thus a new term in the vocabulary of the human race came into existence at Antioch about the year 44. Thus Jews and Gentiles, who, under the teaching of St. Paul,[5] believed that Jesus of Nazareth was the Saviour of the world, "were first called Christians."

[1] Chrysostom says that Barnabas brought Saul from Tarsus to Antioch:—*ὅτι ἐνταῦθα καὶ ἐλπίδες χρησταὶ, καὶ μείζων ἡ πόλις, καὶ πόλυ τὸ πλῆθος.* Of Antioch he says:—*σκόπει, πῶς κάθαπερ γῆ λιπαρὰ τὸν λόγον ἐδέξατο ἡ πόλις αὕτη, καὶ πόλυν τὸν καρπὸν ἐπεδείξατο.* Hom. xxv.

[2] See Acts xi. 26.

[3] See above, pp. 31 and 67.

[4] See above, pp. 34, 35.

[5] Οὐ *μικρὸν τῆς πόλεως ἐγκώμιον*, is the remark of Chrysostom. He goes so far as to say: *Ὄντως διὰ τοῦτο ἐνταῦθα ἐχρηματίσθησαν καλεῖσθαι Χριστιανοὶ, ὅτι Παῦλος ἐνταῦθα τοσοῦτον ἐποίησε χρόνον.* See Hom. xxv., and Cramer's Catena.

It is not likely that they received this name from the Jews. The "Children of Abraham"[1] employed a term much more expressive of hatred and contempt. They called them "the sect of the Nazarenes."[2] These disciples of Jesus traced their origin to Nazareth in Galilee; and it was a proverb, that nothing good could come from Nazareth.[3] Besides this, there was a further reason why the Jews would not have called the disciples of Jesus by the name of "Christians." The word "Christ" has the same meaning with "Messiah." And the Jews, however blinded and prejudiced on this subject, would never have used so sacred a word to point an expression of mockery and derision; and they could not have used it in grave and serious earnest, to designate those whom they held to be the followers of a false Messiah, a fictitious Christ. Nor is it likely that the "Christians" gave this name to themselves. In the Acts of the Apostles, and in their own letters, we find them designating themselves as "brethren," "disciples," "believers," "saints."[4] Only in two places[5] do we find the term "Christians;" and in both instances it is implied to be a term used by those who are without. There is little doubt that the name originated with the Gentiles,[6] who began to see now that this new sect was so far distinct from the Jews, that they might naturally receive a new designation. And the form of the word implies that it came from the Romans,[7] not from the Greeks. The word "Christ" was often in the conversation of the believers, as we know it to have been constantly in their letters. "Christ" was the title of Him, whom they avowed as their leader and their chief. They confessed that this Christ had been crucified, but they asserted that He was risen from the dead, and that He guided them by His invisible power. Thus "Christian" was the name which naturally found its place in the reproachful language of their enemies.[8] In the first

[1] Mat. iii. 9. Luke iii. 8. John viii. 39. [2] Acts xxiv. 5.

[3] John i. 46. See John vii. 41, 52. Luke xiii. 2, &c.

[4] Acts xv. 23. ix. 26. v. 14. ix. 32. Rom. xv. 25. Col. i. 2, &c.

[5] Acts xxvi. 28, and 1 Pet. iv. 16.

[6] All this is well argued by Hemsen, pp. 45–47, and note.

[7] So we read in the Civil Wars of "Marians" and "Pompeians," for the partizans of Marius and Pompey; and, under the Empire, of "Othonians" and "Vitellians," for the partizans of Otho and Vitellius. The word "Herodians" (Mat. xxii. 16. Mark iii. 6. xii. 13. See p. 34) is formed exactly in the same way.

[8] It is a Latin derivative from the Greek term for the Messiah of the Jews. It is connected with the office, not the name, of our Saviour: which harmonises with the important fact, that in the Epistles He is usually called not "Jesus" but "Christ." (See a good paper in the North British Review on the Antiquity of the Gospels.) The word "Jesuit" (which, by the way, is rather Greek than Latin) did not come into the vocabulary of the Church till after the lapse of 1500 years. It is not a little remarkable that the word "Jesuit" is a proverbial term of reproach, even in Roman Catholic countries; while the word "Christian" is used so proverbially for all that is good, that it has been applied to benevolent actions, in which Jews have participated. (See Bishop Wilberforce's speech in the House of Lords on the Jews in 1848.) This reminds

instance, we have every reason to believe that it was a term of ridicule and derision.[1] And it is remarkable that the people of Antioch were notorious for inventing names of derision, and for turning their wit into the channels of ridicule.[2] And in every way there is something very significant in the place where we first received the name we bear. Not in Jerusalem, the city of the Old Covenant, the city of the people who were chosen to the exclusion of all others, but in a Heathen city, the Eastern centre of Greek fashion and Roman luxury; and not till it was shown that the New Covenant was inclusive of all others, then and there we were first called Christians, and the Church received from the World its true and honourable name.[3]

us of the old play on the words *Χριστὸς* and *Χρηστὸς*, which was not unfrequent in the early Church.

[1] See Tac. Ann. xv. 44. It is needless to remark that it soon became a title of glory. Julian tried to substitute the term "Galilean" for "Christian." Mr. Humphry quotes the following remarkable words from the Liturgy of St. Clement:—*εὐχαριστοῦμέν σοι, ὅτι τὸ ὄνομα τοῦ Χριστοῦ σου ἐπικέκληται ἐφ' ἥμας, καὶ σοι προσῳκειώμεθα.*

[2] Apollonius of Tyana was driven out of the city by their insults, and sailed away (like St. Paul) from Seleucia to Cyprus, where he visited Paphos. Philost. Vit. iii. 16. See Julian's Misopogen, and what Zosimus says of this emperor's visit to Antioch (iii. 11, p. 140 of the Bonn ed.). See also Chrysostom's first homily on Dives and Lazarus, and the account which Zosimus gives of the breaking of the statues in the reign of Theodosius (iv. 41, p. 223). One of the most remarkable is mentioned in the Persian War under Justinian, where Procopius says, *Ἀντιοχέων ὁ δῆμος (εἰσὶ γὰρ οὐ κατεσπουδασμένοι, ἀλλὰ γελοίοις τε καὶ ἀταξίᾳ ἱκανῶς ἔχονται) πολλὰ εἰς τὸν Χοσρόην ὑβριζόν τε ἀπὸ τῶν ἐπάλξεων καὶ ξὺν γέλωτι ἀκόσμῳ ἐτώθαζον* (Bell. Pers. ii. 8); the consequence of which was the destruction both of themselves and their city.

[3] Malalas says (Chronog. x.) that the name is given by Evodius, "who succeeded St. Peter as bishop of Antioch." *Ἐπὶ αὐτοῦ Χριστιανοὶ ὠνομάσθησαν, τοῦ αὐτοῦ ἐπισκοποῦ Εὐόδου προσομιλήσαντος αὐτοῖς καὶ ἐπιθήσάντος αὐτοῖς τὸ ὄνομα τοῦτο. Πρῴην γὰρ Ναζωραῖοι καὶ Γαλιλαῖοι ἐκαλοῦντο οἱ Χριστιανοί*, p. 247 of the Bonn Edition. There is another tradition that a council was held for the specific purpose of giving a name to the body of believers. The following passage from William of Tyre exhibits, in a short compass, several of the medieval ideas concerning this passage of the Sacred History. It will be observed, that St. Peter is made bishop of Antioch, that the great work of building up the Church there is assigned to him and not to St. Paul, and the relation of St. Luke and Theophilus is absolutely determined:—

"In hac Apostolorum Princeps cathedram obtinuit sacerdotalem, et pontificali primum functus est dignitate: viro venerabili Theophilo, qui erat in eadem civitate potentissimus, in proprio dogmate basilicam dedicante. Cui Lucas, ex eadem urbe trahens originem, tam Evangelium suum, quam Actus Apostolorum scripsit: qui et beato Petro, septimus in ordine Pontificum, in eadem Ecclesia successit. In hac etiam primus fidelium habitus est conventus, in qua et Christianorum nomen dedicatum est. Prius enim qui Christi sequebantur doctrinam, Nazareni dicebantur: postmodum verò a Christo deducto nomine, auctoritate illius Synodi, Christiani sunt dicti fideles universi. Unde etiam, quia gens sine difficultate prædicantem suscepit Apostolum, ad Christi fidem unanimiter conversa, et nomen, quod sicut unguentum effusum longè lateque redolet, prima invenit et docuit, nomen ejus designatum est novum, et Theopolis est appellata: ut quæ prius hominis nequam et impii [*i. e.* Antiochi] nomen pertulerat

In narrating the journeys of St. Paul, it will now be our duty to speak of Antioch, not Jerusalem, as his point of departure and return. Let us look, more closely than has hitherto been necessary, at its character, its history, and its appearance. The position which it occupied near the abrupt angle formed by the coasts of Syria and Asia Minor, and in the opening where the Orontes passes between the ranges of Lebanon and Taurus, has already been noticed.[1] And we have mentioned the numerous colony of Jews which Seleucus introduced into his capital, and raised to an equality of civil rights with the Greeks.[2] There was everything in the situation and circumstances of this city, to make it a place of concourse for all classes and kinds of people. By its harbour of Seleucia it was in communication with all the trade of the Mediterranean; and, through the open country behind the Lebanon, it was conveniently approached by the caravans from Mesopotamia and Arabia. It united the inland advantages of Aleppo with the maritime opportunities of Smyrna. It was almost an oriental Rome, in which all the forms of the civilised life of the empire found some representative. Through the first two centuries of the Christian era, it was what Constantinople became afterwards, "the Gate of the East." And, indeed, the glory of the city of Ignatius was only gradually eclipsed by that of the city of Chrysostom. That great preacher and commentator himself, who knew them both by familiar residence, always speaks of Antioch with peculiar reverence,[3] as the patriarchal city of the Christian name.

There is something curiously prophetic in the stories which are told of the first founding of this city. Like Romulus on the Palatine, Seleucus is said to have watched the flight of birds from the summit of Mount Casius. An eagle took a fragment of the flesh of his sacrifice, and carried

ejus qui eam ad fidem vocaverat, domicilium et civitas deinceps appellaretur, super hoc condignam recipiens a Domino retributionem."—Gul. Tyr. iv. 9.

When the Crusaders were besieged in turn, Peter the Hermit went to the Mahometan commander and appealed as follows (vi. 15):—

"Hanc urbem Apostolorum princeps Petrus, nostræ fidei fidelis et prudens dispensator, verbi sui virtute, et exhortationis qua preeminebat gratia, sed et signorum magnitudine ab idololotria revocans, ad fidem Christi convertit, nobis eam reddens peculiarem."

[1] P. 20. [2] P. 17.

[3] See especially Hom vii. on St. Matthew (p. 98, Field's Ed.) where he tells the people of Antioch, that though they boasted of their city's preeminence in having first enjoyed the Christian name, they were willing enough to be surpassed in Christian virtue by more homely cities. The writers of the Middle Ages use the strongest language concerning Antioch. Thus, Leo Diaconus, in the tenth century;—*Τρίτη τῶν περὶ τὴν οἰκουμένην πόλεων, τῷ τε κάλλει καὶ τῷ μεγέθει τῶν περιβόλων, ἔτι δὲ πλήθει τοῦ δήμου, καὶ τῶν οἰκιῶν ἀμηχάνοις κατασκευαῖς* (iv. 11, p. 73 of the Bonn Edition): and William of Tyre in the twelfth;—Civitas gloriosa et nobilis, tertium vel potius secundum (nam de hoc maxima quæstio est) post urbem Roman dignitatis gradum sortita; omnium provinciarum quas tractus orientalis continet, princeps et moderatrix, iv. 9.

it to a point on the sea-shore, a little to the north of the mouth of the Orontes. There he founded a city, and called it *Seleucia*[1] after his own name. This was on the 23d of April. Again, on the 1st of May, he sacrificed on the hill Silphius; and then repeated the ceremony and watched the auguries at the city of Antigonia, which his vanquished rival, Antigonus, had begun and left unfinished. An eagle again decided that this was not to be his own metropolis, and carried the flesh to the hill Silphius, which is on the south side of the river, about the place where it turns from the north to the west. Five or six thousand Athenians and Macedonians were ordered to convey the stones and timber of Antigonia down the river; and *Antioch* was founded by Seleucus, and called after his father's name.[2]

This fable, invented perhaps to give a mythological sanction to what was really an act of sagacious prudence and princely ambition, is well worth remembering. Seleucus was not slow to recognise the wisdom of Antigonus in choosing a site for his capital, which should place it in ready communication both with the shores of Greece and with his eastern territories on the Tigris and Euphrates; and he followed the example promptly, and completed his work with sumptuous magnificence. Few princes have ever lived with so great a passion for the building of cities;[3] and this is a feature of his character which ought not to be unnoticed in this narrative. Two at least of his cities in Asia Minor have a close connexion with the life of St. Paul. These are the Pisidian Antioch[4] and the Phrygian Laodicea,[5] one called by the name of his father, the other of his mother. He is said to have built in all nine Seleucias, sixteen Antiochs, and six Laodiceas.[6] This love of commemorating the members of his family was conspicuous in his works by the Orontes. Besides Seleucia and Antioch, he built in the immediate neighbourhood, a Laodicea in honour of his mother, and an Apamea[7] in honour of his wife. But by far the most famous of these four cities was the Syrian Antioch.

We must allude to its edifices and ornaments only so far as they are due to the Greek kings of Syria and the first five Cæsars of Rome.[8] If

[1] See Acts xiii. 4.

[2] The story is told by Malalas at the beginning of the eighth book. See it also in Vaillant's Seleucidarum Imperium. Some say that Seleucus called the city after his father, some after his son.

[3] Mannert, p. 363.

[4] Acts xiii. 14. xiv. 21. 2 Tim. iii. 11.

[5] Coloss. iv. 13, 15, 16. See Rev. i. 11. iii. 14.

[6] See Vaillant, as above.

[7] There was another Apamea, much mentioned by Cicero, in Asia Minor, not far from the Phrygian Laodicea and Pisidian Antioch.

[8] The authorities principally referred to for the history and topography of Antioch, have been the Chronographia of John Malalas (Ed. Bonn), and the History of William of Tyre. Other sources of information are Libanius and Julian's Misopogon. A vast amount of learning is collected together in C. O. Müller's "Antiquitates Antiochenæ:" Göttingen. 1839.

we were to allow our description to wander to the times of Justinian or the Crusaders, though these are the times of Antioch's greatest glory, we should be transgressing on a period of history which does not belong to us. Strabo, in the time of Augustus, describes the city as a Tetrapolis, or union of four cities.[1] The two first were erected by Seleucus Nicator himself, in the situation already described, between Mount Silphius and the river, on that wide space of level ground where a few poor habitations still remain, by the banks of the Orontes. The river has gradually changed its course and appearance, as the city has decayed. Once it flowed round an island, which, like the island in the Seine,[2] by its thoroughfares and bridges, and its own noble buildings, became part of a magnificent whole. But, in Paris, the Old City is on the island; in Antioch, it was the New City, built by the second Seleucus and the third Antiochus. Its chief features were a palace, and an arch like that of Napoleon. The fourth and last part of the Tetrapolis was built by Antiochus Epiphanes, where Mount Silphius rises abruptly on the south. On one of its craggy summits he placed, in the fervour of his Romanising mania,[3] a temple dedicated to Jupiter Capitolinus; and on another, a strong citadel, which dwindled to the Saracen Castle of the first Crusade. At the rugged bases of the mountain, the ground was levelled for a glorious street, which extended for four miles across the length of the city, and where sheltered crowds could walk through continuous colonnades from the eastern to the western suburb. The whole was surrounded by a wall, which, ascending to the heights and returning to the river, does not deviate very widely in its course from the wall of the Middle Ages, which can still be traced by the fragments of ruined towers. This wall is assigned by a Byzantine writer to Tiberius, but it seems more probable that the emperor only repaired what Antiochus Epiphanes had built.[4] Turning now to the period of the Empire, we find that Antioch had memorials of all the great Romans whose names have been mentioned as yet in this biography. When Pompey was defeated by Cæsar, the Conqueror's name was perpetuated in this Eastern city by an aqueduct and by baths, and by a basilica called Cæsarium. In the reign of Augustus, Agrippa[5] built in all cities of the

[1] After having said that the district of Seleucis is a Tetrapolis, as containing the four cities, Antioch, Seleucia, Apamea, and Laodicea, he says of Antioch; *ἔστι δὲ καὶ αὕτη Τετράπολις*, xvi. 2.

[2] Julian the Apostate suggests a parallel between Paris and Antioch. See the Misopogon, and compare Gibbon's 19th and 23rd chapters.

[3] See above, p. 27, n. 1.

[4] See Müller Antiq. Antioch, pp. 54, and 81.

[5] This friend of Augustus and Mæcenas must be carefully distinguished from that grandson of Herod who bore the same name, and whose death is one of the subjects of this chapter. For the works of Herod the Great at Antioch see Joseph. Ant. xvi. 5, 3 B. J. i. 21, 11.

empire, and Herod of Judæa followed the example to the utmost of his power. Both found employment for their munificence at Antioch. A gay suburb rose under the patronage of the one, and the other contributed a road and a portico. The reign of Tiberius was less remarkable for great architectural works; but the Syrians by the Orontes had to thank him for many improvements and restorations in their city. Even the four years of his successor left behind them the aqueduct and the baths of Caligula.

The character of the inhabitants is easily inferred from the influences which presided over the city's growth. Its successive enlargement by the Seleucidæ proves that their numbers rapidly increased from the first. The population swelled still further, when, instead of the metropolis of the Greek kings of Syria, it became the residence of Roman governors. The mixed multitude received new and important additions in the officials who were connected with the details of provincial administration. Luxurious Romans were attracted by its beautiful climate. New wants continually multiplied the business of its commerce. Its gardens and houses grew and extended on the north side of the river. Many are the allusions to Antioch, in the history of those times, as a place of singular pleasure and enjoyment. Here and there, an elevating thought is associated with its name. Poets have spent their young days at Antioch,[1] great generals have died there,[2] emperors have visited and admired it.[3] But, for the most part, its population was a worthless rabble of Greeks and Orientals. The frivolous amusements of the theatre were the occupation of their life. Their passion for races, and the ridiculous party-quarrels[4] connected with them, were the patterns of those which afterwards became the disgrace of Byzantium. The oriental element of superstition and imposture was not less active. The Chaldean astrologers found their most credulous disciples in Antioch.[5] Jewish impostors,[6] sufficiently common throughout the East,

[1] See Cic. pro Archia Poeta.

[2] All readers of Tacitus will recognize the allusion. (See Ann. ii.) It is not possible to write about Antioch without some allusion to Germanicus and his noble-minded wife. And yet they were the parents of Caligula.

[3] For all that long series of emperors whose names are connected with Antioch, see Müller.

[4] See especially what Malalas says of the *Blue Faction* and the *Green Faction* under the reigns of Caligula and Claudius. Both Emperors patronized the latter. Mal. pp. 244, and 246.

[5] Chrysostom complains that even Christians in his day, were led away by this passion for horoscopes. See Hom iv. on 1 Cor. Compare the "Ambubaiarum Collegia" of Horace. Juvenal traces the superstitions of heathen Rome to Antioch, "In Tiberim defluxit Orontes."

[6] Compare the cases of Simon Magus (Acts viii.), Elymas the Sorcerer (Acts xiii.), and the sons of Sceva (Acts xix.). We shall have occasion to return to this subject again.

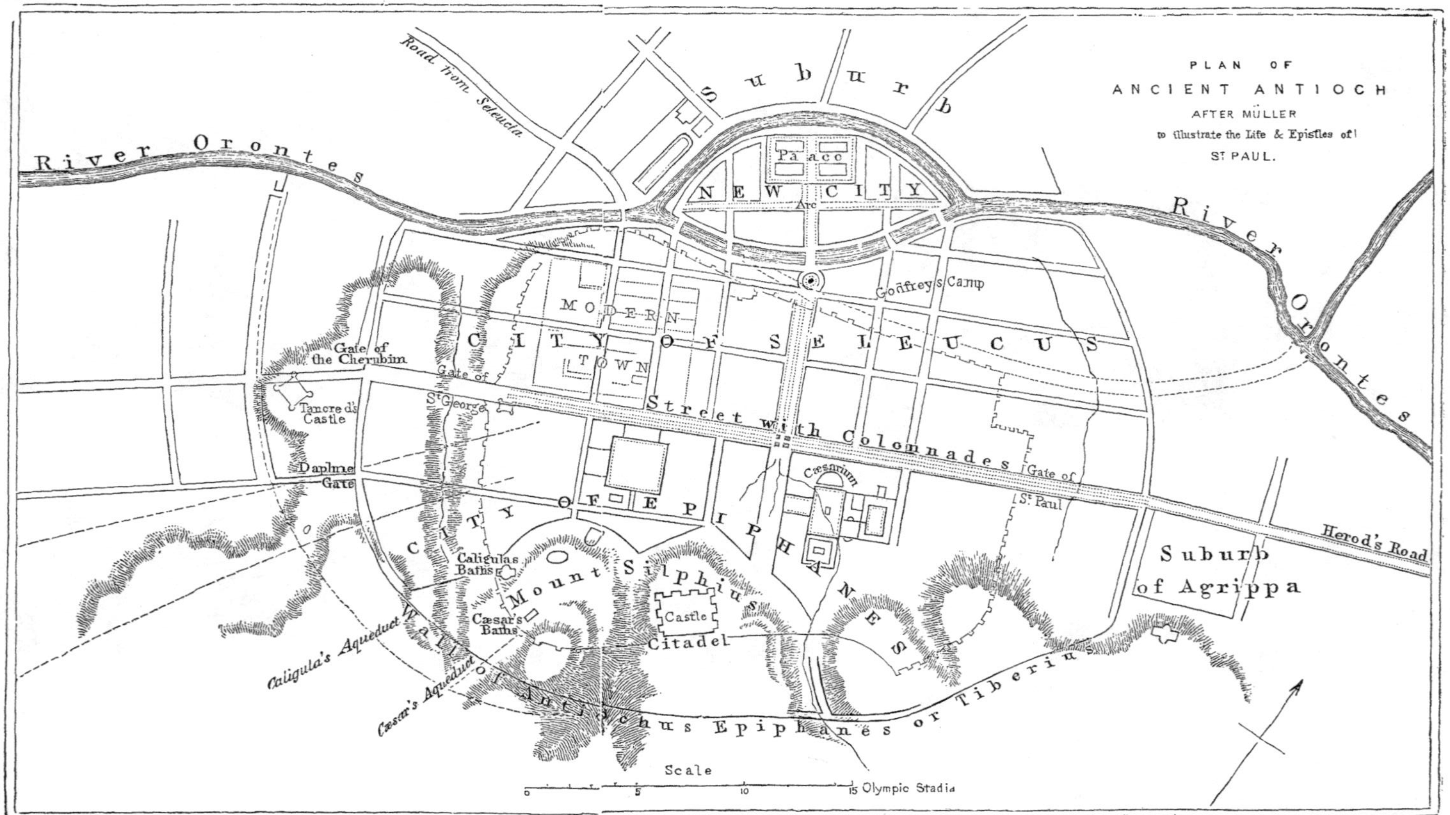

PLAN OF
ANCIENT ANTIOCH
AFTER MÜLLER
to illustrate the Life & Epistles of
St PAUL.
River Orontes
River Orontes
Road from Seleucia
Suburb
Palace
NEW CITY
Arc
Godfrey's Camp
MODERN
TOWN
CITY OF SELEUCUS
Gate of the Cherubim
Tancred's Castle
Gate of St George
Street with Colonnades
Daphne Gate
CITY OF EPIPHANES
Cæsarium
Gate of St Paul
Herod's Road
Suburb of Agrippa
Caligulas Baths
Cæsar's Baths
Mount Silphius
Castle
Citadel
Caligula's Aqueduct
Cæsar's Aqueduct
Wall of Antiochus Epiphanes or Tiberius
Scale
0 5 10 15 Olympic Stadia

found their best opportunities here. It is probable that no populations have ever been more abandoned than those of oriental Greek cities under the Roman Empire, and of these cities Antioch was the greatest and the worst.[1] If we wish to realise the appearance and reality of the complicated heathenism of the first Christian century, we must endeavour to imagine the scene of that suburb, the famous Daphne,[2] with its fountains and groves of bay trees, its bright buildings, its crowds of licentious votaries, its statue of Apollo,—where, under the climate of Syria and the wealthy patronage of Rome, all that was beautiful in nature and in art had created a sanctuary for a perpetual festival of vice.

Thus, if any city, in the first century, was worthy to be called the Heathen Queen and Metropolis of the East, that city was Antioch. She was represented, in a famous allegorical statue, as a female figure, seated on a rock and crowned, with the river Orontes at her feet.[3] With this image, which art has made perpetual, we conclude our description. There is no excuse for continuing it to the age of Vespasian and Titus, when Judæa was taken, and the Western Gate, decorated with the spoils, was called the [4]"Gate of the

ALLEGORICAL STATUE OF ANTIOCH.

[1] Ausonius (Ordo Nob. Urb. iii.) hesitates between the rank of Antioch and Alexandria, in eminence and vice.

"Tertia Phæbeæ lauri domus Antiochia,
Vellet Alexandri si quarta colonia poni.
Ambarum locus unus: et has furor ambitionis
In certamen agit vitiorum. Turbida vulgo
Utraque, et amentis populi malesana tumultu."

[2] Gibbon's description of Daphne (ch. xxiii.) is well known. For more exact details see Müller, pp. 42–49. The sanctuary was on the high ground, four or five miles to the S. W. of Antioch. The road led through the suburb of Heraclea.

[3] For this celebrated statue of the Τύχη 'Αντιοχείας, or Genius of Antioch, so constantly represented on coins, see Müller, Antiq. Antioch, pp. 35–41, and his Archäologie, p. 165. The engraving here given is from Pistolesi's Vaticano.

[4] See Malalas (book x. p. 261), who adds that Titus built a theatre at Antioch where

Cherubim,"—or to the Saracen age, when, after many years of Christian history and Christian mythology, we find the "Gate of St. Paul" placed opposite the "Gate of St. George," and when Duke Godfrey pitched his camp between the river and the city-wall.[1] And there is reason to believe that earthquakes,[2] the constant enemy of the people of Antioch, have so altered the very appearance of its site, that such a description would be of little use. As the Vesuvius of Virgil or Pliny[3] would hardly be recognised in the angry neighbour of modern Naples, so it is more than probable that the dislocated crags, which still rise above the Orontes, are greatly altered in form from the fort-crowned heights of Seleucus or Tiberius, Justinian or Tancred.[4]

Earthquakes occurred in each of the reigns of Caligula and Claudius.[5] And it is likely that, when Saul and Barnabas were engaged in their apostolic work, parts of the city had something of that appearance, which still makes Lisbon dreary, new and handsome buildings being raised in close proximity to the ruins left by the late calamity. It is remarkable how often great physical calamities are permitted by God to follow in close succession to each other. That age, which, as we have seen, had been visited by earthquakes,[6] was presently visited by famine. The reign of Claudius, from bad harvests or other causes, was a period of general distress and scarcity "over the whole world."[7] In the fourth year of his reign, we are told by Josephus that the famine was so severe, that the price of food became enormous, and great numbers perished.[8] At this time it happened that Helena, the mother of Izates, king of Adiabene, and a recent convert to Judaism, came to worship at Jerusalem. Moved

a synagogue had been. On the theatre was the inscription "Ex præda Judæa" 'Eξ πραίδα 'Ιουδαία.)

1 The description of the ground in William of Tyre (iv. 10, 13, 14, &c.) is deserving of careful attention. He frequently mentions the gate of St. Paul.

2 Müller Antiq. Antioch, pp. 13–17.

3 Georg. ii. 224. Plin. Epp. vi. 16 & 20.

4 See William of Tyre, besides the passages above referred to, in his description of the taking of the city, v. 23. vi. 1. Many of those who were ignorant of the nature of the ground fled to the heights, and "confractis cervicibus et membris contritis, vix de seipsis reliquerunt aliquam memoriam."

5 "Early in the morning on March 23, in the year 37,"—*ἔπαθεν ὑπὸ θεομηνίας 'Αντιόχεια ἡ μεγάλη . . . ἔπαθε δὲ καὶ μέρος Δάφνης*. Malalas, x. p. 243. And again under Claudius,—*'Εσείσθη δὲ τότε καὶ ἡ μεγάλη 'Αντιοχεία πόλις, καὶ διεῤῥάγη ὁ ναὸς τῆς 'Αρτέμιδος καὶ τοῦ Ἄρεως καὶ τοῦ Ηρακλέος καὶ οἶκοι φανεροὶ ἔπεσαν*, p. 246.

6 Malalas, in the passage last referred to, mentions an earthquake in Asia Minor, and a grant of money by the Emperor Claudius for the restoration of the injured cities. For aid rendered to certain cities of Asia Minor after a similar catastrophe (Tac. A. ii. 47, Plin. N. H. ii. 86), Tiberius was honoured with a commemorative statue, the pedestal of which has been discovered at Puteoli. See Müller, Arch. p. 231.

7 Besides the famine in Judæa, we read of three others in the reign of Claudius; one in Greece, mentioned by Eusebius, and two in Rome, the first mentioned by Dio Cassius (lx. 11), the second by Tacitus (A. xii. 43).

8 Antiq. iii. 15, 3. xx. 2, 5, and 5, 2.

with compassion for the misery she saw around her, she sent to purchase corn from Alexandria and figs from Cyprus, for distribution among the poor. Izates himself (who had also been converted by one who bore the same name[1] with him who baptized St. Paul) shared the charitable feelings of his mother, and sent large sums of money to Jerusalem.

While this relief came from Assyria, from Cyprus, and from Africa, to the Jewish sufferers in Judæa, God did not suffer His own Christian people, probably the poorest and certainly the most disregarded in that country, to perish in the general distress. And their relief also came from nearly the same quarters. While Barnabas and Saul were evangelizing the Syrian capital, and gathering in the harvest, the first seeds of which had been sown by "men of Cyprus and Cyrene," certain prophets came down from Jerusalem to Antioch, and one of them named Agabus announced that a time of famine was at hand.[2] The Gentile disciples felt that they were bound by the closest link to those Jewish brethren whom though they had never seen they loved. "For if the Gentiles had been made partakers of their spiritual things, their duty was also to minister unto them in carnal things."[3] No time was lost in preparing for the coming calamity. All the members of the Christian community, according to their means, "determined to send relief," Saul and Barnabas being chosen to take the contribution to the elders at Jerusalem.[4]

About the time when these messengers came to the Holy City on their errand of love, a worse calamity than that of famine had fallen upon the Church. One Apostle had been murdered, and another was in prison There is something touching in the contrast between the two brothers, James and John. One died before the middle of the first Christian century; the other lived on to its close. One was removed just when his Master's kingdom, concerning which he had so eagerly enquired,[5] was beginning to show its real character; he probably never heard the word "Christian" pronounced. Zebedee's other son remained till the antichristian[6] enemies of the faith were "already come," and was labouring against them when his brother had been fifty years at rest in the Lord. He who had foretold the long service of St. John, revealed to St. Peter that he should die by a violent death.[7] But the time was not yet come. Herod had bound him with two chains. Besides the soldiers who watched his sleep, guards were placed before the door of the prison. And "after the

[1] This Ananias was a Jewish merchant, who made proselytes among the women about the court of Adiabene, and thus obtained influence with the king. (Jos. Ant. xx. 2, 3.) See what has been said above (pp. 19 and 100. n. 3) about the female proselytes at Damascus and Iconium.

[2] Acts xi. 28.
[3] Rom. xv. 27.
[4] Acts xi. 29, 30.
[5] See Mark x. 35–45. Acts i. 6.
[6] 1 John ii. 18. iv. 3. 2 John 7
[7] John xxi. 18–22. See 2 Pet. i. 14.

passover"[1] the king intended to bring him out and gratify the people with his death. But Herod's death was nearer than St. Peter's. For a moment we see the Apostle in captivity[2] and the king in the plenitude of his power. But before the autumn a dreadful change had taken place. On the 1st of August (we follow a probable calculation,[3] and borrow some circumstances from the Jewish historian[4]) there was a great commemoration in Cæsarea. Some say it was in honour of the emperor's safe return from the island of Britain.[5] However this might be, the city was crowded, and Herod was there. On the second day of the festival he came into the theatre. That theatre had been erected by his grandfather,[6] who had murdered the Innocents; and now the grandson was there, who had murdered an Apostle. The stone seats, rising in a great semicircle, tier above tier, were covered with an excited multitude. The king came in, clothed in magnificent robes, of which silver was the costly and brilliant material. It was early in the day, and the sun's rays fell upon the king, so that the eyes of the beholders were dazzled with the brightness which surrounded him. Voices from the crowd, here and there, exclaimed that it was the apparition of something divine. And when he spoke and made an oration to the people, they gave a shout, saying, "It is the voice of a God and not of a man." But in the midst of this idolatrous ostentation the angel of God suddenly smote him. He was carried out of the theatre a dying man, and on the 6th of August he was dead.

[1] *μετὰ τὸ πάσχα*, Acts xii. 4. The traditional places of St. James' martyrdom and of the house of St. Mark (mentioned below) are both in the Armenian quarter. One is the Armenian, the other the Syrian, convent. See Mr. Williams' "Memoir of Jerusalem," printed as a Supplement to the "Holy City," the second edition of which (1849) had not appeared when our earlier chapters were written.

[2] For the tradition concerning these chains, see Platner's Account of the Church of San Pietro in Vincoli in the Beschreibung Roms. By a curious coincidence, the festival is on August 1st; the first day of that festival of Cæsarea, at which Agrippa died. The Chapel of the Tower of London is dedicated to St. Peter ad Vincula. See Cunningham's Handbook for London, and Macaulay's History, i. 628.

[3] That of Wieseler, pp. 132–136.

[4] Compare Acts xii. 20–24, with Josephus, Ant. xix. 8, 2.

[5] This is Anger's view. Others think it was in honour of the birthday of Claudius (Aug. 1). Wieseler has shown that it was more probably the festival of the Quinquennalia, observed on the same day of the same month in honour of Augustus. The observance dated from the taking of Alexandria, when the month Sextilis received the emperor's name.

[6] See Joseph. Ant. xv. 9, 6. It is from his narrative (xix. 8, 2) that we know the theatre to have been the scene of Agrippa's death-stroke. The "throne" (Acts xii. 21) is the tribunal (*βῆμα*) prætoris or sedes prætorum (Suet. Aug. 44. Ner. 12. See Dio Cass. lix. 14). Josephus says nothing of the quarrel with the Tyrians and Sidonians. Probably it arose simply from mercantile relations (see 1 Kings v. 11. Ezek. xxvii. 17), and their desire for reconciliation (Acts xii. 20) would naturally be increased by the existing famine. Baronius strangely traces the misunderstanding to St. Peter's having formed Christian churches in Phœnicia. See the next note.

This was that year, 44,[1] on which we have already said so much. The country was placed again under Roman governors, and hard times were at hand for the Jews. Herod Agrippa had courted their favour. He had done much for them, and was preparing to do more. Josephus tells us, that "he had begun to encompass Jerusalem with a wall, which, had it been brought to perfection, would have made it impracticable for the Romans to take it by siege: but his death, which happened at Cæsarea, before he had raised the walls to their due height, prevented him."[2] That part of the city, which this boundary was intended to inclose, was a suburb when St. Paul was converted. The work was not completed till the Jews were preparing for their final struggle with the Romans:[3] and the Apostle, when he came from Antioch to Jerusalem, must have noticed the unfinished wall to the north and west of the old Damascus gate. We cannot determine the season of the year when he passed this way. We are not sure whether the year itself was 44 or 45. It is not probable that he was in Jerusalem at the passover, when St. Peter was in prison, or that he was praying with those anxious disciples at the "house of Mary the mother of John, whose surname was Mark."[4] But there is this link of interesting connection between that house and St. Paul, that it was the familiar home of one who was afterwards (not always[5] without cause for anxiety or reproof) a companion of his journeys. When Barnabas and Saul returned to Antioch, they were attended by "John, whose surname was Mark." With the affection of Abraham towards Lot, his uncle[6] Barnabas withdrew from the scene of persecution. We need not doubt that higher motives were added,—that at the first, as at the last,[7] St. Paul regarded him as "profitable to him for the ministry."

Thus attended, he willingly retraced his steps towards Antioch. A field of noble enterprise was before him. He could not doubt that God, who had so prepared him, would work by his means great conversions among the Heathen. At this point of his life, we cannot avoid noticing

[1] See Baronius, under this year, for various passages of the traditionary life of St. Peter; his journey from Antioch through Asia Minor to Rome; his meeting with Simon Magus, &c.; and the other Apostles; their general separation to preach the Gospel to the Gentiles in all parts of the world: the formation of the Apostles' Creed, &c. St. Peter is alleged to have held the See of Antioch for seven years before that of Rome. (See under year 39.) The meeting ("in qua neuter errasse monstratur") of St. Paul and St. Peter at Antioch (Gal. ii. 11) is connected with Acts xv. 35 (year 51) The same want of criticism is apparent in modern Roman Catholic historians, *e. g* Röhrbacher, Histoire Universelle de l'Eglise Catholique, liv. xxiv. vol. 4.

[2] B. J. ii. 11, 6.

[3] See Robinson, vol. i. pp. 411 and 465; Williams' Memoir, p. 84; and Schulz' Jerusalem.

[4] Acts xii. 12.

[5] See Acts xiii. 13. xv. 37–39.

[6] It should be observed that ἀνεψιὸς (Col. iv. 10) does not necessarily mean "nephew.

[7] See 2 Tim. iv. 11.

those circumstances of inward and outward preparation, which fitted him for his peculiar position of standing between the Jews and Gentiles. He was not a Sadducee, he had never Hellenised,—he had been educated at Jerusalem,—everything conspired to give him authority, when he addressed his countrymen as a "Hebrew of the Hebrews." At the same time, in his apostolical relation to Christ, he was quite disconnected with the other Apostles; he had come in silence to a conviction of the truth at a distance from the Judaising Christians, and had early overcome those prejudices which impeded so many in their approaches to the Heathen. He had just been long enough at Jerusalem to be recognised and welcomed by the apostolic college,[1] but not long enough even to be known by face "unto the churches in Judæa."[2] He had been withdrawn into Cilicia till the baptism of the Gentiles was a notorious and familiar fact to those very churches.[3] He could hardly be blamed for continuing what St. Peter had already begun.

And if the Spirit of God had prepared him for building up the United Church of Jews and Gentiles, and the Providence of God had directed all the steps of his life to this one result, we are called on to notice the singular fitness of this last employment, on which we have seen him engaged, for assuaging the suspicious feeling which separated the two great branches of the Church. In quitting for a time his Gentile converts at Antioch, and carrying a contribution of money to the Jewish Christians at Jerusalem, he was by no means leaving the higher work for the lower. He was building for after-times. The interchange of mutual benevolence was a safe foundation for future confidence. Temporal comfort was given in gratitude for spiritual good received. The Church's first days were christened with charity. No sooner was its new name received, in token of the union of Jews and Gentiles, than the sympathy of its members was asserted by the work of practical benevolence. We need not hesitate to apply to that work the words which St. Paul used, after many years, of another collection for the poor Christians in Judæa:—"The administration of this service not only supplieth the want of the Saints, but is abundant also by many thanksgivings unto God; whiles by the experiment of this ministration they glorify God for your professed subjection unto the Gospel of Christ, and for your liberal distribution unto them."[4]

[1] Acts ix. 27. [2] Gal. i. 22.

[3] These were the churches of Lydda, Saron, Joppa, &c., which Peter had been visiting when he was summoned to Cæsarea. Acts ix. 32–43.

[4] 2 Cor. ix. 12–14.

CHAPTER V.

"Saulus qui fuerat fit adempto lumine Paulus:
Mox recipit visum, fit Apostolus, ac populorum
Doctor."—PRUDENTIUS, *Vas Electionis.*

SECOND PART OF THE ACTS OF THE APOSTLES.—REVELATION AT ANTIOCH.—PUBLIC DEVOTIONS.—DEPARTURE OF BARNABAS AND SAUL.—THE ORONTES.—HISTORY AND DESCRIPTION OF SELEUCIA.—VOYAGE TO CYPRUS.—SALAMIS.—ROMAN PROVINCIAL SYSTEM.—PROCONSULS AND PROPRÆTORS.—SERGIUS PAULUS.—ORIENTAL IMPOSTORS AT ROME AND IN THE PROVINCES.—ELYMAS BARJESUS.—HISTORY OF JEWISH NAMES.—SAUL AND PAUL.

THE second part of the Acts of the Apostles is generally reckoned to begin with the thirteenth chapter. At this point St. Paul begins to appear as the principal character; and the narrative, gradually widening and expanding with his travels, seems intended to describe to us, in minute detail, the communication of the Gospel to the Gentiles. The thirteenth and fourteenth chapters embrace a definite and separate subject; and this subject is the first journey of the first Christian missionaries to the Heathen. These two chapters of the inspired record are the authorities for the present and the succeeding chapters of this work, in which we intend to follow the steps of Paul and Barnabas, in their circuit through Cyprus and the southern part of Lesser Asia.

The history begins suddenly and abruptly. We are told that there were in the Church at Antioch,[1] "prophets and teachers," and among the rest "Barnabas," with whom we are already familiar. The others were "Simeon, who was surnamed Niger," and "Lucius of Cyrene," and "Manaen, the foster-brother of Herod the Tetrarch,"—and "Saul," who still appears under his Hebrew name. We observe, moreover, not only that he is mentioned after Barnabas, but that he occupies the lowest place in this enumeration of "prophets and teachers." The distinction between these two offices in the Apostolic Church will be discussed hereafter. At present it is sufficient to remark that the "prophecy" of the New Testament does not necessarily imply a knowledge of things to come, but rather a gift of exhorting with a peculiar force of inspiration. In the Church's early miraculous days the "prophet" appears to have been ranked higher

[1] Ἐν Ἀντιοχείᾳ κατὰ τὴν οὖσαν ἐκκλησίαν. Acts xiii. 1.

than the "teacher."[1] And we may perhaps infer that, up to this point of the history, Barnabas had belonged to the rank of "prophets," and Saul to that of "teachers;" which would be in strict conformity with the inferiority of the latter to the former, which, as we have seen, has been hitherto observed.

Of the other three who are grouped with these two chosen missionaries we do not know enough to justify any long disquisition. But we may remark in passing that there is a certain interest attaching to each one of them. Simeon is one of those Jews who bore a Latin surname in addition to their Hebrew name, like "John whose surname was Mark," mentioned in the last verse of the preceding chapter, and like Saul himself, whose change of appellation will presently be brought under notice.[2] Lucius, probably the same who is mentioned in the Epistle to the Romans,[3] is a native of Cyrene, that African city which has already been mentioned as abounding in Jews, and which sent to Jerusalem our Saviour's cross-bearer.[4] Manaen is spoken of as the foster-brother of Herod the Tetrarch: this was Herod Antipas, the Tetrarch of Galilee; and since we learn from Josephus[5] that this Herod and his brother Archelaus were children of the same mother, and afterwards educated together at Rome, it is probable that this Christian prophet or teacher had spent his early childhood with those two princes, who were now both banished from Palestine to the banks of the Rhone.[6]

These were the most conspicuous persons in the Church of Antioch, when a revelation was received of the utmost importance. The occasion on which the revelation was made seems to have been a fit preparation for it. The Christians were engaged in religious services of peculiar solemnity. The Holy Ghost spoke to them "as they ministered unto the Lord

[1] Compare Acts xiii. 1 with 1 Cor. xii. 28, 29. Eph. iv. 11.

[2] See Acts xiii. 9. Compare Col. iv. 11.

[3] Rom. xvi. 21. There is no reason whatever for supposing that St. Luke (Lucanus) is meant, though Wetstein ingeniously quotes Herodotus in commendation of the *physicians of Cyrene:* Πρῶτοι *μὲν* Κροτωνιῆται *ἰητροὶ ἐλέγοντο ἀνὰ τὴν* Ἑλλαδα *εἶναι, δεύτεροι δὲ* Κυρηναῖοι, iii. 131.

[4] See above, p. 17, n. 6.

[5] Their mother's name was Malthace, a Samaritan. B. J. i. 28, 4. See Ant. xvii. 1, 3. Ὁ *δὲ* Ἀρχέλαος *καὶ* Ἀντίπας *παρὰ τινὶ ἰδιώτῃ τροφὰς εἶχον ἐπὶ* Ῥώμης. Compare *ἀνατεθραμμένος*, Acts xxii. 3. The word *σύντροφος*, xiii. 1, refers to an earlier period. One of the sect of the Essenes (see pp. 34, 35), who bore the name of Manaen or Manaem, is mentioned by Josephus (Ant. xv. 10, 5), as having foretold to Herod the Great, in the days of his obscurity, both his future power and future wickedness. The historian adds, that Herod afterwards treated the Essenes with great kindness. Nothing is more likely than that this Manaen was the father of the companion of Herod's children. Another Jew of the same name is mentioned, at a later period (B. J. ii. 17, 8, 9. Life 5), as having encouraged robberies, and come to a violent end. The name is the same with that of the king of Israel. 2 Kings xv. 14–22. See the LXX.

[6] See above, pp. 29 and 54.

and fasted." The word[1] here translated "ministered," has been taken by opposite controversialists to denote the celebration of the "sacrifice of the mass" on the one hand, or the exercise of the office of "preaching" on the other. It will be safer if we say simply that the Christian community at Antioch were engaged in one united act of prayer and humiliation. That this solemnity would be accompanied by words of exhortation, and that it would be crowned and completed by the holy communion, is more than probable; that it was accompanied with fasting[2] we are expressly told. These religious services might have had a special reference to the means which were to be adopted for the spread of the Gospel now evidently intended for all; and the words, "separate me *now*[3] Barnabas and Saul for the work whereunto I have called them," may have been an answer to specific prayers. How this revelation was made, whether by the mouth of some of the prophets who were present, or by the impulse of a simultaneous and general inspiration,—whether the route to be taken by Barnabas and Saul was at this time precisely indicated,[4]—and whether they had previously received a conscious personal call, of which this was the public ratification,[5]—it is useless to inquire. A definite work was pointed out, as now about to be begun under the counsel of God; two definite agents in this work were publicly singled out: and we soon see them sent forth to their arduous undertaking, with the sanction of the Church at Antioch.

Their final consecration and departure was the occasion of another religious solemnity. A fast was appointed, and prayers were offered up; and, with that simple ceremony of ordination[6] which we trace through the earlier periods of Jewish history, and which we here see adopted, under the highest authority, in the Christian Church, "they laid their hands on them, and sent them away." The words are wonderfully simple; but

1 Λειτουργούντων, v. 2. Chrysostom considers it equivalent to κηρυττόντων, Hom. XXVII. So Erasmus: "Proprium est *operantium sacris.* Nullum autem sacrificium Deo gratius quàm impertiri doctrinam Evangelicam." Fleury says, "Comme ils célébroient le service divin:" Tillemont, "Ils estoient occupez aux diverses fonctions de leur ministère, comme à offrir le sacrifice, et à prescher:" Baronius, more positively, "Quòd habet Latina versio *ministrantibus illis*, Græcè legitur *λειτουργούντων*, id est, *sacrificantibus.* Certè quidem non sine sacrificii incruenti ministerio ejusmodi sacras ordinationes celebrari, antiqui omnium Ecclesiarum Rituales libri significant."

2 For the association of Fasting with Ordination, see Bingham. IV. vi. 6. XXI. ii. 8.

3 This word δή is quite unnoticed by many of the commentators, and is untranslated in the Vulgate and the English. See its use in the following passages: Luke ii. 15. Acts xv. 36. 1 Cor. vi. 20.

4 It is evident that the course of St. Paul's journeys was often indeterminate, and regulated either by convenient opportunities (as in Acts xxi. 2. xxviii. 11), or by compulsion (as in xiv. 6. xvii. 14) or by supernatural admonitions (xxii. 21. xvi. 6-10).

5 St. Paul at least had long been conscious of his own vocation, and could only be waiting to be summoned to his work.

6 It forms no part of the plan of this work to enter into ecclesiastical controversies. It is sufficient to refer to Acts vi. 6. 1 Tim. iv. 14. v. 22. 2 Tim. i. 6 Heb. vi. 2.

those who devoutly reflect on this great occasion, and on the position of the first Christians at Antioch, will not find it difficult to imagine the thoughts which occupied the hearts of the disciples during the first "Ember Days" of the Church,[1]—their deep sense of the importance of the work which was now beginning,—their faith in God, on whom they could rely in the midst of such difficulties,—their suspense during the absence of those by whom their own faith had been fortified,—their anxiety for the intelligence they might bring on their return.

Their first point of destination was the island of Cyprus. It is not necessary, though quite allowable, to suppose that this particular course was divinely indicated in the original revelation at Antioch. Four reasons at least can be stated, which may have induced the Apostles, in the exercise of a wise discretion, to turn in the first instance to this island. It is separated by no great distance from the mainland of Syria; its high mountain-summits are easily seen[2] in clear weather from the coast near the mouth of the Orontes; and in the summer-season many vessels must often have been passing and repassing between Salamis and Seleucia. Besides this, it was the native place of Barnabas.[3] Since the time when "Andrew found his brother Simon, and brought him to Jesus,"[4] and the Saviour was beloved in the house of "Martha and her sister and Lazarus,"[5] the ties of family relationship had not been without effect on the progress of the Gospel.[6] It could not be unnatural to suppose that the truth would be welcomed in Cyprus, when it was brought by Barnabas and his kinsman Mark[7] to their own connections or friends. Moreover, the Jews were numerous in Salamis.[8] By sailing to that city they were following the track of the synagogues. Their mission, it is true, was chiefly to the Gentiles: but their surest course for reaching them was through the medium of the proselytes and the Hellenising Jews. To these considerations we must add, in the fourth place, that some of the Cypriotes were already Christians. No one place out of Palestine, with the exception of Antioch, had been so honourably associated with the work of successful evangelisation.[9]

The palaces of Antioch were connected with the sea by the river Orontes. Strabo[10] says that in his time they sailed up the stream in one day;

1 See Bingham, as above.

2 Colonel Chesney speaks of "the lofty island of Cyprus as seen to the S. W. in the distant horizon," from the bay of Antioch.—Paper on the Bay of Antioch and the ruins of Seleucia Pieria in the Journal of the Royal Geographical Society, vol. viii. p. 228.

3 Acts iv. 36. 4 John i. 41, 42. 5 John xi. 5.

6 See an instance of this in the life of St. Paul himself. Acts xxiii. 16-33. Compare 1 Cor. vii. 16.

7 Εἶχον δὲ καὶ Ἰωάννην ὑπηρέτην. Acts xiii. 5. See xii. 25, and p. 129, n. 6, above.

8 xiii. 5. See below, p. 140.

9 See Acts iv. 36. xi. 19, 20. xxi. 16.

10 'Ανάπλους ἐκ θαλάττης ἐστὶν εἰς τὴν 'Αντιόχειαν αὐθημερόν, xvi. 2.

and Pausanias[1] speaks of great Roman works which had improved the navigation of the channel. Probably it was navigable by vessels of some considerable size, and goods and passengers were conveyed by water between the city and the sea. Even in our own day, though there is now a bar at the mouth of the river, there has been a serious project of uniting it by a canal with the Euphrates, and so of re-establishing one of the old lines of commercial intercourse between the Mediterranean and the Indian Sea. The Orontes comes from the valley between Lebanon and Anti-Lebanon, and does not, like many rivers, vary capriciously between a winter-torrent and a thirsty watercourse, but flows on continually to the sea. Its waters are not clear, but they are deep and rapid.[2] Their course has been compared to that of the Wye. They wind round the bases of high and precipitous cliffs, or by richly cultivated banks, where the vegetation of the south, the vine and the fig-tree, the myrtle, the bay, the ilex, and the arbutus, are mingled with dwarf oak and English sycamore.[3] If Barnabas and Saul came down by water from Antioch, this was the course of the boat which conveyed them. If they travelled the five or six leagues[4] by land, they crossed the river at the north side of Antioch, and came along the base of the Pierian hills by a route which is now roughly covered with fragrant and picturesque shrubs, but which then doubtless was a track

[1] His words are very vague, and no date is given. *'Ορόντην τὸν Σύρων ποταμὸν οὐ τὰ πάντα ἐν ἰσοπέδῳ μέχρι θαλάσσης ῥέοντα, ἀλλ' ἐπὶ κρημνόν τε ἀποῤῥῶγα καὶ ἐς κάταντες ἀπ' αὐτοῦ φερόμενον, ἠθέλησεν ὁ 'Ρωμαίων βασιλεὺς* [?] *ἀναπλεῖσθαι ναυσὶν ἐκ θαλάσσης ἐς 'Αντιόχειαν πόλιν· ἔλυτρον οὖν σὺν πόνῳ τε καὶ δαπάνῃ χρημάτων ὀρυξάμενος ἐπιτήδειον ἐς τὸν ἀνάπλουν, ἐξέτρεψεν ἐς τοῦτο τὸν ποταμόν.* Paus Arcad. viii. 29.

[2] Colonel Chesney found the river rapid, and impeded by fish-weirs. He adds, "Ibrahim Pacha talked of making the river navigable, which might be done by blasting some rocks in its bed, and by removing the wooden fish-weirs which traverse the river in several places near Antioch; it would only be necessary to cut a towing-path for horses through the woods along its banks. Lieutenant Cleaveland and the other officers were of opinion that a short tug-steamer of sufficient power would certainly go up the river to Antioch; which was in fact done by the Columbine's boat for the greater part of the way: and if a row of piles were to be driven into the sea in the line of the river, extending beyond the bar, so as to enable the current of the river to carry the sand and mud farther out into deep water, the Orontes would then admit vessels of 200 tons, instead of being obstructed by a bar, over which there is a depth of water of from three and a half to nine feet in winter. At any rate, it might be made navigable for boats, as the average fall of the river, between Antioch and the sea, scarcely exceeds five feet and a half per mile; and boats would then go twenty-seven miles above the town to Murad Pacha and different parts of the lake of Antioch." R. G. J. viii. p. 230.

[3] For views, with descriptions, see Fisher's Syria, I. 5, 19, 77. II. 28.

[4] Colonel Chesney says, "The windings give a distance of about forty-one miles, whilst the journey by land is only sixteen miles and a half.' —R. G. J. viii. p. 230 Strabo (xvi. 2) makes the distance from Antioch to Seleucia one hundred and twenty stadia. Forbiger (Handbuch der Alten Geographie, ii. 645) calls it three [German] geographical miles.

well worn by travellers, like the road from the Piræus to Athens, or from Ostia to Rome.

Seleucia united the two characters of a fortress and a seaport. It was situated on a rocky eminence, which is the southern extremity of an elevated range[1] of hills projecting from Mount Amanus. From the south-east, where the ruins of the Antioch Gate[2] are still conspicuous, the ground rose towards the north-east into high and craggy summits; and round the greater part of the circumference of four miles[3] the city was protected by its natural position. The harbour and mercantile suburb were on level ground towards the west; but here, as on the only weak point at Gibraltar, strong artificial defences had made compensation for the weakness of nature.[4] Seleucus, who had named his metropolis in his father's honour (p. 122), gave his own name to this maritime fortress;[5] and here, around his tomb,[6] his successors contended for the key of Syria.[7] "Seleucia by the sea" was a place of great importance under the Seleucidæ and the Ptolemies; and so it remained under the sway of the Romans. In consequence of its bold resistance to Tigranes, when he was in possession of all the neighbouring country, Pompey gave it the privileges of a "Free City;"[8] and a contemporary of St. Paul speaks of it as having those privileges still.[9]

[1] This hilly range was called Pieria. Hence the city was called, to distinguish it from others of the same name, Seleucia Pieria (Plin. v. 18. Strabo xvi. 2). For the same reason it was sometimes called Seleucia ad Mare.

[2] "On the south side of the city there was a strong gate, adorned with pilasters, and defended with round towers. This gate is still standing, almost entire, and is called the gate of Antioch."—Pococke. "On the S. E. side of the walls is the gate of Antioch, adorned with pilasters and defended by towers; this entrance must have been very handsome. Near it, and parallel to the walls, are the remains of a double row of marble columns."—Chesney.

[3] "The space within the walls of the town and suburbs, which have a circumference altogether of about *four miles*, is filled with the ruins of houses."—Chesney.

[4] *Ὑπὸ τὴν ἐπὶ θάλατταν αὐτῆς νεύουσαν πλευρὰν ἐν τοῖς ἐπιπέδοις, τά τ' ἐμπορεῖα καὶ τὸ προάστειον κεῖται, διαφερόντως τετειχισμένον.* Polybius, v. 59.

[5] Strabo says of the two cities, Ἡ *μεγίστη τοῦ πατρὸς αὐτοῦ ἐπώνυμος, ἡ δ' ἐρυμνοτάτη αὐτοῦ·* xvi. 2. A little below he says of Seleucia, *Ἐρυμά ἐστιν ἀξιόλογον καὶ κρείττων βίας ἡ πόλις.*

[6] Seleucus was buried here. Appian. Syr. 63.

[7] See especially the account given by Polybius of the siege of Seleucia in the war of Antiochus the Great with Ptolemy, Book v. ch. 58, 59, 60. In these chapters we find the clearest description both of its military importance and of its topography. The authors owe their best acknowledgments to Colonel Chesney for two obliging communications in January and February 1850, containing notes on Seleucia, and especially a plan of the inner basin and the pier. Since that time, Colonel Chesney's volumes on the Euphrates Expedition have appeared: and more recently a valuable paper on "Seleucia Pieria," by Dr. Yates, has been published in the *Museum of Classical Antiquities*, Part VI.

[8] *Ἐλευθέραν αὐτὴν ἔκρινε Πομπήϊος, ἀποκλείσας Τιγράνην.* Strabo xvi. 2. Tarsus had the same privileges. See p. 45. Compare p. 25, note.

[9] Plin. v. 18.

EXCAVATION AT SELEUCIA. (From Laborde).

The most remarkable work among the extant remains of Seleucia, is an immense excavation,—probably the same with that which is mentioned by Polybius,[1]—leading from the upper part of the ancient city to the sea. It consists alternately of tunnels and deep open cuttings. It is difficult to give a confident opinion as to the uses for which it was intended. But the best conjecture seems to be that it was constructed for the purpose of drawing off the water, which might otherwise have done mischief to the houses and shipping in the lower part of the town; and so arranged at the same time, as when needful, to supply a rush of water to clear out the port. The inner basin, or dock, is now a morass; but its dimensions can be measured, and the walls that surrounded it can be distinctly traced.[2] The position of the ancient-flood-gates, and the passage through which the vessels were moved from the inner to the outer harbour, can be accurately marked. The very piers of the outer harbour are still to be seen under the water. The southern jetty takes the wider sweep, and overlaps the northern, forming a secure entrance and a well protected basin. The stones are of great size, "some of them twenty feet long, five feet deep, and six feet wide;" and they were fastened to each other with iron cramps. The masonry of ancient Seleucia is still so good, that not long since a Turkish Pasha[4] conceived the idea of clearing out and repairing the harbour.

[1] *Πρόσβασιν δὲ μίαν ἔχει κατὰ τὴν ἀπὸ θαλάττης πλευρὰν κλιμακωτὴν καὶ χειροποίητον, ἐγκλίμασι καὶ σκαλώμασι πυκνοῖς καὶ συνεχέσι διειλημμένην.* Polyb. v. 59.

[2] Pococke gives a rude plan of Seleucia, with the harbour, &c. The more exact and minute description of Colonel Chesney is as follows:—"On the south side of the entrance there is a substantial jetty, formed of large blocks of stone, secured by iron cramps. It runs N. W. for seventy yards to the sea, and it may still be traced curving more to the N. under water, and overlapping the northern jetty, which is in a more ruinous state, but appears to have taken the direction of W. S. W., forming a kind of basin, with a narrow entrance tolerably well protected, and altogether suited for the Roman galleys. The ancient flood-gates are about fifty yards E. of the south pier. The passage for the galleys, &c., is cut through the solid rock, on which are the remains of a defensive tower on each side. Apartments below, with the remains of staircases to the top of each, are sufficiently distinct, as well as the places where the gates had been suspended between the towers. Immediately on passing the gateway, the passage widens to about one hundred yards; it takes the direction of S. E. by E., between two solid walls of masonry for three hundred and fifty yards, to the entrance of the great basin, which is now closed by a garden wall. The port or basin is an irregular oval of about four hundred and fifty yards long by three hundred and fifty in width at the southern extremity, and rather more than two hundred at the northern. The surrounding wall is formed of large cut stones solidly put together, and now rising only about seven feet above the mud, which during the lapse of ages has gradually accumulated, so as to cover probably about eight feet above the original level. The exterior side of the basin is about one-third of a mile from the sea; the interior is close to the foot of the hill," pp. 230, 231.

[3] Pococke.

[4] Ali Pasha, governor of Bagdad in 1835, once governor of Aleppo. "The foundation of his plan (when he turned his thoughts to the means of increasing the commercial prosperity of this part of Turkey), was to be the restoration of the once magnifi

These piers were unbroken when Saul and Barnabas came down to Seleucia, and the large stones fastened by their iron cramps protected the vessels in the harbour from the swell of the western sea. Here, in the midst of unsympathising sailors, the two missionary Apostles, with their younger companion, stepped on board the vessel which was to convey them to Salamis. As they cleared the port, the whole sweep of the bay of Antioch opened on their left,—the low ground by the mouth of the Orontes,—the wild and woody country beyond it,—and then the peak of Mount Casius, rising symmetrically from the very edge of the sea to a height of five thousand feet.[1] On the right, in the south-west horizon, if the day was clear, they saw the island of Cyprus from the first.[2] The current sets northerly and north-east between the island and the Syrian coast.[3] But with a fair wind, a few hours would enable them to run down from Seleucia to Salamis; and the land would rapidly rise in forms well-known and familiar to Barnabas and Mark.

Until the present year (1850) we have not been in possession of accurate charts of the coast near Salamis. Almost every island of the Mediterranean, except Crete and Cyprus, has been minutely surveyed and described by British naval officers. The soundings of the coast of Crete are as yet comparatively unknown: but the charts of Cyprus are on the

cent port of Seleucia, the masonry of which is still in so good a state that it merely requires trifling repairs in some places, and to be cleared out, which might have been done for £31,000, and partially for £10,000."—Chesney.

[1] "The lofty Jebel-el-Akrab, rising 5318 feet above the sea, with its abutments extending to Antioch."—Chesney, p. 228. Pliny's language concerning this mountain is absurdly extravagant: "In promontorio Seleucia. Super eam mons Casius. Cujus excelsa altitudo quarta vigilia orientem per tenebras Solem adspicit, brevi circumactu corporis diem noctemque pariter ostendens. Ambitus ad cacumen XIX. M. pass. est, altitudo per directum IV."—N. H. v. 18. Mount Casius is, however, a conspicuous and beautiful feature of this bay. St. Paul must have seen it in all his voyages to and from Antioch, and we shall often have occasion to allude to it.

[2] See above, p. 134, n. 2.

[3] "In sailing from the southern shores of Cyprus, with the winds adverse, you should endeavour to obtain the advantage of the set of the current, which between Cyprus and the mouths of the Nile always runs to the eastward, changing its direction to the N. E. and N. as you near the coast of Syria."—Norie, p. 149. "The current, in general, continues easterly along the Libyan coast, and E. N. E. off Alexandria; thence, advancing to the coast of Syria, it sets N. E. and more northerly; so that country vessels bound from Damietta to an eastern port of Cyprus, have been carried by the current past the island."—Purdy, p. 276. After leaving the Gulph of Scanderoon, the current sets to the westward along the south coast of Asia Minor, as we shall have occasion to notice hereafter. A curious illustration of the difficulty sometimes experienced in making this passage will be found in Meursius, Cyprus, &c., p. 158; where the decree of an early council is cited, directing the course to be adopted on the death of a bishop in Cyprus, if the vessel which conveyed the news could not cross to Antioch.

CAPE GREGO, N.W. BY W. SIX MILES.

eve of publication.[1] From Cape St. Andrea,[2] the north-eastern point of the island, the coast trends rapidly to the west, till it reaches Cape Grego,[3] the south-east extremity. The wretched modern town of Famagousta is nearer the latter point than the former, and the ancient Salamis was situated a short distance to the north of Famagousta. Near Cape St. Andrea are two or three small islands, anciently called "The Keys."[4] These, if they were seen at all, would soon be lost to view. Cape Grego is distinguished by a singular promonotory of table land. And there is little doubt that the woodcut here given from our English sailing directions, represents that very "rough, lofty, table-shaped eminence" which Strabo mentions in his description of the coast, and which has been identified with the Idalium of the classical poets.[5]

The ground lies low in the neighbourhood of Salamis; and the town was situated on a bight of the coast to the north of the river Pediæus.

[1] Captain Graves returned from the survey of Cyprus while these sheets were passing through the press. His kindness has enabled us to give the accompanying *Map of Cyprus* and *Plan of Salamis*, before the publication of the Government Charts. Some further information will be embodied in a supplementary note; and we hope that, as Captain Graves is about to proceed to the survey of Crete, we shall soon be in possession of abundant information with regard to that island.

[2] The *Dinaretum* of Pliny, v. 35. This north-eastern extremity of the island, per haps from being long and narrow (*καθ' ὁ στενὴ ἡ νῆσος*, Strabo xiv. 6), was called *Οὐρὰ βοὸς*, or the ox's tail. Ptolem. v. 14, § 3.

[3] The *Pedalium* of Strabo and Ptolemy.

[4] Κλεῖδες, mentioned by Strabo, Ptolemy, and Pliny. See what Herodotus says (v. 108) concerning the Phœnician fleet cruising about the Keys. These islands are mentioned by Pococke (ii. 219) as follows: "Opposite to the north-east corner are the isles called Clides by the ancients; the largest of which is not a mile in circumference. Authors differ about the number of them; those who name but two, probably took notice only of the two largest; there are two more that appear only as rocks, the farthest of which is not a mile from the land. There is another, which has some herbage on it, and may be the second as to its dimensions; it is so very near to the land that it may have been separated from it since those authors wrote."

[5] *Λόφος τραχὺς, ὑψηλὸς, τραπεζοειδής.* Strabo xiv. 6. There is a similar eminence on the Spanish coast near Cape de Gat, called Roldan's Table (la Mesa de Roldan). See Purdy, Pt. i. p. 23. For the identification of this place in Cyprus with Idalium, see Mannert, vi. 444. Pococke (p. 214) mentions a village called Trapeza near this point of the coast.

This low land is the largest plain in Cyprus, and the Pediæus is the only true river in the island, the rest being only winter-torrents, flowing in the wet season from the two mountain ranges which intersect it from east to west. This plain probably represents the kingdom of Teucer, which is familiar to us in the early stories of legendary Greece. It stretches inwards between the two mountain ranges to the very heart of the country, where the modern Turkish capital, Nicosia, is situated.[1] In the days of historical Greece, Salamis was the capital. Under the Roman Empire, if not the seat of government, it was at least the most important mercantile town. We have the best reasons for believing that the harbour was convenient and capacious.[2] Thus we can form to ourselves some idea of the appearance of the place in the reign of Claudius. A large city by the sea-shore, a wide spread plain with cornfields and orchards, and the blue distance of mountains beyond, composed the view on which the eyes of Barnabas and Saul rested when they came to anchor in the bay of Salamis.

The Jews, as we should have been prepared to expect, were numerous in Salamis. This fact is indicated to us in the sacred narrative ; for we learn that this city had several synagogues, while other cities had often only one.[3] They had doubtless been established here in considerable numbers in the active period, which succeeded the death of Alexander.[4] The unparalleled productiveness of Cyprus, and its trade in fruit, wine, flax, and honey, would naturally attract them to the mercantile port. The farming of the copper mines by Augustus to Herod may probably have swelled their numbers.[5] One of the most conspicuous passages in the history of Salamis was the insurrection of the Jews in the reign of Trajan, when great part of the city was destroyed.[6] Its demolition was com-

[1] See Pococke's description, vol. ii. pp. 214–217. He gives a rude plan of ancient Salamis. (See above, p. 139, n. 1.) The ruined aqueduct which he mentions appears to be subsequent to the time of St. Paul. We have not had the opportunity of consulting a more recent work, Von Hammer's Topographische Ansichten aus der Levante.

[2] See especially the account in Diodorus Siculus (Book xx. pp. 759–761) of the great naval victory of Salamis, won by Demetrius Poliorcetes over Ptolemy. Scylax also says that Salamis had a good harbour. His expression is, λιμένα ἔχουσα κλειστὸν χειμερινόν. See Gail.

[3] Acts xiii. 5. Compare v. 9. ix. 20, and contrast xvii. 1. xviii. 4.

[4] Philo (Legat. ad Cai.) speaks of the Jews of Cyprus.

[5] See above, p. 17, n. 3.

[6] "The flame spread to Cyprus, where the Jews were numerous and wealthy. One Artemio placed himself at their head. They rose and massacred 240,000 of their fellow-citizens; the whole populous city of Salamis became a desert. The revolt of Cyprus was first suppressed; Hadrian, afterwards emperor, landed on the island, and marched to the assistance of the few inhabitants who had been able to act on the defensive. He defeated the Jews, expelled them from the island, to whose beautiful coasts no Jew was ever after permitted to approach. If one were accidentally wrecked on the inhospitable shore, he was instantly put to death."—Milman, iii. 111, 112. The author says

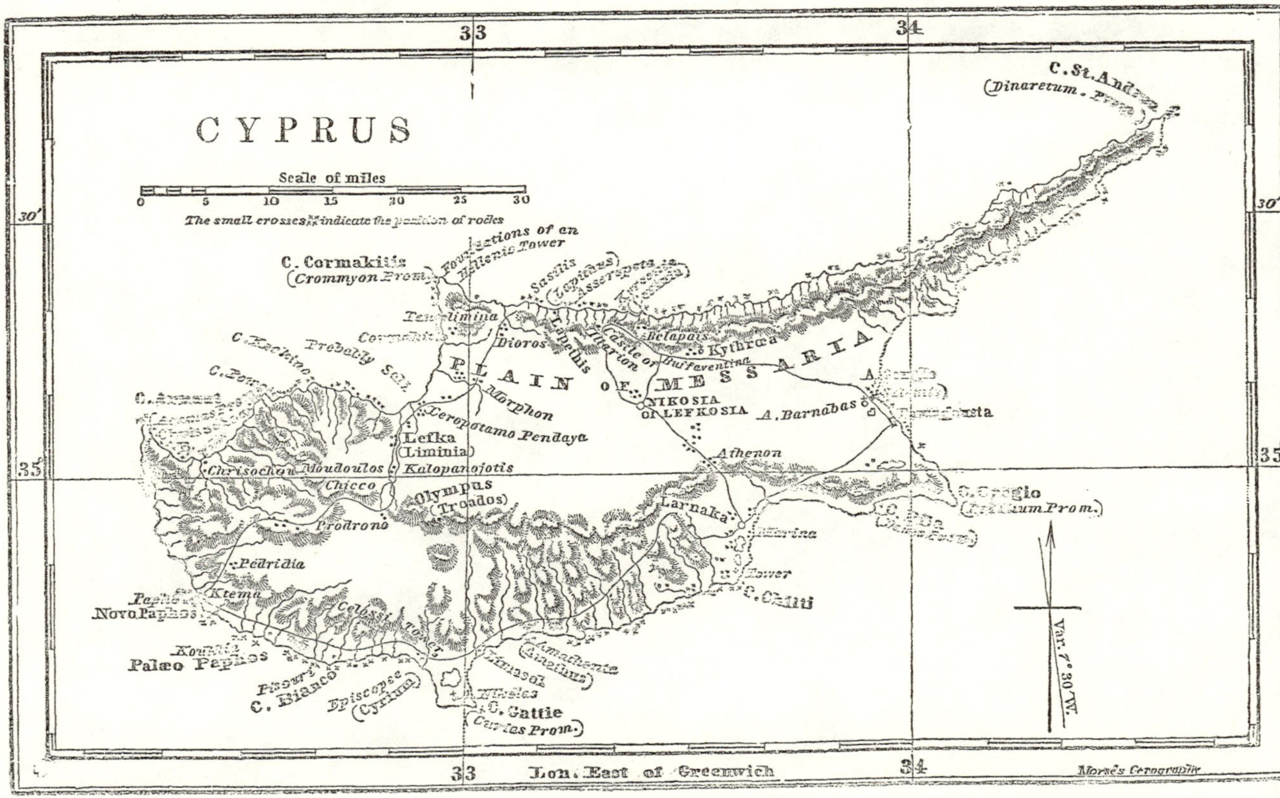
CYPRUS
Scale of miles
0 5 10 15 20 25 30
The small crosses indicate the position of rocks
C. Cormakitis
(Crommyon Prom.)
Foundations of an Hellenic Tower
Sasilis
Asserapeta
Belapais
Kythræa
PLAIN OF MESSARIA
Dioros
Morphon
Ceropotamo Pendaya
Lefka
(Liminia)
Kalopanojotis
NIKOSIA
or LEFKOSIA
A. Barnabas
Athenon
Larnaka
C. Gregio
C. Chiti
Tower
Olympus
(Troados)
Chicco
Chrisochou
Moudoulos
Prodromo
Pedridia
Ktema
Novo Paphos
Palæo Paphos
C. Bianco
Episcopee
(Cyrium)
Limasol
C. Gattie
(Curias Prom.)
Amathonte
(Amathus)
C. St. Andrea
(Dinaretum. Prom.)
Probably Salt
C. Kormakiti
30′
35
33
34
Lon. East of Greenwich
Var. 7° 30′ W.
Morse's Cerographic

pleted by an earthquake. It was rebuilt by a Christian emperor, from whom it received its medieval name of Constantia.[1]

It appears that the proclamation of the Gospel was confined by Barnabas and Saul to the Jews and the synagogues. We have no information of the length of their stay, or the success of their labours. Some stress seems to be laid on the fact that John (*i. e.* Mark), "was their minister." Perhaps we are to infer from this, that his hands baptized the Jews and proselytes, who were convinced by the preaching of the Apostles.[2]

From Salamis they travelled to Paphos, at the other extremity of the island. The two towns were probably connected together by a well travelled and frequented road.[3] It is indeed likely that, even under the Empire, the islands of the Greek part of the Mediterranean, as Crete and Cyprus, were not so completely provided with lines of internal communication as those which were nearer the metropolis, and had been longer under Roman occupation, such as Corsica and Sardinia. But we cannot help believing that Roman roads were laid down in Cyprus and Crete, after the manner of the modern English roads in Corfu and the other Ionian islands, which islands, in their social and political condition, present many points of resemblance to those which were under the Roman sway in the time of St. Paul. On the whole, there is little doubt that his journey from Salamis to Paphos, a distance from east to west of not more than an hundred miles, was accomplished in a short time and without difficulty.

Paphos was the residence of the Roman governor. The appearance of the place (if due allowance is made for the differences of the nineteenth century and the first) may be compared with that of the town of Corfu in the present day, with its strong garrison of imperial soldiers in the midst of a Greek population, with its mixture of two languages, with its symbols of a strong and steady power side by side with frivolous amusements, and with something of the style of a court about the residence of its governor. All the occurrences, which are mentioned at Paphos as taking place on the arrival of Barnabas and Saul, are grouped so entirely

above (109), that the Rabbinical traditions are full of the sufferings of the Jews in this period. In this island there was massacre before the time of the rebellion, "and the sea that broke upon the shores of Cyprus was tinged with the red hue of carnage."

1 Jerome speaks of it under this name: "Salamis, quæ nunc Constantia dicitur."—Ep. Philem.

2 See 1 Cor. xiv. 16.

3 On the west of Salamis, in the direction of Paphos, Pococke saw a church and monastery dedicated to Barnabas, and a grotto where he is said to have been buried, after suffering martyrdom in the reign of Nero (P. 217). There is a legend in Cedrenus and Nicephorus Calistus of the discovery of his relics, with the Gospel of St. Matthew on his breast, in the reign of Anastasius or Zeno.—See Meursius. A road is marked between Salamis and Paphos in the Peutingerian Table.

round the governor's person, that our attention must be turned for a time to the condition of Cyprus as a Roman province, and the position and character of Sergius Paulus.

From the time when Augustus united the world under his own power, the provinces were divided into two different classes. The business of the first Emperor's life was to consolidate the imperial system under the show of administering a republic. He retained the names and semblances of those liberties and rights which Rome had once enjoyed. He found two names in existence, the one of which was henceforth inseparably blended with the Imperial dignity and Military command, the other with the authority of the Senate and its Civil administration. The first of these names was "Prætor," the second was "Consul." Both of them were retained in Italy; and both were reproduced in the Provinces as "Proprætor" and "Proconsul."[1] He told the Senate and people that he would relieve them of all the anxiety of military proceedings, and that he would resign to them those provinces, where soldiers were unnecessary to secure the fruits of a peaceful administration. He would take upon himself all the care and risk of governing the other provinces, where rebellion might be apprehended, and where the proximity of warlike tribes made the presence of the legions perpetually necessary. These were his professions to the Senate: but the real purpose of this ingenious arrangement was the disarming of the republic, and the securing to himself the absolute control of the whole standing army of the empire.[2] The scheme was sufficiently transparent; but there was no sturdy national life in

[1] *Τῶν δύο τούτων ὀνομάτων ἐπὶ πλεῖστον ἐν τῇ δημοκρατίᾳ ἀνθησάντων, τὸ μέν τοῦ Στρατηγοῦ, τοῖς αἱρετοῖς, ὡς καὶ τῷ πολέμῳ ἀπὸ τοῦ πάνυ ἀρχαίου προσῆκον, ἔδωκεν, Ἀντιστρατήγους σφᾶς προσειπών· τὸ δὲ δὴ τῶν Ὑπάτων, τοῖς ἑτέροις, ὡς καὶ εἰρηνικωτέροις, Ἀνθυπάτους αὐτοὺς ἐπικαλέσας. Αὐτὰ μὲν γὰρ τὰ ὀνόματα, τό τε τοῦ Στρατηγοῦ καὶ τὸ τοῦ Ὑπάτου, ἐν τῇ Ἰταλίᾳ, ἐτήρησε, τοὺς δὲ ἔξω πάντας, ὡς καὶ ἀντ' ἐκείνων ἄρχοντας προσηγόρευσε.* Dio Cass. liii. 13. It is very important, as we shall see presently, to notice the accompanying statement, that *all governors of the Senate's provinces were to be called Proconsuls, whatever their previous office might have been* (*καὶ ἀνθυπάτους καλεῖσθαι μὴ ὅτι τοὺς δύο τοὺς ὑπατευκότας, ἀλλὰ καὶ τοὺς ἄλλους τῶν ἐστρατηγηκότων ἢ δοκούντων γε ἐστρατηγηκέναι μόνον ὄντας*): *and all governors of the Emperor's provinces were to be styled Legati or Proprætors, even if they had been Consuls* (*τοὺς δὲ ἑτέρους ὑπό τε ἑαυτοῦ αἱρεῖσθαι, καὶ Πρεσβευτὰς αὐτοῦ Ἀντιστρατηγούς τε ὀνομάζεσθαι, κἂν ἐκ τῶν ὑπατευκότων ὦσι, διέταξε*).

[2] Provincias validiores, et quas annuis magistratuum imperiis regi nec facile nec tutum erat, ipse suscepit; cætera Proconsulibus sortito permisit, et tamen nonnullas commutavit interdum. Sueton. Aug. 47.—*Τὰ μὲν ἀσθενέστερα, ὡς καὶ εἰρηναῖα καὶ ἀπόλεμα, ἀπέδωκε τῇ Βουλῇ· τὰ δὲ ἰσχυρότερα, ὡς καὶ σφαλερὰ καὶ ἐπικίνδυνα, καὶ ἤτοι πολεμίους τινὰς προσοίκους ἔχοντα, ἢ καὶ αὐτὰ καθ' ἑαυτὰ μέγα τι νεωτερίσαι δυνάμενα, κάτεσχε· λόγῳ μὲν, ὅπως ἡ μὲν Γερουσία ἀδεῶς τὰ κάλλιστα τῆς ἀρχῆς καρπῶτο, αὐτὸς δὲ τούς τε πόνους καὶ κινδύνους ἔχοι·—ἔργῳ δε, ἵνα ἐπὶ τῇ προφάσει ταύτῃ ἐκεῖνοι μὲν καὶ ἄοπλοι καὶ ἄμαχοι ὦσιν, αὐτὸς δὲ δὴ μόνος καὶ ὅπλα ἔχῃ, καὶ στρατιώτας τρέφῃ* Dio Cass. liii. 12.

Italy to resist his despotic innovations, and no foreign civilised powers to arrest the advance of imperial aggrandisement; and it thus came to pass that Augustus, though totally destitute of the military genius either of Cromwell or Napoleon, transmitted to his successors a throne guarded by an invincible army, and a system of government destined to endure through several centuries.

Hence we find in the reign, not only of Augustus but of each of his successors from Tiberius to Nero, the provinces divided into these two classes. On the one side we have those which are supposed to be under the Senate and people. The governor is appointed by lot, as in the times of the old republic. He carries with him the lictors and fasces, the insignia of a Consul; but he is destitute of military power. His office must be resigned at the expiration of a year. He is styled "Proconsul," and the Greeks, translating the term, call him 'Ανθύπατος.[1] On the other side are the provinces of Cæsar. The governor may be styled "Proprætor," or 'Αντιστράτηγος; but he is more properly "Legatus," or Πρεσβευτής,—the representative or "commissioner" of the Emperor. He goes out from Italy with all the pomp of a military commander, and he does not return till the Emperor recalls him.[2] And to complete the symmetry and consistency of the system, the subordinate districts of these imperial provinces are regulated by the Emperor's "Procurator" ('Επίτροπος[3]), or "High Steward." The New Testament, in the strictest conformity with the other historical authorities of the period, gives us examples of both kinds of provincial administration. We are told by Strabo, and by Dio Cassius, that "Asia" and "Achaia" were assigned to the Senate;[4] and the title, which in each case is given to the governor in the Acts of the Apostles, is "Proconsul."[5] The same authorities inform us that Syria was an imperial province,[6] and no such title as "Proconsul" is assigned by the sacred writers to "Cyrenius governor of Syria,"[7] or to Pilate, Festus and Felix,[8] the Procurators of Judæa, which, as we have seen (p. 25), was a dependency of that great and unsettled province.

[1] Which our English translators have rendered by the ambiguous word "deputy." Acts xiii. 7. "The *deputy* of the country, Sergius Paulus." "Gallio was the *deputy* of Achaia," xviii. 12. "There are *deputies*," xix. 38.

[2] All these details are stated, and the two kinds of governors very accurately distinguished in the 53d Book of Dio Cassius, ch. 13. It should be remarked, that ἐπαρχία (the word still used for the subdivisions of the modern Greek Kingdom) is applied indiscriminately to both kinds of provinces.

[3] See Dio Cass. liii. 15.

[4] Strabo xvii. 3. Dio Cass. liii. 12. The latter uses 'Ελλὰς instead of 'Αχαία. as in Acts xx. 2.

[5] 'Ανθύπατος, xviii. 12. xix. 38.

[6] Strabo and Dio. ibid.

[7] Luke ii. 2.

[8] The word invariably used in the New Testament is 'Ηγεμὼν. This is a general term, like the Roman "Præses" and the English "Governor;" as may be seen by

PROCONSUL OF CYPRUS.[1]

Dio Cassius informs us, in the same passage where he tells us that Asia and Achaia were provinces of the Senate, that Cyprus was retained by the Emperor for himself.[2] If we stop here, we naturally ask the question,—and some have asked the question rather hastily,[3]—how it comes to pass that St. Luke speaks of Sergius Paulus by the style of "Proconsul?" But any hesitation concerning the strict historical accuracy of the sacred historian's language, is immediately set at rest by the very next sentence

comparing Luke ii. 2 with iii. 1, and observing that the very same word is applied to the offices of the Procurator of Judæa, the Legatus of Syria, and the Emperor himself. Josephus generally uses Ἐπίτροπος for the Procurator of Judæa, and Ἡγεμὼν for the Legatus of Syria.

[1] The woodcut is from Akerman's Numismatic Illustrations, p. 41. Specimens of the coin are in the Imperial Cabinet at Vienna, and in the Bibliothèque du Roi. There are other Cyprian coins of the Imperial age, with PROCOS in Roman characters. See Eckhel and Akerman's Numismatic Illustrations. Pellerini says that many coins of the reign of Claudius, with KOINON KYΠΡΙΩΝ, are of the red copper of the island: a fact peculiarly interesting to us, if the notion, mentioned p. 17, n. 3, and p. 141, be correct.

[2] Along with Syria and Cilicia. Ἡ Συρία, ἡ κοίλη καλουμένη, ἥ τε Φοινίκη, καὶ Κιλικία, καὶ Κύπρος, καὶ Αἰγύπτιοι, ἐν τῇ τοῦ Καίσαρος μερίδι τότε ἐγένοντο. Dio Cass. liii. 12.

[3] Thus Baronius (sub anno 46) conjectures that Cyprus must have been at this time under the Proconsul of Cilicia. "Cum Sergius Paulus hic dicatur Proconsul; et auctore Strabone (lib. 14, in fine) et aliis [?] exploratum habeatur, Cyprum non proconsularem sed prætoriam factam esse provinciam; cur a Luca non Prætor [Proprætor] sed Proconsul nominetur, ea videtur esse ratio, quòd eadem prætoria provincia sæpe honoris causa data est administranda Ciliciæ Proconsuli." Grotius thinks the word is inaccurately used by St. Luke by a sort of catachresis. "Propriè qui Cypro præerat vocabatur ἀντιστρατηγός. Sed non mirum est Græcos ista permiscuisse, aut potius, ut egregii erant adulatores, nomen quam honorificentissimum dedisse provinciarum rectoribus. Generale nomen est Præsidis: quo et hic Latinè uti licet." Hammond (Annot. on Acts xiii., not in the ed. of 1653) refutes Baronius, and takes the view of Grotius. The whole mistake has arisen from the following words in the last paragraph of Strabo's fourteenth book:—γέγονε στρατηγικὴ ἐπαρχία καθ' αὑτὴν . . . ἐγένετο ἐπαρχία ἡ νῆσος, καθάπερ καὶ νῦν ἐστὶ, στρατηγική. And the whole explanation is to be found in the clear statement of Dio Cassius (given above, p. 142, n. 1), that all governors of the Senate's provinces had the *title* of Proconsul, though they were often only of Prætorian rank. Thus we find Tacitus calling Cæsius Cordus Proconsul of Crete (Ann. iii. 38), and T. Vinius Proconsul of Narbonensian Gaul (Hist. i. 48), though we know that Africa and Asia were the only Senatorian provinces governed by men of Proconsular rank. See Dio Cass. liii. 14, and Strabo xvii. 3.

of the secular historian,[1]—in which he informs us that Augustus restored Cyprus to the Senate in exchange for another district of the empire,—a statement which he again repeats in a later passage of his work.[2] It is evident, then, that the governor's style and title from this time forward would be "Proconsul." But this evidence, however satisfactory, is not all that we possess. The coin, which is here engraved, distinctly presents to us a Cyprian Proconsul of the reign of Claudius. And the inscription, which will be found at the end of this chapter, supplies us with the names of two additional governors, who were among the predecessors or successors of Sergius Paulus.[3]

It is remarkable that two men called Sergius Paulus are described in very similar terms by two physicians who wrote in Greek, the one a heathen, the other a Christian. The heathen writer is Galen. He speaks of his contemporary as a man interested and well-versed in philosophy.[4] The Christian writer is St. Luke, who tells us here that the governor of Cyprus was a "prudent" man, who "desired to hear the word of God." This governor seems to have been of a candid and inquiring mind: nor will this philosophical disposition be thought inconsistent with his connection with the Jewish impostor, whom Saul and Barnabas found at the Paphian court, by those who are acquainted with the intellectual and religious tendencies of the age.

For many years before this time, and many years after, impostors from the East, pretending to magical powers, had great influence over the Roman mind. All the Greek and Roman literature of the empire, from Horace to Lucian,[5] abounds in proof of the prevalent credulity of this sceptical period. Unbelief, when it has become conscious of its weakness, is often glad to give its hand to superstition. The faith of educated Romans was utterly gone. We can hardly wonder, when the East was thrown open,—

1 *Ὕστερον τὴν μὲν Κύπρον καὶ τὴν Γαλατίαν τὴν περὶ Νάρβωνα τῷ δήμῳ ἀπέδωκεν, αὐτὸς δὲ τὴν Δαλματίαν ἀντέλαβε.* Dio, liii. 12.

2 *Τότε δ' οὖν καὶ τὴν Κύπρον καὶ τήν Γαλατίαν τὴν Ναρβωνησίαν ἀπέδωκε τῷ δήμῳ, ὡς μηδὲν τῶν ὅπλων αὐτοῦ δεομένας.* Dio, liv. 4.

3 If Baur had lived in the age of Baronius or Grotius he would have adduced this passage as an argument against the historical accuracy of this part of the Acts.

4 *Τοῦδε τοῦ νῦν ἐπάρχου τῆς Ῥωμαίων πόλεως, ἀνδρὸς τὰ πάντα πρωτεύοντος ἔργοις τε καὶ λόγοις τοῖς ἐν φιλοσοφίᾳ, Σεργίου Παύλου ὑπάτου.* De Anatom. Administr. i. 1. t. ii. p. 218, ed. Kühn.—*Σέργιος τὲ ὁ καὶ Παῦλος, ὃς οὐ μετὰ πολὺν χρόνον ἔπαρχος ἐγένετο τῆς πόλεως, καὶ Φλάβιος . . . . ἐσπευκῶς [ἐσπουδακῶς?] δὲ περὶ τὴν Ἀριστοτέλους φιλοσοφίαν, ὥσπερ καὶ ὁ Παῦλος.*—De Prænot. ad Epig. c. 2. t. xiv. p. 612. The Sergius Paulus here spoken of was *ἔπαρχος* of Rome about the year 177 A. D., and was personally known to Galen. The passages are adduced by Wetstein without any remark; and from him they are quoted by Dr. Bloomfield, in his Recensio Synoptica, as if they referred to the Sergius Paulus of the Acts, who lived more than a hundred years earlier. We owe the correction of this mistake to Dr. Greenhill, who wrote the life of Galen in Smith's Dictionary of Biography.

5 See Horace's Odes, I. XI., and Lucian's Life of Alexander of Abonoteichus.

the land of mystery,—the fountain of the earliest migrations,—the cradle of the earliest religions,—that the imagination both of the populace and the aristocracy of Rome became fanatically excited, and that they greedily welcomed the most absurd and degrading superstitions. Not only was the metropolis of the empire crowded with "hungry Greeks," but "Syrian fortune-tellers" flocked into all the haunts of public amusement. Athens and Corinth did not now contribute the greatest or the worst part of the "dregs" of Rome; but (to adopt Juvenal's use of that river of Antioch we have lately been describing) "the Orontes itself flowed into the Tiber."[1]

Every part of the East contributed its share to the general superstition. The gods of Egypt and Phrygia found unfailing votaries. Before the close of the republic, the temples of Isis and Serapis had been more than once erected, destroyed and renewed.[2] Josephus tells us that certain disgraceful priests of Isis[3] were crucified at Rome by the second emperor; but this punishment was only a momentary check to their sway over the Roman mind. The more remote districts of Asia Minor sent their itinerant soothsayers;[4] Syria sent her music and her medicines; Chaldæa her "Babylonian numbers" and "mathematical calculations."[5] To these corrupters of the people of Romulus we must add one more Asiatic nation,—the nation of the Israelites;—and it is an instructive employment to observe that, while some members of the Jewish people were rising, by the Divine power, to the highest position ever occupied by men on earth, others were sinking themselves, and others along with them, to the lowest and most contemptible degradation. The treatment and influence of the Jews at Rome were often too similar to those of other Orientals. One year we find them banished;[6] another year we see them quietly re-established.[7] The Jewish beggar-woman was the gipsy of the first century,

[1] Ambubaiarum collegia, pharmacopolæ,
Mendici, mimæ, balatrones, hoc genus omne.—Hor. I. Sat. ii. 1.

Non possum ferre, Quirites,
Græcam Urbem: quamvis quota portio fæcis Achæi?
Jam pridem Syrus in Tiberim defluxit Orontes,
Et linguam, et mores, et cum tibicine chordas
Obliquas, nec non gentilia tympana secum
Vexit, et ad Circum, &c.—Juv. Sat. iii. 60.

[2] Lucan, viii. 830.

[3] Ant. xviii. 3, 4.

[4] Alexander of Abonoteichus, whose life was written by Lucian, and Apollonius of Tyana, whose adventures are recorded by Philostratus, might be adduced as specimens of the "Phryx augur" (Juv. vi. 584) and the "Commagenus haruspex" (ib. 549).

[5] Babylonii Numeri, Hor. I. Od. xi. 2. Chaldaicæ rationes, Cic. Div. ii. 47. See the whole passage 42–47. The Chaldæan astrologers were called "Mathematici" (Juv. vi. 562, xiv. 248). See the definition in Aulus Gellius, i. 9: "Vulgus, quos gentilitio vocabulo Chaldæos dicere oportet, mathematicos dicit." There is some account of their proceedings at the beginning of the fourteenth book of the Noctes Atticæ.

[6] Acts xviii. 2.

[7] Acts xxviii. 17.

shivering and crouching in the outskirts of the city, and telling fortunes, as Ezekiel said of old, "for handfuls of barley, and for pieces of bread."[2] All this catalogue of Oriental impostors, whose influx into Rome was a characteristic of the period, we can gather from that revolting satire of Juvenal, in which he scourges the follies and vices of the Roman women. But not only were the women of Rome drawn aside into this varied and multiplied fanaticism; but the eminent men of the declining republic, and the absolute sovereigns of the early empire, were tainted and enslaved by the same superstitions. The great Marius had in his camp a Syrian, probably a Jewish[3] prophetess, by whose divinations he regulated the progress of his campaigns. As Brutus, at the beginning of the republic, had visited the oracle of Delphi, so Pompey, Crassus, and Cæsar, at the close of the republic, when the oracles were silent,[4] sought information from Oriental astrology. No picture in the great Latin satirist is more powerfully drawn than that in which he shows us the Emperor Tiberius "sitting on the rock of Capri, with his flock of Chaldæans round him."[5] No sentence in the great Latin historian is more bitterly emphatic than that in which he says that the astrologers and sorcerers are a class of men who "will always be discarded and always cherished."[6]

What we know, from the literature of the period, to have been the case in Rome and in the empire at large, we see exemplified in a province in the case of Sergius Paulus. He had attached himself to "a certain sorcerer, a false prophet, a Jew, whose name was Barjesus," and who had

[1] Arcanam Judæa tremens mendicat in aurem,
Interpres legum Solymarum, et magna Sacerdos
Arboris, ac summi fida internuncia cœli.
Implet et illa manum sed parcius: ære minuto
Qualiacunque voles Judæi somnia vendunt.
Juv. vi. 542–546.

Nunc sacri fontis nemus, et delubra locantur
Judæis; quorum cophinus, fœnumque supellex.
Omnis enim populo mercedem pendere jussa est
Arbor, et ejectis mendicat silva Camœnis.—iii. 13–16.

[2] Ezek. xiii. 19.

[3] Niebuhr (Lect. vol. i. p. 363) thinks she was a Jewess. Her name was Martha. See Long's Plutarch, § 17.

[4] Cic. Div. ii. 47. Compare Juvenal (vi. 553).
Chaldæis sed major erit fiducia: quicquid
Dixerit astrologus, credent a fonte relatum
Hammonis; quoniam Delphis oracula cessant,
Et genus humanum damnat caligo futuri.

[5] Principis angusta Caprearum in rupe sedentis
Cum grege Chaldæo.—Juv. x. 93.
See Gifford's note. Suetonius and Dio Cassius give us similar information concerning the superstition of Tiberius.

[6] Genus hominum potentibus infidum, sperantibus fallax, quod in civitate nostra et vitabitur semper et retinebitur.—Tac. Hist.

given himself the Arabic name of "Elymas," or "The Wise." But the Proconsul was not so deluded by the false prophet[1] as to be unable, or unwilling, to listen to the true. "He sent for Barnabas and Saul," of whose arrival he was informed, and whose free and public declaration of the "Word of God" attracted his inquiring mind. Elymas used every exertion to resist them, and to hinder the Proconsul's mind from falling under the influence of their divine doctrine. Truth and falsehood were brought into visible conflict with each other. It is evident, from the graphic character of the narrative,—the description of Paul "setting his eyes,"[2] on the sorcerer,—"the mist and darkness" which fell on Barjesus, —the "groping about for some one to lead him,"[3]—that the opposing wonder-workers stood face to face in the presence of the Proconsul,—as Moses and Aaron withstood the magicians at the Egyptian court,—Sergius Paulus being in this respect different from Pharaoh, that he did not "harden his heart."

The miracles of the New Testament are generally distinguished from those of the Old, by being for the most part works of mercy and restoration, not of punishment and destruction. Two only of our Lord's miracles were inflictions of severity, and these were attended with no harm to the bodies of men. The same law of mercy pervades most of those interruptions of the course of nature, which He gave His servants, the Apostles, power to effect. One miracle of wrath is mentioned as worked in His name by each of the great Apostles, Peter and Paul; and we can see sufficient reasons why liars and hypocrites, like Ananias and Sapphira, and powerful impostors, like Elymas Barjesus, should be publicly punished in the face of the Jewish and Gentile worlds, and made the examples and warnings of every subsequent age of the Church.[4] A different passage in

[1] For the good and bad senses in which the word *Μάγος* was used, see Professor Trench's recent book on the Second Chapter of St. Matthew. It is worth observing, that Simon Magus was a Cyprian, if he is the person mentioned by Josephus. A. xx. 5, 2.

[2] *'Ατενίζειν*, "to look intently." Acts xiii. 10. The same word which is used in xxiii. 1. Our first impression is, that there was something searching and commanding in St. Paul's eye. But if the opinion is correct, that he suffered from an affection of the eyes, this word may express a peculiarity connected with his defective vision. See the Bishop of Winchester's note (Ministerial Character of Christ, p. 555), who compares the LXX. in Numb. xxxiii. 55, Josh. xxiii. 13, and applies this view to the explanation of the difficulty in Acts xxiii. 1–5. And it is remarkable that, in both the traditional accounts of Paul's personal appearance which we possess, he is said to have had contracted eye-brows. Malalas (x. p. 257, Ed. Bonn.) calls him *σύνοφρυς*; and Nicephorus (H. E. ii. 37) says *κάτω τὰς ὀφρῦς εἶχε νενούσας*. Many have thought that "the thorn in his flesh," 2 Cor. xii. 7, was an affection of the eyes. Hence, perhaps, the statement in Gal. iv. 14–16, and the *πήλικα γράμματα*, Gal. vi. 11. (See our Preface, p. xvii. note.)

[3] It may be added that these phrases seem to imply that the person from whence they came was an eye-witness. Some have inferred that Luke himself was present.

[4] It is not necessary to infer from these passages, or from 1 Cor. v. 3–5. 1 Tim. i

the life of St. Peter presents a parallel which is closer in some respects with this interview of St. Paul with the sorcerer in Cyprus. As Simon Magus, —who had "long time bewitched the people of Samaria with his sorceries,"—was denounced by St. Peter "as still in the gall of bitterness and bond of iniquity," and solemnly told that "his heart was not right in the sight of God;"[1]—so St. Paul, conscious of his apostolic power, and under the impulse of immediate inspiration, rebuked Barjesus, as a child of that Devil who is the father of lies,[2] as a worker of deceit and mischief,[3] and as one who sought to pervert and distort that which God saw and approved as right.[4] He proceeded to denounce an instantaneous judgment; and, according to his prophetic word, the "hand of the Lord" struck the sorcerer as it had once struck the Apostle himself on the way to Damascus;—the sight of Elymas began to waver,[5] and presently a darkness settled on it so thick, that he ceased to behold the sun's light. This blinding of the false prophet opened the eyes of Sergius Paulus.[6] That which had been intended as an opposition to the Gospel, proved the means of its extension. We are ignorant of the degree of this extension in the island of Cyprus. But we cannot doubt that when the Proconsul was converted, his influence would make Christianity reputable; and that from this moment the Gentiles of the island, as well as the Jews, had the news of salvation brought home to them.

And now, from this point of the Apostolical History, PAUL appears as the great figure in every picture. Barnabas, henceforward, is always in the background. The great Apostle now enters on his work as the preacher to the Gentiles; and simultaneously with his active occupation of the field in which he was called to labour, his name is suddenly changed. As "Abram" was changed into "Abraham," when God promised that he should be the "father of many nations;" as "Simon" was changed into "Peter," when it was said, "On this rock I will build my church;"—so "Saul" is changed into "Paul," at the moment of his first great victory among the Heathen. That "the plains of Mamre by Hebron"

20, that Peter and Paul had power to inflict these judgments at their will. Though, even if they had this power, they had also the spirit of love and supernatural knowledge to guide them in the use of it.

1 Acts viii. 21–23.

2 John viii. 44.

3 Ῥαδιουργία (xiii. 10), expresses the cleverness of a successful imposture.

4 Notice *εὐθείας*, xiii. 10, and *εὐθεῖα*, viii. 21.

5 Ἀχλὺς καὶ σκότος, xiii. 11. This may be used, in Luke's medical manner, to express the stages of the blindness. Compare *ἔστη καὶ περιέπατει* in the account of the recovery, iii. 8.

6 "Durch das Erblinden des Magiers dem Proconsul die Augen geöffnet werden." These are the words of Schrader, who yet exercises his utmost ingenuity to explain away everything supernatural in the occurrence. See Schrader's Paulus, ii. p. 170–175. Baur's notion of course is, that the whole story was invented or embellished. Baur's Paulus, Pt. I. ch. iv.

were to the patriarch,—what "Cæsarea Philippi,"[1] by the fountains of the Jordan, was to the fisherman of Galilee,—that was the city of Paphos, on the coast of Cyprus, to the tent-maker of Tarsus. Are we to suppose that the name was now really given him for the first time,—that he adopted it himself as significant of his own feelings,—or that Sergius Paulus conferred it on him in grateful commemoration of the benefits he had received,—or that "Paul," having been a Gentile form of the Apostle's name in early life conjointly with the Hebrew "Saul," was now used to the exclusion of the other, to indicate that he had receded from his position as a Jewish Christian, to become the friend and teacher of the Gentiles? All these opinions have found their supporters both in ancient and modern times.[2] The question has been alluded to before in this work (p. 46). It will be well to devote some further space to it now, once for all.

It cannot be denied that the words in Acts xiii. 9—"Saul, who is also Paul"—are the line of separation between two very distinct portions of St. Luke's biography of the Apostle, in the former of which he is uniformly called "Saul," while in the latter he receives, with equal consistency, the name of "Paul." It must also be observed that the Apostle always speaks of himself under the latter designation in every one of his Epistles, without any exception; and not only so, but the Apostle St. Peter, in the only passage where he has occasion to allude to him,[3] speaks of him as "our beloved brother Paul." We are, however, inclined to adopt the opinion that the Cilician Apostle had this Roman name, as well as his other Hebrew name, in his earlier days, and even before he was a Christian. This adoption of a Gentile name is so far from being alien to the spirit of a Jewish family, that a similar practice may be traced through all the periods of Hebrew History.[4] Beginning with the *Persian* epoch (B.C. 550–350) we find such names as "Nehemiah," "Schammai," "Belteshazzar," which betray an oriental origin,[5] and show that Jewish appellatives followed the growth of the living language. In the *Greek* period we encounter the names of "Philip,"[6] and his son "Alexander,"[7] and of Alexander's successors, "Antiochus," "Lysima-

[1] See Gen. xiii. 18. xvii. 5. Mat. xvi. 13-18, and Mr. Stanley's Sermon on St. Peter.

[2] Olshausen, among the moderns, follows the opinion of Jerome.

[3] 2 Pet. iii. 15.

[4] The following remarks are taken from Zunz, "Namen der Juden," Leipsig, 1837,—a work which arose out of political circumstances in Germany.

[5] See what Zunz says of the terminations ja, ài, and the article Ha, as in Pedaja, Sakkai, Hakatan, Hakoz, &c.

[6] Mat. x. 3. Acts vi. 5. xxi. 8. Joseph. Ant. xiv. 10, 22.

[7] Acts xix. 33, 34. See 2 Tim. iv. 14. Alexander was a common name among the Asmonæans. It is said that when the great conqueror passed through Judæa, a promise was made to him that all the Jewish children born that year should be called "Alexander."

chus," "Ptolemy," "Antipater;"[1] the names of Greek philosophers, such as "Zeno" and "Epicurus;"[2] even Greek mythological names, as "Jason" and "Menelaus."[3] Some of these words will have been recognised as occurring in the New Testament itself. When we mention ***Roman*** names adopted by the Jews, the coincidence is still more striking. "Crispus,"[4] "Justus,"[5] "Niger,"[6] are found in Josephus[7] as well as in the Acts. "Drusilla" and "Priscilla" might have been Roman matrons. The "Aquila" of St. Paul is the counterpart of the "Apella" of Horace.[8] Nor need we end our survey of Jewish names with the early Roman empire; for, passing by the destruction of Jerusalem, we see Jews, in the earlier part of the *Middle Ages*, calling themselves "Basil," "Leo," "Theodosius," "Sophia;" and, in the latter part, "Albert," "Benedict," "Crispin," "Denys."[9] We might pursue our inquiry into the nations of modern Europe; but enough has been said to show, that as the Jews have successively learnt to speak Chaldee, Greek, Latin, or German, so they have adopted into their families the appellations of those Gentile families among whom they have lived. It is indeed remarkable that the Separated Nation should bear, in the very names recorded in its annals, the trace of every nation with whom it has come in contact and never united.

It is important to our present purpose to remark that double names often occur in combination, the one national, the other foreign. The earliest instances are "Belteshazzar-Daniel," and "Esther-Hadasa."[10] Frequently there was no resemblance or natural connection between the two words, as in "Herod-Agrippa," "Salome-Alexandra," "Juda-Aristobulus," "Simon-Peter." Sometimes the meaning was reproduced, as in "Malich-Kleodemus." At other times an alliterating resemblance of sound[11] seems to have dictated the choice, as in "Jose-Jason," "Hillel-Julus," "*Saul-Paulus*,"—"*Saul, who is also Paul.*"

1 1 Mac. xii. 16. xvi. 11. 2 Mac. iv. 29. Joseph. Ant. xiv. 10.

2 Zunz adduces these names from the Mischna and the Berenice Inscription.

3 Jason, Joseph. Ant. xii. 10, 6, perhaps Acts xvii. 5-9. Rom. xvi. 21. Menelaus, Joseph. Ant. xii. 5, 1. See 2 Mac. iv. 5.

4 Acts xviii. 8.

5 Acts i. 23.

6 Acts xiii. 1.

7 Joseph Vit. 68, 65. B. J. iv. 6, 1. Compare 1 Cor. i. 14. Acts xviii. 7. Col. iv. 11.

8 Hor. I. Sat. v. 100. Priscilla appears under the abbreviated form "Prisca," 2 Tim. iv. 19.

9 See further details in Zunz.

10 *Δανιὴλ οὗ τὸ ὄνομα ἐπεκλήθη* Βαλτάσαρ. Dan. x. 1. LXX. See the Hebrew in Esther ii. 7, הדסה היא אסתר. So Zerubbabel was called Sheshbazzar. Compare Ezra v. 16 with Zech. iv. 9. The Oriental practice of adopting names which were significant must not be left out of view. See Parkhurst, and his quotation from the Targum on הדס.

11 Perhaps the best note among the commentators is that of Grotius. "*Saulus qui et Paulus;* id est, qui, ex quo cum Romanis conversari cœpit, hoc nomine a suo non abludente, cæpit a Romanis appellari. Sic qui Jesus Judæis, Græcis *Jason*· Hillel,

Thus it seems to us that satisfactory reasons can be adduced for the double name borne by the Apostle,—without having recourse to the hypothesis of Jerome, who suggests that, as Scipio was called Africanus from the conquest of Africa, and Metellus Creticus from the conquest of Crete, so Saul carried away his new name as a trophy of his victory over the heathenism of the Proconsul Paulus[1]—or to that notion, which Augustine applies with much rhetorical effect in various parts of his writings,[2] where he alludes to the literal meaning of the word "*Paulus*," and

Pollio: Onias, *Menelaus:* Jakin, *Alcimus.* Apud Romanos Silas, *Silvanus*, ut notavit Hieronymus: Pasides, *Pansa*, ut Suetonius in Crassitio; Diocles, *Diocletianus;* Biglinitza, soror Justiniani, Romane *Vigilantia.*" See Joseph. Ant. xii. 5, 1. Compare Jesus Justus, Col. iv. 11.

[1] Diligenter attende, quod hic primum Pauli nomen inceperit. Ut enim Scipio, subjecta Africa, Africani sibi nomen assumpsit, et Metellus, Creta insula subjugata, insigne Cretici suæ familiæ reportavit; et imperatores nunc usque Romani ex subjectis gentibus Adiabenici, Parthici, Sarmatici, nuncupantur: ita et Saulus ad prædicationem gentium missus, a primo ecclesiæ spolio Proconsule Sergio Paulo victoriæ suæ trophæa retulit, erexitque vexillum, ut Paulus diceretur e Saulo." —Hieron. in Ep. Philem. Augustine, in one passage, takes the same view. "Ipse minimus Apostolorum tuorum (1 Cor. xv. 9) cum Paulus Proconsul, per ejus militiam debellata superbia, sub lene jugum Christi tui missus est, regis magni provincialis effectus (Acts xiii. 7, 12), ipse quoque ex priore Saulo Paulus vocari amavit, ob tam magnæ insigne victoriæ."—Conf. viii. 4. It is impossible not to feel that this theory is very inconsistent with the humility of St. Paul. Baronius, who sees this objection, gives a conjecture which is more probable: "Saulo cognomen suum, quod etiam Æmiliorum familiæ fuit, quo sibi magis arctiusque eo vinculo Apostolum vinciret, Sergius Paulus indidit." And again below "A Sergio Paulo, amicitiæ gratia, familiæ suæ cognomine nobilitatus est Apostolus."

[2] "Vox illa de cœlo prostravit persecutorem, et erexit prædicatorem; occidit Saulum, et vivificavit Paulum (Acts ix). Saül enim persecutor erat sancti viri (1 Sam. xix.); inde nomen habebat iste quando persequebatur Christianos: postea de Saulo factus est Paulus (Acts xiii). Quid est Paulus? Modicus. Ergo quando Saulus, superbus, elatus: quando Paulus, humilis, modicus. Ideo sic loquimur, Paulo post videbo te, id est, post modicum. Audi quia modicus factus est: *Ego enim sum minimus Apostolorum* (1 Cor. xv. 9); et *Mihi, minimo omnium Sanctorum*, dicit alio loco (Ephes. iii. 8). Sic erat inter Apostolos tanquam fimbria vestimenti; sed tetigit Ecclesia gentium tanquam fluxum patiens, et sanata est. (Matt. ix. 20–22.) Tract. viii. in Ep. Jo. The same train of thought is found, often in the same words, in the following places: Enarr. in Ps. lxxii. 4. Serm. ci. on Luke x. 2–6. Serm. clxviii. on Eph. vi. 23. Serm. cclxxix. de Paulo Apostolo. In one passage he gives point to the contrast by alluding to the tall stature of the first king of the Jews. "Saulus a Saüle nomen derivatur. Qui fuerit Saül, notis. Ipsius electa est statura proceris [procera]. Sic enim describit Scriptura, quod supereminens esset omnibus, quando electus est ut ungeretur in regem (1 Sam. ix. 2). Non fuit sic Paulus [Saulus], sed factus Paulus. Paulus enim parvus."—Serm. clxix. in Philip. iii. 3–16. In these passages the notion may be used only rhetorically. In another place he gives it as an opinion. "Non ob aliud, quantum mihi videtur, hoc nomen elegit, nisi ut se ostenderet tanquam minimum Apostolorum"—De Sp. et Lit. xii. At one time he finds in Stephen the counterpart of David: "Talis fuerat Saül in David, qualis Saulus in Stephanum."—Serm. cccxv. in Sol. Steph. Mart. At another, David prefigures our Lord himself· "Saül erat ille persecutor David. In David Christus erat, in David Christus præfigurabatur: tanquam David Saüli de Cœlo, *Saule, Saule, quid me persequeris?*" Serm. clxxv in 1 Tim. i. 15.

contrasts Saul, the unbridled king, the proud self-confident persecutor of David, with Paul, the lowly, the penitent,—who deliberately wished to indicate, by his very name, that he was "the *least* of the Apostles,"[1] and "*less than the least* of all Saints."[2] Yet we must not neglect the coincident occurrence of these two names in this narrative of the events which happened in Cyprus. We need not hesitate to dwell on the associations which are connected with the name of "Paulus," or on the thoughts which are naturally called up, when we notice the critical passage in the sacred history, where it is first given to Saul of Tarsus. It is surely not unworthy of notice that, as Peter's first Gentile convert was a member of the *Cornelian House* (p. 116), so the surname of the noblest family of the *Æmilian House*[3] was the link between the Apostle of the Gentiles and his convert at Paphos. Nor can we find a nobler Christian version of any line of a Heathen poet, than by comparing what Horace says of him who fell at Cannæ,—"*animæ magnæ prodigum Paulum*,"—with the words of him who said at Miletus, "*I count not my life dear unto myself*, so that I might finish my course with joy, and the ministry which I have received of the Lord Jesus."[4]

And though we imagine, as we have said above, that Saul had the name of Paul at an earlier period of his life, and should be inclined to conjecture that the appellation came from some connection of his ancestors (perhaps as manumitted slaves) with some member of the Roman family of the Æmilian Pauli;[5]—yet we cannot believe it accidental that the words,[6] which have led to this discussion, occur at this particular point of the inspired narrative. The Heathen name rises to the surface at the moment when St. Paul visibly enters on his office as the Apostle of the Heathen. The Roman name is stereotyped at the moment when he converts the Roman governor. And the place where this occurs is Paphos, the favourite sanctuary of a shameful idolatry. At the very spot which was notorious throughout the world for that which the Gospel forbids and destroys,—there, before he sailed for Perga, having achieved his victory, the Apostle erected his trophy,[7]—as Moses, when Amalek was discom-

1 1 Cor. xv. 9.

2 Eph. iii. 8.

3 Paulus was the cognomen of a family of the Gens Æmilia. The stemma is given in Smith's Dictionary of Classical Biography, under Paulus Æmilius. The name must of course have been given to the first individual who bore it from the smallness of his stature: it is a contraction of Pauxillus: see Donaldson's Varronianus. It should be observed, that both Malalas and Nicephorus (quoted above) speak of St. Paul as short of stature.

4 Hor. I. Od. xii. 37. Acts xx. 24. Compare Phil. iii. 8.

5 Compare the case of Josephus, alluded to above, p. 46.

6 Acts xiii. 9.

7 See the words of Jerome quoted above, p, 151, n. 3. "Victoriæ suæ *tropæa* retulit, erexitque *vexillum*."

fited, "built an altar, and called the name of it Jehovah-Nissi,—the Lord my Banner."[1]

ΚΛΑΥΔΙΩΙ ΚΑΙΣΑΡΙ ΣΕΒΑΣΤΩΙ
ΓΕΡΜΑΝΙΚΩΙ ΑΡΧΙΕΡΕΙ ΜΕΓΙΣΤΩΙ
ΔΗΜΑΡΧΙΧΗΣ ΕΞΟΥΣΙΑΣ ΑΥΤΟΚΡΑΤΟΡΙ
ΠΑΤΡΙ ΠΑΤΡΙΔΟΣ ΚΟΥΡΙΕΩΝ Η ΠΟΛΙΣ
ΑΠΟ ΤΩΝ ΠΡΟΚΕΚ[Ρ]ΙΜΕΝΩ[Ν Υ]ΠΟ ΙΟΥΛΙΟΥ
ΚΟΡΔΟΥ ΑΝΘΥΠΑΤΟΥ ΛΟΥΚΙΟΣ ΑΝΝΙΟΣ ΒΑΣ[ΣΟΣ ΑΝΘ]Υ
ΠΑΤΟΣ ΚΑΘΙΕΡΩΣΕΝ· ΙΒ.

INSCRIPTION FOUND AT CURIUM, IN CYPRUS.[2]

[1] Exod. xvii. 15.

[2] Boeckh. Corpus Inscriptionum (No. 2632). This inscription has been selected because of its allusion to the Emperor Claudius. The year is 52 A. U. C. 805. Of the two proconsuls here mentioned, Julius Cordus and L. Annius Bassus, the former is mentioned in another inscription (No. 2631, found at Citium). See the inscriptions and other evidence collected by Engel in his work on Cyprus. Kypros. Berlin, 1843, I. pp. 459–463.

CHAPTER VI.

> "Paulus præco Dei, qui fera gentium
> Primus corda sacro perdomuit stilo,
> Christum per populos ritibus asperis
> Immanes placido dogmate seminat."
>
> PRUDENTIUS, *Cont. Symm.* Præf.

OLD AND NEW PAPHOS.—DEPARTURE FROM CYPRUS.—COAST OF PAMPHYLIA.—PERGA.—MARK'S RETURN TO JERUSALEM.—MOUNTAIN-SCENERY OF PISIDIA.—SITUATION OF ANTIOCH.—THE SYNAGOGUE.—ADDRESS TO THE JEWS.—PREACHING TO THE GENTILES.—PERSECUTION BY THE JEWS.—HISTORY AND DESCRIPTION OF ICONIUM.—LYCAONIA.—DERBE AND LYSTRA.—HEALING OF THE CRIPPLE.—IDOLATROUS WORSHIP OFFERED TO PAUL AND BARNABAS.—ADDRESS TO THE GENTILES.—ST. PAUL STONED.—TIMOTHEUS.—THE APOSTLES RETRACE THEIR JOURNEY.—PERGA AND ATTALEIA.—RETURN TO SYRIA.

THE banner of the Gospel was now displayed on the coasts of the heathen The glad tidings had "passed over to the isles of Chittim,"[1] and had found a willing audience in that island, which, in the vocabulary of the Jewish Prophets, is the representative of the trade and civilisation of the Mediterranean Sea. Cypras was the early meeting-place of the Oriental and Greek forms of social life. Originally colonised from Phœnicia, it was successively subject to Egypt, to Assyria, and to Persia; the settlements of the Greeks on its shores had begun in a remote period, and their influence gradually advanced, till the older links of connection were entirely broken by Alexander and his successors. But not only in political and social relations, by the progress of conquest and commerce, was Cyprus the meeting-place of Greece and the East. Here also their forms of idolatrous worship met and became

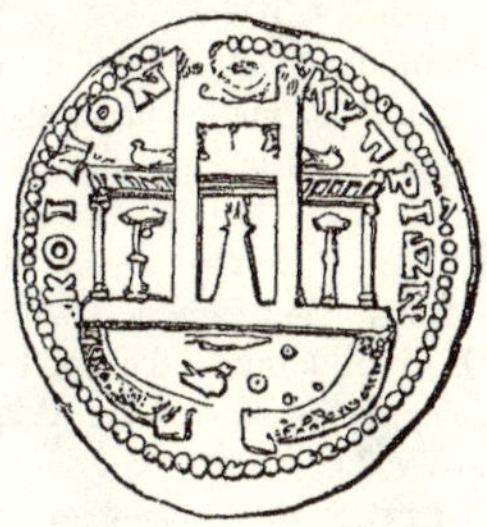

COIN OF PAPHOS.[2]

[1] The general notion intended by the phrases "isles" and "coasts" of "Chittim," seems to have been "the islands and coasts of the Mediterranean to the west and north-west of Judæa." Numb. xxiv. 24. Jer. ii. 10. Ezek. xxvii. 6. See Gen. x. 4, 5. Isai. xxiii. 1. Dan. xi. 30. But primarily the name is believed to have been connected with *Citium* (see note 2, p. 154), which was a Phœnician colony. See Gesenius, under כתים. Epiphanius (himself a Cyprian bishop) says, *Κίτιον ἡ Κυπρίων νῆσος καλεῖται· Κίτιοι γὰρ Κύπριοι.* Hær. xxx. 25.

[2] From the British Museum: see below, p. 156, n. 7.

blended together. Paphos was, indeed, a sanctuary of Greek religion: on this shore the fabled goddess first landed, when she rose from the sea:[1] this was the scene of a worship celebrated in the classical poets, from the age of Homer,[2] down to the time when Titus, the son of Vespasian, visited the spot with the spirit of a heathen pilgrim, on his way to subjugate Judæa.[3] But the polluted worship was originally introduced from Assyria or Phœnicia:[4] the Oriental form under which the goddess was worshipped, is represented on Greek coins:[5] the Temple bore a curious resemblance to those of Astarte at Carthage or Tyre:[6] and Tacitus pauses to describe the singularity of the altar and the ceremonies, before he proceeds to narrate the campaign of Titus.[7] And here it was that we have seen Christianity firmly established by St. Paul,—in the very spot where the superstition of Syria had perverted man's natural veneration and love of mystery, and where the beautiful creations of Greek thought had administered to what Athanasius, when speaking of Paphos, well describes as the "deification of lust."[8]

The Paphos of the poets, or *Old Paphos*, as it was afterwards called, was situated on an eminence at a distance of nearly two miles from the sea. *New Paphos* was on the sea-shore, about ten miles to the north.[9] But the old town still remained as the sanctuary which was visited by

[1] Deam ipsam conceptam mari huc appulsam. Tac. Hist. ii. 3. See P. Mela, ii. 7.

[2] Odyss. viii. 362. See Eurip. Bacch. 400. Virg. Æn. i. 415. Hor. Od. I. xxx Lucan. Phars. viii. 456.

[3] Tac. Hist. ii. 2–4. Compare Suet. Tit. 5. Tacitus speaks of magnificent offerings presented by kings and others to the temple at Old Paphos.

[4] Pausanias traces the steps of the worship from Assyria to Paphos and Phœnicia, and ultimately to Cythera. Attic. xiv. 6. Tacitus connects Cilicia with some of the religious observances.

[5] See below, n. 7.

[6] See Müller's Archäologie, § 239 (p. 298).

[7] Sanguinem aræ obfundere vetitum: precibus et igne puro altaria adolentur, nec ullis imbribus, quanquam in aperto, madescunt. Simulacrum Deæ non effigie humana, continuus orbis latiore i nitio tenuem in ambitum metæ modo exsurgens: et ratio in obscuro. Tac. H. ii. 3. See Max. Tyr. *Παφίοις ἡ μὲν 'Αφροδίτη τὰς τιμὰς ἔχει· τὸ δὲ ἄγαλμα οὐκ ἂν εἰκάσαις ἄλλῳ τῳ ἢ πυραμίδι λευκῇ, ἡ δὲ ὕλη ἀγνοεῖται.* Diss. viii. 8. Also Clem. Alex. Coh. ad Gentes. III. iv.

[8] He is alluding to the worship of Venus at Paphos, and says: *τὴν ἐπιθυμίαν θεοποιήσαντες προσκυνοῦσιν.* Athan. Cont. Græcos, p. 10, ed. Col. 1686. Compare Arnob. v. 19.

[9] Or rather the north-west. See the Chart, which is due to the kindness of Captain Graves. R. N. The words of Strabo are: *Εἶθ' ἡ Πάφος . . . . λιμένα ἔχουσα . . . . διέχει δὲ πεζῇ σταδιους ἑξήκοντα τῆς Παλαιπάφου· καὶ πανηγυρίζουσι διὰ τῆς ὁδοῦ ταύτης κατ' ἔτος ἐπὶ τὴν Παλαίπαφον, ἄνδρες ὁμοῦ γυναιξὶν ἐκ τῶν ἄλλων πόλεων συνιόντες.* xiv. 6. The following is an extract from some MSS. notes by Captain Graves: "Kouklia (Old Paphos) is three hours' ride from Ktema (near New Paphos) along a bridle-path, with corn-fields on either side. The ruins are extensive, particularly a Cyclopean wall . . . with inscriptions of an early date. There are also very extensive catacombs." The Peut. Table makes the distance eleven miles. Forbiger (Alte Geographie, iii. 1049) says incorrectly, that Old Paphos was according to Strabo sixty stadia "weiter landeinwärts" from New Paphos.

heathen pilgrims; profligate processions, at stated seasons, crowded the road between the two towns, as they crowded the road between Antioch and Daphne (p. 125); and small models of the mysterious image[1] were sought as eagerly by strangers as the little "silver shrines" of Diana at Ephesus.[2] Doubtless the position of the old town was an illustration of the early custom, mentioned by Thucydides, of building at a safe distance from the shore, at a time when the sea was infested by pirates; and the new town had been established in a place convenient for commerce, when navigation had become more secure. It was situated on the verge of a plain, smaller than that of Salamis, and watered by a scantier stream than the Pediæus (see p. 139). Not long before the visit of Paul and Barnabas it had been destroyed by an earthquake. Augustus had rebuilt it, and from him it had received the name of Augusta, or Sebaste.[3] But the old name still retained its place in popular usage, and has descended to modern times. The "Paphos" of Strabo, Ptolemy, and St. Luke,[4] became the "Papho" of the Venetians and the "Baffa" of the Turks. A second series of *Latin*[5] architecture has crumbled into decay. Mixed up with the ruins of palaces and churches are the poor dwellings of the Greek and Mahomedan inhabitants, partly on the beach, but chiefly on a low ridge of sandstone rock, about two miles[6] from the ancient port, for the

[1] See the story in Athenæus, xv. 18. Ὁ Ἡρόστρατος, *ἐμπορίᾳ χρώμενος καὶ χώραν πολλὴν περιπλέων, προσσχών ποτε καὶ* Πάφῳ *τῆς* Κύπρου, *ἀγαλμάτιον* Ἀφροδίτης *σπιθαμιαῖον, ἀρχαῖον τῇ τέχνῃ, ὠνησάμενος, ᾔει φέρων εἰς* Ναύκρατιν. *κ. τ. λ.* The narrative goes on to say that the merchant was saved by the miraculous image from shipwreck.

[2] Acts xix. 24.

[3] We learn this from Dio Cassius. *Παφίοις σεισμῷ πονήσασι καὶ χρήματα ἐχαρίσατο, καὶ τὴν πόλιν* Αὔγουσταν *καλεῖν, κατὰ δόγμα ἐπέτρεψε*, liv. 23. See also Senec. Ep. 91. N. Q. vi. 26. The Greek form *Sebaste*, instead of *Augusta*, occurs in an inscription found on the spot, which is further interesting as containing the name of another *Paulus*. Μαρκίᾳ Φιλίππου *θυγατρί, ἀνεψιᾷ* Καίσαρος *θεοῦ* Σεβαστοῦ, *γυναικὶ* Παύλου Φαβίου Μαξίμου, Σεβαστῆς Πάφου *ἡ βουλὴ καὶ ὁ δῆμος*. Boeckh. No. 2629. So Antioch in Pisidia was called Cæsarea. See below, p. 170.

[4] Strab. xiv. 6. Ptol. v. 14, 1.

[5] The following passage from a traveller about the time of the Reformation, is a curious instance of the changes of meaning which the same words may undergo. "Paphos ruinis plena videtur, templis tamen frequens, inter quæ *Latina* sunt præstantiora, in quibus ritu *Romano* divina peraguntur. et Gallorum legibus vivitur." Itin. Hieros. Bartæi. de Salignaco, 1587.

[6] This is the distance between the Ktema and the Marina given by Captain Graves. In Purdy's Sailing Directions (p. 251), it is stated to be only half a mile. Captain Graves says: "In the vicinity are numerous ruins and ancient remains; but when so many towns have existed, and so many have severally been destroyed, all must be left to conjecture. A number of columns broken and much mutilated are lying about, and some substantial and well-built vaults, or rather subterraneous communications, under a hill of slight elevation, are pointed out by the guides as the remains of a temple dedicated to Venus. Then there are numerous excavations in the sandstone hills, which probably served at various periods the double purpose of habitations and tombs. Sev-

marsh, which once formed the limit of the port, makes the shore unhealthy during the heats of summer by its noxious exhalations. One of the most singular features of the neighbourhood consists of the curious caverns excavated in the rocks, which have been used both for tombs and for dwellings. The port is now almost blocked up, and affords only shelter for boats. "The Venetian stronghold, at the extremity of the Western mole, is now fast crumbling into ruins. The mole itself is broken up, and every year the massive stones of which it was constructed are rolled over from their original position into the port."[1] The approaches to the harbour can never have been very safe, in consequence of the ledge of rocks[2] which extends some distance into the sea. At present, the eastern entrance to the anchorage is said to be the safer of the two. The western, under ordinary circumstances, would be more convenient for a vessel clearing out of the port, and about to sail for the Gulf of Pamphylia.

We have remarked in the last chapter, that it is not difficult to imagine the reasons which induced Paul and Barnabas, on their departure from Seleucia, to visit first the island of Cyprus. It is not quite so easy to give an opinion upon the motives which directed their course to the coast of Pamphylia, when they had passed through the native island of Barnabas, from Salamis to Paphos. It might be one of those circumstances which we call accidents, and which, as they never influence the actions of ordinary men without the predetermining direction of Divine Providence, so were doubtless used by the same Providence to determine the course even of Apostles. As St. Paul, many years afterwards, joined at Myra that vessel in which he was shipwrecked,[3] and then was conveyed to Puteoli in a ship which had accidentally wintered at Malta[4]—so on this occasion there might be some small craft in the harbour at Paphos, bound for the opposite gulf of Attaleia, when Paul and Barnabas were thinking of their future progress. The distance is not great, and frequent communication, both political and commercial, must have taken place between the towns of Pamphylia and those of Cyprus.[5] It is possible that St. Paul, having

eral monasteries and churches now in ruins, of a low Gothic architecture, are more easily identified; but the crumbling fragments of the sandstone with which they are constructed, only add to the incongruous heap around, that now covers the palace of the Paphian Venus."—MS. note by Captain Graves, R. N.

[1] Captain Graves. MS.

[2] "A great ledge of rocks lies in the entrance to Papho, extending about a league; you may sail in either to the eastward or westward of it, but the eastern passage is the widest and best." Purdy, p. 251. The soundings may be seen in our copy of Captain Graves' Chart.

[3] Acts xxvii. 5, 6.

[4] Acts xxviii. 11–13.

[5] And perhaps Paphos more especially, as the seat of government. At present Khalandri (Gulnar), to the south-east of Attaleia and Perga, is the port from which the Tatars from Constantinople, conveying government despatches, usually cross to Cyprus. See Purdy, p. 245, and the reference to Irby and Mangles.

already preached the Gospel in Cilicia,[1] might wish now to extend it among those districts which lay more immediately contiguous, and the population of which was, in some respects, similar to that of his native province.[2] He might also reflect that the natives of a comparatively unsophisticated district might be more likely to receive the message of salvation, than the inhabitants of those provinces which were more completely penetrated with the corrupt civilisation of Greece and Rome. Or his thoughts might be turning to those numerous families of Jews, whom he well knew to be settled in the great towns beyond Mount Taurus, such as Antioch in Pisidia, and Iconium in Lycaonia, with the hope that his Master's cause would be most successfully advanced among those Gentiles, who flocked there, as everywhere, to the worship of the synagogue. Or, finally, he may have had a direct revelation from on high, and a vision, like that which had already appeared to him in the Temple,[3] or like that which he afterwards saw on the confines of Europe and Asia,[4] may have directed the course of his voyage. Whatever may have been the calculations of his own wisdom and prudence, or whatever supernatural intimations may have reached him, he sailed, with his companions Barnabas and John, in some vessel, of which the size, the cargo, and the crew, are unknown to us, past the promontories of Drepanum and Acamas, and then across the waters of the Pamphylian Sea, leaving on the right the cliffs[5] which are the western boundary of Cilicia, to the innermost bend of the bay of Attaleia.

This bay is a remarkable feature in the shore of Asia Minor, and it is not without some important relations with the history of this part of the world. It forms a deep indentation in the general coast-line, and is bordered by a plain, which retreats itself like a bay into the mountains. From the shore to the mountains, across the widest part of the plain, the distance is a journey of eight or nine hours. Three principal rivers intersect this level space : the Catarrhactes, which falls over the sea-cliffs near Attaleia, in the waterfalls which suggested its name ; and farther to the east the Cestrus and Eurymedon, which flow by Perga and Aspendus to a low and sandy shore. About the banks of these rivers, and on the open waters of the bay, whence the eye ranges freely over the ragged mountain summits which inclose the scene, armies and fleets had engaged in some of those battles of which the results were still felt in the day of St. Paul. From the base of that steep shore on the west, where a rugged knot of mountains is piled up into snowy heights above the rocks of Phaselis, the

[1] See pp. 104–106 and 117.

[2] Strabo's expression is, Οἱ Πάμφυλοι, πολὺ τοῦ Κιλικίου φύλου μετέχοντες, xii. 7.

[3] Acts xxii. 17–21. See p. 104. [4] Acts xvi. 9.

[5] About C. Anamour (Anemurium, the southernmost point of Asia Minor), and Alaya (the ancient Coracesium), there are cliffs of 500 and 600 feet high. See Purdy, p. 244. Compare our Map of the N. E. corner of the Mediterranean.

united squadron of the Romans and Rhodians sailed across the bay in the year 190 B.C.; and it was in rounding that promontory near Side on the east, that they caught sight of the fleet of Antiochus, as they came on by the shore with the dreadful Hannibal on board.[1] And close to the same spot where the Latin power had defeated the Greek king of Syria, another battle had been fought at an earlier period, in which the Greeks gave one of their last blows to the retreating force of Persia, and the Athenian Cimon gained a victory both by land and sea; thus winning, according to the boast of Plutarch, in one day the laurels of Platæa and Salamis.[2] On that occasion a large navy sailed up the river Eurymedon as far as Aspendus. Now, the bar at the mouth of the river would make this impossible.[3] The same is the case with the river Cestrus, which, Strabo says, was navigable in his day for sixty stadia, or seven miles, to the city of Perga.[4] Ptolemy calls this city an inland town of Pamphylia; but so he speaks of Tarsus in Cilicia.[5] And we have seen that Tarsus, though truly called an inland town, as being some distance from the coast, was nevertheless a mercantile harbour. Its relation with the Cydnus was similar to that of Perga with the Cestrus; and the vessel which brought St. Paul to win more glorious victories than those of the Greek and Roman battles of the Eurymedon,—came up the course of the Cestrus to her moorings near the Temple of Diana.

All that Strabo tells us of this city is that the Temple of Diana was on an eminence at some short distance, and that an annual festival was held in honour of the goddess.[6] The chief associations of Perga are with

COIN OF PERGA.[7]

[1] The description in Livy is as vivid as if it proceeded from an eye-witness: "In confinio Lyciæ et Pamphyliæ *Phaselis* est: prominet penitus in altum, conspiciturque prima terrarum Rhodum a Cilicia petentibus, et procul navium præbet prospectum .... Postquam superavere Rhodii promontorium, quod ab *Sida* prominet in altum, extemplo et conspecti ab hostibus sunt, et ipsi eos viderunt." xxxvii. 23. Compare the English Sailing Directions.

[2] Plut. Cim.

[3] See Beaufort's Karamania, p. 135.

[4] Εἶθ' ὁ Κέστρος ποταμὸς, ὃν ἀναπλεύσαντι σταδίους ἑξήκοντα Πέργη πόλις. xiv. 4.

[5] Perga is reckoned among the Παμφυλίας μεσόγειοι. Ptol. v. 5, 7. So Tarsus among the Κιλικίας μεσογ. v. 8, 7.

[6] Πλησίον ἐπὶ μετεώρου τόπου τὸ τῆς Περγαίας Ἀρτέμιδος ἱερὸν, ἐν ᾧ πανήγυρις κατ' ἔτος συντελεῖται. xiv. 4.

[7] From the British Museum.

the Greek rather than the Roman period: and its existing remains are described as being "purely Greek, there being no trace of any later inhabitants."[1] Its prosperity was probably arrested by the building of Attaleia[2] after the death of Alexander, in a more favourable situation on the shore of the bay. Attaleia has never ceased to be an important town since the day of its foundation by Attalus Philadelphus. But when the traveller pitches his tent at Perga, he finds only the encampments of shepherds, who pasture their cattle amidst the ruins. These ruins are walls and towers, columns and cornices, a theatre and a stadium, a broken aqueduct encrusted with the calcareous deposit of the Pamphylian streams, and tombs scattered on both sides of the site of the town. Nothing else remains of Perga, but the beauty of its natural situation, "between and upon the sides of two hills, with an extensive valley in front, watered by the river Cestrus, and backed by the mountains of the Taurus."[3]

The coins of Perga are a lively illustration of its character as a city of the Greeks. We have no memorial of its condition as a city of the Romans; nor does our narrative require us to delay any longer in describing it. The Apostles made no long stay in Perga. This seems evident, not only from the words used at this point of the history,[4] but from the marked manner in which we are told that they *did* stay,[5] on their return from the interior. One event, however, is mentioned as occurring at Perga, which, though noticed incidentally and in a few words, was attended with painful feelings at the time, and involved the most serious consequences. It must have occasioned deep sorrow to Paul and Barnabas, and possibly even then some mutual estrangement: and afterwards it became the cause of their quarrel and separation.[6] Mark "departed from them from Pamphylia, and went not with them to the work." He came with them up the Cestrus as far as Perga, but there he forsook them, and, taking advantage of some vessel which was sailing towards Palestine, he "returned to Jerusalem,"[7] which had been his home in earlier years.[8] We are not to suppose that this implied an absolute rejection of Christianity. A soldier who has wavered in one battle may live to obtain a glorious vic-

[1] Fellows. See Note 3. [In a letter received from E. Falkener, Esq., Architect, it is stated that though the theatre is disposed after the Greek manner, its architectural details (as well as those of the stadium) are all Roman.]

[2] Acts xiv. 25.

[3] This description is quoted or borrowed from Sir C. Fellow's "Asia Minor, 1839," pp. 190-193. Gen. Köhler appears to have seen these ruins in 1800, on "a large and rapid stream" between Stavros and Adalia, but without identifying them with Perga. Leake's Asia Minor, p. 132. See Cramer, ii. 280.

[4] *Διελθόντες ἀπὸ τῆς Πέργης*, xiii. 14. On their return it is said, *διελθόντες τὴν Πισιδίαν*, xiv. 24. Similarly, a rapid journey is implied in *διοδεύσαντες τὴν* Α. *καὶ* Α., xvii. 1.

[5] *Λαλήσαντες ἐν Πέργῃ τὸν λόγον, κατέβησαν, κ. τ. λ.* xiv 25.

[6] Acts xv. 37-39. [7] Acts xiii. 13. [8] Acts xii. 12, 25

tory. Mark was afterwards not unwilling to accompany the Apostles on a second missionary journey;[1] and actually did accompany Barnabas again to Cyprus.[2] Nor did St. Paul always retain his unfavourable judgment of him (Acts xv. 38), but long afterwards, in his Roman imprisonment, commended him to the Colossians, as one who was "a fellow-worker unto the kingdom of God," and "a comfort" to himself:[3] and in his latest letter, just before his death, he speaks of him again as one "profitable to him for the ministry."[4] Yet if we consider all the circumstances of his life, we shall not find it difficult to blame his conduct in Pamphylia, and to see good reasons why Paul should afterwards, at Antioch, distrust the steadiness of his character. The child of a religious mother, who had sheltered in her house the Christian disciples in a fierce persecution, he had joined himself to Barnabas and Saul, when they travelled from Jerusalem to Antioch, on their return from a mission of charity. He had been a close spectator of the wonderful power of the religion of Christ,—he had seen the strength of faith under trial in his mother's home,—he had attended his kinsman Barnabas in his labours of zeal and love,—he had seen the word of Paul sanctioned and fulfilled by miracles,—he had even been the "minister" of Apostles in their successful enterprize:[5] and now he forsook them, when they were about to proceed through greater difficulties to more glorious success. We are not left in doubt as to the real character of his departure. He was drawn from the work of God by the attraction of an earthly home.[6] As he looked up from Perga to the Gentile mountains, his heart failed him, and turned back with desire towards Jerusalem. He could not resolve to continue persevering, "in journeyings often, in perils of rivers, in perils of robbers."[7]

"Perils of rivers" and "perils of robbers"—these words express the very dangers which St. Paul would be most likely to encounter on his journey from Perga in Pamphylia to Antioch in Pisidia. The lawless and maurauding habits of the population of those mountains which separate the table-land in the interior of Asia Minor from the plains on the south coast, were notorious in all parts of ancient history. Strabo uses the same strong language both of the Isaurians[8] who separated Cappadocia from Cilicia, and of their neighbours the Pisidians, whose native fortresses were the barrier between Phrygia and Pamphylia.[9] We have the

[1] Acts. xv. 37. [2] Acts xv. 39. [3] Col. iv. 10.

[4] 2 Tim. iv. 11. [5] See Acts xiii. 5.

[6] Matthew Henry pithily remarks: "Either he did not like the work, or he wanted to go and see his mother."

[7] 2 Cor. xi. 26.

[8] See p. 20.

[9] Of Isauria he says, *λῃστῶν ἅπασαι κατοικίαι.* xii. 6. Of the Pisidians he says that *καθάπεο οἱ Κίλικες, λῄστρικῶς ἤσκηνται.* Ib. 7. He adds that even the Pamphylians,

same character of the latter of these robber tribes in Xenophon, who is the first to mention them ;[1] and in Zosimus, who relieves the history of the later empire by telling us of the adventures of a robber chief, who defied the Romans and died a desperate death in these mountains.[2] Alexander the Great, when he heard that Memnon's fleet was in the Ægean, and marched from Perga to rejoin Parmenio in Phrygia, found some of the worst difficulties of his whole campaign in penetrating through this district.[3] The scene of one of the roughest campaigns connected with the wars of Antiochus the Great was among the hill-forts near the upper waters of the Cestrus and Eurymedon.[4] No population through the midst of which St. Paul ever travelled, abounded more in those "perils of robbers," of which he himself speaks, than the wild and lawless clans of the Pisidian Highlanders.

And if on this journey he was exposed to dangers from the attacks of men, there might be other dangers, not less imminent, arising from the natural character of the country itself. To travellers in the East there is a reality in "perils of rivers," which we in England are hardly able to understand. Unfamiliar with the sudden flooding of thirsty water-courses, we seldom comprehend the full force of some of the most striking images in the Old and New Testaments.[5] The rivers of Asia Minor, like all the rivers in the Levant, are liable to violent and sudden changes.[6] And no district in Asia Minor is more singularly characterised by its "water floods" than the mountainous tract of Pisidia, where rivers burst out at the bases of huge cliffs, or dash down wildly through narrow ravines. The very notice of the *bridges* in Strabo, when he tells us how the Cestrus

"though living on the south side of Taurus, had not quite given up their robber habits and did not always allow their neighbours to live in peace."

[1] Xen. Anab. I. i. 11. ix. 9. III. ii. 14.

[2] His name was Lydius—τὸ γένος Ἴσαυρος, ἐντεθραμμένος τῇ συνήθει λῃστείᾳ. Zos. pp. 59–61, in the Bonn Ed. The scene is at Cremna. See the Map. Compare what Zosimus says of the robbers near Selge, 265. The beautiful story of St. John and the robber (Euseb. Eccl. Hist. iii. 23) will naturally occur to the reader. See also the frequent mention of Isaurian robbers in the latter part of the life of Chrysostom, prefixed to the Benedictine edition of his works.

[3] See the account of Arrian, I. 27, 28, and especially the notices of Selge and Sagalassus; and compare the accounts of these cities by modern travellers, P. Lucas, Arundel, and Fellows.

[4] See especially the siege of Selge by Achæus in Polybius, v. 72–77. Compare the account of Sagalassus in the narrative of the Campaign of Manlius. Liv. xxxviii. 15, and see Cramer's Asia Minor.

[5] Thus the true meaning of 2 Cor. xi. 26 is lost in the English translation. Similarly, in the Sermon on the Mount (Matt. vii. 25, 27), ποταμὸι is translated "floods," and the image confused. See Ps. xxxii. 6.

[6] The crossing of the Halys by Crœsus (Herod. i. 75) is an illustration of the difficulties presented by the larger rivers of Asia Minor. Vonones, when attempting to escape from Cilicia (Tac. Ann. ii. 68), lost his life in consequence of not being able to cross the Pyramus.

and Eurymedon tumble down from the heights and precipices of Selge to the Pamphylian Sea, is more expressive than any elaborate description.[1] We cannot determine the position of any bridges which the Apostle may have crossed, but his course was never far from the channels of these two rivers: and it is an interesting fact, that his name is still traditionally connected with one of them, as we learn from the information recently given to an English traveller by the Archbishop of Pisidia.[2]

Such considerations respecting the physical peculiarities of the country now traversed by St. Paul, naturally lead us into various trains of thought concerning the scenery, the climate, and the seasons.[3] And there are certain probabilities in relation to the time of the year when the Apostle may be supposed to have journeyed this way, which may well excuse some remarks on these subjects. And this is all the more allowable, because we are absolutely without any data for determining the year in which this first missionary expedition was undertaken. All that we can assert with confidence is that it must have taken place somewhere in the interval between the years 45 and 50.[4] But this makes us all the more desirous to determine, by any reasonable conjectures, the movements of the Apostle in reference to a better chronology than that which reckons by successive years,—the chronology which furnishes us with the real imagery round his path,—the chronology of the seasons.

Now we may well suppose that he might sail from Seleucia to Salamis at the beginning of spring. In that age and in those waters, the commencement of a voyage was usually determined by the advance of the season. The sea was technically said to be "open" in the month of March.[5]

[1] Τὴν χώραν τὴν Σελγέων ὀρεινὴν· κρημνῶν καὶ χαραδρῶν οὖσαν πλήρη, ἃς ποιοῦσιν ἄλλοι τε ποταμοὶ, καὶ ὁ Εὐρυμέδων, καὶ ὁ Κέστρος, ἀπὸ τῶν Σελγικῶν ὀρῶν εἰς τὴν Παμφυλίαν ἐκπίπτοντες θάλατταν· γέφυραι δ' ἐπίκεινται ταῖς ὁδοῖς. Strabo, xii. 7.

[2] "About two hours and a half from Isbarta, towards the south-east, is the village of Sav, where is the source of a river called the Sav-Sou. Five hours and a half beyond, and still towards the south-east, is the village of *Paoli* (*St. Paul*), and here the river, which had continued its course so far, is lost in the mountains, &c." Arundell's Asia Minor, vol. ii. p. 31. Isbarta is near Sagalassus. The river is probably the Eurymedon. See Arundell's Map in the first volume.

[3] The descriptive passages which follow are chiefly borrowed from "Asia Minor, 1839," and "Lycia, 1841," by Sir C. Fellows, and "Travels in Lycia, 1847," by Lieutenant Spratt, R. N., and Professor E. Forbes. The writer desires also to acknowledge his obligations to various travellers, especially Professor Forbes, Mr. Falkener, and Dr. Wolff.

[4] See Wieseler, pp. 222–226. Anger, pp. 188, 189. The extent of the interval is much the same on Mr. Greswell's system (Diss. vol. iv. p. 138); on that of Mr. Browne (Ordo Sæclorum, p. 120) somewhat less.

[5] Ex die tertio iduum Novembris, usque in diem sextum iduum Martiarum, maria clauduntur. Nam lux minima noxque prolixa, nubium densitas, aeris obscuritas, ventorum imbrium, vel nivium geminata sævitia. Vegetius, quoted in Smith's "Shipwreck. &c.," p. 45. See Hor. Od. I. iv. III. vii.

If St. Paul began his journey in that month, the lapse of two months might easily bring him to Perga, and allow sufficient time for all that we are told of his proceedings at Salamis and Paphos. If we suppose him to have been at Perga in May, this would have been exactly the most natural time for a journey to the mountains. Earlier in the spring, the passes would have been filled with snow.[1] In the heat of summer the weather would have been less favourable for the journey. In the autumn the disadvantages would have been still greater, from the approaching difficulties of winter. But again, if St. Paul was at Perga in May, a further reason may be given why he did not stay there, but seized all the advantages of the season for prosecuting his journey to the interior. The habits of a people are always determined or modified by the physical peculiarities of their country; and a custom prevails among the inhabitants of this part of Asia Minor, which there is every reason to believe has been unbroken for centuries. At the beginning of the hot season they move up from the the plains to the cool basin-like hollows on the mountains. These *yailahs* or summer retreats are always spoken of with pride and satisfaction, and the time of the journey anticipated with eager delight. When the time arrives, the people may be seen ascending to the upper grounds, men, women, and children, with flocks and herds, camels and asses, like the patriarchs of old.[2] If then St. Paul was at Perga in May, he would find the inhabitants deserting its hot and silent streets. They would be moving in the direction of his own intended journey. He would be under no temptation to stay. And if we imagine him as joining[3] some such compa-

[1] "*March* 4.—The passes to the Yailahs from the upper part of the valley being still shut up by snow, we have no alternative but to prosecute our researches amongst the low country and valleys which border the coast."—Sp. and F. i. p. 48. The valley referred to is that of the Xanthus, in Lycia.

[2] "*April* 30.—We passed many families *en route* from Adalia to the mountain plains for the summer." Sp. and F. i. p. 242. Again, p. 248. (*May* 3.) See p. 57. During a halt in the valley of the Xanthus (*May* 10), Sir C. Fellows says that an almost uninterrupted train of cattle and people (nearly twenty families) passed by. "What a picture would Landseer make of such a pilgrimage. The snowy tops of the mountains were seen through the lofty and dark-green fir-trees, terminating in abrupt cliffs. . . . . From clefts in these gushed out cascades . . . and the waters were carried away by the wind in spray over the green woods. . . . In a zigzag course up the wood lay the track leading to the cool places. In advance of the pastoral groups were the straggling goats, browsing on the fresh blossoms of the wild almond as they passed. In more steady courses followed the small black cattle . . . then came the flocks of sheep, and the camels . . . bearing piled loads of ploughs, tent-poles, kettles . . . and amidst this rustic load was always seen the rich Turkey carpet and damask cushions, the pride even of the tented Turk." Lycia, pp. 238, 239.

[3] It has always been customary for travellers in Asia Minor, as in the patriarchal East, to join caravans if possible. So P. Lucas, on his second journey, waited at Broussa (ch. 13); and on another occasion at Smyrna (ch. 32), for the caravan going to Satalia (Attalcia); and on a later journey could not leave the caravan to visit some ruins between Broussa and Smyrna (i. 134).

ny of Pamphylian families on his way to the Pisidian mountains, it gives much interest and animation to the thought of this part of his progress.

Perhaps it was in such company that the Apostle entered the first passes of the mountainous district, along some road formed partly by artificial pavement, and partly by the native marble, with high cliffs frowning on either hand, with tombs and inscriptions, even then ancient, on the projecting rocks around, and with copious fountains bursting out "among thickets of pomegranates and oleanders."[1] The oleander, "the favourite flower of the Levantine midsummer," abounds in the lower watercourses, and in the month of May it borders all the banks with a line of brilliant crimson.[2] As the path ascends, the rocks begin to assume the wilder grandeur of mountains, the richer fruit-trees begin to disappear, and the pine and walnut succeed; though the plane-tree still stretches its wide leaves over the stream which dashes wildly down the ravine, crossing and recrossing the dangerous road.[3] The alteration of climate which attends on the traveller's progress, is soon perceptible. A few hours will make the difference of weeks or even months. When the corn is in the ear on the lowlands, ploughing and sowing are hardly well begun upon the highlands.

[1] In ascending from Limyra, a small plain on the coast not far from Phaselis, Spratt and Forbes mention "a rock-tablet with a long Greek inscription .. by the side of an ancient paved road, at a spot where numerous and copious springs gush out among thickets of pomegranates and oleanders." (i. p. 160.) Fellows, in coming to Attaleia from the north, "suddenly entered a pass between the mountains, which diminished in width until cliffs almost perpendicular inclosed us on either side. The descent became so abrupt that we were compelled to dismount and walk for two hours, during which time we continued rapidly descending an ancient paved road, formed principally of the native marble rock, but which had been perfected with large stones at a very remote age; the deep ruts of chariot-wheels were apparent in many places. The road is much worn by time; and the people of a later age, diverging from the track, have formed a road with stones very inferior both in size and arrangement. About half an hour before I reached the plain ... a view burst upon me through the cliffs ... I looked down from the rocky steps of the throne of winter upon the rich and verdant plain of summer, with the blue sea in the distance.... Nor was the foreground without its interest; on each projecting rock stood an ancient sarcophagus, and the trees half concealed the lids and broken sculptures of innumerable tombs." A. M. pp. 174, 175. This may very probably have been the pass and road by which St. Paul ascended. P. Lucas, on his second voyage (1705), met with a paved road between Buldur and Adalia. "Nous commençâmes à remonter, mais par un chemin magnifique et pavé de longues pierres de marbre blanc."—Ch. xxxiii. p. 310. See Gen. Koehler's Itinerary, in Leake's Asia Minor. "*March* 20 (16 *hours from Adalia*).—The two great ranges on the west and north of the plains now approach each other, and at length are only divided by the passes through which the river finds its way. The road, however, leaves this gorge to the right, and ascends the mountain by a paved winding causeway, a work of great labour and ingenuity. At the foot of it are ruins ... cornices, capitals, and fluted columns ... sarcophagi, with their covers beside them ... many with inscriptions." p. 134.

[2] See the excellent Chapter on the Botany of Lycia in Spratt and Forbes, vol. ii. ch. xiii.

[3] See the animated description of the ascent from Myra in Fellows' Lycia, p. 221.

Spring flowers may be seen in the mountains by the very edge of the snow,[1] when the anemone is withered in the plain, and the pink veins in the white asphodel flower are shrivelled by the heat. When the cottages are closed and the grass is parched, and everything is silent below in the purple haze and stillness of midsummer, clouds are seen drifting among the Pisidian precipices, and the cavern is often a welcome shelter from a cold and penetrating wind.[2] The upper part of this district is a wild region of cliffs, often isolated and bare, and separated from each other by valleys of sand, which the storm drives with blinding violence among the shivered points.[3] The trees become fewer and smaller at every step. Three belts of vegetation are successively passed through in ascending from the coast: first the oak woods, then the forests of pine, and lastly the dark scattered patches of the cedar-juniper:[4] and then we reach the treeless plains of the interior, which stretch in dreary extension to the north and the east.

After such a journey as this, separating, we know not where, from the companions they may have joined, and often thinking of that Christian companion who had withdrawn himself from their society when they needed him most, Paul and Barnabas emerged from the rugged mountain passes, and came upon the central table-land of Asia Minor. The whole interior region of the peninsula may be correctly described by this term; for, though intersected in various directions by mountain-ranges, it is, on the whole, a vast plateau, elevated higher than the summit of Ben Nevis above the level of the sea.[5] This is its general character, though a long journey across the district brings the traveller through many varieties of scenery. Sometimes he moves for hours along the dreary margin of an

1 "*May* 7.—Close to the snow many beautiful plants were in flower, especially *Anemone Appenina,* and several species of violet, squill, and fritillary." Sp. and F. i. p. 261. This was near Cibyra, "the Birmingham of Asia Minor." "*May* 9.—Ascending through a winterly climate, with snow by the side of our path, and only the crocus and anemones in bloom . . . we beheld a new series of cultivated plains to the west, being in fact table-lands, nearly upon a level with the tops of the mountains which form the eastern boundary of the valley of the Xanthus. . . . . Descending to the plain, probably 1000 feet, we pitched our tent, after a ride of 7¾ hours. . . . . Upon boiling the thermometer, I found that we were more than 4000 feet above the sea, and cutting down some dead trees, we provided against the coming cold of the evening by lighting three large fires around our encampment." Fell. Lycia, p. 234. This was in descending from Almalee, in the great Lycian yailah, to the south-east of Cibyra.

2 For further illustrations of the change of season caused by difference of elevation, see Sp. and F. i. p. 242. Again, p. 293, "Every step led us from spring into summer;" and the following pages. See also Fellows: "Two months since at Syra the corn was beginning to show the ear, whilst here they have only in a few places now begun to plough and sow." A. M. 158. "The corn, which we had the day before seen changing colour for the harvest, was here not an inch above the ground, and the buds of the bushes were not yet bursting." Lycia, p. 226.

3 See Sp. and F. i. pp. 195–202. Fell. A. M. pp. 165–174. Also Sp. and F. ii. ch. ix.

4 Sp. and F. ii. ch. xiii.

5 The yailah of Adalia is 3500 feet above the sea: Sp. and F. i. p. 244. The vast

inland sea of salt,[1]—sometimes he rests in a cheerful hospitable town by the shore of a freshwater lake.[2] In some places the ground is burnt and volcanic, in others green and fruitful. Sometimes it is depressed into watery hollows, where wild swans visit the pools, and storks are seen fishing and feeding among the weeds :[3] more frequently it is spread out into the broad open downs, like Salisbury Plain, which afford an interminable pasture for flocks of sheep.[4] To the north of Pamphylia, the elevated plain stretches through Phrygia for a hundred miles from Mount Olympus to Mount Taurus.[5] The southern portion of these bleak uplands was crossed by St. Paul's track, immediately before his arrival at Antioch, in Pisidia. The features of human life which he had around him are probably almost as unaltered as the scenery of the country,—dreary villages with flat-roofed huts and cattle-sheds in the day, and at night an encampment of tents of goats' hair,—tents of *cilicium* (see p. 47),—a blazing fire in the midst,—horses fastened around,—and in the distance the moon shining on the snowy summits of Taurus.[6]

The *Sultan Tareek*, or Turkish Royal Road from Adalia to Kiutayah and Constantinople, passes nearly due north by the beautiful lake of Buldur.[7] The direction of Antioch in Pisidia bears more to the east. After passing somewhere near Selge and Sagalassus, St. Paul approached by the margin of the much larger, though perhaps not less beautiful, lake of Eyerdir.[8] The position of the city is not far from the northern shore of this lake, at the base of a mountain range which stretches through Phrygia

plain, "at least 50 miles long and 20 wide," south of Kiutaya in Phrygia, is about 6000 feet above the sea. Fell. A. M. p. 155. This may be overstated, but the plain of Erzeroum is quite as much.

[1] We shall have occasion to mention the salt lakes hereafter.

[2] The two lakes of Buldur and Eyerdir are mentioned below. Both are described as very beautiful. The former is represented in the Map to the south of Lake Ascania, the latter is the large lake to the south of Antioch. That of Buldur is slightly brakish. Hamilton, I. 494.

[3] "*March* 27 (*near Kiutaya*).—I counted 180 storks fishing or feeding in one small swampy place not an acre in extent. The land here is used principally for breeding and grazing cattle, which are to be seen in herds of many hundreds." Fell. Asia Minor, p. 155. "*May* 8.—The shrubs are the rose, the barbary, and wild almond, but all are at present fully six weeks later than those in the country we have lately passed. I observed on the lake many stately wild swans, (*near Almalee,* 3000 feet above the sea)."—Fell. Lycia, p. 228.

[4] We shall have occasion to return presently to this character of much of the interior of Asia Minor when we come to the mention of Lycaonia (Acts xiv. 6).

[5] Fellows' Asia Minor, p. 155, &c.

[6] See Fellows' Asia Minor, p. 177, and especially the mention of the goats' hair tents.

[7] See above, n. 2.

[8] See the descriptions in Arundell's Asia Minor, ch. xiii., and especially ch. xv. It is singular that this sheet of water is unnoticed by the classical writers. Mr. Arundell is of opinion that it is the lake Pusgusa mentioned by Nicetas in his account of the war of John Commenus with the Turks of Iconium (Bonn. Ed. p. 50).

in a south-easterly direction. It is, however, not many years since the statement could be confidently made. Strabo, indeed, describes its position with remarkable clearness and precision. His words are as follows:— "In the district of Phrygia called Paroreia, there is a certain mountain-ridge, stretching from east to west. On each side there is a large plain below this ridge: and it has two cities in its neighbourhood; Philomelium on the north, and on the other side Antioch, called Antioch near Pisidia. The former lies entirely in the plain, the latter (which has a Roman colony) is on a height."[1] With this description before him, and taking into account certain indications of distance furnished by ancient authorities, Colonel Leake, who has perhaps done more for the elucidation of Classical Topography than any other man, felt that Ak-Sher, the position assigned to Antioch by D'Anville and other geographers, could not be the true place: Ak-Sher is on the north of the ridge, and the position could not be made to harmonise with the Tables.[2] But he was not in possession of any information which could lead him to the true position; and the problem remained unsolved till Mr. Arundell started from Smyrna, in 1833, with the deliberate purpose of discovering the scene of St. Paul's labours. He successfully proved that Ak-Sher is Philomelium, and that Antioch is at Jalobatch, on the other side of the ridge. The narrative of his successful journey is very interesting: and every Christian ought to sympathise in the pleasure with which, knowing that Antioch was seventy miles from Apamea, and forty-five miles from Apollonia, he first succeeded in identifying Apollonia; and then, exactly at the right distance, perceived, in the tombs near a fountain, and the vestiges of an ancient road, sure indications of his approach to a ruined city; and then saw, across the plain, the remains of an aqueduct at the base of the mountain; and, finally, arrived at Jalobatch, ascended to the elevation described by Strabo, and felt, as he looked on the superb ruins around, that he was "really on the spot consecrated by the labours and persecution of the Apostles Paul and Barnabas."[3]

The position of the Pisidian Antioch being thus determined by the convergence of ancient authority and modern investigation, we perceive that it lay on an important line of communication, westward by Apamea

[1] Ἡ παρώρεια ὀρεινήν τινα ἔχει ῥάχιν, ἀπὸ τῆς ἀνατολῆς ἐκτεινομένην ἐπὶ δύσιν· ταύτῃ δ' ἑκατέρωθεν ὑποπέπτωκε τὶ πεδίον μέγα, καὶ πόλεις πλησίον αὐτῆς, πρὸς ἄρκτον μὲν Φιλομήλιον, ἐκ θατέρου δὲ μέρους Ἀντιόχεια, ἡ πρὸς Πισιδίᾳ καλουμένη· ἡ μὲν, ἐν πεδίῳ κειμένη πᾶσα, ἡ δ' ἐπὶ λόφου, ἔχουσα ἐποικίαν Ῥωμαίων. xii. 8.

[2] See Leake's Asia Minor, p. 41. The same difficulties were perceived by Mannert, p. 179.

[3] See Arundell's Asia Minor, ch. xii. xiii. xiv. and the view. There is also a view in Laborde. The opinion of Mr. Arundell is fully confirmed by Mr. Hamilton. Researches in Asia Minor, vol. I. ch. xxvii. The aqueduct conveyed water to the town from the Sultan Dagh (Strabo's ὀρεινη ῥάχις).

with the valley of the Mæander, and eastward by Iconium with the coun try behind the Taurus. In this general direction, between Smyrna and Ephesus on the one hand, and the Cilician Gates which lead down tc Tarsus on the other, conquering armies and trading caravans, Persian satraps, Roman proconsuls, and Turkish pachas, have travelled for centuries.[1] The Pisidian Antioch was situated about half-way between these extreme points. It was built (as we have seen in an earlier chapter, IV. p. 122) by the founder of the Syrian Antioch; and in the age of the Greek kings of the line of Seleucus it was a town of considerable importance. But its appearance had been modified, since the campaigns of Scipio and Manlius, and the defeat of Mithridates,[2] by the introduction of Roman usages, and the Roman style of building. This was true to a certain extent, of all the larger towns of Asia Minor: but this change had probably taken place in the Pisidian Antioch, more than in many cities of greater importance; for, like Philippi,[3] it was a Roman *Colonia.*[4] Without delaying, at present, to explain the full meaning of this term, we may say that the character impressed on any town in the Empire which had been made subject to military colonisation was particularly *Roman*, and that all such towns were bound by a tie of peculiar closeness to the Mother City. The insignia of Roman power were displayed more conspicuously than in other towns in the same province. In the provinces where Greek was spoken, while other towns had Greek letters on their coins, the money of the colonies was distinguished by Latin superscriptions. Antioch must have had some eminence among the eastern colonies, for it was founded by Augustus, and called Cæsarea.[5] Such coins as those

COIN OF ANT. PIS.[6]

[1] In illustration of this we may refer to the caravan routes and Persian military roads as indicated in Kieppert's Hellas, to Xenophon's Anabasis, to Alexander's campaign and Cicero's progress, to the invasion of Tamerlane, and the movements of the Turkish and Egyptian armies in 1832 and 1833.

[2] See p. 14.

[3] Acts xvi. 12.

[4] Ἔχουσα ἐποικίαν Ῥωμαίων: Strabo xii. 8. Pisidarum colonia Cæsarea, eadem Antiochia: Plin. N. H. v. 24. In Pisidia juris Italici est colonia Antiochensium: Paulus in Digest. Lib. l. tit. xv. (de colonis et jure Italico).

[5] We should learn this from the inscription on the coins, COL. CÆS. ANTIOCHIÆ,

[6] From the British Museum.

COIN OF ANT. PI.[1]

described and represented on this page, were in circulation here, though not at Perga or Iconium, when St. Paul visited these cities: and, more than at any other city visited on this journey, he would hear Latin spoken side by side with the Greek, and the ruder Pisidian dialect.[2]

Along with this population of Greeks, Romans, and native Pisidians, a greater or smaller number of Jews was intermixed. They may not have been a very numerous body, for only one synagogue[3] is mentioned in the narrative. But it is evident, from the events recorded, that they were an influential body, that they had made many proselytes, and that they had obtained some considerable dominion (as in the parallel cases of Damascus recorded by Josephus,[4] and Berœa and Thessalonica in the Acts of the Apostles[5]) over the minds of the Gentile women.

On the sabbath days the Jews and the proselytes met in the synagogue. It is evident that at this time full liberty of public worship was permitted to the Jewish people in all parts of the Roman empire, whatever limitations might have been enacted by law or compelled by local opposition, as relates to the form and situation of the synagogues. We infer from Epiphanius that the Jewish places of worship were often erected in open and conspicuous positions.[6] This natural wish may frequently

if we did not learn it from Pliny, quoted in the preceding note. Mr. Hamilton found an inscription at Yalobatch, with the letters ANTIOCH EAE CAESARE. (p. 474.)

1 From the British Museum.

2 Strabo, speaking of Cibyra in Lycia, says, *τέτταρσι γλώτταις ἐχρῶντο οἱ Κιβυράται, τῇ Πισιδικῇ, τῇ Σολύμων, τῇ Ἑλληνίδι, τῇ Λυδῶν.* xiii. 4. Again, he mentions thirteen "barbarous" tribes as opposed to the Greeks, and among these the Pisidians. xiv. 5. We shall have to return to this subject of language again, in speaking of the speech of Lycaonia." Acts xiv. 11.

3 See remarks on Salamis, p. 141.

4 The people of Damascus were obliged to use caution in their scheme of assassinating the Jews;—*ἐδεδοίκεσαν γὰρ τὰς ἑαυτῶν γυναῖκας ἁπάσας πλὴν ὀλίγων ὑπηγμένας τῇ Ἰουδαϊκῇ θρησκείᾳ.* B. J. ii. 20, 2.

5 Acts xvii. 4. 12.

6 He is speaking of the synagogue at Nablous, and says: *Προσευχῆς τόπος ἐν Σικίμοις, ἐν τῇ νυνὶ καλουμένῃ Νεαπόλει, ἔξω τῆς πόλεως ἐν τῇ πεδιάδι ὡς ἀπὸ σημείων δύο, θεατροειδής, οὕτως ἐν ἀέρι καὶ αἰθρίῳ τόπῳ ἐστὶ κατασκευασθεὶς ὑπὸ τῶν Σαμαρειτῶν*

have been checked by the influence of the heathen priests, who would not willingly see the votaries of an ancient idolatry forsaking the temple for the synagogue: and feelings of the same kind may probably have hindered the Jews, even if they had the ability or desire, from erecting religious edifices of any remarkable grandeur and solidity. No ruins of the synagogues of imperial times have remained to us, like those of the temples in every province, from which we are able to convince ourselves of the very form and size of the sanctuaries of Jupiter, Apollo, and Diana. There is little doubt that the sacred edifices of the Jews have been modified by the architecture of the remote countries through which they have been dispersed, and the successive centuries through which they have continued a separate people. Under the Roman Empire it is natural to suppose that they must have varied, according to circumstances, through all gradations of magnitude and decoration, from the simple *proseucha* at Philippi[1] to the magnificent prayer-houses at Alexandria.[2] Yet there are certain traditional peculiarities which have doubtless united together by a common resemblance the Jewish synagogues of all ages and countries.[3] The arrangement for the women's places in a separate gallery, or behind a partition of lattice-work,[4]—the desk in the centre, where the Reader, like Ezra in ancient days, from his "pulpit of wood," may "open the book in the sight of all the people . . . and read in the book the law of God distinctly, and give the sense, and cause them to understand the reading,"[5]—the carefully closed Ark on the one side of the building nearest to Jerusalem, for the preservation of the rolls or manuscripts of the Law,[6]—the seats all round the building, whence "the eyes of all them that are in the synagogue" may be "fastened" on him who speaks,[7]—the "chief seats,"[8] which were appropriated to the "ruler" or "rulers" of the synagogue, according as its organisation might be more or less complete,[9] and which were so dear to the hearts of those who professed to be

πάντα τὰ τῶν Ἰουδαίων μιμουμένων.—Hær. lxxx. 1. Frequently they were built by the waterside for the sake of ablution. Compare Acts xvi. 13 with Joseph. Ant. xiv. 10, 23.

1 Acts xvi. 13. The question of the identity or difference of the *proseucha* and *synagogue* will be considered hereafter. Probably προσευχή is a general term. See Juv. Sat. iii. 296. Joseph. Vit. § 54. We find in Philo the words προσευκτήριον (de Vit. Mos. iii. 685) and συναγώγιον (Legat. p. 1035).

2 See Philo Legat. ad Cai. p. 1011.

3 Besides the works referred to in the notes to Ch. II., Allen's "Modern Judaism" and Bernard's "Synagogue and Church" may be consulted with advantage on subjects connected with the synagogue.

4 See Philo, as referred to by Winer.

5 Nehem. viii. 4–8.

6 This "Armarium Judaicum" is mentioned by Tertullian. De Cultu Fœm. i. 3.

7 See Luke iv. 20.

8 These πρωτοκαθέδριαι (Mat. xxiii. 6) seem to have faced the rest of the congregation. See Jam. ii. 3.

9 Ἀρχισυναγωγός, Luke xiii. 14. Acts xviii. 8. 17. πρεσβύτεροι, Luke vii. 3. ἀρχισυναγωγοί, Mark v. 22. Acts xiii. 15. Some are of opinion that the smaller synagogue

peculiarly learned or peculiarly devout,—these are some of the features of a synagogue, which agree at once with the notices of Scripture, the descriptions in the Talmud, and the practice of modern Judaism.

The meeting of the congregations in the ancient synagogues may be easily realised, if due allowance be made for the change of costume, by those who have seen the Jews at their worship in the large towns of Modern Europe. On their entrance into the building, the four-cornered Tallith [1] was first placed like a veil over the head, or like a scarf over the shoulders. The prayers were then recited by an officer called the "Angel," or "Apostle," of the Assembly.[2] These prayers were doubtless many of them identically the same with those which are found in the present service-books of the German and Spanish Jews, though their liturgies, in the course of ages, have undergone successive developments, the steps of which are not easily ascertained. It seems that the prayers were sometimes read in the vernacular language [3] of the country where the synagogue was built; but the Law was always read in Hebrew. The sacred roll [4] of manuscript was handed from the Ark to the Reader by the Chazan, or "Minister;" [5] and then certain portions were read according to a fixed cycle, first from the Law and then from the Prophets. It is impossible to determine the period when the sections from these two divisions of the Old Testament were arranged as in use at present; [6] but the same necessity for translation and explanation existed then as now. The Hebrew and English are now printed in parallel columns. Then, the reading of the Hebrew was elucidated by the Targum or the Septuagint, or followed by a paraphrase in the spoken language of the country.[7] The Reader stood [8] while thus employed, and all the congregation sat around. The manuscript was rolled up and returned to the Chazan.[9]

had one "ruler," the larger many. It is more probable that the "chief ruler" with the "elders" formed a congregational council, like the kirk-session in Scotland.

1 The use of the Tallith is said to have arisen from the Mosaic commandment directing that fringes should be worn on the four corners of the garment.

2 "R. Gamaliel dicit: Legatus ecclesiæ fungitur officio pro omnibus, et officio hoc rite perfunctus omnes ab obligatione liberat." Vitringa, who compares Rev. ii. 1.

3 See Winer's Realwörterbuch, art. Synagogen.

4 See the words *ἀναπτύξας* and *πτύξας*, Luke iv. 17, 20. In 1 Mac. iii. 48 the phrase is *ἐξεπέτασαν τὸ βίβλιον τοῦ νόμου.*

5 Luke iv. 17, 20.

6 A full account both of the *Paraschioth* or Sections of the Law, and the *Haphtaroth* or Sections of the Prophets, as used both by the Portuguese and German Jews, may be seen in Horne's Introduction, vol. iii. pp. 254–258.

7 See pp. 35, 36. In Palestine the Syro-Chaldaic language would be used; in the Dispersion, usually the Greek. Lightfoot (Exerc. on Acts) seems to think that the Pisidian language was used here. See the passage of Strabo quoted above.

8 'Αναστὰς, Acts xiii. 16. On the other hand, *ἐκάθισε* is said of Our Lord's solemn teaching, Luke iv. 20.

9 See Luke iv. 20.

Then followed a pause, during which strangers or learned men, who had "any word of consolation" or exhortation, rose and addressed the meeting. And thus, after a pathetic enumeration of the sufferings of the chosen people [1] or an allegorical exposition [2] of some dark passage of Holy Writ, the worship was closed with a benediction and a solemn "Amen." [3]

To such a worship in such a building a congregation came together at Antioch in Pisidia, on the sabbath which immediately succeeded the arrival of Paul and Barnabas. Proselytes came and seated themselves with the Jews: and among the Jewesses behind the lattice were "honourable women" [4] of the colony. The two strangers entered the synagogue, and, wearing the Tallith, which was the badge of an Israelite,[5] "sat down" [6] with the rest. The prayers were recited, the extracts from "the Law and the Prophets" were read; [7] the "Book" returned to the "Minister," [8] and then we are told that "the rulers of the synagogue" sent to the new comers, on whom many eyes had already been fixed, and invited them to address the assembly, if they had words of comfort or instruction to speak to their fellow Israelites.[9] The very attitude of St. Paul, as he answered the invitation, is described to us. He "rose" from his seat, and with the animated and emphatic gesture which he used on other occasions,[10] "beckoned with his hand." [11]

After thus graphically bringing the scene before our eyes, St. Luke gives us, if not the whole speech delivered by St. Paul, yet at least the substance of what he said. For into however short a space he may have condensed the speeches which he reports, yet it is no mere outline, no dry analysis of them which he gives. He has evidently preserved, if not *all* the words, yet the *very* words uttered by the Apostle; nor can we fail to recognise in all these speeches a tone of thought, and even of expression, which stamps them with the individuality of the speaker.

On the present occasion we find St. Paul beginning his address by connecting the Messiah whom he preached, with the preparatory dispensation which ushered in His advent. He dwells upon the previous history of the Jewish people, for the same reasons which had led St. Stephen to

[1] The sermon in the synagogue in "Helon's pilgrimage" is conceived in the true Jewish feeling. Compare the address of St. Stephen.

[2] We see how an inspired Apostle uses allegory. Gal. iv. 21–31.

[3] See Neh. viii. 6. 1 Cor. xiv. 16. [4] Acts xiii. 50.

[5] "As I entered the synagogue [at Blidah in Algeria], they offered me a Tallith, saying in French, 'Etes-vous Israëlite?' I could not wear the Tallith, but I opened my English Bible and *sat down*, thinking of Paul and Barnabas at Antioch in Pisidia." —Extract from a private journal.

[6] Acts xiii. 14. [7] Acts xiii. 15. [8] Luke iv. 20.

[9] *Λόγος παρακλήσεως*. Acts xiii. 15.

[10] *Ἐκτείνας τὴν χεῖρα*. Acts xxvi. 1. *Κατέσεισε τῇ χειρὶ τῷ λαῷ*. xxi. 40. *Αἱ χεῖρες αὗται*. xx. 34.

[11] Acts xiii. 16.

do the like in his defence before the Sanhedrin. He endeavours to conciliate the minds of his Jewish audience by proving to them that the Messiah whom he proclaimed, was the same whereto their own prophets bare witness; come, not to destroy the law, but to fulfil; and that His advent had been duly heralded by His predicted messenger. He then proceeds to remove the prejudice which the rejection of Jesus by the authorities at Jerusalem (the metropolis of their faith) would naturally raise in the minds of the Pisidian Jews against His divine mission. He shows that Christ's death and resurrection had accomplished the ancient prophecies, and declares this to be the "glad tiding" which the Apostles were charged to proclaim. Thus far the speech contains nothing which could offend the exclusive spirit of Jewish nationality. On the contrary, St. Paul has endeavoured to carry his hearers with him by the topics on which he has dwelt; the Saviour whom he declares is "a Saviour unto Israel;" the Messiah whom he announces is the fulfiller of the Law and the Prophets. But having thus conciliated their feelings, and won their favourable attention, he proceeds in a bolder tone, to declare the Catholicity of Christ's salvation, and the antithesis between the Gospel and the Law. His concluding words, as St. Luke relates them, might stand as a summary representing in outline the early chapters of the Epistle to the Romans; and therefore, conversely, those chapters will enable us to realise the manner in which St. Paul would have expanded the heads of argument which his disciple here records. The speech ends with a warning against the bigoted rejection of Christ's doctrine, which this latter portion of the address was so likely to call forth.

The following were the words (so far as they have been preserved to us) spoken by St. Paul on this memorable occasion:—

Address to Jews and Proselytes.

"Men of Israel, and ye, proselytes of the Gentiles, who worship the God of Abraham, give audience.

God's choice of Israel to be His people, and of David to be the progenitor of the Messiah.

"The God of this people Israel chose our fathers, and raised them up into a mighty nation, when they dwelt as strangers in the land of Egypt; and with an high arm brought He them out therefrom. And about the time of forty years, even as a nurse beareth her child, so bare He them[1] through the wilderness. And He destroyed

[1] The beauty of this metaphor has been lost to the authorized version on account of the reading (ἐτροποφόρησεν instead of ἐτροφοφόρησεν) adopted in the Textus Receptus. Griesbach, Scholz, and Lachman restored the latter reading, on the authority of the Uncial MSS., A. C. E. We regret to see that Tischendorf has reinstated the former reading (because it has a somewhat greater weight of MSS. of the Greek Testament in its favour), without taking into account the evident allusion to Deut. i. 31 where τροφοφορῆσαι is acknowledged to be the correct reading.

seven nations in the land of Canaan, and gave their land as a portion unto His people. And after that He gave unto them Judges about the space[1] of four hundred and fifty years, until Samuel the Prophet; then desired they a king, and He gave unto them Saul, the son of Cis, a man of the tribe of Benjamin, to rule them forty years. And when He had removed Saul, He raised up unto them David to be their king; to whom also He gave testimony, and said: *I have found David, the son of Jesse, a man after my own heart, which shall fulfil all my will.*[2] Of this man's seed hath God, according to His promise, raised unto Israel a Saviour Jesus.

John the Baptist was His predicted forerunner.

"And John was *the messenger who went before His face*[3] *to prepare His way before Him*, and he preached the baptism of repentance to all the people of Israel. And as John fulfilled his course his[4] saying was, 'Whom think ye that I am? I am not He. But behold there cometh one after me whose shoes' latchet I am not worthy to loose.'

The rulers of Jerusalem fulfilled the Prophets by causing the death of Jesus.

"Men and Brethren, whether ye be children of the stock of Abraham, or proselytes of the Gentiles, to you hath been sent the tiding of this salvation, which Jerusalem hath cast out: for the inhabitants thereof, and their rulers, because they knew Him not, nor yet the voices of the prophets which are read in their synagogues every Sabbath day, have fulfilled the Scriptures in condemning Him. And though they found in Him no cause of death, yet desired they Pilate that He should be slain. And when they had fulfilled all which was written of Him, they took Him down from the tree, and laid Him in a sepulchre.

HIS RESURRECTION.

"But God raised Him from the dead.

Attested by

"And He was seen for many days by them who

[1] We need not trouble our readers with the difficulties which have been raised concerning the chronology of this passage. Supposing it could be proved that St. Paul's knowledge of ancient chronology was imperfect, this need not surprise us; for there seems no reason to suppose (and we have certainly no right to assume *à priori*) that divine inspiration would instruct the Apostles in truth discoverable by uninspired research, and non-essential to their religious mission.

[2] Compare Ps. lxxxix. 20, with 1 Sam. xiii. 14.

[3] Mal. iii. 1, as quoted Mat. xi. 10, not exactly after the LXX., but with *πρὸ προσώπου* introduced, as here, according to the literal translation of the Hebrew לִפְנֵי.

[4] Observe *ἔλεγε* not *ἔλεξε*, and *ἐπλήρου* not *ἐπλήρωσε*.

came up with Him from Galilee to Jerusalem, who are now[1] His witnesses to the people of Israel.[2]

many witnesses.

"And while they[3] proclaim it in Jerusalem, we declare unto you the same Glad Tiding concerning the promise which was made to our fathers; even that God hath fulfilled the same unto us their children, in that He hath raised up Jesus from the dead;[4] as it is also written in the second psalm, *Thou art my Son, this day have I begotten thee.*[5] And whereas He hath raised Him from the grave, no more to return unto corruption, He hath said on this wise, *The blessings of David will I give you, even the blessings which stand fast in holiness.*[6] Wherefore it is written also in another psalm, *Thou shalt not suffer thine Holy One to see corruption.*[7] Now David, after he had ministered in his own generation to the will of God, fell asleep, and was laid unto his fathers, and saw corruption; but He whom God raised from the dead saw no corruption.

The Glad Tiding of the Apostles is the announcement that Christ's resurrection had fulfilled God's promises.

"Be it known unto you, therefore, men and brethren, that through this Jesus is declared unto you the forgiveness of sins. And in Him all who have faith are justified from all transgressions, wherefrom in the Law of Moses ye could not be justified.[8]

Catholicity of Christ's salvation. Antithesis between the Gospel and the Law.

"Beware, therefore, lest that come upon you which is spoken in the Prophets, *Behold, ye despisers, and wonder, and perish; for I work a work in your days, a work which ye shall in no wise believe, though a man declare it unto you.*"[9]

Final warning.

This address made a deep and thrilling impression on the audience. While the congregation were pouring out of the synagogue, many of

[1] This νῦν, which is here very important, is erroneously omitted by the Textus Receptus.

[2] 'Ο λαός always means the *Jewish* people.

[3] Observe ἡμεῖς ὑμας, emphatically contrasted with the preceding οἵτινες . . . πρὸς τὸν λαόν (Humphry).

[4] 'Αναστήσας scilicet ἐκ νεκρῶν (De Wette). We cannot agree with Mr. Humphry that it can here (consistently with the context) have the same meaning as in vii. 37.

[5] Ps. ii. 7.

[6] Isaiah lv. 3; observe τὰ ὅσια, and compare with τὸν ὅσιον, which follows.

[7] Ps. xvi. 10.

[8] We are here reminded of the arguments of St. Peter on the day of Pentecost, just as the beginning of the speech recals that of St. Stephen before the Sanhedrin. Possibly, St. Paul himself had been an auditor of the first, as he certainly was of the last.

[9] Habak. i. 5.

them[1] crowded round the speaker, begging that "these words," which had moved their deepest feelings, might be repeated to them on their next occasion of assembling together.[2] And when at length the mass of the people had dispersed, singly or in groups, to their homes, many of the Jews and proselytes still clung to Paul and Barnabas, who earnestly exhorted them (in the form of expression which we could almost recognise as St. Paul's, from its resemblance to the phraseology of his Epistles,) "to abide in the grace of God."[3]

"With what pleasure can we fancy the Apostles to have observed these hearers of the Word, who seemed to have heard it in such earnest. How gladly must they have talked with them,—entered into various points more fully than was possible in any public address,—appealed to them in various ways which no one can touch upon who is speaking to a mixed multitude. Yet with all their pleasure and their hope, their knowledge of man's heart must have taught them not to be over confident; and therefore they would earnestly urge them to continue in the grace of God; to keep up the impression which had already outlasted their stay within the synagogue;—to feed it, and keep it alive, and make it deeper and deeper, that it should remain with them for ever. What the issue was we know not,—nor does that concern us,—only we may be sure that here, as in other instances, there were some in whom their hopes and endeavours were disappointed; there were some in whom they were to their fullest extent realised."[4]

The intervening week between this Sabbath and the next had not only its days of meeting in the synagogue,[5] but would give many opportunities for exhortation and instruction in private houses; the doctrine would be noised abroad, and, through the proselytes, would come to the hearing of the Gentiles. So that "on the following Sabbath almost the whole city came together to hear the Word of God." The synagogue was crowded.[6] Multitudes of Gentiles were there in addition to the proselytes. This was

[1] The words *τὰ ἔθνη* ("Gentiles," Eng. Trans.) in the Textus Receptus have caused a great confusion in this passage. They are omitted in the best MSS. The authorities may be seen in Tischendorf. See below, p. 183, note.

[2] It is not quite certain whether we are to understand *εἰς τὸ μεταξὺ σάββατον* (xiii. 42) to mean "the next Sabbath" (like *τῷ ἐρχομένῳ σαββάτῳ*, v. 44), or some *intermediate* days of meeting during the week. The Jews were accustomed to meet in the synagogues on Monday and Thursday as well as on Saturday. Rabbinical authorities attribute this arrangement to Ezra. These intermediate days (*Zwischentage*) were called ימים שבינתיים. Hence the Greek *μεταξύ*, used by the Hellenistic Jews, which Hesychius explains by *μετ' ὀλίγον, ἀνὰ μέσον*. See Schöttgen, Horæ Hebraicæ, and Nork's Rabbinische Quellen u. Parallelen, Leips. 1839.

[3] *Ἔπειθον αὐτοὺς ἐπιμένειν τῇ χάριτι τοῦ Θεοῦ.* xiii. 43. Compare Acts xx. 24. 1 Cor. xv. 10. 2 Cor. vi. 1. Gal. ii. 21.

[4] Dr. Arnold's Twenty-fourth Sermon on the Interpretation of Scripture.

[5] See above, note 2.

[6] Acts xiii. 44.

more than the Jews could bear. Their spiritual pride and exclusive bigotry was immediately roused. They could not endure the notion of others being freely admitted to the same religious privileges with themselves. This was always the sin of the Jewish people. Instead of realising their position in the world as the prophetic nation for the good of the whole earth, they indulged the self-exalting opinion, that God's highest blessings were only for themselves. Their oppressions and their dispersions had not destroyed this deeply-rooted prejudice; but they rather found comfort under the yoke, in brooding over their religious isolation: and even in their remote and scattered settlements, they clung with the utmost tenacity to the feeling of their exclusive nationality. Thus, in the Pisidian Antioch, they who on one Sabbath had listened with breathless interest to the teachers who spoke to them of the promised Messiah, were on the next Sabbath filled with the most excited indignation, when they found that this Messiah was "a light to lighten the Gentiles," as well as "the glory of His people Israel." They made an uproar, and opposed the words of Paul[1] with all manner of calumnious expressions, "contradicting and blaspheming."

And then the Apostles, promptly recognising in the willingness of the Gentiles and the unbelief of the Jews the clear indications of the path of duty, followed that bold[2] course which was alien to all the prejudices of a Jewish education. They turned at once and without reserve to the Gentiles. St. Paul was not unprepared for the events which called for this decision. The prophetic intimations at his first conversion, his vision in the Temple at Jerusalem, his experience at the Syrian Antioch, his recent success in the island of Cyprus, must have led him to expect the Gentiles to listen to that message which the Jews were too ready to scorn. The words with which he turned from his unbelieving countrymen were these: "It was needful that the Word of God should first be spoken unto you: but inasmuch as ye reject it, and deem yourselves unworthy of eternal life, lo! we turn to the Gentiles." And then he quotes a prophetical passage from their own Sacred Writings. "For thus hath the Lord commanded us, saying, I have set thee for a light to the Gentiles, that thou shouldest be for salvation to the ends of the earth."[3] This is the first recorded instance of a scene which was often reenacted. It is the course which St. Paul himself defines in his Epistle to the Romans, when he describes the Gospel as coming first to the Jew and then to the Gentile;[4]

[1] Τοῖς ὑπὸ τοῦ Παύλου λεγομένοις, xiii. 45. This implies indirectly that Paul was the "chief speaker," as we are told, xiv. 12.

[2] Παῤῥησιασάμενοι. Compare ἐπαῤῥησιασάμεθα, 1 Thess. ii. 2, where the circumstances appear to have been very similar.

[3] Isai. xlix. 6, quoted with a slight variation from the LXX. See Isai. xlii. 6. Luke ii. 32.

[4] Rom. i. 16. ii. 9. Compare xi. 12, 25.

and it is the course which he followed himself on various occasions of his life, at Corinth,[1] at Ephesus,[2] and at Rome.[3]

That which was often obscurely foretold in the Old Testament,—that those should "seek after God who knew Him not," and that He should be honoured by "those who were not a people:"[4]—that which had already seen its first fulfilment in isolated cases during Our Lord's life, as in the centurion and the Syrophenican woman, whose faith had no parallel in all the people of "Israel:"[5]—that which had received an express accomplishment through the agency of two of the chiefest of the Apostles, in Cornelius, the Roman officer at Cæsarea, and in Sergius Paulus, the Roman governor at Paphos,—began now to be realised on a large scale in a whole community. While the Jews blasphemed and rejected Christ, the Gentiles "rejoiced and glorified the Word of God" The counsels of God were not frustrated by the unbelief of His chosen people. A new "Israel," a new "election," succeeded to the former.[6] A church was formed of united Jews and Gentiles; and all who were destined to enter the path of eternal life[7] were gathered into the Catholic[8] brotherhood of the hitherto separated races. The synagogue had rejected the inspired missionaries, but the apostolic instruction went on in some private house or public building belonging to the heathen. And gradually the knowledge of Christianity began to be disseminated through the whole vicinity.[9]

The enmity of the Jews, however, was not satisfied by the expulsion of the Apostles from the synagogue. What they could not accomplish by violence and calumny, they succeeded in effecting by a pious intrigue. That influence of women in religious questions, to which our attention will be repeatedly called hereafter, is here for the first time brought before our notice in the sacred narrative of St. Paul's life. Strabo, who was intimately acquainted with the social position of the female sex in the towns of Western Asia, speaks in strong terms of the power which they possessed and exercised in controlling and modifying the religious opinions of the men.[10] This general fact received one of its most striking illustrations in

1 Acts xviii. 6.
2 Acts xix. 9.
3 Acts xxviii. 28.
4 See Hosea i. 10. ii. 23, as quoted in Rom. ix. 25, 26.
5 Mat. viii. 5–10. xv. 21–28.
6 See Rom. xi. 7, and Gal. vi. 16.

7 *'Επίστευσαν ὅσοι ἦσαν τεταγμένοι εἰς ζωὴν αἰώνιον.* xiii. 48. It is well known that this passage has been made the subject of much controversy with reference to the doctrine of predestination. Its bearing on the question is very doubtful. See how *διατεταγμένος* is used, Acts xx. 13. On the other hand, see *τὸ διαδεταγμένον*, Luke iii. 13, and *τεταγμέναι*, Rom. xiii. 1. For Markland's translation, "fidem professi sunt, quotquot (tempus, diem) constituerant, in vitam æternam," see Winer's Grammatik, p. 304.

8 Mr. Tate (Cont. Hist. p. 19) says, that this was "the first Christian church, gathered in part from among the idolatrous Gentiles." This is on the supposition that the *'Ελληνες* (Acts xi. 20, 21) were all "Greek proselytes."

9 Acts xiii. 49.

10 *῞Απαντες τῆς δεισιδαιμονίας ἀρχηγοὺς οἴονται τὰς γυναῖκας· αὗται δὲ καὶ τοὺς ἄνδρας*

the case of Judaism. We have already more than once alluded to the influence of the female proselytes at Damascus:[1] and the good services which women contributed towards the early progress of Christianity is abundantly known both from the Acts and the Epistles.[2] Here they appear in a position less honourable, but not less influential. The Jews contrived, through the female proselytes at Antioch, to win over to their cause some ladies of high respectability, and through them to gain the ear of men who occupied a position of eminence in the city. Thus a systematic persecution was excited against Paul and Barnabas. Whether the supreme magistrates of the colony were induced by this unfair agitation to pass a sentence of formal banishment, we are not informed;[3] but for the present the Apostles were compelled to retire from the colonial limits.

In cases such as these, instructions had been given by our Lord Himself how His Apostles were to act. During His life on earth, He had said to the Twelve, "Whosoever shall not receive you, nor hear you, when ye depart thence, shake off the dust under your feet for a testimony against them. Verily, I say unto you, it shall be more tolerable for Sodom and Gomorrah in the day of judgment, than for that city."[4] And while Paul and Barnabas thus fulfilled Our Lord's words, shaking off from their feet the dust of the dry and sunburnt road,[5] in token of God's judgment on wilful unbelievers, and turning their steps eastwards in the direction of Lycaonia, another of the sayings of Christ was fulfilled, in the midst of those who had been obedient to the faith: "Blessed are ye, when men shall revile you and persecute you, and shall say all manner of evil against you falsely, for my sake. Rejoice and be exceeding glad: for great is your reward in heaven; for so persecuted they the prophets which were before you."[6] Even while their faithful teachers were removed from them, and travelling across the bare uplands[7] which separate

προκαλοῦνται, πρὸς τὰς ἐπὶ πλέον θεραπείας τῶν θεῶν, καὶ ἑορτὰς καὶ ποτνιασμούς. vii. 3.

1 See above, p. 19, and p. 171, n. 4.

2 See Acts xvi. 14. xvii. 2. Philipp. iv. 3. 1 Cor. vii. 16.

3 We should rather infer the contrary, since they revisited the place on their return from Derbe (xiv. 21).

4 Mark vi. 11. Matt. x. 14, 15. Luke ix. 5. For other symbolical acts expressing the same thing, see Nehem. v. 13. Acts xviii. 6. It was taught in the schools of the Scribes that the dust of a heathen land defiled by the touch. Lightf. on Matt. x. 14, and Harm. of N. T., Acts xiv. Hence the shaking of the dust off the feet implied that the city was regarded as profane.

5 "Literally may they have shaken off the dust of their feet, for even now (Nov. 9) the roads abound with it, and in the summer months it must be a plain of dust." Arundell's Asia Minor, vol. i. p. 319.

6 Matt. v. 11, 12.

7 Leake approached Iconium from the northern side of the mountains which separate Antioch from Philomelium (see p. 169). He says: "On the descent from a ridge branching eastward from these mountains, we came in sight of the vast plain around

Antioch from the plain of Iconium, the disciples of the former city received such manifest tokens of the love of God, and the power of the "Holy Ghost," that they were "filled with joy" in the midst of persecution.

Iconium has obtained a place in history far more distinguished than that of the Pisidian Antioch. It is famous as the cradle of the rising power of the conquering Turks.[1] And the remains of its Mahomedan architecture still bear a conspicuous testimony to the victories and strong government of a tribe of Tartar invaders. But there are other features in the view of modern *Konieh* which to us are far more interesting. To the traveller in the footsteps of St. Paul, it is not the armorial bearings of the Knights of St. John, carved over the gateways in the streets of Rhodes, which arrest the attention, but the ancient harbour and the view across the sea to the opposite coast. And at Konieh his interest is awakened, not by minarets and palaces and Saracenic gateways, but by the vast plain and the distant mountains.[2]

These features remain what they were in the first century, while the town has been repeatedly destroyed and rebuilt, and its architectural character entirely altered. Little, if anything, remains of Greek or Roman Iconium, if we except the ancient inscriptions and the fragments of sculptures which are built into the Turkish walls.[3] At a late period of the Empire it was made a Colonia, like its neighbour, Antioch: but it was not so in the time of St. Paul.[4] There is no reason to suppose that its

Konieh, and of the lake which occupies the middle of it; and we saw the city with its mosques and ancient walls, still at the distance of twelve or fourteen miles from us." p. 45. Ainsworth travelled in the same direction, and says: "We travelled three hours along the plain of Konieh, always in sight of the city of the Sultans of Roum, before we reached it." Trav. in Asia Minor, II. p. 58. P. Lucas, who approached from Eregli, beyond Lystra and Derbe (see below), speaks of Iconium as "presque au bout de la plaine." Second Voyage, ch. xx.

[1] Iconium was the capital of the Seljukian Sultans, and had a great part in the growth of the Ottoman empire.

[2] "Konieh extends to the east and south over the plain far beyond the walls, which are about two miles in circumference. . . . . Mountains covered with snow rise on every side, excepting towards the east, where a plain, as flat as the desert of Arabia, extends far beyond the reach of the eye." Capt. Kinneir.

[3] "The city wall is said to have been erected by the Seljukian Sultans: it seems to have been built from the ruins of more ancient buildings, as broken columns, capitals, pedestals, bas-reliefs, and other pieces of sculpture, contribute towards its construction. It has eighty gates, of a square form, each known by a separate name, and, as well as most of the towers, embellished with Arabic inscriptions. . . . I observed a few Greek characters on the walls, but they were in so elevated a situation that I could not decypher them." Capt. Kinneir. See Col. Leake's description; and also the recently published work of Col. Chesney (1850) on the Euphrates Expedition, vol. i. p. 348, 349.

[4] Hence we have placed this coin of Iconium in the note, lest the Latin letters and the word COL. should lead the reader to suppose its political condition in the time of St. Paul resembled that of Antioch in Pisidia. (See p. 170, note.) These coins were

character was different from that of the other important towns on the principal lines of communication through Asia Minor. The elements of its population would be as follows :—a large number of trifling and frivolous Greeks, whose principal places of resort would be the theatre and the market-place ; some remains of a still older population, coming in occasionally from the country, or residing in a separate quarter of the town : some few Roman officials, civil or military, holding themselves proudly aloof from the inhabitants of the subjugated province ; and an old established colony of Jews, who exercised their trade during the week, and met on the Sabbath to read the law in the Synagogue.

The same kind of events took place here as in Antioch, and almost in the same order.[1] The Apostles went first to the Synagogue, and the effect of their discourses there was such, that great numbers both of the Jews and Greeks (*i. e.* proselytes or heathens, or both[2]) believed the Gospel. The unbelieving Jews raised up an indirect persecution by exciting the minds of the Gentile population against those who received the Christian doctrine. But the Apostles persevered and lingered in the city some considerable time, having their confidence strengthened by the miracles[3] which God worked through their instrumentality, in attestation of the truth of His Word. There is an apocryphal narrative of certain events assigned to this residence at Iconium :[4] and we may innocently adopt so

COIN OF ICONIUM.

not found before the reign of Gallienus, and Iconium is not mentioned by any writer as a Colonia ; hence Mannert (p. 195) conjectures that it was made a garrison-town and took the title as an empty honour. Mythological derivations were suggested by the ancients for the name : thus it was said that after the deluge Prometheus and Minerva made images of clay (*εἰκόνια*), and breathed life into them. Hence, says Stephanus Byzantinus, it ought to be written Εἰκόνιον (*ἔδει διὰ διφθόγγου*), as it is sometimes on coins. Another story (Eustath. in Dionys. Perieg. v. 856) is connected with an image of Medusa set up by Perseus. For the relation of the city to Lycaonia in Phrygia, see below, p. 186, n. 3.

1 See Acts xiv. 1–5.

2 Perhaps Ἑλλήνων (v. 1) may mean "proselytes," as opposed to "Gentiles," ἐθνῶν (v. 2).

3 The distinct appeal to miracles (v. 3) should be especially noticed.

4 It would have been a mischievous confusion of history and legend to have introduced St. Thecla of Iconium into the text. But her story has so prominent a place in all Roman Catholic histories, that it cannot be altogether omitted. See Baronius (sub anno 47), Fleury (i. 28), and Röhrbacher (Hist. de l'Egl. Cath., liv. xxv.), who write

much of the legendary story, as to imagine St. Paul preaching long and late to crowded congregations, as he did afterwards at Assos,[1] and his enemies bringing him before the civil authorities, with the cry that he was disturbing their households by his sorcery, or with complaints like those at

as if the "Acta Pauli et Theclæ" rested on the same foundation with the inspired narrative of the "Acts of the Apostles.". These apocryphal Acts were edited by Grabe (Spicil. vol. i.) in Greek and Latin from MSS. in the Bodleian Library. They are also in the Bibliotheca Patrum., vol I., and they are noticed by Fabricius, Cod. Apoc. N. T. vol. ii. In Jones on the Canon (vol. ii. p. 353–403) they are given both in Greek and English.

The outline of the story is as follows. On the arrival of St. Paul at Iconium, Thecla was betrothed to Thamyris. To his despair, and to the mother's perplexity, she forgets her earthly attachments, and remains night and day at a window, riveted by the preaching of St. Paul, which she hears in a neighbouring house (*ἐπὶ τῆς θυρίδος τῆς οἴκου αὐτῆς καθεσθεῖσα ἀπὸ τῆς σύνεγγυς θυρίδος ἤκουεν νυκτὸς καὶ ἡμέρας τὸ λεγόμενον ὑπὸ τοῦ Παύλου*, Grabe, p. 97; and again, *ὡς ἀράχνη ἐπὶ τῆς θυρίδος δεδεμένη, τοῖς Παύλου λόγοις κρατεῖται*, p. 98). [Cf. Acts, xx. 9.] By the contrivance of the false disciples, Demas and Hermogenes, (who say that they will prove the resurrection of those who know God to consist in their offspring,—*διδάξομεν ὅτι ἣν λέγει οὗτος ἀνάστασιν γένεσθαι, ἤδη γέγονεν ἐφ' οἷς ἔχομεν τέκνοις, καὶ ἀνέστημεν, θεὸν ἐπιγνόντες*, p. 101). [See 2 Tim. i. 15. iv. 10, also ii. 18.] St. Paul is brought before Castellius the Proconsul, and by his orders, with cries of *Μάγος ἐστίν· ἄπαγε τὸν μάγον* cast into prison. Thecla bribes the jailer with her ear-rings, visits the Apostle, and is instructed by him. St. Paul is scourged and banished. Thecla is condemned to be burnt, because she refuses to marry Thamyris; but her life is saved by a miraculous earthquake and storm of rain. Meanwhile St. Paul, with Onesiphorus [2 Tim. i. 16], who had been his host at Iconium, is in a tomb on the road to Daphne. There he is rejoined by Thecla, and they travel together to Antioch. In consequence of the admiration of a certain citizen called Alexander, a scene similar to that on Abraham's visit to Egypt is enacted; and ultimately Thecla is condemned to the wild beasts. But the lioness crouches at her feet, and the monsters in the water (*αἱ φῶκαι*, p. 111), die when she enters it, and float to the surface. Thecla is thus preserved. A lady called Tryphæna [Rom. xvi. 12], receives her into her house and is instructed by her. Thecla rejoins St. Paul at Myra, in Lycia. Thence she travels to Iconium, where she finds Thamyris dead, and endeavours in vain to convert her mother. She goes by Daphne to Seleucia, and leads an ascetic life in the neighbourhood of that city. Here miracles rouse the jealousy of the physicians, but their conspiracy against her chastity is defeated Finally, she dies at the age of ninety, having left Iconium at eighteen.

Though she was rescued from a violent death, Röhrbacher reckons her in the rank of Stephen as the first of the female martyrs. Grabe seems to be of opinion that the story has a basis of truth,—"argumentis nescio quomodo haud usquequaque sufficientibus ad narrationes adeo parum verisimiles lectori cordato pervadendas," as Fabricius says. Cod. Apoc. N. T. II. p. 796. Jones criticises the whole document at great length, and decides strongly against the veracity of the story. It may be worth while to notice one error in geography in the Greek narrative. St. Paul is said to have gone from Antioch to Iconium (as in the Acts) and Onesiphorus (who had been informed by Titus of the personal appearance of St. Paul) to have gone with his family to meet him on the royal road, which leads to Lystra (Grabe, p. 95). Now Lystra is on the contrary side of Iconium from Antioch. On the whole, the mythical character of the narrative, whatever basis of truth it may have, is very apparent.

Thecla is often alluded to by the Fathers, especially those of the fourth century,—

[[1] Acts xx. 7–11.]

Philippi and Ephesus, that he was "exceedingly troubling their city," and "turning away much people."[1] We learn from an inspired source[2] that the whole population of Iconium was ultimately divided into two great factions (a common occurrence, on far less important occasions, in these cities of Oriental Greeks), and that one party took the side of the Apostles, the other of the Jews. But here, as at Antioch, the influential classes were on the side of the Jews. A determined attempt was at last made to crush the Apostles, by loading them with insult and actually stoning them. Learning this wicked conspiracy, in which the magistrates themselves were involved,[3] they fled to some of the neighbouring districts of Lycaonia, where they might be more secure, and have more liberty in preaching the Gospel.

It would be a very natural course for the Apostles, after the cruel treatment they had experienced in the great towns on a frequented route, to retire into a wilder district and among a ruder population. In any country, the political circumstances of which resemble those of Asia Minor under the early emperors, there must be many districts, into which the civilisation of the conquering and governing people has hardly penetrated. We have an obvious instance in our Eastern presidencies, in the Hindoo villages which have retained their character without alteration, notwithstanding the successive occupations by Mahomedans and English. Thus, in the Eastern provinces of the Roman Empire there must have been many towns and villages where local customs were untouched, and where Greek, though certainly understood, was not commonly spoken. Such, perhaps, were the places which now come before our notice in the Acts of the Apostles,—small towns, with a rude dialect and primitive superstition[4]— "Lystra and Derbe, cities of Lycaonia."[5]

The district of Lycaonia extends from the ridges of Mount Taurus and the borders of Cilicia, on the south; to the Cappadocian hills, on the north. It is a bare and dreary region, unwatered by streams, though in parts liable to occasional inundations. Strabo mentions one place where water was even sold for money. In this respect there must be a close resemblance between this country and large tracts of Australia. Nor is this the only particular in which the resemblance may be traced. Both regions afford excellent pasture for flocks of sheep, and give opportunities for ob-

Jerome, Augustine, Ambrose, Eusebius, Epiphanius, Chrysostom, Gregory of Nyssa, and Gregory of Nazianzus. The references may be seen in Grabe and Jones. The passages adduced from Cyprian appear to be spurious, and some doubt rests on Tertull. de Bapt. c. 17. The life of Thecla was written in Greek verse by Basil of Seleucia (pub. 1622, with Gregory Thaumaturgus).

[1] Acts xvi. 20. xix. 26. [2] Acts xiv. 4.

[3] It is impossible to determine exactly the meaning of ἄρχουσι.

[4] Acts xiv. 11, 12, &c. [5] Acts xiv. 6.

taining large possessions by trade in wool.[1] It was here, on the downs of Lycaonia, that Amyntas, while he yet led the life of a nomad chief, before the time of his political elevation,[2] fed his three hundred flocks. Of the whole district Iconium[3] was properly the capital: and the plain round Iconium may be reckoned as its great central space, situated midway between Cilicia and Cappadocia. This plain is spoken of as the largest in Asia Minor.[4] It is almost like the steppes of Great Asia, of which the Turkish invaders must often have been reminded,[5] when they came to these level spaces in the west; and the camels which convey modern travellers to and from Konieh, find by the side of their path tufts of salt and prickly herbage, not very dissimilar to that which grows in their native deserts.[6]

Across some portion of this plain Paul and Barnabas travelled both before and after their residence in Iconium. After leaving the high land to the north-west,[7] during a journey of several hours before arriving at the city, the eye ranges freely over a vast expanse of level ground to the south and the east. The two most eminent objects in the view are the snowy summits of Mount Argæus, rising high above all the intervening hills in the direction of Armenia,—and the singular mountain mass called the "Kara-Dagh," or "Black Mount," south-eastwards in the direction of Cilicia.[8] And still these features continue to be conspicuous, after Iconium

[1] *Καίπερ ἄνυδρος οὖσα ἡ χώρα πρόβατα ἐκτρέφει θαυμαστῶς, τραχείας δὲ ἐρέας· καί τινες ἐξ αὐτῶν τούτων μεγίστον πλούτον ἐκτήσαντο.* Strabo xii. 6. He speaks also of "wild asses" as roaming over the district. The rest of his description is as follows: *Τὰ τῶν Λυκαόνων ὀροπέδια ψυχρὰ καὶ ψιλὰ καὶ ὀναγρόβοτα, ὑδάτων τε σπάνις πολλή· ὅπου δὲ καὶ εὑρεῖν δυνατὸν, βαθύτατα φρέατα τῶν πάντων, κάθαπερ ἐν Σοάτροις, ὅπου καὶ πιπράσκεται τὸ ὕδωρ. . . . Ἀμύντας δ' ὑπὲρ τριακοσίας ἔσχε ποίμνας ἐν τοῖς τόποις τούτοις. . . . Ἐνταῦθα δέ που καὶ τὸ Ἰκόνιόν ἐστι, πολίχνιον εὖ συνῳκισμένον καὶ χώραν εὐτυχεστέραν ἔχον τῆς λεχθείσης ὀναγροβότου. Πλησιάζει δ' ἤδη τούτοις τοῖς τόποις ὁ Ταῦρος, ὁ τὴν Καππαδοκίαν ὁρίζων καὶ τὴν Λυκαονίαν πρὸς τοὺς ὑπερκειμένους Κίλικας τοὺς Τραχειώτας.*

[2] See above, Ch. I. p. 23.

[3] See the Synecdemus of Hierocles. Steph. Byz. says it is—*πόλις Λυκαονίας πρὸς τοῖς ὅροις τοῦ Ταύρου.* Basil of Seleucia, in his life of St. Thecla, says: *πόλις αὕτη Λυκαονίας, τῆς μὲν Ἑώας οὐ πολὺ ἀπέχουσα, τῇ δὲ Ἀσιανῶν μᾶλλόν τι προσορμίζουσα, καὶ τῆς Πισιδῶν καὶ Φρυγῶν χώρας ἐν προοιμίᾳ κειμένη.* Xenophon, who is the first to mention Iconium, calls it "the last city of Phrygia" (*τῆς Φρυγίας πόλις ἐσχάτη*, Anab I. 2, 19) in the direction of "Lycaonia."

[4] See Leake, p. 93.

[5] The remark is made by Texier in his "Asie Mineure."

[6] Ainsworth (II. p. 68) describes the camels, as he crossed this plain, eagerly eating the tufts of Mesembryanthemum and Salicornia, "reminding them of plains with which they were probably more familiar than those of Asia Minor." The plain, however, is naturally rich. See Strabo, and Col. Leake.

[7] See above, p. 169, n. 1.

[8] See Leake, p. 45. "(*Between Ladik and Konieh*). To the north-east nothing appeared to interrupt the vast expanse but two very lofty summits covered with snow, at a great distance. They can be no other than the summits of Mount Argæus, above Cæsarea. [This is doubtful; see Ham. A. M. II. p. 305, and Trans. of Geog. Soc. viii.

is left behind, and the traveller moves on over the plain towards Lystra and Derbe. Mount Argæus still rises far to the north-east, at the distance of one hundred and fifty miles. The Black Mountain is gradually approached, and discovered to be an isolated mass, with reaches of the plain extending round it like channels of the sea.[1] The cities of Lystra and Derbe were somewhere about the bases of the Black Mountain. We have dwelt thus minutely on the physical characteristics of this part of Lycaonia, because the positions of its ancient towns have not been determined. We are only acquainted with the general features of the scene. While the site of Iconium has never been forgotten, and that of Antioch in Pisidia has now been clearly identified, those of Lystra and Derbe remain unknown, or at best are extremely uncertain.[2] No conclusive coins or inscriptions have been discovered; nor has there been any such con-

145.] To the south-east the same plains extend as far as the mountains of Karaman (Laranda). At the south-east extremity of the plains beyond Konieh, we are much struck with the appearance of a remarkable insulated mountain called Kara-Dagh (Black Mountain), rising to a great height, covered at the top with snow [Jan. 31,] and appearing like a lofty island in the midst of the sea. It is about sixty miles distant." The lines marked on the Map are the Roman roads mentioned in the Itineraries.

[1] See Leake, pp. 93–97. "(*Feb.* 1. *From Konieh to Tshumra.*)—Our road pursues a perfect level for upwards of twenty miles. (*Feb.* 2. *From Tshumra to Kassaba.*)—Nine hours over the same uninterrupted level of the finest soil, but quite uncultivated, except in the immediate neighbourhood of a few widely dispersed villages. It is painful to behold such desolation in the midst of a region so highly favoured by nature. Another characteristic of these Asiatic plains is the exactness of the level, and the peculiarity of their extending, without any previous slope, to the foot of the mountains, which rise from them like lofty islands out of the surface of the ocean. The Karamanian ridge seems to recede as we approach it, and the snowy summits of Argæus [?] are still to be seen to the north-east. . . . . At three or four miles short of Kassaba, we are abreast of the middle of the very lofty insulated mountain already mentioned, called Kara-Dagh. It is said to be chiefly inhabited by Greek Christians, and to contain 1001 churches; but we afterwards learnt that these 1001 churches (Binbir-Kilisseh) was a name given to the extensive ruins of an ancient city at the foot of the mountain. (*Feb.* 3. *From Kassaba to Karaman.*)—Four hours; the road still passing over a plain, which towards the mountains begins to be a little intersected with low ridges and ravines. . . . Between these mountains and the Kara-Dagh there is a kind of strait, which forms the communication between the plain of Karaman and the great levels lying eastward of Konieh. . . . Advancing towards Karaman, I perceive a passage into the plains to the north-west, round the northern end of Kara-Dagh, similar to that on the south, so that this mountain is completely insulated. We still see to the north-east the great snowy summit of Argæus, [?] which is probably the highest point of Asia Minor." See a similar description of the isolation of the Kara-dagh in Hamilton (II. 315, 320), who approached it from the East.

[2] Col. Leake wrote thus in 1824: "Nothing can more strongly show the little progress that has hitherto been made in a knowledge of the ancient geography of Asia Minor, than that, of the cities which the journey of St. Paul has made so interesting to us, the site of one only (Iconium) is yet certainly known. Perga, Antioch of Pisidia, Lystra, and Derbe, remain to be discovered." p. 103. We have seen that two of these four towns have been fully identified,—Perga by Sir C. Fellows and Antioch by Mr Arundel. It is to be hoped that the other two will yet be clearly ascertained.

vergence of modern investigation and ancient authority as leads to an infallible result. Of the different hypotheses which have been proposed, we have been content in the accompanying map to indicate those[1] which appear as most probable.

We resume the thread of our narrative with the arrival of Paul and Barnabas at Lystra. One peculiar circumstance strikes us immediately in what we read of the events in this town; that no mention occurs of any synagogue or of any Jews. It is natural to infer that there were few Israelites in the place, though (as we shall see hereafter) it would be a mistake to imagine that there were none. We are instantly brought in contact with a totally new subject,—with Heathen superstition and mythology; yet not the superstition of an educated mind, as that of Sergius Paulus,—nor the mythology of a refined and cultivated taste, like that of the Athenians,—but the mythology and superstition of a rude and unsophisticated people. Thus does the Gospel, in the person of St. Paul, successively clash with opposing powers, with sorcerers and philosophers, cruel magistrates and false divinities. Now it is the rabbinical master of the synagogue, now the listening proselyte from the Greeks, that is resisted or convinced,—now the honest inquiry of a Roman officer, now the

[1] The general features of the map on the opposite page are copied from Kiepert's large map of Asia Minor, and his positions for Lystra and Derbe are adopted. Lystra is marked near the place where Leake (p. 102) conjectured that it might be, some twenty miles S. of Iconium. It does not appear, however, that he saw any ruins on the spot. There are very remarkable Christian ruins on the N. side of the Kara-dagh, at Bin-bir-Kilisseh ("The 1001 churches"), and Leake thinks that they may mark the site of Derbe. We think Mr. Hamilton's conjecture much more probable, that they mark the site of Lystra, which has a more eminent ecclesiastical reputation than Derbe. See Ham. A. M. II 319, and Trans. of Georg. Soc. vol. viii. [While this was passing through the press, the writer received an indirect communication from Mr. Hamilton, which will be the best commentary on the map. The communication says, "there are *ruins* (though slight) at the spot where Derbe is marked on Kiepert's map, and as this spot is *certainly on a line of Roman road*, it is not unlikely that it may represent Derbe. He did not actually visit Divlé, but the coincidence of name led him to think it might be Derbe. He does not know of any ruins at the place where Kiepert writes Lystra, but was not on that spot. There may be ruins there, but he thinks they cannot be of importance, as he did not hear of them, though in the neighbourhood; and he prefers Bin-bir-Kilisseh as the site of Lystra."] The following description of the Bin-bir-Kilisseh is supplied by a letter from Mr. E. Falkner. "The principal group of the Bin-bir-Kilisseh lies at the foot of Kara-Dagh . . . Perceiving ruins on the slope of the mountain, I began to ascend, and on reaching these discovered they were churches; and, looking upwards, descried others yet above me, and climbing from one to the other I at length gained the summit, where I found two churches. On looking down, I perceived churches on all sides of the mountain, scattered about in various positions. The number ascribed to them by the Turks is of course metaphorical; but including those in the plain below, there are about two dozen in tolerable preservation, and the remains of perhaps forty may be traced altogether . . . The mountain must have been considered sacred, all the ruins are of Christian epoch, and, with the exception of a huge palace, every building is a church."

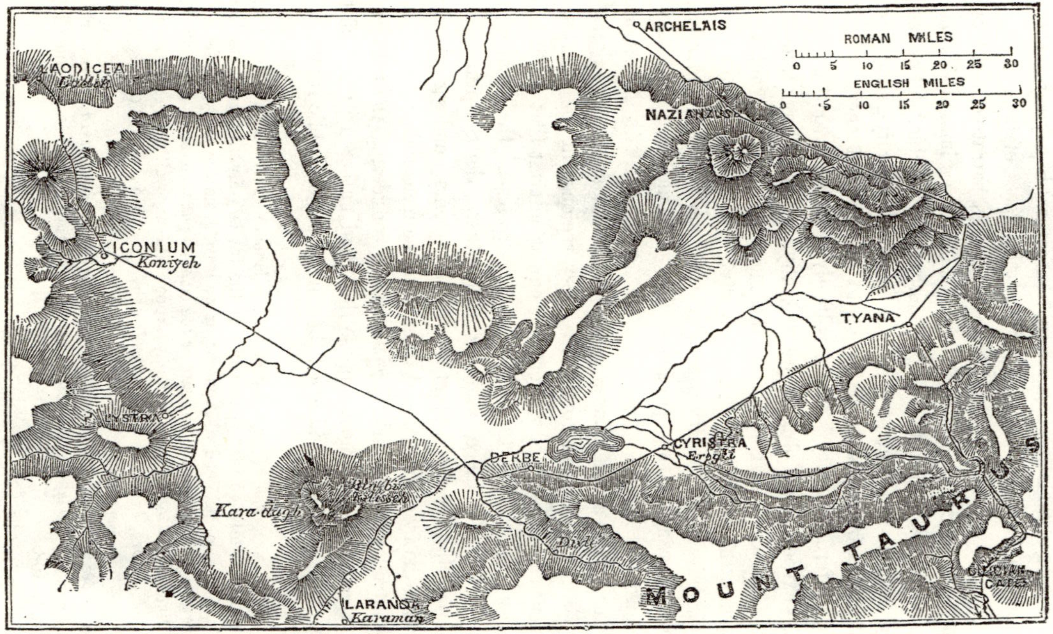
ARCHELAIS
ROMAN MILES
0 5 10 15 20 25 30
ENGLISH MILES
0 5 10 15 20 25 30
NAZIANZUS
LAODICEA
ICONIUM
Koniyeh
TYANA
LYSTRA
CYRISTRA
DERBE
Kara-dagh
Divl
MOUNT TAURUS
LARANDA
Karaman

wild fanaticism of a rustic credulity, that is addressed with bold and persuasive eloquence.

It was a common belief among the ancients that the gods occasionally visited the earth in the form of men. Such a belief with regard to Jupiter, "the father of gods and men," would be natural in any rural district: but nowhere should we be prepared to find the traces of it more than at Lystra; for Lystra, as it appears from St. Luke's narrative,[1] was under the tutelage of Jupiter, and the tutelary divinities were imagined to haunt the cities under their protection, though elsewhere invisible.[2] The temple of Jupiter was a conspicuous object in front of the city-gates:[3] what wonder if the citizens should be prone to believe that their "Jupiter, which was before the city," would willingly visit his favourite people? Again, the expeditions of Jupiter were usually represented as attended by Mercury. He was the companion, the messenger, the servant of the gods.[4] Thus the notion of these two divinities appearing together in Lycaonia is quite in conformity with what we know of the popular belief. But their appearance in that particular district would be welcomed with more than usual credulity. Those who are acquainted with the literature of the Roman poets are familiar with a beautiful tradition of Jupiter and Mercury visiting in human form these very regions[5] in the interior of Asia Minor. And it is not without a singular interest that we find one of Ovid's stories reappearing in the sacred pages of the Acts of the Apostles. In this instance, as in so many others, the Scripture, in its incidental descriptions of the Heathen world, presents "undesigned coincidences" with the facts ascertained from Heathen memorials.

These introductory remarks prepare us for considering the miracle recorded in the Acts. We must suppose that Paul gathered groups of the Lystrians about him, and addressed them in places of public resort, as a

[1] *Τοῦ Διος τοῦ ὄντος πρὸ τῆς πόλεως αὐτῶν;* It is more likely that a *temple* than a *statue* of Jupiter is alluded to. The temple of the tutelary divinity was outside the walls at Perga (see p. 161) and at Ephesus, as we learn from the story in Herodotus (I. 26), who tells us that in a time of danger the citizens put themselves under the protection of Diana, by attaching her temple by a rope to the city-wall (*ἀνέθεσαν τὴν πόλιν τῇ Ἀρτέμιδι, ἐξάψαντες ἐκ τοῦ νηοῦ σχοίνιον ἐς τὸ τεῖχος*). So Pallas is called, Ἀνασσ' Ὄγκα *πρὸ πόλεως*. Sept. c. Theb. 164.

[2] *Καί φασι τοὺς οἰκιστὰς ἥρωας ἢ θεοὺς πολλάκις ἐπιστρέφεσθαι τὰς αυτων πόλεις τοῖς αλλοις ὄντας ἀφανεῖς, ἔν τε θυσίας καὶ τίσιν ἑορταῖς δημοτελέσιν.* Dio. Chrys. Orat. XXXIII. p. 408.

[3] Acts xiv. 13.

[4] See the references in Smith's Dictionary of Classical Biography and Mythology under "Hermes."

[5] See the story of Baucis and Philemon, Ovid. Met. viii. 611, &c. Even if the Lycaonians were a Semitic tribe, it is not unnatural to suppose them familiar with Greek mythology. An identification of classical and "barbarian" divinities had taken place in innumerable instances, as in the case of the Tyrian Hercules and Paphian Venus.

modern missionary might address the natives of a Hindoo village.[1] But it would not be necessary in his case, as in that of Schwartz or Martyn, to have learnt the primitive language of those to whom he spoke. He addressed them in Greek, for Greek was well understood in this border country of the Lystrians, though their own dialect was either a barbarous corruption of that noble language, or the surviving remainder of some older tongue. He used the language of general civilisation, as English may be used now in a Welch country-town like Dolgelly or Carmarthen. The subjects he brought before these illiterate idolaters of Lycaonia were doubtless such as would lead them, by the most natural steps, to the knowledge of the true God, and the belief in His Son's resurrection. He told them, as he told the educated Athenians,[2] of Him whose worship they had ignorantly corrupted, whose unity, power, and goodness they might have discerned through the operations of nature; whose displeasure against sin had been revealed to them by the admonitions of their natural conscience.

On one of these occasions[3] St. Paul observed a cripple, who was earnestly listening to his discourse. He was seated on the ground, for he had an infirmity in his feet, and had never walked from the hour of his birth. St. Paul looked at him attentively, with that remarkable expression of the eye which we have already noticed (p. 148). The same Greek word is used as when the Apostle is described as "earnestly beholding the council," and as "setting his eyes on Elymas the sorcerer."[4] On this occasion that penetrating glance saw, by the power of the Divine Spirit, into the very secrets of the cripple's soul. Paul perceived "that he had faith to be saved."[5] These words, implying so much of moral preparation in the heart of this poor Heathen, rise above all that is told us of the lame Jew, whom Peter, "fastening his eyes upon him with John," had once healed at the temple gate in Jerusalem.[6] In other respects the parallel between the two cases is complete. As Peter said in the presence of the Jews, "In the name of Jesus Christ of Nazareth, rise up and walk," so Paul said before his idolatrous audience at Lystra, "Stand upright on thy feet." And in this case, also, the word which had been suggested to the speaker by a supernatural intuition was followed by a supernatural result. The obedient alacrity in the spirit, and the new strength in the body, rushed together simultaneously. The lame man sprang up in the joyful

[1] See for instance Fox's "Chapters on Missions," p. 153, &c.

[2] It is very important to compare together the speeches at Lystra and Athens, and both with the first chapter of the Romans. See pp. 193, 194.

[3] *Καί τις ἀνὴρ ἐν Λύστροις ἀδύνατος τοῖς ποσὶν ἐκάθητο, κ. τ. λ.* Acts xiv. 8, &c.

[4] Acts xxiii. 1. xiii. 9.

[5] *Σωθῆναι* is the word in the original. xiv. 9.

[6] Acts iii. Wetstein remarks on the greater faith manifested by the heathen at Lystra than the Jew at Jerusalem.

consciousness of a power he had never felt before, and walked like those who had never had experience of infirmity.

And now arose a great tumult of voices from the crowd. Such a cure of a congenital disease, so sudden and so complete, would have confounded the most skilful and skeptical physicians. An illiterate people would be filled with astonishment, and rush immediately to the conclusion that supernatural powers were present among them. These Lycaonians thought at once of their native traditions, and crying out vociferously in their mother-tongue,[1]—and we all know how the strongest feelings of an excited people find vent in the language of childhood,—they exclaimed that the gods had again visited them in the likeness of men,—that Jupiter and Mercury were again in Lycaonia,—that the persuasive speaker was Mercury and his companion Jupiter. They identified Paul with Mercury, because his eloquence corresponded with one of that divinity's attributes. Paul was the "chief speaker," and Mercury was the god of eloquence.[2] And if it be asked why they identified Barnabas with Jupiter, it is evidently a sufficient answer to say that these two divinities were always represented as companions[3] in their terrestrial expeditions, though we may well believe (with Chrysostom and others[4]) that there was something majestically benignant in his appearance, while the personal aspect of St. Paul (and for this we can quote his own statements[5]) was comparatively insignificant.

How truthful and how vivid is the scene brought before us! and how many thoughts it suggests to those who are at once conversant with Heathen mythology and disciples of Christian theology! Barnabas, identified with the Father of Gods and Men, seems like a personification of mild beneficence and provident care;[6] while Paul appears invested with more active attributes, flying over the world on the wings of faith and love, with quick words of warning and persuasion, and ever carrying in his hand the purse of the "unsearchable riches."[7]

[1] Some are of opinion that the "speech of Lycaonia" was a Semitic language; others that it was a corrupt dialect of Greek. See the Dissertations of Jablonski and Gühling in Iken's Thesaurus.

[2] Acts xiv. 12. Hor. Od. I. x. Ov. Fast. v. 668. Hence *λόγου θνητοῖσι προφῆτα.* Orph. Hymn. 28, 4. So Lucian: *Ἑρμοῦ λαλιστάτου καὶ λογιωτάτου θεῶν ἁπάντων.* Gallus 2, and Macrobius; "Scimus Mercurium vocis et sermonis potentum." Sat. I. 8.

[3] See, for instance, Ovid. Fast. v. 495:—

"Jupiter et lato qui regnat in æquore frater
Carpebant socias Mercuriusque vias."

[4] *Ἐμοὶ δοκεῖ καὶ ἀπὸ τῆς ὄψεως ἀξιοπρεπὴς εἶναι ὁ Βαρνάβας.* Chrys. Hom. xxx.

[5] See 2. Cor. x. 1, 10, where we must remember that he is quoting the statements of his adversaries.

[6] See Acts iv. 36, 37. ix. 27. xi. 22–25, 30. It is also very possible that Barnabas was *older*, and therefore more *venerable* in appearance, than St. Paul.

[7] For one of the most beautiful representations of Mercury, with all his well-known insignia, see the Museo Borbonico, vol. vi. No. 2.

The news of a wonderful occurrence is never long in spreading through a small country-town. At Lystra the whole population was presently in an uproar. They would lose no time in paying due honour to their heavenly visitants. The priest attached to that temple of Jupiter before the city gates, to which we have before alluded,[1] was summoned to do sacrifice to the god whom he served. Bulls and garlands, and whatever else was requisite to the performance of the ceremony, were duly prepared, and the procession moved amidst crowds of people to the residence of the Apostles. They, hearing the approach of the multitude, and learning their idolatrous intention, were filled with the utmost horror. They "rent their clothes," and rushed out[2] of the house in which they lodged, and met the idolaters approaching the vestibule.[3] There, standing at the doorway, they opposed the entrance of the crowd; and Paul expressed his abhorrence of their intention, and earnestly tried to prevent their fulfilling it, in a speech of which only the following short outline is recorded by St. Luke :—

"Ye men of Lystra, why do ye these things? We also are men, of like passions with you; and we are come to preach to you the Glad Tiding, that you may turn from these vain idols to the living God, who made the heavens, and the earth, and the sea, and all things that are therein. For in the generations that are past, He suffered all the nations of the Gentiles to walk in their own ways. Nevertheless He left not Himself without witness, in that He blessed you,[4] and gave you rain from heaven, and fruitful seasons, filling your[5] hearts with food and gladness."

This address held them listening, but they listened impatiently. Even with this energetic disavowal of his divinity, and this strong appeal to their reason, St. Paul found it difficult to disturb the Lycaonians from offering to him and Barnabas an idolatrous worship.[6] There is no doubt that St.

[1] P. 190.

[2] 'Εξεπήδησαν, not εἰσεπήδησαν, is the reading sanctioned by the later critics on full manuscript authority. See Tischendorf.

[3] Πυλῶνες does not mean the gate of the city (which would be πύλη), but the vestibule or gate which gave admission from the public street into the court of the Atrium. So the word is used, Matt. xxvi. 71, for the vestibule of the high-priest's palace; Luke xvi. 20, for that of Dives: Acts x. 17, of the house where Peter lodged at Joppa; Acts xii. 13, of the house of Mary the mother of John Mark. It is nowhere used for the gate of a city except in the Apocalypse. Moreover, it seems obvious that if the priest had only brought the victims to sacrifice them at the city gates, it would have been no offering to Paul and Barnabas.

[4] Read ὑμῖν (with Griesbach, Lachman, &c.) instead of ἡμῖν; or else omit the word altogether (with Tischendorf), which gives the same sense.

[5] 'Υμῶν, not ἡμῶν, is the right reading.

[6] Acts xiv. 18.

ANCIENT SACRIFICE.—DRAWING BY G. SCHARF, JR., FROM THE ANCIENT SCULPTURE, COPIED BY RAPHAEL FOR HIS CARTOON

Paul was the speaker, and before we proceed further in the narrative, we cannot help pausing to observe the essentially Pauline character which this speech manifests, even in so condensed a summary of its contents. It is full of undesigned coincidences in argument, and even in the expressions employed, with St. Paul's language in other parts of the Acts, and in his own Epistles. Thus, as here he declares the object of his preaching to be that the idolatrous Lystrians should "turn from these vain idols to the living God," so he reminds the Thessalonians how they, at his preaching, had "turned from idols to serve the living and true God."[1] Again, as he tells the Lystrians that "God had in the generations that were past, suffered the nations of the Gentiles to walk in their own ways;" so he tells the Romans that "God in His forbearance had passed over the former sins of men, in the times that were gone by;"[2] and so he tells the Athenians,[3] that "the past times of ignorance God had overlooked." Lastly, how striking is the similarity between the natural theology with which the present speech concludes, and that in the Epistle to the Romans, where, speaking of the heathen, he says that atheists were without excuse; "for that which can be known of God is manifested in their hearts, God Himself having shown it to them. For His being and His might, though they be invisible, yet are seen ever since the world was made, being understood by His works, which prove His eternal power and Godhead."[4]

The crowd reluctantly retired, and led the victims away without offering them in sacrifice to the Apostles. It might be supposed that at least a command had been obtained over their gratitude and reverence, which would not easily be destroyed; but we have to record here one of those sudden changes of feeling, which are humiliating proofs of the weakness of human nature and of the superficial character of religious excitement. The Lycaonians were proverbially fickle and faithless;[5] but we may not too

[1] 1 Thess. i. 9. The coincidence is more striking in the Greek, because the very same verb, *ἐπιστρέφειν*, is used in each passage, and is intransitive in both.

[2] Rom. iii. 25: *Τὴν πάρεσιν τῶν προγεγονότων ἁμαρτημάτων ἐν τῇ ἀνοχῇ τοῦ Θεοῦ*,—the mis-translation of which in the authorised version entirely alters its meaning.

[3] Acts xvii. 30.

[4] Rom. i. 19, 20. We ought not to leave this speech without noticing Mr. Humphrey's conjecture that the conclusion of it is a quotation from some lyric poet. We cannot think this at all probable; the fact that the passage from *οὐρανόθεν* to *καρδιάς* can be broken up into a system of irregular lines, consisting of dochmiac and choriambic feet, proves nothing; because there is scarcely any passage in Greek prose which might not be resolved into lyrical poetry by a similar method; just as, in English, the columns of a newspaper may be read off as hexameters (spondaic, or otherwise), quite as good as most of the so-called English hexameters which are published. It seems very unlikely that St. Paul, in addressing the simple and illiterate inhabitants of Lystra (whose vernacular language was not even Greek), should quote a lyrical poem. It would have been as improbable as that John Wesley, when trying to pacify the Welsh mob at Brecon, should have quoted one of Gray's odes.

[5] The Schol. on Il. IV. 88, 92 says: *Ἄπιστο γὰρ Λυκάονες, ὡς καὶ Ἀριστοτέλης μαρτυρεῖ.*

hastily decide that they were worse than many others might have been under the same circumstances. It would not be difficult to find a parallel to their conduct among the modern converts from idolatry to Christianity. And certainly no later missionaries have had more assiduous enemies than the Jews, whom the Apostles had everywhere to oppose. Certain Jews from Iconium, and even from Antioch,[1] followed in the footsteps of Paul and Barnabas, and endeavoured to excite the hostility of the Lystrians against them. When they heard of the miracle worked on the lame man, and found how great an effect it had produced on the people of Lystra, they would be ready with a new interpretation of this occurrence. They would say that it had been accomplished, not by Divine agency, but by some diabolical magic; as once they had said at Jerusalem, that He who came "to destroy the works of the devil," cast out devils "by Beelzebub the prince of the devils."[2] And this is probably the true explanation of that sudden change of feeling among the Lystrians, which at first sight is very surprising. Their own interpretation of what they had witnessed having been disavowed by the authors of the miracle themselves, they would readily adopt a new interpretation, suggested by those who appeared to be well acquainted with the strangers, and who had followed them from distant cities. Their feelings changed with a revulsion as violent as that which afterwards took place among the "barbarous people" of Malta,[3] who first thought St. Paul was a murderer, and then a god. The Jews, taking advantage of the credulity of a rude tribe, were able to accomplish at Lystra the design they had meditated at Iconium.[4] St. Paul was stoned,—not hurried out of the city to execution like St. Stephen,[5] the memory of whose death must have come over St. Paul at this moment with impressive force,—but stoned somewhere in the streets of Lystra, and then dragged through the city gate, and cast outside the walls, under the belief that he was dead. This is the occasion to which the Apostle afterwards alluded in the words, "once I was stoned,"[6] in that long catalogue of sufferings,

[1] Acts xiv. 19.
[2] Matt. xii. 24.
[3] Acts xxviii. 4–6.
[4] Acts xiv. 5.

[5] See the end of Ch. II. At Jerusalem the law required that these executions should take place outside the city. It must be remembered that stoning was a Jewish punishment, and that it was proposed by Jews at Iconium, and instigated and begun by Jews at Lystra.

[6] See Paley's remark on the expression "*once* I was stoned," in reference to the previous *design* of stoning St. Paul at Iconium. "Had the assault been completed, had the history related that a stone was thrown, as it relates that preparations were made both by Jews and Gentiles to stone Paul and his companions, or even had the account of this transaction stopped, without going on to inform us that Paul and his companions were 'aware of the danger and fled,' a contradiction between the history and the epistles would have ensued. Truth is necessarily consistent; but it is scarcely possible that independent accounts, not having truth to guide them, should thus advance to the very brink of contradiction without falling into it." Horæ Paulinæ, p. 69

to which we have already referred in this chapter.[1] Thus was he "in perils by his own countrymen, in perils by the heathen,"—"in deaths oft,"—"always bearing about in the body the dying of the Lord Jesus, that the life also of Jesus might be made manifest in his body. . . . . Alway delivered unto death for Jesus' sake, that the life also of Jesus might be made manifest in his mortal flesh."[2]

On the present occasion these last words were literally realised, for by the power and goodness of God he rose from a state of apparent death as if by a sudden resurrection.[3] Though "persecuted," he was not "forsaken,"—though "cast down" he was "not destroyed." "As the disciples stood about him, he rose up, and came into the city."[4] We see from this expression that his labours in Lystra had not been in vain. He had found some willing listeners to the truth, some "disciples" who did not hesitate to show their attachment to their teacher by remaining near his body, which the rest of their fellow-citizens had wounded and cast out. These courageous disciples were left for the present in the midst of the enemies of the truth. Jesus Christ had said,[5] "when they persecute you in one city, flee to another," and the very "next day"[6] Paul "departed with Barnabas to Derbe."

But before we leave Lystra, we must say a few words on one spectator of St. Paul's sufferings, who is not yet mentioned by St. Luke, but who was destined to be the constant companion of his after years, the zealous follower of his doctrine, the faithful partner of his danger and distress. St. Paul came to Lystra again after the interval of one or two years, and on that occasion we are told[7] that he found a certain Christian there, "whose name was Timotheus, whose mother was a Jewess, while his father was a Greek," and whose excellent character was highly esteemed by his fellow Christians of Lystra and Iconium. It is distinctly stated that at the time of this second visit Timothy was already a Christian; and since we know from St. Paul's own expression,—"my own son in the faith,"[8]—that he was converted by St. Paul himself, we must suppose this change to have taken place at the time of the first visit. And the reader will remember that St. Paul in the second Epistle to Timothy

See pp. 163, 164.

Compare 2 Cor. iv. 8–12 and xi. 23–27.

3 The natural inference from the narrative is, that the recovery was miraculous; and it is evident that such a recovery must have produced a strong effect on the minds of the Christians who witnessed it.

4 Acts xiv. 20. 5 Matt. x. 23. 6 Acts xiv. 20. 7 Acts xvi. 1.

8 1 Tim. i. 2. Compare i. 18 and 2 Tim. ii. 1. It is indeed possible that these expressions might be used, if Timothy became a Christian by his mother's influence, and through the recollection of St. Paul's sufferings; but the common view is the most natural. See what is said 1 Cor. iv. 14, 15: "As my beloved sons I warn you; for though ye have ten thousand instructors in Christ, yet have ye not many fathers; for in Christ Jesus I have begotten you through the gospel."

(iii. 10, 11) reminds him of his own intimate and personal knowledge of the sufferings he had endured, "*at Antioch, at Iconium, at Lystra,*"—the places (it will be observed) being mentioned in the exact order in which they were visited, and in which the successive persecutions took place. We have thus the strongest reasons for believing that Timothy was a witness of St. Paul's injurious treatment: and this too at a time of life when the mind receives its deepest impressions from the spectacle of innocent suffering and undaunted courage. And it is far from impossible that the generous and warm-hearted youth was standing in that group of disciples, who surrounded the apparently lifeless body of the Apostle at the outside of the walls of Lystra.

We are called on to observe at this point, with a thankful acknowledgment of God's providence, that the flight from Iconium, and the cruel persecution at Lystra, where events which involved the most important and beneficial consequences to universal Christianity. It was here, in the midst of barbarous idolaters, that the Apostle of the Gentiles found an associate, who became to him and the Church far more than Barnabas, the companion of his first mission. As we have observed above,[1] there appears to have been at Lystra no synagogue, no community of Jews and proselytes, among whom such an associate might naturally have been expected. Perhaps Timotheus and his relations may have been almost the only persons of Jewish origin in the town. And his "grandmother Lois" and "mother Eunice"[2] may have been brought there originally by some accidental circumstance, as Lydia[3] was brought from Thyatira to Philippi.[4] And, though there was no synagogue at Lystra, this family may have met with a few others in some *proseucha*, like that in which Lydia and her fellow-worshippers met "by the river side."[5] Whatever we may conjecture concerning the congregational life to which Timotheus may have been accustomed, we are accurately informed of the nature of that domestic life which nurtured him for his future labours. The good soil of his heart was well prepared before Paul came, by the instructions[6] of Lois and Eunice, to receive the seed of Christian truth, sown at the Apostle's first visit, and to produce a rich harvest of faith and good works before the time of his second visit.

Derbe, as we have seen, is somewhere[7] not far from the "Black

[1] See p. 188. [2] 2 Tim. i. 5. [3] Acts xvi. 14.

[4] See also the remarks on the Jews settled in Asia Minor, ch. I. pp. 17, 18; and on the Hellenistic and Aramæan Jews, ch. II. p. 37.

[5] Acts xvi. 13. [6] 2 Tim. i. 5.

[7] See the note on Lystra. Strabo says of Derbe:—Τῆς Ἰσαυρικῆς ἐστιν ἐν πλευραῖς, μάλιστα τῇ Καππαδοκίᾳ ἐπιπεφυκός, κ. τ. λ. xii. 6. Stephanus Byzantinus says that Derbe was φρούριον Ἰσαυρίας καὶ λιμήν [the last word is evidently a mistake; perhaps, as the French translators of Strabo suggest, it ought to be λίμνη]; but he implies that it was closely connected with Lycaonia, and at the same time that "the speech of

Mountain," which rises like an island in the south-eastern part of the plain of Lycaonia. A few hours would suffice for the journey between Lystra and its neighbour-city. We may, perhaps, infer from the fact that Derbe is not mentioned in the list of places which St. Paul[1] brings to the recollection of Timothy as scenes of past suffering and distress, that in this town the Apostles were exposed to no persecution. It may have been a quiet resting-place after a journey full of toil and danger. It does not appear that they were hindered in "evangelising"[2] the city: and the fruit of their labours was the conversion of "many disciples."[3]

And now we have reached the limit of St. Paul's first missionary journey. About this part of the Lycaonian plain, where it approaches, through gradual undulations,[4] to the northern bases of Mount Taurus, he was not far from that well-known pass[5] which leads down from the central table-land to Cilicia and Tarsus. But his thoughts did not centre in an earthly home. He turned back upon his footsteps; and revisited the places, Lystra, Iconium, and Antioch,[6] where he himself had been reviled and persecuted, but where he had left, as sheep in the desert, the disciples whom his Master had enabled him to gather. They needed building up and strengthening in the faith,[7] comforting in the midst of their inevitable sufferings, and fencing round by permanent institutions. Therefore Paul and Barnabas revisited the scenes of their labours, undaunted by the dangers which awaited them, and using words of encouragement, which none but the founders of a true religion would have ventured to address to their earliest converts, that "we can only enter the kingdom of God by passing through much tribulation." But not only did they fortify their faith by passing words of encouragement; they ordained elders in every church after the pattern of the first Christian communities in Palestine,[8] and with that solemn observance which had attended their own consecration,[9] and

Lycaonia" was in some way peculiar, when he says that some called it Δελβεία, ὅ ἐστ. τῇ τῶν Λυκαόνων φωνῇ ἄρκουθος. This variety in the form of the name, added to the proximity of lake Ak Göl, induced Mr. Hamilton to think Divlé might be Derbe.—Researches, vol. II. p. 313.

[1] 2 Tim. iii. 11.

[2] Εὐαγγελισάμενοι τὴν πόλιν ἐκείνην. xiv. 21.

[3] Μαθητεύσαντες ἱκάνους. Ibid.

[4] So Leake describes the neighbourhood of Karaman (Laranda), pp. 96, 97. Hamilton, speaking of the same district, mentions 'low ridges of cretaceous limestone, extending into the plain from the mountains." II. 324.

[5] The "Cilician Gates," to which we shall return at the beginning of the second missionary journey (Acts xv. 41). See the Map.

[6] Mentioned (Acts xiv. 21) in the inverse order from that in which they had been visited before (xiii. 14, 51. xiv. 6).

[7] Ἐπιστηρίζοντες τὰς ψυχὰς τῶν μαθητῶν, παρακαλοῦντες ἐμμένειν τῇ πίστει. xiv. 22.

[8] The first mention of presbyters in the Christian, opposed to the Jewish sense, occurs Acts xi. 30, in reference to the church at Jerusalem.

[9] Ch. V pp. 133, 134.

which has been transmitted to later ages in connection with ordination,—"with fasting and prayer"—they "made choice of fit persons to serve in the sacred ministry of the Church."[1]

Thus, having consigned their disciples to Him "in whom they had believed," and who was "able to keep that which was entrusted to Him,"[2] Paul and Barnabas descended through the Pisidian mountains to the plain of Pamphylia. If our conjecture is correct (see p. 165), that they went up from Perga in spring, and returned at the close of autumn,[3] and spent all the hotter months of the year in the elevated districts, they would again pass in a few days through a great change of seasons, and almost from summer to winter. The people of Pamphylia would have returned from their cold residences to the warm shelter of the plain by the sea-side; and Perga would be full of its inhabitants. The Gospel was preached within the walls of this city, through which the Apostles had merely passed[4] on their journey to the interior. But from St. Luke's silence it appears that the preaching was attended with no marked results. We read neither of conversions nor persecutions. The Jews, if any Jews resided there, were less inquisitive and less tyrannical than those at Antioch and Iconium; and the votaries of "Diana before the city" at Perga (see p. 160) were less excitable than those who worshipped "Jupiter before the city" at Lystra.[5] When the time came for returning to Syria, they did not sail down the Cestrus, up the channel of which river they had come on their arrival from Cyprus,[6] but travelled across the plain to Attaleia, which was situated on the edge of the Pamphylian gulf.

Attaleia had something of the same relation to Perga, which Cadiz has to Seville. In each case the latter city is approached by a river-voyage, and the former is more conveniently placed on the open sea. Attalus Philadelphus, king of Pergamus, whose dominions extended from the north-western corner of Asia Minor to the Sea of Pamphylia, had built this city in a convenient position for commanding the trade of Syria or Egypt. When Alexander the Great passed this way, no such city was in existence: but since the days of the kings of Pergamus, who inherited a fragment of his vast empire, Attaleia has always existed and flourished, retaining the name of the monarch who built it.[7] Behind it is the plain,

[1] First Collect for the Ember Weeks. [2] Acts xiv. 23. Compare 2 Tim. i. 12

[3] Wieseler (p. 224) thinks the events on this journey must have occupied more than one year. It is evident that the case does not admit of any thing more than conjecture.

[4] See above, pp. 160, and notes. [5] Acts xiv. 13. [6] Pp. 160, 161.

[7] See Strab. xiv. 4 and Ptol. v. 5, 2. Strabo places Attaleia to the west of the Catarrhactes, Ptolemy to the east. Admiral Beaufort (Karamania, ch. vi.) was of opinion that the modern *Satalia* is the site of the ancient Olbia, and that *Laara* is the true Attaleia. Mannert (Georg. der G. und R. vi. 130) conjectures that Olbia may have been the ancient name of the city which Attalus rebuilt and called after his own name:

WALL OF PERGA.

through which the calcareous waters of the Catarrhactes flow, perpetually constructing and destroying and reconstructing their fantastic channels.[1] In front of it, and along the shore on each side, are long lines of cliffs,[2] over which the river finds its way in waterfalls to the sea, and which conceal the plain from those who look toward the land from the inner waters of the bay, and even encroach on the prospect of the mountains themselves.

When this view is before us, the mind reverts to another band of Christian warriors, who once sailed from the bay of Satalia to the Syrian Antioch. Certain passages, in which the movements of the Crusaders and Apostles may be compared with each other are among the striking contrasts of history. Conrad and Louis, each with an army consisting at first of 70,000 men, marched through part of the same districts[3] which were traversed by Paul and Barnabas alone and unprotected. The shattered remains of the French host had come down to Attaleia through "the abrupt mountain-passes and the deep vallies "which are so well described by the contemporary historian.[4] They came to fight the battle of the Cross

and Forbiger (Alte Geographie, ii. 268) inclines to think the opinion is very probable. The perpetual changes in the river-bed of the Catarrhactes have necessarily caused some difficulty in the identification of ancient sites in this part of the Pamphylian plain. Spratt and Forbes, however ("Lycia," &c., ch. vi.), seems to have discovered the true Olbia further to the west, and to have proved that Satalia is Attaleia. They add that the style of its relics is invariably Roman, agreeing with the date of its foundation.

1 See Spratt and Forbes for a full account of the irregular deposits and variations of channel observable in this river.

2 There are also ancient sea-cliffs at some distance behind the present coast line. See Fellows, and Spratt and Forbes.

3 See the Maps in Michaud's Histoire des Croisades and Milman's Gibbon.

4 Tandem vero Pamphyliam ingressi, *per abrupta montium*, *per devexa vallium*, *cum difficultate nimia* . . . . usque Attaleiam, ejusdem regionis metropolim pervenerunt."—William of Tyre, xvi. 26. The passage which follows is worth quoting, both for the account of Satalia as it was in the twelfth century, and the description of the voyage to Antioch on the Orontes. "Est autem Attaleia civitas in littore maris sita, Imperatoris Constantinopolitani subjecta imperio, agrum habens opimum, et tamen civibus suis inutilem. Nam angustiantibus eos undique hostibus, nec permittentibus agrorum cultui vacare, jacet ager infructuosus, dum non est qui exercendo fœcunditatem possit procreare: alias tamen multa habens commoditates, gratum se solet præbere hospitibus. Nam aquas emanans perspicuas et salutares, pomeriis est obsita fructiferis, situ placens amœnissimo: trajectarum tamen frequens et per mare devectarum solent habere copias, et transeuntibus sufficientem ciborum commoditatem ministrare Quia vero hostibus nimis est contermina, eorum non valens indesinenter sustinere molestias, facta est eis tributaria, per hoc necessariorum cum hostibus commercium.

"Hanc nostri idiomatis Græci non habentes peritiam, corrupto vocabulo *Satalium* appellant. Unde et totus ille maris sinus, a promontorio Lissidora, usque in insulam Cyprum, Attalicus dicitur, qui vulgari appellatione *Gulphus Sataliæ* nuncupatur.

"Ad hanc perveniens Rex Francorum cum suis, ob multitudinem concurrentium tantum passus est alimentorum penuriam quod pene residuum exercitus, et maxime pauperes consumerentur inedia. Ipse vero cum suis principibus, relictis pedestribus

with a great multitude, and with the armour of human power; their journey was encompassed with defeat and death; their arrival at Attaleia was disastrous and disgraceful; and they sailed to Antioch a broken and dispirited army. But the Crusaders of the first century, the Apostles of Christ, though they too passed "through much tribulation," advanced from victory to victory. Their return to the place "whence they had been recommended to the grace of God for the work which they fulfilled,"[1] was triumphant and joyful, for the weapons of their warfare were "not carnal."[2] The Lord Himself was their tower and their shield.

turmis maturat navigio, Isauriam Ciliciamque a læva deserens: a dextris autem Cypro relicta, prosperis actus flatibus, fauces Orontis fluminis, quod Antiochiam prælabitur, qui locus hodie dicitur Symeonis portus, juxta antiquam urbem Seleuciam, et ab Antiochia decem plus minusve paulo distat miliaribus, ingreditur."

[1] Acts xiv. 26. [2] See 2 Cor. x. 4.

From Fellows' Asia Minor, p. 191. This sculpturing of a shield upon a tower may also be seen in a drawing of Isaura in Hamilton's Researches, vol. ii. p. 332.

CHAPTER VII.

"Inter hos scopulus et sinus, inter hæc vada et freta . . . velificata Spiritu Dei fides navigat. . . . Propterea Spiritus Sanctus consultantibus tunc Apostolis vinculum et jugum nobis relaxavit, ut idololatriæ devitandæ vacaremus."—*Tertull. de Idoll.* § 24.

CONTROVERSY IN THE CHURCH.—SEPARATION OF JEWS AND GENTILES.—OBSTACLES TO UNION, BOTH SOCIAL AND RELIGIOUS.—DIFFICULTY IN THE NARRATIVE.—SCRUPLES CONNECTED WITH THE CONVERSION OF CORNELIUS.—LINGERING DISCONTENT.—FEELINGS EXCITED BY THE CONDUCT AND SUCCESS OF ST. PAUL,—ESPECIALLY AT JERUSALEM.—INTRIGUES OF THE JUDAIZERS AT ANTIOCH.—CONSEQUENT ANXIETY AND PERPLEXITY.—MISSION OF PAUL AND BARNABAS TO JERUSALEM.—DIVINE REVELATION TO ST. PAUL.—TITUS.—JOURNEY THROUGH PHŒNICE AND SAMARIA.—THE PHARISEES.—PRIVATE CONFERENCES.—PUBLIC MEETING.—SPEECH OF ST. PETER.—NARRATIVE OF BARNABAS AND PAUL.—SPEECH OF ST. JAMES.—THE DECREE.—CHARITABLE NATURE OF ITS PROVISIONS.—IT INVOLVES THE ABOLITION OF JUDAISM.—PUBLIC RECOGNITION OF ST PAUL'S MISSION TO THE HEATHEN.—ST. JOHN.—RETURN TO ANTIOCH WITH JUDAS, SILAS, AND MARK.—READING OF THE LETTER.—WEAK CONDUCT OF ST. PETER AT ANTIOCH.—HE IS REBUKED BY ST. PAUL.—PERSONAL APPEARANCE OF THE TWO APOSTLES.—THEIR RECONCILIATION.

If, when we contrast the voyage of Paul and Barnabas across the bay of Attaleia, with the voyage of those who sailed over the same waters in the same direction, eleven centuries later, our minds are powerfully drawn towards the pure age of early Christianity, when the power of faith made human weakness irresistibly strong;—the same thoughts are not less forcibly presented to us, when we contrast the reception of the Crusaders at Antioch, with the reception of the Apostles in the same city. We are told by the Chroniclers[1], that Raymond, "Prince of Antioch," waited with much expectation for the arrival of the French King; and that, when he heard of his landing at Seleucia, he gathered together all the nobles and chief men of the people, and went out to meet him, and

[1] Raymond . . . princeps Antiochenus . . . adventum diebus multis ante expectaverat, cum desiderio sustinens, convocatis nobilibus totius regionis, et populi primoribus, cum electo comitatu ei occurrens, in urbem Antiochenam, omnem ei exhibens reverentiam, occurrente ei universo clero et populo, magnificentissime introduxit. Will. of Tyr. xvi. 27.

brought him into Antioch with much pomp and magnificence, showing him all reverence and homage, in the midst of a great assemblage of the clergy and people. All that St. Luke tells us of the reception of the Apostles after their victorious campaign, is, that they entered into the city and "gathered together the church, and told them how God had worked with them and how He had opened a door of faith to the Gentiles."[1] Thus the kingdom of God came at the first "without observation,"[2]—with the humble acknowledgment that all power is given from above,—and with a thankful recognition of our Father's merciful love to all mankind.

No age, however, of Christianity, not even the earliest, has been without its difficulties, controversies, and corruptions. The presence of Judas among the apostles, and of Ananias and Sapphira among the first disciples,[3] were proofs of the power which moral evil possesses to combine itself with the holiest works. The misunderstanding of "the Grecians and Hebrews" in the days of Stephen,[4], the suspicion of the apostles, when Paul came from Damascus to Jerusalem,[5] the secession of Mark at the beginning of the first missionary journey,[6] were symptoms of the prejudice, ignorance, and infirmity, in the midst of which the Gospel was to win its way in the hearts of men. And the arrival of the apostles at Antioch at the close of their journey was presently followed by a troubled controversy, which involved the most momentous consequences to all future ages of the Church; and which led to that visit to Jerusalem which, next after his conversion, is perhaps the most important passage in St. Paul's life.

We have seen (Ch. I.) that great numbers of Jews had long been dispersed beyond the limits of their own land, and were at this time distributed over every part of the Roman Empire. "Moses had of old time, in every city, them that preached him, being read in the Synagogues every Sabbath-day."[7] In every considerable city, both of the East and West, were established some members of that mysterious people,—who had a written law, which they read and re-read, in the midst of the contempt of those who surrounded them, week by week, and year by year,—who were bound everywhere by a secret link of affection to one city in the world, where alone their religious sacrifices could be offered,—whose whole life was utterly abhorrent from the temples and images which crowded the neighbourhood of their Synagogues, and from the gay and licentious festivities of the Greek and Roman worship.

In the same way it might be said that Plato and Aristotle, Zeno and Epicurus,[8] "had in every city those that preached them." Side by side with the doctrines of Judaism, the speculations of Greek philosophers

[1] Acts xiv. 27 [2] Luke xvii. 20. [3] Acts v. [4] P. 66. [5] P. 102.
[6] P. 163. [7] Acts xv. 21. [8] See Acts xvii. 18.

TOMBS AT SELEUCIA.

were—not indeed read in connection with religious worship—but orally taught and publicly discussed in the schools. Hence the Jews, in their foreign settlements, were surrounded, not only by an idolatry which shocked all their deepest feelings, and by a shameless profligacy unforbidden by, and even associated with, that which the Gentiles called religion,—but also by a proud and contemptuous philosophy that alienated the more educated classes of society to as great a distance as the unthinking multitude.

Thus a strong line of demarcation between the Jews and Gentiles ran through the whole Roman empire. Though their dwellings were often contiguous, they were separated from each other by deep-rooted feelings of aversion and contempt. The "middle wall of partition"[1] was built up by diligent hands on both sides. This mutual alienation existed, notwithstanding the vast number of proselytes, who were attracted to the Jewish doctrine and worship, and who, as we have already observed (Ch. I.), were silently preparing the way for the ultimate union of the two races. The breach was even widened, in many cases, in consequence of this work of proselytism: for those who went over to the Jewish camp, or hesitated on the neutral ground, were looked on with some suspicion by the Jews themselves, and thoroughly hated and despised by the Gentiles.

It must be remembered that the separation of which we speak was both religious and social. The Jews had a divine law, which sanctioned the principle, and enforced the practice, of national isolation. They could not easily believe that this law, with which all the glorious passages of their history were associated, was meant only to endure for a limited period: and we cannot but sympathise in the difficulty they felt in accepting the notion of a cordial union with the uncircumcised, even after idolatry was abandoned and morality observed. And again, the peculiar character of the religion which isolated the Jews was such as to place insuperable obstacles in the way of social union with other men. Their ceremonial observances precluded the possibility of their eating with the Gentiles. The nearest parallel we can find to this barrier between the Jews and Gentiles, is the institution of *caste* among the ancient populations of India, which presents itself to our politicians as a perplexing fact in the government of the presidencies, and to our missionaries as the great obstacle to the progress of Christianity in the East.[2] A Hindoo cannot eat with a Parsee, or a Mahomedan,—and among the Hindoos themselves

[1] Eph. ii. 14.

[2] See for instance the memoir of the Rev. H. W. Fox (1850), pp. 123–125. A short statement of the strict regulations of the modern Jews, in their present dispersed state concerning the slaughtering of animals for food and the sale of the meat, is given in Allen's Modern Judaism, ch. xxii.

the meals of a Brahmin are polluted by the presence of a Pariah,—though they meet and have free intercourse in the ordinary transaction of business. And so it was in the patriarchal age. It was "an abomination for the Egyptians to eat bread with the Hebrews."[1] The same principle was divinely sanctioned for a time in the Mosaic Institutions. The Israelites, who lived among the Gentiles, met them freely in the places of public resort, buying and selling, conversing and disputing: but their families were separate: in the relations of domestic life, it was "unlawful," as St. Peter said to Cornelius, "for a man that was a Jew to keep company or come unto one of another nation."[2] When St. Peter returned from the centurion at Cæsarea to his brother-christians at Jerusalem, their great charge against him was that he had "gone in to men uncircumcised, and had eaten with them:"[3] and the weak compliance of which he was guilty, after the true principle of social unity had been publicly recognised, and which called forth the stern rebuke of his brother-apostles, was that, after eating with the Gentiles, he "withdrew and separated himself, fearing them which were of the circumcision."[4]

How these two difficulties, which seemed to forbid the formation of an united Church on earth, were ever to be overcome,—how the Jews and Gentiles were to be religiously united, without the enforced obligation of the whole Mosaic Law,—how they were to be socially united as equal brethren in the family of a common Father,—the solution of this problem must in that day have appeared impossible. And without the direct intervention of Divine grace it would have been impossible. We now proceed to consider how that grace gave to the minds of the Apostles, the wisdom, discretion, forbearance, and firmness which were required; and how St. Paul was used as the great instrument in accomplishing a work necessary to the very existence of the Christian Church.

We encounter here a difficulty, well known to all who have examined this subject, in combining into one continuous narrative the statements in the Epistle to the Galatians and in the Acts of the Apostles. In the latter book we are informed of five distinct journeys made by the Apostle to Jerusalem after the time of his conversion;—first, when he escaped from Damascus, and spent a fortnight with Peter;[5] secondly, when he took the collection from Antioch with Barnabas in the time of famine;[6] thirdly, on the occasion of the Council, which is now before us in the fifteenth chapter of the Acts; fourthly, in the interval between his second and third missionary journeys;[7] and, fifthly, when the uproar was made in the Temple, and he was taken into the custody of the Roman garrison.[8] In the Epistles to the Galatians, St. Paul speaks of two journeys to Jeru-

[1] Gen. xliii. 32.
[2] Acts x. 28.
[3] Acts xi. 3.
[4] Gal. ii. 12.
[5] P. 101
[6] P. 127.
[7] Acts xviii. 22.
[8] Acts xxi. &c.

salem,—the first being "three years" after his conversion,[1] the second "fourteen years" later,[2] when his own apostleship was asserted and recognised in a public meeting of the other apostles.[3] Now, while we have no difficulty in stating, as we have done,[4] that the first journey of one account is the first journey of the other, theologians have been variously divided in opinion, as to whether the second journey of the Epistle must be identified with the second, third, or fourth of the Acts; or whether it is a separate journey, distinct from any of them. It is agreed by all that the fifth cannot possibly be intended.[5] The view we have adopted, that the second journey of the Epistle is the third of the Acts, is that of a majority of the best critics and commentators. For the arguments by which it is justified, and for a full discussion of the whole subject, we must refer the reader to the note at the end of this Chapter. Some of the arguments will be indirectly presented in the following narrative. So far as the circumstances combined together in the present Chapter appear natural, consecutive and coherent, so far some reason will be given for believing that we are not following an arbitrary assumption or a fanciful theory.

It is desirable to recur at the outset to the first instance of a Gentile's conversion to Christianity.[6] After the preceding remarks, we are prepared to recognise the full significance of the emblematical[7] vision which St. Peter saw at Joppa. The trance into which he fell at the moment of his hunger,—the vast sheet descending from heaven,—the promiscuous assemblage of clean and unclean animals[8]—the voice from heaven which said, "Arise, Peter, kill and *eat*,"—the whole of this imagery is invested with the deepest meaning, when we recollect all the details of religious and social life, which separated, up to that moment, the Gentile from the Jew. The words heard by St. Peter in his trance came like a shock on all the prejudices of his Jewish education.[9] He had never so

1 Gal. i. 18.

2 We take the δεκατεσσάρων (Gal. ii. 1) to refer to the preceding journey, and not to the conversion. This question, as well as that of the reading τεσσάρων, will be discussed in a future note.

3 Gal. ii. 1–10.

4 P. 101.

5 Some writers, *e. g.* Paley and Schrader, have contended that an entirely different journey, not mentioned in the Acts, is alluded to. This also will be discussed hereafter.

6 Acts x. xi.

7 The last emblematical visions (properly so called) were those seen by the prophet Zachariah.

8 See Levit. xi.

9 The feeling of the Jews in all ages is well illustrated by the following extract from a modern Jewish work: "If we disregard this precept, and say, 'What difference can it make to God if I eat the meat of an ox or swine,' we offend against His will, we pollute ourselves by what goes into the mouth, and can consequently lay no longer a claim to holiness; for the term 'holiness,' applied to mortals, means only a framing of our desires by the will of God. . . . . Have we not enough to eat without touching forbidden things? Let me beseech my dear fellow-believers not to deceive themselves by

broken the law of his forefathers as to eat any thing it condemned as unclean. And though the same voice spoke to him "a second time,"[1] and "answered him from heaven,"[2]—"What God has made clean that call not thou common,"—it required a wonderful combination of natural[3] and supernatural evidence to convince him that God is "no respecter of persons," but "in every nation" accepts him that "feareth Him and worketh righteousness,"[4]—that all such distinctions as depend on "meat and drink," on "holydays, new moons, and sabbaths," were to pass away,—that these things were only "a shadow of things to come,"—that "the body is of Christ,"—and that "in Him we are complete . . . circumcised with a circumcision not made with hands . . . buried with Him in baptism," and risen with Him through faith.[5]

The Christians "of the circumcision,"[6] who travelled with Peter from Joppa to Cæsarea, were "astonished" when they saw "the gift of the Holy Ghost poured out" on the uncircumcised Gentiles: and much dissatisfaction was created in the Church, when intelligence of the whole transaction came to Jerusalem. On Peter's arrival, his having "gone in to men uncircumcised, and eaten with them," was arraigned as a serious violation of religious duty. When St. Peter "rehearsed the matter from the beginning, and expounded it by order," appealing to the evidence of the "six brethren" who had accompanied him,—his accusers were silent, and so much conviction was produced at the time, that they expressed their gratitude to God, for His mercy in "granting to the Gentiles repentance unto life."[7] But subsequent events too surely proved that the discontent at Jerusalem was only partially allayed. Hesitation and perplexity began to arise in the minds of the Jewish Christians, with scrupulous misgivings concerning the rectitude of St. Peter's conduct, and an uncomfortable jealousy of the new converts. And nothing could be more natural than all this jealousy and perplexity. To us, with our present knowledge, it seems that the slightest relaxation of a ceremonial law should have been willingly and eagerly welcomed. But the view from the Jewish standing-point was very different. The religious difficulty in the mind of a Jew was greater than we can easily imagine. We can well believe that the minds of many may have been perplexed by the words and the conduct of our Lord Himself: for He had not been sent "save to the lost sheep of the house of Israel," and He said that it was "not meet to

saying, 'there is no sin in eating of aught that lives;' on the contrary, there is sin and contamination too." Leeser's Jews and the Mosaic Law; ch. on "The forbidden Meats." Philadelphia, 5594.

1 Acts x. 15. 2 Acts xi. 9.

3 The coincidence of outward events and inward admonitions was very similar to the circumstances connected with St. Paul's baptism by Ananias at Damascus.

4 Acts x. 34, 35. 5 See Col. ii. 8–23. 6 Acts x. 45, with xi. 12.

7 Acts xi. 1–18.

take the children's bread and cast it to dogs."[1] Until St. Paul appeared before the Church in his true character as the Apostle of the uncircumcision, few understood that "the law of the commandments contained in ordinances" had been abolished by the cross of Christ;[2] and that the "other sheep," not of the Jewish fold, should be freely admitted into the "one fold" by the "One Shepherd."[3]

The smouldering feeling of discontent which had existed from the first increased and became more evident as new Gentile converts were admitted into the Church. To pass over all the other events of the interval which had elapsed since the baptism of Cornelius, the results of the recent journey of Paul and Barnabas through the cities of Asia Minor must have excited a great commotion among the Jewish Christians. "A door of faith" had been opened "unto the Gentiles."[4] "He that wrought effectually in Peter to the apostleship of the circumcision, the same had been mighty in Paul toward the Gentiles."[5] And we cannot well doubt that both he and Barnabas had freely joined in social intercourse with the Gentile Christians, at Antioch in Pisidia, at Iconium, Lystra, and Derbe, as Peter "at the first"[6] "a good while ago"[7] had eaten with Cornelius at Cæsarea. At Antioch in Syria, it seems evident that both parties lived together in amicable intercourse and in much "freedom."[8] Nor, indeed, is this the city where we should have expected the Jewish controversy to have come to a crisis: for it was from Antioch that Paul and Barnabas had first been sent as missionaries to the heathen:[9] and it was at Antioch that Greek proselytes had first accepted the truth,[10] and that the united body of believers had first been called "Christians."[11]

Jerusalem was the metropolis of the Jewish world. The exclusive feelings which the Jews carried with them wherever they were diffused, were concentrated in Jerusalem in their most intense degree. It was there, in the sight of the Temple, and with all the recollections of their ancestors surrounding their daily life, that the impatience of the Jewish Christians kindled into burning indignation. They saw that Christianity, instead of being the purest and holiest form of Judaism, was rapidly becoming a universal and indiscriminating religion, in which the Jewish element would be absorbed and lost. This revolution could not appear to them in any other light than as a rebellion against all that they had been taught to hold inviolably sacred. And since there was no doubt that the great instigator of this change of opinion was that Saul of Tarsus whom they had once known as a young Pharisee at the "feet of Gamaliel," the contest took the form of an attack made by "certain of the sect of the

[1] Matt. xv. 24, 26. [2] Eph. ii. 15.
[3] John x. 16. [4] Acts xiv. 27. [5] Gal. ii. 8.
[6] Acts xv. 14. [7] Acts xv. 7. [8] See Gal. ii. 4.
[9] Acts xiii. 1, &c. [10] Acts xi. 19–21. [11] Acts xi. 26.

Pharisees" upon St. Paul. The battle which had been fought and lost in the "Cilician synagogue" was now to be renewed within the Church itself.

Some of the "false brethren" (for such is the name which St. Paul gives to the Judaizers [1]) went down "from Judæa" to Antioch.[2] The course they adopted, in the first instance, was not that of open antagonism to St. Paul, but rather of clandestine intrigue. They came as "spies" into an enemy's camp,[3] creeping in "unawares,"[4] that they might ascertain how far the Jewish Law had been relaxed by the Christians at Antioch; their purpose being to bring the whole Church, if possible, under the "bondage" of the Jewish yoke. It appears that they remained some considerable time at Antioch,[5] gradually insinuating, or openly inculcating, their opinion that the observance of the Jewish Law was *necessary to salvation.* It is very important to observe the exact form which their teaching assumed. They did not merely recommend or enjoin, for prudential reasons, the continuance of certain ceremonies in themselves indifferent: but they said, "Except ye be circumcised after the manner of Moses, *ye cannot be saved.*" Such a doctrine must have been instantly opposed by St. Paul with his utmost energy. He was always ready to go to the extreme verge of charitable concession when the question was one of peace and mutual understanding: but when the very foundations of Christianity were in danger of being undermined, when the very continuance of "the truth of the Gospel"[6] was in jeopardy, it was impossible that he should "give place by subjection," even "for an hour."

The "dissension and disputation,"[7] which arose between Paul and Barnabas and the false brethren from Judæa, resulted in a general anxiety and perplexity among the Syrian Christians. The minds of "those who from among the Gentiles were turned unto God" were "troubled" and unsettled.[8] Those "words" which "perverted the Gospel of Christ" tended also to "subvert the souls" of those who heard them.[9] It was determined, therefore, "that Paul and Barnabas, with certain others, should go up to Jerusalem unto the Apostles and elders about this question." It was well known that those who were disturbing the peace of the Church had their head-quarters in Judæa. Such a theological party could only be successfully met in the stronghold of Jewish nationality. Moreover, the residence of the principal Apostles was at Jerusalem, and the community over which "James" presided was still regarded as the Mother-Church of Christendom.

[1] Gal. ii. 4. [2] Acts xv. 1.

[3] *Κατασκοπῆσαι.* "Verbum Castrense." Grotius. See Chrys. on Gal. ii. 4.

[4] See *παρεισάκτους* and *παρεισῆλθον.* Gal. ii. 4.

[5] This may be inferred from the imperfect *ἐδίδασκον.* Compare xiv. 28.

[6] Gal. ii. 5. [7] Acts xv. 2. [8] Acts xv. 19. [9] Gal. i. 7. Acts. xv. 24.

In addition to this mission with which St. Paul was entrusted by the Church at Antioch, he received an intimation of the Divine Will communicated by direct revelation. Such a revelation at so momentous a crisis must appear perfectly natural to all who believe that Christianity was introduced into the world by the immediate power of God. If "a man of Macedonia" appeared to Paul in the visions of the night, when he was about to carry the Gospel from Asia into Europe:[1] if "the angel of God" stood by him in the night when the ship that was conveying him to Rome was in danger of sinking;[2] we cannot wonder when he tells us that, on this occasion, when he "went up to Jerusalem with Barnabas," he went "by revelation."[3] And we need not be surprised, if we find that St. Paul's path was determined by two different causes; that he went to Jerusalem partly because the Church deputed him, and partly because he was divinely admonished. Such a combination and co-operation of the natural and the supernatural we have observed above,[4] in the case of that vision which induced St. Peter to go from Joppa to Cæsarea. Nor need we feel any great difficulty in adopting this view of St. Paul's journey from Antioch to Jerusalem,—from this circumstance, that the two motives which conspired to direct him are separately mentioned in different parts of Scripture. It is true that we are told in the Acts[5] simply that it was "determined" at Antioch that Paul should go to Jerusalem; and that in Galatians,[6] we are informed by himself that he went "by revelation." But we have an exact parallel in an earlier journey, already related,[7] from Jerusalem to Tarsus. In St. Luke's narrative[8] it is stated that "the brethren," knowing that the conspiracy against his life, "brought him down to Cæsarea and sent him forth;" while in the speech of St. Paul himself,[9] we are told that in a trance he saw Jesus Christ, and received from Him a command to depart "quickly out of Jerusalem."

Similarly directed from without and from within, he travelled to Jerusalem on the occasion before us. It would seem that his companions were carefully chosen with reference to the question in dispute. On the one hand was Barnabas,[10] a Jew and "a Levite" by birth,[11] a good representative of the church of the circumcision. On the other hand was Titus,[12] now first mentioned[13] in the course of our narrative, a

[1] Acts xvi. 9.
[2] Acts xxvii. 23.
[3] Gal. ii. 2. Schrader (who does not however identify this journey with that in Acts xv.) translates *κατὰ ἀποκάλυψιν*—"to make a revelation," which is a meaning the words can scarcely bear.
[4] Pp. 207, 208.
[5] xv. 2.
[6] ii. 2.
[7] Ch. III. p. 104.
[8] Acts ix. 30.
[9] Acts xxii. 17, 18.
[10] Acts xv. 2.
[11] Acts iv. 36.
[12] Gal. ii. 1–5.
[13] Titus is not mentioned at all in the Acts of the Apostles, unless the reading *Τίτου Ἰούστου* in xviii. 7 be correct, which is not probable (see below, p. 229, note). Besides the present Epistle and that to Titus himself, he is only mentioned in 2 Cor. and 2 Tim.

convert from heathenism, an uncircumcised "Greek." From the expression used of the departure of this company it seems evident that the majority of the Christians at Antioch were still faithful to the truth of the Gospel. Had the Judaizers triumphed, it would hardly have been said that Paul and his fellow-travellers were "brought on their way by the Church."[1] Their course was along the great Roman Road, which followed the Phœnician coast-line, and traces of which are still seen on the cliffs overhanging the sea,[2] and thence through the midland districts of Samaria and Judæa. When last we had occasion to mention Phœnice,[3] we were alluding to those who were dispersed on the death of Stephen, and preached the Gospel "to Jews only" on this part of the Syrian coast. Now it seems evident that many of the heathen Syro-Phœnicians had been converted to Christianity: for as Paul and Barnabas passed through, "declaring the conversion of the Gentiles, they caused great joy unto all the brethren." As regards the Samaritans,[4] we cannot be surprised that they who, when Philip first "preached Christ unto them," had received the glad tidings with "great joy," should be ready to express their sympathy in the happiness of those who, like themselves, had recently been "aliens from the commonwealth of Israel."

Fifteen years[5] had now elapsed since that memorable journey, when

In a later part of this work he will be noticed more particularly as St. Paul's συνεργός (2 Cor. viii. 23).

[1] Προπεμφθέντες ὑπὸ τῆς ἐκκλησίας. Acts xv. 3. So the phrase παραδοθεὶς τῇ χάριτι τοῦ Κυρίου ὑπὸ τῶν ἀδελφῶν (xv. 40), may be reasonably adduced as a proof that the feeling of the majority was with Paul rather than Barnabas.

[2] Dr. Robinson passed two Roman milestones between Tyre and Sidon (iii. 415), and observed traces of a Roman road between Sidon and Beyrout. See also Fisher's Syria (i. 40) for a notice of the Via Antonina between Beyrout and Tripoli.

[3] P. 116. Acts xi. 19, 20. It may be interesting here to allude to the journey of a Jew in the Middle Ages from Antioch to Jerusalem. It is probable that the stations, the road, the rate of travelling were the same, and the distribution of the Jews not very different. We find the following passage in the Itinerary of Benjamin of Tudela, who travelled in 1163. "Two days bring us from Antioch to Lega, which is Latachia, and contains about 200 Jews, the principal of whom are R. Chiia and R. Joseph. . . . One day's journey to Gebal of the children of Ammon; it contains about 150 Jews. . . . . Two days hence is Beyrut. The principal of its 50 Jewish inhabitants are R. Solomon, R. Obadiah, and R. Joseph. It is hence one day's journey to Saida, which is Sidon of Scripture [Acts xxvii. 3], a large city, with about 20 Jewish families. . . . . One day's journey to New Sur [Tyre, Acts xxi. 3], a very beautiful city. . . . . The Jews of Sur are ship-owners and manufacturers of the celebrated Tyrian glass. . . . . It is one day hence to Acre [Ptolemais, Acts xxi. 7]. It is the frontier town of Palestine; and, in consequence of its situation on the shore of the Mediterranean, and of its large port, it is the principal place of disembarcation of all pilgrims who visit Jerusalem by sea." Early Travels to Palestine, pp. 78–81.

[4] See pp. 79, 80.

[5] Gal. ii. 1, where we ought probably to reckon inclusively. See note at the end of this Chapter.

St. Paul left Jerusalem, with all the zeal of a Pharisee, to persecute and destroy the Christians in Damascus.[1] He had twice entered, as a Christian, the Holy City again. Both visits had been short and hurried, and surrounded with danger. The first was three years after his conversion, when he spent a fortnight with Peter, and escaped assassination by a precipitate flight to Tarsus.[2] The second was in the year 44, when Peter himself was in imminent danger, and when the messengers who brought the charitable contribution from Antioch were probably compelled to return immediately.[3] Now St. Paul came at a more peaceful period of the Church's history, to be received as the successful champion of the Gospel, and as the leader of the greatest revolution which the world has seen. It was now undeniable that Christianity had spread to a wide extent in the Gentile world, and that he had been the great instrument in advancing its progress. He came to defend his own principles and practice against an increasing torrent of opposition, which had disturbed him in his distant ministrations at Antioch, but the fountain-head of which was among the Pharisees at Jerusalem.

The Pharisees had been the companions of St. Paul's younger days. Death had made many changes in the course of fifteen years; but some must have been there who had studied with him "at the feet of Gamaliel." Their opposition was doubtless embittered by remembering what he had been before his conversion. Nor do we allude here to those Pharisees who opposed Christianity. These were not the enemies whom St. Paul came to resist. The time was past when the Jews, unassisted by the Roman power, could exercise a cruel tyranny over the Church. Its safety was no longer dependent on the wisdom or caution of Gamaliel. The great debates at Jerusalem are no longer between Jews and Christians in the Hellenistic synagogues, but between the Judaising and spiritual parties of the Christians themselves. Many of the Pharisees, after the example of St. Paul, had believed that Jesus was Christ.[4] But they had not followed the example of their school-companion in the surrender of Jewish bigotry. The battle, therefore, which had once been fought without, was now to be renewed within the Church. It seems that, at the very first reception of Paul and Barnabas at Jerusalem, some of these Pharisaic Christians "rose up," and insisted that the observance of Judaism was necessary to salvation. They said that it was absolutely "needful to circumcise" the new converts, and to "command them to keep the Law of Moses." The whole course of St. Paul's procedure among the Gentiles was here openly attacked. Barnabas was involved in the same suspicion and reproach; and with regard to Titus, who was

[1] See Ch. III. [2] P. 101. Compare p. 206. [3] P. 127. Compare p. 206
[4] Acts xv. 5.

with them as the representative of the Gentile Church, it was asserted that, without circumcision, he could not hope to be partaker of the blessings of the Gospel.

But far more was involved than any mere opposition, however factious, to individual missionaries, or than the severity of any conditions imposed on individual converts. The question of liberty or bondage for all future ages was to be decided ; and a convention of the whole Church at Jerusalem was evidently called for. In the meantime, before "the Apostles and elders came together to consider of this matter,"[1] St. Paul had private conferences with the more influential members of the Christian community,[2] and especially with James, Peter, and John,[3] the great Apostles and "Pillars" of the Church. Great caution and management were required, in consequence of the intrigues of the "false brethren," both in Jerusalem and Antioch. He was, moreover, himself the great object of suspicion, and it was his duty to use every effort to remove the growing prejudice. Thus, though conscious of his own inspiration and tenaciously holding the truth which he knew to be essential, he yet acted with that prudence which was characteristic of his whole life,[4] and which he honestly avows in the Epistle to the Galatians.

If we may compare our own feeble imitations of Apostolic zeal and prudence with the proceedings of the first founders of the Church of Christ, we may say that these preliminary conferences were like the private meetings which prepare the way for a great religious assembly in England. Paul and Barnabas had been deputed from Antioch ; Titus was with them as a sample of Gentile conversions, and a living proof of their reality ; and the great end in view was to produce full conviction in the Church at large. At length the great meeting was summoned[5] which was to settle the principles of missionary action among the Gentiles. It was a scene of earnest debate, and perhaps, in its earlier portion, of angry "disputing :"[6] but the passages which the Holy Spirit has caused to be recorded for our instruction are those which relate to the Apostles themselves,—the address of St. Peter, the narrative of Barnabas and Paul, and the concluding speech of St. James. These three passages must be separately considered in the order of Scripture.

[1] Acts xv. 6. [2] Gal. ii. 2.

[3] Gal. ii. 9. [4] See, for instance, the sixth and seventeenth verses of Acts xxi

[5] This meeting is described (Acts xv. 6) as consisting of the "Apostles and Elders ;' but the decision afterwards given is said to be the decision of "the Apostles and Elders with the whole Church" (v. 22), and the decree was sent in the names of "the Apostles, and Elders, and Brethren" (v. 23). Hence we must suppose, either that the decision was made by the synod of the Apostles and Elders, and afterwards ratified by another larger meeting of the whole Church, or that there was only one meeting, in which the whole Church took part, although only the "Apostles and Elders" are mentioned.

[6] Acts xv. 7

St. Peter was the first of the Apostles who rose to address the assembly.[1] He gave his decision against the Judaizers, and in favour of St. Paul. He reminded his hearers of the part which he himself had taken in admitting the Gentiles into the Christian Church. They were well aware, he said, that these recent converts in Syria and Cilicia were not the first heathens who had believed the Gospel, and that he himself had been chosen by God to begin the work which St. Paul had only been continuing. The communication of the Holy Ghost was the true test of God's acceptance; and God had shown that He was no respecter of persons, by shedding abroad the same miraculous gifts on Jew and Gentile, and purifying by faith the hearts of both alike. And then St. Peter went on to speak, in touching language, of the yoke of the Jewish law. Its weight had pressed heavily on many generations of Jews, and was well known to the Pharisees who were listening at that moment. They had been relieved from legal bondage by the salvation offered through faith; and it would be tempting God to impose on others a burden which neither they nor their fathers had ever been able to bear.

The next speakers were Paul and Barnabas. There was great silence through all the multitude,[2] and every eye was turned on the missionaries while they gave the narrative of their journeys. Though Barnabas is mentioned here before Paul,[3] it is most likely that the latter was "the chief speaker." But both of them appear to have addressed the audience.[4] They had much to relate of what they had done and seen together: and especially they made appeal to the miracles which God had worked among the Gentiles by them. Such an appeal must have been a persuasive argument to the Jew, who was familiar, in his ancient Scriptures, with many divine interruptions of the course of nature. These interferences had signalised all the great passages of Jewish history. Jesus Christ had proved His divine mission in the same manner. And the events at Paphos,[5] at Iconium,[6] and Lystra,[7] could not well be regarded in any other light than as a proof that the same Power had been with Paul and Barnabas, which accompanied the words of Peter and John in Jerusalem and Judæa.[8]

But the opinion of another speaker still remained to be given. This was James, the brother of the Lord,[9] who, from the austere sanctity of his

[1] Acts xv. 7–11.

[2] Ἐσίγησε πᾶν τὸ πλῆθος κ. τ. λ. Acts xv. 12. The imperfect ἤκουον implies attention to a continued narrative.

[3] This order of the names in the narrative, xv. 12, and in the letter below, v. 25 (not in v. 22), is a remarkable exception to the phrase "Paul and Barnabas," which has been usual since Acts xiii. See below, p. 221, note 5.

[4] See v. 13, μετὰ τὸ σιγῆσαι αὐτούς.

[5] Acts xiii. 11.

[6] Acts xiv. 3.

Acts xiv. 8.

[8] Acts ii. v. ix.

[9] See Acts xv. 13–32. It is well known that there is much perplexity connected

character, was commonly called, both by Jews and Christians, "James the Just." No judgment could have such weight with the Judaising party as his. Not only in the vehement language in which he denounced the sins of the age, but even in garb and appearance, he resembled John the Baptist, or one of the older prophets, rather than the other apostles of the new dispensation. "Like the ancient saints, even in outward aspect, with the austere features, the linen ephod, the bare feet, the long locks and unshorn beard of the Nazarite,"[1]—such, according to tradition, was the man who now came forward, and solemnly pronounced the Mosaic rites were not of eternal obligation. After alluding to the argument of Peter (whose name we find him characteristically quoting in its Jewish form[2]), he turns to the ancient prophets, and adduces a passage from Amos[3] to prove that Christianity is the fulfilment of Judaism. And then he passes to the historical aspect of the subject, contending that this fulfilment was predetermined by God himself, and that the Jewish dispensation was in truth the preparation for the Christian.[4] Such a decision, pronounced by one who stood emphatically on the confines of the two dispensations, came with great force on all who heard it, and carried with it the general opinion of the assembly to the conclusion that those "who from among the Gentiles had turned unto God" should not be "troubled" with any Jewish obligations, except such as were necessary for peace and the mutual good understanding of the two parties.

The spirit of charity and mutual forbearance is very evident in the decree which was finally enacted. Its spirit was that expressed by St. Paul in his Epistles to the Romans and Corinthians. He knew, and was persuaded by the Lord Jesus, that nothing is unclean of itself: but to him that esteemeth anything to be unclean, to him it is unclean. He knew that an idol is nothing in the world, and that there is none other God but one: but all men have not this knowledge: some could not eat that which had been offered in sacrifice to an idol without defiling their conscience. It is good to abstain from everything whereby a weaker brother may be led to

with those apostles who bore the name of James. Neander (Pfl. u. L. p. 554) says the question is one of the most difficult in the New Testament. Wieseler has written an essay on the subject in the St. u. K. We are not required here to enter into the investigation, and are content to adopt the opinion which is most probable.

[1] Stanley's Sermons and Essays, &c., p. 295. We must refer here to the whole of the "Sermon on the Epistle of St. James," and of the "Essay on the Traditions of James the Just," especially pp. 292, 302, 327.

[2] *Συμεὼν ἐξηγήσατο.* Acts xv. 14. So St. Peter names himself at the beginning of his Second Epistle, *Συμεὼν Πέτρος δοῦλος, κ. τ. λ.*

[3] Amos ix. 11, 12. We are not required to express any opinion on the application of prophecy to the future destiny of the Jews; but we must observe, that the Apostles themselves apply such prophecies as this to the Christian Dispensation. See Acts ii. 17

[4] *Γνωρτὰ ἀπ' αἰῶνος, κ. τ. λ.* v. 18. Compare Acts xvii. 26. Rom. i. 2. Eph. i. 10 iii. 9, 10. Col. i. 26.

stumble. To sin thus against our brethren is to sin against Christ.[1] In accordance with these principles it was enacted that the Gentile converts should be required to abstain from that which had been polluted by being offered in sacrifice to idols, from the flesh of animals which had been strangled, and generally from the eating of blood. The reason for these conditions is stated in the verse to which particular allusion has been made at the beginning of the present chapter.[2] The Law of Moses was read every Sabbath in all the cities, where the Jews were dispersed.[3] A due consideration for the prejudices of the Jews made it reasonable for the Gentile converts to comply with some of the restrictions which the Mosaic Law and ancient custom had imposed on every Jewish meal. In no other way could social intercourse be built up and cemented between the two parties. If some forbearance were requisite on the part of the Gentiles in complying with such conditions, not less forbearance was required from the Jews in exacting no more. And to the Gentiles themselves the restrictions were a merciful condition : for it helped them to disentangle themselves more easily from the pollutions connected with their idolatrous life. We are not merely concerned here with the question of social separation, the food which was a delicacy[4] to the Gentile being abominated by the Jew,—nor with the difficulties of weak and scrupulous consciences, who might fear too close a contact between "the table of the Lord" and "the table of Demons,"[5]—but this controversy had an intimate connection with the principles of universal morality. The most shameless violations of purity took place in connection with the sacrifices and feasts celebrated in honour of heathen divinities.[6] Everything, therefore, which tended to keep the Gentile converts even from accidental or apparent association with these scenes of vice, made their own recovery from pollution more easy, and enabled the Jewish converts to look on their new Christian brethren with less suspicion and antipathy. This seems to be the reason why we find an acknowledged sin mentioned in the decree

[1] Rom. xiv. 1 Cor. viii.

[2] Above, p. 204. There is some difference of opinion as to the connection of this verse with the context. Some consider it to imply that while it was necessary to urge these conditions on the Gentiles, it was needless to say any thing to the Jews on the subject, since they had the Law of Moses, and knew its requirements. Dean Milman infers that the regulations were made because the Christians in general met in the same places of religious worship with the Jews. "These provisions were necessary, because the Mosaic Law was universally read, and from immemorial usage in the synagogue The direct violation of its most vital principles by any of those who joined in the common worship would be incongruous, and of course highly offensive to the more zealous Mosaists." Hist. of Christianity, vol. i. p. 426, n.

[3] Acts xv. 21.

[4] We learn from Athenæus that τὸ πνικτὸν was regarded as a delicacy among the Greeks.

[5] 1 Cor. x. 21.

[6] See Tholuck in his "Nature and Moral Influence of Heathenism," part iii.

along with ceremonial observances which were meant to be only temporary[1] and perhaps local.[2] We must look on the whole subject from the Jewish point of view, and consider how violations of morality and contradictions of the ceremonial law were associated together in the Gentile world. It is hardly necessary to remark that much additional emphasis is given to the moral part of the decree, when we remember that it was addressed to those who lived in close proximity to the profligate sanctuaries of Antioch and Paphos.[3]

We have said that the ceremonial part of the decree was intended for a temporary and perhaps only a local observance. It is not for a moment implied that any Jewish ceremony is necessary to salvation. On the contrary, the great principle was asserted, once for all, that man is justified, not by the law, but by faith: one immediate result was that Titus, the companion of Paul and Barnabas, "was not compelled to be circumcised."[4] His case was not like that of Timothy at a later period,[5] whose circumcision was a prudential accommodation to circumstances, without endangering the truth of the Gospel. To have circumcised Titus at the time of the meeting in Jerusalem, would have been to have asserted that he was "bound to keep the whole law."[6] And when the alternative was between "the liberty wherewith Christ has made us free," and the reimposition of "the yoke of bondage," Paul's language always was,[7] that if Gentile converts were circumcised, Christ could "profit them nothing." By seeking

[1] We cannot, however be surprised that one great branch of the Christian Church takes a different view. The doctrine of the Greek Church, both Ancient and Modern, may be seen in the *Πηδάλιον*, or Greek Book of Canon Law (Athens, 1841). In the Apostolic Constitutions we find the following:—*Εἴτις 'Επίσκοπος ἢ Πρεσβύτερος ἢ Διάκονος φάγῃ κρέα ἐν αἵματι ψυχῆς αὐτοῦ, ἢ θηριάλωτον ἢ θνησιμαῖον, καθαιρείσθω. τοῦτο γὰρ ὁ Νόμος ἀπεῖπεν. Εἰ δὲ Λαϊκὸς εἴη, ἀφοριζέσθω.* The modern comment, after adducing Gen. ix. and Levit. xvii., proceeds: *'Αλλὰ γὰρ καὶ εἰς τὸν νέον Νόμον τοῦ Εὐαγγελίου τὰ τοιαῦτα ἐμποδίζονται νὰ μὴν τρώγωνται. Συναχθέντες γὰρ οἱ ἴδιοι οὗτοι 'Απόστολοι ἔγραψαν, κ. τ. λ.* (Acts xv. 18, 19.) *'Η αἰτία δὲ διὰ τὴν ὁποίαν ἐμποδίζονται τὰ θηριάλωτα ἢ ὀρνεοπύτακτα ζῶα ἢ θνησιμαῖα, ἢ πνικτὰ, εἶναι, διὰ τι δὲν χύνεται ὅλον τὸ αἷμα αὐτῶν ἀλλὰ ηένει μέσα εἰς αὐτὰ, διασκορπιζόμενον εἰς τὰ φλεβίδια ὅλα τοῦ κρέατος, ἀπὸ τὰ ὁποῖα νὰ εὐγῇ δὲν εἶναι τρόπος.* (pp. 45, 46.) Again, in one of the Canons of the Trullian Council, we find: *'Η Θεία ἡμῖν γραφὴ ἐνετείλατο, ἀπέχεσθαι, κ. τ. λ. Τοῖς οὖν διὰ τὴν λίχνον γαστέρα, αἷμα οἱουδήποτε ζώου τέχνῃ τινὶ κατασκευάζουσιν ἐδώδιμον καὶ οὕτω τοῦτο ἐσθίουσι, προσφορῶς ἐπιτιμῶμεν.* (p. 160.) And in the Council of Gaggra, in a decree alluding to 1 Tim. iv. 3, the same condition is introduced: *Εἴ τις ἐσθιόντα κρέα (χωρὶς αἵματος καὶ εἰδωλοθύτου καὶ πνικτοῦ) μετ' εὐλαβείας καὶ πιστέως, κατακρίνοι . . . ἀνάθεμα ἔστω.* (p. 230.) The practice of the modern Greeks is strictly in accordance with these decisions.

[2] At least the decree (Acts xv. 23) is addressed only to the churches of "Syria and Cilicia," and we do not see the subject alluded to again after xvi. 4.

[3] See above, pp. 135 and 168, and Lucian's Treatise de Deâ Syriâ."

[4] Gal. ii. 3. [5] Acts xvi. 3. [6] Gal. v. 3.

[7] *'Ιδε ἐγὼ Παῦλος λέγω ὑμῖν, ὅτι ἐὰν περιτέμνησθε, Χριστὸς ὑμᾶς οὐδὲν ὠφελήσει* Gal. v. 2.

to be justified in the law they fell from grace.[1] In this firm refusal to comply with the demand of the Judaizers, the case of all future converts from heathenism was virtually involved. It was asserted once for all that in the Christian Church there is "neither Greek nor Jew, circumcision nor uncircumcision, barbarian, Scythian, bond, nor free: but that Christ is all and in all."[2] And St. Paul obtained the victory for that principle which, we cannot doubt, will hereafter destroy the distinctions that are connected with the institution of slavery in America and of caste in India.

Certain other points decided in this meeting had a more direct personal reference to St. Paul himself. His own independent mission had been called in question. Some, perhaps, said that he was antagonistic to the Apostles at Jerusalem, others that he was entirely dependent on them.[3] All the Judaizers agreed in blaming his course of procedure among the Gentiles. This course was now entirely approved by the other Apostles. His independence was fully recognised. Those who were universally regarded as "pillars of the truth," James, Peter, and John,[4] gave to him and Barnabas the right hand of fellowship, and agreed that they should be to the heathen what themselves were to the Jews. Thus was St. Paul publicly acknowledged as the Apostle of the Gentiles, and openly placed in that position from which "he shall never more go out," as a pillar of the temple of the "New Jerusalem," inscribed with the "New Name" which proclaims the union of all mankind in one Saviour.[5]

One of those who gave the right hand of fellowship to St. Paul, was the "beloved disciple" of that Saviour.[6] This is the only meeting of St. Paul and St. John recorded in Scripture. It is, moreover, the last notice which we find there of the life of St. John, until the time of the apocalyptic vision in the island of Patmos. For both these reasons the mind eagerly seizes on the incident, though it is only casually mentioned in the Epistle to the Galatians. Like other incidental notices contained in Scripture, it is very suggestive of religious thoughts. St. John had been silent during the discussion in the public assembly; but at the close of it he ex-

[1] Gal. v. 4. [2] Col. iii. 11.

[3] The charges brought against St. Paul by the Judaizers were very various at different times.

[4] It should be carefully observed here that James is mentioned first of these *Säulenaposteln* (to quote a phrase from the German commentators), and that Peter is mentioned by the name of Cephas, as in 1 Cor. i. 12.

[5] See Rev. iii. 12. The same metaphor is found in 1 Tim. iii. 15, where Timothy is called (for this seems the natural interpretation), "a pillar and support of the truth." In these passages it is important to bear in mind the peculiarity of ancient architecture, which was characterised by vertical columns, supporting horizontal entablatures. Inscriptions were often engraved on these columns. Hence the words in the passage quoted from Revelations: *γράψω ἐπ' αὐτὸν . . . τὸ ὄνομά μου τὸ καινόν.*

[6] Gal. ii. 9.

pressed his cordial union with St. Paul in "the truth of the Gospel."[1] That union has been made visible to all ages by the juxtaposition of their Epistles in the same Sacred Volume. They stand together among the pillars of the Holy Temple; and the Church of God is thankful to learn how Contemplation may be united with Action, and Faith with Love, in the spiritual life.

To the decree with which Paul and Barnabas were charged, one condition was annexed, with which they gladly promised to comply. We have already had occasion to observe (p. 66) that the Hebrews of Judæa were relatively poor, compared with those of the dispersion, and that the Jewish Christians in Jerusalem were exposed to peculiar suffering from poverty; and we have seen Paul and Barnabas once before the bearers of a contribution from a foreign city for their relief.[2] They were exhorted now to continue the same charitable work, and in their journeys among the Gentiles and the dispersed Jews, "to remember the poor" at Jerusalem.[3] In proof of St. Paul's faithful discharge of this promise, we need only allude to his zeal in making "the contribution for the poor saints at Jerusalem," in Galatia, Macedonia and Achaia;[4] and to that last journey to the Holy Land, when he went, "after many years," to take "alms to his nation."[5] It is more important here to consider (what indeed we have mentioned before) the effect which this charitable exertion would have in binding together the divided parties in the Church. There cannot be a doubt that the Apostles had this result in view. Their anxiety on this subject is the best commentary on the spirit in which they had met on this great occasion; and we may rest assured that the union of the Gentile and Jewish Christians was largely promoted by the benevolent efforts which attended the diffusion of the Apostolic Decree.

Thus the controversy being settled, Paul's mission to the Gentiles being fully recognised, and his method of communicating the Gospel approved of by the other Apostles, and the promise being given, that in their journeys among the heathen, they would remember the necessities of the Hebrew Christians in Judæa, the two missionaries returned from Jerusalem to Antioch. They carried with them the decree which was to give peace to the consciences that had been troubled by the Judaising agitators; and the two companions, Judas and Silas,[6] who travelled with them, were empowered to accredit their commission and character. It seems also that Mark

[1] Gal. ii. 5. [2] See pp. 127, 128.

[3] Μόνον τῶν πτωχῶν ἵνα μνημονεύωμεν, ὁ καὶ ἐσπούδασα αὐτὸ τοῦτο ποιῆσαι. Gal. ii. 10. Where the change from the plural to the singular should be noticed. Is this because Barnabas was soon afterwards separated from St. Paul (Acts xv. 39), who had thenceforth to prosecute the charitable work alone?

[4] "As I have given order to the Churches of Galatia, &c.," 1 Cor. xv. 1–4. "It hath pleased them of Macedonia and Achaia, &c." Rom. xv. 25, 26. See 2 Cor. viii. ix.

[5] Acts xxiv. 17 [6] Acts xv. 22. 27. 32.

was another companion of Paul and Barnabas on this journey; for the last time we had occasion to mention his name was when he withdrew from Pamphylia to Jerusalem (p. 162), and presently we see him once more with his kinsman at Antioch.[1]

The reception of the travellers at Antioch was full of joy and satisfaction.[2] The whole body of the Church was summoned together to hear the reading of the letter; and we can well imagine the eagerness with which they crowded to listen, and the thankfulness and "consolation" with which such a communication was received, after so much anxiety and perplexity. The letter indeed is almost as interesting to us as to them, not only because of the principle asserted and the results secured, but also because it is the first document preserved to us from the acts of the Primitive Church. The words of the original document, literally translated, are as follows:—

THE APOSTLES AND THE ELDERS, AND THE BRETHREN, TO THE GENTILE BRETHREN IN ANTIOCH, AND SYRIA, AND CILICIA, GREETING.[3]

"Whereas we have heard that certain men who went out from us have troubled you with words, and unsettled your souls[4] by telling you to circumcise yourselves and keep the Law, although we gave them no such commission:

"It has been determined by us, being assembled with one accord, to choose some from amongst ourselves and send them to you with our beloved[5] Barnabas and Saul, men that have hazarded their lives for the name of our Lord Jesus Christ. We have sent therefore Judas and Silas, who themselves also[6] will tell you by word the same which we tell you by letter.

"For it has been determined by the Holy Ghost and by us, to lay upon you no greater burden than these necessary things: that ye abstain from meats offered to idols, and

[1] Acts xv. 37. [2] Acts xv. 31.

[3] *Χαίρειν*. The only other place where this salutation occurs is James i. 1; an undesigned coincidence tending to prove the genuineness of this document.

[4] Although the best MSS. omit the words from *λέγοντες* to *νόμον*, yet we cannot but agree with De Wette that they cannot possibly be an interpolation.

[5] It is another undesigned coincidence that the names of these two Apostles are here in the reverse order to that which, in St. Luke's *narrative* (except when he speaks of Jerusalem), they have assumed since chap. xiii. In the view of the Church at Jerusalem, Paul's name would naturally come after that of Barnabas. See above, p. 215, n. 3.

[6] *'Απαγγέλλοντας*. The present participle may be explained by the ancient idiom of letter writing, by which the writer transferred himself into the time of the reader This seems a more natural explanation than that given by Winer, Gramk. sect. 46. 5.

from blood, and from things strangled, and from fornication. Wherefrom if ye keep yourselves it shall be well with you. FAREWELL."

The encouragement inspired by this letter would be increased by the sight of Judas and Silas, who were ready to confirm its contents by word of mouth. These two disciples remained some short time at Antioch. They were possessed of that power of "prophecy," which was one of the forms in which the Holy Spirit made His presence known: and the Syrian Christians were "exhorted and confirmed" by the exercise of this miraculous gift.[1] The minds of all were in great tranquillity when the time came for the return of these messengers "to the Apostles" at Jerusalem. Silas, however, either remained at Antioch, or soon came back.[2] He was destined, as we shall see, to become the companion of St. Paul, and to be at the beginning of the second missionary journey what Barnabas had been at the beginning of the first.

Two painful scenes were witnessed at Antioch before the Apostle started on that second journey. We are informed[3] that Paul and Barnabas protracted their stay in this city, and were diligently occupied, with many others, in making the glad tidings of the Gospel known, and in the general work of Christian instruction. It is in this interval of time that we must place that visit of St. Peter to Antioch,[4] which St. Paul mentions in the Epistle to the Galatians,[5] immediately after his notice of the affairs of the Council. It appears that Peter, having come to Antioch for some reason which is unknown to us,[6] lived at first in free and unrestrained intercourse with the Gentile converts, meeting them in

[1] *Ἰούδας τε καὶ Σίλας, καὶ αὐτοὶ προφῆται ὄντες. κ. τ. λ.* Acts xv. 32. Compare xiii. 1.

[2] Acts xv. 34. The reading is doubtful. Some MSS. add the words *μόνος δὲ Ἰούδας ἐπορεύθη·*, but the best omit the verse altogether. The question is immaterial. If the verse is genuine, it modifies the word *ἀπελύθησαν* in the preceding verse; if not, we have merely to suppose that Silas went to Jerusalem and then returned.

[3] Acts xv. 35.

[4] Neander (Pfl. und L.) places this meeting of Peter and Paul later, but his reasons are far from satisfactory. From the order of narration in the Epistle to the Galatians, it is most natural to infer that the meeting at Antioch took place soon after the Council at Jerusalem. Some writers wish to make it anterior to the Council, from an unwillingness to believe that St. Peter would have acted in this manner after the Decree. But it is a sufficient answer to this objection to say that his conduct was equally inconsistent with his own previous conduct in the case of Cornelius.

[5] ii. 11, &c.

[6] The tradition which represents Peter as having held the See of Antioch before that of Rome has been mentioned before, p. 128, note. Tillemont (S. Pierre xxvii. xxviii. and notes) places the period of this Episcopate about 36–42. He says it is "une chose assez embarrassée," and it is certainly difficult to reconcile it with Scripture. For the Festivals of the Chair of Peter at Antioch and Rome, see the Bollandists under Feb. 22, and Jan. 18.

social friendship, and eating with them, in full consistency with the spirit of the recent Decree, and with his own conduct in the case of Cornelius. At this time certain Jewish brethren came "from James," who presided over the Church at Jerusalem. Whether they were really sent on some mission by the Apostle James, or we are merely to understand that they came from Jerusalem, they brought with them their old Hebrew repugnance against social intercourse with the uncircumcised, and Peter in their society began to vacillate. In weak compliance with their prejudices, he "withdrew and separated himself" from those whom he had lately treated as brethren and equals in Christ. Just as in an earlier part of his life he had first asserted his readiness to follow his Master to death, and then denied him through fear of a maid-servant; so now, after publicly protesting against the notion of making any difference between the Jew and the Gentile, and against laying on the neck of the latter a yoke which the former had never been able to bear,[1] we find him contradicting his own principles, and "through fear of those who were of the circumcision,"[2] giving all the sanction of his example to the introduction of *caste* into the Church of Christ.

Such conduct could not fail to excite in St. Paul the utmost indignation. St. Peter was not simply yielding a non-essential point, through a tender consideration for the consciences of others. This would have been quite in accordance with the principle so often asserted by his brother-Apostle, that "it is good neither to eat flesh nor drink wine, nor any thing whereby thy brother stumbleth, or is made weak." Nor was this proceeding a prudent and innocent accommodation to circumstances for the sake of furthering the Gospel, like St. Paul's conduct in circumcising Timothy at Iconium;[3] or, indeed, like the Apostolic Decree itself. St. Peter was acting under the influence of a contemptible and sinful motive, —the fear of man: and his behaviour was giving a strong sanction to the very heresy which was threatening the existence of the Church; namely, the opinion that the observance of Jewish ceremonies was necessary to salvation. Nor was this all. Other Jewish Christians, as was naturally to be expected, were led away by his example: and even Barnabas, the chosen companion of the Apostle of the Gentiles, who had been a witness and an actor in all the great transactions in Cyprus, in Pisidia, and Lycaonia,—even Barnabas, the missionary, was "carried away" with the dissimulation of the rest.[4] When St. Paul was a spectator of such inconsistency, and perceived both the motive in which it originated and the results to which it was leading, he would have been a traitor[5] to his Master's cause, if he had hesitated (to use his own

[1] Acts xv. 9, 10. [2] Gal. ii. 12. [3] Acts xvi. 3.
[4] Gal. ii. 13.
[5] We can only allude to the opinion of some early writers, that the whole scene was

emphatic words) to rebuke Peter "before all," and to "withstand him to the face."[1]

It is evident from St. Paul's expression that it was on some public occasion that this open rebuke took place. The scene, though slightly mentioned, is one of the most remarkable in Sacred History: and the mind naturally labors to picture to itself the appearance of the two men. It is, therefore, at least allowable to mention here that general notion of the forms and features of the two Apostles, which has been handed down in tradition, and was represented by the early artists.[2] St. Paul[3] is set before us as having the strongly marked and prominent features of a Jew, yet not without some of the finer lines indicative of Greek thought. His stature was diminutive, and his body disfigured by some lameness or distortion, which may have provoked the contemptuous expressions of his enemies.[4] His beard was long and thin. His head was bald. The characteristics of his face were, a transparent complexion, which visibly

pre-arranged between Peter and Paul, and that there was no real misunderstanding. Even Chrysostom advocates this unchristian view.

[1] Gal. ii. 14, 11.

[2] For the representations of St. Peter and St. Paul in early pictures and mosaics, see the first volume of Mrs. Jameson's "Sacred and Legendary Art," especially pp. 145, 159, 161, 162, 201. They correspond with the traditionary descriptions quoted in the next note. "St. Peter is a robust old man, with a broad forehead, and rather coarse features, an open undaunted countenance, short grey hair, and short thick beard, curled, and of a silvery white. Paul was a man of small and meagre stature, with an aquiline nose, and sparkling eyes: in the Greek type the face is long and oval, the forehead high and bald; the hair brown, the beard long, flowing, and pointed. . . . These traditional characteristic types of the features and persons of the two greatest apostles were long adhered to. We find them most strictly followed in the old Greek mosaics, in the early Christian sculpture, and the early pictures; in all which the sturdy dignity and broad rustic features of St. Peter, and the elegant contemplative head of St. Paul, who looks like a Greek philosopher, form a most interesting and suggestive contrast." The dispute at Antioch is the subject of a picture by Guido. See p. 199.

[3] The descriptions of St. Paul's appearance by Malalas and Nicephorus have been alluded to before, p. 148. Quoted at length they are as follows:—Τῇ ἡλικίᾳ κονδοειδής· φαλακρὸς, μιξοπόλιος τὴν κάραν καὶ τὸ γένειον, εὔρινος, ὑπόγλαυκος, σύνοφρυς, λευκόχρους, ἀνθηροπρόσωπος, εὐπώγων, ὑπογελῶντα ἔχων τὸν χαρακτῆρα, φρόνιμος, ἠθικὸς, εὐόμιλος, γλυκύς. Mal. Chronog. x. p. 257, ed. Bonn. Παῦλος μικρὸς ἦν καὶ συνεσταλμένος τὸ τοῦ σώματος μέγεθος καὶ ὥσπερ ἀγκύλον αὐτὸ κεκτημένος· σμικρὸν καὶ κεκυφὼς, τὴν ὄψιν λευκὸς καὶ τὸ πρόσωπον προφερής· ψίλὸς τὴν κεφαλήν· χαροποὶ δὲ αὐτῷ ἦσαν οἱ ὀφθαλμοί· κάτω δὲ καὶ τὰς ὀφρῦς εἶχε νευούσας· εὐκαμπῆ καὶ ῥέπουσαν ὅλῳ τῷ προσώπῳ περιφέρων τὴν ῥῖνα, τὴν ὑπήνην δασεῖαν καὶ καθειμένην ἀρκούντως ἔχων, ῥαινομένην δὲ ταύτην καὶ τὴν κεφαλὴν ὑπὸ πολιαῖς ταῖς θριξίν. Niceph. H. E. ii. 37. In accordance with these notices, St. Paul is described in the Actæ Pauli et Theclæ, as μικρὸς τῷ μεγέθει, ψιλὸς τῆν κεφαλὴν, ἀγκύλος ταῖς κνήμαις, εὔκνημος, συνόφρυς ἐπίῤῥινος, χάριτος πλήρης (Grabe, p. 95); and so the Γαλιλαῖος ἐς τρίτον οὐρανὸν ἀεροβατήσας in Lucian's Philopatris is said to have been ἀναφαλαντίας and ἐπίῤῥινος. Ed. Tauch. iv. 318.

[4] See above, p. 192.

betrayed the quick changes of his feelings, a bright grey eye under thickly overhanging united eyebrows,[1] a cheerful and winning expression of countenance, which invited the approach and inspired the confidence of strangers. It would be natural to infer,[2] from his continual journeys and manual labour, that he was possessed of great strength of constitution. But men of delicate health have often gone through the greatest exertions:[3] and his own words on more than one occasion show that he suffered much from bodily infirmity.[4] St. Peter[5] is represented to us as a man of larger and stronger form, as his character was harsher and more abrupt. The quick impulses of his soul revealed themselves in the flashes of a dark eye. The complexion of his face was pale and sallow: and the short hair, which is described as entirely grey at the time of his death, curled black and thick round his temples and his chin, when the two Apostles stood together at Antioch, twenty years before their martyrdom.

Believing, as we do, that these traditionary pictures have probably some foundation in truth, we gladly take them as helps to the imagination. And they certainly assist us in realizing a remarkable scene, where Judaism and Christianity, in the persons of two Apostles, are for a moment brought before us in strong antagonism. The words addressed by St. Paul to St. Peter before the assembled Christians at Antioch, contain the full statement of the Gospel as opposed to the Law. "If thou, being born a Jew, art wont to live according to the customs of the Gentiles, and not of the Jews, why wouldst thou now constrain the Gentiles to keep the ordinances of the Jews? We are by birth the seed of Abraham, and not unhallowed Gentiles; yet, knowing that a man is not counted righteous by the works of the law, but by the faith of Jesus Christ, we ourselves also have put our faith in Christ Jesus, that we might be counted righteous by the faith of Christ, and not by the works of the law. For by the works of the law *shall no man living be counted righteous.*"[6]

[1] See above, p. 148, n. 2.

[2] So Winer says: "Eine feste Constitution dürfen wir dem Manne zutrauen, welcher so viel und unter zum Theil so ungünstigen Umständen reiste (2 Cor. xi. 23, ff.) auch neben geistiger Anstrengung (vgl. Act. xx. 7. 2 Cor. xi. 28) noch körperliche Arbeit verrichten konnte (1 Thess. ii. 9. 2 Thess. iii. 8)." Realwörterbuch, II. 222. See Tholuck's Essay on St. Paul's early Life for some speculations on the Apostle's temperament.

[3] The instance of Alfred the Great may be rightly alluded to. His biographer, Asser, says that from his youth to his death he was always either suffering pain or expecting it.

[4] See 2 Cor. xii. 7. Gal. iv. 13, 14.

[5] The picture in Malalas (Chronog. p. 256) relates to the time of his martyrdom. *Γέρων ὑπῆρχε τῇ ἡλικίᾳ, διμοιριαῖος, ἀναφάλας, κονδόθριξ, ὁλοπόλιος τὴν κάραν καὶ γένειον, λευκὸς, ὑπόχλωρος, οἰνοπαὴς τοὺς ὀφθαλμοὺς, εὐπώγων, μακρόρινος, σύνοφους ἀνακαθήμενος, φρόνιμος, ὀξύχολος, εὐμετάβλητος, δειλός.* See also Niceph. H. E. ii. 37.

[6] The quotation is from Psalm cxliii. 2, which is also quoted in the same connection, Rom. iii. 20. There is much difference of opinion among commentators on Gal. ii. as

These sentences contain in a condensed form the whole argument of the Epistles to the Galatians and Romans.

Though the sternest indignation is expressed in this rebuke, we have no reason to suppose that any actual quarrel took place between the two Apostles. It is not improbable that St. Peter was immediately convinced of his fault, and melted at once into repentance. His mind was easily susceptible of quick and sudden changes; his disposition was loving and generous: and we should expect his contrition, as well as his weakness, at Antioch to be what it was in the high-priest's house at Jerusalem. Yet, when we read the narrative of this rebuke in St. Paul's epistle, it is a relief to turn to that passage at the conclusion of one of St. Peter's letters, where, in speaking of the "long-suffering of our Lord" and of the prospect of sinless happiness in the world to come, he alludes, in touching words, to the Epistles of "*our beloved brother Paul.*"[1] We see how entirely all past differences are forgotten,—how all earthly misunderstandings are absorbed and lost in the contemplation of Christ and eternal life. Not only did the Holy Spirit overrule all contrarieties, so that the writings of both Apostles teach the Church the same doctrine: but the Apostle who was rebuked "is not ashamed to call the attention of the Church to epistles in one page of which his own censure is recorded."[2] It is an eminent triumph of Christian humility and love. We shall not again have occasion to mention St. Peter and St. Paul together until we come to the last scene of all.[3] But, though they might seldom meet while laboring in their Master's cause, their lives were united, "and in their deaths they were not divided."

COIN OF ANTIOCH.[4]

to the point where Paul's address to Peter terminates. Many writers (see especially Usteri) think it continues to the end of the chapter. We are inclined to believe that it ends at v. 16; and that the words εἰ δὲ ζητοῦντες, κ. τ. λ. are intended to meet doctrinal objections (similar to those in Rom. iii. 3, 5. vi. 1, 15. vii. 7, 13) which the Galatians might naturally be supposed to make.

[1] 2 Pet. iii. 15, 16.

[2] See Sermons by Dr. Vaughan of Harrow (1846), p. 410.

[3] The martyrdom at Rome. See Mrs. Jameson's Work, especially pp. 180–183, 193–195.

[4] From the British Musuem. See Mr. Scharf's drawing above, p. 125, and what is said there of the emblematical representation of Antioch. On this coin the seated figure bears a palm branch, as the emblem of victory.

NOTE.

On the Time of the Visit to Jerusalem mentioned in Galatians (Chap. ii.)[1]

To avoid circumlocution we shall call the visit mentioned in Galatians ii. 1 the *Galatian Visit*, and we shall designate the visit mentioned in Acts ix. as *visit* (1), that in Acts xi. and xii. as *visit* (2), that in Acts xv. as *visit* (3), that in Acts xviii. as *visit* (4), that in Acts xxi. as *visit* (5).

I. The *Galatian Visit* was not the same with *visit* (1), because it is mentioned as subsequent by St. Paul.[2]

II. Was the *Galatian Visit* the same with *visit* (2) ?[3] The first impression from reading the end of Gal. i. and beginning of Gal. ii. would be that it was ; for St. Paul seems to imply that there had been no intermediate visit between the one mentioned in Gal. i. 18, which was *visit* (1), and that in Gal. ii. 1, which we have called the *Galatian Visit*.[4] On the other side, however, we must observe that St. Paul's object in this passage is not to enumerate all his visits to Jerusalem. His opponents had told his converts that Paul was no true Apostle, that he was only a Christian teacher authorised by the Judæan Apostles, that he derived his authority and his knowledge of the Gospel from Peter, James, and the rest of "the twelve." St. Paul's object is to refute this statement. This he does by declaring firstly that his commission was not from men but from God ; secondly, that he had taught Christianity for three years without seeing any of "the twelve" at all ; thirdly, that at the end of that time he had only spent one fortnight at Jerusalem with Peter and James, and

[1] This question is one of the most important, both chronologically and historically, in the life of St. Paul. Perhaps its discussion more properly belongs to the Epistle to the Galatians than to this place; but it has been given here as a justification of the view taken in the preceding chapter. It is treated of by Paley (*Horæ Paulinæ*), Winer (*Ep. ad Galatas*, Lips. 1829, Exc. II.), Anger (*De Temporum in Actis ratione*, Lips. 1833, ch. IV.), Hemsen (*Leben des Ap. Paulus*, pp. 52–69), Neander (*Pflanz. und Leit.* I. pp. 183–189), Böttger (*Beiträge*, &c., Göttingen, 1837, p. 14 *et seq.*), Wieseler (*Chronologie*, pp. 176–208), Schrader (*Der Apost. Paulus*); also by Burton, Browne, and Greswell. Of these, all except Paley, Böttger, Wieseler, Browne, and Schrader, adopt our view. The opinions of the latter five writers are referred to below.

[2] Gal. ii. 1.

[3] This is Böttger's view; but he is obliged to alter δεκατεσσάρων into τεσσάρων in Gal. ii. 1 to support his opinion. See note on p. 233. It is also the view of Mr. Browne (*Ordo Sæclorum*); but he places the conversion much earlier than we think probable.

[4] We must certainly acknowledge that St. Paul appears to say this; and some commentators have avoided the difficulty by supposing that, although Paul and Barnabas were commissioned to convey the alms from Antioch to Jerusalem, yet that St. Paul was prevented (by some circumstances not mentioned) from going the whole way to Jerusalem. For example, it might be too hazardous for him to appear within the walls of the city at such a time of persecution. For further explanation, see Neander *Pfl und Leit.* p. 188.

then had gone to Cilicia and remained personally unknown to the Judæan Christians; fourthly, that fourteen years afterwards he had undertaken a journey to Jerusalem, and that he then obtained an acknowledgment of his independent mission from the chief apostles. Thus we see that his object is not to enumerate every occasion where he might possibly have been instructed by "the twelve," but to assert (an assertion which he confirms by oath, Gal. i. 20) that his knowledge of Christianity was not derived from their instruction. A short visit to Jerusalem which produced no important results he might naturally pass over, and especially if he saw none of "the twelve" at Jerusalem when he visited it. Now this was probably the case at *visit* (2), because it was just at the time of Herod Agrippa's persecution, which would naturally disperse the Apostles from Jerusalem, as the persecution at Stephen's death did; with regard to St. Peter it is expressly said that, after his miraculous escape from prison, he quitted Jerusalem.[1] This supposition is confirmed by finding that Barnabas and Saul were sent to the *Elders* (πρεσβυτέρους) of the church at Jerusalem, and not to the *Apostles.*

A further objection to supposing the *Galatian Visit* identical with *visit* (2) is that, at the time of the Galatian Visit, Paul and Barnabas are described as having been already extensively useful as missionaries to the Heathen; but this they had not been in the time of *visit* (2).

Again, St. Paul could not have been, at so early a period, considered on a footing of equality with St. Peter. Yet this he was at the time of the *Galatian Visit.*[2]

Again, *visit* (2) could not have been so long as fourteen years[3] after *visit* (1). For *visit* (2) was certainly not later than 45 A. D., and if it was the same as the *Galatian Visit*, *visit* (1) must have been not later than from 31 to 33 A. D. (allowing the inclusive Jewish mode of reckoning to be possibly employed). But Aretas (as we have seen, p. 81) was not in possession of Damascus till about 37.

Again, if *visit* (2) were fourteen years after *visit* (1), we must suppose nearly all this time spent by St. Paul at Tarsus, and yet that all his long residence there is unrecorded by St. Luke, who merely says that he went to Tarsus and from thence to Antioch.[4]

III. The *Galatian Visit* not being identical with (1) or (2), was it identical with (3), (4), or (5)? We may put (5) at once out of the question, because St. Paul did not return to Antioch after (5), whereas he did return after the *Galatian Visit.* There remain therefore (3) and (4) to be considered. We shall take (4) first.

IV. Wieseler has lately argued very ingeniously that the *Galatian*

[1] Acts xii. 17. [2] See Gal. ii. 9.

[3] On this fourteen years, see note in p. 233.

[4] Acts ix. 30 and xi. 26. See what Prof. Burton says on this interval.

Visit was the same with (4). His reasons are, firstly, that at the *Galatian Visit* the Apostles allowed unlimited freedom to the Gentile converts, *i. e.* imposed no conditions upon them, such as those in the decrees of the Council passed at *visit* (3). This, however, is an inference not warranted by St. Paul's statement, which speaks of the acknowledgment of his personal independence, but does not touch the question of the converts. Secondly, Wieseler urges that, till the time of *visit* (4), St. Paul's position could not have been so far on a level with St. Peter's as it was at the *Galatian Visit.* Thirdly, he thinks that the condition of making a collection for the poor Christians in Jerusalem, which St. Paul says[1] he had been forward to fulfil, must have been fulfilled in that great collection which we know that St. Paul set on foot immediately after *visit* (4), because we read of no other collection made by St. Paul for this purpose.[2] Fourthly, Wieseler argues that St. Paul would not have been likely to take an uncircumcised Gentile, like Titus, with him to Jerusalem at a period earlier than *visit* (4). And moreover, he conceives Titus to be the same with the Corinthian Justus,[3] who is not mentioned as one of St. Paul's companions till Acts xviii. 7, that is, not till after *visit* (3).

It is evident that these arguments are not conclusive in favor of *visit* (4), even if there were nothing on the other side; but there are, moreover, the following objections against supposing the *Galatian Visit* identical with (4). Firstly, Barnabas was St. Paul's companion in the *Galatian Visit;* he is not mentioned as being with him at *visit* (4). Secondly, had so important a conference between St. Paul and the other Apostles taken place at *visit* (4), it would not have been altogether passed over by St. Luke, who dwells so fully upon the Council held at the time of *visit* (3), the decrees of which (on Wieseler's view) were inferior in importance to the *concordat* between St. Paul and the other Apostles which he supposes to have been made at *visit* (4). Thirdly, the whole tone of the second chapter of Galatians is against Wieseler's hypothesis; for in that chapter St. Paul plainly seems to speak of the *first* conference which he had held after his success among the heathen, with the chief apostles at Jerusalem, and he had certainly seen and conferred with them during *visit* (3).

V. We have seen, therefore, that *if the Galatian Visit be mentioned at all in the Acts*, it must be identical with *visit* (3), at which the (so called) Council of Jerusalem took place. We will now consider the objections

[1] Gal. ii. 9.

[2] The collection carried up to Jerusalem at *visit* (2) might, however, be cited as an exception to this remark; for (although not expressly stated) it is most probable that St. Paul was active in forwarding it, since he was selected to carry it to Jerusalem.

[3] Many of the most ancient MSS. and versions read *Titus Justus* (Τίτου Ἰούστου) in Acts xviii. 7. Tischendorf, however, prefers Ἰούστου. See above, p. 211, n. 13.

against the identity of these two visits urged by Paley and others, and then the arguments in favour of the identity.

Objections to the Identity of the Galatian Visit *with* Visit (3).	*Answers to the Objections.*
1. St. Paul in Gal. (ii. 1) mentions this journey as if it had been the next visit to Jerusalem after the time which he spent there on his return from Damascus; he does not say anything of any intermediate visit. This looks as if he were speaking of the journey which he took with Barnabas to Jerusalem (Acts xi. 30), to convey alms to the Jewish Christians in the famine.	1. This objection is answered above, pp. 227, 228.
2. In the Galatians, the journey is said to have taken place κατ' ἀποκάλυψιν (Gal. ii. 2); but in Acts xv. 2–4, 6–12, a public mission is mentioned.	2. The journey may have taken place in consequence of a revelation, and yet may also have been agreed to by a vote of the church at Antioch. Thus in St. Paul's departure from Jerusalem (Acts ix. 29, 30), he is said to have been sent by the brethren in consequence of danger feared; and yet (Acts xxii. 17–21) he says that he had taken his departure in consequence of a vision on the very same occasion (see pp. 211, 12).
3. In the Galatians Barnabas and Titus are spoken of as St. Paul's companions; in the Acts, Barnabas and others (τινὲς ἄλλοι), Acts xv. 2; but Titus is not mentioned.	3. This argument is merely *ex silentio*, and therefore inconclusive. In the Acts, Paul and Barnabas are naturally mentioned, as being prominent characters in the history. Whereas in the Epistle, Titus would naturally be mentioned by St. Paul as a personal friend of his own, and also because of his refusal to circumcise him.
4. The object of the visit in Acts xv. is different from that of the *Galatian Visit*. The object in Acts xv. was to seek relief from the imposition of the Mosaic Law, that of the *Galatian Visit* was to obtain the recognition of St. Paul's independent apostleship.	4. Both these objects are implied in each narrative. The recognition of St. Paul's apostleship is implied in Acts xv. 25: συν τοῖς ἀγαπητοῖς ἡμῶν Βαρνάβᾳ καὶ Παυλῷ ἀνθρώποις παραδεδωκόσι τὰς ψυχὰς αὐτῶν ὑπὲρ τοῦ ὀνόματος τοῦ Κυρίου ἡμῶν Ἰησοῦ Χριστοῦ. And the relief from the imposition of the Mosaic Law is implied, Gal. ii. 7, ἰδόντες ὅτι πεπίστευμαι τὸ εὐαγγέλιον τῆς ἀκροβυστίας, where the word ἀκροβυστίας shows that the Apostles at the time of St. Paul's visit to Jerusalem, mentioned in the Epistle, acknowledged that the uncircumcised might partake of τὸ εὐαγγέλιον The same thing is shown by the fact that the circumcision of Titus was not insisted on. We must remember also that the

transactions recorded are looked upon from different points of view, in the Acts, and in the Epistle; for Acts xv. contains a narrative of a great transaction in the history of the Church, while St. Paul, in the Epistle, alludes to this transaction with the object of proving the recognition of his independent authority.

5. In Acts xv. a public assembly of the Church in Jerusalem is described, while in the Galatians only private interviews with the leading Apostles are spoken of.

5. The private interviews spoken of in the Epistle do not exclude the supposition of public meetings having also taken place; and a communication to the *whole Church* (αὐτοῖς, Gal. ii. 2) is expressly mentioned.

6. The narrative in the Epistle says nothing of the decision of the Council of Jerusalem, as it is commonly called, mentioned Acts xv. Now this decision was conclusive of the very point disputed by the Judaising teachers in Galatia, and surely therefore would not have been omitted by St. Paul in an argument involving the question, had he been relating the circumstances which happened at Jerusalem when that decision was made.

6. The narrative in Galatians gives a statement intended to prove the recognition of St. Paul's independent authority, which is sufficient to account for this omission. Moreover if St. Paul's omission of reference to the decision of the Council proved that the journey he speaks of was prior to the Council, it must equally prove that the whole Epistle was written before the Council of Jerusalem; yet it is generally acknowledged to have been written long after the Council. The probable reason why St. Paul does not refer to the decision of the Council is this:—that the Judaising teachers did not absolutely dispute that decision; they probably did not declare the absolute necessity of circumcision, but spoke of it as admitting to greater privileges, and a fuller covenant with God. The Council had only decided that *Gentile* Christians need not observe the law. The Judaising party might still contend that *Jewish* Christians ought to observe it (as we know they did observe it till long afterwards). And also the decrees of the council left Gentile Christians subject to the same restrictions with the Proselytes of the Gate. Therefore the Judaising party would naturally argue that they were still not more fully within the pale of the Christian Church than the Proselytes of the Gate were within that of the Jewish Church. Hence they would urge them to submit to circumcision, by way of placing themselves in full membership with the Church; just as they would have urged a Proselyte of the Gate to become a Proselyte of Righteousness. Also St. Paul might assume that the decision of the

Council was well known to the churches of Galatia, for Paul and Silas had carried it with them there.

7. It is inconsistent to suppose that after the decision of the Council of Jerusalem, St. Peter could have behaved as he is described doing (Gal. ii. 12); for how could he refuse to eat with the uncircumcised Christians, after having advocated in the Council their right of admission to Christian fellowship?

7. This objection is founded on a misunderstanding of St. Peter's conduct. His withdrawal from eating at the same table with the uncircumcised Christians did not amount to a denial of the decision of the Council. His conduct showed a weak fear of offending the Judaising Christians who came from Jerusalem; and the practical effect of such conduct would have been, if persisted in, to separate the Church into two divisions. Peter's conduct was still more inconsistent (see Winer, p. 157) with the consent which he had certainly given previously (Gal. ii. 7–9) to the εὐαγγέλιον of Paul; and with his previous conduct in the case of Cornelius (see pp. 223, 224). We may add that whatever difficulty may be felt in St. Paul's not alluding to the decrees of the Council in his Epistle to the Galatians, must also be felt in his total silence concerning them when he treats of the question of εἰδωλόθυτα in the Epistles to Corinth and Rome, for that question had been explicitly decided by the Council. The fact is, that the Decrees of the Council were not designed as of permanent authority, but only as a temporary and provisional measure; and their authority was superseded as the Church gradually advanced towards true Christian freedom.

8. The Epistle mentions St. Paul as conferring with James, Peter, and John, whereas in Acts xv. John is not mentioned at all, and it seems strange that so distinguished a person, if present at the Council, should not have been mentioned.

8. This argument is only *ex silentio*, and obviously inconclusive.

9. Since in the Galatians St. Paul mentions James, Peter, and John, it seems most natural to suppose that he speaks of the well-known apostolic triumvirate so often classed together in the Gospels. But if so, the James mentioned must be James the Greater, and hence the journey mentioned in the Galatians must have been before the death of James the Greater, and therefore before the Council of Jerusalem.

9. This objection proceeds on the mere assumption that because James is mentioned first he must be James the Greater, whereas James the Less became even a more conspicuous leader of the Church at Jerusalem than James the Greater had previously been, as we see from Acts xv.; hence he might be very well mentioned with Peter and John, and the fact of his name coming first in St. Paul's narrative agrees better with this supposition, for James the Greater is never mentioned the

	first in the Apostolic triumvirate, the order of which is Peter, James, and John; but James the Less would naturally be mentioned first, if the Council at Jerusalem was mentioned, since we find from Acts xv. that he took the part of president in that Council.
10. St. Paul's refusal to circumcise Titus (Gal. ii.), and voluntary circumcising of Timothy (Acts xviii. 21), so soon afterwards.	10. Timothy's mother was a Jewess, and he had been brought up a Jew;[1] whereas Titus was a Gentile. The circumstances of Timothy's circumcision will be more fully discussed hereafter.

Thus we see that the objections against the identity of the *Galatian visit* with *visit* (3), are inconclusive. Consequently we might at once conclude (from the obvious circumstances of identity between the two visits), that they were actually identical. But this conclusion is further strengthened by the following arguments.

1.[2] The *Galatian visit* could not have happened *before visit* (3); because, if so, the Apostles at Jerusalem had already granted to Paul and Barnabas[3] the liberty which was sought for the εὐαγγέλιον τῆς ἀκροβυστίας; therefore there would have been no need for the Church to send them again to Jerusalem upon the same cause. And again, the *Galatian visit* could not have happened *after visit* (3); because, almost immediately after that period, Paul and Barnabas ceased to work together as missionaries to the Gentiles; whereas, up to the time of the *Galatian visit*, they had been working together.[4]

2. The *Chronology* of St. Paul's life (so far as it can be ascertained) agrees better with the supposition that the *Galatian visit* was *visit* (3), than with any other supposition.

Reckoning backwards from the ascertained epoch of 60 A.D., when St. Paul was sent to Rome, we find that he must have begun his second missionary journey in 51, and that, therefore, the Council (i. e. *visit* (3)) must have been either in 50 or 51. This calculation is based upon the history in the Acts. Now, turning to the Epistle to the Galatians we find the following epochs—

A.—Conversion.

B.—3 years' interval (probably Judaically reckoned=2 years).

C.—Flight from Damascus, and *visit* (1).

D.—[5] 14 years' interval (probably Judaically reckoned=13 years).

[1] See 2 Tim. iii. 15. We may remark that this difficulty (which is urged by Wieseler) is quite as great on his own hypothesis; for, according to him, the refusal happened only about two years after the consent.

[2] See Winer's Galatians, pp. 141 & 144. [3] Gal. ii. 3–6. [4] Gal. ii. 1, 9.

[5] The reading δεκατεσσάρων (Gal. ii. 1) is undoubtedly to be retained. It is the reading of all the ancient MSS. which contain the passage. Neander (*Pfl. und Leit* i. p. 187), by mistake asserts that the Chronicon Paschale reads τεσσάρων; but the

E.—*Galatian visit.*

And since Aretas was supreme at Damascus[1] at the time of the flight, and his supremacy there probably began about 37 (see pages 81 and 100), we could not put the flight at a more probable date than 38. If we assume this to have been the case, then the *Galatian visit* was 38+13=51, which agrees with the time of the Council (i. e. *visit* (3)) as above.

VI. Hence we need not farther consider the views of those writers who (like Paley and Schrader) have resorted to the hypothesis that the *Galatian visit* is some supposed journey not recorded in the Acts at all; for we have proved that the supposition of its identity with the third visit there recorded satisfies every necessary condition. Schrader's notion is, that the *Galatian visit* was between *visit* (4) and *visit* (5). Paley places it between *visit* (3) and *visit* (4). A third view is ably advocated in a discussion of the subject (not published) which has been kindly communicated to us. The principal points in this hypothesis are, that the Galatians were converted in the *first* missionary journey, that the *Galatian visit* took place between *visit* (2) and *visit* (3), and that the Epistle to the Galatians was written after the *Galatian visit* and before *visit* (3). This hypothesis certainly obviates some difficulties,[2] and it is quite possible (see next Chapter) that the Galatian churches might have been formed at the time supposed: but we think the "fourteen years" inconsistent with this view, and we are strongly of opinion that a much later date must be assigned to the Epistle.[3]

reverse is the fact. The words of the Chronicon are: Τῷ *εἰπεῖν αὐτὸν διὰ δεκατεσσάρων ἐτῶν δοκεῖ μοι τοὺς χρόνους τῶν ἀποστόλων τοὺς ἀπὸ τῆς ἀναλήψεως ἀριθμεῖν αὐτόν.* (*Chronic.* ed. Bonn. I. p. 436.) The mistake has probably arisen from the words *ἔτη τέσσαρα*, which relate to a different subject, in the sentence below (see Wieseler, p. 207). Διά, of time, means "after an interval of." (See *Winer's Grammatik*, p. 363, and *Winer's Galat.* p. 162. Also *Anger*, pp. 159, 160.) But it may be used, according to the Jewish way of reckoning time, *inclusively;* thus Jesus is said to have risen from the dead *διὰ τρίων ἡμερῶν* (*Ignat. ad Trall.* c. 9). So in the Gospels *μετά* is used (Mark viii. 31). The fourteen years must be reckoned *from the epoch last mentioned*, which is the *visit* (1) to Jerusalem, and not the Conversion; at least this is the most natural way, although the other interpretation might be justified, if required by the other circumstances of the case.

[1] 2 Cor. xi. 32.

[2] Especially the difficulties which relate to the apparent discrepancies between the *Galatian visit* and *visit* (3), and to the circumstance that the Apostle does not allude to the Council in his argument with the Galatians on the subject of circumcision. The MS. to which we allude is by T. F. Ellis, Esq., formerly Fellow of Trinity College, Cambridge.

[3] Since these pages were printed, we have seen, in Dr. Davidson's Introduction to the N. T. (vol. ii.), a good statement of the principal arguments for the view we have advocated. We may add also the authority of Dr. H. Thiersch, in favour of our view of this Council. See the recently published English translation of his History of the Christian Church, p. 120.

ST. PAUL'S SECOND MISSIONARY JOURNEY,
REPRESENTING
THE ROMAN PROVINCES, ABOUT 50 A. D.

CHAPTER VIII.

ΠΑΥΛΟΣ *καὶ* ΣΙΛΟΥΑΝΟΣ *καὶ* ΤΙΜΟΘΕΟΣ.—1 Thess. i. 1.

POLITICAL DIVISIONS OF ASIA MINOR.—DIFFICULTIES OF THE SUBJECT.—PROVINCES IN THE REIGNS OF CLAUDIUS AND NERO.—I. ASIA. II. BITHYNIA.—III. PAMPHYLIA.—IV. GALATIA.—V. PONTUS.—VI. CAPPADOCIA.—VII. CILICIA.—VISITATION OF THE CHURCHES PROPOSED.—QUARREL AND SEPARATION OF PAUL AND BARNABAS.—PAUL AND SILAS IN CILICIA.—THEY CROSS THE TAURUS.—LYSTRA.—TIMOTHY.—HIS CIRCUMCISION.—JOURNEY THROUGH PHRYGIA.—SICKNESS OF ST. PAUL.—HIS RECEPTION IN GALATIA.—JOURNEY TO THE ÆGEAN.—ALEXANDRIA TROAS.—ST. PAUL'S VISION.

THE life of St. Paul being that of a traveller, and our purpose being to give a picture of the circumstances by which he was surrounded, it is often necessary to refer to the geography, both physical and political, of the countries through which he passed. This is more needful in the case of Asia Minor, not only because it was the scene of a very great portion of his journeys, but because it is less known to ordinary readers than Palestine, Italy, or Greece. We have already described, at some length, the physical geography of those southern districts which are in the immediate neighbourhood of Mount Taurus.[1] And now that the Apostle's travels take a wider range, and cross the Asiatic peninsula from Syria to the frontiers of Europe, it is important to take a general view of the political geography of this part of the Roman empire. Unless such a view is obtained in the first place, it is impossible to understand the topographical expressions employed in the narrative, or to conjecture the social relations into which St. Paul was brought in the course of his journeys[2] through Asia Minor.

It is, however, no easy task to ascertain the exact boundaries of the Roman provinces in this part of the world at any given date between Augustus and Constantine.[3] In the first place, these boundaries were contin-

[1] Ch. I. pp. 20–22. Ch. VI. p. 159.

[2] *i. e.* the journeys in Acts xvi. and Acts xviii.

[3] So far as we know, the only attempt to ascertain and describe the political divisions of Asia Minor in the time of St. Paul, is that of Böttger in the first of his Beiträge (Gött. 1837.) He has brought together a great number of references, but the essay is confused, and some of his conclusions are strangely destitute of proof.

ually changing. The area of the different political districts was liable to sudden and arbitrary alterations. Such terms as "Asia,"[1] "Pamphylia,"[2] &c., though denoting the extent of a true political jurisdiction, implied a larger or smaller territory at one time than another. And again, we find the names of earlier and later periods of history mixed up together in inextricable confusion. Some of the oldest geographical terms, such as "Æolis," "Ionia," "Caria," "Lydia," were disappearing from ordinary use in the time of the Apostles:[3] but others, such as "Mysia"[4] and "Lycaonia,"[5] still remained. Obsolete and existing divisions are presented to us together: and the common maps of Asia Minor[6] are as unsatisfactory as if a map of France was set before us, distributed half into provinces and half into departments. And in the third place, some of the names have no political significance at all, but express rather the ethnographical relations of ancient tribes. Thus, "Pisidia"[7] denotes a district which might partly be in one province and partly in another; and "Phrygia"[8] reminds us of the diffusion of an ancient people, the broken portions of whose territory were now under the jurisdiction of three or four distinct governors. Cases of this kind are, at first sight, more embarrassing than the others. They are not merely similar to the two-fold subdivision of Ireland, where a province, like Ulster, may contain several definite counties: but a nearer parallel is to be found in Scotland, where a geographical district, associated with many historical recollections,—such as Galloway or Lothian,—may be partly in one county and partly in another.

Our purpose is to elucidate the political subdivisions of Asia Minor

[1] Acts ii. 9. vi. 9. xvi. 6. xix. 10, 27, 31. xx. 16, 18. xxvii. 2. 1 Cor. xvi. 19. 2 Cor. i. 8. 2 Tim. i. 15. 1 Pet. i. 1.

[2] Acts ii. 10. xiii. 13. xv. 38. xxvii. 5.

[3] See Böttger, § 13. He remarks that Tacitus, Vitruvius, Justin, &c. speak of Pergamus, Ephesus, Cnidus, Thyatira, &c. as towns of *Asia*, not of Æolis, Ionia, Caria, Lydia, &c., respectively. See Acts xxvii. 2. Rev. i. 11.

[4] Acts xvi. 7, 8.

[5] Acts xiv. 6, 11.

[6] In the ordinary maps, ethnographical and political divisions of three or four different periods are confused together. Spruner's new "Atlas Antiquus" is, we believe, the only one which exhibits the provincial divisions of the "Imperium Romanorum;" and it relates to the age of Trajan, when many changes had been made. Observe, for instance, the union of Crete as one province with Achaia and Macedonia. Under the earlier emperors it was united with Cyrene. See map of St. Paul's second journey.

A map of this kind belongs to a period too late for Kiepert's "Hellas," and too early for Wiltsch's "Atlas Ecclesiasticus." In the map published by Neander to illustrate the first planting of the Church, the provinces are not shown; and it is to be regretted that the ancient terms, such as Caria, Lydia, &c., have been introduced. Of the English maps, that of Colonel Leake is invaluable for its clear representation of the ancient roads, and those of Major Rennell are very important for elucidating general geographical relations; but neither of them shows the ancient political divisions.

[7] Acts xiii. 14. xiv. 24.

[8] Acts ii. 10. xvi. 6. xviii. 23.

as they were in the reigns of Claudius and Nero,—or, in other words, to enumerate the provinces which existed, and to describe the boundaries which were assigned to them, in the middle of the first century of the Christian era. The order we shall follow is from West to East, and in so doing we shall not deviate widely from the order in which the provinces were successively incorporated as substantive parts of the Roman empire. We are not, indeed, to suppose that St. Luke and St. Paul used all their topographical expressions in the strict political sense, even when such a sense was more or less customary. There was an exact usage and a popular usage of all these terms. But the first step towards fixing our geographical ideas of Asia Minor, must be to trace the boundaries of the provinces. When this is done, we shall be better able to distinguish those terms which, about the year 50 A. D., had ceased to have any true political significance, and to discriminate between the technical and the popular language of the sacred writers.

I. Asia.—There is sometimes a remarkable interest associated with the history of a geographical term. One case of this kind is suggested by the allusion which has just been made to the British islands. Early writers speak of Ireland under the appellation of "Scotia." Certain of its inhabitants crossed over to the opposite coast:[1] their name spread along with their influence: and at length the title of Scotland was entirely transferred from one island to the other. In classical history we have a similar instance in the name of "Italy," which at first only denoted the southernmost extremity of the peninsula: then it was extended so as to include the whole with the exception of Cisalpine Gaul: and finally, crossing the Rubicon, it advanced to the Alps; while the name of "Gaul" retreated beyond them. Another instance, on a larger scale, is presented to us on the south of the Mediterranean. The "Africa" of the Romans spread from a limited territory on the shore of that sea, till it embraced the whole continent which was circumnavigated by Vasco di Gama. And similarly the term, by which we are accustomed to designate the larger and more celebrated continent of the ancient world, traces its derivation to the "Asian meadow by the streams of the Cayster,"[2] celebrated in the poems of Homer.

This is the earliest occurrence of the word "Asia." We find, however, even in the older poets,[3] the word used in its widest sense to

1 See what Bede says of Ireland (i. 1):—"Hæc proprie patria Scotorum est: ab hac egressi tertiam in Britannia Britonibus et Pictis gentem addiderunt."

2 'Ασίῳ ἐν λειμῶνι, Καϋστρίου ἀμφὶ ῥέεθρα. Il. ii. 461. See Virg. Georg. i. 383, which is copied from Homer. It does not appear that the Roman prose writers ever used the word in its primitive and narrowest sense.

3 As in Æschylus, Persæ and Prom. V.

denote all the countries in the far East. Either the Greeks, made familiar with the original Asia by the settlement of their kindred in its neighbourhood, applied it as a generic appellation to all the regions beyond it: or the extension of the kingdom of Lydia from the banks of the Cayster to the Halys as its eastern boundary, diffused the name of Asia as far as that river, and thus suggested the division of Herodotus into "Asia within the Halys" and "Asia beyond the Halys."[2] However this might be, the term retained, through the Greek and Roman periods, both a wider and a narrower sense; of which senses we are concerned only with the latter. The Asia of the New Testament is not the continent which stretches into the remote East from the Black Sea and the Red Sea, but simply the western portion of that peninsula which, in modern times, has received the name of "Asia Minor."[3] What extent of country, and what political significance we are to assign to the term, will be shown by a statement of a few historical changes.

The fall of Crœsus reduced the Lydian kingdom to a Persian satrapy. With the rest of the Persian empire, this region west of the Halys fell before the armies of Alexander. In the confusion which followed the conqueror's death, an independent dynasty established itself at Pergamus, not far from the site of ancient Troy. At first their territory was narrow, and Attalus I. had to struggle with the Gauls who had invaded the peninsula, and with the neighbouring chieftains of Bithynia, who had invited them.[4] Antagonists still more formidable were the Greek kings of Syria, who claimed to be "Kings of Asia," and aimed at the possession of the whole of the peninsula.[5] But the Romans appeared in the

[1] Having the same general meaning as our phrase "The East." This is Mannert's opinion, Geog. der G. und R. VI. ii. 16. The words "Levant" and "Anadoli" (the modern name of Asia Minor) have come into use in the same way.

[2] This is the view of Wieseler, who refers to a passage in Callinus quoted by Strabo, where the Lydians of Sardis are called Ἀσιονεῖς; and compares the parallel case of "Palestine," which at first meant only the country of the Philistines, and then was used by the Greeks and Romans to designate the whole of the land of Canaan. Chronologie, p. 32.

[3] The peninsula which we call Asia Minor was never treated by the ancients as a geographical whole. The common divisions were, "Asia within the Halys" and "Asia beyond the Halys" (as above); or, "Asia within the Taurus" and "Asia beyond the Taurus." It is very important to bear this in mind: for some interpreters of the New Testament imagine that the Asia there spoken of is the peninsula of Lesser Asia. The term "Asia Minor" is first found in Orosius (i. 2), a writer of the fourth century, though "Asia Major" is used by Justin (xv. 4, 1) to denote the remote and eastern parts of the continent.

[4] See below, p. 241.

[5] In the first book of Maccabees (viii. 6) we find Antiochus the Great called by this title. And even after his successors were driven beyond the Taurus by the Romans, we see it retained by them, as the title of the king of France was retained by our own monarchs until a very recent period. See 1 Mac. xi. 13. xii. 39. xiii. 32. 2 Mac. iii. 3.

East, and ordered Antiochus to retire beyond the Taurus,[1] and then conferred substantial rewards on their faithful allies. Rhodes became the mistress of Caria and Lycia, on the opposite coast;[2] and Eumenes, the son of Attalus, received, in the West and North-west, Lydia and Mysia, and a good portion of that vague region in the interior which was usually denominated "Phrygia,"[3]—stretching in one direction over the district of Lycaonia.[4] Then it was that, as 150 years since the Margraves of Brandenburg became Kings of Prussia, so the Princes of Pergamus became "Kings of Asia." For a time they reigned over a highly-civilised territory, which extended from sea to sea. The library of Pergamus was the rival of that of Alexandria: and Attaleia, from whence we have lately seen the Apostle sailing to Syria[5] (Acts xiv. 25, 26), and Troas, from whence we shall presently see him sailing to Europe (Acts xvi. 11), were the southern and northern (or rather the eastern and western) harbours of King Attalus II. At length the debt of gratitude to the Romans was paid by King Attalus III., who died in the year 133, and left by testament the whole of his dominions to the benefactors of his house.[6] And now the "*Province of Asia*" appears for the first time as a new and significant term in the history of the world. The newly acquired possession was placed under a prætor, and ultimately a

[1] Excedito urbibus, agris, vicis, castellis cis Taurum montem usque ad Halyn (?) flumen, et a valle Tauri usque ad juga qua ad Lycaoniam vergit. Liv. xxxviii. 38. Compare 1 Mac. viii. 8.

[2] Polyb. xxii. 7, 7. 27, 8. Liv. xxxvii. 54–56. xxxviii. 39. Strabo, xiv. App. Syr. 44.

[3] Livy's words are:—"In Asia Phrygiam utramque (alteram ad Hellespontum, majorem alteram vocant) et Mysiam, quam Prusias rex ademerat, Eumeni restituerunt." xxxviii. 39. (See xxxvii. 56.) "Phrygia Major" was the great central space of Asia Minor, which retained the name of its earliest inhabitants. It was subdivided, like Poland, among the contiguous provinces, and it is useless to attempt to determine its limits in this passage. (See below, 240, n. 5 and 249, note.) "Phrygia Minor" was an outlying district on the Hellespont, inhabited at some period by the same race. The case of Mysia, in consequence of the difficulties of Acts xvi. 7, 8, will be examined particularly, when we come to this part of St. Paul's journey.

[4] Thus Iconium, Lystra, and Derbe were probably once in "Asia." See below, under Galatia. [In Van Kapelle, Comment. de Regibus et Antiquit. Pergam. (Amstel. 1842), is a map showing the extent of the Kingdom of Pergamus in the reign of Eumenes II. It assigns to him the whole of Phrygia, with Milyas, which is represented as a narrow strip running down from the North towards the sea, and terminating in a straight line a little to the N. of Attaleia.]

[5] Pp. 200–203. Another Scripture city, the Philadelphia of Rev. i. 11. iii. 7, was also built by Attalus II. (Philadelphus).

[6] Attali ignotus hæres regiam occupavit. Hor. Od. II. xviii. "Eo tempore Attalus, rex Asiæ, mortuus est, hæredemque populum Romanum reliquit. Ita imperio Romano per testamentum Asia accessit." Eutrop. iv. 19. *Κατέλιπε κληρονόμους Ῥωμαίους. οἱ δ' ἐπαρχίαν ἀπέδειξαν τὴν χώραν, Ἀσίαν προσαγορεύσαντες, ὁμώνυμον τῇ ἠπείρῳ.* Strabo, xiii. 4. Also Justin, xxxvi. 4. Florus, ii. 20.

proconsul.[1] The letters and speeches of Cicero make us familiar with the names of more than one who enjoyed this distinction. One was the orator's brother, Quintus;[2] another was Flaccus, whose conduct as governor he defended before the Senate.[3] Some slight changes in the extent of the province may be traced. Pamphylia was withdrawn from this jurisdiction.[4] Rhodes lost her continental possessions, and Caria was added to Asia, while Lycia was declared independent.[5] The boundary on the side of Phrygia is not easily determined, and was probably variable.[6] But enough has been said to give a general idea of what is meant in the New Testament by that "*Asia*" which St. Paul attempted to enter,[7] after passing through Phrygia and Galatia; which St. Peter addressed in his First Epistle,[8] along with Pontus, Cappadocia, Galatia, and Bithynia; and which embraced the "seven churches,"[9] whose angels are mentioned in the Revelation of St. John.

II. Bithynia.—Next to Asia, both in proximity of situation and in the order of its establishment, was the province of Bithynia. Nor were the circumstances very different under which these two provinces passed

COIN OF BITHYNIA.[10]

[1] We learn from Acts xix. 38—"there are proconsuls (deputies)"—that it was a proconsular or senatorial province. The important distinction between the emperor's and the senate's provinces has been carefully stated in Ch. V. pp. 141–145. The incidental proof in the Acts is confirmed by Strabo (xvii. 3) and Dio (liii. 12), who tell us that Augustus made Asia a proconsular province.

[2] See Cic. ad Q. fratrem, i. 2, and C. Nepos, Att. For the first governors of the new province, and the treatment it received from them, see Justin, xxxvi. 4.

[3] Orat. pro L. Flacco. He was the immediate predecessor of Q. Cicero.

[4] See below, under Pamphylia.

[5] Polyb. xxx. 5, 12. Liv. xlv. 25. Thus Cicero, in his speech for Flaccus, says (c. 27):—"Asia vestra constat ex Phrygia, Mysia, Caria, Lydia." See Cramer's Asia Minor under Rhodes, &c.

[6] Hence we find both the sacred and heathen writers of the period sometimes including Phrygia in Asia and sometimes excluding it. In 1 Pet. i. 1 it seems to be included; in Acts ii. 9, 10. xvi. 6 it is expressly excluded. See what Wieseler says (pp. 32–35) on Plin. v. 28.

[7] Acts xvi. 6. [8] 1 Pet. i. 1. [9] Rev. i. 11.

[10] From the British Museum. These coins—one of Claudius, struck at Nicæa, the other of Nero and Agrippina, struck at Nicomedia—show, by the word ΑΝΘΥΠΑΤΟΣ, that Bithynia, like Asia, was a senatorial province. We learn the same fact from Strabo (xvii. 3) and Dio (liii. 12).

COIN OF BITHYNIA.

under the Roman sceptre. As a new dynasty established itself after the death of Alexander on the north-eastern shores of the Ægean, so an older dynasty[1] secured its independence at the Western edge of the Black Sea. Nicomedes I. was the king who invited the Gauls with whom Attalus I. had to contend: and as Attalus III., the last of the House of Pergamus, paid his debt to the Romans by making them his heirs, so the last of the Bithynian House, Nicomedes III., left his kingdom as a legacy to the same power in the year 75.[2] It received some accessions on the east after the defeat of Mithridates;[3] and in this condition we find it in the list given by Dio of the provinces of Augustus;[4] the intermediate land between it and Asia being the district of Mysia, through which it is neither easy nor necessary to draw the exact frontier-line.[5] Stretching inland from the shores of the Propontis and Bosphorus, beyond the lakes near the cities of Nicæa and Nicomedia, to the upper ravines of the Sangarius, and the snowy range of Mount Olympus, it was a province rich in all the changes of beauty and grandeur. Its history is as varied as its scenery, if we trace it from the time when Hannibal was an exile at the court of Prusias, to the establishment of Othman's Mahommedan capital in the city which still bears that monarch's name. It was Hadrian's favourite province, and many monuments remain of that emperor's partiality.[6] But we cannot say more of it without leaving our proper subject. We have no reason to believe that St. Paul ever entered it, though once he made the attempt.[7] Except the passing mention of Bithynia in this and one other place,[8] it has no connection with the apostolic writings. The first great passage of its ecclesiastical history is

1 See their history in Mannert, III. ix. and the Appendix to Clinton's Fasti Hellenici.

2 Anno urbis conditæ DCLXXVI. mortuus est Nicomedes, rex Bithyniæ, et per testamentum populum Romanum fecit hæredem. Eutrop. vi. 6. Cf. Liv. Epit. xciii.

3 *Τῶν τοῦ Πόντου πόλεών τινες τῷ τῆς Βιθυνίας νομῷ προσετετάχατο.* Dio Cass. xlii. 45. See Strabo, xii. 3.

4 *Βιθυνία μετὰ τοῦ προσκειμένου οἱ Πόντου* is reckoned by him among the Senatorian provinces. liii. 12. See Liv. Epit. cii. There is some inaccuracy in Forbiger, p. 376.

5 See below, on Acts xvi. 7, 8.

6 It was the birthplace of his favourite Antinous. He took it from the senate, and placed it under his own jurisdiction. (Dio, lxix. 14.) But when St. Paul passed this way, it was under the senate, as we see by the coins of Claudius and Nero above.

7 Acts xvi. 7. 8 1 Pet. i. 1.

found in the correspondence of Trajan with its governor Pliny, concerning the persecution of the Christians. The second is the meeting of the first general council, when the Nicene Creed was drawn up on the banks of the Lake Ascanius.

III. Pamphylia.—This province has already been mentioned (Chap. VI.) as one of the regions traversed by St. Paul in his first missionary journey. But though its physical features have been described, its political limits have not been determined. The true Pamphylia of the earliest writers is simply the plain which borders the Bay of Attaleia, and which, as we have said,[1] retreats itself like a bay into the mountains. How small and insignificant this territory was, may be seen from the records of the Persian war, to which Herodotus says that it sent only thirty ships; while Lycia, on one side, contributed fifty, and Cilicia, on the other, a hundred.[2] Nor do we find the name invested with any wider significance, till we approach the frontier of the Roman period. A singular dispute between Antiochus and the king of Pergamus, as to whether Pamphylia was really within or beyond Mount Taurus, was decided by the Romans in favour of their ally.[3] This could only be effected by a generous inclusion of a good portion of the mountainous country within the range of this geographical term.[4] Henceforward, if not before,[5] Pamphylia comprehended some considerable part of what was anciently called Pisidia. We have seen that the Romans united it to the kingdom of Asia. It was, therefore, part of the province of Asia at the death of Attalus. It is difficult to trace the steps by which it was detached from that province. We find it (along with certain districts of Asia) included in the military jurisdiction of Cicero, when he was governor of Cilicia.[6] It is spoken of as a separate province in the reign of Augustus.[7] Its boundary on the Pisidian side, or in the direction of Phrygia,[8] must be left indeterminate. Pisidia was included in this province: but, again, Pisidia is itself indeterminate; and we have good reasons for believing that Antioch in Pisidia[9]

[1] P. 159.

[2] Herod. vii. 91, 92.

[3] Polyb. xxii. 27, 11. Liv. xxxviii. 39.

[4] Insident verticem Pisidæ. Plin. H. N. v. 24. Strabo (xii.) even says that some *Pisidian* towns were *south* of Taurus. See Cramer.

[5] Ἡ Πισιδική is spoken of, as if it were a province of Pamphylia, by Diodorus and Polybius. See Mannert.

[6] Ep. ad Att. v. 21.

[7] Dio Cassius, liii. 26, where we are told that the Pamphylian districts bestowed on Amyntas were restored by Augustus to their own province. So also in the reign of Claudius, lx. 17, quoted below, p. 243, n. 4.

[8] Pisidia was often reckoned as a part of Phrygia, under the name of *Φρυγία Πισιδική* or *Φρυγία πρὸς Πισιδίαν*. See Forbiger, p. 322.

[9] See Mannert, pp. 117, 169, 178. The Pisidian mountaineers had overrun this part of Phrygia, and their name remained there. See, however, Plin. H. N. v. 25.

was really under the governor of Galatia.[1] Cilicia was contiguous to Pamphylia on the east. Lycia was a separate region on the west, first as an appendage to Rhodes[2] in the time of the Republic, and then as a free state[3] under the earliest emperors; but about the very time when Paul was travelling in these countries, Claudius brought it within the provincial system, and united it to Pamphylia:[4] and monuments make us acquainted with a public officer who bore the title of "Proconsul of Lycia and Pamphylia."[5]

IV. Galatia.—We come now to a political division of Asia Minor, which demands a more careful attention. Its sacred interest is greater than that of all the others, and its history is more peculiar. The Christians of Galatia were they who received the Apostle "as if he had been an angel,"—who, "if it had been possible, would have plucked out their eyes and given them to him,"—and then were "so soon removed" by new teachers "from him that called them, to another Gospel,"—who began to "run well," and then were hindered,—who were "bewitched" by that zeal which compassed sea and land to make one proselyte,—and who were as ready, in the fervour of their party spirit, to "bite and devour one another," as they were willing to change their teachers and their gospels.[6] It is no mere fancy which discovers, in these expressions of St Paul's Epistle, indications of the character of that remarkable race of mankind, which all writers, from Cæsar to Thierry,[7] have described as susceptible of quick impressions and sudden changes, with a fickleness equal to their courage and enthusiasm, and a constant liability to that disunion which is the fruit of excessive vanity,—that race, which has not only pro-

[1] In the division of the fourth century, Pisidia became a province, and Antioch was its capital. See the Notitia.

[2] See above, p. 239, n. 2.

[3] Polyb. xxx. 5, 12. Liv. xlv. 25. See Cramer.

[4] Lyciis ob exitiabiles inter se discordias libertatem ademit. Suet. Claud. 25. Τοὺς Λυκίους στασιάσαντας, ὥστε καὶ Ῥωμαίους τινὰς ἀποκτεῖναι, ἐδουλώσατό τε, καὶ ἐς τὸν τῆς Παμφυλίας νομὸν ἐσέγραψεν. Dio Cass. lx. 17. Suetonius says, just above, that about the same time Claudius made over to the senate the provinces of Macedonia and Achaia. Hence we find a *proconsul* at Corinth. Acts xviii. 12.

[5] The inscription is adduced from Gruter by Mannert (p. 159) and Forbiger (p. 250, n. 95). At a later period Lycia was a distinct province, with Myra as its capital.

[6] Gal. iv. 14, 15. i. 6. v. 7. iii. 1. i. 7. v. 15.

[7] Cæsar, infirmitatem Gallorum veritus, quod sunt in consiliis capiendis mobiles, et novis plerumque rebus student, nihil his committendum existimavit. Cæs. B. G. iv. 5. Les traits saillans de la famille gauloise, ceux qui la différencient le plus, à mon avis, des autres familles humaines, peuvent se résumer ainsi: une bravoure personelle que rien n'égale chez les peuples anciens; un esprit franc, impétueux, ouvert à toutes les impressions, éminemment intelligent; mais, à côté de cela, une mobilité extrême, point de constance, une répugnance marquée aux idées de discipline et d'ordre si puissantes chez les races germaniques, beaucoup d'ostentation, enfin une désunion perpetuelle, fruit de l'excessive vanité. Thierry, Hist. des Gaulois, Introd iv., v

duced one of the greatest nations of modern times,[1] but which, long before the Christian era, wandering forth from their early European seats, burnt Rome and pillaged Delphi, founded an empire in Northern Italy more than co-extensive with Austrian Lombardy, and another in Asia Minor, equal in importance to one of the largest pachalicks.

For the "*Galatia*" of the New Testament was really the "*Gaul*" of the East. The "Epistle to the Galatians" would more literally and more correctly be called the "Epistle to the Gauls." When Livy, in his account of the Roman campaigns in Galatia, speaks of its inhabitants, he always calls them "Gauls."[2] When the Greek historians speak of the inhabitants of ancient France, the word they use is "Galatians."[3] The two terms are merely the Greek and Latin forms of the same "barbarian" appellation.[4]

That emigration of the Gauls, which ended in the settlement in Asia Minor, is less famous than those which led to the disasters in Italy and Greece: but it is, in fact, identical with the latter of these two emigrations, and its results were more permanent. The warriors who roamed over the Cevennes, or by the banks of the Garonne, reappear on the Halys and at the base of Mount Dindymus. They exchange the superstitions of Druidism for the ceremonies of the worship of Cybele. The very name of the chief Galatian tribe is one with which we are familiar in the earliest history of France;[5] and Jerome says that, in his own day, the language spoken at Ancyra was almost identical with that of Trêves.[6]

The French travellers (as Tournefort and Texier) seem to write with patriotic enthusiasm when they touch Galatia; and we have found our best materials in Thierry's history.

[2] Galli. Liv. xxxviii. 12–27. Once indeed, in the speech of Manlius (c. 17), the Roman general is introduced as saying, "Hi jam degeneres sunt; mixti, et Gallogræci vere, quod appellantur." The country of the Galatians was called Gallogræcia (c. 12, 18). See Justin, xxv. 2.

[3] Γαλάτια; as in Polybius, for instance, and Dio Cassius. Some have even thought that Γαλατίαν in 2 Tim. iv. 10 means the country commonly called Gaul; and some MSS. have Γαλλίαν.

[4] And we may add that "Galatæ" and "Keltæ" are the same word. See Arnold's Rome, i. 522.

[5] See Thierry, ch. iv., on the Tectosages. The Galatians, like the Belgians of Northern France, seem to have belonged to the Kymry, and not the Gael. Diod. Sic. v. 32, referred to by Arnold, p. 522; also Appian. See Thierry, pp. 131, 132.

[6] Unum est quod inferimus . . . . Galatas excepto sermone græco, quo omnis oriens loquitur, propriam linguam eandem habere quam Treviros. Hieron. Prol. in Ep. Gal. It is very likely that there was some Teutonic element in these emigrating tribes, but it is hardly possible now to distinguish it from the Keltic. The converging lines of distinct nationalities become more faint as we ascend towards the point where they meet. Thierry considers the Tolistoboii, whose leader was Lutarius (Luther or Clothair?), to have been a Teutonic tribe. The departure of new German colonies to Asia Minor is again advocated after 2100 years. See Prof. Ross's Deutschland und Kleinasien.

The Galatians were a stream from that torrent of barbarians which poured into Greece in the third century before our era, and which recoiled in confusion from the cliffs of Delphi. Some tribes had previously separated from the main army, and penetrated into Thrace. There they were joined by certain of the fugitives, and together they appeared on the coasts, which are separated by a narrow arm of the sea from the rich plains and valleys of Bithynia.[1] The wars with which that kingdom was harassed, made their presence acceptable. Nicomedes was the Vortigern of Asia Minor: and the two Gaulish chieftains, Leonor and Lutar, may be fitly compared to the two legendary heroes of the Anglo-Saxon invasion. Some difficulties occurred in the passage of the Bosphorus, which curiously contrast with the easy voyages of our piratic ancestors.[2] But once established in Asia Minor, the Gauls lost no time in spreading over the whole peninsula with their arms and devastation. In their first crossing over we have compared them to the Saxons. In their first occupation they may be more fitly compared to the Danes.[3] For they were a moveable army rather than a nation,—encamping, marching, and plundering at will. They stationed themselves on the site of ancient Troy, and drove their chariots in the plain of the Cayster.[4] They divided nearly the whole peninsula among their three tribes. They levied tribute on cities, and even on kings. The wars of the east found them various occupation. They hired themselves out as mercenary soldiers. They were the royal guards of the kings of Syria, and the mamelukes of the Ptolemies in Egypt.[5]

[1] Liv. xxxviii. 16, and Polyb.

[2] Lutarius Macedonibus duas tectas naves et tres lembos adimit; his, alios atque alios dies noctesque transvehendo, intra paucos dies omnes copias trajecit. Liv. xxxviii. 16.

[3] Compare the Saxon Chronicle, for instance, with what Livy says:—Profecti ex Bithynia in Asiam processerunt . . . Tantum terroris omnibus, quæ cis Taurum incolunt, gentibus injecerunt, ut quas adissent, quasque non adissent, pariter ultimæ propinquis, imperio parerent . . . Tantus terror eorum nominis erat, ut Syriæ quoque ad postremum reges stipendium dare non abnuerent. xxxviii. 16. And Justin:—Gallorum ea tempestate tantæ fœcunditatis juventus fuit, ut Asiam omnem velut examine aliquo implerent. xxv. 2.

[4] *Εἰς τὴν πόλιν Ἴλιον.* Strabo, xiii. *Ἐν λειμῶνι Καϋστρίῳ ἔσταν ἅμαξαι.* Callim. Hym. ad. Dian. v. 257, quoted by Thierry, p. 191. See the beautiful lines he quotes in the following page, from the anthology on the death of the maidens of Miletus (*ἃς ὁ βιαστὸς Κελτῶν εἰς ταύτην μοῖραν ἔτρεψεν Ἄρης*).

[5] Denique neque reges Orientis sine mercenario Gallorum exercitu ulla bella gesserunt; neque pulsi regno ad alios quam ad Gallos confugerunt. Tantus terror Gallici nominis, et armorum invicta felicitas erat, ut aliter neque majestatem suam tutari neque amissam reciperare se posse nisi Gallica virtute arbitrarentur. Justin, l. c.; and further references in Thierry, pp. 196–200. Even in the time of Julius Cæsar, we find 400 Gauls (Galatians), who had previously been part of Cleopatra's body-guard, given for the same purpose to Herod. Joseph. B. J. xx. 3.

The surrounding monarchs gradually curtailed their power, and repressed them within narrower limits. First Antiochus Soter drove the Tectosages,[1] and then Eumenes drove the Trocmi and Tolistoboii,[2] into the central district which afterwards became Galatia. Their territory was definitely marked out and surrounded by the other states of Asia Minor, and they retained a geographical position similar to that of Hungary in the midst of its Sclavonic neighbours. By degrees they coalesced into a number of small confederate states, and ultimately into one united kingdom.[3] Successive circumstances brought them into contact with the Romans in various ways; first, by a religious embassy sent from Rome to obtain peaceful possession of the sacred image of Cybele;[4] secondly, by the campaign of Manlius, who reduced their power and left them a nominal independence;[5] and then through the period of hazardous alliance with the rival combatants in the civil wars. The first Deiotarus was made king by Pompey, fled before Cæsar at the battle of Pharsalia, and was defended before the conqueror by Cicero, in a speech which still remains to us.[6] The second Deiotarus, like his father, was Cicero's friend, and took charge of his son and nephew during the Cilician campaign.[7] Amyntas, who succeeded him, owed his power to Antony,[8] but prudently went over to Augustus in the battle of Actium. At the death of Amyntas, Augustus made some modifications in the extent of Galatia, and placed it under a governor. It was now a province, reaching from the borders of Asia and Bithynia to the neighbourhood of Iconium, Lystra, and Derbe, "cities of Lycaonia."[9]

Henceforward, like the Western Gaul, this territory was a part of the Roman empire, though retaining the traces of its history in the character and language of its principal inhabitants. There was this difference, however, between the Eastern and Western Gaul, that the latter

[1] His appellation of "the Saviour" was derived from this victory. App. Syr. 65.

[2] Liv. xxxviii. 16. See 40.

[3] This does not seem to have been effectually the case till after the campaign of Manlius. The nation was for some time divided into four tetrarchies. Deiotarus was the first sole ruler; first as tetrarch, then as king.

[4] Liv. xxix. 10, 11.

[5] Liv. xxxviii. 16, &c.

[6] See Cic. de Div. ii. 37. Ep. ad Fam. xv. 2, &c.

[7] Ep. ad Att. v. 17.

[8] He received some parts of Lycaonia and Pamphylia in addition to Galatia Proper. Dio Cass. xlix. 32. See above, Ch. I. p. 23.

[9] The Pamphylian portion was removed (see above), but the Lycaonian remained. Τοῦ 'Αμύντου τελευτήσαντος, ἡ Γαλατία μετὰ τῆς Λυκαονίας 'Ρωμαῖον ἄρχοντα ἔσχε. Dio. C. liii. 26. See Eutrop. vii. 8. Thus we find Pliny (H. N. v. 42) reckoning the Lystreni in Galatia, though he seems to imply (ib. 25) that the immediate neighbourhood of Iconium was in Asia. It is therefore quite possible, so far as geographical difficulties are concerned, that the Christian communities in the neighbourhood of Lystra might be called "Churches of Galatia." See p. 234. We think, however, as we have said, that other difficulties are decisive against the view there mentioned.

was more rapidly and more completely assimilated to Italy. It passed from its barbarian to its Roman state, without being subjected to any intermediate civilisation.[1] The Gauls of the East, on the other hand, had long been familiar with the Greek language and the Greek culture. St. Paul's Epistle was written in Greek. The contemporary inscriptions of the province are usually in the same language.[2] The Galatians themselves are frequently called Gallo-Græcians;[3] and many of the inhabitants of the province must have been of pure Grecian origin. Another section of the population, the early Phrygians, were probably numerous, but in a lower and more degraded position. The presence of great numbers of Jews[4] in the province implies that it was, in some respects, favourable for traffic; and it is evident that the district must have been constantly intersected by the course of caravans from Armenia, the Hellespont, and the South.[5] The Roman itineraries inform us of the lines of communication between the great towns near the Halys and the other parts of Asia Minor. These circumstances are closely connected with the spread of the Gospel, and we shall return to them again when we describe St. Paul's first reception in Galatia.

V. Pontus.—The last independent dynasties in the north of the Peninsula have hitherto appeared as friendly or subservient to the Roman power. Asia and Bithynia were voluntarily ceded by Attalus and Nicomedes; and Galatia, on the death of Amyntas, quietly fell into the station of a province. But when we advance still further to the East, we are reminded of a monarch who presented a formidable and protracted opposition to Rome. The war with Mithridates was one of the most serious wars in which the Republic was ever engaged; and it was not till after a long struggle that Pompey brought the kingdom of Pontus under the Roman yoke. In placing Pontus among the provinces of Asia Minor at this exact point of St. Paul's life, we are (strictly speaking) guilty of an anachronism. For long after the western portion of the

1 The immediate neighbourhood of Marseilles, which was thoroughly imbued with a knowledge of Greek, must of course be excepted.

2 See Boëckh's Corpus Inscriptionum.

3 See above, p. 244, note 2.

4 See in Josephus (Ant. xvi. 6) the letter which Augustus wrote in favour of the Jews of Ancyra, and which was inscribed on a pillar in the temple of Cæsar. We shall have occasion hereafter to mention the Monumentum Ancyranum.

5 See what Livy says of Gordium, one of the minor towns near the western frontier:—"Haud magnum quidem oppidum est, sed plus quam mediterraneum celebre et frequens emporium. Tria maria pari ferme distantia intervallo habet." xxxviii. 18. Again, Strabo says of Tavium,—ἐμπορεῖον τῶν ταύτῃ. xii. 5. This last city was the capital of the Eastern Galatians, the Trocmi, who dwelt beyond the Halys. The Tolistoboii were the western tribe, near the Sangarius, with Pessinus as their capital. The chief town of the Tectosages in the centre, and the metropolis of the nation, was Ancyra.

empire of Mithridates was united partly with Bithynia and partly with Galatia,[1] the region properly called Pontus[2] remained under the government of independent chieftains. Before the Apostle's death, however, it was really made a province by Nero.[3] Its last king was that Polemo II., who was alluded to at the beginning of this work, as the contemptible husband of one of Herod's grand-daughters.[4] In himself he is quite unworthy of such particular notice, but he demands our attention, not only because, as the last independent king in Asia Minor, he stands at one of the turning points of history, but also because through his marriage with Berenice, he must have had some connection with the Jewish population of Pontus, and therefore probably with the spread of the Gospel on the shores of the Euxine. We cannot forget that Jews of Pontus were at Jerusalem on the day of Pentecost,[5] that the Jewish Christians of Pontus were addressed by St. Peter in his first Epistle,[6] and that "a Jew born in Pontus"[7] became one of the best and most useful associates of the Apostle of the Gentiles.

VI. Cappadocia.—Crossing the country southwards from the birthplace of Aquila towards that of St. Paul, we traverse the wide and varied region which formed the province of Cappadocia, intermediate between Pontus and Cilicia. The period of its provincial existence began in the reign of Tiberius. Its last king was Archelaus,[8] the contemporary of the

[1] See above, under Pamphylia, for the addition to that province. A tract of country, near the Halys, henceforward called Pontus Galaticus, was added to the kingdom of Deiotarus.

[2] Originally, this district near the Euxine was considered a part of Cappadocia, and called "Cappadocia on the sea (Pontus)." The name Pontus gradually came into use, with the rising power of the ancestors of Mithridates the Great.

[3] Ponti regnum, concedente Polemone, in provinciæ formam redegit. Suet. Nero, c. 18. See Eutrop. vii. 13; Aur. Vict. Cæs. 5. The statements of Forbiger (p. 292) are not quite in harmony with those in p. 413. It is probably impossible to determine the boundary which was ultimately arranged between the two contiguous provinces of Pontus and Cappadocia, when the last of the independent monarchs had ceased to reign. In the division of Constantine, Pontus formed two provinces, one called Helenopontus in honour of his mother, the other still retaining the name of Pontus Polemoniacus.

[4] P. 24 and p. 25, n. 3. In or about the year 60 A. D. we find Berenice again with Agrippa in Judæa, on the occasion of St. Paul's defence at Cæsarea. Acts xxv., xxvi. It is probable that she was with Polemo in Pontus about the year 52, when St. Paul was travelling in the neighbourhood.

[5] Acts ii. 9. [6] 1 Pet. i. 1. [7] Acts xviii. 2.

[8] He was made king by Antony, and, fifty years afterwards, was summoned to Rome by Tiberius, who had been offended by some disrespect shown to himself in the island of Rhodes. "Rex Archelaus quinquagesimum annum Cappadocia potiebatur, invisus Tiberio, quod eum Rhodi agentem nullo officio coluisset . . . regnum in provinciam reductum est." Tac. Ann. ii. 42. Cappadoces in formam provinciæ reducti. Ib. 56. See Dio Cass. lvii. 17. Strabo, xii. 1. Suet. Tib. c. 37. Eutrop. vii. 9.

Jewish tetrarch of the same name.[1] Extending from the frontier of Galatia to the river Euphrates, and bounded on the South by the chain of Taurus, it was the largest province of Asia Minor.[2] Some of its cities are celebrated in ecclesiastical history.[3] But in the New Testament it is only twice alluded to, once in the Acts,[4] and once in the Epistles.[5]

VII. Cilicia.—A single province yet remains, in one respect the most interesting of all, for its chief city was the Apostle's native town. For this reason the reader's attention was invited long ago to its geography and history.[6] It is therefore unnecessary to dwell upon them further. We need not go back to the time when Servilius destroyed the robbers in the mountains, and Pompey the pirates on the coast.[7] And enough has been said of the conspicuous period of its provincial condition, when Cicero came down from Cappadocia through the great pass of Mount Taurus,[8] and the letters of his correspondents in Rome were forwarded from Tarsus to his camp on the Pyramus.[9] Nearly all the light we possess concerning the fortunes of Roman Cilicia is concentrated on that particular time. We know the names of few of its later governors. Perhaps the only allusion to its provincial condition about the time of Claudius and Nero, which we can adduce from any ancient writer, is that passage in the Acts, where Felix is described as enquiring "of what province" St. Paul was. The use of the strict political term,[10] informs us that it was a separate province; but we are not able to state whether it was under the jurisdiction of the senate or the Emperor.[11]

1 Mat. ii. 22.

2 The Lesser Armenia was politically united with it. For details, see Forbiger, p. 292.

3 Especially Nyssa, Nazianzus, and Neocæsarea, the cities of the three Gregories, and Cæsarea, the city of Basil,—to say nothing of Tyana and Samosata.

4 ii. 9. 5 1 Pet. i. 1. 6 Pp. 20–26. See also 48, 49.

7 Pp. 20, 21. 8 See below, p. 257, note.

9 Quum essem in castris ad fluvium Pyramum, redditæ mihi sunt uno tempore a te epistolæ duæ, quas ad me Q. Servilius Tarso miserat. Ep. ad Fam. iii. 11.

10 Επαρχία. Acts xxiii. 34, the only passage where the word occurs in the New Testament. For the technical meaning of the term see above, p. 143, n. 2. It is strange that Böttger (Beitr. I.) should have overlooked this passage. He says (§ 7), that the *Province of Cilicia* ceased to exist at the death of Amyntas, and afterwards makes it to be included in the province of Cappadocia; a mistake which has, perhaps, arisen from the fact that a small district to the north of Taurus was called Cilicia. Another mistake is still more unaccountable, viz. the construction of a *Province of Phrygia* (§ 4, 10). The only authority adduced is a single phrase from the epitome of a lost book of Livy: whereas there is not a trace in history of any such province before the time of Constantine. Then, it is true, we find Phrygia Salutaris and Phrygia Pacatiana as two of the eleven provinces of the Diocese of Asia; but under the earlier emperors the term is simply ethnographical.

11 Spruner's map in the Atlas Antiquus leaves this point undecided. Can we infer from a passage in Agrippa's speech to the Jews (Joseph. B. J. ii. 16, 4), where he says

With this last division of the Heptarchy of Asia Minor we are brought to the starting-point of St. Paul's second missionary journey. Cilicia is contiguous to Syria, and indeed is more naturally connected with it than with the rest of Asia Minor.[1] We might illustrate this connection from the letters of Cicero;[2] but it is more to our purpose to remark that the Apostolic Decree, recently enacted at Jerusalem, was addressed to the Gentile Christians "in Antioch, and Syria, and Cilicia,"[3] and that Paul and Silas travelled "through Syria and Cilicia"[4] in the early part of their progress.

This second missionary journey originated in a desire expressed by Paul to Barnabas, that they should revisit all the cities where they had preached the Gospel and founded churches.[5] He felt that he was not called to spend a peaceful, though laborious, life at Antioch, but that his true work was "far off among the Gentiles."[6] He knew that his campaigns were not ended,—that as the soldier of Jesus Christ, he must not rest from his warfare, but must "endure hardness," that he might please Him who had called him.[7] As a careful physician, he remembered that they, whose recovery from sin had been begun, might be in danger of relapse; or, to use another metaphor, and to adopt the poetical language of the Old Testament, he said,—"Come, let us get up early to the vineyards: let us see if the vine flourish."[8] The words actually recorded as used by St. Paul on this occasion, are these:—"Come, let us turn back and visit our brethren in every city, where we have announced the word of the Lord, and let us see how they fare."[9] We notice here, for the first time, a trace of that tender solicitude concerning his converts, that earnest longing to behold their faces, which appears in the letters which he wrote afterwards, as one of the most remarkable, and one of the most attractive, features of his character. Paul was the speaker, and not Barnabas. The feelings of Barnabas might not be so deep, nor his anxiety so urgent.[10] Paul thought doubtless of the Pisidians and Lycaonians, as he thought afterwards at Athens and Corinth of the Thessalonians, from whom he

that Cilicia, as well as Bithynia, Pamphylia, &c., was "kept tributary to the Romans without an army," that it was one of the senate's provinces?

1 See p. 105, comparing Acts ix. 30 with Gal. i. 21.

2 Ep. ad Fam. xv. 2, ad Att. v. 20.

3 Acts xv. 23. 4 Acts xv. 41. 5 Acts xv. 36. 6 Acts xxii. 21.

7 2 Tim. ii. 3, 4.

8 Cant. vii. 12, quoted by Matthew Henry. See his excellent remarks on the whole passage.

9 There is much force in the particle δὴ, which is almost unnoticed by the commentators. It seems to express something like impatience, especially when we compare it with the words μετά τινας ἡμέρας, which precede. The tender feeling implied in the phrase πῶς ἔχουσι fully justifies what we have said in the text.

10 We might almost be inclined to suspect that Paul had previously urged the same proposal on Barnabas, and that he had hesitated to comply.

had been lately "taken,—in presence not in heart,—endeavouring to see their face with great desire—night and day praying exceedingly that he might see their face, and might perfect that which was lacking in their faith."[1] He was "not ignorant of Satan's devices."[2] He feared lest by any means the Tempter had tempted them, and his labour had been in vain.[3] He "stood in doubt of them," and desired to be "present with them" once more.[4] His wish was to revisit every city where converts had been made. We are reminded here of the importance of continuing a religious work when once begun. We have had the institution of presbyters,[5] and of councils[6] brought before us in the sacred narrative; and now we have an example of that system of church visitation,[7] of the happy effects of which we have still some experience, when we see weak resolutions strengthened, and expiring faith rekindled, in confirmations at home, or in missionary settlements abroad.

This plan, however, of a combined visitation of the churches was marred by an outbreak of human infirmity. The two apostolic friends were separated from each other by a quarrel, which proved that they were indeed, as they had lately told the Lystrians, "men of like passions" with others.[8] Barnabas was unwilling to undertake the journey unless he were accompanied by his relation Mark. Paul could not consent to the companionship of one who "departed from them from Pamphylia, and went not with them to the work:"[9] and neither of them could yield his opinion to the other. This quarrel was much more closely connected with personal feelings than that which had recently occurred between St. Peter and St. Paul,[10] and it was proportionally more violent. There is little doubt that severe words were spoken on the occasion. It is unwise to be over-anxious to dilute the words of Scripture, and to exempt even Apostles from blame. By such criticism we lose much of the instruction which the honest record of their lives was intended to convey. We are taught by this scene at Antioch, that a good work may be blessed by God, though its agents are encompassed with infirmity, and that changes, which are violent in their beginnings, may be overruled for the best results. Without attempting to balance too nicely the faults on either side, our simplest course is to believe that, as in most quarrels, there was blame with both. Paul's natural disposition was impetuous and impatient, easily kindled to indignation, and (possibly) overbearing. Barnabas had shown his

[1] 1 Thess. ii. 17. iii. 10. [2] 2 Cor. ii. 11. [3] 1 Thess. iii. 5.
[4] Gal. iv. 20. [5] Acts xiv. 23. See p. 199.
[6] Acts xv. See Ch. VII.
[7] See the remarks on this subject in Menken's Blicke in das Leben des Apostels Paulus (Bremen, 1828), p. 96.
[8] Acts xiv. 15. [9] Acts xv. 38, with xiii. 13. See pp. 161, 162.
[10] Pp. 222–224.

weakness when he yielded to the influence of Peter and the Judaizers. The remembrance of the indirect censure he then received may have been perpetually irritated by the consciousness that his position was becoming daily more and more subordinate to that of the friend who rebuked him. Once he was spoken of as chief of those "prophets at Antioch,"[2] among whom Saul was the last: now his name was scarcely heard, except when he was mentioned as the companion of Paul.[3] In short, this is one of those quarrels in which, by placing ourselves in imagination on the one side and the other, we can alternately justify both, and easily see that the purest Christian zeal, when combined with human weakness and partiality, may have led to the misunderstanding. How could Paul consent to take with him a companion who would really prove an embarrassment and a hindrance? Such a task as that of spreading the Gospel of God in a hostile world needs a resolute will and an undaunted courage. And the work is too sacred to be put in jeopardy by any experiments.[4] Mark had been tried once and found wanting. "No man, having put his hand to the plough, and looking back, is fit for the kingdom of God."[5] And Barnabas would not be without strong arguments to defend the justice of his claims. It was hard to expect him to resign his interest in one who had cost him much anxiety and many prayers. His dearest wish was to see his young kinsman approving himself as a missionary of Christ. Now, too, he had been won back to a willing obedience,—he had come from his home at Jerusalem,—he was ready now to face all the difficulties and dangers of the enterprise. To repel him in the moment of his repentance was surely "to break a bruised reed" and to "quench the smoking flax."[6]

It is not difficult to understand the obstinacy with which each of the disputants, when his feelings were once excited, clung to his opinion as to a sacred truth.[7] The only course which now remained was to choose two different paths and to labour independently; and the Church saw the humiliating spectacle of the separation of its two great missionaries to the Heathen. We cannot, however, suppose that Paul and Barnabas parted,

[1] Gal. ii. 13. P. 224.

[2] Acts xiii. Pp. 131, 132. Moreover, as a friend suggests at the moment of these pages going to press, St. Paul was under personal obligations to Barnabas for introducing him to the Apostles (Acts ix. 27), and the feelings of Barnabas would be deeply hurt if he thought his friendship slighted.

[3] See p. 149.

[4] A timid companion in the hour of danger is one of the greatest evils. Matthew Henry quotes Prov. xxv. 19: "Confidence in an unfaithful man in time of trouble, is like a broken tooth and like a foot out of joint."

[5] Luke ix. 62. [6] Matt. xii. 20.

[7] Jerome says: "Paulus severior, Barnabas clementior; uterque in suo sensu abundat, et tamen dissensio habet aliquid humanæ fragilitatis." Contra Pelag. ii. 522 And Chrysostom says:) Παῦλος ἐζήτει τὸ δίκαιον, ὁ Βαρνάβας τὸ φιλάνθρωπον.

like enemies, in anger and hatred. It is very likely that they made a deliberate and amicable arrangement to divide the region of their first mission between them, Paul taking the continental, and Barnabas the insular, part of the proposed visitation.[1] Of this at least we are certain, that the quarrel was overruled by Divine Providence to a good result. One stream of missionary labour had been divided, and the regions blessed by the waters of life were proportionally multiplied. St. Paul speaks of Barnabas afterwards[2] as of an Apostle actively engaged in his Master's service. We know nothing of the details of his life beyond the moment of his sailing for Cyprus; but we may reasonably attribute to him not only the confirming of the first converts,[3] but the full establishment of the Church in his native island. At Paphos the impure idolatry gradually retreated before the presence of Christianity; and Salamis, where the tomb of the Christian Levite[4] is shown,[5] has earned an eminent place in Christian history, through the writings of its bishop, Epiphanius.[6] Mark, too, who began his career as a "minister" of the Gospel in this island,[7] justified the good opinion of his kinsman. Yet, the severity of Paul may have been of eventual service to his character, in leading him to feel more deeply the serious importance of the work he had undertaken. And the time came when Paul himself acknowledged, with affectionate tenderness, not only that he had again become his "fellow-labourer,"[8] but that he was "profitable to the ministry,"[9] and one of the causes of his own "comfort."[10]

It seems that Barnabas was the first to take his departure. The feeling of the majority of the Church was evidently with St. Paul, for when he had chosen Silas for his companion and was ready to begin his journey, he was specially "commended by the brethren to the grace of God."[11] The visitation of Cyprus having now been undertaken by others, his obvious course was not to go by sea in the direction of Perga or Attaleia,"[12]

[1] If Barnabas visited Salamis and Paphos, and if Paul, after passing through Derbe, Lystra, and Iconium, went as far as Antioch in Pisidia (see below), the whole circuit of the proposed visitation was actually accomplished, for it does not appear that any converts had been made at Perga and Attaleia.

[2] 1 Cor. ix. 6: whence also it appears that Barnabas, like St. Paul, supported himself by the labour of his hands.

[3] Paul took the copy of the Apostolic Decree into Cilicia. If the Judaizing tendency had shown itself in Cyprus, Barnabas would still be able to refer to the decision of the council, and Mark would stand in the same relation to him as a witness in which Silas did to Paul.

[4] Acts iv. 36. [5] MS. note from Capt. Graves, R. N.

[6] The name of this celebrated father has been given to one of the promontories of the island, the ancient Acamas.

[7] Acts xiii. 5. [8] Philemon, 24. [9] 2 Tim. iv. 11.

[10] Col. iv. 10, 11. [11] Acts xv. 40.

[12] If no other causes had occurred to determine the direction of his journey, there

but to travel by the Eastern passes directly to the neighbourhood of Iconium. It appears, moreover, that he had an important work to accomplish in Cilicia. The early fortunes of Christianity in that province were closely bound up with the city of Antioch and the personal labours of St. Paul. When he withdrew from Jerusalem, "three years" after his conversion, his residence for some time was in "the regions of Syria and Cilicia."[1] He was at Tarsus in the course of that residence, when Barnabas first brought him to Antioch.[2] The churches founded by the Apostle in his native province must often have been visited by him; for it is far easier to travel from Antioch to Tarsus, than from Antioch to Jerusalem, or even from Tarsus to Iconium. Thus the religious movements in the Syrian metropolis penetrated into Cilicia. The same great "prophet" had been given to both, and the Christians in both were bound together by the same feelings and the same doctrines. When the Judaizing agitators came to Antioch, the result was anxiety and perplexity, not only in Syria, but also in Cilicia. This is nowhere literally stated; but it can be legitimately inferred. We are, indeed, only told that certain men came down with false teaching from Judæa to Antioch.[3] But the Apostolic Decree is addressed to "the Gentiles of *Cilicia*"[4] as well as those of Antioch, thus implying that the Judaizing spirit, with its mischievous consequences, had been at work beyond the frontier of Syria. And, doubtless, the attacks on St. Paul's apostolic character had accompanied the attack on apostolic truth,[5] and a new fulfilment of the proverb was nearly realised, that a prophet in his own country is without honour. He had, therefore, no ordinary work to accomplish as he went "through Syria and Cilicia confirming the churches;"[6] and it must have been with much comfort and joy that he was able to carry with him a document, emanating from the Apostles at Jerusalem, which justified the doctrine he had taught, and accredited his personal character. Nor was he alone as the bearer of this letter, but Silas was with him also, ready "to tell the same things by mouth."[7] It is a cause for thankfulness that God put it into the heart of Silas to "abide still at Antioch"[8] when Judas returned to Jerusalem, and to accompany St. Paul[9] on his northward journey. For when the Cilician Christians saw their countryman arrive without

might be no vessel at Antioch or Seleucia bound for Pamphylia; a circumstance not always sufficiently taken into account by those who have written on St. Paul's voyages.

[1] Gal. i. 21. Acts ix. 30. See pp. 104–106.

[2] Acts xi. 25. See p. 118.

[3] Acts xv. 1.

[4] Acts xv. 23.

[5] Pp. 210, 219.

[6] Acts xv. 41. The work of allaying the Judaizing spirit in Cilicia would require some time. Much might be accomplished during the residence at Antioch (xv. 36) which might very well include journeys to Tarsus. But we are distinctly told that the churches of Cilicia were "confirmed" by St. Paul, when he was on his way to those of Lycaonia.

[7] Acts xv. 27.

[8] See p. 222, n. 3

[9] Acts xv. 40.

his companion Barnabas, whose name was coupled with his own in the apostolic letter,[1] their confidence might have been shaken, occasion might have been given to the enemies of the truth to slander St. Paul, had not Silas been present, as one of those who were authorised to testify that both Paul and Barnabas were "men who had hazarded their lives for the name of our Lord Jesus Christ."[2]

Where "the churches" were, which he "confirmed" on his journey,—in what particular cities of "Syria and Cilicia,"—we are not informed. After leaving Antioch by the bridge over the Orontes,[3] he would cross Mount Amanus by the gorge which was anciently called the "Syrian Gates," and is now known as the Beilan Pass.[4] Then he would come to Alexandria and Issus, two cities that were monuments of the Macedonian conqueror; one as retaining his name, the other as the scene of his victory. After entering the Cilician plain, he may have visited Adana, Ægæ, or Mopsuetia, three of the conspicuous cities on the old Roman roads.[5] With all these places St. Paul must have been more or less familiar: probably there were Christians in all of them, anxiously waiting for the decree, and ready to receive the consolation it was intended to bring. And one other city must certainly have been visited. If there were churches anywhere in Cilicia, there must have been one at Tarsus. It was the metropolis of the province; Paul had resided there, perhaps for some years, since the time of his conversion; and if he loved his native place well enough to speak of it with something like pride to the Roman officer at Jerusalem,[6] he could not be indifferent to its religious welfare. Among the "Gentiles of Cilicia," to whom the letter which he carried

[1] Acts xv. 25. [2] Acts xv. 26.

[3] See the description of ancient Antioch above, Ch. IV. p. 123; also p. 136.

[4] The "*Syrian Gates*" are the entrance into Cilicia from Syria, as the "*Cilician Gates*" are from Cappadocia. The latter pass, however, is by far the grander and more important of the two. Intermediate between these two, in the angle where Taurus and Amanus meet, is the pass into Syria by which Darius fled after the battle of Issus. Both entrances from Syria into Cilicia are alluded to by Cicero (Fam. xv. 4), as well as the great entrance from Cappadocia (Att. v. 20, quoted below).

For a complete account of the geography of this district, see Mr. Ainsworth's paper in the eighth volume of the Geographical Society's Transactions. The Beilan Pass is a long valley, by which Amanus is crossed at a height of near 3000 feet above the level of the Mediterranean. To the N. of this is a *minor pass*, marked by an ancient ruin called the "Pillars of Jonas," which Alexander had to retrace when he turned back to meet Darius at Issus. Beyond Issus, on the Cilician shore, is another *minor pass*, where an ancient gate-way remains.

[5] If the itineraries are examined and compared together, the Roman roads will be observed to diffuse themselves among these different towns in the Cilician plain, and then to come together again at the bend of the bay, before they enter the Syrian Gates. Mopsuetia and Adana were in the direct road from Issus to Tarsus; Ægæ was on the coast-road to Soli. Baiæ also was an important town situated to the S. of Issus.

[6] Acts xxi. 39.

was addressed, the Gentiles of Tarsus had no mean place in his affections. And his heart must have overflowed with thankfulness, if, as he passed through the streets which had been familiar to him since his childhood, he knew that many households were around him where the Gospel had come "not in word only but in power," and the relations between husband and wife, parent and child, master and slave, had been purified and sanctified by Christian love. No doubt the city still retained all the aspect of the cities of that day, where art and amusement were consecrated to a false religion. The symbols of idolatry remained in the public places,—statues, temples, and altars,—and the various "objects of devotion," which in all Greek towns, as well as in Athens (Acts xvii. 23), were conspicuous on every side. But the silent revolution was begun. Some families had already turned "from idols to serve the living and true God."[1] The "dumb idols" to which, as Gentiles, they had been "carried away even as they were led,"[2] had been recognised as "nothing in the world,"[3] and been "cast to the moles and to the bats."[4] The homes which had once been decorated with the emblems of a vain mythology, were now bright with the better ornaments of faith, hope, and love. And the Apostle of the Gentiles rejoiced in looking forward to the time when the grace which had been triumphant in the household should prevail against principalities and powers,—when "every knee should bow at the name of Jesus, and every tongue confess that He is Lord, to the glory of God the Father."[5]

But it has pleased God that we should know more of the details of

[1] 1 Thess. i. 9. [2] 1 Cor. xii. 2. [3] 1 Cor. viii. 4.

[4] Isai. ii. 20. These remarks have been suggested by a recent discovery of much interest at Tarsus. In a mound which had formerly rested against a portion of the city wall, since removed, was discovered a large collection of terracotta figures and lamps. At first these were thought to be a sherd-wreck, or the refuse of some Ceramicus or pottery-work. But on observing that the lamps had been used and that the earthenware gods (*Dî fictiles*) bore no trace of having been rejected because of defective workmanship, but on the contrary, had evidently been used, it has been imagined that these terracottas must have been thrown away, as connected with idolatry, on the occasion of some conversion to Christianity. The figures are such as these,—a head of Pan, still showing the mortar by which it was set up in some garden or vineyard; the boy Mercury; Cybele, Jupiter, Ceres crowned with corn, Apollo with rays, a lion devouring a bull (precisely similar to that engraved, p. 22), with other symbols of general or local mythology. There are, moreover, some ears, legs, &c., which seem to have been votive offerings, and which, therefore, it would have been sacrilege to remove; and a great number of lamps or incense burners, with a carbonaceous stain on them. The date when these things were thrown to the "moles and bats" seems to be ascertained by the dressing of the hair in one of the female figures, which is that of the period of the early emperors, as shown in busts of Domitia, or Julia, the wife of Titus, the same that is censured by the Roman satirist and by the Christian Apostle. Some of them are undoubtedly of an earlier period. We owe the opportunity of seeing these remains, and the foregoing criticisms on them (by Mr. Abington, of Hanley, in Staffordshire), to the kindness of W. B. Barker, Esq., who was for many years a resident at Tarsus, and who is preparing a work on the history of Cilicia.

[5] Phil. ii. 10, 11.

early Christianity in the wilder and remoter regions of Asia Minor. To these regions the footsteps of St. Paul were turned, after he had accomplished the work of confirming the churches in Syria and Cilicia. The task now before him was the visitation of the churches he had formed in conjunction with Barnabas. We proceed to follow him in his second journey across Mount Taurus.

The vast mountain-barrier which separates the sunny plains of Cilicia and Pamphylia from the central table-land, has frequently been mentioned.[1] On the former journey[2] St. Paul travelled from the Pamphylian plain to Antioch in Pisidia, and thence by Iconium to Lystra and Derbe. His present course across the mountains was more to the eastward; and the last-mentioned cities were visited first. More passes than one lead down from Lycaonia and Cappadocia through the chain of Taurus into Cilicia.[3] And it has been supposed[4] that the Apostle travelled through one of the minor passes, which quits the lower plain at Pompeiopolis,[5] and enters the upland plain of Iconium, not far from the conjectural site of Derbe. But there is no sufficient reason to suppose that he went by any other than the ordinary road. A traveller wishing to reach the Valais conveniently from the banks of the Lago Maggiore would rather go by the Simplon, than by the difficult path across the Monte Moro; and there is one great pass in Asia Minor which may be called the Simplon[6] of Mount Taurus, described as a rent or fissure in the mountain-chain, extending from north to south through a distance of eighty miles,[7] and known in ancient days by the name of the "Cilician Gates,"[8] —which has been, in all ages, the easiest and most convenient entrance

1 Especially pp. 20, 48, 105, 162–170, 186, 199, 200.

2 Acts xiii. 14. Pp. 163–169.

3 The principal passes are enumerated in the "Modern Traveller." For ancient notices of them see Forbiger.

4 By Wieseler in his Chronologie. He refers to Hamilton's notice of the pass, and infers that this would be the route adopted, because it leads most directly to Derbe (Divle). But, in the first place, the site of Derbe suggested by Hamilton is (as we have seen, pp. 190, 198) very doubtful; and, secondly, the shortest road across a mountain-chain is not necessarily the best. The road by the Cilician Gates was carefully made and kept up, and enters the Lycaonian plain near where Derbe must have been situated. A recent traveller, the Rev. G. F. Weston, vicar of Crosby Ravensworth, went by a pass from Lycaonia into Cilicia, which seems to be the same as that alluded to by Hamilton and Wieseler, and, from the account in his journal, to be very rough and difficult. It seems likely that this was the pass by which Cyrus sent Syennesis. Anab. I. ii. See Ainsworth's Travels in the Track of the Ten Thousand Greeks (1844).

5 For Pompeiopolis or Soli, see p. 21 and the note.

6 Mr. Ainsworth points out some interesting particulars of resemblance and contrast between the Alps and this part of the Taurus. Travels and Researches in Asia Minor, &c. (1842), II. 80.

7 Col. Chesney in the Euphrates Expedition, i. 353.

8 Besides the passages quoted below, see Polyb. xii. Diod. xiv. p 406.

from the northern and central parts of the peninsula to the level by the sea-shore, where the traveller pauses before he enters Syria. The securing of this pass was the greatest cause of anxiety to Cyrus, when he marched into Babylonia to dethrone his brother.[1] Through this gorge Alexander descended to that Cilician plain,[2] which has been finely described by a Greek historian as a theatre made by Nature's hand for the drama of great battles.[3] Cicero followed in the steps of Alexander, as he tells his friend Atticus in a letter written with characteristic vanity.[4] And to turn to the centuries which have elapsed since the time of the Apostles and the first Roman emperors: twice, at least, this pass has been the pivot on which the struggle for the throne of the East seemed to turn,—once, in the war described by obscure historians,[5] when a pretender at Antioch made the Taurus his defence against the Emperor of Rome; and once, in a war which we remember, when a pretender at Alexandria fortified it and advanced beyond it in his attempt to dethrone the Sultan.[6] In the wars between the Crescent and the Cross, which have filled up much of the intervening period, this defile has decided the fate of many an army. The Greek historians of the first Saracen invasions describe it by a word, unknown to classical Greek, which denotes that when this passage (between Cappadocia and Cilicia) was secure, the

[1] Xen. Anab. i. 4. Mannert and Forbiger both think that he went by a pass more to the east; but the arguments of Mr. Ainsworth for the identity of Dana with Tyana, and the coincidence of the route of Cyrus with the "Cilician Gates," appear to be conclusive. Travels in the Track, &c., p. 40.

[2] See Arrian, ii. 7 and Quintus Curtius, iii. 4.

[3] *Πεδίον πλατύτατόν τε καὶ ἐπιμηκέστατον· ᾧ περίκειται μὲν λόφος εἰς θεάτρου σχῆμα, αἰγιαλὸς δε ἐπὶ θαλάσσης μέγιστος ἐκτείνεται· ὥσπερ τῆς φύσεως ἐργασαμένης στάδιον μάχης.* Herodian. iii. 4.

[4] Iter in Ciliciam feci per Tauri pylas. Tarsum veni a. d. iii. non. Octob. Inde ad Amanam contendi, qui Syriam a Cilicia aquarum divortio dividit. . . . . Castra paucos dies habuimus, ea ipsa, quæ contra Darium habuerat apud Issum Alexander, imperator haud paulo melior, quam aut tu aut ego. Ep. ad Att. v. 20.

[5] The war between Severus and Pescennius Niger. Herodian, iii. 1–4. He says of Niger, on the approach of Severus:—*'Εκέλευε τοῦ Ταύρου ὄρους τὰ στενὰ καὶ κρημνώδη διαφράττεσθαι . . . . πρόβλημα ὀχυρὸν νομίζων τῶν ἐν τῇ ἀνατολῇ ὁδῶν, τὸ δύσβατον τοῦ ὄρους· ὁ γὰρ Ταῦρος μεταξὺ ὢν Καππαδοκίας καὶ Κιλικίας, διακρίνει τά τε τῇ ἄρκτῳ καὶ τὰ τῇ ἀνατολῇ ἔθνη προσκείμενα*, iii. 1. When his advanced troops were defeated near the Bosphorus, some of them fled *περὶ τὴν ὑπωρείαν ἐπί Γαλατίας τε καὶ 'Ασίας, φθάσαι θέλοντες τὸν Ταῦρον ὑπερβῆναι, καὶ ἔντος τοῦ ἐρύματος γένεσθαι.* Ib. 2.

[6] This was emphatically the case in the first war between Mahomet Ali and the Sultan, when Ibrahim Pasha crossed the Taurus and fought the battle of Konieh, in December, 1832. In the second war, the decisive battle was fought at Nizib, in June, 1839, further to the East: but even then, while the negociations were pending, this pass was the military boundary between the opposing powers. See Mr. Ainsworth's Travels and Researches, quoted below. He was arrested in his journey by the battle of Nizib. For a slight notice of the two campaigns, see Yates' Egypt, I. xv. In the second volume (ch. v.) is a curious account of an interview with Ibrahim Pasha at Tarsus. in 1833, with notices of the surrounding country.

frontier was closed.[1] The Crusaders, shrinking from the remembrance of its precipices and dangers, called it by the more awful name of the "Gates of Judas."[2]

Through this pass we conceive St. Paul to have travelled on his way from Cilicia to Lycaonia. And if we say that the journey was made in the spring of the year 51, we shall not deviate very far from the actual date.[3] By those who have never followed the Apostle's footsteps, the successive features of the scenery through which he passed may be compiled from the accounts of recent travellers, and arranged in the following order.[4] After leaving Tarsus, the road ascends the valley of the Cydnus, which, for some distance, is nothing more than an ordinary mountain valley, with wooded eminences and tributary streams.[5] Beyond the point where the road from Adanah comes in from the right,[6] the hills suddenly draw together and form a narrow pass, which has always been guarded by precipitous cliffs, and is now crowned by the ruins of a medieval castle.[7] In some places the ravine contracts to a width of ten or twelve paces,[8] leaving room for only one chariot to pass.[9] It is an anxious place to any one in command

[1] The word *κλεισούρα* (clausura). Scylitzes Curopalates, published in the Bonn edition of Cedrenus, vol. ii. pp. 677, 703. For the history of the word, see the glossary to Cedrenus; where we find also the word *κλεισουριάρχης*. "Gregorius Cappadox, qui et clusuriarches." In both passages, Scylitzes alludes to the difference of climate between Cilicia and the interior. See, especially, p. 677: *Τὸν Ταῦρον τὸ ὄρος ὑπερβὰς πανστρατίᾳ εἰσβάλλει τῇ Ῥωμαίων· ἐντυχόντες δ' ἄθροοι τόποις ψυχροῖς ἐξ ἄγαν ἀλεεινῶν καὶ θερμῶν πολλῆς μεταβολῆς ᾔσθοντο· διὸ καὶ ἄνθρωποι πολλοὶ ἀπέθανον καὶ ζῶα πολλὰ ἐναπέψυσαν.* Compare the Claustra Caspiarum of Tacitus, Hist. i. 6 and the Claustra Montium, Ib. iii. 2.

[2] See Michaud's Histoire des Croisades, i. p. 141. Correspondence d'Orient, viii. p. 6.

[3] We have no means of exactly determining either the year or the season. He left Corinth in the spring (Acts xviii. 21) after staying there a year and a half (Acts xviii. 11). He arrived, therefore, at Corinth in the autumn; and probably, as we shall see, in the autumn of the year 52. Wieseler (pp. 36, 44) calculates that a year might be occupied in the whole journey from Antioch through Asia Minor and Macedonia to Corinth. Perhaps it is better to allow a year and a half; and the spring is the more likely season to have been chosen for the commencement of the journey. See p. 165.

[4] Very full descriptions may be seen in Ainsworth and in Capt. Kinneir's Travels.

[5] See Colonel Chesney's description of the valley.

[6] Mr. Ainsworth says the road which he followed to Adanah turns off from that to Tarsus, about five miles from the rocky gap mentioned. There is another mountain track from Adanah, mentioned by Captain Kinneir, which comes into the pass at a higher point.

[7] "On the right hand, or south side, of this pass are two bold rocky summits, towering, bare and precipitous, over the surrounding forest: the more western of these bears the ruins of a castle, with crumbling walls and round towers, said to be Genoese." Ainsworth's Travels and Researches II. 77.

[8] This gorge is called the Golek Boghaz. It is, as Capt. Kinneir says, "the part of the pass most capable of defence, and where a handful of determined men, advantageously posted, might bid defiance to the most numerous armies."

[9] The general phrase of Xenophon concerning the Cilician Gates is, *ὁδὸς ἁμαξιτὸς ὀρθία ἰσχυρῶς καὶ ἀμήχανος εἰσελθεῖν στρατεύματι, εἴ τις ἐκώλυεν.* Anab. I. ii. Mr

of a military expedition. To one who is unburdened by such responsibility, the scene around is striking and impressive. A canopy of fir-trees is high overhead. Bare limestone cliffs rise above on either hand to an elevation of many hundred feet. The streams which descend towards the Cydnus are closed by the road, and here and there undermine it or wash over it.[1] When the higher and more distant of these streams are left behind, the road emerges upon an open and elevated region, 4000 feet above the level of the sea.[2] This space of high land may be considered as dividing the whole mountain journey into two parts. For when it is passed, the streams are seen to flow in a new direction. Not that we have attained the point where the highest land of Asia Minor[3] turns the waters north and south. The torrents which are seen descending to the right, are merely the tributaries of the Sarus, another river of Cilicia.[4] The road is conducted northwards through this new ravine; and again the rocks close in upon it, with steep naked cliffs, among cedars and pines, forming "an intricate defile, which a handful of men might convert into another Thermopylæ."[5] When the highest peaks of Taurus are left behind, the road to Tyana is continued in the same northerly

Ainsworth regards this as applying to the Golek Boghaz; but it may be referred with equal propriety to the other narrow defile in the higher part of the pass, and this reference is more agreeable to the context.

1 See the descriptions in Ainsworth and Kinneir.

2 "The plain, if it may be so called, which occupies the level summit between the waters of the Seihun and the river of Tarsus is about an English mile in width, the approach to it being uphill and through a broken and woody country." Ainsw. Trav. and Res. p. 75. He then proceeds to describe the Egyptian batteries (this was soon after the battle of Nizib), and adds that the height of this upland, according to his observations, was 3812 feet.

3 This is the Anti-Taurus, which, though far less striking in appearance than the Taurus, is really higher, as is proved by the course of the Sarus and other streams.

4 See this veryclearly described by Ainsworth in each of his works. "The road is carried at first over low undulating ground, the waters of which flow towards the mountains. It enters them with the rivulets tributary to the Sarus, which have an easterly flow, and follows the waters for some distance, amid precipitous cliffs and wooded abutments, till they sever the main chain. . . . Beyond this, the road turns off to the south, up the course of a tributary. . . . An expansive upland here presents itself [see n. 2]. . . . . Beyond this the waters flow no longer to the Sarus, but to the Cydnus." —Travels in the Track, &c., pp. 44, 45. "Sixteen miles from Eregli [Cybistra] the waters begin to flow eastward, and soon collect in a small rivulet, which finds its way through Taurus to the bed of the Seihun [Sarus]. This is a peculiarity in the hydrographical features of this part of Taurus not hitherto pointed out." Trav. and Res. p. 71. The fact, however, is implied by Captain Kinneir, who says that, after travelling some miles from Tyana, he found "the Sihoun flowing through the valley parallel with the road."

5 These are Ainsworth's words of the Golek Boghaz (Trav. and Res. p. 77), but they must be true also of this portion of the pass; though he says in his other work that three chariots might pass abreast (Trav. in the Track, p. 45). In this part the chief *Turkish* defences were erected (Trav. and Res. p. 72.)

direction;[1] while that to Iconium takes a turn to the left, and passes among wooded slopes with rocky projections, and over ground comparatively level, to the great Lycaonian plain.[2]

The whole journey from Tarsus to Konieh is enough, in modern times, to occupy four laborious days;[3] and, from the nature of the ground, the time required can never have been much less. The road, however, was doubtless more carefully maintained in the time of St. Paul than at the present day, when it is only needed by Tartar couriers and occasional traders. Antioch and Ephesus had a more systematic civilisation than Aleppo or Smyrna; and the governors of Cilicia, Cappadocia, and Galatia, were more concerned than a modern pacha in keeping up the lines of internal communication.[4] At various parts of the journey from Tarsus to Iconium traces of the old military way are visible, marks of ancient chiseling, substructions, and pavement; stones that have fallen over into the rugged river-bed, and sepulchres hewn out in the cliffs, or erected on the level ground.[5] Some such traces still follow the ancient line of road where it enters the plain of Lycaonia, beyond Cybistra,[6] near the spot where we conceive the town of Derbe to have been formerly situated.[7]

[1] The roads towards Syria and Cæsarea in Cappadocia, and Angora in Galatia, both meet at Tyana. See the Map. p. 189. The place is worthy of notice as the native city of Apollonius, the notorious philosopher and traveller. This is carefully remarked by the author of the Jerusalem Itinerary.

[2] See Colonel Chesney's description, and above, p. 199, for the remarks of Leake and Hamilton on the neighbourhood of Karaman (Laranda). Neither of those travellers passed through the Cilician Gates. For further topographical details, see Kiepert's large Map of Asia Minor. Colonel Chesney's general map is also useful; and another of his maps, in which a delineation of the southern part of the pass is given.

[3] Mr. Ainsworth, in the month of November, was six days in travelling from Iconium to Adanah. Major Rennell, who enters very fully into all questions relating to distances and rates of travelling, says that more than forty hours are taken in crossing the Taurus from Eregli to Adanah, though the distance is only 78 miles; and he adds, that fourteen more would be done on common ground in the same time. Geog. of Western Asia.

[4] Inscriptions in Asia Minor, relating to the repairing of roads by the governors of provinces and other officials, are not infrequent. See those on public works in Gruter, p. 149, &c.; also Boeckh and Texier.

[5] See Ainsworth and Kinneir.

[6] See the Map with the line of Roman road, p. 189. Cybistra (Eregli) was one of Cicero's military stations. Its relation to the Taurus is very clearly pointed out in his letters. "Cum exercitu per Cappadociæ partem eam, quæ cum Cilicia continens est, iter feci, contraque ad Cybistra, quod oppidum est ad montem Taurum, locavi." Ad Fam. xv. 2. "In Cappadocia extrema non longe a Tauro apud oppidum Cybistra castra feci, ut et Ciliciam tuerer et Cappadociam tenens," &c. Ib. 4. At this point he was very near Derbe. He had come from Iconium, and afterwards went through the pass to Tarsus; so that his route must have nearly coincided with that of St. Paul. The bandit-chief Antipater of Derbe, is one of the personages who plays a considerable part in this passage of Cicero's life.

[7] See above, p. 188, n. 1, and p. 198, n. 7 Mr. Hamilton (A. M. vol. ii.) gives a de-

As St. Paul emerged from the mountain-passes, and came along the lower heights through which the Taurus recedes to the Lycaonian levels, the heart, which had been full of affection and anxiety all through the journey, would beat more quickly at the sight of the well-known objects before him. The thought of his disciples would come with new force upon his mind, with a warm thanksgiving that he was at length allowed to revisit them, and to "see how they fared."[1] The recollection of friends, from whom we have parted with emotion, is often strongly associated with natural scenery, especially when the scenery is remarkable. And here the tender-hearted Apostle was approaching the home of his Lycaonian converts. On his first visit, when he came as a stranger, he had travelled in the opposite direction:[2] but the same objects were again before his eyes, the same wide-spreading plain, the same black summit of the Kara-Dagh. In the further reach of the plain, beyond the "Black Mount," was the city of Iconium; nearer to its base was Lystra; and nearer still to the traveller himself was Derbe,[3] the last point of his previous journey. Here was his first meeting now with the disciples he had then been enabled to gather. The incidents of such a meeting,—the inquiries after Barnabas,—the welcome given to Silas,—the exhortations, instructions, encouragements, warnings, of St. Paul,—may be left to the imagination of those who have pleasure in picturing to themselves the features of the Apostolic age, when Christianity was new.

This is all we can say of Derbe, for we know no details either of the former or present visit to the place. But when we come to Lystra, we are at once in the midst of all the interest of St. Paul's public ministry and private relations. Here it was that Paul and Barnabas were regarded as heathen divinities;[4] that the Jews, who had first cried "Hosanna" and then crucified the Saviour, turned the barbarians from homage to insult;[5] and that the little church of Christ had been fortified by the assurance that the kingdom of heaven can only be entered through "much tribulation."[6] Here too it was that the child of Lois

tailed account of his journey in this direction, and of the spots where he saw ruins, inscriptions, or tombs. He heard of Divle when he was in a yailah on the mountains, but did not visit it in consequence of the want of water. There was none within eight hours. See Trans. of Geog. Soc. viii. 154, and compare what is said of the drought of Lycaonia by Strabo, as quoted above, p. 186.

Texier is of opinion that the true site of Derbe is Divle, which he describes as a village in a wild valley among the mountains, with Byzantine remains. Asie Mineure, ii. 129, 130. The same view seems to be taken by Dr. Bailie, who adduces an inscription from "Devlê or Devrê" in his second Fasciculus of Inscriptions (1847), p. 264. g

[1] See above, p. 250.

[2] Compare Acts xiv. with 2 Tim iii. 10, 11.

[3] See the account of the topography of this district, Ch. VI. pp. 182, &c.

[4] Acts xiv. 12–18. pp. 192, &c. [5] Acts xiv. 19. pp. 195, 196

[6] Acts xiv. 22, p. 199.

KARA—DAGH. NEAR LYSTRA.

and Eunice, taught the Holy Scriptures from his earliest years, had been trained to a religious life, and prepared, through the Providence of God, by the sight of the Apostle's sufferings, to be his comfort, support, and companion.[1]

Spring and summer had passed over Lystra, since the Apostles had preached there. God had continued to "bless" them, and given them "rain from heaven and fruitful seasons, filling their hearts with food and gladness."[2] But still "the living God, who made the heavens, and the earth, and the sea, and all things that are therein," was only recognised by a few. The temple of the Lystrian Jupiter still stood before the gate, and the priest still offered the people's sacrifices to the imaginary protector of the city.[3] Heathenism was invaded, but not yet destroyed. Some votaries had been withdrawn from that polytheistic religion, which wrote and sculptured in stone its dim ideas of "present deities;"[4] crowding its thoroughfares with statues and altars,[5] ascribing to the King of the Gods the attributes of beneficent protection and the government of atmospheric changes,[6] and vaguely recognizing Mercury as the dispenser of fruitful seasons and the patron of public happiness.[7] But many years of difficulty and persecution were yet to elapse before Greeks and barbarians fully learnt, that the God whom St. Paul preached was a Father everywhere present to his children, and the One Author of every "good and perfect gift."

1 See pp. 197, 198.

2 See the words used in St. Paul's address to the Lystrians, Acts xiv. and the remarks made pp. 193, 195. New emphasis is given to the Apostle's words, if we remember what Strabo says of the absence of water in the pastures of Lycaonia. Mr. Weston found that water was dearer than milk at Bin-bir-Kilisseh, and that there was only one spring, high up the Kara-Dagh.

3 P. 190, n. 1. I. E. I. Walch, in his Spicilegium Antiquitatum Lystrensium (Diss. in Acta Apostolorum, Jena, 1766, vol. iii.), thinks that a *statue* of Jupiter, and not a *temple*, is meant. He adduces many *inscriptions* in illustration of the subject, such as the following: "Jupiter Custos coloniæ Mutinensis," "Serapi conservatori," "Deo in cujus tutela domus est;" and especially one from Gruter, with JUPITER CUSTOS, and the attributes of *Mercury* above. The equivalent Greek terms are πολιοῦχος and προπυλαῖος.

4 Inscriptions with "Dîs præsentibus," or the Greek word ΕΠΙΦΑΝΕΙΑ, were very common. Caligula wished statues to be erected in his honour, with ΔΙΟΣ ΕΠΙΦΑΝΟΥΣ inscribed on them. See Walch. Compare the "Præsens Divus" of Horace, Od. III. v. 2, and see the idea expanded in the fifth ode of the fourth book.

5 See the remarks on Tarsus above, p. 256, and the note.

6 Jupiter was called ἐπικάρπιος and ὄμβριος; and such inscriptions as the following were frequent,—*Jovi O. M. Tempestatum Divinarum potenti.* Compare them with St. Paul's words, Acts xiv. 17. See also Walch's references to Callimachus, Lucian, and Athenæus.

7 Mercury is sometimes represented with a cornucopiæ, ears of corn, &c., and the words "sæculo frugifero." There are also coins with "felicitas publica" and the symbols of Mercury. Walch.

Lystra, however, contributed one of the principal agents in the accomplishment of this result. We have seen how the seeds of Gospel truth were sown in the heart of Timotheus.[1] The instruction received in childhood,—the sight of St. Paul's sufferings,—the hearing of his words,—the example of the "unfeigned faith, which first dwelt in his grandmother Lois and his mother Eunice,"[2]—and whatever other influences the Holy Spirit had used for his soul's good,—had resulted in the full conviction that Jesus was the Messiah. And if we may draw an obvious inference from the various passages of Scripture, which describe the subsequent relation of Paul and Timothy, we may assert that natural qualities of an engaging character were combined with the Christian faith of this young disciple. The Apostle's heart seems to have been drawn towards him with peculiar tenderness. He singled him out from the other disciples. "Him would Paul have to go forth with him."[3] This feeling is in harmony with all we read, in the Acts and the Epistles, of St. Paul's affectionate and confiding disposition. He had no relative ties which were of service in his apostolic work; his companions were few and changing; and though Silas may well be supposed to have supplied the place of Barnabas, it was no weakness to yearn for the society of one who might become, what Mark had once appeared to be, a *son* in the Gospel.[4] Yet how could he consistently take an untried youth on so difficult an enterprize? How could he receive Timothy into "the glorious company of Apostles" when he had rejected Mark? Such questions might be raised, if we were not distinctly told that the highest testimony was given to Timothy's

[1] Pp. 197, 198. It is well known that commentators are not agreed whether Lystra or Derbe was the birthplace of Timothy. But the former opinion is by far the most probable. The latter rests on the view which some critics take of Acts xx. 4. The whole aspect of Acts xvi. 1, 2 is in favour of Lystra. St. Luke mentions Lystra after Derbe, and then says *ἐκεῖ*; and again, when referring to the town where Timothy was well spoken of, he does not mention Derbe at all, but Lystra first and Iconium next. It is quite unnatural, in the other passage, to place the comma after *Γάϊος* with Olshausen, or to read *Τιμόθεός τε Δερβαῖος* with Kuinoel, or *καὶ* Δ. Τ. with Heinrichs. The only motives for the change appear to be the notion that Timothy's birthplace ought to be specified, as in the case of the others, and the wish to identify Caius with the disciple mentioned xix. 29. But to these arguments Meyer and De Wette very justly reply, that it was useless to mention Timothy's birthplace, when it was known already; and that the name Caius was far too common to cause us any difficulty. Wieseler (pp. 25, 26) ingeniously suggests that Timothy might be a native of Derbe, and yet met with by St. Paul at Lystra. He is unwilling to think that a new Caius can be mentioned so soon in company with Aristarchus. But surely we may answer that the very word *Δερβαῖος* may be intended to show that a different person is intended from the Caius of xix. 29.

[2] 2 Tim. i. 5.

[3] *Ἠθέλησεν*, Acts xvi. 3. The wish was spontaneous, not suggested by others.

[4] This is literally what he afterwards said of Timothy: "Ye know that, *as a son with the father*, he has served with me in the Gospel." Philip. ii. 22. Compare also the phrases, "my son," "my own son in the faith" 1 Tim. i. 2, 18, and 2 Tim. ii. 1.

Christian character, not only at Lystra, but Iconium also.[1] We infer from this, that diligent inquiry was made concerning his fitness for the work to which he was willing to devote himself. To omit, at present, all notice of the prophetic intimations which sanctioned the appointment of Timothy,[2] we have the best proof that he united in himself those outward and inward qualifications which a careful prudence would require. One other point must be alluded to, which was of the utmost moment at that particular crisis of the Church. The meeting of the Council at Jerusalem had lately taken place. And, though it had been decided that the Gentiles were not to be forced into Judaism on embracing Christianity, and though St. Paul carried with him[3] the decree, to be delivered "to all the churches,"—yet still he was in a delicate and difficult position. The Jewish Christians had naturally a great jealousy on the subject of their ancient divine law; and in dealing with the two parties the Apostle had need of the utmost caution and discretion. We see, then, that in choosing a fellow-worker for his future labours, there was a peculiar fitness in selecting one, "whose mother was a Jewess, while his father was a Greek."[4]

We may be permitted here to take a short retrospect of the childhood and education of St. Paul's new associate. The hand of the Apostle himself has drawn for us the picture of his early years.[5] That picture represents to us a mother and a grandmother, full of tenderness and faith, piously instructing the young Timotheus in the ancient Scriptures, making his memory familiar with that "cloud of witnesses" which encompassed all the history of the chosen people, and training his hopes to expect the Messiah of Israel.[6] It is not allowed to us to trace the previous history of these godly women of the dispersion. It is highly probable that they may have been connected with those Babylonian Jews whom Antiochus settled in Phrygia three centuries before:[7] or they may have been conducted into Lycaonia by some of those mercantile and other changes which affected the movements of so many families at the epoch we are writing of; such, for instance, as those which brought the household of the Corinthian Chloe into relations with Ephesus,[8] and caused the prose-

[1] Acts xvi. 2.

[2] Τὰς προαγούσας ἐπὶ σὲ προφητείας. 1 Tim. i. 18. See iv. 14. We ought to add, that "the brethren" who gave testimony in praise of Timothy were the very converts of St. Paul himself, and, therefore, witnesses in whom he had good reason to place the utmost confidence.

[3] Acts xvi. 4. [4] Acts xvi. 1. [5] 2 Tim. i. 5. iii. 15, &c.

[6] If it is allowable to allude to an actual picture of a scene of this kind, we may mention the drawing of "Jewish Women reading the Scriptures," in Wilkie's Oriental Sketches.

[7] See Ch. II. p. 38, also Ch. I. pp. 17, 18. The authority for the statement made there is Joseph. Ant. xii. 3 4.

[8] 1 Cor. i. 11.

lyte Lydia to remove from Thyatira to Philippi.[1] There is one difficulty which, at first sight, seems considerable; viz. the fact that a religious Jewess, like Eunice, should have been married to a Greek. Such a marriage was scarcely in harmony with the stricter spirit of early Judaism, and in Palestine itself it could hardly have taken place.[2] But among the Jews of the dispersion, and especially in remote districts, where but few of the scattered people were established, the case was rather different. Mixed marriages, under such circumstances, were doubtless very frequent. We are at liberty to suppose that in this case the husband was a proselyte. We hear of no objections raised to the circumcision of Timothy, and we may reasonably conclude that the father was himself inclined to Judaism:[3] if, indeed, he were not already deceased, and Eunice a widow. This very circumstance, however, of his mixed origin, gave to Timothy an intimate connection with both the Jewish and Gentile worlds. Though far removed from the larger colonies of Israelitish families, he was brought up in a thoroughly Jewish atmosphere: his heart was at Jerusalem while his footsteps were in the level fields near Lystra, or on the volcanic crags of the Black Mount: and his mind was stored with the Hebrew or Greek[4] words of inspired men of old in the midst of the rude idolaters, whose language was "the speech of Lycaonia." And yet he could hardly be called a Jewish boy, for he had not been admitted within the pale of God's ancient covenant by the rite of circumcision. He was in the same position, with respect to the Jewish church, as those, with respect to the Christian church, who, in various ages, and for various reasons, have deferred their baptism to the period of mature life. And "the Jews which were in those quarters,"[5] however much they may have respected him, yet, knowing "that his father was a Greek," and that he himself was uncircumcised, must have considered him all but an "alien from the commonwealth of Israel."

Now, for St. Paul to travel among the synagogues with a companion in this condition,—and to attempt to convince the Jews that Jesus was

[1] Acts xvi. 14.

[2] Selden's language is very strong. "Cum Gentili sive libera sive ancilla Ebræi sponsalia plane irrita erant, uti et Gentilis aut servi cum Ebræa." Uxor Ebraica, II. iv. Michaelis, in his Commentaries on the Laws of Moses, takes a very different view, and seems to think there was little to hinder such marriages. The cases of Esther and of various members of the Herodian family obviously occur to us.

[3] The expression in the original (xvi. 3) is Ελλην ὑπῆρχεν, which means, "he was a born Greek. The most natural inference is, that his father was living, and most probably not a proselyte of righteousness, if a proselyte at all.

[4] We cannot tell how far this family is to be reckoned Hellenistic or Aramaic (see Ch. II.) But the Hellenistic element would be likely to predominate. In reference to this subject, Mr. Grinfield, in his recent work on the Septuagint, p. 53, notices the two passages from that version in St. Paul's letters to Timothy. 1 Tim. v. 18. 2 Tim. ii. 19.

[5] Acts xvi. 3.

the Messiah, when his associate and assistant in the work was an uncircumcised heathen,—would evidently have been to encumber his progress and embarrass his work. We see in the first aspect of the case a complete explanation of what to many has seemed inconsistent, and what some have ventured to pronounce as culpable, in the conduct of St. Paul. "He took and circumcised Timotheus." How could he do otherwise if he acted with his usual far-sighted caution and deliberation? Had Timothy not been circumcised, a storm would have gathered round the Apostle in his further progress. The Jews, who were ever ready to persecute him from city to city, would have denounced him still more violently in every synagogue when they saw in his personal preferences, and in the co-operation he most valued, a visible revolt against the law of his forefathers. To imagine that they could have overlooked the absence of circumcision in Timothy's case, as a matter of no essential importance, is to suppose they had already become enlightened Christians. Even in the bosom of the Church we have seen[1] the difficulties which had recently been raised by scrupulousness and bigotry on this very subject. And the difficulties would have been increased tenfold in the untrodden field before him by proclaiming everywhere on his very arrival that circumcision was abolished. His fixed line of procedure was to act on the cities through the synagogues, and to preach the Gospel first to the Jew and then to the Gentile.[2] He had no intention of abandoning this method, and we know that he continued it for many years.[3] But such a course would have been impossible had not Timothy been circumcised. He must necessarily have been repelled by that people who endeavoured once to murder St. Paul, because they imagined he had taken a Greek into the Temple.[4] The very intercourse of social life would have been hindered, and made almost impossible, by the presence of a half-heathen companion: for, however far the stricter practice may have been relaxed among the Hellenising Jews of the dispersion, the general principle of exclusiveness everywhere remained, and it was still "an abomination" for the circumcised to eat with the uncircumcised.[5]

It may be thought, however, that St. Paul's conduct in circumcising Timothy was inconsistent with the principle and practice he maintained at Jerusalem when he refused to circumcise Titus.[6] But the two cases were entirely different. Then there was an attempt to enforce circumcision as necessary to salvation: now it was performed as a voluntary act, and simply on prudential grounds. Those who insisted on the ceremony in the

[1] Ch. VII.

[2] Acts xiii. 5, 14. xiv. 1 xvii. 1, 2, 10. xviii. 4, 19. xix. 8, 9; and compare Rom. i. 16. ii. 9, 10.

[3] See Acts xxviii.

[4] Acts xxi. 29, with xxii. 22.

[5] See p. 205.

[6] Gal. ii. 3. See p. 218.

case of Titus were Christians, who were endeavouring to burden the Gospel with the yoke of the law: those for whose sakes Timothy became obedient to one provision of the law, were Jews, whom it was desirable not to provoke, that they might more easily be delivered from bondage. By conceding in the present case, prejudice was conciliated and the Gospel furthered: the results of yielding in the former case would have been disastrous, and perhaps ruinous, to the cause of pure Christianity.

If it be said that even in this case there was danger lest serious results should follow,—that doubt might be thrown on the freedom of the Gospel, and that colour might be given to the Judaizing propensity:—it is enough to answer that indifferent actions become right or wrong according to our knowledge their probable consequences,—and that St. Paul was a better judge of the consequences likely to follow from Timothy's circumcision than we can possibly be. Are we concerned about the effects likely to have been produced on the mind of Timothy himself? There was no risk, at least, lest he should think that circumcision was necessary to salvation, for he had been publicly recognised as a Christian before he was circumcised;[1] and the companion, disciple, and minister of St. Paul was in no danger, we should suppose, of becoming a Judaizer. And as for the moral results, which might be expected to follow in the minds of the other Lycaonian Christians,—it must be remembered that at this very moment St. Paul was carrying with him and publishing the decree which announced to all Gentiles that they were not to be burdened with a yoke which the Jews had never been able to bear. St. Luke notices this circumstance in the very next verse after the mention of Timothy's circumcision, as if to call our attention to the contiguity of the two facts.[2] It would seem, indeed, that the very best arrangements were adopted which a divinely enlightened prudence could suggest. Paul carried with him the letter of the Apostles and elders, that no Gentile Christian might be enslaved to Judaism. He circumcised his minister and companion, that no Jewish Christian might have his prejudices shocked. His language was that which he always used,—"Circumcision is nothing, and uncircumcision is nothing. The renovation of the heart in Christ is everything.[3] Let every man be persuaded in his own mind."[4] No innocent prejudice was ever treated roughly by St. Paul. To the Jew he became a Jew, to the Gentile a Gentile: "he was all things to all men, if by any means he might save some."[5]

Iconium appears to have been the place where Timothy was circumcised. The opinion of the Christians at Iconium, as well as those at

[1] Acts xvi. 1–3.

[2] See vv. 3, 4.

[3] Gal. v. 6. vi. 15. St. Paul's own conduct on the confines of Galatia is a commentary on the words he uses to the Galatians.

[4] Rom. xiv. 5.

[5] 1 Cor. ix. 20–22.

Lystra, had been obtained before the Apostle took him as his companion. These towns were separated only by the distance of a few miles ;[1] and constant communication must have been going on between the residents in the two places, whether Gentile, Jewish, or Christian. Iconium was by far the most populous and important city of the two,—and it was the point of intersection of all the great roads in the neighbourhood.[2] For these reasons we conceive that St. Paul's stay in Iconium was of greater moment than his visits to the smaller towns, such as Lystra. Whether the ordination of Timothy, as well as his circumcision, took place at this particular place and time, is a point not easy to determine. But this view is at least as probable as any other that can be suggested : and it gives a new and solemn emphasis to this occasion if we consider it as that to which reference is made in the tender allusions of the pastoral letters,—where St. Paul reminds Timothy of his good confession before "many witnesses,"[3] of the "prophecies" which sanctioned his dedication to God's service,[4] and of the "gifts" received by the laying on of "the hands of the presbyters"[5] and the Apostle's "own hands."[6] Such references to the day of ordination, with all its well-remembered details, not only were full of serious admonition to Timothy, but possess the deepest interest for us.[7] And this interest becomes still greater if we bear in mind that the "witnesses" who stood by were St. Paul's own converts, and the very "brethren" who gave testimony to Timothy's high character at Lystra and Iconium ;[8]—that the "prophecy" which designated him to his office was the same spiritual gift which had attested the commission of Barnabas and Saul at Antioch,[9] and that the College of Presbyters,[10] who,

[1] To what has been said before (pp. 182, 186, &c.), add the following note from a MS. journal already quoted. "*Oct.* 6.—Left Konieh at 12. Traversed the enormous plains for 5½ hours, when we reached a small Turcoman village. . . *Oct.* 7.—At 11.30 we approached the Kara-Dagh, and in about an hour began to ascend its slopes. We were thus about 11 hours crossing the plain from Konieh. This, with 2 on the other side, made in all 13 hours. We were heartily tired of the plain."

[2] Roads from Iconium to Tarsus in Cilicia, Side in Pamphylia, Ephesus in Asia, Angora in Galatia, Cæsarea in Cappadocia, &c., are all mentioned in the ancient authorities.

[3] 1 Tim. vi. 12. [4] 1 Tim. i. 18. [5] 1 Tim. iv. 14. [6] 2 Tim. i. 6.

[7] This is equally true, if the ordination is to be considered coincident with the "laying on of hands," by which the miraculous gifts of the Holy Ghost were first communicated, as in the case of Cornelius (Acts x. 44), the Samaritans (viii. 17), the disciples at Ephesus (xix. 6), and St. Paul himself (ix. 17). See the Essay on the Apostolical Office in Stanley's Sermons and Essays, especially p. 71. These *gifts* doubtless pointed out the *offices* to which individuals were specially called. Compare together the three important passages: Rom. xii. 6–8. 1 Cor. xii. 28-30. Eph. iv 11, 12 ; also 1 Pet. iv. 10, 11.

[8] Compare Acts xvi. 2 with Acts xiii. 51—xiv. 22.

[9] Compare 1 Tim. i. 18 with Acts xiii. 1–3.

[10] Τὸ πρεσβυτέριον. 1 Tim. iv. 14. See 2 Tim. i. 6.

in conjunction with the Apostle, ordained the new minister of the Gospel, consisted of those who had been "ordained in every church"[1] at the close of that same journey.

On quitting Iconium St. Paul left the route of his previous journey; unless indeed he went in the first place to Antioch in Pisidia,—a journey to which city was necessary in order to complete a full visitation of the churches founded on the continent in conjunction with Barnabas. It is certainly most in harmony with our first impressions, to believe that this city was not unvisited. No mention, however, is made of the place, and it is enough to remark that a residence of a few weeks at Iconium as his head-quarters would enable the Apostle to see more than once all the Christians at Antioch, Lystra, and Derbe.[2] It is highly probable that he did so: for the whole aspect of the departure from Iconium, as it is related to us in the Bible, is that of a new missionary enterprise, undertaken after the work of visitation was concluded. St. Paul leaves Iconium, as formerly he left the Syrian Antioch, to evangelize the heathen in new countries. Silas is his companion in place of Barnabas, and Timothy is with him "for his minister," as Mark was with him then. Many roads were before him. By travelling westward he would soon cross the frontier of the province of Asia,[3] and he might descend by the valley of the Mæander to Ephesus, its metropolis:[4] or the roads to the south[5] might have conducted him to Perga and Attaleia, and the other cities on the coast of Pamphylia. But neither of these routes was chosen. Guided by the ordinary indications of Providence, or consciously taught by the Spirit of God, he advanced in a northerly direction, through what is called, in the general language of Scripture, "Phrygia and the region of Galatia."

We have seen[6] that the term "Phrygia" had no political significance

[1] Acts xiv. 23.

[2] It would also be very easy for St. Paul to visit Antioch on his route from Iconium through Phrygia and Galatia. See below, p. 271. The fact that *Pisidia* is not mentioned cannot be used as an argument against a visit to that place. Böttger (§ 18) very forcibly says it is highly improbable that St. Paul should pass by his converts there, and not communicate to them the letter of the Council. But, again, this does not prove that he is right in including Antioch in *Galatia*.

[3] It is impossible, as we have seen (pp. 239, 240) to determine the exact frontier.

[4] The great road from Ephesus to the Euphrates ascended the valley of the Mæander to the neighbourhood of Laodicea, Hierapolis, and Colosse [Col. iv. 13–16], and thence passed by Apamea to Iconium. See the references to Strabo and Cicero in the next note but two.

[5] The Peutinger Table has a direct road from Iconium to Side, on the coast of Pamphylia. Thence another road follows the coast to Perga, and goes thence across Western Pisidia to the valley of the Mæander. None of the Itineraries mention any direct road from Antioch in Pisidia to Perga and Attaleia, corresponding to the journeys of Paul and Barnabas. For an allusion to the importance of Side, see p. 23. n. 2. Compare p. 160.

[6] Pp. 236, 239, 240, 243, 250, &c., and the notes.

in the time of St. Paul. It was merely a geographical expression, denoting a debatable country of doubtful extent, diffused over the frontiers of the provinces of Asia and Galatia, but mainly belonging to the former. We believe that this part of the Apostle's journey might be described under various forms of expression, according as the narrator might speak politically or popularly. A traveller proceeding from Cologne to Hanover might be described as going through Westphalia or through Prussia. The course of the railroad would be the best indication of his real path. So we imagine that our best guide in conjecturing St. Paul's path through this part of Asia Minor is obtained by examining the direction of the ancient and modern roads. We have marked his route in our map along the general course of the Roman military way, and the track of Turkish caravans, which leads by Laodicea, Philomelium, and Synnada,[1] — or, to use the existing terms, by Ladik, Ak-Sher, and Eski-Karahisser.[2] This road follows the northern side of that ridge which Strabo describes as separating Philomelium and Antioch in Pisidia, and which, as we have seen,[3] materially assisted Mr. Arundel in discovering the latter city. If St. Paul revisited Antioch on his way[4] — and we cannot be sure that he did not,—he would follow the course of his former journey,[5] and then regain the road to Synnada by crossing the ridge to Philomelium. We

[1] These are the stages in the great road from Ephesus to Mazaca in the Peutinger Table. At Synnada it meets a road from the north. See them laid down approximately in Colonel Leake's Map of Asia Minor, and compare Major Rennell's work on Western Asia. This was the route of Cicero, when he travelled from Ephesus to Cilicia. Ep. ad Att. v. 20. Fam. III. 8. xv. 4. *Synnada* was a place of considerable importance as the capital of a Conventus Juridicus. (Plin. v. 29.) Compare Cic. Att. v. 21. Liv. xxxviii. 15. xlv. 34. Strabo expressly says, that *Laodicea Combusta* was on the great road from Ephesus to the Euphrates. *Philomelium* is mentioned as an intermediate stage both by Cicero and Strabo (l. c.). For the modern names of these places, and their relation to modern routes, see the next note.

[2] For the modern roads, Murray's Handbook for the East may be consulted: Route 93 (Scutari, by Nicæa and Konieh, to Tarsus and Baias), and Route 94. (Constantinople, by the Rhyndacus and Konieh, to Cæsarea and Cappadocia.) Both these routes coincide between Ak-Sher and Konieh. This line of road was also traversed by Otter, Browne, and Leake (see Leake's map), and by Hamilton Ainsworth, and the author of the MS. journal we have quoted. See, again, the Modern Traveller, p. 311. (Route from Konieh to Kiutaya and Broussa.) *Ladik* is Laodicæa Combusta, situated just beyond the hills which bound the plain of Konieh (see p. 182, and especially p. 186). *Ak-Sher* used to be identified with Antioch in Pisidia, but is now believed to be Philomelium (see the next note). *Eski-Karahissar* is now identified with Synnada. See Franz, Fünf Inschriften u. Fünf Städten in Kleinasien, Berlin, 1840. It is near [possibly identical with ?] *Afium-Karahissar* (so called from its opium plantations), an important town half-way between Angora and Smyrna. It is almost certain that St. Paul must have passed more than once near this place. Mr. Hamilton was there on two journeys, from Angorah to Antioch in Pisidia, and from the valley of the Hermus to Iconium. See his Descriptions, I. xxvi. II. xli.

[3] See pp. 169, 170.

[4] See above, p. 270, n. 2.

[5] Acts xiv

must again repeat that the path marked down here is conjectural. We have nothing either in St. Luke's narrative or in St. Paul's own letters to lead us to any place in Phrygia, as certainly visited by him on this occasion, and as the home of the converts he then made. One city indeed, which is commonly reckoned among the Phrygian cities, has a great place in St. Paul's biography, and it lay on the line of an important Roman road.[1] But it was situated far within the province of Asia, and for several reasons we think it highly improbable that he visited Colosse on this journey, if indeed he ever visited it at all. The most probable route is that which lies more to the northwards in the direction of the true Galatia.

The remarks which have been made on Phrygia must be repeated, with some modification, concerning Galatia. It is true that Galatia was a province: but we can plainly see that the term is used here in its popular sense,—not as denoting the whole territory which was governed by the Galatian proconsul, but rather the primitive region of the tetrarchs and kings, without including those districts of Phrygia or Lycaonia, which were now politically united with it.[2] There is absolutely no city in true Galatia which is mentioned by the Sacred Writers in connection with the first spread of Christianity. From the peculiar form of expression[3] with which the Christians of this part of Asia Minor are addressed by St. Paul in the Epistle which he wrote to them,[4] and alluded to in another of his Epistles,[5]—we infer that "the *churches* of Galatia" were not confined to any one city, but distributed through various parts of the country. If we were to mention two cities, which, both from their intrinsic importance, and from their connection with the leading roads,[6] are likely to have been visited and revisited by the

[1] Xenophon reckons Colosse in Phrygia. Anab. ii. 1. So Strabo, xii. 8. It was on the great road mentioned above, from Iconium to Ephesus. Böttger, who holds "the churches of Galatia" to have been merely the churches at Derbe, Lystra, and Iconium, supposes St. Paul never to have been in northern Galatia, but to have travelled to Colosse, and thence by Sardis to the frontier of Bithynia. See the map attached to his First Essay. We come here upon a question which we need not anticipate; viz. whether St. Paul was *ever* at Colosse. For Böttger's view of Col. ii. 1, see his Third Essay.

[2] See pp. 246, 247, and the notes.

[3] Ταῖς ἐκκλησίαις τῆς Γαλατίας, in the plural. The occurrence of this term in the salutation gives the Epistle to the Galatians the form of a circular letter. The same phrase, in the Second Epistle to the Corinthians, conveys the impression that there was no great central church in Galatia, like that of Corinth in Achaia, or that of Ephesus in Asia.

[4] Gal. i. 2. [5] 1 Cor. xvi. 1.

[6] The route is conjecturally laid down in the map from Synnada to Pessinus and Ancyra. Mr. Hamilton travelled exactly along this line, and describes the bare and dreary country at length (I. xxiv.–xxvii.). Near Pessinus he found an inscription (No. 139) relating to the repairing of the Roman road, on a column which had probably

Apostle, we should be inclined to select Pessinus and Ancyra. The first of these cities retained some importance as the former capital of one of the Galatian tribes,[1] and its trade was considerable under the early emperors.[2] Moreover, it had an ancient and wide-spread renown, as the seat of the primitive worship of Cybele, the Great Mother.[3] Though her oldest and most sacred image (which, like that of Diana at Ephesus,[4] had "fallen down from heaven") had been removed to Rome,—her worship continued to thrive in Galatia, under the superintendence of her effeminate and fanatical priests or Galli,[5] and Pessinus was the object of one of Julian's pilgrimages, when heathenism was on the decline.[6] Ancyra was a place of still greater moment: for it was the capital of the province.[7] The time of its highest eminence was not under the Gaulish but the Roman government. Augustus built there a magnificent temple of marble,[8] and inscribed there a history of his deeds, almost in the style of an Asiatic sovereign.[9] This city was the meeting-place of all the great roads in the north of the peninsula.[10] And, when we add that Jews had been established there from the time of Augustus,[11] and probably earlier, we can hardly avoid the conclusion that the Temple and Inscription at Angora, which successive travellers have described and copied during the last three hundred years, were once seen by the Apostle of the Gentiles.

However this may have been, we have some information from his own pen, concerning his first journey through "the region of Galatia." We

been a milestone. Both the Antonine and Jerusalem Itineraries give the road between Pessinus and Ancyra, with the intermediate stages.

1 The Tolistoboii, or Western Galatians. See Strabo and Livy.

2 Πεσσινοῦς ἐστὶν ἐμπορεῖον τῶν ταύτῃ μεγίστων. Strabo xiii. 5. Its position has been established by Texier and Hamilton. See Franz.

3 See above, p. 246.

4 Compare Herodian's expression of the image of Cybele (i. 11), *Αὐτὸ τὸ ἄγαλμα διοπετὲς, ὡς λέγουσιν*, with that in the Acts (xix. 35), *πόλιν νεωκόρον τοῦ διοπετοῦς*. The ancients had a notion that Pessinus derived its name *ἀπὸ τοῦ πεσεῖν*. Forbiger, p. 366.

5 Jerome connects this term with the name of the Galatians. See, however, Smith's Dictionary of Antiquities, under the word. See also under "Megalesia."

6 Ammian. Marc. xxii. 9.

7 The words ΑΓΚΥΡΑ ΜΗΤΡΟΠΟΛΙΣ appear on its coins at this period. It was also called "Sebaste," from the favour of Augustus. The words ΣΕΒΑΣΤΗΝΩΝ ΤΕΚΤΟΣΑΓΩΝ appear both on coins and inscriptions.

8 This temple has been described by a long series of travellers, from Lucas and Tournefort to Hamilton and Texier.

9 Full comments on this inscription will be found in Boeckh, Texier, and Hamilton, and in the Archäologische Zeitung for Feb. 1843. We may compare it with the recently deciphered record of the victories of Darius Hystaspes on the rock at Behistoun. See Vaux's Nineveh and Persepolis.

10 Colonel Leake's map shows at one glance what we learn from the Itineraries. We see there the roads radiating from it in every direction.

11 See the reference to Josephus, p. 247, n. 4.

know that he was delayed there by sickness, and we know in what spirit the Galatians received him.

St. Paul affectionately reminds the Galatians[1] that it was "*bodily sickness* which caused him to preach the Glad-tidings to them at the first." The allusion is to his first visit: and the obvious inference is, that he was passing through Galatia to some other district (possibly Pontus,[2] where we know that many Jews were established), when the state of his bodily health arrested his progress.[3] Thus he became, as it were, the Evangelist of Galatia against his will. But his zeal to discharge the duty that was laid on him, did not allow him to be silent. He was instant "in season and out of season." "Woe" was on him if he did not preach the Gospel. The same Providence detained him among the Gauls, which would not allow him to enter Asia or Bithynia:[4] and in the midst of his weakness he made the glad-tidings known to all who would listen to him We cannot say what this sickness was, or even confidently identify it with that "thorn in the flesh"[5] to which he feelingly alludes in his Epistles, as a discipline which God had laid on him. But the remembrance of what he suffered in Galatia seems so much to colour all the phrases in this part of the Epistle, that a deep personal interest is connected with the circumstance. Sickness in a foreign country has a peculiarly depressing effect on a sensitive mind. And though doubtless Timotheus watched over the Apostle's weakness with the most affectionate solicitude,—yet those who have experienced what fever is in a land of strangers will know how to sympathise, even with St. Paul, in this human trial. The climate and the prevailing maladies of Asia Minor may have been modified with the lapse of centuries: and we are without the guidance of St. Luke's medical language,[6] which sometimes throws a light on diseases alluded to in Scripture: but two Christian sufferers, in widely different ages of the Church, occur to the memory as we look on the map of Galatia. We could hardly mention any two men more thoroughly imbued with the spirit of St. Paul, than John Chrysostom and Henry Martyn.[7] And

[1] Gal. iv. 13.

[2] See above, pp. 248, 249.

[3] There can be no doubt that the *literal* translation of δι' ἀσθένειαν τῆς σαρκὸς is, "*on account of* bodily weakness." See Winer's Grammatik, § 53. And there seems no good reason why we should translate it differently, though most of the English commentators take a different view. See Meyer and De Wette. Böttger, in harmony with his hypothesis that St. Luke's Galatia means the neighbourhood of Lystra and Derbe, thinks that the bodily weakness here alluded to was the result of the stoning at Lystra. Acts xiv.

[4] Acts xvi. 6, 7.

[5] 2 Cor. xii. 7–10.

[6] See the paper alluded to p. 95, n. 1.

[7] There was a great similarity in the last sufferings of these apostolic men; the same intolerable pain in the head, the same inclement weather, and the same cruelty on the part of those who urged on the journey. We quote the Benedictine life of Chrysostom. "Unus e militibus illud unum satagens ut mala morte Joannem neca

VIEW OF JERUSALEM FROM THE NORTH-EAST.

when we read how these two saints suffered in their last hours from fatigue, pain, rudeness, and cruelty, among the mountains of Asia Minor which surround the place[1] where they rest,—we can well enter into the meaning of St. Paul's expressions of gratitude to those who received him kindly in the hour of his weakness.

The Apostle's reception among the frank and warm-hearted Gauls was peculiarly kind and disinterested. No Church is reminded by the Apostle so tenderly of the time of their first meeting.[2] The recollection is used by him to strengthen his reproaches of their mutability, and to enforce the pleading with which he urges them to return to the true Gospel. That Gospel had been received in the first place with the same affection which they extended to the Apostle himself. And the subject, the manner, and the results of his preaching are not obscurely indicated in the Epistle itself. The great topic there, as at Corinth and everywhere, was "*the Cross of Christ*"—"*Christ crucified*" set forth among them.[3] The Divine evidence of the Spirit followed the word, spoken by the mouth of the Apostle, and received by "the hearing of the ear."[4] Many were converted, both Greeks and Jews, men and women, free men and slaves.[5] The worship of false divinities, whether connected with the old superstition at Pessinus, or the Roman idolatry at Ancyra, was forsaken for that of the true and living God.[6] And before St. Paul left the "region of Galatia" on his onward progress, various Christian communities[7] were added to those of Cilicia, Lycaonia, and Phrygia.

In following St. Paul on his departure from Galatia, we come to a

ret. . . . Cum pluvia vehemens decideret, id nihil curans proficiscebatur ille; ita ut in dorso et in pectore aquarum rivi decurrerent. Ingentem rursus solis æstum pro deliciis habebat, cum nosset B. Joannis caput, Elisæi instar calvum, æstu vexari. . . . Unde discesserant redire coacti sunt, quod ille ægrotaret; capitis enim dolore laborabat, quod solis radios ferre non posset. Sic igitur reversus . . . appositus est ad patres suos et ad Christum transiit." Compare this with the account of H. Martyn's last hours. "*Oct.* 2.—In the night Hassan sent to summon me away, but I was quite unable to move. . . . We travelled all the rest of the day and all night; it rained most of the time. Soon after sunset the ague came on again. . . . My fever increased to a violent degree; the heat in my eyes and forehead was so great that the fire almost made me frantic. . . . *Oct.* 5.—The sleep had refreshed me, but I was feeble and shaken; yet the merciless Hassan hurried me off." The last words in his journal were written the next day. He died on the 16th.

1 It is remarkable that Chrysostom and Martyn are buried in the same place. They both died on a journey, at Tocat or Comana in Pontus.

2 The references have been given above in the account of Galatia, p. 243.

3 Compare Gal. iii. 1, with 1 Cor. i. 13, 17. ii. 2, &c.

4 Τὸ πνεῦμα ἐλάβετε ἐξ ἀκοῆς πίστεως. Gal. iii. 2. See v. 5. So at Thessalonica 1 Thess. ii. 13.

5 Gal. iii. 27, 28.

6 See the remarks above (p. 256) in reference to Tarsus.

7 The plural ἐκκλήσιαι (Gal. i. 2, and 1 Cor. xvi. 1) implies this. See p. 272.

passage of acknowledged difficulty in the Acts of the Apostles.[1] Not that the words themselves are obscure. The difficulty relates, not to grammatical construction, but to geographical details. The statement contained in St. Luke's words is as follows :—After preaching the Gospel in Phrygia and Galatia, they were hindered from preaching it in Asia; accordingly, when in Mysia or its neighbourhood, they attempted to penetrate into Bithynia ; and this also being forbidden by the Divine Spirit, they passed by Mysia and came down to Troas.[2] Now everything depends here on the sense we assign to the geographical terms. What is meant by the words "Mysia," "Asia," and "Bithynia?" It will be remembered that all these words had a wider and a more restricted sense.[3] They might be used popularly and vaguely; or they might be taken in their exacter political meaning. It seems to us that the whole difficulty disappears by understanding them in the former sense, and by believing (what is much the more probable, *à priori*) that St. Luke wrote in the usual popular language, without any precise reference to the provincial boundaries. We need hardly mention *Bithynia;* for, whether we speak of it traditionally or politically, it was exclusive both of Asia and Mysia.[4] In this place it is evident that *Mysia* is excluded also from Asia, just as Phrygia, is above ;[5] not because these two districts were not parts of it in its political character of a province,[6] but because they had a history and a traditional character of their own, sufficiently independent to give them a name in popular usage. As regards *Asia*, it is simply viewed as the western portion of Asia Minor. Its relation to the peninsula has been very well described by saying that it occupied the same relative position

[1] Acts xvi. 6, 7. For a similar accumulation of participles, see Acts xxv. 6–8.

[2] See Wieseler's remarks on this passage, p. 31, &c.

[3] See above, p. 237.

[4] Mysia was at one time an apple of discord between the kings of Pergamus and Bithynia; and at one time the latter were masters of a considerable tract on the shore of the Propontis. But this was at an end when the Romans began to interfere in the affairs of the east. See Livy's words of the *kingdom* of Asia: "Mysiam, quam Prusias rex ademerat, Eumeni restituerunt ;" and Cicero's on the *province* of Asia: "Asia vestra constat ex Phrygia, Mysia," &c., pp. 239, 240. It may be well to add a few words on the history of Mysia, which was purposely deferred to this place. See p. 239, n. 3. Under the Persians this corner of Asia Minor formed the satrapy of *Little Phrygia:* under the Christian emperors it was the province of *The Hellespont.* In the intermediate period we find it called "Mysia," and often divided into two parts: viz. *Little Mysia* on the north, called also Mysia on the Hellespont, or Mysia Olympene, because it lay to the north of Mount Olympus; and *Great Mysia,* or Mysia Pergamene, to the south and east, containing the three districts of Troas, Æolis, and Teuthrania. See Forbiger, p. 110.

[5] Acts xvi. 6.

[6] Böttger, in his First Essay (§ 16) says that *Little Mysia* is meant, and that this district was in the province of *Bithynia;* and de Wette seems to take the same view. But this is rather like cutting the knot; and, after all, there is no knot to be cut There appears to be no good proof that Little Mysia was in Bithynia.

which Portugal occupies with regard to Spain.[1] The comparison would be peculiarly just in the passage before us. For the Mysia of St. Luke is to Asia what Gallicia is to Portugal; and the journey from Galatia and Phrygia to the city of Troas has its European parallel in a journey from Castile to Vigo.

We are evidently destitute of materials for laying down the route of St. Paul and his companions. All that relates to Phrygia and Galatia must be left vague and blank, like an unexplored country in a map (as in fact this region itself is in the maps of Asia Minor),[2] where we are at liberty to imagine mountains and plains, rivers and cities, but are unable to furnish any proofs. As the path of the Apostle, however, approaches the Ægean, it comes out into comparative light: the names of places are again mentioned, and the country and the coast have been explored and described. The early part of the route then must be left indistinct. Thus much, however, we may venture to say,—that since the Apostle usually turned his steps towards the large towns, where many Jews were established, it is most likely that Ephesus, Smyrna, or Pergamus was the point at which he aimed, when he sought "to preach the word in Asia." There is nothing else to guide our conjectures, except the boundaries of the provinces and the direction of the principal roads.[3] If he moved from Angora[4] in the general direction above pointed out, he would cross the river Sangarius near Kiutaya,[5] which is a great modern thoroughfare, and has been mentioned before (Ch. VI. p. 168) in connection with the route from Adalia to Constantinople; and a little further to the west, near Aizani, he would be about the place where the boundaries of Asia, Bithynia, and Mysia meet together, and on the watershed which separates the waters flowing northwards to the Propontis, and those which feed the rivers of the Ægean.

Here then we may imagine the Apostle and his three companions to pause,—uncertain of their future progress,—on the chalk downs which lie

1 Paley's Horæ Paulinæ.

2 See Kiepert's map. Hardly any region in the peninsula has been less explored than Galatia and Northern Phrygia.

3 The *roads* in this part of Asia Minor are most effectively laid down in the map accompanying Franz's Fünf Städten, &c. But the *boundaries* of Galatia, Phrygia, Mysia, &c., there given, are not *provincial.*

4 Mr. Ainsworth mentions a hill near Angora in this direction, the Baulos-Dagh, which is named after the Apostle.

5 Kiutaya (the ancient Cotyæum) is now one of the most important towns in the peninsula. See Routes 99 and 100 in Murray's Handbook. It lies too on the ordinary road between Broussa and Konieh. Dorylæum (Eski-Sher) seems to have had the same relation to the ancient roads. One of those in the Peut. Table strikes off at this point into Bithynia, meeting that from Ancyra at Nicæa. Mr. Ainsworth (II. 46–62) travelled from Nicæa by Dorylæum, Mr. Weston by Broussa and Kiutaya. The two routes meet near Synnada, and coincide as far as Konieh. See p. 271.

between the fountains of the Rhyndacus and those of the Hermus,—in the midst of scenery not very unlike what is familiar to us in England. The long range of the Mysian Olympus to the north is the boundary of Bithynia. The summits of the Phrygian Dindymus on the south are on the frontier of Galatia and Asia. The Hermus flows through the province of Asia to the islands of the Ægean. The Rhyndacus flows to the Propontis, and separates Mysia from Bithynia. By following the road near the former river they would easily arrive at Smyrna or Pergamus By descending the valley of the latter and then crossing Olympus,[2] they would be in the richest and most prosperous part of Bithynia. In which direction shall their footsteps be turned? Some divine intimation, into the nature of which we do not presume to inquire, told the Apostles that the Gospel was not yet to be preached in the populous cities of Asia.[3] The time was not yet come for Christ to be made known to the Greeks and Jews of Ephesus,—and for the churches of Sardis, Pergamus, Philadelphia, Smyrna, Thyatira, and Laodicea, to be admitted to their period of privilege and trial, for the warning of future generations. Shall they turn, then, in the direction of Bithynia?[4] This also is forbidden. St. Paul (so far as we know) never crossed the Mysian Olympus, or entered the cities of Nicæa and Chalcedon, illustrious places in the Christian history of a later age. By revelations, which were anticipative of the fuller and clearer communication at Troas, the destined path of the Apostolic

[1] See Mr. Hamilton's account of the course of the Rhyndacus (I. v. vi. viii.); his comparison of the district of Azanitis to the chalk scenery of England (p. 100); and his notice of Dindymus (p. 105), which seems to be part of the watershed that crosses the country from the Taurus towards Ida, and separates the waters of the Mediterranean and Ægean from those of the Euxine and Propontis. In the course of his progress up the Rhydancus he frequently mentions the aspect of Olympus, the summit of which could not be reached at the end of March in consequence of the snow.

[2] The ordinary road from Broussa to Kiutayah crosses a part of the range of Olympus. The Peut. Table has a road joining Broussa with Pergamus.

[3] It will be observed that they were merely forbidden to *preach the Gospel* (λαλῆσαι τὸν λόγον) in Asia. We are not told that they did not *enter* Asia. Their road lay entirely through Asia (politically speaking) from the moment of leaving Galatia till their arrival at Troas. On the other hand, they were not allowed to *enter* Bithynia at all (εἰς τὴν B. πορευθῆναι). Meyer's view of the word "Asia" in this passage is surprising. He holds it to mean the eastern continent as opposed to "Europe." [See p. 237, &c.] He says that the travellers, being uncertain whether Asia in the more limited sense were not intended, made a vain attempt to enter Bithynia, and finally learned at Troas that Europe was their destination.

[4] The route is drawn in the map past Aizani into the valley of the Hermus, and then northwards towards Hadriani on the Rhyndacus. This is merely an imaginary line, to express to the eye the changes of plan which occurred successively to St. Paul. The scenery of the Rhyndacus, which is interesting as the frontier river, has been fully explored and described by Mr. Hamilton, who ascended the river to its source, and then crossed over to the fountains of the Hermus and Mæander, near which he saw an ancient road (p. 104), probably connecting Smyrna and Philadelphia with Angora.

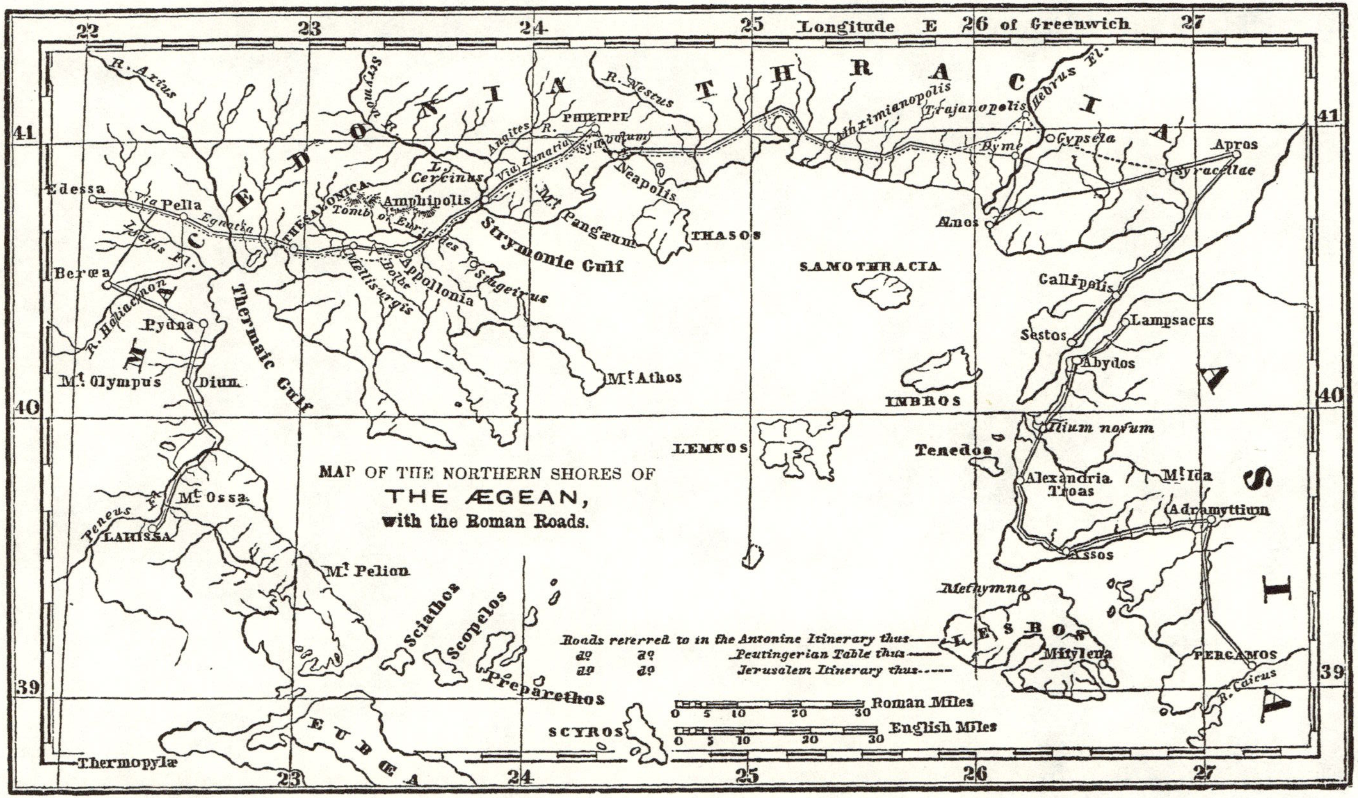
MAP OF THE NORTHERN SHORES OF
THE ÆGEAN,
with the Roman Roads.
Longitude E 26 of Greenwich
MACEDONIA
THRACIA
ASIA
R. Axius
Strymon R.
R. Nestus
Hebrus Fl.
Edessa
Via Pella Egnatia
Ludias Fl.
Beræa
R. Haliacmon
Pydna
Mt. Olympus
Dium
Thermaic Gulf
THESSALONICA
Tomb of Euripides
Amphipolis
L. Cercinus
Angites R.
Via Egnatia
PHILIPPI
Symbolum
Neapolis
Mt. Pangæum
Strymonic Gulf
Mellisurgis
Bolbe
Appollonia
Stageirus
Mt. Athos
THASOS
SAMOTHRACIA
Maximianopolis
Trajanopolis
Dyme
Gypsela
Ænos
Apros
Syracellae
Callipolis
Sestos
Lampsacus
Abydos
IMBROS
LEMNOS
Tenedos
Ilium novum
Alexandria Troas
Mt. Ida
Adramyttium
Assos
Methymna
LESBOS
Mitylena
PERGAMOS
R. Caicus
Mt. Ossa
Peneus Fl.
LARISSA
Mt. Pelion
Sciathos
Scopelos
Peparethos
SCYROS
EUBŒA
Thermopylæ
Roads referred to in the Antonine Itinerary thus
do. do. Peutingerian Table thus
do. do. Jerusalem Itinerary thus
Roman Miles
English Miles

Company was pointed out through the intermediate country, directly to the West. Leaving the greater part of what was popularly called Mysia to the right,[1] they came to the shores of the Ægean, about the place where the deep gulf of Adramyttium, over against the island of Lesbos, washes the very base of Mount Ida.[2]

At Adramyttium, if not before, St. Paul is on the line of a great Roman road.[3] We recognise the place as one which is mentioned again in the description of the voyage to Rome. (Acts xxvii. 2.) It was a mercantile town, with important relations both with foreign harbours, and the towns of the interior of Asia Minor.[4] From this point the road follows the northern shore of the gulf,—crossing a succession of the streams which flow from Ida,[5]—and alternately descending to the pebbly beach and rising among the rocks and evergreen brushwood,—while Lesbos appears and reappears through the branches of the rich forest trees,[6]—till the sea is left behind at the city of Assos. This also is a city of St. Paul. The nineteen miles of road[7] which lie between it and Troas is the distance which he travelled by land before he rejoined the ship which had brought him from Philippi (Acts xx. 13): and the town across the strait, on the shore of Lesbos, is Mitylene,[8] whither the vessel proceeded when the Apostle and his companions met on board.

1 Hence *παρελθόντες τῆς Μυσιαν*, which need not be pressed too closely. They passed along the frontier of Mysia, as it was popularly understood, and they *passed by* the whole district, without staying to evangelise it. One MS. (D.) has *διελθόντες*. It is not necessary to suppose, with Böttger and De Wette, that *Little Mysia* is meant. (Above, p. 276, n. 6.) Wieseler's remark is more just: that they hurried through Mysia, because they knew that they were not to preach the Gospel in Asia.

2 Hence it was sometimes called the Gulf of Ida. *Καλοῦσι δ' οἱ μὲν 'Ιδαῖον κόλπον, οἱ δ' 'Αδραμύττηνον.* Strabo xiii. 1.

3 The characteristics of this bay, as seen from the water, will be mentioned hereafter when we come to the voyage from Assos to Mitylene, (Acts xx. 14). At present we allude only to the *roads* along the coast. Two roads converge at Adramyttium: one which follows the shore from the south, mentioned in the Peutingerian Table; the other from Pergamus and the interior, mentioned also in the Antonine Itinerary. The united route then proceeds by Assos to Alexandria Troas, and so to the Hellespont. They are marked in our map of the northern part of the Ægean.

4 Plin. H. N. v. 30. xiii. 1. Fellows says that there are no traces of antiquities to be found there now, except a few coins. He travelled in the direction just mentioned, from Pergamus by Adramyttium and Assos to Alexandria Troas.

5 Poets of all ages—Homer, Ovid, Tennyson,—have celebrated the streams which flow from the "many-fountained" cliffs of Ida. Strabo says: *Πολυπίδακον τὴν 'Ιδῃ ἰδίως οἴονται λέγεσθαι, διὰ τὸ πλῆθος τῶν ἐξ αὐτῆς ῥεόντων ποταμῶν.* xiii. 1.

6 See the description in Fellows. He was two days in travelling from Adramit to Assos. He says that the hills are clothed with evergreens to the top, and therefore vary little with the season; and he particularly mentions the flat stones of the shingle, and the woods of large trees, especially planes.

7 This is the distance given in the Antonine Itinerary.

8 The strait between Assos and Methymna is narrow. Strabo calls it 60 stadia; Pliny 7 miles. Mitylene is further to the south.

But to return to the present journey. Troas is the name either of a district or a town. As a district it had a history of its own. Though geographically a part of Mysia, and politically a part of the province of Asia, it was yet usually spoken of as distinguished from both.[1] This region,[2] extending from Mount Ida to the plain watered by the Simois and Scamander, was the scene of the Trojan war; and it was due to the poetry of Homer that the ancient name of Priam's kingdom should be retained. This shore has been visited on many memorable occasions by the great men of this world. Xerxes passed this way when he undertook to conquer Greece. Julius Cæsar was here after the battle of Pharsalia.[3] But, above all, we associate the spot with a European conqueror of Asia, and an Asiatic conqueror of Europe; with Alexander of Macedon and Paul of Tarsus. For here it was that the enthusiasm of Alexander was kindled at the tomb of Achilles, by the memory of his heroic ancestors; here he girded on their armour; and from this goal he started to overthrow the august dynasties of the East. And now the great Apostle rests in his triumphal progress upon the same poetic shore: here he is armed by heavenly visitants with the weapons of a warfare that is not carnal; and hence he is sent forth to subdue all the powers of the West, and bring the civilization of the world into captivity to the obedience of Christ.

Turning now from the district to the city of Troas, we must remember that its full and correct name was Alexandria Troas. Sometimes, as in the New Testament, it is simply called Troas;[4] sometimes, as by Pliny and Strabo, simply Alexandria.[5] It was not, however, one of those cities (amounting in number to nearly twenty[6]) which were built and named by the conqueror of Darius. This Alexandria received its population and its name under the successors of Alexander. It was an instance of that centralisation of small scattered towns into one great mercantile city, which was characteristic of the period. Its history was as follows:[7] — Antigonus, who wished to leave a monument of his name on this classical ground, brought together the inhabitants of the neighbouring towns to one point on the coast, where he erected a city, and called it Antigonia Troas. Lysimachus, who succeeded to his power on the Dardanelles, increased

[1] Thus Ptolemy treats it as distinct from Great Mysia and Little Mysia. He calls it also by the name of Little Phrygia. See above, p. 239, n. 3. For the retreat of the Phrygians from the Dardanelles, see Mannert, p. 406, and Scylax as quoted by him.

[2] If we are not needlessly multiplying topographical illustrations, we may compare the three principal districts of the province of Asia, viz. Phrygia, Lydia, and Mysia, to the three Ridings of Yorkshire. Troas will then be in Mysia what Craven is in the West Riding, a district which has retained a distinctive name, and has found its own historian.

[3] Lucan. Pharsal. ix. 960. See the notes on Julius Cæsar below.

[4] Acts xvi. 8, 11. xx. 5. 2 Cor. ii. 12. 2 Tim. iv. 13.

[5] Strabo xiii. Plin. H. N. v.

[6] Steph. Byz. art. Ἀλεξάνδρεια.

[7] It is given at length by Mannert, III. 471–475.

and adorned the city, but altered its name, calling it in honour of "the man of Macedonia"[1] (if we may make this application of a phrase which Holy Writ[2] has associated with the place), Alexandria Troas. This name was retained ever afterwards. When the Romans began their eastern wars, the Greeks of Troas espoused their cause, and were thence forward regarded with favour at Rome. But this willingness to recompense useful service was combined with other feelings, half-poetical, half-political, which about this time took possession of the mind of the Romans. They fancied they saw a primeval Rome on the Asiatic shore. The story of Æneas in Virgil, who relates in twelve books how the glory of Troy was transferred to Italy,[3]—the warning of Horace, who admonishes his fellow-citizens that their greatness was gone if they rebuilt the ancient walls,[4]—reveal to us the fancies of the past and the future, which were popular at Rome. Alexandria Troas was a recollection of the city of Priam, and a prophecy of the city of Constantine. The Romans regarded it in its best days as a "New Troy:"[5] and the Turks even now call its ruins "Old Constantinople."[6] It is said that Julius Cæsar, in his dreams of a monarchy which should embrace the East and the West, turned his eyes to this city as his intended capital:[7] and there is no doubt that Constantine, "before he gave a just preference to the situation of Byzantium, had conceived the design of erecting the seat of empire on this celebrated spot, from whence the Romans derived their fabulous origin."[8] Augustus brought the town into close and honourable connection with Rome by

[1] Not the *Vir Macedo* of Horace (Od. III. xvi. 14), the Ἀνὴρ Μακεδὼν of Demosthenes (*τί γένοιτ' ἂν νεώτερον, κ. τ. λ.* Phil. I. and Orat. ad Ep. Phil.), but his more eminent son.

[2] See Acts xvi. 9.

[3] See especially Book VI.

[4] "Ne nimium pii
Tecta velint reparare Trojæ."—Od. III. iii.

[5] This name applies more strictly to *New Ilium*, which, after many vicissitudes, was made a place of some importance by the Romans, and exempted from all imposts. The strong feeling of Julius Cæsar for the people of Ilium, his sympathy with Alexander, and the influence of the tradition which traced the origin of his nation, and especially of his own family, to Troy, are described by Strabo (xiii. 1): Καθ' *ἡμᾶς Καῖσαρ ὁ θεὸς πολὺ πλέον αὐτῶν προὐνόησε, ζηλώσας, ἅμα καὶ* Ἀλέξανδρον . . . . *φιλαλέξανδρος ὢν, καὶ τῆς πρὸς τοὺς Ἰλιᾶς συγγενείας γνώριμώτατα ἔχων τεκμήρια, ἐπεῤῥώσθη πρὸς τὴν ἐνεργεσίαν νεανικῶς. κ. τ. λ.* New Ilium, however, gradually sank into insignificance, and Alexandria Troas remained as the representative of the Roman partiality for the Troad.

[6] Eski-Stamboul.

[7] "Quin etiam varia fama percrebruit, migraturum Alexandriam vel Ilium, translatis simul opibus imperii, exhaustaque Italia delectibus, et procuratione Urbis amicis permissa." Suet. Cæs. 79.

[8] Gibbon, ch. XVII. He adds that, "though the undertaking was soon relinquished, the stately remains of unfinished walls and towers attracted the notice of all who sailed through the Hellespont." The authorities are Zosimus, Sozomen, Theophanes, Nicephorus Callistus, and Zonaras. The references are in Gibbon's note.

making it a *colonia*,[1] and assimilated its land to that of Italy by giving it the *jus Italicum.*[2] When St. Paul was there, it had not attained its utmost growth as a city of the Romans. The great aqueduct was not yet built, by which Herodes Atticus brought water from the fountains of Ida, and the piers of which are still standing.[3] The enclosure of the walls, extending above a mile from east to west, and near a mile from north to south, may represent the limits of the city in the age of Claudius.[4] The ancient harbour,[5] even yet distinctly traceable, and not without a certain desolate beauty, when it is the foreground of a picture with the hills of Imbros and the higher peak of Samothrace in the distance,[6] is an object of greater interest than the aqueduct and the walls. All further allusions to the topography of the place may be deferred till we describe the Apostle's subsequent and repeated visits.[7] At present he is hastening towards Europe. Everything in this part of our narrative turns our eyes to the West.

[1] Νῦν δὲ καὶ Ῥωμαίων ἀποικίαν δέδεκται. Strabo. Troas Antigonia dicta, nunc Alexandria, colonia Romana. Plin v. 30. The full name on coins of the Antonines is, "Col. Alexandria Augusta Troas."

[2] Deferring the consideration of *colonial* privileges to its proper place, in connection with Philippi (Acts xvi. 12), we may state here the general notion of the *Jus Italicum.* It was a privilege entirely relating to the *land.* The maxim of the Roman law was: "Ager Italicus immunis est: ager provincialis vectigalis est." The Jus Italicum raised provincial land to the same state of immunity from taxation which belonged to land in Italy. But this privilege could only be enjoyed by those who were citizens. Therefore it would have been an idle gift to any community not possessing the *civitas;* and we never find it given except to a *colonia.* Conversely, however, all colonies did not possess the Jus Italicum. Carthage was a colony for two centuries before it received it. See Hoeck's Römische Geschichte, I. ii. pp. 238–242. This reference cannot be made without an acknowledgement of the writer's personal obligations to Professor Hoeck, and of the advantages derived from the University Library at Göttingen, of which he is director.

[3] See Cramer and Clarke.

[4] See Pococke, II. 110.

[5] We shall hereafter recur to the descriptions in Pococke's and Chandler's Travels, in Walpole's Memoirs, Fellows, &c. At present we quote the following from the Sailing Directory. "The ancient port is a basin, about 400 feet long and 200 broad, now entirely shut out from the sea by a narrow strip of the land. Many vestiges of the ancient town remain on and about the shore. On a hill near it are the ruins of the theatre, once a magnificent building, 180 feet from one end of the semicircle to the other; and being on the side of the hill, the highest seats command an extensive view of the sea, Tenedos, Lemnos, and, in clear weather, Mount Athos, 28 leagues distant." P. 157.

[6] The author of Eōthen was much struck by the appearance of Samothrace seen aloft over Imbros, when he recollected how Jupiter is described in the Iliad as watching from thence the scene of action before Troy. "Now I knew," he says, "that Homer had passed along here,—that this vision of Samothrace overtowering the nearer island was common to him and to me." P. 64. The same train of thought may be extended to our present subject, and we may find a sacred pleasure in looking at any view which has been common to St. Paul and to us.

[7] Acts xvi. xx. 2 Cor. ii. 2 Tim. iv.

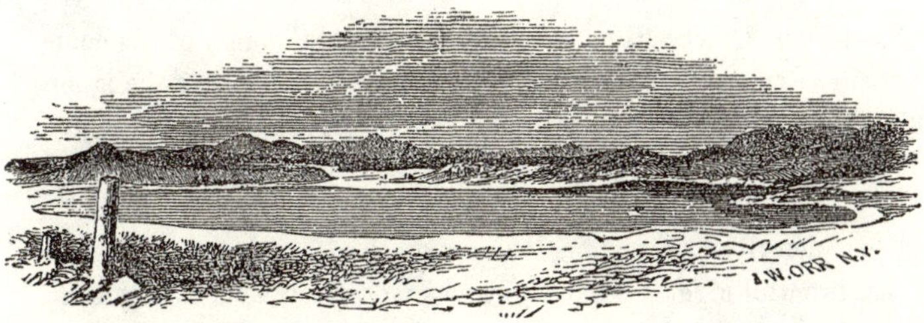

HARBOUR OF TROAS.[1]

When St. Paul's eyes were turned towards the West, he saw the view which is here delineated. And what were the thoughts in his mind when he looked towards Europe across the Ægean? Though ignorant of the precise nature of the supernatural intimations which had guided his recent journey, we are led irresistibly to think that he associated his future work with the distant prospect of the Macedonian hills. We are reminded of another journey, when the Prophetic Spirit gave him partial revelations on his departure from Corinth, and on his way to Jerusalem. "After I have been there I must also see Rome[2]—I have no more place in these parts[3]—I know not what shall befall me, save that the Holy Ghost witnesseth that bonds and afflictions abide me."[4]

Such thoughts, it may be, had been in the Apostle's mind at Troas, when the sun set behind Athos and Samothrace,[5] and the shadows fell on Ida and settled dark on Tenedos and the deep. With the view of the distant land of Macedonia imprinted on his memory, and the thought of Europe's miserable heathenism deep in his heart, he was prepared, like Peter at Joppa,[6] to receive the full meaning of the voice which spoke to him in a dream. In the visions of the night, a form appeared to come and stand by him;[7] and he recognized in the supernatural visitant "a

1 Engraved from a drawing by the Rev. G. Weston. The view is towards the N.W., and includes Tenedos and Imbros, and possibly Samothrace.

2 Acts xix. 21.

3 Rom. xv. 23. It will be remembered that the Epistle to the Romans was written just before this departure from Corinth.

4 Acts xx. 22, 23.

5 Athos and Samothrace are the highest points in this part of the Ægean. They are the conspicuous points from the summit of Ida, along with Imbros, which is nearer. (Walpole's Memoirs, p. 122.) See the notes at the beginning of the next Chapter. "Mount Athos is plainly visible from the Asiatic coast at sunset, but not at other times. Its distance hence is about 80 miles. Reflecting the red rays of the sun, it appears from that coast like a huge mass of burnished gold. . . . Mr. Turner, being off the N. W. end of Mytilen (Lesbos) 22d June, 1814, says, 'The evening being clear, we plainly saw the immense Mount Athos, which appeared in the form of an equilateral triangle.'" Sailing Directory, p. 150. In the same page a sketch is given of Mount Athos, N. by W. ¼ W., 45 miles.

6 See the remarks on St. Peter's vision, p. 92. See also p. 104, n. 1; and p. 207.

7 Ἀνήρ Μακεδών τις. Acts xvi. 9.

man of Macedonia,"[1] who came to plead the spiritual wants of his country. It was the voice of the sick inquiring for a physician,—of the ignorant seeking for wisdom,—the voice which ever since has been calling on the Church to extend the Gospel to Heathendom,—"Come over and help us."

Virgil has described an evening[2] and a sunrise[3] on this coast, before and after an eventful night. That night was indeed eventful in which St. Paul received his commission to proceed to Macedonia. The commission was promptly executed.[4] The morning-star appeared over the cliffs of Ida. The sun rose and spread the day over the sea and the islands as far as Athos and Samothrace. The men of Troas awoke to their trade and their labour. Among those who were busy about the shipping in the harbour were the newly arrived Christian travellers, seeking for a passage to Europe,— Paul, and Silas, and Timotheus,—and that new companion, "Luke[5] the beloved Physician," who, whether by prearrangement, or by a providential meeting, or (it may be) even in consequence of the Apostle's delicate health,[6] now joined the mission, of which he afterwards wrote the history. God provided a ship for the messengers He had chosen: and (to use the language of a more sacred poetry than that which has made these coasts illustrious)[7] "He brought the wind out of his treasuries, and by His power He brought in the south wind,"[8] and prospered the voyage of His servants.

[1] St. Paul may have known, by his dress, or by his words, or by an immediate intuition, that he was "a man of Macedonia." Grotius suggests the notion of a representative or guardian angel of Macedonia—*angelus Macedoniam curans*; as the "prince of Persia," &c., in Dan. x.

[2] Vertitur interea cœlum, et ruit Oceano nox,
Involvens umbra magna terramque polumque,
. . . . . .
Et jam Argiva phalanx instructis navibus ibat
A Tenedo, tacitæ per amica silentia lunæ.
Æn. II. 250.

[3] Jamque jugis summæ surgebat Lucifer Idæ,
Ducebatque diem.—Æn. II. 801.

[4] Εὐθέως ἐζητήσαμεν Acts xvi. 10.

[5] We should notice here not only the change of *person* from the third to the first, but the simultaneous transition (as it has been well expressed) from the *historical* to the *autoptical* style, as shown by the fuller enumeration of details. We shall return to this subject again, when we come to the point where St. Luke parts from St. Paul at Philippi: meantime we may remark that it is highly probable that they had already met and laboured together at Antioch.

[6] This suggestion is made by Wieseler.

[7] The classical reader will remember that the throne of Neptune in Homer, whence he looks over Ida and the scene of the Trojan war, is on the peak of Samothrace (Il. XIII. 10–14), and his cave deep under the water between Imbros and Tenedos (Il. XIII 32–35).

[8] Ps. cxxxv. 7. lxxviii. 26. For arguments to prove that the wind was literally a *south wind* in this case, see the beginning of the next Chapter.

CHAPTER IX.

Πρόσεσχε τῇ Τρῳάδι—εἶτα ἐκεῖθεν καταχθεὶς ἐπὶ τὴν Νεάπολιν, διὰ Φιλίππων παρώδευεν Μακεδονίαν.—*Martyrium S. Ignatii.*

"La religion du Christ ne pouvait demeurer plus long temps circonscrite dans l'Orient; bien qu'elle y eût pris naissance, son avenir était ailleurs. Déjà l'Occident exerçait sur les destinées du monde cette influence qui dès-lors a toujours grandi, en sorte que le Christianisme devait se faire Européen, pour devenir universel."—*Rilliet on the Philippians.*

VOYAGE BY SAMOTHRACE TO NEAPOLIS.—PHILIPPI.—CONSTITUTION OF A COLONY.—LYDIA.—THE DEMONIAC SLAVE.—PAUL AND SILAS ARRESTED.—THE PRISON AND THE JAILOR.—THE MAGISTRATES.—DEPARTURE FROM PHILIPPI.—ST. LUKE.—MACEDONIA DESCRIBED.—ITS CONDITION AS A PROVINCE.—THE VIA EGNATIA.—ST. PAUL'S JOURNEY THROUGH AMPHIPOLIS AND APOLLONIA.—THESSALONICA.—THE SYNAGOGUE.—SUBJECTS OF ST PAUL'S PREACHING.—PERSECUTION, TUMULT, AND FLIGHT.—THE JEWS AT BERŒA.—ST. PAUL AGAIN PERSECUTED.—PROCEEDS TO ATHENS.

THE weather itself was propitious to the voyage from Asia to Europe. It is evident that Paul and his companions sailed from Troas with a fair wind. On a later occasion we are told that five days were spent on the passage from Philippi to Troas.[1] On the present occasion the same voyage, in the opposite direction, was made in two. If we attend to St. Luke's technical expression,[2] which literally means that they "sailed before the wind," and take into account that the passage to the west, between Tenedos and Lemnos, is attended with some risk,[3] we may infer that the wind

[1] Compare Acts xvi. 11, 12, with xx. 6. For the expression, "sailed from Philippi" (xx. 6), and the relation of Philippi with its harbour, Neapolis, see below, p. 286, n. 10.

[2] Εὐθυδρομέω. It occurs again in Acts xxi. 1, evidently in the same sense.

[3] "All ships should pass to the eastward of Tenedos. . . . . Ships that go to the westward in calms may drift on the shoals of Lemnos, and the S. E. end of that island being very low is not seen above nine miles off. . . . . It is also to be recollected, that very dangerous shoals extend from the N. W. and W. ends of Tenedos." Purdy's Sailing Directory, pp. 158, 189. See again under Tenedos, p. 157, and under Lemnos, p. 153; also p. 160. Captain Stewart says (p. 63): "To work up to the Dardanelles, I prefer going inside of Tenedos . . . . you can go by your lead, and during light winds, you may anchor any where. If you go outside of Tenedos, and it falls calm, the current sets you towards the shoal off Lemnos." [The writer has heard this and what follows confirmed by those who have had practical experience in the merchant service in the Levant.]

blew from the southward.[1] The southerly winds in this part of the Archipelago do not usually last long, but they often blow with considerable force. Sometimes they are sufficiently strong to counteract the current which sets to the southward from the mouth of the Dardanelles.[2] However this might be on the day when St. Paul passed over these waters, the vessel in which he sailed would soon cleave her way through the strait between Tenedos and the main, past the Dardanelles, and near the eastern shore of Imbros. On rounding the northern end of this island, they would open Samothrace, which had hitherto appeared as a higher and more distant summit over the lower mountains of Imbros.[3] The distance between the two islands is about twelve miles.[4] Leaving Imbros, and bearing now a little to the west, and having the wind still (as our sailors say) two or three points abaft the beam, the helmsman steered for Samothrace; and, under the shelter of its high shore, they anchored for the night.[5]

Samothrace is the highest land in the north of the Archipelago, with the exception of Mount Athos.[6] These two eminences have been in all ages the familiar landmarks of the Greek mariners of the Ægean. Even from the neighbourhood of Troas, Mount Athos is seen towering over Lemnos, like Samothrace over Imbros.[8] And what Mount

COIN OF SAMOTHRACE.[7]

[1] The same inference may be drawn from the fact of their going to Samothrace at all. Had the wind blown from the northward or the eastward, they probably would not have done so. Had it blown from the westward, they could not have made the passage in two days, especially as the currents are contrary. This consistency in minute details should be carefully noticed, as tending to confirm the veracity of the narrative.

[2] "The current from the Dardanelles begins to run strongly to the southward at Tenedos, but there is no difficulty in turning over it with a breeze." Purdy, p. 159. "The current in the Archipelago sets almost continually to the southward, and is increased or retarded according to the winds. In lying at Tenedos, near the north of the Dardanelles, I have observed a strong southerly wind entirely stop it; but it came strong to the southward the moment the gale from that point ceased." Captain Stewart, ib. p. 62. For the winds, see pp. 63 and 163.

[3] "The island Imbro is separated from Samothraki by a channel twelve miles in breadth. It is much longer and larger, but not so high as that island." Purdy, p. 152.

[4] See the preceding note. [5] Acts xvi. 11.

[6] "Samothraki is the highest land in the Archipelago, except Candia and Mount Athos." Purdy, p. 152.

[7] From the British Museum.

[8] An evening view has been quoted before (p. 283, n. 5). The following is a morning view. "*Nov.* 26, 1828, 8 A. M.—Morning beautifully clear. Lemnos just opening. Mount Athos was at first taken for an island about five leagues distant, the outline and shades appearing so perfectly distinct, though nearly fifty miles off. The base of

Athos is, in another sense, to the superstitious Christian of the Levant,[1] the peak of Samothrace was, in the days of heathenism, to his Greek ancestors in the same seas. It was the "Monte Santo," on which the Greek mariner looked with awe, as he gazed on it in the distant horizon, or came to anchor under the shelter of its coast. It was the sanctuary of an ancient superstition, which was widely spread over the neighbouring continents, and the history of which was vainly investigated by Greek and Roman writers.[2] If St. Paul had staid here even a few days, we might be justified in saying something of the "Cabiri;" but we have no reason to suppose that he even landed on the island. At present it possesses no good harbour, though many places of safe anchorage:[3] and if the wind was from the southward, there would be smooth water anywhere on the north shore. The island was, doubtless, better supplied with artificial advantages in an age not removed by many centuries from the flourishing period of that mercantile empire which the Phœnicians founded, and the Athenians inherited, in the Ægean Sea. The relations of Samothrace with the opposite coast were close and frequent, when the merchants of Tyre had their miners at work in Mount Pangæus,[4] and when Athens diffused her citizens as colonists or exiles on all the neighbouring shores.[5] Nor can those relations have been materially altered when both the Phœnician and Greek settlements on the sea were absorbed in the wider and continental dominion of Rome. Ever since the day when Perseus fled to Samothrace from the Roman conqueror,[6] frequent vessels had been passing and repassing between the island and the coasts of Macedonia and Thrace.

The Macedonian harbor at which St. Paul landed was Neapolis. Its

it was covered with haze, as was the summit soon afterward; but toward sunset it became clear again. It is immensely high; and, as there is no other mountain like it to the northward of Negropont, it is an excellent guide for this part of the coast." Purdy, p. 150.

[1] See the account of Mount Athos (Monte Santo) in Curzon's Monasteries of the Levant, Pt. IV., and the view, p. 327. In his sail from the Dardanelles to the mountain,—the breeze, the shelter and smooth water on the shore of Lemnos, &c.,—there are points of resemblance with St. Paul's voyage. For another account of Mount Athos, see the second volume of Urquhart's Spirit of the East.

[2] For a mass of references to those who have written concerning Cybele and the Cabiri, and the Samothracian mysteries, see Hermann's Lehrbuch der gottesdienstlichen Alterthümer der Griechen, § 65 (Gött. 1846).

[3] See Purdy, p. 152.

[4] Τὸ Πάγγαιον οὖρος, ἐν τῷ χρύσεά τε καὶ ἀργύρεα ἔνι μέταλλα. Herod. vii. 112. Thasos was the head-quarters of the Phœnician mining operations in this part of the Ægean. Herodotus visited the island, and was much struck with the traces of their work. vi. 47.

[5] It is hardly necessary to refer to the formation of the commercial empire of Athens before the Peloponnesian war, to the mines of Scapte Hyle, and the exile of Thucydides. See Grote's Greece, ch. xxvi., xlvii., &c.

[6] Liv. xlv. 6.

direction from Samothrace is a little to the north of east. But a southerly breeze would still be a fair wind, though they could not literally "run before it." A run of seven or eight hours, notwithstanding the easterly current,[1] would bring the vessel under the lee of the island of Thasos, and within a few miles of the coast of Macedonia. The shore of the mainland in this part is low, but mountains rise to a considerable height behind.[2] To the westward of the channel which separates it from Thasos, the coast recedes and forms a bay, within which, on a promontory with a port on each side,[3] the ancient Neapolis was situated.

Some difference of opinion has existed concerning the true position of this harbour:[4] but the traces of paved military roads approaching the promontory we have described, in two directions corresponding to those indicated in the ancient itineraries; the Latin inscriptions which have been found on the spot; the remains of a great aqueduct on two tiers of Roman arches, and of cisterns like those at Baiæ near the other Neapolis on the Campanian shore,[5] seem to leave little doubt that the small Turkish village of Cavallo is the Naples[6] of Macedonia, the "Neapolis" at which St. Paul landed, and the sea-port of Philippi, the "first city"[7] which the traveller reached on entering this "part of Macedonia," and a city of no little importance as a Roman military "colony."[8]

A ridge of elevated land, which connects the range of Pangæus with the higher mountains in the interior of Thrace, is crossed between Neapolis and Philippi.[9] The whole distance is about ten miles.[10] The ascent of

[1] "Inside of Thasso, and past Samothraki, the current sets to the eastward." Purdy, p. 62. "The current at times turns by Monte Santo (Athos), from the S.W., strong toward the eastward, by Thasso." p. 152.

[2] See Purdy, p. 152, and the accurate delineation of the coast in the Admiralty charts.

[3] Clarke's Travels, ch. xii. and xiii. For a more exact description of the place as a harbour, in its present condition, see Purdy, p. 152.

[4] Cousinéry, in his Voyage dans la Macédoine, identifies Neapolis with Eski-Cavallo, a harbour more to the west (perhaps the ancient Galepsus, or Æsyme), of which he gives an interesting description; but his arguments are not satisfactory. Colonel Leake whose opinion is of great weight, though he did not personally visit Philippi and Neapolis, agrees with Dr. Clarke, vol. iii. p. 180.

[5] All these remains are mentioned at length in Dr. Clarke's Travels, at the end of ch. xii. and the beginning of ch. xiii. For the mention of the two paved roads (which are, in fact, parts of the Via Egnatia), see the extracts quoted below, p. 289, n. 1.

[6] A singular mistake is made by Hoog (De Cœtus Christianorum Philippensis Conditione primæva. Lug. Bat. 1825), who says that *this* Neapolis was called Parthenopa, and erroneously quotes Cellarius.

[7] Acts xvi. 12.

[8] For the meaning of πρώτη πόλις and of κολωνία, see p. 290, &c.

[9] This is the Mount Symbolum mentioned by Dio Cassius in his account of the battle. See Leake, pp. 214–225.

[10] Hence it was unnecessary for Meyer to deride Olshausen's remark, that Philippi was the "*first city*" in Macedonia visited by the Apostle, because Neapolis was its harbour. Olshausen was quite right. The distance of Neapolis from Philippi is only

the ridge is begun immediately from the town, through a defile formed by some precipices almost close upon the sea. When the higher ground is attained, an extensive and magnificent sea-view is opened towards the south. Samothrace is seen to the east; Thasos to the south-east; and, more distant and farther to the right, the towering summit of Athos.[1] When the descent on the opposite side begins and the sea is lost to view, another prospect succeeds, less extensive, but not less worthy of our notice. We look down on a plain, which is level as an inland sea, and which, if the eye could range over its remoter spaces, would be seen winding far within its mountain-enclosure, to the west and the north.[2] Its appearance is either exuberantly green,—for its fertility has been always famous,[3]—or cold and dreary,—for the streams which water it are often diffused into marshes,[4]—according to the season when we visit this corner of Macedonia; whether it be when the snows are white and chill on the summits of the Thracian Hæmus,[5] or when the roses, of which Theophrastus and Pliny speak, are displaying their bloom on the warmer slopes of the Pangæan hills.[6]

This plain, between Hæmus and Pangæus, is the plain of Philippi, where the last battle was lost by the republicans of Rome. The whole re-

twice as great as that from the Piræus to Athens, not much greater than that from Cenchreæ to Corinth, and less than that from Seleucia to Antioch, or from Ostia to Rome.

[1] We may quote here two passages from Dr. Clarke, one describing this approach to Neapolis from the neighbourhood, the other his departure in the direction of Constantinople. "Ascending the mountainous boundary of the plain on its north-eastern side by a broad ancient paved way, we had not daylight enough to enjoy the fine prospect of the sea and the town of Cavallo upon a promontory. At some distance lies the isle of Thasos, now called Tasso. It was indistinctly discerned by us; but every other object, excepting the town, began to disappear as we descended toward Cavallo." Ch. xii. "Upon quitting the town, we ascended a part of Mount Pangæus by a paved road, and had a fine view of the bay of Neapolis. The top of the hill, towards the left, was covered with ruined walls, and with the ancient aqueduct, which here crosses the road. From hence we descended by a paved road as before . . . the isle of Thasos being in view towards the S. E. Looking to the E., we saw the high top of Samothrace, which makes such a conspicuous figure from the plains of Troy. To the S., towering above a region of clouds, appeared the loftier summit of Mount Athos." Ch. xiii.

[2] See the very full descriptions of the plain of Serrés, in the various parts of its extension, given by Leake (ch. xxv.) and Cousinéry.

[3] For its present productiveness, see Leake and Cousinéry as before.

[4] See Leake and Cousinéry.

[5] Lucan's view is very winterly :—

"Video Pangæa nivosis
Cana jugis, latosque Hæmi sub rupe Philippos."—Phars. i. 680.

[6] The "Rosa centifolia," which he mentions as cultivated in Campania [compare Virgil's "Biferi rosaria Pæsti"] and in Greece, near Philippi. "Pangæus mons in vicino fert," he continues, "numerosis foliis ac parvis; unde accolæ transferentes conserunt, ipsaque plantatione proficiunt." Plin. H. N. xxi. 10. See Theoph. Hist. vi. 6. Athen. xv. 29.

gion around is eloquent of the history of this battle. Among the mountains on the right was the difficult path by which the republican army penetrated into Macedonia;[1] on some part of the very ridge on which we stand were the camps of Brutus and Cassius;[2] the stream before us is the river which passed in front of them;[3] below us, "upon the left hand of the even field,"[4] is the marsh[5] by which Antony crossed as he approached his antagonist; directly opposite is the hill of Philippi, where Cassius died; behind us is the narrow strait of the sea, across which Brutus sent his body to the island of Thasos, lest the army should be disheartened before the final struggle.[6] The city of Philippi was itself a monument of the termination of that struggle. It had been founded by the father of Alexander, in a place called, from its numerous streams, "The Place of Fountains," to commemorate the addition of a new province to his kingdom, and to protect the frontier against the Thracian mountaineers.[7] For similar reasons the city of Philip was gifted by Augustus with the privileges of a *colonia*. It thus became at once a border-garrison of the province of Macedonia, and a perpetual memorial of his victory over Brutus.[8] And now a Jewish Apostle came to the same place, to win a greater victory than that of Philippi, and to found a more durable empire than that of Augustus. It is a fact of deep significance, that the "first city" at which St. Paul arrived,[9] on his entrance into Europe, should be that "colony," which was more fit than any other in the empire to be considered the representative of Imperial Rome.

The characteristic of a *colonia* was, that it was a miniature resemblance of Rome. Philippi is not the first city of this kind to which we have traced the footsteps of St. Paul; Antioch in Pisidia,[10] and Alexandria Troas,[11] both possessed the same character: but this is the first place where Scripture calls our attention to the distinction; and the events which befell the Apostle at Philippi were directly connected with the

1 See Plutarch's Life of Brutus, with Mr. Long's notes, and Leake, p. 215.

2 This is the Mount Symbolum of Dio Cassius. The republicans were so placed as to be in communication with the sea. The triremes were at Neapolis.

3 The Gangas or Gangites. Leake, p. 217.

4 Julius Cæsar, Act v. sc. i. The topography of Shakspere is perfectly accurate. In this passage Octavius and Antony are looking at the field from the opposite side.

5 The battle took place in autumn, when the plain would probably be inundated.

6 Plutarch's Life of Brutus.

7 Diod. Sic. xvi. pp. 511–514.

8 The full and proper Roman name was *Colonia Augusta Julia Philippensis*. See the coin here engraved, and the inscriptions in Orelli.

9 Πρώτη τῆς μερίδος τῆς Μακεδονίας πόλις (Acts xvi. 12), which must certainly mean the first city in its geographical relation to St. Paul's journey; not the first politically ("chief city," Eng. Vers.), either of Macedonia or a part of it. The chief city of the province was Thessalonica; and, even if we suppose the subdivisions of Macedonia Prima, Secunda, &c., to have subsisted at this time, the chief city of Macedonia Prima was not Philippi, but Amphipolis. See Wieseler's discussion of the subject.

10 See above, p. 171.

11 See pp. 281, 2.

COIN OF PHILIPPI.[1]

privileges of the place as a Roman colony, and with his own privileges as a Roman citizen. It will be convenient to consider these two subjects together. A glance at some of the differences which subsisted among individuals and communities in the provincial system will enable us to see very clearly the position of the *citizen* and of the *colony*.

We have had occasion (Ch. I. p. 26) to speak of the combination of actual provinces and nominally independent states through which the power of the Roman emperor was variously diffused; and, again (Ch. V. p. 142), we have described the division of the provinces by Augustus into those of the Senate, and those of the Emperor. Descending now to examine the component population of any one province, and to inquire into the political condition of individuals and communities, we find here again a complicated system of rules and exceptions. As regards individuals, the broad distinction we must notice is that between those who were citizens and those who were not citizens. When the Greeks spoke of the inhabitants of the world, they divided them into "Greeks" and "Barbarians,"[2] according as the language in which poets and philosophers had written was native to them or foreign. Among the Romans the phrase was different. The classes into which they divided mankind consisted of those who were politically "Romans,"[3] and those who had no link (except that of subjection) with the city of Rome. The technical words were *Cives* and *Peregrini*,[4]—"citizens" and "strangers." The inhabitants of Italy were "citizens;" the inhabitants of all other parts of the empire (until Caracalla extended to the provinces[5] the same privileges which Julius Cæsar

[1] From the British Museum.

[2] Thus St. Paul, in writing his Greek epistles, uses this distinction. Rom. i. 14. Col. iii. 11. Hence also, Acts xxviii. 2, 4. 1 Cor. xiv. 11.

[3] The word "Roman" is always used *politically* in the New Testament. John xi. 48. Acts xvi. xxii. xxiii. xxviii.

[4] "Die Einwohner der Provinzen waren entweder Römische Bürger oder Latinen oder Peregrinen. Erstere bestanden theils aus den Bürgern der Municipien u. Colonien, theils aus den Provinzialen, die einzeln die Civität erhalten hatten. Sie hatten mit den Italikern die gewöhnlichen Bürgerrechte gemein, das Connubium, Commercium, den Schutz gegen Leibestrafen vor förmlichen Urtheils-spruch, und die Provocation an den Kaiser wider Strafsentenzen des Magistrats." Walther's Geschichte des Röm. Rechts. Die Provinzen unter den Kaisern, p. 329 (ed. 1840). See Joseph. A. xiv. 10 11-19.

[5] See Milman's Gibbon, i. p. 281 and the note.

had granted to the peninsula[1]) were naturally and essentially "strangers." Italy was the Holy Land of the kingdom of this world. We may carry the parallel further, in order to illustrate the difference which existed among the citizens themselves. Those true-born Italians, who were diffused in vast numbers through the provinces, might be called Citizens of the Dispersion; while those Strangers who, at various times, and for various reasons, had received the gift of citizenship, were in the condition of political Proselytes. Such were Paul and Silas,[2] in their relation to the empire, among their fellow-Romans in the colony of Philippi. Both these classes of citizens, however, were in full possession of the same privileges; the most important of which were exemption from scourging, and freedom from arrest, except in extreme cases; and in all cases the right of appeal from the magistrate to the emperor.[3]

The remarks which have been made concerning individuals may be extended, in some degree, to *communities* in the provinces. The city of Rome might be transplanted, as it were, into various parts of the empire, and reproduced as a *colonia;* or an alien city might be adopted, under the title of a *municipium,*[4] into a close political communion with Rome. Leaving out of view all cities of the latter kind (and indeed they were limited entirely to the western provinces), we will confine ourselves to what was called a *colonia*. A Roman colony was very different from anything which we usually intend by the term. It was no mere mercantile

[1] By the Julia Lex de Civitate (B. C. 90), supplemented by other laws.

[2] We can hardly help inferring, from the narrative of what happened at Philippi, that Silas was a Roman citizen as well as St. Paul. As to the mode in which he obtained the citizenship, we are more ignorant than in the case of St. Paul himself, whose father was a citizen (Acts xxii. 28). All that we are able to say on this subject has been given before, pp. 45, 46.

[3] Two of these privileges will come more particularly before us, when we reach the narrative of St. Paul's arrest at Jerusalem. To the extract given above from Walther, add the following:—"Körperliche Züchtigungen waren unter der Republik nicht gegen Bürger, und auch später nur an geringen Leuten erlaubt. Gegen Freie wurde dazu der Stock, gegen Knechte die schimpflichere Geissel gebraucht." P. 848. Thus it appears that Paul and Silas were treated with a cruelty which was only justifiable in the case of a slave, and was not usually allowed in the case of any freeman. From pp. 883–885, it would seem, that an accused citizen could only be imprisoned before trial for a very heinous offence, or when evidently guilty. Bail was generally allowed, or retention in a magistrate's house was held sufficient.

[4] The privilege of a colonia was transplanted citizenship, that of a municipium was engrafted citizenship. The distinction is stated very precisely by Aulus Gellius: "Municipia extrinsecus in civitatem (Romanam) veniunt, coloniæ ex civitate Romana propagatæ sunt." N. A. xvi. 13. We have nothing to do, however, with municipia in the history of St. Paul. We are more concerned with *liberæ civitates*, and we shall presently come to one of them in the case of Thessalonica. Probably the best view, in a small compass, of the status of the different kinds of cities in the provinces, is that given in the 7th chapter of the 5th book of Hoeck's Römische Geschichte. Free use has been made of the help this chapter affords.

factory, such as those which the Phœnicians established in Spain,[1] or on those very shores of Macedonia with which we are now engaged; or such as modern nations have founded in the Hudson's Bay territory or on the coast of India. Still less was it like those incoherent aggregates of human beings which *we* have thrown, without care or system, on distant islands and continents. It did not even go forth, as a young Greek republic left its parent state, carrying with it, indeed, the respect of a daughter for a mother, bnt entering upon a new and independent existence. The Roman colonies were primarily intended as military safeguards of the frontiers, and as checks upon insurgent provincials.[2] Like the military roads, they were part of the great system of fortification by which the empire was made safe. They served also as convenient possessions for rewarding veterans who had served in the wars, and for establishing freedmen and other Italians whom it was desirable to remove to a distance The colonists went out with all the pride of Roman citizens, to represent and reproduce the city in the midst of an alien population. They proceeded to their destination like an army with its standards;[3] and the limits of the new city were marked out by the plough. Their names were still enrolled in one of the Roman tribes. Every traveller who passed through a *colonia* saw there the insignia of Rome. He heard the Latin language, and was amenable, in the strictest sense, to the Roman law. The coinage of the city, even if it were in a Greek province, had Latin inscriptions.[4] Cyprian tells us that in his own episcopal city, which once had been Rome's greatest enemy, the Laws of the XII Tables were inscribed on brazen tablets in the market-place.[5] Though the colonists, in addition to the poll-tax, which they paid as citizens, were compelled to pay a ground-tax (for the land on which their city stood was provincial land, and therefore tributary, unless it were assimilated to Italy by a special exemption);[6] yet they were entirely free from any intrusion by the

1 Especially in the mountains on the coast between Cartagena and Almeria.

2 "—— Colonus,
Missus ad hoc, pulsis (vetus est ut fama) Sabellis,
Quo ne per vacuum Romano incurreret hostis."
HORACE, Sat. ii. 1.

3 See the standards on one of the coins of Antioch in Pisidia, p. 170. The wolf, with Romulus and Remus, which will be observed on the other coin, was common on colonial money. Philippi was in the strictest sense a military colony, formed by the establishment of a *cohors prætoria emerita*. Plin. H. N. iv. 18; Eckhel, II. 75.

4 This has been noticed before, p. 170. Compare the coin of Philippi with that of Thessalonica engraved below.

5 Speaking of the prevalent sins of Carthage, he says: "Incisæ sint licet leges duodecim tabulis, et publice ære præfixo jura præscripta sint, inter leges ipsas delinquitur, inter jura peccatur." De Grat. Dei. 10.

6 Philippi had the *Jus Italicum*, like Alexandria Troas. This is explained above p. 282.

governor of the province. Their affairs were regulated by their own magistrates. These officers were named Duumviri; and they took a pride in calling themselves by the Roman title of Prætors (*στρατηγοί*).[1] The primary settlers in the colony were, as we have seen, real Italians; but a state of things seems to have taken place, in many instances, very similar to what happened in the early history of Rome itself. A number of the native provincials grew up in the same city with the governing body; and thus two (or sometimes three)[2] co-ordinate communities were formed, which ultimately coalesced into one, like the Patricians and Plebeians. Instances of this state of things might be given from Corinth and Carthage, and from the colonies of Spain and Gaul; and we have no reason to suppose that Philippi was different from the rest.

Whatever the relative proportion of Greeks and Romans at Philippi may have been, the number of Jews was small. This is sufficiently accounted for, when we remember that it was a military, and not a mercantile, city. There was no synagogue in Philippi, but only one of those buildings called *Proseuchæ*, which were distinguished from the regular places of worship by being of a more slight and temporary structure, and frequently open to the sky.[3] For the sake of greater quietness, and free-

[1] An instance of this is mentioned by Cicero in the case of Capua: "Cum in cæteris coloniis *Duumviri* appellentur, hi se *Prætores* appellari volebant." Agr. ii. 34.

[2] This was the case at Emporiæ in Spain. See Hoeck, pp. 227, 228.

[3] See the passage quoted from Epiphanius, p. 184, and another extract from the same writer given by Hemsen (note, p. 114): *τινὰς δὲ οἴκους ἑαυτοῖς κατασκευάσαντες, ἢ τόπους πλατεῖς, φόρων δίκην, προσευχὰς ταύτας ἐκάλουν· καὶ ἦσαν μὲν τὸ παλαιὸν προσευχῶν τόποι ἔν τε τοῖς Ἰουδαίοις ἔξω πολέως, καὶ ἐν τοῖς Σαμαρείταις.* A Proseucha may be considered as a *place of prayer*, as opposed to a synagogue, or a *house of prayer*. It appears, however. that the words were more or less convertible, and Grotius and Vitringa consider them nearly equivalent. Josephus (Vit. § 54) describes a Proseucha as *μέγιςτον οἴκημα πολὺν ὄχλον ἐψιδέξασθαι δυνάμενον:* and Philo (Leg. ad Cai. p. 1011) mentions, under the same denomination, buildings at Alexandria, which were so strong that it was difficult to destroy them. Probably, as Winer says, it was the usual name of the meeting-place of Jewish congregations in Greek cities.

Other passages in ancient writers, which bear upon the subject, are alluded to in the following extract from Biscoe: "The seashore was esteemed by the Jews a place most pure, and therefore proper to offer up their prayers and thanksgivings to Almighty God. Philo tells us that the Jews of Alexandria, when Flaccus the governor of Egypt, who had been their great enemy, was arrested by order of the Emperor Caius, not being able to assemble at their synagogues, which had been taken from them, crowded out at the gates of the city early in the morning, went to the neighbouring shores, and standing in a most pure place, with one accord lifted up their voices in praising God. (In Flac. p. 982, D.) Tertullian says, that the Jews in his time, when they kept their great fast, left their synagogues, and on every shore sent forth their prayers to heaven (De Jejun. c. 16): and in another place, among the ceremonies used by the Jews, mentions *orationes littorales* the prayers they made upon the shores (Adv. Nat. i. 13). And long before Tertullian's time there was a decree made at Halicarnassus in favour of the Jews, which, among other privileges, allows them to say their prayers near the shore, according to the custom of their country. (Jos. A. xiv. 10 -23.) It is

dom from interruption, this place of prayer was "outside the gate;" and, in consequence of the ablutions[1] which were connected with the worship, it was "by the river side," on the bank of the Gaggitas,[2] the fountains of which gave the name to the city before the time of Philip of Macedon,[3] and which, in the great battle of the Romans, had been polluted by the footsteps and blood of the contending armies.[4]

The congregation which met here for worship on the Sabbath consisted chiefly, if not entirely, of a few women;[5] and these were not all of Jewish birth, and not all residents of Philippi. Lydia, who is mentioned by name, was a proselyte;[6] and Thyatira, her native place, was a city of the province of Asia.[7] The business which brought her to Philippi was connected with the dyeing trade, which had flourished from a very early period, as we learn from Homer,[8] in the neighbourhood of Thyatira, and is permanently commemorated in inscriptions which relate to the "guild of dyers" in that city, and incidentally give a singular confirmation of the veracity of St. Luke in his casual allusions.[9]

In this unpretending place, and to this congregation of pious women, the Gospel was first preached within the limits of Europe.[10] St. Paul and his companions seem to have arrived in the early part of the week, for "some days" elapsed before "the Sabbath." On that day the stran-

hence abundantly evident, that it was common with the Jews to choose the shore as a place highly fitting to offer up their prayers." P. 251. He adds that the words in Acts xvi. 13 "may signify nothing more than that the Jews of Philippi were wont to go and offer up their prayers at a certain place by the river side, as other Jews, who lived near the sea, were accustomed to do upon the sea-shore." See Acts xxi. 5.

[1] Τὰς προσευχὰς ποιεῖσθαι πρὸς τῇ θαλάσσῃ, κατὰ τὸ πάτριον ἔθος. Joseph. Ant. xiv. 10, 23.

[2] Both Meyer and De Wette made a mistake here in saying that the river was the Strymon. The nearest point on the Strymon was many miles distant. This mistake is the more marked when we find that πύλης, and not πόλεως, is probably the right reading. No one would describe the Strymon as a stream outside the gate of Philippi. We may add that the mention of the *gate* is an instance of St. Luke's autoptical style in this part of the narrative. It is possible that the Jews worshipped outside the gate at Philippi, because the people would not allow them to worship within. Compare what Juvenal says of the Jews by the fountain outside the Porta Capena at Rome (iii. 11).

[3] Crenides was the ancient name.

[4] See Plutarch's Brutus, and Appian.

[5] Ταῖς συνελθούσαις γυναιξίν. Acts xvi. 13.

[6] Σεβομένη τὸν Θεόν. Acts xvi. 14.

[7] See Rev. i. 11.

[8] Il. iv. 141.

[9] Several of the inscriptions will be found in Boeckh. Some were first published by Spon and Wheler. We may observe that the communication at this period between Thyatira and Philippi was very easy, either directly from the harbour of Pergamus, or by the road mentioned in the last chapter, which led through Adramyttium to Troas.

[10] At least this is the first historical account of the preaching of an apostle in Europe. The traditions concerning St. Peter rest on no real proof. We do not here inquire into the knowledge of Christianity which may have spread, even to Rome, through those who returned from Pentecost (Acts ii.), or those who were dispersed in Stephen's persecution (Acts viii.), or other travellers from Syria to the West.

gers went and joined the little company of worshippers at their prayer by the river side. Assuming at once the attitude of teachers, they "sat down,"[1] and spoke to the women who were assembled together. The Lord, who had summoned his servants from Troas to preach the Gospel in Macedonia,[2] now vouchsafed to them the signs of His presence, by giving divine energy to the words which they spoke in His name. Lydia "was one of the listeners,"[3] and the Lord "opened her heart, that she took heed to the things that were spoken of Paul."[4]

Lydia, being convinced that Jesus was the Messiah, and having made a profession of her faith, was forthwith baptized. The place of her baptism was doubtless the stream which flowed by the proseucha. The waters of Europe were "sanctified to the mystical washing away of sin." With the baptism of Lydia that of her "household" was associated. Whether we are to understand by this term her children, her slaves, or the workpeople engaged in the manual employment connected with her trade, or all these collectively, cannot easily be decided.[5] But we may observe that it is the first passage in the life of St. Paul where we have an example of that *family religion* to which he often alludes in his Epistles. The "connexions of Chloe"[6] the "household of Stephanas,"[7] the "Church in the house" of Aquila and Priscilla,[8] are parallel cases, to which we shall come in the course of the narrative. It may also be rightly added, that we have here the first example of that Christian *hospitality* which was so emphatically enjoined,[9] and so lovingly practised, in the Apostolic Church. The frequent mention of the "hosts," who gave shelter to the Apostles,[10] reminds us that they led a life of hardship and poverty, and were the followers of Him "for whom there was *no room in the inn.*" The Lord had said to His Apostles, that, when they entered

[1] Καθίσαντες. Acts xvi. 13. Compare ἐκάθισαν, Acts xiii. 14; and ἐκάθισε, Luke iv. 20.

[2] v. 10.

[3] Ἤκουεν. Acts xvi. 14. From the words ἐλαλοῦμεν and ταῖς λαλουμέναις we infer that Lydia was listening to *conversation* rather than *preaching*. The whole narrative gives us the impression of the utmost modesty and simplicity in Lydia's character.

Another point should be noticed, which exemplifies St. Luke's abnegtion of self, and harmonizes with the rest of the Acts; viz. that, after saying "*we* spake" (v. 13), he sinks his own person, and says that Lydia took heed "to what was spoken by *Paul*" (v. 14). Paul was the chief speaker. The phrase and the inference are the same at Antioch in Pisidia (Acts xiii. 45), when Barnabas was with St. Paul. See p. 179, n. 1.

[4] v. 14.

[5] Meyer thinks they were female assistants in the business connected with her trade. It is well known that this is one of the passages often adduced in the controversy concerning infant baptism. We need not urge this view of it: for belief that infant baptism is "most agreeable with the institution of Christ" does not rest on this text.

[6] 1 Cor. i. 11.

[7] 1 Cor. i. 16. xvi. 15.

[8] Rom. xvi. 5. Compare Philem. 2

[9] Heb. xiii. 2. 1 Tim. v. 10. &c.

[10] Rom. xvi. 23, &c.

into a city, they were to seek out "those who were worthy," and with them to abide. The search at Philippi was not difficult. Lydia voluntarily presented herself to her spiritual benefactors, and said to them, earnestly and humbly,[1] that, "since they had regarded her as a believer on the Lord," her house should be their home. She admitted of no refusal to her request, and "their peace was on that house."[2]

Thus the Gospel had obtained a home in Europe. It is true that the family with whom the Apostles lodged was Asiatic rather than European; and the direct influence of Lydia may be supposed to have contributed more to the establishment of the church of Thyatira, addressed by St. John,[3] than to that of Philippi, which received the letter of St. Paul. But still the doctrine and practice of Christianity were established in Europe; and nothing could be more calm and tranquil than its first beginnings on the shore of that continent, which it has long overspread. The scenes by the river-side, and in the house of Lydia, are beautiful prophecies of the holy influence which women,[4] elevated by Christianity to their true position, and enabled by divine grace to wear "the ornament of a meek and quiet spirit," have now for centuries exerted over domestic happiness and the growth of piety and peace. If we wish to see this in a forcible light, we may contrast the picture which is drawn for us by St. Luke—with another representation of women in the same neighbourhood given by the heathen poets, who tell us of the frantic excitement of the Edonian matrons, wandering, under the name of religion, with dishevelled hair and violent cries, on the banks of the Strymon.[5]

Thus far all was peaceful and hopeful in the work of preaching the Gospel to Macedonia: the congregation met in the house or by the river-side; souls were converted and instructed; and a Church, consisting both of men and women,[6] was gradually built up. This continued for "many days." It was difficult to foresee the storm which was to overcast so fair a prospect. A bitter persecution, however, was unexpectedly provoked: and the Apostles were brought into collision with heathen superstition in one of its worst forms, and with the rough violence of the colonial authorities. As if to show that the work of divine grace is advanced by difficulties and discouragements, rather than by ease and prosperity, the

[1] See above, p. 296, n. 3. [2] Matt. x. 13. [3] Rev. ii.

[4] Observe the frequent mention of women in the salutations in St. Paul's epistles. and more particularly in that to the Philippians. Rilliet, in his Commentary, makes a just remark on the peculiar importance of female agency in the then state of society — "L'organisation de la société civile faisait des femmes un intermédiaire nécessaire pour que la prédication de l'Evangile parvînt jusqu'aux personnes de leur sexe."

[5] Hor. Od. II. vii. 27, &c.

[6] This is almost necessarily implied in "the brethren" (τοὺς ἀδελφοὺς, v. 40) whom Paul and Silas visited and exhorted in the house of Lydia, after their release from prison.

Apostles, who had been supernaturally summoned to a new field of labour, and who were patiently cultivating it with good success, were suddenly called away from it, silenced, and imprisoned.

In tracing the life of St. Paul we have not as yet seen Christianity directly brought into conflict witn heathenism. The sorcerer who had obtained influence over Sergius Paulus in Cyprus was a Jew, like the Apostle himself.[1] The first impulse of the idolaters of Lystra was to worship Paul and Barnabas; and it was only after the Jews had perverted their minds, that they began to persecute them.[2] But as we travel further from the East, and especially through countries where the Israelites were thinly scattered, we must expect to find Pagan creeds in immediate antagonism with the Gospel; and not merely Pagan creeds, but the evil powers themselves which give Paganism its supremacy over the minds of men. The questions which relate to evil spirits, false divinities, and demoniacal possessions, are far too difficult and extensive to be entered on here.[3] We are content to express our belief, that in the demoniacs of the New Testament allusion is really made to personal spirits who exercised power for evil purposes on the human will. The unregenerate world is represented to us in Scripture as a realm of darkness, in which the invisible agents of wickedness are permitted to hold sway under conditions and limitations which we are not able to define. The degrees and modes in which their presence is made visibly apparent may vary widely in different countries and in different ages.[4] In the time of Jesus Christ and His Apostles, we are justified in saying that their workings in one particular mode were made peculiarly manifest.[5] As it was in the life of our Great Master, so

[1] Ch. V. p. 147. [2] Ch. VI. pp. 192, &c.

[3] The arguments on the two sides of this question—one party contending that the demoniacs of Scripture were men afflicted with insanity, melancholy, and epilepsy, and that the language used of them is merely an accommodation to popular belief; the other, that these unhappy sufferers were really possessed by evil spirits—may be seen in a series of pamphlets (partly anonymous) published in London in 1737 and 1738. For a candid statement of both views, see the article on "Demoniacs" in Dr. Kitto's Cyclopedia of Biblical Literature. Compare that on the word "Besessene," in Winer's Real-Wörterbuch; and, above all, Professor Trench's profound remarks in his work on the Miracles, pp. 150, &c.

[4] For some suggestions as to the probable reasons why demoniacal possession is seldom witnessed now, see Trench, p. 162.

[5] Trench says, that "if there was any thing that marked the period of the Lord's coming in the flesh, and that immediately succeeding, it was the wreck and confusion of men's spiritual life . . . . . . the sense of utter disharmony. . . . . . . The whole period was the hour and power of darkness; of a darkness which then, immediately before the dawn of a new day, was the thickest. It was exactly the crisis for such soul-maladies as these, in which the spiritual and bodily should be thus strangely interlinked; and it is nothing wonderful that they should have abounded at that time." P. 162. Neander and Trench, however, both refer to modern missionary accounts of something like the same possession among heathen nations, and of their cessation on conversion to Christianity.

it was in that of His immediate followers. The dæmons recognised Jesus as "the Holy One of God;" and they recognised His Apostles as the "bondsmen of the Most High God, who preach the way of salvation." Jesus "cast out dæmons;" and, by virtue of the power which he gave, the Apostles were able to do in His name what He did in His own.

If in any region of heathendom the evil spirits had pre-eminent sway, it was in the mythological system of Greece, which, with all its beautiful imagery and all its ministrations to poetry and art, left man powerless against his passions, and only amused him while it helped him to be unholy. In the lively imagination of the Greeks, the whole visible and invisible world was peopled with spiritual powers or *dæmons*.[1] The same terms were often used on this subject by Pagans and by Christians. But in the language of the Pagan the dæmon might be either a beneficent or malignant power;[2] in the language of the Christian it always denoted what was evil.[3] When the Athenians said[4] that St. Paul was introducing "new dæmons" among them, they did not necessarily mean that he was in league with evil spirits; but when St. Paul told the Corinthians[5] that though "idols" in themselves were nothing, yet the sacrifices offered to them were, in reality, offered to "dæmons," he spoke of those false divinities which were the enemies of the True.[6]

Again, the language concerning physical changes, especially in the human frame, is very similar in the sacred and profane writers. Sometimes it contents itself with stating merely the facts and symptoms of disease; sometimes it refers the facts and symptoms to invisible personal

[1] For the classical use of the word *δαιμὼν*, Trench refers to a chapter in Creuzer's Symbolik. See the note, p. 155.

[2] Compare, for instance, *δαίμονα δέξιον* (Callim. Hymn. vi.) with *δαίμονα κακὸν* (Hom. Od. xx. 64).

[3] Thus Augustine says: "Nos autem, sicut S. Scriptura loquitur, secundum quam Christiani sumus, *Angelos* quidem partim bonos, partim malos, nunquam vero bonos *Dæmones* legimus. Sed ubicunque illarum literarum hoc nomen positum reperitur, sive dæmones sive dæmonia dicantur, non nisi maligni significantur, spiritus." De Civ. Dei, ix. 19. So Origen: Τὸ *τῶν δαιμόνων ὄνομα οὐ μέσον ἐστὶν, ὡς τὸ τῶν ἀνθρώπων, ἐν οἷς τινες μὲν ἀστεῖοι, τινὲς δὲ φαῦλοι εἰσίν ...... ἀεὶ δ' ἐπὶ τῶν φαύλων ἔξω τοῦ παχυτέρου δώματος δυνάμεως τάσσεται τὸ τῶν δαιμόνων ὄνομα, πλανώντων καὶ περισπώντων τοὺς ἀνθώπους καὶ καθελκόντων ἀπὸ τοῦ Θεοῦ, κ. τ. λ.* For more examples of the use in the Fathers, see Suicer's Thesaurus. Josephus takes the same view: Τὰ *γὰρ καλούμενα δαιμόνια, ταῦτα δὲ πονηρῶν ἐστιν ἀνθρώπων πνεύματα, τοῖς ζῶσιν εἰσδυόμενα καὶ κτείνοντα τοὺς βοηθείας μὴ τυγχάνοντας.* B. J. vii. 6, 3, where he is speaking of a plant alleged to cure those who are thus affected.

[4] Acts xvii. 18.

[5] 1 Cor. x. 20.

[6] It is very important to distinguish the word *Διάβολος* ("Devil") from *δαίμων* or *δαιμόνιον* ("dæmon"). The former word is used, for instance, in Matt. xxv. 41. John viii. 44. Acts xiii. 10. 1 Pet. v. 8, &c.; the latter in John vii. 20. Luke x. 17. 1 Tim. iv. 1. Rev. ix. 20, also James iii. 15. For further remarks on this subject see below on Acts xvii. 18.

agency.[1] One class of phenomena, affecting the mind as well as the body, was more particularly referred to preternatural agency. These were the prophetic states of mind, showing themselves in stated oracles or in more irregular manifestations, and accompanied with convulsions and violent excitement, which are described or alluded to by almost all heathen authors. Here again we are brought to a subject which is surrounded with difficulties. How far, in such cases, imposture was combined with real possession; how we may disentangle the one from the other; how far the supreme will of God made use of these prophetic powers and overruled them to good ends; such questions inevitably suggest themselves, but we are not concerned to answer them here. It is enough to say that we see no reason to blame the opinion of those writers, who believe that a wicked spiritual agency was really exerted in the prophetic sanctuaries and prophetic personages of the heathen world. The heathens themselves attributed these phenomena to the agency of Apollo,[2] the deity of Pythonic spirits; and such phenomena were of very frequent occurrence, and displayed themselves under many varieties of place and circumstance. Sometimes those who were possessed were of the highest condition; sometimes they went about the streets like insane impostors of the lowest rank. It was usual for the prophetic spirit to make itself known by an internal muttering of ventriloquism.[3] We read of persons in this miserable condition used by others for the purpose of gain. Frequently they were slaves;[4] and there were cases of joint proprietorship in these unhappy ministers of public superstition.[5]

In the case before us it was a "female slave"[6] who was possessed

[1] This will be observed in the Gospels, if we carefully compare the different accounts of Our Lord's miracles. Among heathen writers we may allude particularly to Hippocrates, since he wrote against those who treated epilepsy as the result of supernatural possession. Some symptoms, he says, were popularly attributed to Apollo, some to the Mother of the Gods, some to Neptune, &c. *Αἴγα μιμῶνται κῆν βρύχωνται κῆν τὰ δεξιὰ σπῶνται, Μητῆρα θεῶν φασὶν αἰτίην εἶναι· ἢν δὲ ὀξύτερον καὶ εὐτονώτερον φθέγγηται, ἵππῳ εἰκάζουσι, καὶ φασὶ Ποσειδῶνα αἴτιον εἶναι . . . ἢν δὲ λεπτότερον καὶ πυκνότερον οἷον ὄρνιθες, Ἀπόλλων Νόμιος.* Hippoc. de Morbo Sacro.

[2] *Πύθων* is the name of Apollo in his oracular character. Hence *πυθωνικός* and *πυθολήπτος.*

[3] They were the *ἐγγαστρίμυθοι* who spoke with the mouth closed, and who were called *Πύθωνες* (the very word used here by St. Luke, Acts xvi. 16). *Τοὺς ἐγγαστριμύθους νυνὶ Πύθωνας προσαγορευομένους.* Plut. de Def. Orac. p. 414. See Galen and the Scholiast on Aristoph. Vesp. 1014, as referred to by Wetstein. Augustine calls this girl "ventriloqua fœmina" (De Civ. Dei, ii. 23); but Walch thinks from her articulate exclamations, that this was not the case.

[4] Walch refers to Arr. iv. 13.

[5] Many details on these subjects are brought together by Walch, in his Essays "De Servis Fatidicis," at the end of his Dissertationes in Acta Apostolorum, Jena, 1766. The book is very scarce, and we have not had an opportunity of reading these essays with care.

[6] *Παιδίσκη.* Acts xvi. 16, as in xii. 13

with "a spirit of divination;"[1] and she was the property of more than one master, who kept her for the purpose of practising on the credulity of the Philippians, and realised "much profit" in this way. We all know the kind of sacredness with which the ravings of common insanity are apt to be invested by the ignorant; and we can easily understand the notoriety which the gestures and words of this demoniac would obtain in Philippi.[2] It was far from a matter of indifference, when she met the members of the Christian congregation on the road to the proseucha, and began to follow St. Paul, and to exclaim (either because the words she had overheard mingled with her diseased imaginations, or because the evil spirit in her was compelled[2] to speak the truth): "These men are the bondsmen of the Most High God, who are come to announce unto you the way of salvation." This was continued for "several days," and the whole city must soon have been familiar with her words. Paul was well aware of this; and he could not bear the thought that the credit even of the Gospel should be enhanced by such unholy means. Possibly one reason why our Blessed Lord Himself forbade the demoniacs to make Him known, was, that His Holy cause would be polluted by resting on such evidence. And another of our Saviour's feelings must have found an imitation in St. Paul's breast,—that of deep compassion for the poor victim of demoniac power. At length he could bear this Satanic interruption no longer, and, "being grieved, he commanded the evil spirit to come out of her." It would be profaneness to suppose that the Apostle spoke in mere irritation, as it would be ridiculous to imagine that divine help would have been vouchsafed to gratify such a feeling. No doubt there was grief and indignation, but the grief and indignation of an Apostle may be the impulses of divine inspiration. He spoke, not in his own name, but in that of Jesus Christ, and power from above attended his words. The prophecy and command of Jesus concerning his Apostles

[1] Ἔχουσα πνεῦμα πύθωνος (like "Pythia mente incitata." Cic. de Div. ii. 87). Some of the Uncial MSS. read πνεῦμα πύθωνα, which is adopted by Lachmann and Tischendorf. The reading is immaterial to the meaning of the passage. Πύθων is not exactly synonymous with Apollo, but rather, as it is explained in Suidas and Hesychius, δαιμόνιον μαντικόν. See the quotation in De Wette: Τάς τε πνεύματι πύθωνος ἐνθουσιώσας, καὶ φαντασίαν μνήσεως παρεχομένας τῇ τοῦ δαιμονίου περιφορᾷ ἠξίου τὸ ἐσόμενον παραγορεῦσαι· οἱ δὲ τῶν δαιμόνων κάτοχοι ἔφασκον, τὴν νίκην Μήδοις παρέσεσθαι.

[2] See what Trench says on the demoniacs in the country of the Gadarenes. "We find in the demoniac the sense of a misery in which he does not acquiesce, the deep feeling of inward discord, of the true life utterly shattered, of an alien power which has mastered him wholly, and now is cruelly lording over him, and ever drawing further away from him in whom only any created intelligence can find rest and peace. His state is, in the truest sense, "a possession;" another is ruling in the high places of his soul, and has cast down the rightful lord from his seat; and he knows this: and out of his consciousness of it there goes forth from him a cry for redemption, so soon as ever a glimpse of hope is afforded, an unlooked-for Redeemer draws near" P. 159

were fulfilled: that "in His name they should cast out dæmons." It was as it had been at Jericho and by the sea of Gennesareth. The demoniac at Philippi was restored "to her right mind." Her natural powers resumed their course; and the gains of her masters were gone.

Violent rage on the part of these men was the immediate result. They saw that their influence with the people, and with it "all hope"[1] of any future gain, was at end. They proceeded therefore to take a summary revenge. Laying violent hold[2] of Paul and Silas (for Timotheus and Luke were not so evidently concerned in what had happened), they dragged them into the forum[3] before the city authorities. The case was brought before the Prætors (so we may venture to call them, since this was the title which colonial Duumviri were fond of assuming);[4] but the complainants must have felt some difficulty in stating their grievance. The slave that had lately been a lucrative possession had suddenly become valueless; but the law had no remedy for property depreciated by exorcism. The true state of the case was therefore concealed, and an accusation was laid before the prætors in the following form. "These men are throwing the whole city into confusion; moreover they are Jews;[5] and they are attempting to introduce new religious observances,[6] which we, being Roman citizens, cannot legally receive and adopt." The accusation was partly true and partly false. It was quite false that Paul and Silas were disturbing the colony, for nothing could have been more calm and orderly than their worship and teaching at the house of Lydia, or in the synagogue by the water side. In the other part of the indictment there was a certain amount of truth. The letter of the Roman law, even under the republic,[7] was opposed to the introduction of foreign religions; and though exceptions were allowed, as in the case of the Jews themselves, yet the spirit of the law entirely condemned such changes in worship as were likely to unsettle the minds of the citizens, or to produce any tumultuous uproar;[8] and the advice given to Augustus, which both he and his

[1] Ἐξῆλθεν ἡ ἐλπὶς τῆς ἐργασίας αὐτῶν. v. 19.

[2] Ἐπιλαβόμενοι εἵλκυσαν. Compare "obtorto collo rapere ad prætorem," in Terence. The Greek word ἐπιλάβεσθαι does not necessarily denote violence. It is used in a friendly sense, ix. 27.

[3] Εἰς τὴν ἀγόραν ἐπὶ τοὺς ἄρχοντας, v. 19. The word ἄρχοντες is a general term.

[4] See above, p. 294, n. 1. The word στρατηγὸς is the usual Greek translation of *prætor*. It is, however, often used generally for the supreme magistrates of Greek towns. Wetstein tells us that the mayor in Messina was in his time still called *stradigo*.

[5] Ἰουδαῖοι ὑπάρχοντες (v. 20), "being Jews to begin with," as Mr. Humphry very well translates it. Compare Ἰουδαῖος ὑπάρχων, "being born a Jew," in Gal. ii. 14, p. 225.

[6] Ἔθη. The word is similarly used Acts vi. 14. xxvi. 3. xxviii. 17.

[7] "Quoties hoc patrum ævorumque ætate negotium est magistratibus datum, ut sacra externa fieri vetarent, sacrificulos vatesque foro, circo, urbe prohiberent. . omnem disciplinam sacrificandi præterquam more Romano, abolerent." Liv. xxxix. 16.

[8] "Qui novas et usu vel ratione incognitas religiones inducunt, ex quibus animi

successors had studiously followed, was, to check religious innovations as promptly as possible, lest in the end they should undermine the monarchy.[1] Thus Paul and Silas had undoubtedly been doing what in some degree exposed them to legal penalties ; and were beginning a change which tended to bring down, and which ultimately did bring down, the whole weight of the Roman law on the martyrs of Christianity.[2] The force of another part of the accusation, which was adroitly introduced, namely, that the men were "Jews to begin with," will be fully apprehended, if we remember, not only that the Jews were generally hated, suspected, and despised,[3] but that they had lately been driven out of Rome in consequence of an uproar,[4] and that it was incumbent on Philippi, as a colony, to copy the indignation of the mother city.

Thus we can enter into the feelings which caused the mob to rise against Paul and Silas,[5] and tempted the prætors to dispense with legal formalities and consign the offenders to immediate punishment. The mere loss of the slave's prophetic powers, so far as it was generally known, was enough to cause a violent agitation ; for mobs are always more fond of excitement and wonder than of truth and holiness. The Philippians had been willing to pay money for the demoniac's revelations, and now strangers had come and deprived them of that which gratified their superstitious curiosity. And when they learned, moreover, that these strangers were Jews, and were breaking the laws of Rome, their discontent became fanatical. It seems that the prætors had no time to hesitate, if they would retain their popularity. The rough words were spoken :[6]

hominum moveantur, honestiores deportantur, humiliores capite puniuntur." Paulus, Sentent. v. 21, 2, quoted by Rosenmüller.

[1] Dio Cassius tells us that Mæcenas gave the following advice to Augustus :—*Τὸ μὲν ϑεῖον πάντη πάντως αὐτός τε σέβου κατὰ τὰ πάτρια, καὶ τοὺς ἄλλους τιμᾷν ἀνάγκαζε· τοὺς δὲ ξενίζοντάς τι περὶ αὐτὸ καὶ μίσει καὶ κόλαζε;* and the reason is given, viz. that such innovations lead to secret associations, conspiracies, and cabals, *ἅπερ ἥκιστα μοναρχίᾳ συμφέρει.*

[2] See the account of the martyrs of Gaul in Eusebius, v. 1. The governor, learning that Attalus was a Roman citizen, ordered him to be remanded to prison till he should learn the emperor's commands. Those who had the citizenship were beheaded. The rest were sent to the wild beasts.

[3] Cicero calls them "suspiciosa ac maledica civitas." Flacc. 28. See the passages quoted p. 19, n. 1.

[4] Acts xviii. 2 ; which is probably the same occurrence as that which is alluded to by Suetonius, Claud. 25 :—"Judæos impulsore Christo assidue tumultuantes Roma expulit."

[5] *Καὶ συνεπέστη ὁ ὄχλος κατ' αὐτῶν.* v. 22.

[6] The official order is given by Seneca :—"Summove, lictor, despolia, verbera. See again Livy : "Consules spoliari hominem et virgas expediri jussit ;" and Dion Halic. : *Τοῖς ῥαβδούχοις ἐκέλευσαν τὸν ἐσθῆτά τε περικαταῤῥῆξαι καὶ ταῖς ῥάβδοις τὸ σῶμα ξαίνειν*, quoted by Grotius. Some commentators suppose that the duumviri tore off the garments of Paul and Silas with their own hands ; but this supposition is unne

"*Go, lictors: strip off their garments: let them be scourged.*" The order was promptly obeyed, and the heavy blows descended. It is happy for us that few modern countries know, by the example of a similar punishment, what the severity of a Roman scourging was. The Apostles received "many stripes;" and when they were consigned to prison, bleeding and faint from the rod, the jailor received a strict injunction "to keep them safe." Well might St. Paul, when at Corinth, look back to this day of cruelty, and remind the Thessalonians how he and Silas had "suffered before, and were shamefully treated, at Philippi."[1]

The jailor fulfilled the directions of the magistrates with rigorous and conscientious cruelty.[2] Not content with placing the Apostles among the other offenders against the law who were in custody at Philippi, he "thrust them into the inner prison,"[3] and then forced their limbs, lacerated as they were, and bleeding from the scourge, into a painful and constrained posture, by means of an instrument employed to confine and torture the bodies of the worst malefactors.[4] Though we are ignorant of the exact relation of the outer and inner prisons,[5] and of the connexion of the jailor's "house" with both, we are not without very good notions of the misery endured in the Roman places of captivity. We must picture to ourselves something very different from the austere comfort of an English jail. It is only since that Christianity for which the Apostles bled has had influence on the hearts of men, that the treatment of felons has been a distinct subject of philanthropic inquiry, and that we have learnt to pray "for all prisoners and captives." The inner prisons of which we read in the ancient world were like that "dungeon in the court of the prison" into which Jeremiah was let down with cords, and where

cessary. It is quite a mistake to imagine that they rent *their own* garments, like the high-priest at Jerusalem.

1 1 Thess. ii. 2.

2 As in the Captivi of Plautus (iii. 70), quoted by Mr. Humphry. "A. Ne tu istunc hominem perduis. B. Curabitur nam noctu nervo vinctus custodibitur."

3 Ἔβαλον αὐτοὺς εἰς τὴν ἐσωτέραν φυλακήν. v. 24.

4 The ξύλον was what the Romans called *nervus* (Ἠσφαλίσατό, φησιν, εἰς τὸ ξύλον, ὡς ἂν εἴποι τις, εἰς τὸ νέρβον. Chrys. in loc.). Isidore describes it (Orig. ix.) as "vinculum ferreum, quo pedes vel cervices impediuntur." Plautus calls it "lignea custodia;" which, as Dr. Bloomfield justly says, is exactly the "wooden Bastille" of Hudibras. Rec. Synopt. See the note in the Pictorial Bible on Job xiii. 27, and the woodcut of stocks used in India from Roberts's Oriental Illustrations.

5 One of Walch's dissertations is written *De Vinculis Apostoli Pauli.* He says that in a Roman prison there were usually three distinct parts: (1) the *communiora*, where the prisoners had light and fresh air; (2) the *interiora*, shut off by iron gates with strong bars and locks; (3) the *Tullianum*, or dungeon. If this was the case at Philippi, Paul and Silas were perhaps in the second, and the other prisoners in the first part. The third was rather a place of execution than imprisonment. Walch says that in the provinces the prisons were not so systematically divided into three parts. He adds that the jailor or *commentariensis* had usually *optiones* to assist him. In Acts xvi. only one jailor is mentioned.

"he sank in the mire."[1] They were pestilential cells, damp and cold, from which the light was excluded, and where the chains rusted on the limbs of the prisoners. One such place may be seen to this day on the slope of the Capitol at Rome.[2] It is known to the readers of Cicero and Sallust as the place where certain notorious conspirators were executed. The *Tullianum* (for so it was called) is a type of the dungeons in the provinces; and we find the very name applied, in one instance, to a dungeon in the province of Macedonia.[3] What kind of torture was inflicted by the "stocks," in which the arms and legs, and even the necks, of offenders were confined and stretched, we are sufficiently informed by the allusions to the punishment of slaves in the Greek and Roman writers;[4] and to show how far the cruelty of heathen persecution, which may be said to have begun at Philippi, was afterwards carried in this peculiar kind of torture, we may refer to the sufferings "which Origen endured under an iron collar, and in the deepest recesses of the prison, when, for many days, he was extended and stretched *to the distance of four holes on the rack.*"[5]

A few hours had made a serious change from the quiet scene by the water side to the interior of a stifling dungeon. But Paul and Silas had learnt, "in whatever state they were, therewith to be content."[6] They were even able to "rejoice" that they were "counted worthy to suffer" for the name of Christ.[7] And if some thoughts of discouragement came over their minds, not for their own sufferings, but for the cause of their Master; and if it seemed "a strange thing" that a work to which they had been beckoned by God should be arrested in its very beginning; yet they had faith to believe that His arm would be revealed at the appointed time. Joseph's feet, too, had been "hurt in the stocks,"[8] and he became a prince in Egypt. Daniel had been cast into the lions' den, and he

[1] "Then took they Jeremiah and cast him into the dungeon of Malchiah, the son of Hammelech, *which was in the court of the prison;* and they let down Jeremiah with cords. And in the dungeon there was no water, but mire; so Jeremiah sunk in the mire." Jer. xxxviii. 6. See the note in the Pictorial Bible.

[2] For an account of it, see Rich's Companion to the Latin Dictionary.

[3] "Statimque vinctos in Tullianum compingunt." Apul. Met. ix. 183, where the allusion is to Thessaly.

[4] Especially in Plautus.

[5] Euseb. Hist. Eccl. vi. 39. See also what he says of the martyrs in Gaul. Τὰς κατὰ τὴν εἱρκτὴν ἐν τῷ σκότει καὶ τῷ χαλεπωτάτῳ χωρίῳ συγκλείσεις, καὶ τὰς ἐν τῷ ξύλῳ διατάσεις τῶν ποδῶν ἐπὶ πέμπτον διατεινομένων τρύπημα. v. 1. Other extracts from Christian writers are given in Suicer's Thesaurus. Compare the word πεντεσύριγγος in the Schol. on Aristoph. Eq. 1046.

[6] Phil. iv. 11.

[7] Acts v. 41.

[8] Ps. cv. 18, Prayer-Book Version. Philo, writing on the history of Joseph (Gen. xxxix. 21), has some striking remarks on the cruel character of jailors, who live among thieves, robbers, and murderers, and never see anything that is good. They are quoted by Wetstein.

was made ruler of Babylon. Thus Paul and Silas remembered with joy the "Lord our Maker, *who giveth songs in the night.*"[1] Racked as they were with pain, sleepless and weary, they were heard "about midnight," from the depth of their prison-house, "praying and singing hymns to God."[2] What it was that they sang, we know not; but the Psalms of David have ever been dear to those who suffer; they have instructed both Jew and Christian in the language of prayer and praise. And the psalms abound in such sentences as these:—"The Lord looketh down from His sanctuary: out of heaven the Lord beholdeth the earth: that He might hear the mournings of such as are in captivity, and deliver the children appointed unto death."—"O let the sorrowful sighing of the prisoners come before thee: according to the greatness of thy power, preserve thou those that are appointed to die."—"The Lord helpeth them to right that suffer wrong: the Lord looseth men out of prison: the Lord helpeth them that are fallen: the Lord careth for the righteous."[3] Such sounds as these were new in a Roman dungeon. Whoever the other prisoners might be, whether they were the victims of oppression, or were suffering the punishment of guilt,—debtors, slaves, robbers, or murderers,—they listened with surprise to the voices of those who filled the midnight of the prison with sounds of cheerfulness and joy. Still the Apostles continued their praises, and the prisoners listened.[4] "They that sit in darkness, and in the shadow of death: being fast bound in misery and iron; when they cried unto the Lord in their trouble, He delivered them out of their distress. For He brought them out of darkness, and out of the shadow of death: and brake their bonds in sunder. O that men would therefore praise the Lord for His goodness, and declare the wonders that He doeth for the children of men: for He hath broke the gates of brass, and smitten the bars of iron in sunder."[5] When suddenly, as if in direct answer to the prayer of His servants, an earthquake shook the very foundations of the prison,[6] the gates were broken, the bars smitten asunder, and the bands of the prisoners loosed. Without striving to draw a line between the natural and supernatural in this occurrence, and still less endeavoring to resolve what was evidently miraculous into the results of

[1] Job xxxv. 10.

[2] *Προσευχόμενοι ὕμνουν τὸν Θεόν.* Acts xvi. 25. For *ὑμνεῖν*, see Matt. xxvi. 30. Mark xiv. 26. The psalms sung on that occasion are believed to be Ps. cxiii.–cxviii. The word *ὕμνος* is found Eph. v. 19. Col. iii. 16. Compare Heb. ii. 12.

[3] Ps. cii. 19, 20. lxxix. 12. cxlvi. 6–8. See also Ps. cxlii. 8, 9. lxix. 34. cxvi. 14. lxviii. 6.

[4] The imperfects *ὕμνουν* and *ἐπηκροῶντο* imply continuance. The Apostles were singing, and the prisoners were listening, when the earthquake came.

[5] Ps. cvii. 10–16.

[6] *Ἄφνω δὲ σεισμὸς ἐγένετο μέγας, ὥστε σαλευθῆναι τὰ θεμέλια τοῦ δεσμωτηρίου.* v. 26.

ordinary causes, we turn again to the thought suggested by that single but expressive phrase of Scripture, "*the prisoners were listening.*"[1] When we reflect on their knowledge of the Apostles' sufferings (for they were doubtless aware of the manner in which they had been brought in and thrust into the dungeon),[2] and on the wonder they must have experienced on hearing sounds of joy from those who were in pain, and on the awe which must have overpowered them when they felt the prison shaken and the chains fall from their limbs; and when to all this we add the effect produced on their minds by all that happened on the following day, and especially the fact that the jailor himself became a Christian; we can hardly avoid the conclusion that the hearts of many of those unhappy bondsmen were prepared that night to receive the Gospel, that the tidings of spiritual liberty came to those whom, but for the captivity of the Apostles, it would never have reached, and that the jailor himself was their evangelist and teacher.

The effect produced by that night on the jailor's own mind has been fully related to us. Awakened in a moment by the earthquake, his first thought was of his prisoners:[3] and in the shock of surprise and alarm,—"seeing the doors of the prison open, and supposing that the prisoners were fled,"—aware that inevitable death awaited him,[4] with the stern and desperate resignation of a Roman official, he resolved that suicide was better than disgrace, and "drew his sword."

Philippi is famous in the annals of suicide. Here Cassius, unable to survive defeat, covered his face in the empty tent, and ordered his freedman to strike the blow.[5] His messenger Titinius held it to be "a Roman's part"[6] to follow the stern example. Here Brutus bade adieu to his friends, exclaiming, "Certainly we must fly, yet not with the feet, but with the hands;"[7] and many, whose names have never reached us, ended their last struggle for the republic by self-inflicted death.[8] Here, too, another despairing man would have committed the same crime, had not his hand been arrested by an Apostle's voice. Instead of a sudden and hopeless death, the jailor received at the hands of his prisoner the gift both of temporal and spiritual life.

The loud exclamation[9] of St. Paul, "Do thyself no harm: for we are

1 See above, note on ἐπηκροῶντο.

2 See above, on the form of ancient prisons.

3 Ἔξυπνος γενόμενος . . . καὶ ἰδών. κ. τ. λ. v. 27.

4 By the Roman law, the jailor was to undergo the same punishment which the malefactors who escaped by his negligence were to have suffered. Biscoe (p. 330), who refers to the law, L. 4 De Custod. Reor.

5 Plut. Brutus, 43. 6 Julius Cæsar, Act v. Sc. iii. 7 Plut. Brutus, 52.

8 "The majority of the proscribed who survived the battles of Philippi put an end to their own lives, as they despaired of being pardoned." Niebuhr's Lectures, ii. 118.

9 Ἐφώνησε δὲ φωνῇ μεγάλῃ ὁ. Il. v. 28.

all here," gave immediate reassurance to the terrified jailor. He laid aside his sword, and called for a light, and rushed [1] to the "inner prison," where Paul and Silas were confined. But now a new fear of a higher kind took possession of his soul. The recollection of all he had heard before concerning these prisoners and all that he had observed of their demeanour when he brought them into the dungeon, the shuddering thought of the earthquake, the burst of his gratitude towards them as the preservers of his life, and the consciousness that even in the darkness of midnight they had seen his intention of suicide,—all these mingling and conflicting emotions made him feel that he was in the presence of a higher power. He fell down before them, and brought them out, as men whom he had deeply injured and insulted, to a place of greater freedom and comfort; [2] and then he asked them, with earnest anxiety, what he must do to be saved. We see the Apostle here self-possessed in the earthquake, as afterwards in the storm at sea,[3] able to overawe and control those who were placed over him, and calmly turning the occasion to a spiritual end. It is surely, however, a mistake to imagine that the jailor's inquiry had reference merely to temporal and immediate danger. The awakening of his conscience, the presence of the unseen world, the miraculous visitation, the nearness of death,—coupled perhaps with some confused recollection of the "*way of salvation*" which these strangers were said to have been proclaiming,—were enough to suggest that inquiry which is the most momentous that any human soul can make: "*What must I do to be saved?*"[4] Their answer was that of faithful Apostles. They preached "not themselves, but Christ Jesus the Lord."[5] "Believe, not in us, but *in the Lord Jesus, and thou shalt be saved;* and not only thou, but the like faith shall bring salvation to *all thy house.*" From this last expression, and the words which follow, we infer that the members of the jailor's family had crowded round him and the Apostles.[6] No time was lost in making known to them "the word of the Lord." All thought of bodily

[1] The word is *εἰσπηδήσας*, which, as well as *ἀναγάγων* below, seems to imply that the dungeon was subterraneous.

[2] Either the outer prison or the space about the entrance to the jailor's dwelling, if indeed they were not identical.

[3] Acts xxvii. 20–25.

[4] Τί *με δεῖ ποιεῖν ἵνα σωθῶ.* v. 30. The word *σωθῶ* should be compared with *ὁδὸν σωτηρίας*, v. 17. These words must have been frequently in the mouth of St. Paul. It is probable that the demoniac, and possible that the jailor, might have heard them. See p. 301.

[5] 2 Cor. iv. 5.

[6] The preaching of the Gospel to the jailor and his family (*τοις ἐν τῇ οἰκίᾳ αὐτοῦ*), seems to have taken place immediately on coming out of the prison (vv. 30–32); then the baptism of the converts, and the washing of the Apostles' stripes (v. 33); and finally the going up into the house (*εἰς τὸν οἶκον*), and the hospitable refreshment there afforded. It does not appear certain that they returned from the jailor's house into the dungeon before they were taken out of custody (*ἐκ τῆς φυλακῆς.* v. 40).

comfort and repose was postponed to the work of saving the soul. The meaning of "faith in Jesus" was explained, and the Gospel was preached to the jailor's family at midnight, while the prisoners were silent around, and the light was thrown on anxious faces and the dungeon-wall.

And now we have an instance of that sympathetic care, that interchange of temporal and spiritual service, which has ever attended the steps of true Christianity. As it was in the miracles of our Lord and Saviour, where the soul and the body were regarded together, so has it always been in His Church. "In the same hour of the night"[1] the jailor took the Apostles to the well or fountain of water which was within or near the precincts of the prison, and there he washed their wounds, and there also he and his household were baptized. He did what he could to assuage the bodily pain of Paul and Silas, and they admitted him and his, by the "laver of regeneration,"[2] to the spiritual citizenship of the kingdom of God. The prisoners of the jailor were now become his guests. His cruelty was changed into hospitality and love. "He took them up[3] into his house," and, placing them in a posture of repose, set food before them,[4] and refreshed their exhausted strength. It was a night of happiness for all. They praised God that His power had been made effectual in their weakness; and the jailor's family had their first experience of that joy which is the fruit of believing in God.

At length morning broke on the eventful night. In the course of that night the greatest of all changes had been wrought in the jailor's relations to this world and the next. From being the ignorant slave of a heathen magistracy he had become the religious head of a Christian family. A change, also, in the same interval of time, had come over the minds of the magistrates themselves. Either from reflecting that they had acted more harshly than the case had warranted, or from hearing a more accurate statement of facts, or through alarm caused by the earthquake, or through that vague misgiving which sometimes, as in the case of Pilate and his wife,[5] haunts the minds of those who have no distinct religious convictions, they sent new orders in the morning to the jailor. The message conveyed by the lictors was expressed in a somewhat contemptuous form, "*Let those men go.*"[6] But the jailor received it with the utmost joy. He felt his infinite

[1] Παραλαβὼν αὐτοὺς ἐν ἐκείνῃ τῇ ὥρᾳ τῆς νυκτός. v 33. The word παραλαβὼν implies a change of place, as again ἀναγαγὼν below.

[2] Tit. iii. 5.

[3] V. 34. The word ἀναγαγὼν implies at least that the house was higher than the prison. See p. 308, n. 1.

[4] Παρέθηκεν τραπέζαν. v. 34. The custom of Greek and Roman meals must be borne in mind. Guests were placed on couches, and tables, with the different courses of food, were brought and removed in succession.

[5] Matt. xxvii. 19.

[6] Or, as it might be translated, "Let those fellows go:"—'Απόλυσον τοὺς ἀνθρώπους ἐκείνους. v. 35.

debt of gratitude to the Apostles, not only for his preservation from a violent death, but for the tidings they had given him of eternal life. He would willingly have seen them freed from their bondage; but he was dependent on the will of the magistrates, and could do nothing without their sanction. When, therefore, the lictors brought the order, he went with them [1] to announce the intelligence to the prisoners, and joyfully told them to leave their dungeon and "go in peace."

But Paul, not from any fanatical love of braving the authorities, but calmly looking to the ends of justice and the establishment of Christianity, refused to accept his liberty without some public acknowledgement of the wrong he had suffered. He now proclaimed a fact which had hitherto been unknown,—that he and Silas were Roman citizens. Two Roman laws had been violated by the magistrates of the colony in the scourging inflicted the day before.[2] And this, too, with signal aggravations. They were "uncondemned." There had been no form of trial, without which, in the case of a citizen, even a slighter punishment would have been illegal.[3] And it had been done "publicly." In the face of a colonial population, an outrage had been committed on the majesty of the name in which they boasted, and Rome had been insulted in her citizens. "No," said St. Paul; "they have oppressed the innocent and violated the law. Do they seek to satisfy justice by conniving at a secret escape? Let them come themselves and take us out of prison. They have publicly treated us as guilty; let them publicly declare that we are innocent." [4]

"How often," says Cicero,[5] "has this exclamation, *I am a Roman citizen*, brought aid and safety even among barbarians in the remotest parts of the earth."—The lictors returned to the prætors, and the prætors were alarmed. They felt that they had committed an act which, if divulged at Rome, would place them in the utmost jeopardy. They had good reason to fear even for their authority in the colony; for the people of Philippi, "being Romans," might be expected to resent such a viola-

[1] It is evident from v. 37 that they came into the prison with the jailor, or found them in the jailor's house (p. 308, n. 6), for St. Paul spoke "to *them*" (πρὸς αὐτοὺς); on which they went and told the magistrates (v. 38).

[2] The Lex Valeria (B. C. 508) and the Lex Porcia (B. C. 300). See Liv. x. 9. Compare Cicero in the Verrine Orations. "Cædebatur virgis in medio foro Messanæ civis Romanus, judices; cum interea nullus gemitus, nulla vox alia istius miseri inter dolorem crepitumque plagarum audiebatur, nisi hæc, *Civis Romanus sum*. Hac se commemoratione civitatis omnia verbera depulsurum, cruciatumque a corpore dejecturum arbitrabatur." v. 62. "Facinus est vinciri civem Romanum, scelus verberari, prope parricidium necari." v. 66.

[3] "Causa cognita multi possunt absolvi [compare Acts xxvi. 32], incognita quidem nemo condemnari potest." Verr. i. 9. "Inauditi atque indefensi tanquam innocentes perierant. Tac. H. i. 6.

[4] V. 37.

[5] "Illa Vox et imploratio *Civis Romanus sum*, quæ sæpe multis in ultimis terris opem inter barbaros et salutem tulit." Cic. Verr. v. 57.

tion of the law. They hastened, therefore, immediately to the prisoners, and became the suppliants of those whom they had persecuted. They brought them at once out of the dungeon, and earnestly "besought them to depart from the city."[1]

The whole narrative of St. Paul's imprisonment at Philippi sets before us in striking colours his clear judgment and presence of mind. He might have escaped by help of the earthquake and under the shelter of the darkness; but this would have been to depart as a runaway slave. He would not do secretly what he knew he ought to be allowed to do openly. By such a course his own character and that of the Gospel would have been disgraced, the jailor would have been cruelly left to destruction, and all religious influence over the other prisoners would have been gone. As regards these prisoners, his influence over them was like the sway he obtained over the crew in the sinking vessel.[2] It was so great, that not one of them attempted to escape. And not only in the prison, but in the whole town of Philippi, Christianity was placed on a high vantage-ground by the Apostle's conduct that night. It now appeared that these persecuted Jews were themselves sharers in the vaunted Roman privilege. Those very laws had been violated in their treatment, which they themselves had been accused of violating. That no appeal was made against this treatment, might be set down to the generous forbearance of the Apostles. Their cause was now, for a time at least, under the protection of the law, and they themselves were felt to have a claim on general sympathy and respect.

They complied with the request of the magistrates. Yet, even in their departure, they were not unmindful of the dignity and self-possession which ought always to be maintained by innocent men in a righteous cause. They did not retire in any hasty or precipitate flight, but proceeded "from the prison to the house of Lydia;"[3] and there they met the Christian brethren, who were assembled to hear their farewell words of exhortation; and so they departed from the city. It was not, however, deemed sufficient that this infant church at Philippi should be left alone with the mere remembrance of words of exhortation. Two of the Apostolic company remained behind: Timotheus, of whom the Philippians "learned the proof" that he honestly cared for their state, that he was truly like-minded with St. Paul, "serving him in the Gospel as a son serves his father;"[4] and "Luke the Evangelist, whose praise is in the Gospel," though he never praises himself, or relates his own labours, and though we only trace his movements in connexion with St. Paul by the change of a pronoun,[5] or the unconscious variation of his style.

[1] Vv. 38, 39. [2] Acts xxvii. [3] Acts xvi. 40. [4] Phil. ii. 19–25.

[5] In ch. xvii. the narrative is again in the third person; and the pronoun is not

Timotheus seems to have rejoined Paul and Silas, if not at Thessalonica, at least at Berœa.[1] But we do not see St. Luke again in the Apostle's company till the third missionary journey and the second visit to Macedonia.[2] At this exact point of separation, we observe that he drops the style of an eye-witness and resumes that of a historian, until the second time of meeting, after which he writes as an eye-witness till the arrival at Rome and the very close of the Acts. To explain and justify the remark here made, we need only ask the reader to contrast the detailed narrative of events at Philippi with the more general account of what happened at Thessalonica.[3] It might be inferred that the writer of the Acts was an eye-witness in the former city and not in the latter, even if the pronoun did not show us when he was present and when he was absent. We shall trace him again, in the same manner, when he rejoins St. Paul in the same neighbourhood. He appears again on a voyage from Philippi to Troas (Acts xx. 56), as now he has appeared on a voyage from Troas to Philippi. It is not an improbable conjecture that his vocation as a physician[4] may have brought him into connection with these contiguous coasts of Asia and Europe. It has even been imagined, on reasonable grounds,[5] that he may have been in the habit of exercising his professional skill as a surgeon at sea. However this may have been, we have no reason to question the ancient opinion, stated by Eusebius and Jerome,[6] that St. Luke was a native of Antioch. Such a city was a likely place for the education of a physician.[7] It is also natural to suppose that he may have met with St. Paul there, and been converted at an earlier period of the

changed again till we come to xx. 5. The modesty with which St. Luke leaves out all mention of his own labours need hardly be pointed out.

[1] Acts xvii. 14. He is not mentioned in the journey to Thessalonica, nor in the account of what happened there.

[2] Acts xx. 4–6.

[3] Observe, for instance, his mention of running before the wind, and staying for the night at Samothrace. Again he says that Philippi was the first city they came to, and that it was a colony. He tells us that the place of prayer was outside the gate and near a river-side. There is no such particularity in the account of what took place at Thessalonica. See above, p. 284, n. 5. Similar remarks might be made on the other *autoptic* passages of the Acts, and we shall return to the subject again. A careful attention to this difference of style is enough to refute a theory lately advanced (Dr. Kitto's Biblical Review, Sept. 1850) that Silas was the author of the Acts. Silas was at Thessalonica as well as Philippi. Why did he write so differently concerning the two places?

[4] See Tate's Continuous History.

[5] This suggestion is made by Mr. Smith in his work on the Shipwreck, &c., p. 8. It is justly remarked, that the ancient ships were often so large that they may reasonably be supposed to have sometimes had surgeons on board.

[6] Euseb. iii. 4. Hieron. de Sc. Ec. 7.

[7] Alexandria was famous for the education of physicians, and Antioch was in many respects a second Alexandria.

history of the Church.[1] His medical calling, or his zeal for Christianity, or both combined (and the combination has ever been beneficial to the cause of the Gospel), may account for his visits to the North of the Archipelago:[2] or St. Paul may himself have directed his movements, as he afterwards directed those of Timothy and Titus.[3] All these suggestions, though more or less conjectural, are worthy of our thoughts, when we remember the debt of gratitude which the Church owes to this Evangelist, not only as the historian of the Acts of the Apostles, but as an example of long continued devotion to the truth, and of unshaken constancy to that one Apostle, who said with sorrow, in his latest trial, that others had forsaken him, and that "only Luke" was with him.[4]

Leaving their first Macedonian converts to the care of Timotheus and Luke, aided by the co-operation of godly men and women raised up among the Philippians themselves,[5] Paul and Silas set forth on their journey. Before we follow them to Thessalonica, we may pause to take a general survey of the condition and extent of Macedonia, in the sense in which the term was understood in the language of the day. It has been well said that the Acts of the Apostles have made Macedonia a kind of Holy Land;[6] and it is satisfactory that the places there visited and revisited by St. Paul and his companions are so well known, that we have no difficulty in representing to the mind their position and their relation to the surrounding country.

Macedonia, in its popular sense, may be described as a region bounded by a great semicircle of mountains, beyond which the streams flow westward to the Adriatic, or northward and eastward to the Danube and the Euxine.[7] This mountain barrier sends down branches to the sea on the

[1] The conjecture that Lucius of Cyrene (Acts xiii. 1) was the Evangelist, has been mentioned above, p. 132, n. 3.

[2] Compare the case of Democedes in Herodotus, who was established first in Ægina, then in Athens, and finally in Samos. For an account of Greek physicians, see the Appendix to Becker's Charicles. Physicians at Rome were less highly esteemed, and were frequently slaves. At a period even later than St. Luke, Galen speaks of the medical schools of Cos and Cnidus, of Rhodes and of Asia. The passage is quoted in § 38 of the Third Part of Hermann's Lehrbuch der gr. Antiquitäten (1850).

[3] 1 Tim. i. 3. 2 Tim. iv. 9, 21. Tit. i. 5. iii. 12. See above, p. 284.

[4] 2 Tim. iv. 11. See the Christian Year: St. Luke's Day.

[5] The Christian *women* at Philippi have been alluded to before. P 297. See especially Phil. iv. 2, 3 and Rilliet's note. We cannot well doubt that *presbyters* also were appointed, as at Thessalonica. See below. Compare Phil. i. 1.

[6] "The whole of Macedonia, and in particular the route from *Berœa* to *Thessalonica* and *Philippi*, being so remarkably distinguished by St. Paul's sufferings and adventures, becomes as a portion of *Holy Land*." Clarke's Travels, ch. xi.

[7] The mountains on the north, under the names of Scomius, Scordus, &c., are connected with the Hæmus or Balkan. Those on the west run in a southerly direction and are continuous with the chain of Pindus.

eastern or Thracian frontier, over against Thasos and Samothrace;[1] and on the south shuts out the plain of Thessaly, and rises near the shore to the high summits of Pelion, Ossa, and the snowy Olympus.[2] The space thus enclosed is intersected by two great rivers. One of these is Homer's "wide-flowing Axius,"[3] which directs its course past Pella, the ancient metropolis of the Macedonian kings, and the birthplace of Alexander, to the low levels in the neighbourhood of Thessalonica, where other rivers[4] flow near it into the Thermaic gulf. The other is the Strymon, which brings the produce of the great inland level of Serres[5] by Lake Cercinus to the sea at Amphipolis, and beyond which was Philippi, the military outpost that commemorated the successful conquests of Alexander's father. Between the mouths of these two rivers a remarkable tract of country, which is insular, rather than continental,[6] projects into the Archipelago, and divides itself into three points, on the furthest point of which Mount Athos rises nearly into the region of perpetual snow.[7] Part of St. Paul's path between Philippi and Berœa lay across the neck of this peninsula The whole of his route was over historical ground. At Philippi he was close to the confines of Thracian barbarism, and on the spot where the last battle was fought in defence of the republic. At Berœa he came near the mountains, beyond which is the region of Classical Greece, and close to the spot where the battle was fought which reduced Macedonia to a province.[8]

If we wish to view Macedonia as a province, some modifications must

[1] These are the mountains near the river Nestus, which, after the time of Philip, was considered the boundary of Macedonia and Thrace.

[2] The natural boundary between Macedonia and Thessaly is formed by the Cambunian hills, running in an easterly direction from the central chain of Pindus. The Cambunian range is vividly described in the following view from the "giddy height" of Olympus, which rises near the coast. "I seemed to stand perpendicularly over the sea, at the height of 10,000 feet. Salonica was quite distinguishable, lying North-East. Larissa [in Thessaly] appeared under my very feet. The whole horizon from North to South-West was occupied by mountains, *hanging on, as it were, to Olympus*. This is the range that runs Westward along the North of Thessaly, ending in Pindus." Urquhart's Spirit of the East, vol. i. p. 429.

[3] Ἀξιοῦ εὐρὺ ῥέοντος,
Ἀξιοῦ, οὗ κάλλιστον ὕδωρ ἐπικίδναται αἶη.—Il. ii. 849.

[4] The Haliacmon, which flows near Berœa, is the most important of them.

[5] This is the great inland plain at one extremity of which Philippi was situated, and which has been mentioned above (p. 289). Its principal town at present is Serres, the residence of the governor of the whole district, and a place of considerable importance, often mentioned by Cousinéry, Leake, and other travellers.

[6] The peninsula anciently called Chalcidice.

[7] The elevation of Mount Athos is between 4000 and 5000 feet. The writer has heard English sailors say that there is almost always snow on Athos and Olympus, and that, though the land generally is high in this part of the Ægean, these mountains are by far the most conspicuous.

[8] Pydna is within a few miles of Berœa, on the other side of the Haliacmon.

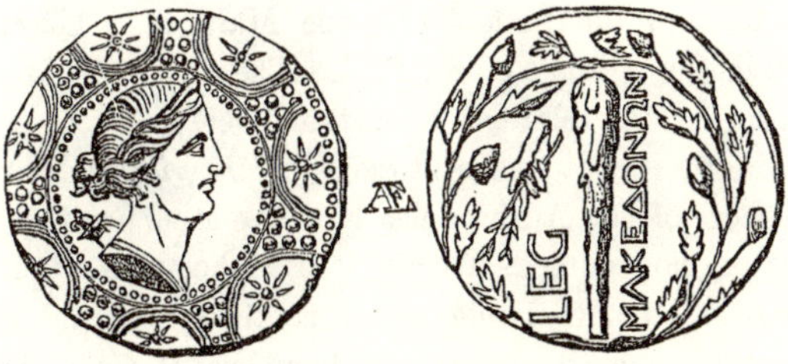

COIN OF ROMAN MACEDONIA.

be introduced into the preceding description. It applies, indeed, with sufficient exactness to the country on its first conquest by the Romans.[2] The rivers already alluded to, define the four districts into which it was divided. *Macedonia Prima* was the region east of the Strymon, of which Amphipolis was the capital;[3] *Macedonia Secunda* lay between the Strymon and the Axius, and Thessalonica was its metropolis; and the other two regions were situated to the south towards Thessaly, and on the mountains to the west.[4] This was the division adopted by Paulus Æmilius after the battle of Pydna. But the arrangement was only temporary. The whole of Macedonia, along with some adjacent territories, was made one province,[5] and centralised under the jurisdiction of a proconsul,[6] who resided at Thessalonica. This province included Thessaly,[7] and extended over the mountain chain which had been the western boundary of ancient Macedonia, so as to embrace a sea-board of considerable length on the shore of the Adriatic.[8] The provincial limits, in this part of the empire, are far more easily discriminated than those with which we have been lately occupied (Ch. VIII.). Three provinces divided the whole surface which

1 From the British Museum. This coin has been selected in consequence of the singular union of Greek and Roman letters. Probably it was struck just before the subdivision, and the letters LEG commemorate the victory of some legion, which is further symbolised by a hand holding a palm-branch. The Diana and the club appear similarly on the coins of *Macedonia Prima*, which are found in great numbers in Wallachia and Transylvania; a fact sufficiently accounted for by the mines which have been mentioned. See Eckhel.

2 See Liv. xlv. 29.

3 See above.

4 *Macedonia Tertia* was between the Axius and Peneus, with Pella for its capital. Pelagonia was the capital of *Macedonia Quarta*. It is remarkable that no coins of the third division have been found, but only of the first, second, and fourth.

5 By Metellus.

6 At first it was one of the emperor's provinces, but afterwards it was placed under the senate.

7 Thessaly was subject to Macedonia when the Roman wars began. At the close of the first war, under Flaminius, it was declared free; but ultimately it was incorporated with the province. See Plin. H. N. and Ptol.

8 Sigonius refers to Dio, Pliny, and Ptolemy. We find Piso the proconsul of Macedonia, who is made notorious by Cicero, having the command of Dyrrhachium on this coast. The same speech informs us that he held parts of Thrace also.

extends from the basin of the Danube to Cape Matapan. All of them are familiar to us in the writings of St. Paul. The extent of *Macedonia* has just been defined. Its relations with the other provinces were as follows. On the north-west it was contiguous to *Illyricum*,[1] which was spread down the shore of the Adriatic nearly to the same point to which the Austrian territory now extends, fringing the Mahometan empire with a Christian border.[2] A hundred miles to the southward, at the Acroceraunian promontory, it touched *Achaia*, the boundary of which province ran thence in an irregular line to the bay of Thermopylæ and the north of Eubœa, including Epirus, and excluding Thessaly.[3] Achaia and Macedonia were traversed many times by the Apostle;[4] and he could say, when he was hoping to travel to Rome, that he had preached the Gospel "round about unto Illyricum."[5]

When we allude to Rome, and think of the relation of the City to the provinces, we are inevitably reminded of the military roads; and here, across the breadth of Macedonia, was one of the greatest roads of the Empire. It is evident that, after Constantinople was founded, a line of communication between the Eastern and Western capitals was of the utmost moment; but the *Via Egnatia*[6] was constructed long before this period Strabo, in the reign of Augustus, informs us that it was regularly made and marked out by milestones, from Dyrrhachium on the Adriatic, to Cypselus on the Hebrus, in Thrace;[7] and even before the close of the republic, we find Cicero speaking, in one of his speeches, of "that military way of ours, which connects us with the Hellespont."[8] Certain districts

1 At first the wars of Rome with the people of this coast merely led to mercantile treaties for the free navigation of the Adriatic. Julius Cæsar and Augustus concluded the series of wars which gradually reduced it to a province.

2 The border town was Lissus, the modern Alessio, not far from Scutari.

3 Except in the western portion, the boundary nearly coincided with that of the modern kingdom of Greece. The provincial arrangements of Achaia will be alluded to more particularly hereafter.

4 Observe how these provinces are mentioned together, Rom. xv. 26. 2 Cor. ix. 2 xi. 9, 10, also 1 Thess. i. 7, 8.

5 Rom. xv. 19. Dalmatia (2 Tim iv. 10) was a district in this province. Nicopolis (Tit. iii. 12) was in Epirus, which, as we have seen, was a district in the province of Achaia, but it was connected by a branch road with the *Via Egnatia* from Dyrrhachium, which is mentioned below.

6 All the details of the Via Egnatia have been carefully elaborated by Tafel in his work on the subject, in two parts. Tübingen, 1841–4.

7 Polybius, in the viith book of Strabo.

8 "Via illa nostra, quæ per Macedoniam est usque ad Hellespontum, militaris." De Prov. Cons. ii. Compare the letters to Atticus, written on the journey from Rome to his province: "Nobis iter est in Asiam, maxime Cyzicum. Dat. xiv. Kal. Mai. de Tarentino." iii. 6. "Aut accedemus in Epirum aut tarde per Candaviam ibimus. Dat. prid. Kal. Mai. Brundisii." iii. 7. "Quum Dyrrachii essemus, duo nuntii. . . . Pellæ mihi præsto fuit Phaetho. . . . Thessalonicam a. d. x. Kal. Jun. venimus. Dat. iiii. Kal. Quint. Thessalonicæ." iii. 8.

on the European side of the Hellespont had been part of the legacy of King Attalus,[1] and the simultaneous possession of Macedonia, Asia, and Bithynia, with the prospect of further conquests in the East, made this line of communication absolutely necessary. When St. Paul was on the Roman road at Troas[2] or Philippi, he was on a road which led to the gates of Rome. It was the same pavement which he afterwards trod at Appii Forum and the Three Taverns.[3] The nearest parallel which the world has seen of the imperial roads is the present European railway system. The Hellespont and the Bosphorus, in the reign of Claudius, were what the Straits of Dover and Holyhead are now; and even the passage from Brundusium in Italy, to Dyrrhachium and Apollonia[4] in Macedonia, was only a tempestuous ferry,—only one of those difficulties of nature which the Romans would have overcome if they could, and which the boldest of the Romans dared to defy.[5] From Dyrrhachium and Apollonia, the Via Egnatia, strictly so called, extended a distance of five hundred miles, to the Hebrus, in Thrace.[6] Thessalonica was about half way between these remote points,[7] and Philippi was the last[8] important town in the province of Macedonia. Our concern is only with that part of the Via Egnatia which lay between the two last-mentioned cities.

The intermediate stages mentioned in the Acts of the Apostles are Amphipolis and Apollonia. The distances laid down in the Itineraries are as follows:—*Philippi to Amphipolis, thirty-three miles; Amphipolis to*

[1] See the preceding Chapter, under "Asia."

[2] See what is said of the road between Troas and Pergamus, &c., p. 278.

[3] Acts xxviii. 15. For notices of the *Via Appia*, where it approaches the Adriatic, in the neighbourhood of *Egnatia* ("Gnatia lymphis iratis extructa"), whence the Macedonian continuation received its name, see Horace's journey, Sat. I. v. Dean Milman's Horace contains an expressive representation of Brundusium, the harbour on the Italian side of the water.

[4] *i. e.* Apollonia on the Adriatic, which must be carefully distinguished from the other town of the same name, and on the same road, between Thessalonica and Amphipolis (Acts xvii. 1).

[5] See the anecdotes of Cæsar's bold proceedings between Brundusium and the opposite side of the sea in Plutarch, 37, 38. The same writer tells us that Cicero, when departing on his exile, was driven back by a storm into Brundusium. See below, p. 322, n. 9. The great landing place on the Macedonian side was Dyrrhachium, the ancient Epidamnus, called by Catullus "Adriæ Tabernæ."

[6] The roads from Dyrrhachium and Apollonia met together at a place called Clodiana, and thence the Via Egnatia passed over the mountains to Heraclea in Macedonia It entered the plain at Edessa (see below), and thence passed by Pella to Thessalonica. The stations, as given by the Antonine and Jerusalem Itineraries and the Peutinger Table, will be found in Cramer's Ancient Greece, v. i. pp. 81–84.

[7] Tafel. Thus Cicero, in the passage above quoted (De Prov. Cons.), speaks of the Thessalonicenses as "positi in gremio imperii nostri."

[8] See above, p. 288, n. 10, and p. 290, n. 9

Apollonia, thirty miles; Apollonia to Thessalonica, thirty-seven miles. These distances are evidently such as might have been traversed each in one day; and since nothing is said of any delay on the road, but everything to imply that the journey was rapid, we conclude (unless, indeed, their recent sufferings made rapid travelling impossible) that Paul and Silas rested one night at each of the intermediate places, and thus our notice of their journey is divided into three parts.

From Philippi to Amphipolis, the Roman way passed across the plain to the north of Mount Pangæus. A traveller, going direct from Neapolis to the mouth of the Strymon, might make his way through an opening in the mountains[2] nearer the coast. This is the route by which Xerxes brought his army,[3] and by which modern journeys are usually made.[4] But Philippi was not built in the time of the Persian War, and now, under the Turks, it is a ruined village. Under the Roman emperors, the position of this *colony* determined the direction of the road. The very productiveness of the soil,[6] and its liability to inundations, must have

COINS OF AMPHIPOLIS [5]

[1] The following is the form in which the distances are given in the Antonine Itinerary, between Edessa and Neapolis:—PELLA. M. P. XXVIII. THESSALONICA. M. P. XXVII. MELLISURGIN. M. P. XX. APOLLONIA. M. P. XVII. AMPHIPOLI. M. P. XXX. PHILIPPIS. M. P. XXXIII. NEAPOLI. M. P. XII. (For Neapolis, see above.) In the other authorities there is a slight difference: the Peutinger Table and the Jerusalem Itinerary give the distance between Thessalonica and Apollonia as thirty-eight miles, and Mellisurgis is not mentioned. See Wesseling. The road, in the Peutinger Table, from Pella by Berœa into Thessaly will be mentioned hereafter.

[2] This opening is the Pieric valley. See Leake, p. 180. "Though the modern route from Cavalla to Orphano and Saloniki, leading by Pravista through the Pieric valley along the southern side of Mount Pangæum, exactly in the line of that of Xerxes, is the most direct, it does not coincide with the Roman road or the Via Egnatia, which passed along the northern base of that mountain, probably for the sake of connecting both these important cities, the former of which was a Roman colony."

[3] Herod. vii.

[4] Dr. Clarke and Cousinéry both took this route. It is described in the Modern Traveller and Murray's Handbook. Leake was at the western opening of the valley when at Orphano.

[5] From the British Museum. One coin bears the name of Claudius; the other belongs to the reign of Trajan, though it bears the name of Hadrian, who was Cæsar when Trajan was emperor.

[6] "The plain is very fertile, and besides yielding abundant harvests of cotton, wheat, barley, and maize, contains extensive pastures peopled with oxen, horses, and

caused this road to be carefully constructed;[1] for the surface of the plain, which is intersected with multitudes of streams, is covered with plantations of cotton and fields of Indian corn,[2] and the villages are so numerous that, when seen from the summits of the neighbouring mountains, they appear to form one continued town.[3] Not far from the coast, the Strymon spreads out into a lake as large as Windermere;[4] and between the lower end of this lake and the inner reach of the Strymonic gulf, where the mountains leave a narrow opening, Amphipolis was situated on a bend of the river.

"The position of Amphipolis is one of the most important in Greece. It stands in a pass which traverses the mountains bordering the Strymonic gulf, and it commands the only easy communication from the coast of that gulf into the great Macedonian plains, which extend, for sixty miles, from beyond Meleniko to Philippi."[5] The ancient name of the place was "Nine Ways," from the great number of Thracian and Macedonian roads which met at this point.[6] The Athenians saw the importance of the position, and established a colony there, which they called Amphipolis, because the river surrounded it.[7] Some of the deepest interest in the history of Thucydides, not only as regards military and political movements,[8] but in reference to the personal experience of the historian himself,[9] is

sheep. No part of the land is neglected; and the district, in its general appearance, is not inferior to any part of Europe." p. 201.

[1] See Leake.

[2] "Des plantes de coton, des rizières immenses, de grandes plantations de tabac, des vignes entrecoupées de terres à blé, formaient sous nos yeux le plus agréable spectacle. . . . . Les produits de cette plaine seraient immenses, si l'activité et l'industrie des habitans répondaient à la liberalité de la nature." Cousinéry, II. 4, 5.

[3] Clarke, ch. xii. At the head of the chapter is a view of the plain as seen from the hills on the south.

[4] The lake *Cercinitis.* Arr. Alex. i. It is about 18 miles long and 6 broad. See *τὸ λιμνῶδες τοῦ Στρυμόνος.* Thuc. v. 7. There is a view of this lake from the north in Cousinéry. Vol. II. p. 3. St. Basil, in writing to his friend Gregory (Ep. 19), describes the Strymon as *σχολαιοτέρῳ ῥεύματι περιλιμνάζων.* This river was celebrated for its eels (*Στουμῶν μεγίστας ἐγχέλεις κεκτημένος.* Athen. vii. 56). Colonel Leake says that "40,000 brace of large eels are caught here annually, besides the smaller ones, and other fish." p. 185.

[5] Leake. For other notices of the importance of this position, see Bp. Thirlwall's Greece, iii. 284, and especially Mr. Grote's Greece, vi. 554–562, and 625–647.

[6] See Herod. vii. 114. Here Xerxes crossed the Strymon, and offered a sacrifice of white horses to the river, and buried alive nine youths and maidens.

[7] Thuc. i. 100. iv. 102.

[8] See especially all that relates to Cleon and Brasidas in the fourth and fifth books.

[9] It was his failure in an expedition against Amphipolis that caused the exile of Thucydides. He had the most intimate personal knowledge of the whole neighbourhood, and yet there is some doubt respecting the topographical details. See the plan in Leake, p. 191, and the Admiralty Chart. But consult especially the memoir and plan at the end of the second volume of Dr. Arnold's Thucydides, and the plan, &c. in Mr. Grote's sixth volume.

concentrated on this spot. And again, Amphipolis appears in the speeches of Demosthenes as a great stake in the latter struggle between Philip of Macedon and the citizens of Athens.[1] It was also the scene of one striking passage in the history of Roman conquest: here Paulus Æmilius, after the battle of Pydna, publicly proclaimed that the Macedonians should be *free;*[2] and now another *Paulus* was here, whose message to the Macedonians was an honest proclamation of a better liberty, without conditions and without reserve.

St. Paul's next stage was to the city of Apollonia. After leaving Amphipolis, the road passes along the edge of the Strymonic gulf, first between cliffs and the sea, and then across a well-wooded maritime plain, whence the peak of Athos is seen far across the bay to the left.[3] We quit the sea-shore at the narrow gorge of Aulon, or Arethusa,[4] and there enter the valley which crosses the neck of the Chalcidic peninsula. Up to this point we have frequent historical land-marks reminding us of Athens. Thucydides has just been mentioned in connection with Amphipolis and the Strymon. As we leave the sea, we have before us on the opposite coast, Stagirus,[5] the birth-place of Aristotle; and in the pass, where the mountains close on the road, is the tomb of Euripides.[6] Thus the steps of our progress, as we leave the East and begin to draw near to Athens, are already among her historians, philosophers, and poets.

Apollonia is somewhere in the inland part of the journey, where the Via Egnatia crosses from the gulf of the Strymon to that of Thessalonica; but its exact position has not been ascertained. We will, therefore, merely allude to the scenery through which the traveller moves, in going from sea to sea. The pass of Arethusa is beautiful and picturesque. A river flows through it in a sinuous course, and abundant oaks

[1] See the passages in the speeches which relate to Philip's encroachment on the Athenian power in the North of the Ægean.

[2] Livy's words (xlv. 30) show that the Romans fully appreciated the importance of the position. "Pars prima habet opportunitatem Amphipoleos; quæ objecta claudit omnes ab oriente sole in Macedoniam aditus."

[3] Dr. Clarke.

[4] This is the place mentioned by Thucydides on the march of Brasidas. Ἀφικόμενος περὶ δείλην ἐπὶ τὸν Αὐλῶνα καὶ Βρομίσκον, ᾗ ἡ Βόλβη λίμνη ἐξίησιν ἐς θάλασσαν. iv. 103. *Aulon* is identified with *Arethusa* by comparing the following passage from Ammianus Marcellinus: "Bromiscus, cui proxima Arethusa convallis et statio est, in qua visitur Euripidis sepulchrum." xxvii. 4. Dr. Clarke, ch. xii., devotes several pages to this tomb. The Jerusalem Itinerary, besides another intermediate station at Pennana, mentions that *at the tomb of Euripides.* Colonel Leake passed this spot on his way from Stavros to Orphano; and he says, "The opening being in the great post road from Saloniki to Constantinople, and in a country which has often been infested with robbers, there is a guard-house in the pass, kept by a few soldiers." p. 170.

[5] Leake identifies Stagirus with Stavros, a little to the south of Aulon, p. 167.

[6] See the last note but one.

AMPHIPOLIS.

and plane trees are on the rocks around.[1] Presently this stream is seen to emerge from an inland lake, whose promontories and villages, with the high mountains rising to the south-west, have reminded travellers of Switzerland.[2] As we journey towards the west, we come to a second lake. Between the two is the modern post-station of Klisali, which may possibly be Apollonia,[3] though it is generally believed to be on the mountain slope to the south of the easternmost lake. The whole region of these two lakes is a long valley, or rather a succession of plains, where the level spaces are richly wooded with forest trees, and the nearer hills are covered to their summits with olives.[4] Beyond the second lake, the road passes over some rising ground, and presently, after passing through a narrow glen, we obtain a sight of the sea once more, the eye ranges freely over the plain of the Axius, and the city of Thessalonica is immediately before us.

Once arrived in this city, St. Paul no longer follows the course of the Via Egnatia. He may have done so at a later period, when he says that he had preached the Gospel "round about unto Illyricum."[5] But at present he had reached the point most favourable for the glad proclamation. The direction of the Roman road was of course determined by important geographical positions; and along the whole line from Dyrrhachium to the Hebrus, no city was so large and influential as Thessalonica.[6]

[1] See Dr. Clarke. Cousinéry writes with great enthusiasm concerning this glen. He is travelling eastwards towards Amphipolis, like Dr. Clarke, and writes thus: "On se trouve bientôt auprès du grand ruisseau, qui, en sortant du lac, va se jeter dans la mer par une vallée étroite. Ses riants ombrages font oublier l'âpreté de la route qu'on vient de parcourir. Ce ruisseau, qui n'a que deux lieux d'étendue, serpente entre la Chalcidique et la Bisaltique: ces deux provinces semblent se séparer au milieu d'une épaisse forêt, pour ouvrir aux voyageurs un chemin qui, de temps immémorial, a conduit de la Macédoine dans la Thrace, à travers des pelouses et des fleurs." p. 116.

[2] See Dr. Clarke. Both he and Cousinéry make mention of the two villages, the Little Bechik and Great Bechik, on its north bank, along which the modern road passes.

[3] This is Tafel's opinion: but Leake and Cousinéry both agree in placing it to the south of Lake Bolbe. Cousinéry, looking from the modern road, which passes on the north side of the lake, says that *Polina* was one of the villages which he saw on the opposite hills. I. 115. [He makes a curious mistake in what follows: "Où nous retrouvons les restes de l'ancienne ville d'Apollonie, que traversait *la voie Appienne*."] Colonel Leake also says that the ruins are to be seen at the right distances from Thessalonica and Amphipolis, but he does not seem to have visited them. See the passage where he points out the difference between the Mygdonian and the Chalcidic Apollonia pp. 457, 458. We ought to add, that the Antonine and Jerusalem Itineraries appear to give two distinct roads between Apollonia and Thessalonica. See Leake, p. 46.

[4] See Clarke's Travels.

[5] See above, p. 316 and the notes. This expression, however, might be used if nothing more were meant than a progress to the very frontier of Illyricum.

[6] The great work on Thessalonica is that by Tafel, the first part of which was published at Tübingen in 1835. This was afterwards reprinted as "Prolegomena" to the Dissertatio de Thessalonica ejusque agro Geographica. Berlin, 1839.

The Apostolic city at which we are now arrived was known in the earliest periods of its history under various names.[1] Under that of Therma[2] it is associated with some interesting recollections. It was the resting-place of Xerxes on his march;[3] it is not unmentioned in the Peloponnesian war;[4] and it was a frequent subject of debate in the last independent assemblies of Athens.[5] When the Macedonian power began to overshadow all the countries where Greek was spoken, this city received its new name, and began a new and more distinguished period of its history. A sister of Alexander the Great was called Thessalonica, and her name was given to the city of Therma when rebuilt and embellished by her husband, Cassander, the son of Antipater.[6] This name, under a form slightly modified, has continued to the present day. The Salneck of the early German poets has become the Saloniki of the modern Levant.[7] Its history can be followed as continuously as its name. When Macedonia was partitioned into four provincial divisions by Paulus Æmilius, Thessalonica was the capital of that which lay between the Axius and the Strymon.[8] When the four regions were united into one Roman province, this city was chosen as the metropolis of the whole. Its name appears more than once in the annals of the civil wars. It was the scene of the exile of Cicero;[9] and one of the stages of his journey between Rome and his province in the East.[10] Antony and Octavius were here after the battle of Philippi:[11] and coins are still extant which allude to the "freedom" granted by the victorious leaders to the city of the Ther-

[1] Emathia and Halia were two of its early names. A good outline of the history is given by Koch in the Einleitung to his Commentar über den ersten Brief des Ap. P. an die Thess. Berlin, 1849.

[2] Hence the gulf continued to be called the Thermaic Gulf. See two of the accentual lines quoted by Tafel from a poem of the middle ages:

Καὶ μέχρι νῦν τὸ πέλαγος τὸ τῆς Θεσσαλονίκης,
Θερμαῖος κόλπος λέγεται, ἀπὸ τῆς Θέρμης κώμης.

[3] Herod. vii. [4] See Thuc. i. 61.

[5] Æsch. Fals. Leg. p. 211. Reiske.

[6] The first author in which the new name occurs is Polybius. Some say that the name was given by Philip in honour of his daughter, and others that it directly commemorated a victory over the Thessalians. But the opinion stated above appears the most probable. See Koch, p. 2. Philip's daughter was called Thessalonica, in commemoration of a victory obtained by her father on the day when he heard of her birth. Cousinéry sees an allusion to this in the Victory on the coins of the city. See below.

[7] See the references to early German poems in Koch's Einleitung, p. 3.

[8] See above, p. 315.

[9] Both in going out and returning he crossed the Adriatic, between Brundusium and Dyrrachium. See p. 317, n. 5. In travelling through Macedonia he would follow the Via Egnatia. Dyrrachium was a "free city," like Thessalonica. "Dyrrachium veni, quod et libera civitas est, et in me officiosa." Ep. Fam. xiv. 1.

[10] Several of his letters were written from Thessalonica on this journey.

[11] Cousinéry.

THESSALONICA, FROM THE SEA.

maic Gulf.[1] Strabo, in the first century, speaks of Thessalonica as the most populous town in Macedonia.[2] Lucian, in the second century, uses similar language.[3] Before the founding of Constantinople, it was virtually the capital of Greece and Illyricum, as well as of Macedonia,[4] and shared the trade of the Ægean with Ephesus and Corinth. Even after the eastern Rome was built and reigned over the Levant, we find both Pagan and Christian writers speaking of Thessalonica as the metropolis of Macedonia,[5] and a place of great magnitude.[6] Through the Middle Ages it never ceased to be important; and it is, at the present day, the second city in European Turkey.[7] The reason of this continued pre-eminence is to be found in its geographical position. Situated on the inner bend of the Thermaic Gulf,[8]—half-way between the Adriatic and the Hellespont,[9]—on the sea-margin of a vast plain watered by several rivers,[10]—and at the entrance of the pass[11] which commands the approach to the other great Macedonian level,—it was evidently destined for a mercantile emporium. Its relation with the inland trade of Macedonia was as close as that of Amphipolis; and its maritime advantages were perhaps even greater. Thus, while Amphipolis decayed under the Byzantine emperors, Thessalonica continued to prosper.[12] There probably never was a time, from the day when it first received its name, that this city, as viewed from the sea, has not had the aspect of a busy commercial town. We see at once how appropriate a place it was for one of the starting points of the Gospel in Europe; and we can appreciate the force of the expression used by St. Paul within a few months of his departure from the Thessalonians,[13] when he says, that "from them the Word of the Lord had

1 Tafel and Cousinéry.

2 *Θεσσαλονικείας, Μακεδονικῆς πόλεως, ἣ νῦν μάλιστα τῶν ἄλλων εὐανδρεῖ.* vii. 7, 4. He seems to be the only writer who uses this form of the name.

3 *Πόλεως τῶν ἐν Μακεδονίᾳ τῆς μεγίστης Θεσσαλονίκης.* Asinus Aureus, 46.

4 Tafel.

5 He calls it *μητρόπολις Μακεδονίας.* See Tafel.

6 *Θεσσαλονίκη πόλις ἐστὶ μεγίστη καὶ πολυάνθρωπος.* Hist. Eccl. v. 17

7 For a very full account of its modern condition, see Dr. Holland's Travels.

8 Medio flexu litoris sinus Thermaici. Plin. H. N. iv. 10. *Εἰς τὸν Θερμαῖον διήκων μυχὸν.* Strabo viii. 1, 3.

9 See above, p. 314.

10 The chief of these are the Axius and Haliacmon. The whole region near the sea consists of low, alluvial soil. See below, on the journey from Thessalonica to Berœa.

11 This is the pass mentioned above, through which the road to Amphipolis passed, and in which Apollonia was situated.

12 Notices of its mercantile relations in the middle ages are given by Tafel. For an account of its modern trade, and the way in which it was affected by the last war, see Holland's Travels.

13 1 Thess. i. 8. The Epistle was written from Corinth very soon after the departure from Thessalonica. See Ch. XI.

sounded forth like a trumpet,[1] not only in Macedonia and Achaia, but in every place."

No city, which we have had occasion to describe, has had so distinguished a Christian history, with the single exception of the Syrian Antioch; and the Christian glory of the Patriarchal city gradually faded before that of the Macedonian metropolis. The heroic age of Thessalonica was the third century.[2] It was the bulwark of Constantinople in the shock of the barbarians; and it held up the torch of the truth to the successive tribes who overspread the country between the Danube and the Ægean,—the Goths and the Sclaves, the Bulgarians of the Greek Church, and the Wallachians,[3] whose language still seems to connect them with Philippi and the Roman colonies. Thus, in the medieval chroniclers, it has deserved the name of "the Orthodox City."[4] The remains of its Hippodrome, which is for ever associated with the history of Theodosius and Ambrose,[5] can yet be traced among the Turkish houses. Its bishops have sat in great councils.[6] The writings of its great preacher and scholar Eustathius[7] are still preserved to us. It is true that the Christianity of Thessalonica, both medieval and modern, has been debased by humiliating

[1] Ἐξήχηται, as Chrysostom says, *δηλῶν ὅτι ὥσπερ σάλπιγγος λαμπρον ἠχούσης ὁ πλήσιον ἅπας πληροῦται τόπος, ὅυτω τῆς ὑμετέρας ἀνδρείας ἡ φήμη καθάπερ ἐκείνη σαλπίζουσα ἱκανὴ τὴν οἰκου μένην ἐμπλῆσαι.*

[2] Tafel traces the history of Thessalonica, in great detail, through the middle ages; and shows how, after the invasion of the Goths, it was the means of converting the Sclaves, and through them the Bulgarians, to the Christian faith. The peasant population to the east of Thessalonica is Bulgarian, to the west it is Greek (Cousinéry, p. 52). Both belong to the Greek Church.

[3] See what Cousinéry says (ch. i.) of the Wallachians, who are intermixed among the other tribes of modern Macedonia. They speak a corrupt Latin, and he thinks they are descended from the ancient colonies. They are a fierce and bold race, living chiefly in the mountains; and when trading caravans have to go through dangerous places they are posted in the front.

[4] See the work of Joh. Cameniata, "De Excidio Thessalonicensi," in the Bonn Edition of the Byzantine writers. The city is described in this account of its being taken by the Arabs in 904. The history of Cameniata is curious. He was crozier-bearer to the archbishop, and was carried off by the Arabs, and landed at Tarsus, where he wrote his book. The narrative of another storming of the city (by the Romans) is alluded to below. There is a third narrative (of its sack by the Turks under Amurath II., in 1430) by M. Anagnostes.

[5] Some accounts say that 15,000 persons were involved in the massacre, for which the archbishop of Milan exacted penance from the emperor. See Gibbon, ch. xxvii. For some notice of the remains of the Hippodrome, which still retains its name, see Cousinéry, ch. ii.

[6] We find the Bishop of Thessalonica in the Council of Sardis, A. D. 347; and a decree of the Council relates to the place.

[7] Eustathius preached and wrote there in the twelfth century. He was highly esteemed by the Comneni, and is held to have been "beyond all dispute the most learned man of his age." Tafel has recently published some of his minor works, among which is an account of the taking of Thessalonica by the Normans in 1185. The sack by the Arabs in 904 is alluded to above, n. 4.

superstition. The glory of its patron saint, Demetrius,[1] has eclipsed that of St. Paul, the founder of its Church. But the same Divine Providence, which causes us to be thankful for the past, commands us to be hopeful for the future; and we may look forward to the time when a new harvest of the "work of faith and labour of love and patience of hope,"[2] shall spring up from the seeds of Divine Truth, which were first sown on the shore of the Thermaic Gulf by the Apostle of the Gentiles.

If Thessalonica can boast of a series of Christian annals, unbroken since the day of St. Paul's arrival, its relations with the Jewish people have continued for a still longer period. In our own day it contains a multitude of Jews[3] commanding an influential position, many of whom are occupied (not very differently from St. Paul himself) in the manufacture of cloth. A considerable number of them are refugees from Spain, and speak the Spanish language. There are materials for tracing similar settlements of the same scattered and persecuted people in this city, at intervals, during the Middle Ages;[4] and even before the destruction of Jerusalem we find them here, numerous and influential, as at Antioch and Iconium. Here, doubtless, was the chief colony of those Jews of Macedonia of whom Philo speaks;[5] for while there was only a *proseucha* at Philippi, and while Amphipolis and Apollonia had no Israelite communities to detain the Apostles, "*the synagogue*"[6] of the neighbourhood was at Thessalonica.

[1] See many allusions to him in Tafel's quotations. Cameniata enumerates Paul first and Demetrius second among the glorious saints of Thessalonica. De Excidio, &c., 3.

[2] 1 Thess. i. 3.

[3] Paul Lucas, in his later journey, says:—"Les Chrétiens y sont environ au nombre de 10,000. On y compte 30,000 Juifs, qui y ont 22 synagogues, et ce sont eux qui y font tout le commerce. Comme ils sont fort industrieux, deux grand vizirs se sont mis successivement en tête de les faire travailler aux manufactures du draps de France, pour mettre la Turquie en état de se passer des étrangers; mais ils n'ont jamais pû réussir: cependant ils vendent assez bien leurs gros draps au grand seigneur, qui en fait habiller ses troupes." P. 37. Hadji Chalfa's Bosna and Rumeli (translated from the Turkish by Von Hammer, and quoted by Tafel,) speaks of the Jews at Thessalonica, in the 17th century, as carpet and cloth makers, of their liberality to the poor, and of their schools, with more than 1000 children. Cousinéry reckons them at 20,000, many of them from Spain. He adds: "Chaque synagogue à Salonique porte le nom de la province d'où sont originaires les familles qui la composent." P. 19. In the "Jewish Intelligence" for 1849 (vol. xv. pp. 374–377), the Jews at Salonica are reckoned at 35,000, being half the whole population, and having the chief trade in their hands. They are said to have thirty-six synagogues, "none of them remarkable for their neatness or elegance of style."

[4] They are alluded to in the 7th century, and again in considerable numbers in the 12th. See Tafel.

[5] See Ch. I. p. 18.

[6] Ἡ συναγωγή, with the article. "Articulus additus significat Philippis, Amphipoli et Apolloniæ nullas fuisse synagogas, sed si qui ibi essent Judæi, eos synagogam adiisse Thessalonicensem." Grotius. There was another synagogue at Berœa. Acts xvii. 10.

The first scene to which we are introduced in this city is entirely Jewish. It is not a small meeting of proselyte women by the river side, but a crowded assembly of true born Jews, intent on their religious worship, among whom Paul and Silas now make their appearance. If the traces of their recent hardships were manifest in their very aspect, and if they related to their Israelitish brethren how they had "suffered before and been cruelly treated at Philippi" (1 Thess. ii. 2), their entrance in among them must have created a strong impression of indignation and sympathy, which explains the allusion in St. Paul's Epistle. He spoke, however, to the Thessalonian Jews with the earnestness of a man who has no time to lose and no thought to waste on his own sufferings. He preached not himself but Christ crucified. The Jewish scriptures were the ground of his argument. He recurred to the same subject again and again. On three successive Sabbaths[1] he argued with them; and the whole body of Jews resident in Thessalonica were interested and excited with the new doctrine, and were preparing either to adopt or oppose it.

The three points on which he insisted were these:—that He who was foretold in prophecy was to be a suffering Messiah,—that after death He was to rise again,—and that the crucified Jesus of Nazareth was indeed the Messiah who was to come. Such is the distinct and concise statement in the Acts of the Apostles (xvii. 3): and the same topics of teaching are implied in the first Epistle, where the Thessalonians are appealed to as men who had been taught to "believe that Jesus had really died and risen again" (iv. 14), and who had turned to serve the true God, and to wait for His Son from heaven, whom he raised from the dead, even Jesus" (i. 10). Of the mode in which these subjects would be presented to his hearers we can form some idea from what was said at Antioch is Pisidia. The very aspect of the worshippers was the same;[2] proselytes were equally attached to the congregations in Pisidia and Macedonia,[3] and the "devout and honourable women" in one city found their parallel in the "chief women" in the other.[4] The impression, too, produced by the address was not very different here from what it had been there. At first

Some MSS. omit the article (see Lachmann). If authority preponderated against it, still the phrase would imply that there was no synagogue in the towns recently passed through.

[1] Ἐπὶ σάββατα τρία διελέγετο (imperf.). Acts xvii. 2.

[2] See the account of the synagogue-worship,—the desk, the ark, the manuscripts, the prayers, the Scripture-reading, the Tallith, &c.,—given in pp. 172–174.

[3] Compare οἱ φοβούμενοι τὸν Θεόν (Acts xiii. 16, 26) with τῶν σεβομένων Ἑλλήνων (Acts xvii. 4). Some MSS. introduce καὶ between the two latter words. See Lachmann; and Paley on 1 Thess.

[4] Compare τὰς σεβομένας γυναῖκας καὶ τὰς εὐσχήμονας (Acts xiii. 50) with γυναικῶν τῶν πρώτων οὐκ ὀλίγαι (Acts xvii. 4). It will be remembered that the women's place in the synagogues was in a separate gallery or behind a lattice. P. 172.

it was favourably received,[1] the interest of novelty having more influence than the seriousness of conviction. Even from the first some of the topics must have contained matter for perplexity or cavilling. Many would be indisposed to believe the fact of Christ's resurrection: and many more who, in their exile from Jerusalem, were looking intently for the restoration of an earthly kingdom,[2] must have heard incredulously and unwillingly of the humiliation of Messiah.

That St. Paul did speak of Messiah's glorious kingdom, the kingdom foretold in the Prophetic Scriptures themselves, may be gathered by comparing together the Acts and the Epistles to the Thessalonians. The accusation brought against him (Acts xvii. 7) was, that he was proclaiming another *king*, and virtually rebelling against the emperor. And in strict conformity to this the Thessalonians are reminded of the exhortations and entreaties he gave them, when among them, that they would "walk worthily of the God who had called them to His *kingdom* and glory" (1 Thess. ii. 12), and addressed as those who had "suffered affliction for the sake of that *kingdom*" (2 Thess. i. 5). Indeed, the royal state of Christ's second advent was one chief topic which was urgently enforced, and deeply impressed, on the minds of the Thessalonian converts. This subject tinges the whole atmosphere through which the aspect of this church is presented to us. It may be said that in each of the primitive churches, which are depicted in the apostolic epistles, there is some peculiar feature which gives it an individual character. In Corinth it is the spirit of party,[3] in Galatia the rapid declension into Judaism,[4] in Philippi it is a steady and self-denying generosity.[5] And if we were asked for the distinguishing characteristic of the first Christians of Thessalonica, we should point to their overwhelming sense of the nearness of the second advent, accompanied with melancholy[6] thoughts concerning those who might die before it, and with gloomy and unpractical views of the shortness of life, and the vanity of the world. Each chapter in the first Epistle to the Thessalonians ends with an allusion to this subject; and it was evidently the topic of frequent conversations, when the Apostle was in Macedonia. But St. Paul never spoke or wrote of the future as though the present was to be forgotten. When the Thessalonians were admonished of Christ's advent,

[1] Acts xvii. 4 compared with xiii. 42–44. [2] Acts i. 6.
[3] 1 Cor. i. 10, &c. [4] Gal. i. 6, &c. [5] Phil. iv. 10–16.
[6] See Trautmann's Apost. Kirche (Leips. 1848). "Der Apostel hatte in Thessalonich, wie es scheint, sein Lieblingsthema, die Herrlichkeit der letzten bevorstehender Erscheinung Jesu Christi (was damals vielleicht ihn selbst sehr beschäftigen mochte) und was dieser vorhergehn werde, ausführlich und tiefer eingehend behandelt (vergl. 2 Thess. ii. 5). Diese geheimnissvolle und dunkle Parthie des christlichen Glaubens und Hoffens hatten denn die Thessalonicher in einer Weise aufgefasst, welche den Grundcharakter dieser Gemeinde offenbar als sinnig und melancholisch darstellt." P. 138.

he told them also of other coming events, full of practical warning to all ages, though to our eyes still they are shrouded in mystery,—of "the falling away," and of "the man of sin."[1] "These awful revelations," he said, "must precede the revelation of the Son of God. *Do you not remember,*" he adds with emphasis in his letter, *that when I was still with you I often*[2] *told you this. You know, therefore,* the hindrance why he is not revealed, as he will be in his own season." He told them, in the words of Christ himself, that "the times and the seasons" of the coming revelations were known only to God:[3] and he warned them, as the first disciples had been warned in Judæa, that the great day would come suddenly on men unprepared, "as the pangs of travail on her whose time is full," and "as a thief in the night;" and he showed them, both by precept and example, that, though it be true that life is short and the world is vanity, yet God's work must be done diligently and to the last.

The whole demeanour of St. Paul among the Thessalonians may be traced by means of these Epistles, with singular minuteness. We see, there, not only what success he had on his first entrance among them,[4] not only how the Gospel came "with power and full conviction of its truth,"[5] but also "*what manner of man* he was among them for their sakes."[6] We see him proclaiming the truth with unflinching courage,[7] endeavouring to win no converts by flattering words,[8] but warning his hearers of all the danger of the sins and pollution to which they were tempted;[9] manifestly showing that his work was not intended to gratify any desire of self-advancement,[10] but scrupulously maintaining an honour-

1 2 Thess. ii.

2 Ἔλεγον (imperf.).

3 "But of the times and seasons, brethren, when these things shall be you need no warning. For yourselves *know perfectly* that the day of the Lord will come as a thief in the night; and while men say, Peace and safety, destruction shall come upon them in a moment, as the pangs of travail on her whose time is full." 1 Thess. v. 1–3. See Acts i. 7. Matt. xxiv. 43. Luke xii. 39. 2 Pet. iii. 10.

4 "*You know yourselves,* brethren, that my coming amongst you was not fruitless." 1 Thess. ii. 1.

5 1 Thess. i. 5.

6 "*You know* the manner in which I behaved myself among you," &c. 1 Thess. i. 5. ("What manner of men we were." Eng. Vers.) Though the words are in the plural, the allusion is to himself only. See the notes on the Epistle itself.

7 "After I had borne suffering and outrage, *as you know,* at Philippi, I *boldly* declared (ἐπαῤῥησιασάμεθα λαλῆσαι) to you God's glad-tiding, though its adversaries contended mightily against me." 1 Thess. ii. 2.

8 "Never did I use flattering words, *as you know.*" 1 Thess. ii. 5.

9 "That you should be consecrated to Him in holiness, and should keep yourselves from fornication . . . . not in lustful passion, like the heathen, who know not God. . . . . All such the Lord will punish, *as I have forwarned you* by my solemn testimony." 1 Thess. iv. 4–6. It is needless to add that such temptations must have abounded in a city like Thessalonica. We know from the Asinus of Lucian that the place had a bad character.

10 1 Thess. ii. 5.

able and unblamable character.[1] We see him rebuking and admonishing his converts with all the faithfulness of a father to his children,[2] and cherishing them with all the affection of a mother for the infant of her bosom.[3] We see in this Apostle at Thessalonica all the devotion of a friend who is ready to devote his life for those whom he loves,[4] all the watchfulness of the faithful pastor, to whom "each one" of his flock is the separate object of individual care.[5]

And from these Epistles we obtain further some information concerning what may be called the outward incidents of St. Paul's residence in this city. He might when there, consistently with the Lord's institution[6] and with the practice of the other Apostles,[7] have been "burdensome" to those whom he taught, so as to receive from them the means of his temporal support. But that he might place his disinterestedness above all suspicion, and that he might set an example to those who were too much inclined to live by the labour of others, he declined to avail himself of that which was an undoubted right. He was enabled to maintain this independent position partly by the liberality of his friends at Philippi, who once and again, on this first visit to Macedonia, sent relief to his necessities (Phil. iv. 15, 16). And the journeys of those pious men who followed the footsteps of the persecuted Apostles along the Via Egnatia by Amphipolis and Apollonia, bringing the alms which had been collected at Philippi, are among the most touching incidents of the Apostolic history. And not less touching is that description which the Apostle himself gives us of that other means of support—"his own labour night and day, that he might not be burdensome to any of them" (1 Thess. ii. 9). He did not merely "rob other churches,"[8] that he might do the Thessalonians service, but the trade he had learnt when a boy in Cilicia[9] justified the old Jewish maxim;[10] "he was like a vineyard that is fenced;" and he was able to show an example, not only to the "disorderly busybodies" of

1 "*You are yourselves witnesses* how holy, and just, and unblamable, were my dealings towards you." 1 Thess. ii. 10.

2 "*You know* how earnestly, *as a father his own children* (ὡς πατὴρ τέκνα ἑαυτοῦ), I exhorted, and intreated, and adjured," &c. 1 Thess. ii. 11.

3 "I behaved myself among you with mildness and forbearance; and as a nurse cherishes *her own children* (τὰ ἑαυτῆς τέκνα) so," &c. 1 Thess. ii. 7. The authorised version is defective. St. Paul compares himself to a mother who is nursing her own child.

4 "It was my joy to give you, not only the Gospel of Christ, but my own life also because ye were dear unto me." 1 Thess. ii. 8.

5 "*You know* how I exhorted *each one* (ἕνα ἕκαστον) among you to walk worthy of God." 1 Thess. ii. 11.

6 Matt. x. 10. Luke x. 7. See 1 Tim. v. 18.

7 1 Cor. ix. 4, &c. 8 2 Cor. xi. 8. 9 Ch. II. p. 47.

10 "He that hath a trade in his hand, to what is he like? He is like a vineyard that is fenced." Ibid.

Thessalonica (1 Thess. iv. 11), but to all, in every age of the Church, who are apt to neglect their proper business (2 Thess. iii. 11), and ready to eat other men's bread for nought (2 Thess. iii. 8). Late at night, when the sun had long set on the incessant spiritual labours of the day, the Apostle might be seen by lamp-light labouring at the rough hair-cloth,[1] "that he might be chargeable to none." It was an emphatic enforcement of the "commands"[2] which he found it necessary to give when he was among them, that they should "study to be quiet and to work with their own hands" (1 Thess. iv. 11), and the stern principle he laid down, that "if a man will not work, neither should he eat." (2 Thess. iii. 10.)

In these same Epistles, St. Paul speaks of his work at Thessalonica as having been encompassed with afflictions,[3] and of the Gospel as having advanced by a painful struggle.[4] What these afflictions and struggles were, we can gather from the slight notices of events which are contained in the Acts. The Apostle's success among the Gentiles roused the enmity of the Jews. Even in the synagogue the proselytes attached themselves to him more readily than the Jews.[5] But he did not merely obtain an influence over the Gentile mind by the indirect means of his disputations on the Sabbath in the synagogue, and through the medium of the proselytes; but on the intermediate days[6] he was doubtless in frequent and direct communication with the heathen. We need not be surprised at the results, even if his stay was limited to the period corresponding to three Sabbaths. No one can say what effects might follow from three weeks of an Apostle's teaching. But we are by no means forced to adopt the supposition that the time was limited to three weeks. It is highly probable that St. Paul remained at Thessalonica for a longer period.[7] At other cities,[8] when he was repelled by the Jews, he became the evangelist of the Gentiles, and remained till he was compelled to depart. The Thessalonian Letters throw great light on the rupture which certainly took place

[1] See Note, p. 47.

[2] Note the phrases,—"*as I commanded you,*" and "*even when I was with you I gave you this precept.*"

[3] 1 Thess. i. 6. [4] Thess. ii. 2.

[5] "*Some* of them [the Jews] believed and consorted with Paul and Silas; and of the devout Greeks *a great multitude*, and of the chief women *not a few.*" Acts xvii. 4.

[6] As at Athens. Acts xvii. 17.

[7] The chief writers on the two sides of this question are enumerated by Anger in a note, p. 69, n. z. Paley, among others, argues for a longer residence than three weeks. Horæ Paulinæ, on 1 Thess. No. vi. Koch, in his recently published commentary, contends, against Schott, &c., that the tumult which caused St. Paul's departure must have taken place immediately after the third Sabbath. Einleitung, pp. 8, 9. Benson argues that the coming of repeated contributions from Philippi implies a longer residence at Thessalonica than three weeks. To this Anger replies, that they might have come within this time, if they were sent by different contributors

[8] Acts xiii. xviii. xix., &c.

with the Jews on this occasion, and which is implied in that one word in the Acts which speaks of their jealousy[1] against the Gentiles. The whole aspect of the Letter shows that the main body of the Thessalonian Church was not Jewish, but Gentile. The Jews are spoken of as an extraneous body, as the enemies of Christianity and of all men, not as the elements out of which the Church was composed.[2] The ancient Jewish Scriptures are not once quoted in either of these Epistles.[3] The converts are addressed as those who had turned, not from Hebrew fables and traditions, but from the practices of heathen idolatry.[4] How new and how comforting to them must have been the doctrine of the resurrection from the dead. What a contrast must this revelation of "life and immortality" have been to the hopeless lamentations of their own pagan funerals, and to the dismal teaching which we can still read in the sepulchral inscriptions[5] of heathen Thessalonica,—such as told the bystander that after death there is no revival, after the grave no meeting of those who have loved each other on earth. How ought the truth taught by the Apostle to have comforted the new disciples at the thought of inevitable, though only temporary, separation from their Christian brethren. And yet how difficult was the truth to realise, when they saw those brethren sink into lifeless forms, and after they had committed them to the earth which had received all their heathen ancestors. How eagerly can we imagine them to have read the new assurances of comfort which came in the letter from Corinth, and which told them "not to sorrow as the rest that have no hope."[6]

But we are anticipating the events which occurred between the Apostle's departure from Thessalonica and the time when he wrote the letter from Corinth. We must return to the persecution that led him to undertake that journey, which brought him from the capital of Macedonia to that of Achaia.

When the Jews saw proselytes and Gentiles, and many of the leading women[7] of the city, convinced by St. Paul's teaching, they must have felt that his influence was silently undermining theirs. In propor-

[1] *Ζηλωσάντες.* Acts xvii. 5.

[2] "You have suffered the like persecution from your own countrymen which they [the Churches in Judæa] endured from the Jews, who killed both our Lord Jesus and their own prophets . . . a people displeasing to God, and enemies to all mankind; who would hinder me from speaking to the Gentiles," &c. 1 Thess. ii. Contrast Rom. ix.

[3] The Epistles to Titus and Philemon, if we mistake not, are the only other instances.

[4] 1 Thess. i. 9.

[5] Some of these inscriptions may be seen in Boeckh, e. g. No. 1973, where the deceased is described as *τέρμ' ἐσιδὼν βιότου ἀλύτοις ὑπὸ νάμασι Μοιρῶν.* See also 1933. In 1988 there is a hint of immortality; but the general feeling of the Greek world concerning the dead is expressed in that one line of Æschylus:—Ἅπαξ θανόντος οὔτις ἔστ' ἀνάστασις.

[6] 1 Thess. iv. 13.

[7] Acts xvii. 4. See above.

tion to his success in spreading Christianity, their power of spreading Judaism declined. Their sensitiveness would be increased in consequence of the peculiar dislike with which they were viewed at this time by the Roman power.[1] Thus they adopted the tactics which had been used with some success before at Iconium and Lystra,[2] and turned against St. Paul and his companions those weapons which are the readiest instruments of vulgar bigotry. They excited the mob of Thessalonica, gathering together a multitude of those worthless idlers about the markets and landing-places[3] which abound in every such city, and are always ready for any evil work.[4] With this multitude they assaulted the house of Jason (perhaps some Hellenistic Jew,[5] whose name had been moulded into Gentile form, and possibly one of St. Paul's relations, who is mentioned in the Epistle to the Romans),[6] with whom Paul and Silas seem to have been lodging. Their wish was to bring Paul and Silas out to the *demus,* or assembly of the people. But they were absent from the house; and Jason and some other Christians were dragged before the city magistrates. The accusation vociferously brought against them was to the following effect: "These Christians, who are setting the whole world in confusion, are come hither at last; and Jason has received them into his house; and they are all acting in the face of the emperor's decrees, for they assert that there is another king, whom they call Jesus." We have seen[7] how some of the parts of St. Paul's teaching at Thessalonica may have given occasion to the latter phrase in this indictment; and we obtain a deeper insight into the cause why the whole indictment was brought forward with so much vehemence, and why it was so likely to produce an effect on the magistrates, if we bear in mind the circumstance alluded to in reference to Philippi,[8] that the Jews were under the ban of the Roman authorities about this time, for having raised a tumult in the metropolis, at the instigation (as was alleged) of one Chrestus, or Christus;[9] and that they

[1] See above, p. 303.

[2] Acts xiv. See pp. 185, 195, &c.; also pp. 180, 181.

[3] Ἀγοραῖοι, like the Lazzaroni at Naples,—"innati triviis ac pæne forenses." Hor. A. P. 245. Such men as are called by Cicero "subrostrani" (Ep. Fam. viii. 1), and by Plautus "subbasilicani" (Capt. 4, 2, 35). See Casaubon on Theophr. Char. 6; or the Archbishop of Thessalonica (p. 348) may explain to us how the word is used. Ἀγοραῖος ἀνὴρ ἢ ὄχλος ἐπὶ σκώμματος λέγεται. Eustath. ad Iliad. ii. 143.

[4] Such men are often πονηροί. Compare Aristoph. Eq. 181, πονηρὸς κἀξ ἀγόρας; and Senec. de Benef. 7,—"Huic homini *malo,* quem invenire in quolibet *foro* possum."

[5] Jason is the form which the name Joshua seems sometimes to have taken. See p. 151, n. 11. It occurs 1 Mac. viii. 17. 2 Mac. ii. 23; also in Josephus, referred to p. 151, n. 5.

[6] Rom. xvi. 21. Tradition says that he became Bishop of Tarsus. For some remarks on St. Paul's kinsmen, see p. 46.

[7] Above, p. 304.

[8] P. 303.

[9] The words of Suetonius are quoted p. 303, n. 4. We shall return to them again

must have been glad, in the provincial cities, to be able to show their loyalty and gratify their malice, by throwing the odium off themselves upon a sect whose very name might be interpreted to imply a rebellion against the emperor.

COIN OF THESSALONICA.

Such were the circumstances under which Jason and his companions were brought before the *politarchs.* We use the Greek the term advisedly; for it illustrates the political constitution of Thessalonica, and its contrast with that of Philippi, which has lately been noticed. Thessalonica was not a colony, like Philippi, Troas, or the Pisidian Antioch, but a *free city*[2] (*Urbs libera*), like the Syrian Antioch, or like Tarsus[3] and Athens. The privilege of what was technically called "freedom" was given to certain cities of the empire for good service in the civil wars, or as a tribute of respect to the old celebrity of the place, or for other reasons of convenient policy. There were few such cities in the western provinces,[4] as there were no *municipia* in the eastern. The free towns were most numerous in those parts of the empire, where the Greek language had long prevailed; and we are generally able to trace the reasons why this privilege was bestowed upon them. At Athens, it was the fame of its ancient eminence, and the evident policy of paying a compliment to the Greeks. At Thessalonica it was the part which its inhabitants had prudently taken in the great struggle of Augustus and Antony against Brutus and Cassius.[5] When the decisive battle had been fought, Philippi was made a military colony, and Thessalonica became *free.*

when we come to Acts xviii. 2. At present we need only point out their probable connection with the word "*Christian.*" See pp. 119, 120, and the notes. We should observe, that St. Paul had proclaimed at Thessalonica that Jesus was the *Christ* (ὁ χριστός). Acts xvii. 3.

1 From the British Museum. For a long series of coins of this character, see Mionnet and the Supplement.

2 For an account of the privileges of *liberæ civitates*, see Hoeck's Römische Geschichte, I. ii. pp. 242–250.

3 See p. 45.

4 There were a few in Gaul and Spain, none in Sardinia. On the other hand, they were very numerous in Greece, the Greek islands, and Asia Minor. Hoeck, p. 249. Such complimentary privileges would have had little meaning if bestowed on a rude people, which had no ancient traditions.

5 See the coins alluded to above, p. 322. Some have the word ΕΛΕΥΘΕΡΙΑΣ with the head of Octavia.

The privilege of such a city consisted in this,—that it was entirely self-governed in all its internal affairs, within the territory that might be assigned to it. The governor of the province had no right, under ordinary circumstances, to interfere with these affairs.[1] The local magistrates had the power of life and death over the citizens of the place. No stationary garrison of Roman soldiers was quartered within its territory.[2] No insignia of Roman office were displayed in its streets. An instance of the care with which this rule was observed is recorded by Tacitus, who tells us, that Germanicus, whose progress was usually distinguished by the presence of twelve lictors, declined to enter Athens attended with more than one.[3] There is no doubt that the magistracies of such cities would be very careful to show their loyalty to the emperor on all suitable occasions, and to avoid every disorder which might compromise their valued dignity, and cause it to be withdrawn. And on the other hand, the Roman State did wisely to rely on the Greek love of empty distinction; and it secured its dominion as effectually in the East by means of these privileged towns, as by the stricter political annexation of the municipia in the West. The form of government in the free cities was very various.[4] In some cases the old magistracies and customs were continued without any material modification. In others, a *senate*, or an *assembly*, were allowed to exist where none had existed before. Here, at Thessalonica, we find an assembly of the people (*Demus*,[5] Acts xvii. 5) and supreme magistrates, who are called *politarchs* (Acts xvii. 8). It becomes an

[1] He might, however, have his residence there, as at Antioch and Tarsus. We find, under the republic, the governor of Asia directed to administer justice to free communities (Cic. pro Font. 32); but usually he did not interfere with the local magistrates. Even his financial officers did not enter the territory to collect the taxes, but the imposts were sent to Rome in some other way. We may add that a free city might have *libertas cum immunitate* (Senec. de Benef. v. 16), *i. e.* freedom from taxation, as a *Colonia* might have the *Jus Italicum*. See these and other details in Hoeck.

[2] Hence such cities were called ἀφρούρητοι. Plut. Flam. 10. App. Mac. 2. See Liv. xlv. 26.

[3] Tacitus says of Germanicus, that, after a bad voyage across the Adriatic, and after visiting the scene of the battle of Actium, "ventum Athenas, fœderique sociæ et vetustæ urbis datum ut uno lictore uteretur." Ann. ii. 53. And yet he was a member of the imperial family. So it is said of Tiberius, during his residence among the Greeks at Rhodes: "genus vitæ civile ad modum instituit, *sine lictore* aut viatore gymnasia interdum obambulans, *mutuaque cum Græculis officia usurpans*, prope *ex æquo*." Suet. Tib. 11. Very severe language is used by Cicero of Piso, governor of Macedonia, for daring to exercise "jurisdictio in libera civitate contra leges senatusque consulta." De Prov. Cons. 3.

[4] The degree of *libertas* was various also. It was settled by a distinct concordat (*fœdus*). Hoeck, p. 242. The granting and withdrawing of this privilege, as well as its amount, was capricious and irregular under the republic, and especially during the civil wars. See Cic. in Pison. 56. Under the emperors it became more regulated, like all the other details of provincial administration.

[5] Tafel seems to think it had also a *senate* (βουλή).

interesting inquiry, whether the existence of this title of the Thessalonian magistracy can be traced in any other source of information. This question is immediately answered in the affirmative, by one of those passages of monumental history which we have made it our business to cite as often as possible in the course of this biography. An inscription which is still legible on an archway in Thessalonica gives this title to the magistrates of the place, informs us of their number, and mentions the very names of some who bore the office not long before the day of St. Paul.

A long street intersects the city from east to west.[1] This is doubtless the very direction which the ancient road took in its course from the Adriatic to the Hellespont; for though the houses of ancient cities are destroyed and renewed, the lines of the great thoroughfares are usually unchanged.[2] If there were any doubt of the fact at Thessalonica, the question is set at rest by two triumphal arches which still, though disfigured by time and injury, and partly concealed by Turkish houses, span the breadth of this street, and define a space which must have been one of the public parts of the city in the apostolic age. One of these arches is at the western extremity, near the entrance from Rome, and is thought to have been built by the grateful Thessalonians to commemorate the victory of Augustus and Antony.[3] The other is further to the east, and records the triumph of some later emperor (most probably Constantine) over enemies subdued near the Danube or beyond. The second of these arches, with its sculptured camels,[4] has altogether an Asiatic aspect, and belongs to a period of the empire much later than that of St. Paul. The first has the representation of consuls with the toga, and corresponds in appearance with that condition of the arts which marks the passing of the republic into the empire. If erected at that epoch, it was undoubtedly existing when the Apostle was in Macedonia. The following inscription[5] in Greek

1 See Cousinéry, ch. ii., and Leake, ch. xxvi.

2 See a traveller's just remark, quoted in reference to Damascus, p. 93, n. 5.

3 A view of the arch is given in Cousinéry, p. 26. See his description. He believes Octavius and Antony to have staid here some time after the victory. The arch is also described by Dr. Holland and Dr. Clarke, who take the same view of its origin. The latter traveller says that its span is 12 feet, and its present height 18 feet, the lower part being buried to the depth of 27 feet more. It is now part of the modern walls, and is called the Vardar Gate, because it leads towards that river (the Axius).

4 There is also a view of this arch in Cousinéry, p. 29. He refers its origin to one of Constantine's expeditions, mentioned by Zosimus. The whole structure formerly consisted of three arches; it is built of brick, and seems to have been faced with marble.

5 From Boeckh, No. 1967. The inscription is given by Leake (p. 236), with a slight difference in one of the names. It goes on to mention the *ταμίας τῆς πόλεως* and the *γυμνασιάρχων*. The names being chiefly Roman, Leake argues for a later date than that which is suggested by Cousinéry. In either case the confirmation of St. Luke's accuracy remains the same.

letters informs us of the magistracy which the Romans recognised and allowed to subsist in the "free city" of Thessalonica:—

ΠΟΛΕΙΤΑΡΧΟΥΝΤΩΝ ΣΩΣΙΠΑΤΡΟΥ ΤΟΥ ΚΛΕΟ
ΠΑΤΡΑΣ ΚΑΙ ΛΟΥΚΙΟΥ ΠΟΝΤΙΟΥ ΣΕΚΟΥΝΔΟΥ
ΠΟΥΒΛΙΟΥ ΦΛΑΟΥΙΟΥ ΣΑΒΕΙΝΟΥ ΔΗΜΗΤΡΙΟΥ
ΤΟΥ ΦΑΥΣΤΟΥ ΔΗΜΗΤΡΙΟΥ ΤΟΥ ΝΙΚΟΠΟΛΕΩΣ
ΖΩΙΛΟΥ ΤΟΥ ΠΑΡΜΕΝΙΩΝΟΣ ΤΟΥ ΚΑΙ ΜΕΝΙΣΚΟΥ
ΓΑΙΟΥ ΑΓΙΛΛΗΙΟΥ ΠΟΤΕΙΤΟΥ. . . . .

These words, engraved on the marble arch,[1] inform us that the magistrates of Thessalonica were called *politarchs*, and that they were seven in number; and it is perhaps worth observing (though it is only a curious coincidence) that three of the names are identical with those of St. Paul's friends in this region,—*Sopater of Beræa*,[2] *Gaius the Macedonian*,[3] and *Secundus of Thessalonica*.[4]

It is at least well worth our while to notice, as a mere matter of Christian evidence, how accurately St. Luke writes concerning the political characteristics of the cities and provinces which he mentions. He takes notice, in the most artless and incidental manner, of minute details which a fraudulent composer would judiciously avoid, and which in the mythical result of mere oral tradition would surely be loose and inexact. Cyprus is a "proconsular" province.[5] Philippi is a "colony."[6] The magistrates of Thessalonica have an unusual title, unmentioned in ancient literature; but it appears, from a monument of a different kind, that the title is perfectly correct. And the whole aspect of what happened at Thessalonica, as compared with the events at Philippi, is in perfect harmony with the ascertained difference in the political condition of the two places. There is no mention of the rights and privileges of *Roman citizenship*;[7] but we are presented with the spectacle of a mixed mob of Greeks and Jews,

[1] The masonry consists of square blocks of marble, six feet thick (Dr. Clarke).

It may be well to mention here some of the other remains at Thessalonica. (1) There are five columns, with an entablature, in the street between the triumphal arches. This ruin is called by the Spanish Jews, *Las Incantadas*. (2) The *Rotunda*, now a mosque, is an ancient temple, similar to the Pantheon at Rome. These two buildings were probably in existence when St. Paul was at Thessalonica. The two following are later. (3) The *Church of St. Sophia*, now a mosque, built under Justinian by the architect of the great church at Constantinople. Here a stone rostrum is shown, from which St. Paul is said to have preached. (4) Another mosque was formerly the *Church of St. Demetrius* [see p. 325], which tradition alleges to have been built near the site of the ancient synagogue where the Apostle reasoned with the Jews.

[2] Acts xx. 4. [3] Acts xix. 29. [4] Acts. xx. 4.

[5] See Ch. V. p. 144. [6] See above, p. 290, &c.

[7] Compare Acts xvi. 21.

who are anxious to show themselves to be "*Cæsar's friends.*"[1] No *lictors*,[2] with rods and fasces, appear upon the scene; but we hear something distinctly of a *demus*,[3] or free assembly of the people. Nothing is said of *religious ceremonies*[4] which the citizens, "being Romans," may not lawfully adopt; all the anxiety, both of people and magistrates, is turned to the one point of showing their loyalty to *the emperor*.[5] And those magistrates by whom the question at issue is ultimately decided, are not Roman *prætors*[6] but Greek *politarchs*.

It is evident that the magistrates were excited and unsettled[7] as well as the multitude. No doubt they were anxious to stand well with the Roman government, and not to compromise themselves or the privileges of their city by a wrong decision in this dispute between the Christians and the Jews.[8] The course they adopted was to "take security" from Jason and his companions. By this expression[9] it is most probably meant that a sum of money was deposited with the magistrates, and that the Christian community of the place made themselves responsible that no attempt should be made against the supremacy of Rome, and that peace should be maintained in Thessalonica itself. By these means the disturbance was allayed.

But though the magistrates had secured quiet in the city for the present, the position of Paul and Silas was very precarious. The lower classes were still excited. The Jews were in a state of fanatical displeasure. It is evident that the Apostles could not appear in public as before, without endangering their own safety, and compromising their fellow-Christians who were security for their good behaviour. The alternatives before them were, either silence in Thessalonica, or departure to some other place. The first was impossible to those who bore the divine commission to preach the Gospel everywhere. They could not hesitate to adopt the second course; and under the watchful care of "the brethren,"

1 The conduct and language of the Jews in Acts xvii. 7 should, by all means, be compared with what was said to Pilate at Jerusalem: "If thou let this man go, thou art not *Cæsar's friend:* whosoever maketh himself a king speaketh against Cæsar." John xix. 12.

2 Ῥαβδοῦχοι. Acts xvi. 35, 38.

3 Acts xvii. 5. 4 Acts xvi. 21. 5 Acts xvii. 7.

6 Στρατηγοί. Acts xvi. 20, 22, 35, &c. See p. 294, and p. 302.

7 The word ἐτάραξαν implies some disturbance of mind on the part of the magistrates.

8 See above.

9 Λαβόντες τὸ ἱκανόν. It is very unlikely that this means, as Grotius supposes, that Jason and his friends gave bail for the appearance of Paul and Silas before the magistrates, for they sent them away the same night. See Meyer. Hemsen thinks (p. 132, note) that Jason pledged himself not to receive them again into his house; and Kuinoel, that he gave a promise of their immediate departure. Neither of these suppositions is improbable; but it is clear that it was impossible for Paul and Silas to stay, if the other Christians were security for the maintenance of the peace.

they departed the same evening from Thessalonica, their steps being turned in the direction of those mountains which are the western boundary of Macedonia.[1] We observe that nothing is said of the departure of Timotheus. If he was at Thessalonica at all, he stays there now, as Luke had staid at Philippi.[2] We can trace in all these arrangements a deliberate care and policy for the well-being of the new churches, even in the midst of the sudden movements caused by the outbreak of persecution. It is the same prudent and varied forethought which appears afterwards in the pastoral epistles, where injunctions are given, according to circumstances,—to "abide" while the Apostle goes to some other region,[3] "hoping that he may come shortly" again,[4]—to "set in order the things that are wanting, and ordain elders,"[5]—or "to use all diligence" to follow[6] and co-operate again in the same work at some new place.

Passing under the Arch of Augustus and out of the Western Gate, the Via Egnatia crosses the plain and ascends the mountains which have just been mentioned,—forming a communication over a very rugged country between the Adriatic and the Hellespont. Just where the road strikes the mountains, at the head of a bay of level ground, the city of Edessa is situated, described as commanding a glorious view of all the country, that stretches in an almost unbroken surface to Thessalonica and the sea.[7] This, however, was not the point to which St. Paul turned his steps. He travelled by a less important road,[8] to the town of Berœa, which was further to the south. The first part of the journey was undertaken at night, but day must have dawned on the travellers long before they reached their place of destination. If the journey was at all like what it is now,[9] it may be simply described as follows. After leaving the

[1] Pp. 313, 314 and the notes.

[2] See p. 313. [3] 1 Tim. i. 3. [4] 1 Tim. iii. 14. [5] Tit. i. 5.

[6] 2 Tim. iv. 9, 21, and especially Tit. iii. 12. The first injunction we read of, after this point, to Timotheus, in conjunction with Silas, is when St. Paul leaves Berœa, and they are told "to come to him with all speed." Acts xvii. 15.

[7] For a description of Edessa (Vodhena) see Cousinéry, p, 75, &c. It seems to be on a plateau at the edge of the mountains, with waterfalls, like Tivoli. He speaks in animated language of the view over fifteen leagues of plain, from the mountains to the sea [what he calls in another place, "les deux vastes plaines cisaxiennes et transaxiennes"], with woods and villages, and a lake in the centre. There is a view of one of the waterfalls, p. 79. See Leake also for a full account of Vodhena, ch. xxvii. He says of this part of the Via Egnatia, that though Polybius states it to have been marked out by milestones all the way, and though the stages are mentioned in all the Itineraries, yet much examination is required before all the details can be determined, p. 279.

[8] The Itineraries give two roads from Thessalonica to Berœa, one passing through Pydna, the other more to the south. See our map of the north of the Ægean. It is conceivable, but not likely, that St. Paul went by water from Thessalonica to the neighbourhood of Pydna. Colonel Leake, after visiting this city, took a boat from Eleftherokhori, and sailed across the gulf to Salonica. Vol. III. pp. 436–438. So Dr. Clarke.

[9] The description of the journey is literally taken from Cousinéry, ch. iii. He was

gardens which are in the immediate neighbourhood of Thessalonica, the travellers crossed a wide tract of corn-fields, and came to the shifting bed of the "wide-flowing Axius." About this part of the journey, if not before, the day must have broken upon them. Between the Axius and the Haliacmon[1] there intervenes another wide extent of the same continuous plain. The banks of this second river are confined by artificial dykes to check its destructive inundations. All the country round is covered with a vast forest, with intervals of cultivated land, and villages concealed among the trees. The road extends for many miles through these woods, and at length reaches the base of the Western Mountains, where a short ascent leads up to the gate of Berœa.[2]

Berœa, like Edessa, is on the eastern slope of the Olympian range, and commands an extensive view of the plain which is watered by the Haliacmon and Axius. It has many natural advantages, and is now considered one of the most agreeable towns in Rumili.[3] Plane-trees spread a grateful shade over its gardens. Streams of water are in every street. Its ancient name is said to have been derived from the abundance of its waters;[4] and the name still survives in the modern Verria, or Kara-Verria.[5] It is situated on the left of the Haliacmon, about five miles from the point where that river breaks through an immense rocky ravine from the mountains to the plain. A few insignificant ruins of the Greek and Roman periods may yet be noticed. The foundations of an ancient bridge are passed on the ascent to the city-gate; and parts of the Greek fortifications may be seen above the rocky bed of a mountain stream. The traces of repairs in the walls, of Roman and Byzantine date,[6] are links between the early fortunes of Berœa and its present condition. It still boasts of eighteen or twenty thousand inhabitants, and is placed in the second rank of the cities of European Turkey.[7]

travelling from Salonica with a caravan to a place called Perlepe, on the mountains to the north-west. The usual road is up the Axius to Gradisca. But one of the rivers higher up was said to be flooded and impassable; hence he went by Caraveria (Berœa), which is fourteen leagues from Salonica. Leake travelled from Salonica to Pella, crossing the Axius on his way. Ch. xxvii.

1 The Haliacmon itself would not be crossed before arriving at Berœa (see below). But there are other large rivers which flow into it, and which are often flooded. Some of the "perils of rivers" (pp. 163, 164) may very possibly have been in this district. See the preceding note. See Leake's remarks on the changing channels of these rivers, p. 437.

2 Compare Leake. 3 See Leake, p. 290, &c.

4 See Tafel (Thessalonica, &c.), who refers to Ælian, H. A. xv. 1, and Cantacuz. iv. 18.

5 Leake uses the former term: Cousinéry calls the town "Caraveria," or "Verria the Black." In the eleventh century we find it called "Verre." See Buchon's French Chronicles, iii. 250.

6 See Leake. It was a fortified city in the eleventh century. Buchon, as above.

7 See Cousinéry (ch. iii.), who reckons the inhabitants at 15,000 or 20,000.

In the apostolic age Berœa was sufficiently populous to contain a colony of Jews.[1] When St. Paul arrived, he went, according to his custom, immediately to the synagogue. The Jews here were of a "nobler"[2] spirit than those of Thessalonica. Their minds were less narrowed by prejudice, and they were more willing to receive "the truth in the love of it." There was a contrast between the two neighbouring communities apparently open to the same religious influences, like that between the "village of the Samaritans," which refused to receive Jesus Christ (Luke ix.), and that other "city" in the same country where "many believed" because of the word of one who witnessed of Him, and "many more because of His own word" (John iv.). In a spirit very different from the ignoble violence of the Thessalonian Jews, the Berœans not only listened to the Apostle's arguments, but they examined the Scriptures themselves, to see if those arguments were justified by prophecy. And, feeling the importance of the subject presented to them, they made this scrutiny of their holy books their "daily" occupation. This was the surest way to come to a strong conviction of the Gospel's divine origin. Truth sought in this spirit cannot long remain undiscovered. The promise that "they who seek shall find" was fulfilled at Berœa; and the Apostle's visit resulted in the conversion of "many." Nor was the blessing confined to the Hebrew community. The same Lord who is "rich unto all that call upon Him,"[3] called many "not of the Jews only, but also of the Gentiles."[4] Both men and women,[5] and those of the highest respectability, among the Greeks,[6] were added to the church founded by St. Paul in that provincial city of Macedonia, which was his temporary shelter from the storm of persecution.

The length of St. Paul's stay in the city is quite uncertain. From the fact that the Berœans were occupied "*daily*" in searching the Scriptures[7] for arguments to establish or confute the Apostle's doctrine, we conclude that he remained there several days at least. From his own assertion in his first letter to the Thessalonians,[8] that, at the time when he had been recently taken away from them, he was very anxious, and used every effort to revisit them, we cannot doubt that he lingered as long as possible in the neighbourhood of Thessalonica.[9] This desire would account for a resi-

[1] Acts xvii. 10.

[2] *Εὐγενέστεροι τῶν ἐν Θεσσ.*, v 11. The Latin word "ingenuus," and the English word "noble," give both the primary and secondary senses. Plutarch says that virtue has its root in *εὐγένεια*, and is developed to perfection by *παίδεια*.

[3] Rom. x. 12. [4] Rom. ix. 24.

[5] Acts xvii. 12.

[6] *Ἑλληνίδων* (v. 12) must be considered as belonging to *ἀνδρῶν* as well as *γυναίκων*.

[7] Acts xvii. 11. [8] 1 Thess. ii. 17.

[9] He says that he made more than one attempt to return: and in this expression he may be referring to what took place at Berœa, as probably as at Athens.

dence of some weeks; and there are other passages[1] in the same Epistle which might induce us to suppose the time extended even to months. But when we find, on the other hand, that the cause which led him to leave Berœa was the hostility of the Jews of Thessalonica, and when we remember that the two cities were only separated by a distance of sixty miles,[2]—that the events which happened in the synagogue of one city would soon be made known in the synagogue of the other,—and that Jewish bigotry was never long in taking active measures to crush its opponents,—we are led to the conclusion that the Apostle was forced to retreat from Berœa after no long interval of time. The Jews came like hunters upon their prey, as they had done before from Iconium to Lystra.[3] They could not arrest the progress of the Gospel,[4] but they "stirred up the people" there, as at Thessalonica before.[5] They made his friends feel that his continuance in the city was no longer safe. He was withdrawn from Berœa and sent to Athens, as in the beginning of his ministry[6] he had been withdrawn from Jerusalem and sent to Tarsus. And on this occasion, as on that,[7] the dearest wishes of his heart were thwarted. The providence of God permitted "Satan" to hinder him from seeing his dear Thessalonian converts, whom "once and again" he had desired to revisit.[8] The divine counsels were accomplished by means of the antagonism of wicked men; and the path of the Apostle was urged on, in the midst of trial and sorrow, in the direction pointed out in the vision at Jerusalem,[9] "*far hence unto the Gentiles.*"

An immediate departure was urged upon the Apostle; and the Church of Berœa suddenly[10] lost its teacher. But Silas and Timotheus remained behind,[11] to build it up in its holy faith, to be a comfort and support in its trials and persecutions, and to give it such organisation as might be neces-

1 Those which relate to the widely extended rumour of the introduction of Christianity into Thessalonica. See below, on 1 Thess. The stay at Athens was short, and the Epistle was written soon after St. Paul's arrival at Corinth; and, if a sufficient time had elapsed for a general knowledge to be spread abroad of what had happened at Thessalonica, we should be inclined to believe that the delay at Berœa was consider able.

2 Wieseler gives a different turn to this consideration, and argues that, because the distance between Berœa and Thessalonica was so great, therefore a long time must have elapsed before the news from the latter place could have summoned the Jews from the former. But we must take into account, not merely the distance between the two cities, but the peculiarly close communication which subsisted among the Jewish synagogues. See, for instance, Acts xxvi. 11.

3 See pp. 195, 196. 4 See Hemsen's Paulus, p. 136.

5 Ἠλθον κακεῖ σαλεύοντες τοὺς ὄχλους. Acts xvii. 13. Compare v. 5.

6 Acts ix. 30.

7 See the remarks on the vision at Jerusalem, p. 104.

8 See above, p. 340. 9 Acts xvii. 17–21. 10 See εὐθέως, v. 14.

11 Acts xvii. 14. The last mention of Timothy was at Philippi; but it is highly pro able that he joined St. Paul at Thessalonica. See above, p. 338. Possibly he brought

sary. Meanwhile some of the new converts accompanied St. Paul on his flight:[1] thus adding a new instance to those we have already seen of the love which grows up between those who have taught and those who have learnt the way of the soul's salvation.[2]

Without attempting to divine all the circumstances which may have concurred in determining the direction of the flight, we can mention some obvious reasons why it was the most natural course. To have returned in the direction of Thessalonica was manifestly impossible. To have pushed over the mountains, by the Via Egnatia, towards Illyricum and the western parts of Macedonia, would have taken the Apostle from those shores of the Archipelago to which his energies were primarily to be devoted. Mere concealment and inactivity were not to be thought of. Thus the Christian fugitives turned their steps towards the sea,[3] and from some point on the coast where a vessel was found, they embarked for Athens. In the ancient tables two roads[4] are marked which cross the Haliacmon and intersect the plain from Berœa, one passing by Pydna,[5] and the other leaving it to the left, and both coming to the coast at Dium near the base of Mount Olympus. The Pierian level (as this portion of the plain was called) extends about ten miles in breadth from the woody falls of the mountain to the sea-shore, forming a narrow passage from Macedonia into Greece.[6] Thus Dium was "the great bulwark of Macedonia on the

some of the contributions from Philippi, p. 329. We shall consider hereafter the movements of Silas and Timothy at this point of St. Paul's journey. Meantime, we may observe that Timotheus was very probably sent to Thessalonica (1 Thess. iii.) from *Berœa*, and not from *Athens*. See Hemsen, pp. 117, 127, 138, 162, and Wieseler, 42–45, 246–249.

[1] Acts xvii. 14, 15.

[2] See above, on the jailor's conversion, pp. 308, 309. Also p. 128.

[3] Ὡς ἐπὶ τὴν θάλασσαν (Acts xvii. 14), translated "as it were to the sea" in the authorised version. This need not at all imply that there was any stratagem. Nor is the word ὡς merely redundant. Viger and Winer have shown that it denotes the intention. The phrase ὡς ἐπὶ is similarly used by Polybius. It seems very likely that in the first instance they had no fixed intention of going to *Athens*, but merely to the *sea*. Their further course was determined by providential circumstances: and, when St. Paul was once arrived at Athens, he could send a message to Timothy and Silas to follow him (v. 15). Those are surely mistaken who suppose that St. Paul travelled from Macedonia to Attica by land.

[4] These roads are clearly laid down in the map of the Northern Ægean. The distance in the Antonine Itinerary is seventeen miles. See Wesseling, p. 328. Nicephorus Gregoras says that Berœa is 160 stadia from the sea (xiii. 8, 3). See also Cantacuz.

[5] Mr. Tate (Continuous History, &c.) suggests that St. Paul may have sailed from Pydna. But Pydna was not a seaport, and, for other reasons, Dium was more conveniently situated for the purpose.

[6] Leake, p. 425. Above (p. 409) he describes the ruins of Dium, among which are probably some remains of the temple of Jupiter Olympius, who was honoured here in periodical games. See Liv. xliv. 6, 7. For Mount Olympus, see pp. 413, 414. He describes it as a conspicuous object for all the country round, as far as Saloniki, and as deriving from its steepness an increase of grandeur and apparent height.

south;" and it was a Roman colony, like that other city which we have described on the eastern frontier.[1] No city is more likely than Dium to have been the last, as Philippi was "the first," through which St. Paul passed in his journey through the province.

Here then,—where Olympus, dark with woods, rises from the plain by the shore, to the broad summit, glittering with snow, which was the throne of the Homeric gods,[2]—at the natural termination of Macedonia,—and where the first scene of classical and poetic Greece opens on our view,—we take our leave, for the present, of the Apostle of the Gentiles. The shepherds from the heights[3] above the vale of Tempe may have watched the sails of his ship that day, as it moved like a white speck over the outer waters of the Thermaic Gulph. The sailors, looking back from the deck, saw the great Olympus rising close above them in snowy majesty.[4] The more distant mountains beyond Thessalonica are already growing faint and indistinct. As the vessel approaches the Thessalian archipelago,[5] Mount Athos begins to detach itself from the isthmus that binds it to the main, and, with a few other heights of Northern Macedonia, appears like an island floating in the horizon.[6]

[1] See above, on Philippi.

[2] The epithets given by Homer to this poetic mountain (μακρός, Il. i. 398; πολυδειράς, i. 44; ἀγάννιφος, Od. ix. 40; αἰγλήεις, Il. i. 530; πολύπτυχος, viii. 410) are as fully justified by the accounts of modern travellers, as the descriptions of the scenery alluded to at the close of the preceding Chapter, p. 282, n. 6.

[3] See Mr. Urquhart's description of the view over the sea and its coasts (mare volivolum terrasque jacentes), from a convent on the face of Mount Olympus. "I might have doubted the reality of its hazy waters, but for the white sails dotted along the frequented course between Salonica and the southern headland of Thessaly. Beyond, and far away to the east, might be guessed or distinguished the peak of Mount Athos, and the distincter lines, between, of the peninsulas Pallene and Sithonia. This glimpse of Mount Athos, at a distance of ninety miles, made me resolve on visiting its shrine and ascending its peak." Spirit of the East, vol. I., p. 426. In the same work (p. 418) are some remarks on the isolation of the mountain. See a passage in Dr. Wordsworth's Greece, p. 197.

[4] Compare p. 314, notes 2 and 7. See also Purdy's Sailing Directory, p. 148. "To the N.W. of the Thessalian Isles the extensive *Gulf of Salonica* extends thirty leagues to the north-westward, before it changes its direction to the north-eastward and forms the port. The country on the west, part of the ancient Thessaly, and now the province of Tricala, exhibits a magnificent range of mountains, which include *Pelion*, now Patras, *Ossa*, now Kissova, and *Olympus*, now Elymbo. The summit of the latter is 6000 feet above the level of the sea."

[5] The group of islands off the north end of Eubœa, consisting of Sciathos, Scopelos, Preparethos, &c. For an account of them, see Purdy, pp. 145–148.

[6] Cousinéry somewhere gives this description of the appearance of heights near Saloniki, as seen from the Thessalian islands. For an instance of a very unfavourable voyage in these seas, in the month of December, thirteen days being spent at sea between Salonica and Zeitun, the reader may consult Holland's Travels ch. xvi.

CHAPTER X.

Ἐς δὲ τον Πειραῖα εἰσπλεύσας ἀνῄει ἀπὸ τῆς νεὼς ἐς τὸ ἄστυ . . . προϊὼν δέ, πολλοις των φιλοσοφούντων ἐνετύγχανε· . . . . . τὴν μὲν δὴ πρώτην διάλεξιν, ἐπειδὴ φιλοθύτας τοὺς Ἀθηναίους εἶδεν, ὑπὲρ ἱερῶν διελέξατο . . . καὶ ταῦτα Ἀθηνῄσιν, οὗ καὶ ἀγνώστων δαιμόνων βωμοὶ ἵδρυνται.—Philost. Vit. Ap. Ty. iv. 6. vi. 2.

ARRIVAL ON THE COAST OF ATTICA.—SCENERY ROUND ATHENS.—THE PIRÆUS AND THE "LONG WALLS."—THE AGORA.—THE ACROPOLIS.—THE "PAINTED PORCH" AND THE "GARDEN."—THE APOSTLE ALONE IN ATHENS.—GREEK RELIGION.—THE UNKNOWN GOD.—GREEK PHILOSOPHY.—THE STOICS AND EPICUREANS.—LATER PERIOD OF THE SCHOOLS.—ST. PAUL IN THE AGORA.—THE AREOPAGUS.—SPEECH OF ST. PAUL.—DEPARTURE FROM ATHENS.

To draw a parallel between a holy Apostle like Paul of Tarsus, and an itinerant magician line Apollonius of Tyana[1] would be unmeaning and profane. But the extract from the biography of that singular man which we have prefixed to this chapter is a suitable and comprehensive motto to that passage in the Apostle's biography on which we are now entering. The sailing into the Piræus,—the entrance into the city of Athens,—the interviews with philosophers,—the devotion of the Athenians to religious ceremonies, the discourse concerning the worship of the Deity,—the

[1] He has been alluded to before, p. 120, n. 2 and p. 146, n. 4. "His life by Philostratus is a mass of incongruities and fables;" but it is an important book, as reflecting the opinions of the age in which it was written. Apollonius himself produced a great excitement in the Apostolic age. See Neander's General Church History (Eng. Trans.), pp. 40–43 and pp. 236–238. It was the fashion among the Antichristian writers of the third century to adduce him as a rival of our Blessed Lord; and the same profane comparison has been renewed by some of our English freethinkers. Without alluding to this any further, we may safely find some interest in putting his life by the side of that of St. Paul. They lived at the same time, and travelled through the same countries; and the life of the magician illustrates that peculiar state of philosophy and superstition which the Gospel preached by St. Paul had to encounter. Apollonius was partly educated at Tarsus; he travelled from city to city in Asia Minor; from Greece he went to Rome, in the reign of Nero, about the time when the magicians had lately been expelled; he visited Athens and Alexandria, where he had a singular meeting with Vespasian: on a second visit to Italy he vanished miraculously from Puteoli: the last scene of his life was Ephesus, or, possibly, Crete or Rhodes. See the Life in Smith's Dictionary of Biography. It is thought by many that St. Paul and Apollonius actually met in Ephesus and Rome. Burton's Lectures on Ecclesiastical History, pp. 157, 240.

ignorance implied by the altars to *unknown Gods*,[1]—these are exactly the subjects which are now before us. If a summary of the contents of the seventeenth chapter of the Acts had been required, it could not have been more conveniently expressed. The city visited by Apollonius was the Athens which was visited by St. Paul: the topics of discussion—the character of the people addressed—the aspect of everything around,—were identically the same. The difference was this, that the Apostle could give to his hearers what the philosopher could not give. The God whom Paul "declared," was worshipped by Apollonius himself as "ignorantly" as by the Athenians.

We left St. Paul on that voyage which his friends induced him to undertake on the flight from Berœa. The vessel was last seen among the Thessalian islands.[2] About that point the highest land in Northern Macedonia began to be lost to view. Gradually the nearer heights of the snowy Olympus[3] itself receded into the distance, as the vessel on her progress approached more and more near to the centre of all the interest of classical Greece. All the land and water in sight becomes more eloquent as we advance: the lights and shadows, both of poetry and history, are on every side; every rock is a monument; every current is animated with some memory of the past. For a distance of ninety miles, from the confines of Thessaly to the middle part of the coast of Attica, the shore is protected, as it were, by the long island of Eubœa. Deep in the innermost gulf, where the waters of the Ægean retreat far within the land, over against the northern parts of this island, is the pass of Thermopylæ, where a handful of Greek warriors had defied all the hosts of Asia. In the crescent-like bay on the shore of Attica, near the southern extremity of the same island, is the maritime sanctuary of Marathon, where the battle was fought which decided that Greece was never to be a Persian Satrapy.[4] When the island of Eubœa is left behind, we soon reach the southern extremity of Attica—Cape Colonna,—Sunium's high promontory, still crowned with the white columns of that temple of Minerva, which was the landmark to Greek sailors, and which asserted the presence of Athens at the very vestibule of her country.[5]

After passing this headland, our course turns to the westward across the waters of the Saronic Gulf, with the mountains of the Morea on our left, and the islands of Ægina and Salamis in front. To one who travels in classical lands no moment is more full of interest and excitement than

[1] This subject is fully entered into below. [2] Above, p. 343.

[3] See the preceding Chapter, p. 342, also 314.

[4] See Quarterly Review, for Sept. 1846, and the first number of the Classical Museum.

[5] See Wordsworth's Athens and Attica, ch. xxvii. A description of the promontory and ruins, will be found in Mure's Journal of a Tour in Greece. See Falconer's Shipwreck, iii. 526.

when he has left the Cape of Sunium behind and eagerly looks for the first glimpse of that city "built nobly on the Ægean shore," which was "the eye of Greece, mother of arts and eloquence."[1] To the traveller in classical times its position was often revealed by the flashing of the light on the armour of Minerva's colossal statue, which stood with shield and spear on the summit of the citadel.[2] At the very first sight of Athens, and even from the deck of the vessel, we obtain a vivid notion of the characteristics of its position. And the place where it stands is so remarkable—its ancient inhabitants were so proud of its climate and its scenery[3]—that we may pause on our approach to say a few words on Attica and Athens, and their relation to the rest of Greece.

Attica is a triangular tract of country, the southern and eastern sides of which meet in the point of Sunium ; its third side is defined by the high mountain ranges of Cithæron and Parnes, which separate it by a strong barrier from Bœotia and Northern Greece. Hills of inferior elevation connect[4] these ranges with the mountainous surface of the south-east,[5] which begins from Sunium itself, and rises on the south coast to the round summits of Hymettus, and the higher peak of Pentelicus near Marathon on the east. The rest of Attica is a plain, one reach of which comes down to the sea on the south, at the very base of Hymettus. Here, about five miles from the shore, an abrupt rock rises from the level, like the rock of Stirling Castle, bordered on the south by some lower eminences, and commanded by a high craggy peak on the north. This rock is the Acropolis of Athens. These lower eminences are the Areopagus, the Pnyx, and the Museum, which determined the rising and falling of the ground in the ancient city. That craggy peak is the hill of Lycabettus,[6] from the summit of which the spectator sees all Athens at his feet,

[1] Paradise Regained, iv. 240.

[2] The expression of Pausanias is,—*Ταύτης τῆς 'Αθηνᾶς ἡ τοῦ δόρατος αἰχμὴ καὶ ὁ λόφος τοῦ κράνους ἀπὸ Σουνίου προσπλέουσιν ἔστιν ἤδη σύνοπτα*, xxviii. 2. This does not mean that it can be seen from Sunium itself, as any one must be aware who is acquainted with the position and height of Hymettus. Colonel Leake says that the view of the Acropolis is open to any vessel sailing towards it up the gulf, on a course of N. 20 W. true, and that it is first distinctly visible without a telescope about Cape Zosta. Addenda, p. 631.

[3] See, especially, Xenophon de Vectigalibus.

[4] The region which connected Parnes and Hymettus, and lay beyond it, was called Diacria.

[5] In this region of the Mesogœa there was an inland plain. The sea-coasts on the east and west, coming down to Sunium, were called Paralia.

[6] The relation of Lycabettus to the crowded buildings below, and to the surrounding landscape, is so like that of Arthur's Seat to Edinburgh and its neighbourhood, and there is so much resemblance between Edinburgh Castle and the Acropolis, that a comparison between the city of the Saronic gulf and the city of the Forth has become justly proverbial.

and looks freely over the intermediate plain to the Piræus and the sea.

Athens and the Piræus must never be considered separately. One was the city, the other was its harbour. Once they were connected together by a continuous fortification. Those who looked down from Lycabettus in the time of Pericles, could follow with the eye all the long line of wall from the temples on the Acropolis to the shipping in the port. Thus we are brought back to the point from which we digressed. We were approaching the Piræus; and, since we must land in maritime Athens before we can enter Athens itself, let us return once more to the vessel's deck, and look round on the land and the water. The island on our left, with steep cliffs at the water's edge, is Ægina. The distant heights beyond it are the mountains of the Morea. Before us is another island, the illustrious Salamis; though in the view it is hardly disentangled from the coast of Attica, for the strait where the battle was fought is narrow and winding. The high ranges behind stretch beyond Eleusis and Megara, to the left towards Corinth, and to the right along the frontier of Bœotia. This last ridge is the mountain line of Parnes, of which we have spoken above. Clouds [1] are often seen to rest on it at all seasons of the year, and in winter it is usually white with snow. The dark heavy mountain rising close to us on the right immediately from the sea, is Hymettus. Between Parnes and Hymettus is the plain; and rising from the plain is the Acropolis, distinctly visible, with Lycabettus behind, and seeming in the clear atmosphere to be nearer than it is.

The outward aspect of this scene is now what it ever was. The lights and shadows on the rocks of Ægina and Salamis, the gleams on the distant mountains, the clouds or the snow on Parnes, the gloom in the deep dells of Hymettus, the temple-crowned rock and the plain beneath it,—are natural features, which only vary with the alternations of morning and evening, and summer and winter.[2] Some changes indeed have taken place: but they are connected with the history of man. The vegetation is less abundant,[3] the population is more scanty. In Greek and Roman times, bright villages enlivened the promontories of Sunium and Ægina, and all the inner reaches of the bay. Some readers will indeed remember a dreary picture which Sulpicius gave his friend Atticus of the deso-

[1] See the passage from the Clouds of Aristophanes quoted by Dr. Wordsworth. Athens and Attica, p. 58. Theophrastus said that the weather would be fine when there was lightning only on Parnes.

[2] This is written under the recollection of the aspect of the coast on a cloudy morning in winter. It is perhaps more usually seen under the glare of a hot sky.

[3] Athens was not always as bare as it is now. See the line quoted by Dio Chrys.: ἄλση δὲ τίς πω τοιαδ' ἔσχ' ἄλλη πόλις; Plato, in the Critias, complains that the wood was diminishing.

lation of these coasts when Greece had ceased to be free;[1] but we must make some allowances for the exaggerations of a poetical regret, and must recollect that the writer had been accustomed to the gay and busy life of the Campanian shore. After the renovation of Corinth,[2] and in the reign of Claudius, there is no doubt that all the signs of a far more numerous population than at present were evident around the Saronic gulf, and that more white sails were to be seen in fine weather plying across its waters to the harbours of Cenchreæ[3] or Piræus.

Now there is indeed a certain desolation over this beautiful bay: Corinth is fallen, and Cenchreæ is an insignificant village. The Piræus is probably more like what it was, than any other spot upon the coast. It remains what by nature it has ever been,—a safe basin of deep water, concealed by the surrounding rock; and now, as in St. Paul's time, the proximity of Athens causes it to be the resort of various shipping. We know that we are approaching it at the present day, if we see, rising above the rocks, the tall masts of an English line-of-battle ship, side by side with the light spars of a Russian corvette or the black funnel of a French steamer. The details were different when the Mediterranean was a Roman lake. The heavy top-gear[4] of corn-ships from Alexandria or the Euxine might then be a conspicuous mark among the small coasting vessels and fishing-boats; and one bright spectacle was then pre-eminent, which the lapse of centuries has made cold and dim, the perfect buildings on the summit of the Acropolis, with the shield and spear of Minerva Promachus glittering in the sun.[5] But those who have coasted along beneath Hymettus,—and past the indentations in the shore,[6] which were sufficient harbours for Athens in the days of her early navigation,—and round by the ancient tomb, which tradition has assigned to Themistocles,[7] into the better and safer harbour of the Piræus,—require no great effort of the imagination to picture the Apostle's arrival. For a moment, as we near the entrance, the land rises and conceals all the plain. Idlers come down upon the rocks to watch the coming vessel. The sailors are all on the alert. Suddenly an opening is revealed; and a sharp turn of the helm brings the ship in between two moles,[8] on which towers are erected. We

[1] "Ex Asia rediens, quum ab Ægina Megaram versus navigarem, cœpi regiones circumcirca prospicere. Post me erat Ægina; ante Megara; dextra Piræus; sinistra Corinthus; quæ oppida quodam tempore florentissima fuerunt, nunc prostrata et diruta ante oculos jacent." Ep. Fam. iv. 5.

[2] Corinth was in ruins in Cicero's time. For the results of its restoration, see the next Chapter.

[3] See Acts xviii. 18. Rom. xvi. 1.

[4] See Smith's Shipwreck, &c.

[5] See above, p. 346.

[6] The harbours of Phalerum and Munychia.

[7] For the sepulchre by the edge of the water, popularly called the "tomb of Themistocles," see Leake, pp. 379, 380, and the notes.

[8] Some parts of the ancient moles are remaining.—Leake, p. 272. See what is said

are in smooth water; and anchor is cast in seven fathoms in the basin of the Piræus.[1]

The Piræus, with its suburbs (for so, though it is not strictly accurate, we may designate the maritime city), was given to Athens as a natural advantage, to which much of her greatness must be traced. It consists of a projecting portion of rocky ground, which is elevated above the neighbouring shore, and probably was originally entirely insulated in the sea. The two rivers of Athens — the Cephisus and Ilissus — seem to have formed, in the course of ages, the low marshy ground which now connects Athens with its port.[2] The port itself possesses all the advantages of shelter and good anchorage, deep water, and sufficient space.[3] Themistocles, seeing that the pre-eminence of his country could only be maintained by her maritime power, fortified the Piræus as the outpost of Athens, and enclosed the basin of the harbour as a dock within the walls.[4] In the long period through which Athens had been losing its political power, these defences had been neglected and suffered to fall into decay, or had been used as materials for other buildings: but there was still a fortress on the highest point;[5] the harbour was still a place of some resort;[6] and a considerable number of seafaring people dwelt in the streets about the sea-shore. When the republic of Athens was flourishing, the sailors

of the colossal lions now removed to Venice, which gave the harbour its modern name, p. 271.

1 "The entrance of the Piræus (Port Leoni) is known by a small obelisk built on a low point by the company of H. M. ship Cambria, in 1820, on the starboard hand going in. . . . The entrance lies E. by. S. and W. by N., and has in it nine and ten fathoms. There are three mole-heads, two of which you have on the starboard hand, and one on the larboard. When past these mole-heads, shorten all sail, luff up, and anchor in seven fathoms. The ground is clear and good. There is room enough for three frigates. As the place is very narrow, great care is required. . . . During the summer months the sea-breezes blow, nearly all day, directly into the harbour. . . . The middle channel of the harbour, with a depth of 9 or 10 fathoms, is 110 feet in breadth; the starboard channel, with 6 fathoms, 40 feet; the larboard, with 2 fathoms, only 28 feet." Purdy's Sailing Directions, p. 83.

2 See the first pages of Curtius, De Portubus Athenarum Commentatio, Hal. 1842.

3 See above, n. 2.

4 For the work of Themistocles, see Thucyd. i. 93. Corn. Nep. Them. 6, and Pausanias. For the completion of the defences during the Peloponnesian war, see Thucyd. ii. 94, and Leake's note, p. 372.

5 The height of Munychia. For the military importance of this position in the Macedonian and Roman periods. see Leake, pp. 401–412. In the same way, the Museum became more important, in the military sense, than the Acropolis, which, in every other respect, was infinitely more illustrious. Pp. 405, 406. Compare p. 429, and the expression of Diodorus, p. 386, n.

6 Strabo speaks of the population living in "villages about the port." One of them was probably near the theatre of Munychia, on the low ground on the east of the main harbour. Leake, p. 396. Even in the time of Alexander, the Piræus had so much declined that a comic writer compared it to a great empty walnut. Leake, p. 402.

were a turbulent and worthless part of its population.[1] And the Piræus under the Romans was not without some remains of the same disorderly class, as it doubtless retained many of the outward features of its earlier appearance :—the landing-places and covered porticos ;[2] the warehouses where the corn from the Black Sea used to be laid up ;[3] the stores of fish brought in daily from the Saronic Gulf and the Ægean ;[4] the gardens in the watery ground at the edge of the plain ;[5] the theatres[6] into which the sailors used to flock to hear the comedies of Menander ; and the temples[7] where they were spectators of a worship which had no beneficial effect on their characters.

Had St. Paul come to this spot four hundred years before, he would have been in Athens from the moment of his landing at the Piræus. At that time the two cities were united together by the double line of fortification, which is famous under the name of the *"Long Walls."* The space included between these two arms[8] of stone might be considered (as, indeed, it was sometimes called) a third city ; for the street of five miles in length thus formed across the plain, was crowded[9] with people, whose habitations were shut out from all view of the country by the vast wall on either side. Some of the most pathetic passages of Athenian history are associ-

[1] The *ναυτικὸς ὄχλος* of Aristophanes.

[2] We read especially of the Μακρὰ Στοά, which was also used as a market. Leake, pp. 367 and 382. See the allusions on the latter page to the meal-bazaar (*στοὰ ἀλφιτοπῶλις*) and the exchange (*δεῖγμα*) ; an armoury also (p. 365) and naval arsenals (p. 374), are mentioned. Some of these had been destroyed by Sulla.

[3] That part of the Peiraic harbour to which the corn-vessels came was called Zea. See Leake, pp. 373–376. Thucydides (viii. 90) mentions the building of some corn-warehouses. Leake, p. 378.

[4] Leake, p. 397. [5] Ibid.

[6] This theatre was on the hill of Phalerum. Leake, p. 386–388. Compare pp. 391, 392 and notes. It is mentioned by Xenophon (Hell. ii. 4, 32) in connection with the affair of Thrasybulus, during which some of the troops were driven into the theatre, like the crowd at Ephesus (Acts xix. 29). There was another theatre in Munychia, mentioned by Lysias and Thucydides ; and there too we have the mention of a great meeting during the Peloponnesian war. Leake, p. 394.

[7] See Pausanias. It is *here* that he mentions the altars to the *unknown gods* (*βωμοὶ θεῶν τε ὀνομαζομένων ἀγνώστων καὶ ἡρώων*). Clemens Alexandrinus mentions some of the statues that were seen here in his time. Leake, p. 369, n. 3, also p. 384. One of the most conspicuous temples was that dedicated to Jupiter and Minerva. Strabo and Liv. xxxi. 30, and Plin. H. N. xxxiv. 8.

[8] "Theseæ brachia longa viæ," as they are called by Propertius (iii. 20, 24) ; and again by Livy,—" Murus qui brachiis duobus Peiræum Athenis jungit " (xxxi. 26). But the name by which they were usually known at Athens, was " the *Long legs*,"—*τὰ μακρὰ σκέλη*.

[9] Andocides distinguishes the three garrisons of Athens as—*οἱ ἐν ἄστει οἰκοῦντες, οἱ ἐν μακρῷ τείχει*, and *οἱ ἐν Πειραιεῖ*. De Myst. p. 22, Reiske. So Polyænus speaks of *οἱ φύλακες τοῦ ἄστεος καὶ τοῦ Πειραιέως καὶ τῶν Σκελῶν*. i 40, 1. That the Longomural space was thickly inhabited is evident from the passages of Thucydides and Xenophon referred to below.

ated with this longomural enclosure: as when, in the beginning of the Peloponnesian war, the plague broke out in the autumn weather among the miserable inhabitants, who were crowded here to suffocation;[1] or, at the end of the same war, when the news came of the defeat on the Asiatic shore, and one long wail went up from the Piræus, "and no one slept in Athens that night."[2] The result of that victory was, that these long walls were rendered useless by being partially destroyed; and though another Athenian admiral and statesman[3] restored what Pericles[4] had first completed, this intermediate fortification remained effective only for a time. In the incessant changes which fell on Athens in the Macedonian period, they were injured and became unimportant.[5] In the Roman siege under Sulla, the stones were used as materials for other military works.[6] So that when Augustus was on the throne, and Athens had reached its ultimate position as a *free city* of the *province* of Achaia, Strabo, in his description of the place, speaks of the Long Walls as matters of past history;[7] and Pausanias, a century later, says simply that "you see the ruins of the walls as you go up from the Piræus."[8] Thus we can easily imagine the aspect of these defences in the time of St. Paul, which is intermediate to these two writers. On each side of the road[9] were the broken fragments of the rectangular masonry[10] put together in the proudest days of Athens; more conspicuous than they are at present (for now[11]

1 Thucyd. ii. 17.

2 Xen. Hell. ii. 2, 3.

3 Leake (p. 428) thinks that the Phaleric wall may have supplied the materials for Conon's restoration. "At least no further notice of the Phaleric wall occurs in history, nor have any vestiges of it been yet discovered."

4 For the progress of the work from its first commencement, see Grote's Greece, vol. v.

5 See what Livy says of their state after the death of Demetrius Poliorcetes. "Inter angustias *semiruti muri*, qui brachiis duobus Piræum Athenis jungit." xxxi. 26. Yet he afterwards speaks of their being objects of *admiration* in the time of Æm. Paulus. "Athenas plenas quidem et ipsas vetustate famæ, multa tamen visenda habentes; arcem, portus, muros Piræum urbi jungentes." xlv. 27.

6 Appian says that Sulla made use of the timber of the Academy and the stones from the Long Walls for his military works. *Ὕλην τῆς Ἀκαδημίας ἔκοπτε καὶ μηχανὰς εἰργάζετο μεγίστας· τά τε μακρὰ σκέλη καθῄρει, λίθους καὶ ξύλα καὶ γῆν ἐς τὸ χῶμα μεταβάλλων.* De Bello Mith. 30.

7 *Τῷ τείχει τούτῳ* (the Peiraic fortification) *συνῆπται τὰ καθειλκυσμένα ἐκ τοῦ ἄστεος σκέλη· ταῦτα δ' ἦν μακρὰ τείχη, τετταράκοντα σταδίων τὸ μῆκος, συνάπτοντα τὸ ἄστυ τῷ Πειραιεῖ.* Strabo, ix. 1. He goes on to say that a succession of wars had had the effect of destroying the defences of the Piræus.

8 *Ἀνιόντων ἐκ Πειραιῶς, ἐρείπια τῶν τειχῶν ἐστιν, ἃ Κόνων, ὕστερον τῆς πρὸς Κνίδῳ ναυμαχίας, ἀνέστησε.* Paus. Att. ii. 2.

9 Leake thinks that the *Hamaxitus* or carriage-way went on the outside of the northern wall (p. 384); but Forchammer has shown that this was not the case, p. 24.

10 Leake, p. 417.

11 See Leake, Wordsworth, and other modern travellers. It seems, from what Spon and Wheler say, that in 1676 the remains were larger and more continuous than at present.

only the foundations can be traced here and there across the plain), but still very different from what they were when two walls of sixty feet high, with a long succession of towers,[1] stood to bid defiance to every invader of Attica.

COIN OF ATHENS.

The consideration of the Long Walls leads us to that of the city walls themselves. Here many questions might be raised concerning the extent of the enclosure,[3] and the positions of the gates,[4] when Athens was under the Roman dominion. But all such enquiries must be entirely dismissed. We will assume that St. Paul entered the city by the gate which led from the Piræus, that this gate was identical with that by which Pausanias entered. and that its position was in the hollow between the outer slopes of the Pnyx and Museum.[5] It is no ordinary advantage that we possess a description of Athens under the Romans, by the traveller and antiquarian whose name has just been mentioned. The work of Pausanias[6] will be our

1 "There is no direct evidence of the height of the Long Walls; but, as Appian (De B. Mith. 30) informs us that the walls of the Peiraic city were forty cubits high, we may presume those of the Long Walls were not less. Towers were absolutely necessary to such a work; and the inscription relating to the Long Walls leaves no question as to their having existed." Leake, p. 424, n. 1. The inscription, to which allusion is made, was published by K. O. Müller, in his work "De Munimentis Athenarum" (Gött. 1836); it is given in Leake's Appendix.

2 From the British Museum.

3 Our plan of Athens is taken from that of Kiepert, which is based on the arguments contained in Forchammer's Topographie von Athen. (Kiel. 1841.) It differs materially from that of Leake, especially in giving a larger area to the city on the east and south, and thus bringing the Acropolis in the centre. Forchammer thinks that the traces of ancient walls, which are found on the Pnyx, &c., do not belong to the fortifications of Themistocles, but to some later defences erected by Valerian.

4 For various discussions on the gates, see Leake, Wordsworth, and Forchammer.

5 Pausanias does not mention the Peiraic gate by that name. See Leake, Wordsworth, and Forchammer. The first of these authorities places it where the modern road from the Piræus enters Athens, beyond all the high ground to the north of the Pnyx; the second places it in the hollow between the Pnyx and the Museum; the third in the same direction, but more remote from the Acropolis, in conformity with his view concerning the larger circumference of the walls.

6 Pausanias visited Athens about fifty years after St. Paul. It is probable that very

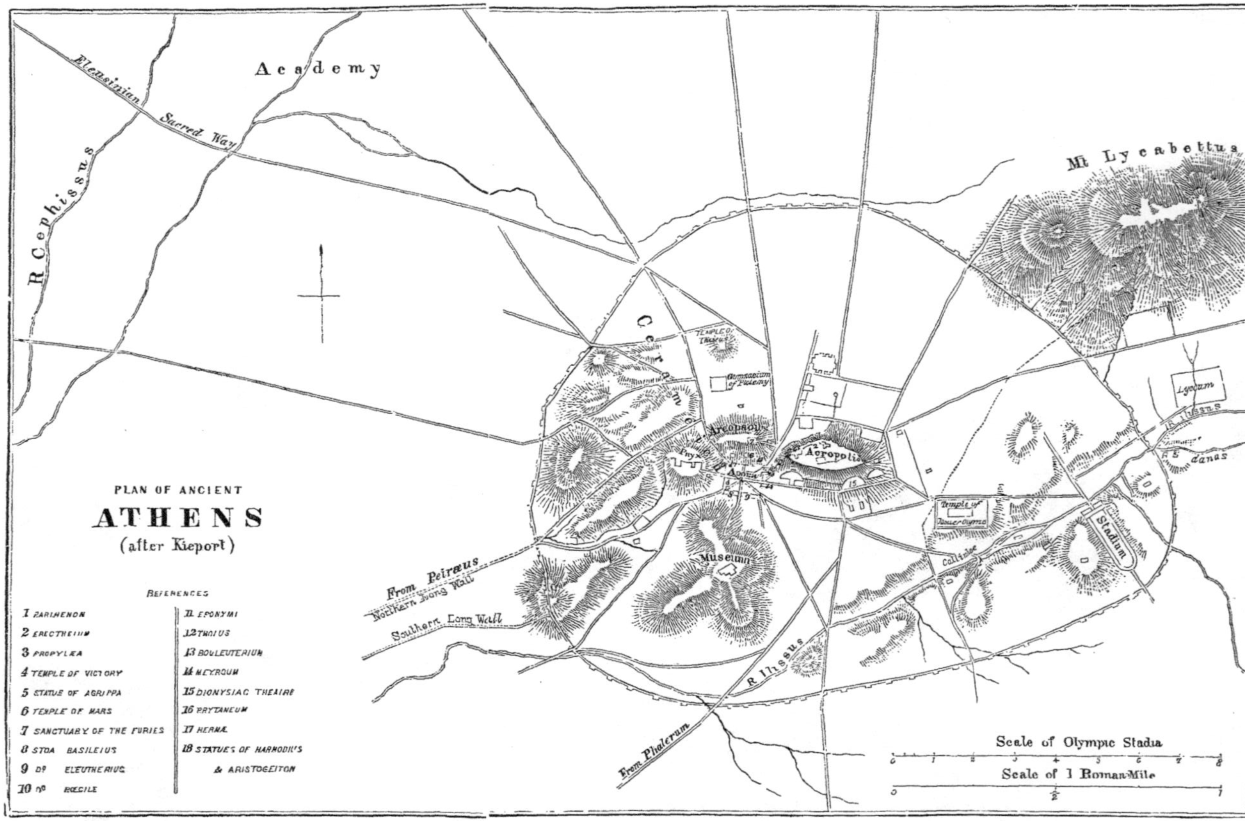

PLAN OF ANCIENT
ATHENS
(after Kiepert)
REFERENCES
1 PARTHENON
2 ERECTHEIUM
3 PROPYLÆA
4 TEMPLE OF VICTORY
5 STATUE OF AGRIPPA
6 TEMPLE OF MARS
7 SANCTUARY OF THE FURIES
8 STOA BASILEIUS
9 Dº ELEUTHERIUS
10 Dº PŒCILE
11 EPONYMI
12 THOLUS
13 BOULEUTERIUM
14 METROUM
15 DIONYSIAC THEATRE
16 PRYTANEUM
17 HERMÆ
18 STATUES OF HARMODIUS & ARISTOGEITON
Academy
Eleusinian Sacred Way
R Cephissus
Mt Lycabettus
Ceramicus
Temple of Theseus
Gymnasium of Ptolemy
Areopagus
Acropolis
Pnyx
Agora
Museum
Temple of Jupiter Olympius
Callirhoe
Stadium
Lyceum
R Ilissus
Eridanus
From Peiræus
Northern Long Wall
Southern Long Wall
From Phalerum
Scale of Olympic Stadia
Scale of 1 Roman Mile

best guide to the discovery of what St. Paul saw. By following his route through the city, we shall be treading in the steps of the Apostle himself, and shall behold those very objects which excited his indignation and compassion.

Taking, then, the position of the Peiraic gate as determined, or at least resigning the task of topographical enquiries, we enter the city, and with Pausanias as our guide, look round on the objects which were seen by the Apostle. At the very gateway we are met with proofs of the peculiar tendency of the Athenians to multiply their objects both of art and devotion.[1] Close by the building where the vestments were laid up which were used in the annual procession of their tutelary divinity Minerva,[2] is an image of her rival Neptune, seated on horseback, and hurling his trident.[3] We pass by a temple of Ceres, on the walls of which an archaic inscription[4] informs us that the statues it contains were the work of Praxiteles. We go through the gate: and immediately the eye is attracted by the sculptured forms of Minerva, Jupiter, and Apollo, of Mercury and the Muses, standing near a sanctuary of Bacchus. We are already in the midst of an animated scene, where temples, statues, and altars are on every side, and where the Athenians, fond of publicity and the open air, fond of hearing and telling what is curious and strange,[5] are enjoying their climate and enquiring for news. A long street is before us, with a colonnade or cloister on either hand, like the covered arcades of Bologna or Turin.[6] At the end of the street, by turning to the left, we might go through the whole Ceramicus,[7] which leads by the tombs of eminent Athenians to the open inland country and the groves of the Academy. But we turn to the right into the *Agora*, which *was* the centre of a glorious public life, when the orators and statesmen, the poets and the artists of Greece, found there all the incentives of their noblest enthusiasm; and still continued to be the meeting-place of philosophy, of idleness, of conversation, and of business, when Athens could only be

few changes had taken place in the city, with the exception of the new buildings erected by Adrian.

1 Acts xvii. 23.

2 This building is the Pompeium (Πομπεῖον). Paus. ii. 4. See Forchammer, p. 31.

3 We have used the terms "Minerva, Neptune," &c., instead of the more accurate terms "Athene, Poseidon," &c., in accommodation to popular language. So before Ch. VI.), in the case of Jupiter and Mercury.

4 Ἀττικοῖς γράμμασιν. Paus.

5 Acts xvii. 21.

6 Forchammer makes this comparison, p. 34. It is probable, however, that these covered walks were not formed with arches, but with pillars bearing horizontal entablatures. The position we have assigned to this street is in accordance with the plan of Forchammer, who places the wall and gate more remotely from the Agora than our English topographers.

7 This term, in its full extent, included not only the road between the city wall and the Academy, but the Agora itself. See Plan of Athens.

proud of her recollections of the past. On the south side is the *Pnyx*,[1] a sloping hill partially levelled into an open area for political assemblies; on the north side is the more craggy eminence of the *Areopagus*,[2] before us, towards the east, is the *Acropolis*,[3] towering high above the scene of which it is the glory and the crown. In the valley enclosed by these heights is the *Agora*,[4] which must not be conceived of as a great "market," (Acts xvii. 17) like the bare spaces in many modern towns, where little attention has been paid to artistic decoration, but is rather to be compared to the beautiful squares of such Italian cities as Verona and Florence, where historical buildings have closed in the space within narrow limits, and sculpture has peopled it with impressive figures. Among the buildings of greatest interest are the porticoes or cloisters, which were decorated with paintings and statuary, like the Campo Santo at Pisa. We think we may be excused for multiplying these comparisons: for though they are avowedly imperfect, they are really more useful than any attempt at description could be, in enabling us to realize the aspect of ancient Athens. Two of the most important of these were the Portico of the King, and the Portico of the Jupiter of Freedom.[5] On the roof of the former were statues of Theseus and the Day: in the front of the latter was the divinity to whom it was dedicated, and within were allegorical paintings illustrating the rise of the Athenian democracy.[6] One characteristic of the Agora was, that it was full of memorials of actual history. Among the plane trees planted by the hand of Cimon,[7] were the statues of the great men of Athens—such as Solon the lawgiver,[8] Conon the admiral,[9] Demosthenes the orator.[10] But among her historical men were her deified heroes, the representatives of her

[1] It is remarkable that the Pnyx, the famous meeting-place of the political assemblies of Athens, is not mentioned by Pausanias. This may be because there were no longer any such assemblies, and therefore his attention was not called to it; or, perhaps, it is omitted because it was simply a level space, without any work of art to attract the notice of an antiquarian.

[2] See this more fully described below. [3] See above, p. 346.

[4] We adopt the view of Forchammer, which is now generally received, that the position of the Agora was always the same. The hypothesis of a *new Agora* to the north of the Areopagus, was first advanced by Meursius and has been adopted by Leake.

[5] In the plan, these two porticoes are placed side by side, after Kiepert. Leake places them to the N. W. of the Areopagus, in accordance with his theory concerning the new Agora. See below. The first of these porticoes was so called because the King Archon held his court there. Pausanias does not give the name of the second; but it is inferred from comparing his description with other authors.

[6] Paus. iii. 2. [7] Plut. Cim. Wordsw. p. 68.

[8] Paus. xvi. 1. This was in front of the Stoa Pœcile, which will be mentioned below.

[9] Paus. iii. 1. [10] Paus. viii. 4.

mythology—Hercules and Theseus,[1]—and all the series of the Eponymi[2] on their elevated platform, from whom the tribes were named, and whom an ancient custom connected with the passing of every successive law And among the deified heroes were memorials of the older divinities,—Mercuries, which gave their name to the street in which they were placed,[3]—statues dedicated to Apollo, as patron of the city,[4] and her deliverer from plague,[5]—and, in the centre of all, the Altar of the Twelve Gods,[6] which was to Athens what the Golden Milestone was to Rome. If we look up to the Areopagus, we see the temple[7] of that deity from whom the eminence had received the name of "Mars' Hill;"[8] and we are aware that the sanctuary of the Furies[9] is only hidden by the projecting ridge beyond the stone steps and the seats of the judges. If we look forward to the Acropolis, we behold there, closing the long perspective, a series of little sanctuaries on the very ledges of the rock,—shrines of Bacchus and Æsculapius, Venus, Earth, and Ceres,[10] ending with the lovely form of that Temple of Unwinged Victory[11] which glittered by the entrance of the Propylæa above the statues of Harmodius and Aristogeiton.[12] Thus, every god in Olympus found a place in the Agora. But the religiousness of the Athenians went even further. For every public place and building was likewise a sanctuary. The Record House was a temple

1 The legends of these two heroes were frequently combined in works of art. See Wordsworth's Greece. Their statues in the Agora are mentioned by Pausanias, viii. 5.

2 Paus. viii.

3 See what Leake says on this street, p. 253. We adopt Kiepert's arrangement.

4 Apollo Patrous. His temple was called Pythium. In this building the naval car, used in the Panathenaic procession, was laid up after its festal voyages, to be exhibited to travellers; "as the Ducal barge of Venice, the Bucentoro, in which the Doge solemnized the annual marriage with the sea, is now preserved for the same purpose in the Venetian arsenal." Wordsworth, p. 189.

5 Apollo Alexicacus, who was believed to have made the plague to cease in the Peloponnesian war.

6 See Wordsworth, p. 169. This is one of the objects not mentioned by Pausanias. It was near the statue of Demosthenes.

7 See the plan.

8 Acts xvii. 22.

9 The sanctuary was in a deep cleft in the front of the Areopagus, facing the Acropolis. See below.

10 For the position of these temples, see Leake, Section VII., on the fourth part of the route of Pausanias.

11 The history of this temple is very curious. In 1676 it was found entire by Spon and Wheler. Subsequent travellers found that it had disappeared. In 1835 the various portions were discovered in an excavation, with the exception of two, which are in the British Museum. It is now entirely restored. The original structure belongs to the period of the close of the Persian wars.

12 For their position, see Pausanias. These statues were removed by Xerxes; and Alexander, when at Babylon, gave an order for their restoration. Images of Brutus and Cassius were at one time erected near them (Dio C. xlvii. 20), but probably they were removed by Augustus.

of the Mother of the Gods.[1] The Council-House held statues of Apollo and Jupiter, with an altar of Vesta.[2] The Theatre at the base of the Acropolis, into which the Athenians crowded to hear the words of their great tragedians, was consecrated to Bacchus.[3] The Pnyx, near which we entered, on whose elevated platform they listened in breathless attention to their orators, was dedicated to Jupiter[4] on High, with whose name those of the Nymphs of the Demus[5] were gracefully associated. And, as if the imagination of the Attic mind knew no bounds in this direction, abstractions were deified and publicly honoured. Altars were erected to Fame, to Modesty, to Energy, to Persuasion, and to Pity.[6] This last altar is mentioned by Pausanias among "those objects in the Agora which are not understood by all men: for," he adds, "the Athenians alone of all the Greeks give divine honour to Pity."[7] It is needless to show how the enumeration which we have made (and which is no more than a selection from what is described by Pausanias) throws light on the words of St. Luke and St. Paul; and especially how the groping after the abstract and invisible, implied in the altars alluded to last, illustrates the inscription "To the Unknown God," which was used by Apostolic wisdom to point the way to the highest truth.

What is true of Agora is still more emphatically true of the *Acropolis*, for the spirit which rested over Athens was concentrated here. The feeling of the Athenians with regard to the Acropolis was well, though fancifully, expressed by the rhetorician who said that it was the middle space of five concentric circles of a shield, whereof the outer four were Athens, Attica, Greece, and the world.[8] The platform of the Acropolis was a museum of art, of history, and of religion. The whole was "one vast

1 The *Μητρῷον*. See the plan. 2 The *Βουλευτήριον*. See the plan.

3 Its position may be seen on the plan, on the south side of the Acropolis.

4 See the inscription in Boeckh. This is attributed to the elevated position of the Pnyx as seen from the Agora. Wordsworth's Athens and Attica, p. 72.

5 See the restored inscription in Wordsworth (p. 70):—ΗΙΕΡΟΝ ΝΥΜΦΑΙΣ ΔΗΜΟΣΙΑΙΣ.

6 It is doubtful in what part of Athens the altars of Fame, Modesty, and Energy (*Αἰδοῦς καὶ Φήμης καὶ Ὁρμῆς*) were placed. Æschines alludes to the altar of Fame. The altar of Persuasion (*Πειθῶ*) was on the ascent of the Acropolis. There were many other memorials of the same kind in Athens. Cicero speaks of a temple or altar to Contumelia and Impudentia. De Leg. ii. 11. In the temple of Minerva Polias, in the Acropolis, was an altar of Oblivion. Plut. Sympos. 9.

7 *Ἐλέου βωμὸς, ᾧ μάλιστα θεῶν, ἐς ἀνθρώπινον βίον καὶ μεταβολὰς πραγμάτων ὅτι ὠφέλιμος, μόνοι τιμὰς Ἑλλήνων νέμουσιν Ἀθηναῖοι.* xvii. 1. He adds that this altar was *not so much due to their human sympathy as to their peculiar piety towards the gods*, and he confirms this opinion by proceeding to mention the altars of Fame, Modesty, and Energy.

8 *Ὥσπερ γὰρ ἐπ' ἀσπίδος κύκλων εἰς ἀλλήλους ἐμβεβηκότων, πέμπτως εἰς ὀμφαλὸν πληροῖ διὰ πάντων ὁ κάλλιστος· εἴπερ ἡ μὲν Ἑλλὰς ἐν μέσῳ τῆς πάσης γῆς· ἡ δὲ Ἀττικὴ τῆς Ἑλλάδος· τῆς δὲ χώρας ἡ πόλις· τῆς δ' αὖ πόλεως ἡ ὁμώνυμος.* Aristid. Panath. i. 99

THE AREOPAGUS.

composition of architecture and sculpture, dedicated to the national glory and to the worship of the gods." By one approach only—through the Propylæa built by Pericles—could this sanctuary be entered. If St. Paul went up that steep ascent on the western front of the rock, past the Temple of Victory, and through that magnificent portal, we know nearly all the features of the idolatrous spectacle he saw before him. At the entrance, in conformity with his attributes, was the statue of Mercurius Propylæus.[1] Further on, within the vestibule of the beautiful enclosure, were statues of Venus and the Graces.[2] The recovery of one of those who had laboured among the edifices of the Acropolis was commemorated by a dedication to Minerva as the goddess of Health.[3] There was a shrine of Diana, whose image had been wrought by Praxiteles.[4] Intermixed with what had reference to divinities, were the memorials of eminent men and of great victories. The statue of Pericles, to whom the glory of the Acropolis was due, remained there for centuries.[5] Among the sculptures on the south wall was one which recorded a victory we have alluded to,—that of Attalus over the Galatians.[6] Nor was the Roman power without its representatives on this proud pedestal of Athenian glory. Before the entrance were statues of Agrippa and Augustus;[7] and at the eastern extremity of the esplanade a temple was erected in honour of Rome and the emperor.[8] But the main characteristics of the place were mythological and religious, and truly Athenian. On the wide levelled area were such groups as the following:—Theseus contending with the Minotaur; Her-

[1] Paus. xxii. 8.

[2] These statues were said to be the work of Socrates. Paus. ib.

[3] The Minerva Hygieia was of bronze, and dedicated by Pericles in memory of the recovery of a favourite workman ot Mnesicles, the architect of the Propylæa. He had fallen from the roof, and Minerva appeared in a dream to Pericles and prescribed a remedy. Plut. Per. 13. Plin. H. N. xxii. 17.

[4] Paus. xxiii. 9.

[5] Pausanias mentions this statue twice, xxv. 1 and xxxviii. 2. It stood by a brazen chariot with four horses, mentioned by Herodotus (v. 79) as on the left hand to those who enter the Acropolis.

[6] See p. 241. Several of the statues seen by Pausanias in Athens were those of the Greek kings who reigned over the fragments of Alexander's empire. See, especially, his mention of the Ptolemies, viii. ix.

[7] One pedestal is still standing in this position, with the name of Agrippa inscribed on it. There is some reason to believe that some earlier Greek statues had been converted in this instance, as in many others, into monuments of Augustus and Agrippa. Cicero, in one of his letters from Athens, speaks indignantly of this custom: "Equidem valde ipsas Athenas amo. Odi inscriptiones alienarum statuarum." Att. vi. 1. Within the enclosure of the Acropolis, Pausanias saw a statue of Hadrian. Unless this also was a Romanized Greek statue, it was not there in St. Paul's time.

[8] This temple is not mentioned by Pausanias. Some fragments remain, and among them the inscription which records the dedication. Augustus did not allow the provinces to dedicate any temple to him except in conjunction with Rome. Suet. Aug 2. There was a temple of this kind at Cæsarea. See p. 115.

cules strangling the serpents; the Earth imploring showers from Jupiter; Minerva causing the olive to sprout while Neptune raises the waves.[1] The mention of this last group raises our thoughts to the *Parthenon*,—the Virgin's House,—the glorious temple which rose in the proudest period of Athenian history to the honour of Minerva, and which ages of war and decay have only partially defaced. The sculptures on one of its pediments represented the birth of the goddess: those on the other depicted her contest with Neptune.[2] Under the outer cornice were groups representing the victories achieved by her champions. Round the inner frieze was the long series of the Panathenaic procession.[3] Within was the colossal statue of ivory and gold, the work of Phidias, unrivalled in the world, save only by the Jupiter Olympus of the same famous artist. This was not the only statue of the Virgin Goddess within the sacred precincts; the Acropolis boasted of three Minervas.[4] The oldest and most venerated was in the small irregular temple called the Erectheium, which contained the mystic olive-tree of Minerva and the mark of Neptune's trident. This statue, like that of Diana at Ephesus (Acts xix. 35), was believed to have fallen from heaven.[5] The third, though less sacred than the Minerva Polias, was the most conspicuous of all.[6] Formed from the brazen spoils of the battle of Marathon, it rose in gigantic proportions above all the buildings of the Acropolis, and stood with spear and shield as the tutelary divinity of Athens and Attica. It was the statue which may have caught the eye of St. Paul himself, from the deck of the vessel in which he sailed round Sunium to the Piræus.[7] Now he had landed in Attica, and beheld all the wonders of that city which divides with one other city all the glory of heathen antiquity. Here, by the statue of *Minerva Promachus*, he could reflect on the meaning of the objects he had seen in his progress. His path had been among the forms of great men and deified heroes, among the temples, the statues, the altars of the gods of Greece. He had seen the creations of mythology represented to the eye, in every form of beauty and grandeur, by the sculptor and the architect. And the one overpowering result was this:—"His spirit was stirred within him, when he saw the city wholly given to idolatry."

1 These groups, among others, are mentioned by Pausanias, xxiv.

2 For descriptive papers on these pediments, see the Classical Museum, Nos. VI., XVIII., and XXII. With the remains themselves, in the Elgin Room at the British Museum, the restoration of Mr. Lucas should be studied.

3 For these sculptures, it is only necessary to refer to the Elgin Room in the British Museum.

4 See here, especially, Dr. Wordsworth's Chapter on the three Minervas.

5 Διόπετες. Its material was not marble nor metal, but olive-wood.

6 The pedestal appears to have been twenty feet, and the statue fifty-five feet, in height. Leake, p. 351. The lower part of the pedestal has lately been discovered.

7 See above, pp. 346, 348.

But we must associate St. Paul, not merely with the religion, but with the philosophy of Greece. And this, perhaps, is our best opportunity for doing so, if we wish to connect together, in this respect also, the appearance and the spirit of Athens. If the Apostle looked out from the pedestal of the Acropolis over the city and the open country, he would see the places which are inseparably connected with the names of those who have always been recognised as the great teachers of the pagan world. In opposite directions he would see the two memorable suburbs where Aristotle and Plato, the two pupils of Socrates, held their illustrious schools. Their positions are defined by the courses of the two rivers to which we have already alluded.[1] The streamless bed of the Ilissus passes between the Acropolis and Hymettus in a south-westerly direction, till it vanishes in the low ground which separates the city from the Piræus. Looking towards the upper part of this channel we see (or we should have seen in the first century) gardens with plane-trees and thickets of agnus-castus, with "others of the torrent-loving shrubs of Greece."[2] At one spot, near the base of Lycabettus, was a sacred enclosure. Here was a statue of Apollo Lycius, represented in an attitude of repose, leaning against a column, with a bow in the left hand and the right hand resting on his head. The god gave the name to the Lyceum.[3] Here among the groves, the philosopher of Stagirus,[4] the instructor of Alexander, used to walk. Here he founded the school of the Peripatetics. To this point an ancient dialogue represents Socrates as coming, outside the northern city-wall, from the grove of the Academy.[5] Following, therefore, this line in an opposite direction, we come to the scene of Plato's school. Those dark olive groves have revived after all the disasters which have swept across the plain. The Cephisus has been more highly favoured than the Ilissus. Its waters still irrigate the suburban gardens of the Athenians.[6] Its nightingales are still vocal among the twinkling olive-branches.[7] The gnarled trunks of the ancient trees of our own day could not be distinguished from those which were familiar with the presence of Plato, and are

[1] Above, p. 349.

[2] Leake, p. 275. See Plato's Phædrus. The Lyceum was remarkable for its plane-trees. Socrates used to discourse under them (Max. Tyr. 24), and Aristotle and Theophrastus afterwards enjoyed their shade (Theoph. H. Plant. i. 11). We cannot tell how far these groves were restored since the time of Sulla who cut them down. Plut. Sull. 12.

[3] Lucian. Gymnas. 7.

[4] See an allusion to his birthplace above, p. 320.

[5] 'Επορευόμην ἐξ 'Ακαδημίας εὐθὺ Λυκείου τὴν ἔξω τείχους ὑπ' αὐτὸ τὸ τεῖχος. Plat. Lys. 1.

[6] The stream is now divided and distributed, in order to water the gardens and olive-trees. Plutarch calls the Academy the best wooded of the suburbs of Athens (δενδροφορώτατον τῶν προαστείων. Sull. 12). Compare Diog. Laert. iii. 7.

[7] See the well-known chorus in Sophocles. Œd. Col. 668.

more venerable than those which had grown up after Sulla's destruction of the woods, before Cicero[1] visited the Academy in the spirit of a pilgrim. But the Academicians and Peripatetics are not the schools to which our attention is called in considering the biography of St. Paul. We must turn our eye from the open country to the city itself, if we wish to see the places which witnessed the rise of the *Stoics* and *Epicureans*. Lucian, in a playful passage, speaks of Philosophy as coming up from the Academy, by the Ceramicus, to the Agora: "and there," he says, "we shall meet her by the Stoa Pœcile."[2] Let us follow this line in imagination, and, having followed it, let us look down from the Acropolis into the Agora. There we distinguish a cloister or colonnade, which was not mentioned before, because it is more justly described in connection with the Stoics. The *Stoa Pœcile*, or the Painted Cloister,[3] gave its name to one of those sects who encountered the Apostle in the Agora. It was decorated with pictures of the legendary wars of the Athenians, of their victories over their fellow Greeks, and of the more glorious struggle at Marathon. Originally the meeting-place of the poets,[4] it became the school where Zeno met his pupils, and founded the system of stern philosophy which found adherents both among Greeks and Romans for many generations. The system of Epicurus was matured nearly at the same time and in the same neighbourhood. The site of the philosopher's garden[5] is now unknown, but it was well known in the time of Cicero;[6] and in the time of

[1] Cicero, at one time, contemplated the erection of a monument to show his attachment to the Academy. Att. vi. 1.

[2] *'Ενταῦθα γὰρ ἐν Κεραμεικῷ ὑπομενοῦμεν αὐτήν· ἡ δὲ ἤδη που ἀφίξεται, ἐπανιοῦσα ἐξ 'Ακαδημίας, ὡς περιπατήσειε καὶ ἐν τῇ Ποικίλῃ· τοῦτο γὰρ ὁσημέραι ἔθος πόιεῖν αὐτῇ.* Piscator. 13.

[3] This Stoa is the subject of a long paragraph (xv.) in Pausanias. It was one of the most famous buildings in Athens. Æschines says distinctly that it was in the Agora: —*Προσέλθετε τῇ διανοίᾳ εἰς τὴν Ποικίλην, ἁπάντων γὰρ ὑμῶν τῶν καλῶν ἔργων τὰ ὑπομνήματα ἐν τῇ ἀγόρᾳ ἀνάκειται.* C. Ctesiph. p. 163.

[4] Ritter's History of Philosophy (Eng. Trans.), vol. iii. p. 452.

[5] This garden was proverbially known among the ancients. See Juvenal, xiii. 172. (Epicurum exigui lætum plantaribus horti), and xiv. 319. (Quantum, Epicure, tibi parvis suffecit in hortis): and compare Cicero's expression, De Nat. Deorum, i. 43. (Democriti fontibus Epicurus hortulos suos irrigavit). Diogenes Laertius (x.) mentions the price at which the garden was bought. Pliny (H. N. xix. 19) traces the love of city gardens to Epicurus (Jam quidem hortorum nomine in ipsa urbe delicias, agros, villasque possident. Primus hoc instituit Athenis *Epicurus otii magister*). Some have thought that the suburb on the Ilissus, mentioned by Pausanias under the name of "the gardens" (*κῆποι*), was the scene of the home of Epicurus. But this is improbable.

[6] On his first visit to Athens, at the age of twenty-eight, Cicero lodged with an Epicurean. On the occasion of his second visit, the attachment of the Epicureans to the garden of their founder was brought before him in a singular manner. "There lived at this time in exile at Athens C. Memmius. . . . . The figure which he had borne in Rome gave him great authority in Athens; and the council of Areopagus had granted

St. Paul it could not have been forgotten, for a peculiarly affectionate feeling subsisted among the Epicureans towards their founder.[1] He left this garden as a legacy to the school, on condition that philosophy should always be taught there, and that he himself should be annually commemorated.[2] The sect was dwindled into smaller numbers than their rivals, in the middle of the first century. But it is highly probable that, even then, those who looked down from the Acropolis over the roofs of the city, could distinguish the quiet garden, where Epicurus lived a life of philosophic contentment, and taught his disciples that the enjoyment of tranquil pleasure was the highest end of human existence.

The spirit in which Pausanias traversed these memorable places and scrutinised everything he saw, was that of a curious and rather superstitious antiquarian. The expressions used by Cicero, when describing the same objects, show that his taste was gratified, and that he looked with satisfaction on the haunts of those whom he regarded as his teachers.[3] The thoughts and feelings in the mind of the Christian Apostle, who came to Athens about the middle of that interval of time which separates the visit of Pausanias from that of Cicero, were very different from those of criticism or admiration. He burned with zeal for that God whom, "as he went through the city," he saw dishonoured on every side. He was melted with pity for those who, notwithstanding their intellectual greatness, were "wholly given to idolatry." His eye was not blinded to the reality of things, by the appearance either of art or philosophy. Forms of earthly beauty and words of human wisdom were valueless in his judgment, and far worse than valueless, if they deified vice and made fasehood attractive. He saw and heard with an earnestness of conviction which no Epicurean

him a piece of ground to build upon, where Epicurus formerly lived, and where there still remained the old ruins of his walls. But this grant had given great offence to the whole body of the Epicureans, to see the remains of their master in danger of being destroyed. They had written to Cicero at Rome, to beg him to intercede with Memmius to consent to a restoration of it; and now at Athens they renewed their instances, and prevailed on him to write about it. . . . . Cicero's letter is drawn with much art and accuracy; he laughs at the trifling zeal of these philosophers for the old rubbish and paltry ruins of their founder, yet earnestly presses Memmius to indulge them in a prejudice contracted through weakness, not wickedness." Middleton's Life of Cicero, Sect. VII.

1 Ritter, iii. 401.

2 Diog. La. x. 18. Cic. de Fin. ii. 31. See Cic. Fam. xiii. 1, in the letter alluded to above, p. 360, n. 6.

3 Valde me Athenæ delectarunt: urs dunbtaxat et urbis ornamentum, et hominum amores in te, et in nos quædam benevolentia. Sed multum et philosophia. Ἄνω κάτω. Si quid est, est in Aristo, apud quem eram." Att. v. 10. If Orelli's reading in the last two clauses is correct, it would seem that the philosophers of Athens were just then all *topsy-turvy*, and that Cicero found the most satisfaction in his Epicurean friend Aristus.

could have understood, as his tenderness of affection was morally far above the highest point of the Stoic's impassive dignity.

It is this tenderness of affection which first strikes us, when we turn from the manifold wonders of Athens to look upon the Apostle himself. The existence of this feeling is revealed to us in a few words in the Epistle to the Thessalonians.[1] He was filled with anxious thoughts concerning those whom he had left in Macedonia, and the sense of solitude weighed upon his spirit. Silas and Timotheus were not arrived, and it was a burden and a grief to him to be "*left in Athens alone*." Modern travellers have often felt, when wandering alone through the streets of a foreign city, what it is to be out of sympathy with the place and the people. The heart is with friends who are far off; and nothing that is merely beautiful or curious can effectually disperse the cloud of sadness. If, in addition to this instinctive melancholy, the thought of an irreligious world, of evil abounding in all parts of society, and of misery following everywhere in its train,—if this thought also presses heavily on the spirit,—a state of mind is realised which may be some feeble approximation to what was experienced by the Apostle Paul in his hour of dejection. But with us such feelings are often morbid and nearly allied to discontent. We travel for pleasure, for curiosity, for excitement. It is well if we can take such depressions thankfully, as the discipline of a worldly spirit. Paul travelled that he might give to others the knowledge of salvation. His sorrow was only the cloud that kindled up into the bright pillar of the divine presence. He ever forgot himself in his Master's cause. He gloried that God's strength was made perfect in his weakness. It is useful, however, to us, to be aware of the human weakness of that heart which God made strong. Paul was indeed one of us. He loved his friends, and knew the trials both of anxiety and loneliness. As we advance with the subject, this and similar traits of the *man* advance more into view,—and with them, and personified as it were in him, touching traits of the *religion* which he preached, come before us,—and we see, as we contemplate the Apostle, that the Gospel has not only deliverance from the coarseness of vice and comfort for ruder sorrows, but sympathy and strength for the most sensitive and delicate minds.

No mere pensive melancholy, no vain regrets and desires, hold sway over St. Paul, so as to hinder him in proceeding with the work appointed to him. He was "in Athens alone," but he was there as the Apostle of

[1] 1 Thess. iii. 1. It may be thought that too much is built here on this one expression. But we think the remarks in the text will be justified by those who consider the tone of the Epistles to the Thessalonians (see next Chapter), and the depression and sense of isolation evidently experienced by St. Paul when he was without companions. See, especially, Acts xxviii. 15, and 2 Cor. ii. 13. vii. 5. Compare the Introduction, xvi.

God. No time was lost; and, according to his custom, he sought out his brethren of the scattered race of Israel. Though moved with grief and indignation when he saw the idolatry all around him, he deemed that his first thought should be given to his own people. They had a synagogue at Athens, as at Thessalonica, and in this synagogue he first proclaimed his Master. Jewish topics, however, are not brought before us prominently here. They are casually alluded to; and we are not informed whether the Apostle was welcomed or repulsed in the Athenian synagogue. The silence of Scripture is expressive: and we are taught that the subjects to which our attention is to be turned, are connected, not with Judaism, but with Paganism. Before we can be prepared to consider the great speech, which was the crisis and consummation of this meeting of Christianity and Paganism, our thoughts must be given for a few moments to the characteristics of Athenian religion and Athenian philosophy.

The mere enumeration of the visible objects with which the city of the Athenians was crowded, bears witness (to use St. Paul's own words) to their "carefulness in religion."[1] The judgment of the Christian Apostle agreed with that of his Jewish contemporary Josephus,[2]—with the proud boast of the Athenians themselves, exemplified in Isocrates and Plato,[3]—and with the verdict of a multitude of foreigners, from Livy to Julian,[4]—all of whom unite in declaring that Athens was peculiarly devoted to religion. Replete as the whole of Greece was with objects of devotion, the antiquarian traveller[5] informs us that there were more gods in Athens than in all the rest of the country; and the Roman satirist[6] hardly exaggerates, when he says that it is easier to find a god there than a man. But the same enumeration which proves the existence of the religious sentiment in this people, shows also the valueless character of the religion which they cherished. It was a religion which ministered to art and amusement, and was entirely destitute of moral power. Taste was gratified by the bright spectacle to which the Athenian awoke every morning of his life.

[1] See below, on the Speech.

[2] Josephus (contra Ap. I. 12) calls the Athenians *τοὺς εὐσεβεστάτους τῶν Ἑλλήνων.*

[3] *Τοὺς πρὸς τὰ τῶν θεῶν εὐσεβέστατα διακειμένους.* Isoc. Paneg. p. 19. *Οἱ πλείστας μὲν θυσίας καὶ καλλίστας τῶν Ἑλλήνων ἄγομεν, ἀναθήμασί τε κεκοσμήκαμεν τὰ ἱερὰ αὐτῶν, ὡς οὐδένες ἄλλοι, πομπάς τε πολυτελεστάτας καὶ σεμνοτάτας ἐδωρούμεθα τοῖς θεοῖς, ἀν' ἕκαστον ἔτος, καὶ ἐτελοῦμεν χρήματα, ὅσα οὐδ' οἱ ἄλλοι ξύμπαντες Ἕλληνες.* Alcib. II. p. 97. Compare Thucyd. ii. 38.

[4] Athenas inde plenas quidem et ipsas vetustate famæ, multa tamen visenda habentes . . . . simulacra Deorum hominumque, omni genere et materiæ et artium insignia. Lib. xlv. 27. *Φιλόθεοι μάλιστα πάντων εἰσι . . . καθόλου μὲν Ἕλληνες πάντες, αὐτῶν δ' Ἑλλήνων πλέον τοῦτο ἔχω μαρτυρεῖν Ἀθηναίοις.* Jul. Misopogon. See also Dionys. Hal. de Thuc. 40. Strabo, x. Lucian, Prom. 180. Æl. v. 17. Philostr. vi. 2.

[5] *Ἀθηναίοις περισσότερόν τι ἢ τοῖς ἄλλοις ἐς τὰ θεῖά ἐστι σπουδῆς.* Paus. xxiv 3. Compare his remark with reference to the altar of Pity, xvii. 1.

[6] Petron. Sat. c. 17.

Excitement was agreeably kept up by festal seasons, gay processions, and varied ceremonies. But all this religious dissipation had no tendency to make him holy. It gave him no victory over himself: it brought him no nearer to God. A religion which addresses itself only to the taste, is as weak as one that appeals only to the intellect. The Greek religion was a mere deification of human attributes and the powers of nature. It was doubtless better than other forms of idolatry which have deified the brutes; but it had no real power to raise him to a higher position than that which he occupied by nature. It could not even keep him from falling continually to a lower degradation.[1] To the Greek this world was everything: he hardly even sought to rise above it. And thus all his life long, in the midst of everything to gratify his taste and exercise his intellect, he remained in ignorance of God. This fact was tacitly recognised by the monuments in his own religious city. The want of something deeper and truer was expressed on the very stones. As we are told by a Latin writer[2] that the ancient Romans, when alarmed by an earthquake, were accustomed to pray, not to some one of the gods individually, but to god in general, *as to the Unknown;* so the Athenians acknowledged their ignorance of the True Deity by the altars "with this inscription, TO THE UNKNOWN GOD," which are mentioned by heathen writers,[3] as well as by the inspired historian. Whatever the origin of these altars may have been,[4] the true significance of the inscription is that which is pointed out by the Apostle himself.[5] The Athenians were ignorant of the right object of worship. But if we are to give a true account of Athenian religion, we must go beyond the darkness of mere ignorance into the deeper darkness of corruption and sin. The most shameless profligacy was encouraged by

[1] See the Introduction to Neander's general Church History.

[2] Aulus Gellius, I. 28, quoted by Tholuck in his Essay on the Nature and Moral Influence of Heathenism, Eng. Trans. p. 23.

[3] The two heathen writers who mention these altars are Pausanias and Philostratus. See above. The passage often quoted from Lucian is not believed to be of any force.

[4] It is very probable that they originated from a desire to dedicate the altar to *the god* under whose censure the dedicator had fallen, whom he had unwittingly offended, or whom, in the particular case, he ought to propitiate (τῷ προσήκοντι θεῷ, as it is expressed in the story of Epimenides. Diog. Laert. L. 1). Eichorn thinks that these altars belonged to a period when writing was unknown, and that the inscription was added afterwards by those who were ignorant of the deity to which they were consecrated. Jerome says that the inscription was not as St. Paul quoted it, but in the form of a general dedication to all unknown gods. "Inscriptio autem aræ non ita erat ut Paulus asseruit, *Ignoto Deo;* sed ita, *Diis Asiæ et Europæ, Diis ignotis et peregrinis.* Verum quia Paulus non pluribus indigebat Diis ignotis sed uno tantum Deo ignoto, singulari verbo usus est." But unless St. Paul quoted the actual words, his application of the inscription would lose nearly all its point. Some have fancifully found in the inscription an allusion to the God of the Jews. For some of the notions of the older antiquarians concerning the "temple" of the Unknown God, see Leake.

[5] Acts xvii. 23

the public works of art, by the popular belief concerning the character of the gods, and by the ceremonies of the established worship. Authorities might be crowded in proof of this statement, both from heathen and Christian writings.[1] It is enough to say with Seneca,[2] that "no other effect could possibly be produced, but that all shame on account of sin must be taken away from men, if they believe in such gods;" and with Augustine,[3] that "Plato himself, who saw well the depravity of the Grecian gods, and has seriously censured them, better deserves to be called a god, than those ministers of sin." It would be the worst delusion to infer any good of the Grecian religion from the virtue and wisdom of a few great Athenians whose memory we revere. The true type of the character formed by the influences which surround the Athenian, was such a man as Alcibiades,—with a beauty of bodily form equal to that of one of the consecrated statues,—with an intelligence quick as that of Apollo or Mercury,—enthusiastic and fickle,—versatile and profligate,—able to admire the good, but hopelessly following the bad. And if we turn to the one great exception in Athenian history,—if we turn from Alcibiades to the friend who nobly and affectionately warned him,—who, conscious of his own ignorance, was yet aware that God was best known by listening to the voice within,—yet even of Socrates we cannot say more than has been said in the following words: His soul was certainly in some alliance with the Holy God; he certainly felt, in his dæmon or guardian spirit, the inexplicable nearness of his Father in heaven; but he was destitute of a view of the divine nature in the humble form of a servant, the Redeemer with the crown of thorns; he had no ideal conception of that true holiness, which manifests itself in the most humble love and the most affectionate humility. Hence, also, he was unable to become fully acquainted with his own heart, though he so greatly desired it. Hence, too, he was destitute of any deep humiliation and grief on account of his sinful wretchedness, of that true humility which no longer allows itself a biting, sarcastic tone of instruction; and destitute, likewise, of any filial, devoted love. These perfections can be shared only by the Christian, who beholds the Redeemer as a wanderer upon earth in the form of a servant; and who receives in his own soul the sanctifying power of that Redeemer by intercourse with Him."[4]

When we turn from the religion of Athens to take a view of its Philosophy, the first name on which our eye rests is again that of Socrates.[5]

[1] A great number of passages are collected together by Tholuck. See the quotations from Augustine and Clemens Alexandrinus, pp. 106–108; and from Martial, Terence, and Athenæus, pp. 125, 126. For practices connected with the temples, see p. 120.

[2] De Vitâ beatâ, c. 26.

[3] De Civ. Dei, ii. 14.

[4] Tholuck, p. 163.

[5] For Socrates, see especially the Eighth Volume of Grote's History, and the Quarterly Review for Dec. 1850.

This is necessarily the case, not only because of his own singular and unapproached greatness; but because he was, as it were, the point to which all the earlier schools converged, and from which the later rays of Greek philosophy diverged again. The earlier philosophical systems, such as that of Thales in Asia Minor, and Pythagoras in Italy, were limited to physical inquiries: Socrates was the first to call man to the contemplation of himself, and became the founder of ethical science.[1] A new direction was thus given to all the philosophical schools which succeeded; and Socrates may be said to have prepared the way for the Gospel, by leading the Greek mind to the investigation of moral truth. He gave the impulse to the two schools which were founded in the Lyceum, and by the banks of Cephisus,[2] and which have produced such vast results on human thought in every generation. We are not called here to discuss the doctrines of the Peripatetics and Academicians. Not that they are unconnected with the history of Christianity: Plato and Aristotle have had a great work appointed to them, not only as the Heathen pioneers of the Truth before it was revealed, but as the educators of Christian minds in every age. The former enriched human thought with appropriate ideas for the reception of the highest truth in the highest form; the latter mapped out all the provinces of human knowledge, that Christianity might visit them and bless them. And the historian of the Church would have to speak of direct influence exerted on the Gospel by the Platonic and Aristotelian systems, in recounting the conflicts of the parties of Alexandria, and tracing the formation of the theology of the Schoolmen. But the biographer of St. Paul has only to speak of the *Stoics* and *Epicureans*. They only, among the various philosophers of the day, are mentioned as having argued with the Apostle; and their systems had really more influence in the period in which the Gospel was established, though, in the Patristic and Medieval periods, the older systems, in modified forms, regained their sway. The Stoic and Epicurean, moreover, were more exclusively limited than other philosophers to moral investigations,[3]—a fact which is tacitly implied by the proverbial application of the two words to moral principles and tendencies, which we recognise as hostile to true Christianity.

Zeno, the founder of the Stoic school, was a native of the same part

[1] "La philosophie grecque avait été d'abord une philosophie de la nature; arrivée à sa maturité, elle change de caractère et de direction, et elle devient une philosophie morale, sociale, humaine. C'est Socrate que ouvre cette nouvelle ère, et qui en représente le caractère en sa personne." V. Cousin, p. 226.

[2] See above, p. 359.

[3] "Aristote et Platon, en restant fidèles à l'esprit de Socrate, en partant de la nature humaine, arrivent bientôt à un système complet qui renferme avec la nature humaine la nature entière, Dieu et le monde. . . . . Le caractère commun du Stoïcisme et de l'Epicuréisme, est de réduire presque entièrement la philosophie à la morale." V. Cousin, p. 250.

of the Levant with St. Paul himself.[1] He came from Cyprus to Athens at a time when patriotism was decayed and political liberty lost, and when a system, which promised the power of brave and self-sustaining endurance amid the general degradation, found a willing acceptance among the nobler minds. Thus, in the Painted Porch, which had once been the meeting-place of the poets,[2] those who, instead of yielding to the prevailing evil of the times, thought they were able to resist it, formed themselves into a school of philosophers. In the high tone of this school, and in some part of its ethical language, Stoicism was an apparent approximation to Christianity; but, on the whole, it was a hostile system, in its physics, its morals, and its theology. The Stoics condemned the worship of images and the use of temples, regarding them as nothing better than the ornaments of art.[3] But they justified the popular polytheism, and in fact, considered the gods of mythology as minor developments of the Great World-God, which summed up their belief concerning the origin and existence of the world. The Stoics were Pantheists;[4] and much of their language is a curious anticipation of the phraseology of modern Pantheism. In their view, God was merely the Spirit or Reason of the Universe. The world was itself a rational soul, producing all things out of itself, and resuming them all to itself again.[5] Matter was inseparable from the Deity.[6] He did not create: He only organised.[7] He merely impressed law and order on the substance, which was, in fact, himself. The manifestation of the Universe was only a period in the development of God.[8] In conformity with these notions of the world, which substitute a sublime destiny for the belief in a personal Creator and Preserver, were the notions which were held concerning the soul and its relation to the body. The soul was, in fact, corporeal.[9] The Stoics said that at death it would be burnt, or return to be absorbed in God. Thus, a resurrection from the dead, in the sense in which the Gospel has revealed it, must have appeared to the Stoics irrational. Nor was their moral system less hostile to "the truth

[1] He was born at Citium in Cyprus. [See p. 155.] His attention was turned to philosophy by the books brought from Athens by his father, who was a merchant. Somewhere between the ages of twenty and thirty he was shipwrecked near the Piræus, and settled in Athens. The exact dates of his birth and death were not known, but he lived through the greater part of the century between B. C. 350 and B. C. 250. A portrait-bust at Naples is assigned to him, but there is some doubt whether it is to be referred to him or to Zeno the Eleatic. See Müller's Handbuch der Archäologie, p. 730.

[2] See above, p. 360.

[3] Ritter, pp. 537, 538.

[4] Ibid., p. 509. Also pp. 515, 516.

[5] Ibid., p. 592.

[6] *'Ουσίαν δὲ Θεοῦ Ζήνων μέν φησι τὸν ὅλον Κόσμον καὶ τὸν ὀυρανόν.* Diog. La. vii. 148. See Plut. de Stoic. Rep. 34.

[7] "Le Dieu des Stoïciens n'a pas créé la nature, il l'a formée et organisée." V. Cousin, who, however, will not allow the Stoical system to be Pantheistic.

[8] Ritter, p. 593.

Ibid. pp. 512, 549. Compare the whole passage, pp. 518–556.

as it is in Jesus." The proud ideal which was set before the disciple of Zeno was, a magnanimous self-denial, an austere apathy, untouched by human passion, unmoved by change of circumstance. To the Wise man all outward things were alike. Pleasure was no good. Pain was no evil. All actions conformable to Reason were equally good; all actions contrary to Reason were equally evil.[1] The Wise man lives according to Reason; and living thus, he is perfect and self-sufficing. He reigns supreme as a king:[2] he is justified in boasting as a god.[3] Nothing can well be imagined more contrary to the spirit of Christianity. Nothing could be more repugnant to the Stoic than the news of a "Saviour," who has atoned for our sin, and is ready to aid our weakness. Christianity is the School of Humility: Stoicism was the Education of Pride. Christianity is a discipline of life: Stoicism was nothing better than an apprenticeship for death.[4] And fearfully were the fruits of its principle illustrated both in its earlier and late disciples. Its two first leaders[5] died by their own hands; like the two Romans[6] whose names first rise to the memory, when the school of the Stoics is mentioned. But Christianity turns the desperate resolution, that seeks to escape disgrace by death, into the anxious question, "What must I do to be saved?"[7] It softens the pride of stern indifference into the consolation of mutual sympathy. How great is the contrast between the Stoic ideal and the character of Jesus Christ! How different is the acquiescence in an iron destiny from the trust in a merciful and watchful Providence! How infinitely inferior is that sublime egotism, which looks down with contempt on human weakness, with the religion which tells us that "they who mourn are blessed," and which commands to "rejoice with them that rejoice, and to weep with them that weep."

If Stoicism, in its full development, was utterly opposed to Christianity, the same may be said of the very primary principles of the Epi-

[1] See the description which a contemporary of St. Paul gives of Stoicism. "Doctores sapientiæ, qui sola bona quæ honesta, mala tantum quæ turpia; potentiam, nobilitatem, cæteraque extra animum, neque bonis neque malis adnumerant." Tac. Hist. iv. 5.

[2] Hor. Sat. I. iii. Ep. I. i.

[3] Plut. de Stoic. Rep. 13. Adv. Stoic. 33.

[4] "Le Stoïcisme est essentiellement solitaire; c'est le soin exclusif de son âme, sans regard à celle des autres; et, comme la seule chose importante est la pureté de l'âme, quand cette pureté est trop en péril, quand on désespère d'être victorieux dans la lutte, on peut la terminer comme l'a terminée Caton. Ainsi la philosophie n'est plus qu'*un apprentissage de la mort* et non de la vie; elle tend à la mort par son image, l'apathie et l'ataraxie, et se résout définitivement en *un égoïsme sublime.*" V. Cousin.

[5] Zeno and Cleanthes. And yet Cleanthes was the author of that hymn which is, perhaps, the noblest approximation to a Christian hymn that heathenism has produced. See p. 5. The hymn is given in Bloomfield's Recensio Synoptica on Acts xvii. 28, where there is some doubt whether the Apostle quotes from Cleanthes or Aratus. See below.

[6] Cato and Seneca.

[7] See p. 308.

curean[1] school. If the Stoics were Pantheists, the Epicureans were virtually Atheists. Their philosophy was a system of materialism, in the strictest sense of the word; in their view, the world was formed by an accidental concourse of atoms, and was not in any sense created, or even modified, by the Divinity. They did indeed profess a certain belief in what were called gods; but these equivocal divinities were merely phantoms,—impressions on the popular mind,—dreams, which had no objective reality, or at least exercised no active influence on the physical world or the business of life. The Epicurean deity, if self-existent at all, dwelt apart, in serene indifference to all the affairs of the universe. The universe was a great accident, and sufficiently explained itself without any reference to a higher power. The popular mythology was derided, but the Epicureans had no positive faith in anything better. As there was no creator, so there was no moral governor: all notions of retribution and of a judgment to come were of course forbidden by such a creed. The principles of the atomic theory, when applied to the constitution of man, must have caused the resurrection to appear an absurdity. The soul was nothing without the body;[2] or rather, the soul was itself a body, composed of finer atoms, or at best an unmeaning compromise between the material and immaterial.[3] Both body and soul were dissolved together and dissipated into the elements; and when this occurred, all the life of man was ended. The moral result of such a creed was necessarily that which the Apostle Paul described:[4]—"If the dead rise not, let us eat and drink: for to-morrow we die." The essential principle of the Epicurean philosopher was that there was nothing to alarm[5] him, nothing to disturb him. His furthest reach was to do deliberately what the animals do instinctively;[6] his highest aim was to gratify himself. With the coarser and more energetic minds, this principle inevitably led to the grossest sensuality and crime; in the case of others, whose temperament was more common-place, or whose taste was more pure, the system took the form of a selfishness more refined. As the Stoic sought to resist the evil which surrounded him, the Epicurean endeavoured to console himself by a tranquil and indifferent life. He avoided the more violent excitements of political and social engagements,[7] to enjoy the seclusion of a calm contentment. But pleasure was still the end at which he aimed; and if we remove this end to its remotest distance, and understand it to mean an

[1] Epicurus, who founded, and indeed matured, this school (for its doctrines were never further developed), was born in Samos, B. C. 342, though his parents were natives of Attica. He died B. C. 270. An authentic bust has been preserved of him, which is engraved in Visconti's Iconographic Grecque, and again in Milman's Horace, p. 391.

[2] Ritter, p. 440.

[3] Colebrook on Indian Philosophy, quoted by Cousin., p. 255.

[4] 1 Cor. xv. 32. [5] Ritter, p. 430. [6] Ritter, p. 408.

[7] The motto of Epicurus was λάθε βιώσας.

enjoyment which involves the most manifold self-denial,—if we give Epicurus credit for taking the largest view of consequences,—and if we believe that the life of his first disciples was purer than there is reason to suppose,[1]—the end remains the same. Pleasure, not duty, is the motive of moral exertion; expediency is the test to which actions are referred; and the self-denial itself, which an enlarged view of expediency requires, will probably be found impracticable without the grace of God. Thus, the Gospel met in the Garden an opposition not less determined, and more insidious, than the antagonism of the Porch. The two enemies it has ever had to contend with are the two ruling principles of the Epicureans and Stoics,—*Pleasure* and *Pride.*

Such, in their original and essential character, were the two schools of philosophy with which St. Paul was brought directly in contact. We ought, however, to consider how far these schools had been modified by the lapse of time, by the changes which succeeded Alexander and accompanied the formation of the Roman Empire, and by the natural tendencies of the Roman character. When Stoicism and Epicureanism were brought to Rome, they were such as we have described them. In as far as they were speculative systems, they found little favour: Greek philosophy was always regarded with some degree of distrust among the Romans. Their mind was alien from science and pure speculation. Philosophy, like art and literature, was of foreign introduction. The cultivation of such pursuits was followed by private persons of wealth and taste, but was little extended among the community at large. There were no public schools of philosophy at Rome. Where it was studied at all, it was studied, not for its own sake, but for the service of the state.[2] Thus, the peculiarly practical character of the Stoic and Epicurean systems recommended them to the notice of many. What was wanted in the prevailing misery of the Roman world was a philosophy of life. There were some who weakly yielded, and some who offered a courageous resistance, to the evil of the times. The former, under the name of Epicureans, either spent their time in a serene tranquillity, away from the distractions and disorders of political life, or indulged in the grossest sensualism, and justified it on principle. The Roman adherents of the school of Epicurus were never numerous, and few great names can be mentioned among them; though one monument remains, and will ever remain, of this phase of philosophy, in the poem of Lucretius. The Stoical school was more congenial to the endurance of the Roman character; and it educated the minds of some of the noblest men of the time, who scorned to be carried away by the stream of vice. Three great names can be mentioned, which divided the period

[1] See what Ritter says of the scenes of sensuality witnessed in the Garden even in the lifetime of Epicurus, p. 402.

[2] See the Fifth Volume of Tennemann's Geschichte der Philosophie, Einl., pp. 1–13.

between the preaching of St. Paul and the final establishment of Christianity,—Seneca, Epictetus, and Antoninus Pius.[1] But such men were few in a time of general depravity and unbelief. And such was really the character of the time. It was a period in the history of the world, when conquest and discovery, facilities of travelling, and the mixture of races, had produced a general fusion of opinions, resulting in an indifference to moral distinctions, and at the same time encouraging the most abject credulity.[2] The Romans had been carrying on the work which Alexander and his successors had begun. A certain degree of culture was very generally diffused. The opening of new countries excited curiosity. New religions were eagerly welcomed; immoral rites found willing votaries. Vice and superstition went hand in hand through all parts of society, and, as the natural consequence, a scornful scepticism held possession of all the higher intellects.

But though the period of which we are speaking was one of general scepticism, for the space of three centuries the old dogmatic schools still lingered on, more especially in Greece.[3] Athens was indeed no longer what she had once been, the centre from which scientific and poetic light radiated to the neighbouring shores of Asia and Europe. Philosophy had found new homes in other cities, more especially in Tarsus and Alexandria.[4] But Alexandria, though she was commercially great and possessed the trade of three continents, had not yet seen the rise of her greatest schools; and Tarsus could never be what Athens was, even in her decay, to those who travelled with cultivated tastes and for the purposes of education. Thus Philosophy still maintained her seat in the city of Socrates. The four great schools, the Lyceum and the Academy, the Garden and the Porch, were never destitute of exponents of their doctrines. When Cicero came, not long after Sulla's siege, he found the philosophers in residence.[5] As the empire grew, Athens assumed more and more the character of an university town. After Christianity was first preached there, this character was confirmed to the place by the embellishments and the benefactions of Hadrian.[6] And before the schools were closed by the orders of Justinian,[7] the city which had received Cicero and Atticus[8] as students together, became the scene of the college friendship of St

[1] The approximation of the later Stoics, especially Epictetus, to Christianity, is remarkable. Hence the emphasis laid by Milton on the Stoic's "philosophick pride, by him called virtue." Paradise Regained, iv. 300.

[2] See Tennemann, Tholuck, and Neander. [3] Tennemann.

[4] For the schools of Tarsus, see pp. 22, 105.

[5] See above, p. 360, and the notes.

[6] Between the visits of St. Paul and Pausanias, Hadrian made vast additions to the buildings of Athens, and made large endowments for the purposes of education.

[7] See Gibbon, xl. [8] See Middleton's Life.

Basil and St. Gregory,[1] one of the most beautiful episodes of primitive Christianity.

Thus, St. Paul found philosophers at Athens, among those whom he addressed in the Agora. This, as we have seen, was the common meeting place of a population always eager for fresh subjects of intellectual curiosity. Demosthenes had rebuked the Athenians for this idle tendency four centuries before, telling them that they were always craving after news and excitement, at the very moment when destruction was impending over their liberties.[2] And they are described in the same manner, on the occasion of St. Paul's visit, as giving their whole leisure to telling and hearing something newer than the latest news.[3] Among those who sauntered among the plane trees[4] of the Agora, and gathered in knots under the porticos, eagerly discussing the questions of the day, were philosophers, in the garb of their several sects, ready for any new question, on which they might exercise their subtlety or display their rhetoric. Among the other philosophers, the Stoics and Epicureans would more especially be encountered; for the "Painted Porch"[5] of Zeno was in the Agora itself, and the "Garden"[6] of the rival sect was not far distant. To both these classes of hearers and talkers—both the mere idlers and the professors of philosophy—any question connected with a new religion was peculiarly welcome; for Athens gave a ready acceptance to all superstitions and ceremonies, and was glad to find food for credulity or scepticism, ridicule or debate. To this motley group of the Agora, St. Paul made known the two great subjects he had proclaimed from city to city. He spoke aloud of "Jesus and the Resurrection,"[7]—of that Name which is above every name,—that consummation which awaits all the generations of men who have successively passed into the sleep of death. He was in the habit of conversing "daily" on these subjects with those whom he met. His varied experience of men, and his familiarity with many modes of thought, enabled him to present these subjects in such a way as to arrest attention. As regards the philosophers, he was providentially prepared for his collision with them. It was not the first time he had encountered

[1] Basil and Gregory Nazianzene were students together at Athens from 351 to 355. Julian was there at the same time.

[2] Ἡμεῖς δὲ, εἰρήσεται γὰρ τἀληθὲς, οὐδὲν ποιοῦντες ἐνθαδε καθήμεθα, μέλλοντες ἀει καὶ ψηφιζόμενοι, καὶ πυνθανόμενοι κατὰ τὴν ἀγόραν, εἴ τι λέγεται νεώτερον. Demosth. ad Ep. Phil., and c. Phil. I. So Thucydides calls his countrymen νεωτεροποιοί; and Dicæarchus says that the people of Attica are περίεργοι ταῖς λαλιαῖς.

[3] Acts xvii. 21.

[4] See above, 354. It is, of course, impossible to prove that Cimon's plane-trees were succeeded by others; but a boulevard is commonly renewed when a city recovers from its disasters.

[5] For the Στόα ποικίλη, see above, p. 360.

[6] See again above, p. 360.

[7] Acts xvii. 18.

them.[1] His own native city was a city of philosophers, and was especially famous (as we have remarked before) for a long line of eminent Stoics, and he was doubtless familiar with their language and opinions.

Two different impressions were produced by St. Paul's words, according to the disposition of those who heard him. Some said that he was a mere "babbler,"[2] and received him with contemptuous derision. Others took a more serious view, and, supposing that he was endeavouring to introduce new objects of worship,[3] had their curiosity excited, and were desirous to hear more. If we suppose a distinct allusion, in these two classes, to the two philosophical sects which have just been mentioned, we have no difficulty in seeing that the Epicureans were those who, according to their habit, received the new doctrine with ridicule,[4]—while the Stoics, ever tolerant of the popular mythology, were naturally willing to hear of the new "dæmons" which this foreign teacher was proposing to introduce among the multitude of Athenian gods and heroes. Or we may imagine that the two classes denote the philosophers on the one hand, who heard with scorn the teaching of a Jewish stranger untrained in the language of the schools,—and the vulgar crowd on the other, who would easily entertain suspicion (as in the case of Socrates) against any one seeking to cast dishonour on the national divinities, or would at least

[1] See Ch. III. p. 105. Two of the most influential of the second generation of Stoics were Antipater of Tarsus and Zeno of Tarsus. Chrysippus also is said by Strabo to have been a native of the same place.

[2] Σπερμολόγος is properly a bird that picks up seeds from the ground, and it is so used in the "Birds" of Aristophanes. Hence, secondarily, it may mean a pauper who prowls about the market-place, or a parasite who lives by his wits (ex alienis victitans), and hence "a contemptible and worthless person." Or, from the perpetual chattering and chirping of such birds, the word may denote an idle "babbler." See Meyer. The former appears the truest view. See the quotations in Suicer's Thesaurus. The primary meaning of the word is given by Chrysostom in a striking sentence in one of his homilies on the Thessalonians *Ἂν μὴ γεωργοὶ, τὴν γῆν ἀναμοχλεύσαντες, περιστείλωσι τὰ καταβαλλόμενα, τοῖς σπερμολόγοις ὀρνέοις ἔσπειραν.*

[3] *Καίνα δαιμόνια* (Acts xvii. 18); the very words used in the accusation against Socrates. *'Αδίκεῖ Σωκράτης, οὒς μὲν ἡ πόλις νομίζει θεοὺς, οὐ νομίζων, ἕτερα δὲ καινὰ δαιμόνια εἰσφέρων.* Xen. Mem. i. 1. The word *δαιμόνιον* is probably here used quite generally. This is the only place where it occurs in the Acts of the Apostles. See the remarks which have been made before on this subject, pp. 298–300. Maximus Tyrius gives the strict definition of *δαιμων* in the following passage. *Τίθεσο θεὸν μὲν, κατὰ τὸ ἀπαθὲς καὶ ἀθάνατον· δαίμονα δὲ, κατὰ τὸ ἀθάνατον καὶ ἐμπαθές· ἄνθρωπον δὲ, κατὰ τὸ ἐμπαθὲς καὶ θνητόν.* Diss. xxiv. In another place he says that the god and the dæmon have this in common, that they are immortal; the dæmon and the man, that they have passion; the man and the animal, that they have sense; the animal and the plant, that they have life. Diss. xv.

[4] See what Lucian says in the Life of Alexander of Abonoteichus: *Οἱ μὲν ἀμφὶ τὸν Πλάτωνα καὶ Χρύσιππον καὶ Πυθαγόραν, φίλοι, καὶ εἰρήνη βαθεῖα πρὸς ἐκείνους ἦν· ὁ δὲ ἄτεγκτος 'Επίκουρος (οὕτω γὰρ αὐτὸν ὠνόμαζεν) ἔχθιστος δικαίως, πάντα ταῦτα ἐν γέλωτι καὶ παιδιᾷ τιθέμενος.* § 25.

be curious to hear more of this foreign and new religion. It is not, however, necessary to make any such definite distinction between those who derided and those who listened. Two such classes are usually found among those to whom truth is presented. When Paul came among the Athenians, he came, "not with enticing words of man's wisdom," and to some of the "Greeks" who heard him, the Gospel was "foolishness;"[1] while in others there was at least that curiosity which is sometimes made the path whereby the highest truth enters the mind; and they sought to have a fuller and more deliberate exposition of the mysterious subjects, which now for the first time had been brought before their attention.

The place to which they took him was the summit of the hill of Areopagus, where the most awful court of judicature had sat from time immemorial, to pass sentence on the greatest criminals, and to decide the most solemn questions connected with religion.[2] The judges sat in the open air, upon seats hewn out in the rock, on a platform, which was ascended by a flight of stone steps immediately from the Agora.[3] On this spot a long series of awful causes, connected with crime and religion, had been determined, beginning with the legendary trial of Mars,[4] which gave to the place its name of "Mars' Hill." A temple of the god,[5] as we have seen, was on the brow of the eminence; and an additional solemnity was given to the place by the sanctuary of the Furies,[6] in a broken cleft of the rock, immediately below the judges' seat. Even in the political decay of

[1] See 1 Cor. i. 18.—ii. 5.

[2] For the early history of the court, see Hermann's Lehrbuch der G. Staatsalterthümer, c. v., and Grote, vol. v. For miscellaneous details, see Meursius in Gronov. Thes.

[3] Ὑπαίθριοι ἐδίκαζον. Julius Pollux. Vitruvius mentions a building which Leake (p. 356) thinks may sometimes have been used by the Areopagites. "Athenis Areopagi antiquitatis exemplar ad hoc tempus luto tectum." Vit. ii. 1. The number of steps is sixteen. See Wordsworth's Athens and Attica, p. 73. "Sixteen stone steps cut in the rock, at its south-east angle, lead up to the hill of the Areopagus from the valley of the Agora, which lies between it and the Pnyx. This angle seems to be the point of the hill on which the council of the Areopagus sat. Immediately above the steps, on the level of the hill, is a bench of stone excavated in the limestone rock, forming three sides of a quadrangle, like a triclinium: it faces the south: on its east and west side is a raised block: the former may, perhaps, have been the tribunal, the two latter the rude stones which Pausanias saw here, and which are described by Euripides (Iph. T. 962) as assigned, the one to the accuser, the other to the criminal, in the causes which were tried in this court." The stone seats are intermediate in position to the sites of the Temple of Mars and the Sanctuary of the Eumenides, mentioned below.

[4] Pausan. xxviii. 5.

[5] This temple is mentioned by Pausanias, viii. 5. It was on the southern slope of the Areopagus, immediately above the Agora, near the Eponymi and the statue of Demosthenes.

[6] The Athenians, according to their usual euphemism, called these dread goddesses by the name of Εὐμένιδες or Σέμναι; and Pausanias says that their statues in this place had nothing ferocious in their aspect. The proximity of this sanctuary to the Areopagite court must have tended to give additional solemnity to the place.

Athens, this spot and this court were regarded by the people with superstitious reverence.[1] It was a scene with which the dread recollections of centuries were associated. It was a place of silent awe in the midst of the gay and frivolous city. Those who withdrew to the Areopagus from the Agora, came, as it were, into the presence of a higher power. No place in Athens was so suitable for a discourse upon the mysteries of religion. We are not, however, to regard St. Paul's discourse on the Areopagus as a formal defence, in a trial before the court.[2] The whole aspect of the narrative in the Acts, and the whole tenor of the discourse itself, militate against this supposition. The words, half derisive, half courteous, addressed to the Apostle before he spoke to his audience, "May we know what this new doctrine is?" are not like the words which would have been addressed to a prisoner at the bar; and still more unlike a judge's sentence are the words with which he was dismissed at the conclusion, "We will hear thee again of this matter?"[3] Nor is there anything in the speech itself of a really apologetic character, as any one may perceive, on comparing it with the defence of Socrates.[4] Moreover, the verse[5] which speaks so strongly of the Athenian love of novelty and excitement is so introduced, as to imply that curiosity was the motive of the whole proceeding. We may, indeed, admit that there was something of a mock solemnity in this adjournment from the Agora to the Areopagus. The Athenians took the Apostle from the tumult of public discussion, to the place which was at once most convenient and most appropriate. There was everything in the place to incline the auditors, so far as they were seriously disposed at all, to a reverent and thoughtful attention. It is probable that Dionysius,[6] with other Areopagites, were on the

[1] See Aulus Gellius in Winer. In some respects it seems that the influence of the court was increased under the Romans. See Hermann, 176, and Cic. pro Balbo.

[2] Some are of opinion that he was forcibly apprehended and put on a formal trial. It may be argued that, if a public address was all that was required, the Pnyx would have been more suitable than the Areopagus. But we need not suppose the crowd about St. Paul to have been very great; and though the Pnyx might be equally accessible from the Agora, and more convenient for a general address, the Areopagus was more *appropriate* for a discourse upon religion. We are disposed too to lay great stress on the verse (21) which speaks of the curiosity of the Athenians. Unless it were meant to be emphatic, it would almost have the appearance of an interpolation. 'Ἐπιλαβόμενοι (v. 19) is a word of general import. See Acts ix. 27.

[3] There is indeed an apparent resemblance between Acts xvii. 32 and Acts xxiv. 25, but even in the latter passage, Felix is rather setting aside an irksome subject than giving a judicial decision.

[4] Xen. Apol. [5] Acts xvii. 21.

[6] Tradition says that he was the first bishop of Athens. The writings attributed to him, which were once so famous, are now acknowledged to be spurious, and believed to have been the work of some Neo-Platonist. See Fabr. Bib. Græca. Malalas calls him a philosopher, and tells the story of his conversion and ordination as follows:—
Ἑωρακὼς αὐτὸν ὁ ἅγιος Παῦλος προσηγόρευσε, καὶ ἐπηρώτα τὸν ἅγιον Παῦλον ὁ Διο-

judicial seats. And a vague recollection of the dread thoughts associated by poetry and tradition with the Hill of Mars, may have solemnised the minds of some of those who crowded up the stone steps with the Apostle, and clustered round the summit of the hill, to hear his announcement of the new divinities.

There is no point in the annals of the first planting of Christianity which seizes so powerfully on the imagination of those who are familiar with the history of the ancient world. Whether we contrast the intense earnestness of the man who spoke, with the frivolous character of those who surrounded him,—or compare the certain truth and awful meaning of the Gospel he revealed, with the worthless polytheism which had made Athens a proverb in the earth,—or even think of the mere words uttered that day in the clear atmosphere, on the summit of Mars' Hill, in connection with the objects of art, temples, statues, and altars, which stood round on every side,—we feel that the moment was, and was intended to be, full of the most impressive teaching for every age of the world. Close to the spot where he stood was the Temple of Mars. The sanctuary "of the Eumenides was immediately below him; the Parthenon of Minerva facing him above. Their presence seemed to challenge the assertion in which he declared here, that *in* TEMPLES *made with hands the Deity does not dwell.* In front of him, towering from its pedestal on the rock of the Acropolis, —as the Borromean Colossus, which at this day, with outstretched hand, gives its benediction to the low village of Arona; or as the brazen statue of the armed angel, which from the summit of the Castel S. Angelo spreads its wings over the city of Rome,—was the bronze Colossus of Minerva, armed with spear, shield, and helmet, as the champion of Athens. Standing almost beneath its shade, he pronounced that the Deity was *not to be likened* either to that, the work of Phidias, or to other forms in *gold, silver, or stone, graven* by art, and *man's device,* which peopled the scene before him."[1] Wherever his eye was turned, it saw a succession of such statues and buildings in every variety of form and situation. On the rocky ledges on the south side of the Acropolis, and in the midst of the hum of the Agora, were the "objects of devotion" already described. And in the northern parts of the city, which are equally visible from the Areopagus, on the level spaces, and on every eminence, were similar objects, to which we have made no allusion,—and especially that Temple

νύσιος, Τίνα κηρύσσεις θεὸν, σπερμολόγε; καὶ ἀκούσας τοῦ ἁγίου Παύλου ὁ αὐτὸς Διονύσιος διδάσκοντος αὐτὸν προσέπεσεν αὐτῷ, αἰτῶν αὐτὸν φωτισθῆναι καὶ γενέσθαι Χριστιανόν· καὶ βαπτίσας αὐτὸν ὁ ἅγιος Παῦλος ἐποίησε Χριστίανον· καὶ ἑωρακὼς ὁ ἁγ. Π. τὸ θερμὸν τῆς πίστεως τοῦ αὐτοῦ Δ. ἐποίησεν αὐτὸν ἐπίσκοποι ἐν τῇ χώρᾳ ἐκείνῃ. Mal. Chronog. pp. 251, 252. Bonn Ed.

[1] Wordsworth's Athens and Attica, p. 77. The word *χαράγματι* (Acts xvii. 29) should be noticed. The Apostle was surrounded by *sculpture* as well as by temples.

THE ACROPOLIS RESTORED, AS SEEN FROM THE AREOPAGUS

of Theseus, the national hero, which remains in unimpaired beauty, to enable us to imagine what Athens was when this temple was only one among the many ornaments of that city which was "*wholly given to idolatry.*"

In this scene St. Paul spoke, probably in his wonted attitude,[1] "stretching out his hand," his bodily aspect still showing what he had suffered from weakness, toil, and pain;[2] and the traces of sadness and anxiety[3] mingled on his countenance with the expression of unshaken faith. Whatever his personal appearance may have been, we know the words which he spoke. And we are struck with the more admiration, the more narrowly we scrutinize the characteristics of his address. To defer for the present all consideration of its manifold adaptations to the various characters of his auditors, we may notice how truly it was the outpouring of the emotions which, at the time, had possession of his soul. The mouth spoke out of the fulness of the heart. With an ardent and enthusiastic eloquence he gave vent to the feelings which had been excited by all that he had seen around him in Athens. We observe, also, how the whole course of the oration was regulated by his own peculiar prudence. He was brought into a position, when he might easily have been ensnared into the use of words, which would have brought down upon him the indignation of all the city. Had he begun by attacking the national gods in the midst of their sanctuaries, and with the Areopagites on the seats near him, he would have been in almost as great danger as Socrates before him. Yet he not only avoids the snare, but uses the very difficulty of his position to make a road to the convictions of those who heard him. He becomes a heathen to the heathen. He does not say that he is introducing new divinities. He rather implies the contrary, and gently draws his hearers away from polytheism, by telling them that he was making known the God whom they themselves were ignorantly endeavouring to worship. And if the speech is characterised by St. Paul's prudence, it is marked by that wisdom of his Divine Master, which is the pattern of all Christian teaching. As our Blessed Lord used the tribute-money for the instruction of His disciples, and drew living lessons from the water in the well of Samaria, so the Apostle of the Gentiles employed the familiar objects of Athenian life to tell them of what was close to them, and yet they knew not. He had carefully observed the outward appearance of the city. He had seen an altar with an expressive, though humiliating, inscription. And, using this inscription as a text,[4] he spoke to them, as follows, the Words of Eternal Wisdom.

[1] See p. 174, and the note.

[2] See the account of what took place at Philippi, and compare p. 326.

[3] See above, p. 326.

[4] The altar erected to Pity, above alluded to, was once used in a similar manner. The Athenians were about to introduce gladiatorial shows, and Demonax the Cynic

Their altars to UNKNOWN GODS prove both their desire to worship and their ignorance in worshipping.

Ye men of Athens, all things which I behold bear witness to your[1] carefulness in religion. For as I passed through your city, and beheld the objects of your worship, I found amongst them an altar with this inscription, TO[2] THE UNKNOWN GOD. Whom, therefore, ye worship, though ye know Him not, Him declare I unto you.

God dwells not in the temples of the Acropolis, nor needs the service of His creatures.

God, who made the world and all things therein, seeing that He is Lord of heaven and earth, dwelleth not in temples made with hands.[3] Neither is He served by the hands of men, as though He needed any thing; for it is He that giveth unto all life, and breath, and all things. And He made of one blood[4] all the nations of mankind, to dwell upon the face of the whole earth; and ordained to each the appointed seasons of their existence, and the bounds of their habitation. That they should seek God,[5] if haply they might feel after Him and find Him, though he be not far from every one of us: for in Him we live and move and have our being; as certain also of your own poets[6] have said

Man was created capable of knowing God, and ought not to have fallen into the follies of idolatry, even where it was adorned by the art of Phidias.

"For we are also His offspring."

said: "Do not do this till you have first thrown down the altar of Pity." Lucian. Demonax, 57.

[1] The mistranslation of this verse in the Authorised Version is much to be regretted, because it entirely destroys the graceful courtesy of St. Paul's opening address, and represents him as beginning his speech by offending his audience.

[2] Although there is no article before ἀγνώστῳ, yet we need not scruple to retain the definite article of the Authorised Version; for although, if we take the expression by itself, "To *AN* Unknown God" would be a more correct translation, yet, if we consider the probable origin (see above) of these altars erected to ἄγνωστοι θεοί, it will be evident that "To *THE* Unknown God" would be quite as near the sense of the inscription upon any particular one of such altars. Each particular altar was devoted to *the* unknown god to whom it properly belonged, though which of the gods it might be the dedicator knew not.

[3] Here again (as at Antioch in Pisidia) we find St. Paul employing the very words of St. Stephen. Acts vii. 48.

[4] "*Of one blood*;" excluding the boastful assumption of a different origin claimed by the Greeks for themselves over the barbarians.

[5] The reading of A. B. G. H. &c. is θεὸν, not κύριον.

[6] The quotation is from Aratus, a Greek poet, who was a native of Cilicia, a circumstance which would, perhaps, account for St. Paul's familiarity with his writings. His astronomical poems were so celebrated that Ovid declares his fame will live as long as the sun and moon endure:—"Cum sole et luna semper Aratus erit." How little did the Athenian audience imagine that the poet's immortality would really be owing to the quotation made by the despised provincial who addressed them. The

Forasmuch, then, as we are the offspring of God, we ought not to think that the Godhead is like unto gold, or silver, or stone, graven by the art and device of man.

Howbeit, those past times of ignorance God hath overlooked;[1] but now He commandeth all men everywhere to repent, because He hath appointed a day wherein He will judge the world in righteousness, by that Man whom He hath ordained; whereof He hath given assurance unto all,[2] in that He hath raised Him from the dead.

God had over looked the past, but now calls the world to prepare for Christ's judgment.

Christ's mission is proved by His resurrection.

St. Paul was here suddenly interrupted, as was no doubt frequently the case with his speeches both to Jews and Gentiles. Some of those who listened broke out into laughter and derision. The doctrine of the "resurrection" was to them ridiculous, as the notion of equal religious rights with the "Gentiles" was offensive and intolerable to the Hebrew audience at Jerusalem.[3] Others of those who were present on the Areopagus said, with courteous indifference, that they would "hear him again on the subject." The words were spoken in the spirit of Felix, who had no due sense of the importance of the matter, and who waited for "a convenient season." Thus, amidst the derision of some, and the indifference of others,[4] St. Paul was dismissed, and the assembly dispersed.

But though the Apostle "departed" thus "from among them," and though most of his hearers appeared to be unimpressed, yet many of them may have carried away in their hearts the seeds of truth, destined to grow up into the maturity of Christian faith and practice. We cannot fail to notice how the sentences of this interrupted speech are constructed to meet the cases in succession of every class of which the audience was composed. Each word in the address is adapted at once to win and to rebuke. The Athenians were proud of everything that related to the origin of their race and the home where they dwelt. St. Paul tells them that he was struck by the aspect of their city; but he shows them that the place and the time appointed for each nation's existence are parts of one great scheme of Providence; and that one God is the common Father of all nations of the earth. For the general and more ignorant population,

same words occur also in the Hymn of Cleanthes [p. 5. n. 3], which is quoted at length in Dr. Bloomfield's Recensio Synoptica.

1 See notes upon St. Paul's speech at Lystra. It should be observed that no such metaphor as "winked at" is to be found in the original.

2 Observe the coincidence between this sentiment and that in Rom. i. 4.

3 Acts xxii. 22.

4 Some commentators find again in these two classes the Stoics and Epicureans. It is not necessary to make so precise a division.

some of whom were doubtless listening, a word of approbation is bestowed on the care they gave to the highest of all concerns; but they are admonished that idolatry degrades all worship, and leads men away from true notions of the Deity. That more educated and more imaginative class of hearers, who delighted in the diversified mythology, that personified the operations of nature, and localised the divine presence[1] in sanctuaries adorned by poetry and art, are led from the thought of their favourite shrines and customary sacrifices, to views of that awful Being who is the Lord of heaven and earth, and the one Author of universal life. "Up to a certain point in this high view of the Supreme Being, the philosopher of the Garden, as well as of the Porch, might listen with wonder and admiration. It soared, indeed, high above the vulgar religion; but in the lofty and serene Deity, who disdained to dwell in the earthly temple, and needed nothing from the hand of man, the Epicurean might almost suppose that he heard the language of his own teacher. But the next sentence, which asserted the providence of God as the active, creative energy,—as the conservative, the ruling, the ordaining principle,—annihilated at once the atomic theory, and the government of blind chance, to which Epicurus ascribed the origin and preservation of the universe."[2] And when the Stoic heard the Apostle say that we ought to rise to the contemplation of the Deity without the intervention of earthly objects, and that we live and move and have our being in Him—it might have seemed like an echo of his own thought[3]—until the proud philosopher learnt that it was no pantheistic diffusion of power and order of which the Apostle spoke, but a living centre of government and love—that the world was ruled, not by the iron necessity of Fate, but by the providence of a personal God—and that from the proudest philosopher repentance and meek submission were sternly exacted. Above all, we are called upon to notice how the attention of the whole audience is concentered at the last upon JESUS CHRIST,[4] though His name is not mentioned in the whole speech. Before St. Paul was taken to the Areopagus, he had been preaching "Jesus and the resurrection;"[5] and though his discourse was interrupted, this was the last impression he left on the minds of those who heard him. And the impression was such as not merely to excite or gratify an intellectual curiosity, but to startle and search the conscience. Not only had a revival from the dead been granted to that man whom God had ordained—but a day

[1] The sacred grottoes in the rocks within view from the Areopagus should be remembered, as well as the temples, &c. See Wordsworth.

[2] Milman's History of Christianity, vol. II. p. 18. See his observations on the whole speech. He remarks, in a note, the coincidence of St. Paul's οὐδὲν προσδεόμενος with the "nihil indiga nostri" of the Epicurean Lucretius.

[3] This strikes us the more forcibly if the quotation is from the Stoic Cleanthes. See above.

[4] See Meyer.

[5] Acts xvii. 18.

bad been appointed on which by Him the world must be judged in righteousness.

Of the immediate results of this speech we have no further knowledge, than that Dionysius,[1] a member of the Court of Areopagus, and a woman whose name was Damaris,[2] with some others, were induced to join themselves to the Apostle, and became converts to Christianity. How long St. Paul staid in Athens, and with what success, cannot possibly be determined. He does not appear to have been driven by any tumult or persecution. We are distinctly told that he waited for some time at Athens, till Silas and Timotheus should join him; and there is some reason for believing that the latter of these companions did rejoin him in Athens, and was dispatched again forthwith to Macedonia.[3] The Apostle himself remained in the province of Achaia, and took up his abode at its capital on the Isthmus. He inferred, or it was revealed to him, that the Gospel would meet with a more cordial reception there than at Athens. And it is a serious and instructive fact that the mercantile population of Thessalonica and Corinth received the message of God with greater readiness than the highly educated and polished Athenians. Two letters to the Thessalonians, and two to the Corinthians, remain to attest the flourishing state of those Churches. But we possess no letter written by St. Paul to the Athenians; and we do not read that he was ever in Athens again.[4]

Whatever may have been the immediate results of St. Paul's sojourn at Athens, its real fruits are those which remain to us still. That speech on the Areopagus is an imperishable monument of the first victory of Christianity over Paganism. To make a sacred application of the words used by the Athenian historian,[5] it was "no mere effort for the moment," but it is a "perpetual possession," wherein the Church finds ever fresh supplies of wisdom and guidance. It is in Athens we learn what is the highest point to which unassisted human nature can attain; and here we learn also the language which the Gospel addresses to man on his proudest eminence of unaided strength. God, in His providence, has preserved to us, in fullest profusion, the literature which unfolds to us all the life of

[1] See above, p. 375, n. 2.

[2] Nothing is known of Damaris. But, considering the seclusion of the Greek women, the mention of her name, and apparently in connection with the crowd on the Areopagus, is remarkable. Stier throws out the suggestion that she might be a *hetæra*, called like Mary Magdalene to repentance. Reden der Apostel. II. 21.

[3] See 1 Thess. iii. 1. For the movements of Silas and Timotheus about this time, see the note at the end of Ch. XI.

[4] The church of Athens appears to have been long in a very weak state. In the time of the Antonines, Paganism was almost as flourishing there as ever. The Christian community seems at one time to have been entirely dispersed, and to have been collected again about A.D. 165. See Leake, p. 60.

[5] Κτῆμα ἐς ἀεὶ μᾶλλον ἢ ἀγώνισμα ἐς τὸ παραχρῆμα ἀκούειν σύγκειται. Thuc. i. 22

the Athenian people, in its glory and its shame ; and He has ordained that one conspicuous passage in the Holy Volume should be the speech, in which His servant addressed that people as ignorant idolaters, called them to repentance, and warned them of judgment. And it can hardly be deemed profane if we trace to the same Divine Providence the preservation of the very imagery which surrounded the speaker—not only the sea, and the mountains, and the sky, which change not with the decay of nations—but even the very temples, which remain, after wars and revolutions, on their ancient pedestals in astonishing perfection. We are thus provided with a poetic and yet a truthful commentary on the words that were spoken once for all at Athens ; and Art and Nature have been commissioned from above to enframe the portrait of that Apostle, who stands for ever on the Areopagus as the teacher of the Gentiles.

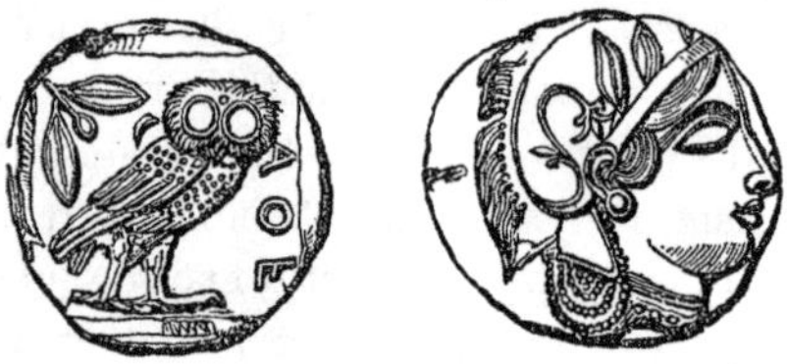

ATHENIAN TETRADRACHM[3]

[3] From the British Museum.

CHAPTER XI.

"I adjure you, in the name of our Lord Jesus, to see that this letter be read to all the brethren."—1 Thess. v. 27.

"I, Paul, add my salutation with my own hand, which is a token whereby all my letters may be known."—2 Thess. iii. 17.

LETTERS TO THESSALONICA WRITTEN FROM CORINTH.—EXPULSION OF THE JEWS FROM ROME.—AQUILA AND PRISCILLA.—ST. PAUL'S LABOURS.—*FIRST EPISTLE TO THE THESSALONIANS.*—ST. PAUL IS OPPOSED BY THE JEWS; AND TURNS TO THE GENTILES.—HIS VISION.—*SECOND EPISTLE TO THE THESSALONIANS.*—CONTINUED RESIDENCE IN CORINTH.

COIN OF CORINTH.[1]

WHEN St. Paul went from Athens to Corinth, he entered on a scene very different from that which he had left. It is not merely that his residence was transferred from a free Greek city to a Roman colony; as would have been the case had he been moving from Thessalonica to Philippi.[2] His present journey took him from a quiet provincial town to the busy metropolis of a province, and from the seclusion of an ancient university to the seat of government and trade.[3] Once there had been a time, in the flourishing age of the Greek republics, when Athens had been politically greater than Corinth; but now that the little territories of the Levantine cities were fused into the larger provincial divisions of the empire, Athens had only the memory of its preeminence, while Corinth held the keys of commerce and swarmed with a crowded population. Both cities had recently experienced severe vicissitudes; but a spell was on the fortunes of the former, and its character remained more entirely Greek than that of any other place:[4] while the latter rose from its ruins, a new and splendid city, on the Isthmus between its two seas, where a

[1] From the British Museum. The emperor is Claudius. See Acts xviii. 2.

[2] See above, p. 333.

[3] A journey in the first century from Athens to Corinth might almost be compared to a journey, in the eighteenth, from Oxford to London.

[4] See the preceding Chapter on Athens.

multitude of Greeks and Jews gradually united themselves with the military colonists sent by Julius Cæsar from Italy,[1] and were kept in order by the presence of a Roman proconsul.[2]

The connection of Corinth with the life of St. Paul and the early progress of Christianity, is so close and eventful, that no student of Holy Writ ought to be satisfied without obtaining as correct and clear an idea as possible of its social condition, and its relation to other parts of the empire. This subject will be considered in a subsequent chapter. At present another topic demands our chief attention. We are now arrived at that point in the life of St. Paul when his first Epistles were written. This fact is ascertained, not by any direct statements either in the Acts or the Epistles themselves, but by circumstantial evidence derived from a comparison of these documents with one another.[3] Such a comparison enables us to perceive that the Apostle's mind, on his arrival at Corinth, was still turning with affection and anxiety towards his converts at Thessalonica. In the midst of all his labours at the Isthmus, his thoughts were continually with those whom he had left in Macedonia; and though the narrative[4] tells us only of his tent-making and preaching in the metropolis of Achaia, we discover, on a closer enquiry, that the Letters to the Thessalonians were written at this particular crisis. It would be interesting in the case of any man whose biography has been thought worth preserving, to discover that letters full of love and wisdom had been written at a time when no traces would have been discoverable, except in the letters themselves, of the thoughts which had been occupying the writer's mind. Such unexpected association of the actions done in one place with affection retained towards another, always seems to add to our personal knowledge of the man whose history we may be studying, and to our interest in the pursuits which were the occupation of his life. This is peculiarly true in the case of the *first Christian correspondence*, which has been preserved to the Church. Such has ever been the influence of letter-writing,—its power in bringing those who are distant near to one another, and reconciling those who are in danger of being estranged;—such especially has been the influence of Christian letters in developing the growth of faith and love, and binding together the dislocated members of the body of Our Lord, and in making each generation in succession the

[1] At the close of the Republic Corinth was entirely destroyed. Thus we find Cicero travelling, not by Corinth, but by Athens. But Julius Cæsar established the city on the Isthmus, in the form of a colony; and the mercantile population flocked back to their old place; so that Corinth rose with great rapidity to the rank of one of the second cities of the Empire. The historical details will be given in the next chapter.

[2] Acts xviii. 12 shows that the province of Achaia was proconsular. See, under Cyprus, pp. 141–145.

[3] See the arguments below, p. 390, n. 3.

[4] Acts xviii. 1–4.

teacher of the next,—that we have good reason to take these Epistles to the Thessalonians as the one chief subject of the present chapter. The earliest occurrences which took place at Corinth must first be mentioned: but for this a few pages will suffice.

The reasons which determined St. Paul to come to Corinth (over and above the discouragement he seems to have met with in Athens) were, probably, twofold. In the first place, it was a large mercantile city, in immediate connection with Rome and the West of the Mediterranean, with Thessalonica and Ephesus in the Ægean, and with Antioch and Alexandria in the East.[1] The Gospel once established in Corinth, would rapidly spread everywhere. And, again, from the very nature of the city, the Jews established there were numerous. Communities of scattered Israelites were found in various parts of the province of Achaia,—in Athens, as we have recently seen,[2]—in Argos, as we learn from Philo,[3]—in Bœotia and Eubœa.[4] But their chief settlement must necessarily have been in that city, which not only gave opportunities of trade by land along the Isthmus between the Morea and the Continent, but received in its two harbours the ships of the Eastern and Western seas. A religion which was first to be planted in the Synagogue, and was thence intended to scatter its seeds over all parts of the earth, could nowhere find a more favourable soil than among the Hebrew families at Corinth.[5]

At this particular time there were a greater number of Jews in the city than usual; for they had lately been banished from Rome by command of the Emperor Claudius.[6] The history of this edict is involved in some obscurity. But there are abundant passages in the contemporary Heathen writers which show the suspicion and dislike with which the Jews were regarded.[7] Notwithstanding the general toleration, they were violently persecuted by three successive emperors;[8] and there is good

[1] For full details, see the next Chapter.

[2] See the preceding Chapter, p. 362.

[3] Philo de Leg. ad Cai. p. 1031. Ed. Francof., adduced in Wiltsch's Handbuch der kirchlichen Geographie, § 9. See also Remond's Versuch einer Geschichte der Ausbreitung des Judenthums, § 15, and § 33.

[4] See p. 18, with Wiltsch and Remond.

[5] See what has been said above on Thessalonica.

[6] Acts xviii. 2.

[7] See, for instance Tacitus and Juvenal, as quoted p. 19, n. 1, and Cicero, p. 303, n. 3, and other passages in Remond.

[8] Four thousand Jews or Jewish proselytes were sent as convicts by *Tiberius* to the island of Sardinia. "Actum et de sacris Ægyptiis Judaicisque pellendis: factumque patrum consultum, ut quatuor milia libertini generis, ea superstitione infecta, in insulam Sardiniam veherentur, coercendis illic latrociniis, et si ob gravitatem cœli interiissent, vile damnum." Tac. An. ii. 85. "Externas cærimonias, Ægyptios Judaicosque ritus compescuit, coactis qui superstitione ea tenebantur, religiosas vestes cum instrumento omni comburere. Judæorum juventutem per speciem sacramenti, in provincias gravioris cœli distribuit; reliquos gentis ejusdem, vel similia sectantes, Urbe submovit,

reason for identifying the edict mentioned by St. Luke with that alluded to by Suetonius, who says that Claudius drove the Jews from Rome because they were incessantly raising tumults at the instigation of a certain *Chrestus*.[1] Much has been written concerning this sentence of the biographer of the Cæsars. Some have held that there was really a Jew called Chrestus, who had excited political disturbances:[2] others that the name is used by mistake for Christus, and that the disturbances had arisen from the Jewish expectations concerning the Messiah, or Christ.[3] It seems to us that the last opinion is partially true; but that we must trace this movement not merely to the vague Messianic idea entertained by the Jews, but to the events which followed the actual appearance of *the Christ*.[4] We have seen how the first progress of Christianity had been the occasion of tumult among the Jewish communities in the provinces;[5] and there is no reason why the same might not have happened in the capital itself.[6] Nor need we be surprised at the inaccurate form in which the same occurs, when we remember how loosely more careful writers than Suetonius write concerning the affairs of the Jews.[7] Chrestus was a common name;[8] Christus was not: and we have a distinct statement by Tertullian and Lactantius[9] that in their day the former was often used for the latter.[10]

Among the Jews who had been banished from Rome by Claudius and had settled for a time at Corinth, were two natives of Pontus, whose names were Aquila and Priscilla.[11] We have seen before (Ch.

sub pœna perpetuæ servitutis, nisi obtemperassent." Suet. Tib. 36. Cf. Joseph. Ant. xviii. 3, 5. The more directly religious persecution of *Caligula* has been mentioned previously, Ch. IV. pp. 110, 111.

1 The words are quoted p. 303, n. 4. Compare p. 332.

2 This is Meyer's view, to which De Wette also inclines.

3 Such seems to be the opinion of Ammon, Paulus, &c. See Meyer *in loc.* Archbishop Usher takes the same view.

4 See Hug and Kuinoel. Orosius (Hist. vii. 6) seems really to have had the reading *Christo* before him. The statement of Dio Cassius (lx. 6) with reference to Claudius and the Jews,—(*τοὺς Ἰουδαίους πλεονάσαντας αὖθις, ὥστε χαλεπῶς ἂν ἄνευ ταραχῆς ὑπὸ τοῦ ὄχλου σφῶν τῆς πόλεως εἰρχθῆναι, οὐκ ἐξήλασε μὲν, τῷ δὲ δὴ πατρίῳ νόμῳ βίῳ χρωμένους ἐκέλευσε μὴ συναθροίζεσθαι*)—seems to refer to a point of time anterior to the edict mentioned by Suetonius and St. Luke.

5 In Asia Minor (Ch. VI.), and more especially in Thessalonica and Berœa (Ch. IX.)

6 Christianity must have been more or less known in Rome, since the return of the Italian Jews from Pentecost (Acts ii.).

7 Even Tacitus.

8 See, for instance, Cic. Fam. ii. 8. Moreover, *Christus* and *Chrestus* are pronounced alike in Romaic. Suetonius, however, was acquainted with the word *Christianus*. Nero, 16.

9 See the passages quoted by Dean Milman (Hist. of Christianity, I. p. 430), who remarks that these tumults at Rome, excited by the mutual hostility of Jews and Christians, imply that Christianity must already have made considerable progress there.

10 See pp. 119, 120, and Tac. Ann. xv. 44.

11 Acts xviii. 2.

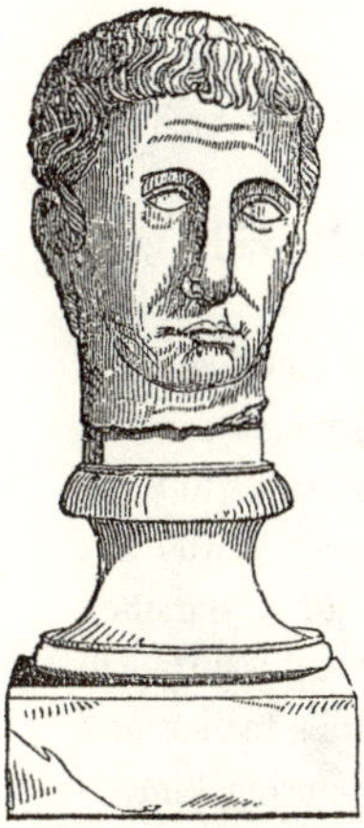
BUST OF CLAUDIUS.[6]

VIII.) that Pontus denoted a province of Asia Minor on the shores of the Euxine, and we have noticed some political facts which tended to bring this province into relations with Judea.[1] Though, indeed, it is hardly necessary to allude to this, for there were Jewish colonies over every part of Asia Minor, and we are expressly told that Jews from Pontus heard St. Peter's first sermon[2] and read his first Epistle.[3] Aquila and Priscilla were, perhaps, of that number. Their names have a Roman form;[4] and, we may conjecture that they were brought into some connection with a Roman family, similar to that which we have supposed to have existed in the case of St. Paul himself.[5] We find they were on the present occasion forced to leave Rome; and we notice that they are afterwards addressed[7] as residing there again; so that it is reasonable to suppose that the metropolis was their stated residence. Yet we observe that they frequently travelled, and we trace them on the Asiatic coast on two distinct occasions, separated by a wide interval of time. First, before their return to Italy (Acts xviii. 18, 26. 1 Cor. xvi. 19), and again, shortly before the martyrdom of St. Paul (2 Tim. iv. 19), we find them at Ephesus. From the manner in which they are referred to as having Christian meetings in their houses, both at Ephesus and Rome,[8] we should be inclined to conclude that they were possessed of some considerable wealth. The trade at which they laboured, or which at least they superintended, was the manufacture of tents,[9] the demand for which must have

[1] Especially the marriage of Polemo with Berenice, p. 25, and p. 248.

[2] Acts ii. 9. [3] 1 Pet. i. 1.

[4] See p. 151, also p. 46. Ἀκύλας is merely the Greek form of Aquila (used by Josephus, Appian, and Dio Cassius). The hypothesis of Reiche, that this Aquila was a freedman of one Pontius Aquila, whose name is mentioned by Greek and Roman writers, and that St. Luke is in error in calling him a native of Pontus, is very gratuitous. Nothing is known of him beyond what we read in the New Testament. The tradition of the Greek Menology is, that he and his wife were beheaded.

From the mention of Priscilla as St. Paul's συνεργός, and as one of the instructors of Apollos, we might naturally infer that she was a woman of good education. Her name appears in 2 Tim. under the form "Prisca." So, in Martial, Tacitus, and Suetonius, "Livia" and "Livilla," "Drusa" and "Drusilla," are used of the same person. See Wetstein on Rom. xvi. Prisca is well known as a Roman name.

Aquila, who made the new translation of the Old Testament into Greek in the reign of Hadrian, was also a native of Pontus.

[5] P. 46. [6] From the Musée des Antiques (Bouillon, Paris, 1812–1817), vol. ii.

[7] Rom. xvi. 3.

[8] Rom. xvi. 3. 1 Cor. xvi. 19.

[9] Many meanings have been given by the commentators to σκηνοποιοὶ,—weavers of tapestry, saddlers, mathematical instrument makers. [Another rendering we have met with somewhere, is "rope-makers;" suggested, perhaps, by the word σχοινοποιοὶ

been continual in that age of travelling,—while the *cilicium*,[1] or hair cloth, of which they were made, could easily be procured at every large town in the Levant.

A question has been raised as to whether Aquila and Priscilla were already Christians, when they met with St. Paul.[2] Though it is certainly possible that they may have been converted at Rome, we think, on the whole, that this was probably not the case. They are simply classed with the other Jews who were expelled by Claudius; and we are told that the reason why St Paul "came and attached himself to them"[3] was not because they had a common religion, but because they had a common trade. There is no doubt, however, that the connection soon resulted in their conversion to Christianity.[4] The trade which St. Paul's father had taught him in his youth[5] was thus made the means of procuring him invaluable associates in the noblest work in which man was ever engaged. No higher example can be found of the possibility of combining diligent labour in the common things of life with the utmost spirituality of mind. Those who might have visited Aquila at Corinth in the working-hours, would have found St. Paul quietly occupied with the same task as his fellow-labourers. Though he knew the Gospel to be a matter of life and death to the soul, he gave himself to an ordinary trade with as much zeal as though he had no other occupation. It is the duty of every man to maintain an honourable independence; and this, he felt, was peculiarly incumbent on him, for the sake of the Gospel he came to proclaim.[6] He knew the obloquy to which he was likely to be exposed, and he prudently prepared for it. The highest motives instigated his diligence in the commonest manual toil. And this toil was no hindrance to that communion with God, which was his greatest joy, and the source of all his peace. While he "laboured, working with his own hands," among the Corinthians, as he afterwards reminded them,[7]—in his heart he was praying continually, with thanksgiving, on behalf of the Thessalonians, as he says to them himself[8] in the letters which he dictated in the intervals of his labour.

This was the first scene of St. Paul's life at Corinth. For the second

which is pronounced by the modern Greeks nearly in the same way.] But nothing is so probable as that they were simply makers of those hair-cloth tents, which are still in constant use in the Levant. That they were manufacturers of the cloth itself is less likely.

1 An account of this cloth is given in Ch. II. p. 47. See p. 168 and p. 329.

2 See the various commentators.

3 Προσῆλθεν αὐτοῖς. Acts xviii. 2.

4 They were Christians, and able to instruct others, when St. Paul left them at Ephesus, on his voyage from Corinth to Syria. See Acts xviii. 18, 26.

5 See p. 46.

6 See what is said above in reference to his labours at Thessalonica, p. 329. We shall meet with the same subject again in the Epistles to the Corinthians.

7 1 Cor. iv. 12.

8 1 Thess. i. 2. ii. 13. 2 Thess. i. 11.

scene we must turn to the synagogue. The Sabbath[1] was a day of rest. On that day the Jews laid aside their tent-making and their other trades, and, amid the derision of their Gentile neighbours, assembled in the house of prayer to worship the God of their forefathers. There St. Paul spoke to them of the "mercy promised to their forefathers," and of the "oath sworn to Abraham," being "performed." There his countrymen listened with incredulity or conviction: and the tent-maker of Tarsus "reasoned" with them and "endeavoured to persuade"[2] both the Jews and the Gentiles who were present, to believe in Jesus Christ as the promised Messiah and the Saviour of the World.

While these two employments were proceeding,—the daily labour in the workshop, and the weekly discussions in the synagogue,—Timotheus and Silas returned from Macedonia.[3] The effect produced by their arrival seems to have been an instantaneous increase of the zeal and energy with which he resisted the opposition, which was even now beginning to hem in the progress of the truth. The remarkable word[4] which is used to describe the "*pressure*" which St. Paul experienced at this moment in the course of his teaching at Corinth, is the same which is employed of our Lord Himself in a solemn passage of the Gospels,[5] when He says, "I have a baptism to be baptized with; and how am I *straitened* till it be accomplished." He who felt our human difficulties has given us human help to aid us in what He requires us to do. When St. Paul's companions rejoined him, he was reinforced with new earnestness and vigour in combating the difficulties which met him. He acknowledges himself that he was at Corinth "in weakness, and in fear and much trembling;"[6] but "God, who comforteth those that are cast down, comforted him by the coming"[7] of his friends. It was only one among many instances we shall be called to notice, in which, at a time of weakness, "he saw the brethren and took courage."[8]

But this was not the only result of the arrival of St. Paul's companions. Timotheus (as we have seen[9]) had been sent, while St. Paul was still at Athens, to revisit and establish the Church of Thessalonica.

[1] See Acts xviii. 4. [2] Ἔπειθε.

[3] Acts xviii. 5. See note at the end of this chapter. We may remark here that Silas and Timotheus were probably the "brethren" who brought the collection mentioned, 2 Cor. xi. 9. Compare Phil. iv. 15.

[4] Συνείχετο. There seems no doubt that the words which succeed should be τῷ λόγῳ and not τῷ πνεύματι. Hammond explains the received reading to mean that Paul was "distressed in spirit," because he produced little effect on his hearers. But the state of mind, whatever it was, is clearly connected with the coming of Timothy and Silas, and seems to imply increasing zeal with increasing opposition. The Vulgate has instabat verbo."

[5] Luke xii. 50. [6] 1 Cor. ii. 3. [7] 2 Cor. vii. 6.

[8] Acts xxviii. 15. See above, on his solitude in Athens, p. 362.

[9] See above.

The news he brought on his return to St. Paul caused the latter to write to these beloved converts; and, as we have already observed,[1] the letter which he sent them is the first of his Epistles which has been preserved to us. It seems to have been occasioned partly by his wish to express his earnest affection for the Thessalonian Christians, and to encourage them under their persecutions; but it was also called for by some errors into which they had fallen. Many of the new converts were uneasy about the state of their relatives or friends, who had died since their conversion. They feared that these departed Christians would lose the happiness of witnessing their Lord's second coming, which they expected soon to behold. In this expectation others had given themselves up to a religious excitement, under the influence of which they persuaded themselves that they need not continue to work at the business of their callings, but might claim support from the richer members of the Church. Others, again, had yielded to the same temptations which afterwards influenced the Corinthian Church, and despised the gift of prophesying[2] in comparison with those other gifts which afforded more opportunity for display. These reasons, and others which will appear in the letter itself, led St. Paul to write to the Thessalonians as follows:[3]—

FIRST EPISTLE TO THE THESSALONIANS.

I.

Salutation. Paul, and Silvanus, and Timotheus, to the Church of 1
the Thessalonians, in the name of God our Father, and
our Lord Jesus Christ;[4] grace be to you and peace.[5]

[1] P. 384. [2] 1 Thess. v. 20.

[3] The correctness of the date here assigned to this Epistle may be proved as follows:—(1) It was written not long after the conversion of the Thessalonians (1 Thess. i. 8, 9), while the tidings of it were still spreading (ἀπαγγέλλουσιν, present) through Macedonia and Achaia, and while St. Paul could speak of himself as only taken from them for a short season (1 Thess. ii. 17). (2) St. Paul had been recently at Athens (iii. 1), and had already preached in Achaia (i. 7, 8). (3) Timotheus and Silas were just returned (ἄρτι, iii. 6) from Macedonia, which happened (Acts xviii. 5) soon after St. Paul's first arrival at Corinth.

We have already observed (Ch. IX. p. 331), that the character of these Epistles to the Thessalonians proves how predominant was the Gentile element in that church, and that they are among the very few letters of St. Paul in which not a single quotation from the Old Testament is to be found. [The use, indeed, of the word Satan (1 Thess. ii. 18) might be adduced as implying some previous knowledge of Judaism in those to whom the letter was addressed. See also the note on 2 Thess. ii. 8.]

[4] Χάρις ὑμῖν καὶ εἰρήνη. This salutation occurs in all St. Paul's Epistles, except the three Pastoral Epistles, where it is changed into Χάρις ἔλεος εἰρήνη.

[5] The remainder of this verse has been introduced into the Textus Receptus by mistake in this place, where it is not found in the best MSS. It properly belongs to 2 Thess. i. 2.

2 I return[1] continual thanks to God for you all, and make mention of you in my prayers without

Thanksgiving for their conversion.

3 ceasing; remembering always, in the presence of our God
and Father, the working of your faith and the labours of
your love, and the patient endurance of your hope, which was
4 fixed on our Lord Jesus Christ. Brethren, beloved by God,
I know how God has chosen you; for the Glad-tidings which I
brought[2] you worked upon you, not only in word, but also in
power; with the might of the Holy Spirit, and with the full
5 assurance of belief. And you, likewise, know the manner in
6 which I behaved myself among you, for your sakes. Moreover, you followed in my steps, and in the steps of our Lord
and Master; and you received His teaching in the midst of
great tribulation,[3] with a joy which came from the Holy Spirit.
7 And thus you have become patterns to all the believers in
8 Macedonia and in Achaia. For from you the word of our
Lord has been sounded forth,[4] and not only has its sound been
heard in Macedonia and Achaia, but also in every place the tidings of your faith towards God have been spread abroad, so that I

[1] It is important to observe in this place, once for all, that St. Paul uses "*we*," according to the idiom of many ancient writers, where a modern writer would use "*I*." Great confusion is caused in many passages by not translating, according to his true meaning, in the first person *singular;* for thus it often happens, that what he spoke of himself individually, appears to us as if it were meant for a general truth: instances will occur repeatedly of this in the Epistles to the Corinthians, especially the Second. It might have been supposed, that when St. Paul associated others with himself in the salutation at the beginning of an epistle, he meant to indicate that the epistle proceeded from them as well as from himself; but an examination of the body of the Epistle will always convince us that such was not the case, but that he was the sole author. For example, in the present Epistle, Silvanus and Timotheus are joined with him in the salutation; but yet we find (ch. iii. 1, 2)—*εὐδοκήσαμεν καταλειφθῆναι ἐν 'Αθήναις μόνοι καὶ ἐπέμψαμεν* Τιμόθεον *τὸν ἀδελφὸν ἡμῶν.* Now, *who* was it who thought fit to be left at Athens alone? Plainly St. Paul himself, and he only; neither Timotheus (who is here expressly excluded) nor Silvanus (who did not rejoin St. Paul till afterwards at Corinth (Acts xviii. 5)), being by possibility included. Ch. iii. 6 is not less decisive *ἄρτι δὲ ἐλθόντος* Τιμοθέον *πρὸς ἡμᾶς ἀφ' ὑμῶν*—when we remember that Silvanus came with Timotheus. Several other passages in the Epistle prove the same thing, but these may suffice.

It is true, that sometimes the ancient idiom in which a writer spoke of himself in the plural is more graceful, and seems less egotistical, than the modern usage; but yet (the modern usage being what it is) a literal translation of the *ἡμεῖς* very often conveys a confused idea of the meaning; and we have thought it better, therefore, to translate according to the modern idom.

[2] St. Paul is here referring to the time when he first visited and converted the Thessalonians; the "hope" spoken of was the hope of our Lord's coming.

[3] This tribulation they brought on themselves by receiving the Gospel.

[4] See p. 324, n. 3.

have no need to speak of it. For others are telling of their own 9
accord,[1] concerning me, how gladly you received me, and how
you forsook your idols, and turned to the service of God, the
living and the true; and that now you wait with eager longing 10
for the return of His Son from the heavens, even Jesus, whom
He raised from the dead, our deliverer from the coming ven-
geance. II.

He reminds them of his own example.

Yea, you know yourselves, brethren, that my 1
coming amongst you was not fruitless; but after I 2
had borne suffering and outrage (as you know) at Philippi,
I trusted in my God, and boldly declared to you God's Glad
tidings, although its adversaries contended mightily against me.
For my exhortations are not prompted[2] by imposture, nor by 3
lasciviousness, nor do I deal deceitfully. But, seeing that God 4
has tried my fitness for His work, and charged me to declare
the Glad-tidings, so I speak, as one who strives to please not
men but God, whose search tries my heart. For never did 5
I use flattering words, as you know; nor hide covetousness un-
der fair pretences, (God is my witness); nor did I seek honour 6
from men, either from you or others; although I might have
been burdensome to you, as being Christ's apostle.[3] But I be- 7
haved myself among you with mildness and forbearance; and
as a nurse cherishes her own children,[4] so in my fond affection 8
it was my joy to give you not only the Glad-tidings of Christ,
but even my own life also, because you were so dear to me.
For you remember, brethren, my toilsome labours; how I 9
worked both night and day, that I might not be burdensome to
any of you, while I proclaimed to you the message which I
bore, the Glad-tidings of God. You are yourselves witnesses, 10

[1] *Αὐτοὶ.*

[2] In this and the following verses, we have allusions to the accusations brought against St. Paul by his Jewish opponents. This very charge of seeking to please men, *ἀνθοώποις ἀρέσκειν*, was repeated by the Judaisers in Galatia. See Gal. i. 10.

[3] One of the grounds upon which St. Paul's Judaising opponents denied his apostolic authority, was the fact that he (in general) refused to be maintained by his converts, whereas Our Lord had given to His apostles the right of being so maintained. St. Paul fully explains his reasons for not availing himself of that right in several passages, especially 1 Cor. ix.; and he here takes care to allude to his possession of the right, while mentioning his renunciation of it. Cf. 2 Thess. iii. 9.

[4] Τὰ *ἑαυτῆς τέκνα*. See p. 329, n. 3. It will be observed, also, that we adopt a different punctuation from that which has led to the received version. In v. 8 it seems very probable that *ὁμειρόμενοι*, and not *ἱμειρόμενοι*, is the correct reading; but the general sense is not altered. See Koch.

and God also is my witness, how holy, and just, and un-
11 blamable, were my dealings towards you who believe. You
know how earnestly, as a father his own children, I exhorted,
and entreated, and adjured each one among you to walk wor-
12 thy of God, by whom you are called into His own kingdom
and glory.

13 Wherefore I also give continual thanks to God, because,
when you heard from me the preaching of God's word, you re-
ceived it not as the word of man, but, as it is in truth, the
word of God; who[1] Himself works inwardly in you that
14 believe. For you, brethren, followed in the steps of the
churches of God in Judea, which are in the fellowship of Christ
Jesus, and suffered the like persecution from your own coun-
15 trymen, which they endured from the Jews; who killed both
our Lord Jesus, and their own prophets, and who have driven
me from city[2] to city; a people displeasing to God, and ene-
16 mies to all mankind, who would hinder me from speaking to
the Gentiles, for their salvation; thus they do, as they have
ever done, to fill up the measure of their sins; but now the
wrath of God has overtaken them to destroy them.[3]

Expresses his desire to see them.

17 But I, brethren, having been torn from you for a
short season (in body, not in heart), have sought
earnestly, with long desire, to behold you again face to face.[4]
18 Wherefore I, Paul (for my own part), would have returned to
visit you, and strove to do so once and again; but Satan hin-
19 dered me. For what is my hope or joy? what is the crown
wherein I glory? what but your own selves, when you shall
20 stand before our Lord Jesus Christ at His appearing. Yea,
III you are my glory and my joy.

And his joy in hearing of their well-doing from Timotheus

1 Therefore, being no longer able to restrain my
2 desire, I determined to be left at Athens alone; and
I sent Timotheus, my brother, and God's servant
and fellow-worker[5] in the Glad-tidings of Christ, that he might
strengthen your constancy, and exhort you concerning your
3 faith, that none of you should suffer himself to be shaken by

[1] We cannot agree with Winer (Grammatik, p. 236) that *ὅς* refers to *λόγον* here *'Εκδιωξάντων*.

[3] *Εἰς τέλος*, "to make an end of them."

[4] See what is said in the preceding chapter in connection with Berœa.

[5] We read, with Griesbach and Tischendorf, *συνεργὸν τοῦ θεοῦ*, which is analogous to (1 Cor. iii. 9) *θεοῦ ἐσμεν συνεργοί*. The boldness of the expression probably led to the variation of reading in the MSS.

these afflictions which have come upon you; for you your-
selves know that such is our appointed lot, and when I was 4
with you, I forewarned you that persecutions awaited us, as
you remember that it befel. For this cause, I also, when I 5
could no longer forbear, sent to learn tidings of your faith; for
I feared lest perchance the tempter had tempted you, and so
my labour among you should be in vain. But now that Timo- 6
theus has returned from you to me, and has brought me the
glad tidings of your faith and love, and that you still keep an
affectionate remembrance of me, longing to see me, as I to see
you—I have been comforted, brethren, on your behalf, and all 7
my own tribulation and distress has been lightened by your
faith. For now, if you be stedfast in the Lord Jesus, I feel 8
myself to live.[1] What thanksgiving can I render to God for 9
you, for all the joy which you cause me in the presence of my
God? Night and day, I pray exceeding earnestly to see you 10
face to face, that I may complete what is yet wanting in your
faith. Now, may God Himself, our Father, and our Lord 11
Jesus Christ, direct my path towards you. Meantime, may 12
our Lord cause you to increase and abound in love to one an-
other and to all men; even such love as I have for you. And 13
so may He keep your hearts stedfast and unblamable in holi-
ness, and present you before our God and Father, with all His
people,[2] at His[3] appearing.
IV

Against sensuality.

It remains, brethren, that I beseech and exhort 1
you in the name of our Lord Jesus, that, as I taught
you what life you must live to please God, so you would walk
thereafter more abundantly. For you know the commands 2
which I delivered to you by the authority of the Lord Jesus. 3
This, therefore, as I then told you, is the will of God; that you 4
should be consecrated unto Him in holiness, and should keep
yourselves from fornication, and that each of you should learn to
get the mastery over his bodily desires[4] in purity and honour;

[1] Ζῶμεν. Compare ἔζων (Rom. vii. 9).

[2] We think it better to place a comma after Χριστοῦ, for our Lord will not *come with all His people*, since some of his people will be on earth.

[3] We substitute the personal pronoun for Ἰησοῦ Χριστοῦ in this and some similar instances, because it is contrary to the English idiom to repeat the noun in such cases.

[4] Κτᾶσθαι cannot mean *to possess;* it means, *to gain possession of*, to *acquire for one's own use.* The use of σκεῦος for *body* is common, and found 2 Cor. iv. 7. Now a man may be said to *gain possession of his own body* when he subdues those lusts which tend to destroy his mastery over it. Hence the interpretation which we have

5 not in lustful passions, like the heathen who know not God.
6 Neither must any man wrong his brother in this matter by his
transgression.[1] All such the Lord will punish, as I have fore-
7 warned you by my solemn testimony. For God has not called
us to a life of uncleanness, but His calling is[2] a holy calling.
8 Wherefore, he that despises these my words, despises not man
but God, who also has given unto me[3] His Holy Spirit.

Exhortation to love, peace, and good order.

9 Concerning brotherly love it is needless that I
should write to you; for ye yourselves are taught of
10 God to love one another; as you show by your deeds towards
all the brethren throughout the whole of Macedonia. I exhort
11 you only, brethren, to abound still more. Seek peaceful quiet-
ness, and give yourselves to the concerns of your private life;
let this be your ambition.[4] Work with your own hands (as I
12 commanded you), for your own support; that the seemly order
of your lives may be manifest to those without the church, and
that you may need no help from others.

Happiness of the Christian dead.

13 Now I desire, brethren, to remove your igno-
rance concerning those who are asleep, that you
14 may not sorrow like other men, who have no hope. For as
surely as we believe that Jesus died and rose again, so surely will
God through Him,[5] bring back those who sleep together with
15 Jesus. This I declare to you, by the authority of the Lord,
that we who are living, who survive to behold the appearing of
our Lord, shall not enter into His presence sooner than the
16 dead. For the Lord himself shall descend from heaven with
the shout of war,[6] the Archangel's voice, and the trumpet of
17 God; and first the dead in Christ[7] shall arise to life; then we

adopted appears justifiable and natural, and is certainly less repugnant to ordinary feelings than that of De Wette,—"Das ein jeglicher wisse sich sein Werkzeug zur Befriedigung des Geschlectstriebes zu verschaffen."

1 The reading τῳ (for τινι), adopted in the Received Text, is allowed by all modern critics to be wrong. The obvious translation of ἐν τῷ πράγματι is, "in the matter in question."

2 Ἐν ἁγιασμῷ, not εἰς ἁγιασμὸν.

3 We retain ἡμᾶς, with Griesbach and the Received Text.

4 Observe the expression φιλοτιμεῖσθαι ἡσυχάζειν, almost equivalent to "be ambitious to be unambitious."

5 Διὰ τοῦ Ἰησοῦ. It is much more natural to connect these words with ἄξει than with κοιμηθέντας, as in the Authorised Version.

6 Ἐν κελεύσματι. The word denotes the shout used in battle. See, for instance, Thucyd. ii. 92. Eur. Hec. 928.

7 Οἱ νεκροὶ ἐν Χριστῷ, equivalent to οἱ κοιμ. ἐν Χ. 1 Cor. xv. 18. Winer's construction (Grammatik, p. 128) is different, and (we think) mistaken.

the living, who remain unto that day, shall be caught up with
them among the clouds to meet the Lord Jesus in the air; and
so both we and they shall be for ever with the Lord. Where- 18
fore comfort one another with these words. V.

The suddenness of Christ's coming a motive to watchfulness.

But of the times and seasons, brethren, when 1
these things shall be, you need no warning. For your- 2
selves know perfectly that the day of the Lord will
come as a thief in the night; and while men say Peace and 3
Safety, destruction shall come upon them in a moment, as the
pangs of travail upon a woman with child; and there shall be
no escape. But you, brethren, are not in darkness, that That 4
day should come upon you as the robber on sleeping men;[1]
for you are all the children of the light and of the day. We 5
are not of the night, nor of darkness; therefore let us not 6
sleep as do others, but let us watch and be sober; for they who 7
slumber, slumber in the night; and they who are drunken, are
drunken in the night; but let us, who are of the day, be 8
sober; arming ourselves with faith and love for a breast-plate;
and wearing for our helmet the hope of salvation. For to ob- 9
tain salvation, not to abide His wrath, hath God ordained us,
through our Lord Jesus Christ, who died for us, that whether 10
we wake or sleep we should live together with Him. Where- 11
fore exhort one another, and build one another up, even as
you already do.

The Presbyters to be duly regarded.

Moreover I beseech you, brethren, to acknowledge 12
those who are labouring among you; who preside over
you in the Lord's name, and give you admonition. I beseech 13
you to esteem them very highly in love, for their work's sake.
And maintain peace among yourselves.

Postscript addressed to the Presbyters.[3]

Duties of the Presbyters.

But you, brethren, I exhort; admonish the dis- 14
orderly, encourage the timid, support the weak, be

[1] There is some authority for the reading κλέπτας, adopted by Lachmann,—"as the daylight surprises robbers;" and this sort of transition, where a word suggests a rapid change from one metaphor to another, is not unlike the style of St. Paul.

[2] Οἰκοδομεῖτε. The full meaning is, "build one another up, that you may all together grow into a temple of God." The word is frequently used by St. Paul in this sense, which is fully explained 1 Cor. iii. 10–17. It is very difficult to express the meaning by any single word in English, and yet it would weaken the expression too much if it were diluted into a periphrasis fully expressing its meaning.

[3] It appears evident that those who are here directed, νουθετεῖτε, are the same who

15 patient with all. Take heed that none of you return evil for
16 evil, but strive to do good always, both to one another and to
17 all men. In every season keep a joyful mind; let nothing
18 cause your prayers to cease; continue to give thanks, whatever
be your lot; for this is the will of God in Christ Jesus concern-
19,20 ing you. Quench not the manifestation of the Spirit; think
21 not meanly of[1] prophesyings; try all [which the prophets
22 utter;] reject the false, but keep the good;[2] hold yourselves
aloof from every form of evil.

Concluding prayers and salutations.

23 Now may the God of peace Himself sanctify you
wholly; and may your whole nature, your spirit and
soul and body, be preserved blameless, when you stand before
24 our Lord Jesus Christ at His appearing. Faithful is He who
calls you; He will fulfil my prayer.
25,26 Brethren, pray for me. Greet all the brethren with the
27 kiss of holiness.[3] I adjure you, in the name of our Lord Jesus,
to see that this letter be read to all the[4] brethren.

Autograph benediction.

28 [5]The grace of our Lord Jesus Christ be with you.[6]

are described immediately before (v. 12) as *νουθετοῦντας*. Also, they are very solemnly directed (v. 27) to see that the letter be read to all the Christians in Thessalonica; which implies that they presided over the Christian assemblies.

1 We know, from the First Epistle to Corinth, that this warning was not unneeded in the early church. (See 1 Cor. xiv.) The gift of prophesying (*i. e.* inspired preaching) had less the appearance of a supernatural gift than several of the other Charisms; and hence it was thought little of by those who sought more for display than edification.

2 *Δοκιμάζειν* includes the notion of rejecting that which does not abide the test.

3 *Φιλήματι ἁγίῳ*. This alludes to the same custom which is referred to in Rom. xvi. 16. 1 Cor. xvi. 20. 2 Cor. xiii. 12. We find a full account of it, as it was practised in the early church, in the Apostolical Constitutions (book ii. ch. 57). The men and women were placed in separate parts of the building where they met for worship; and then, before receiving the Holy Communion, the men kissed the men, and the women the women: before the ceremony, a proclamation was made by the principal deacon:—"Let none bear malice against any: let none do it in hypocrisy." *Μή τις κατά τινος μή τις ἐν ὑποκρίσει· εἶτα καὶ ἀσπαζέσθωσαν ἀλλήλους οἱ ἄνδρες, καὶ ἀλλήλας αἱ γυναῖκες, τὸ ἐν Κυρίῳ φίλημα.* It should be remembered by English readers, that a kiss was in ancient times (as, indeed, it is now in many foreign countries) the ordinary mode of salutation between friends when they met.

4 *'Αγίοις* is omitted in the best MSS.

5 It should be remarked that this concluding benediction is used by St. Paul at the end of the Epistles to the Romans, Corinthians (under a longer form in the 2 Cor.), Galatians, Ephesians, Philippians, and Thessalonians. And, in a shorter form, it is used also at the end of all his other Epistles. It seems (from what he says in 2 Thess. iii 17, 18) to have been always written with his own hand.

6 The "Amen" of the Received Text is a later addition, not found in the best MSS

The strong expressions used in this letter concerning the malevolence of the Jews, lead us to suppose that the Apostle was thinking not only of their past opposition at Thessalonica,[1] but of the difficulties with which they were beginning to surround him at Corinth. At the very time of his writing, that same people who had "killed the Lord Jesus and their own prophets," and had already driven Paul "from city to city," were showing themselves "a people displeasing to God, and enemies to all mankind," by endeavouring to hinder him from speaking to the Gentiles for their salvation (1 Thess. ii. 15, 16). Such expressions would naturally be used in a letter written under the circumstances described in the Acts (xviii. 6), when the Jews were assuming the attitude of an organised and systematic resistance,[2] and assailing the Apostle in the language of blasphemy,[3] like those who had accused our Saviour of casting out devils by Beelzebub.

Now, therefore, the Apostle left the Jews and turned to the Gentiles He withdrew from his own people with one of those symbolical actions, which, in the East, have all the expressiveness of language,[4] and which, having received the sanction of our Lord Himself,[5] are equivalent to the denunciation of woe. He shook the dust off his garments,[6] and proclaimed himself innocent of the blood[7] of those who refused to listen to the voice which offered them salvation. A proselyte, whose name was Justus,[8] opened his door to the rejected Apostle; and that house became thenceforward the place of public teaching. While he continued doubtless to lodge with Aquila and Priscilla (for the Lord had said[9] that His Apostle should abide in the house where the "Son of Peace" was), he met his flock in the house of Justus. Some place convenient for general meeting was evidently necessary for the continuance of St. Paul's work in the cities where he resided. So long as possible, it was the synagogue. When he was exiled from the Jewish place of worship, or unable from other causes to attend it, it was such a place as providential circumstances might suggest. At Rome it was his own hired lodging (Acts xxviii. 30): at Ephesus it was the school of Tyrannus (Acts xix. 9). Here at Corinth it was a house "contiguous to the Synagogue,"[10] offered on the emergency for the Apostle's use by one who had listened and believed. It may

1 See above, Chap. IX.

2 Ἀντιτασσομένων, a military term.

3 Βλασφημούντων. Compare Matt. xii. 24–31.

4 See Acts xiii. 51 [p. 181]. 5 Mark vi. 11.

6 Ἐκτιναξάμενος τὰ ἱμάτια. Acts xviii. 6.

7 See Acts v. 28. xx. 26. Also Ezek. xxxiii. 8, 9, and Mat. xxvii. 24.

8 Nothing more is known of him. The name is Latin.

9 Luke x. 6, 7. We should observe that ἔμενε is the word used (v. 3) of the house of Aquila and Priscilla, ἦλθε (v. 7) of that of Justus.

10 Συνομοροῦσα τῇ συναγωγῇ

readily be supposed that no convenient place could be found in the manufactory of Aquila and Priscilla. There, too, in the society of Jews lately exiled from Rome, he could hardly have looked for a congregation of Gentiles; whereas Justus, being a proselyte, was exactly in a position to receive under his roof indiscriminately, both Hebrews and Greeks.

Special mention is made of the fact, that the house of Justus was "contiguous to the Synagogue." We are not necessarily to infer from this that St. Paul had any deliberate motive for choosing that locality. Though it might be that he would show the Jews, as in a visible symbol, that "by their sin salvation had come to the Gentiles, to provoke them to jealousy,"[1]—while at the same time he remained as near to them as possible, to assure them of his readiness to return at the moment of their repentance. Whatever we may surmise concerning the motive of this choice, certain consequences must have followed from the contiguity of the house and the Synagogue, and some incident resulting from it may have suggested the mention of the fact. The Jewish and Christian congregations would often meet face to face in the street; and all the success of the Gospel would become more palpable and conspicuous. And even if we leave out of view such considerations as these, there is a certain interest attaching to any phrase which tends to localise the scene of Apostolical labours. When we think of events that we have witnessed, we always reproduce in the mind, however dimly, some image of the place where the events have occurred. This condition of human thought is common to us and to the Apostles. The house of John's mother at Jerusalem (Acts xii.), the proseucha by the waterside at Philippi (Acts xvi.), were associated with many recollections in the minds of the earliest Christians. And when St. Paul thought, even many years afterwards, of what occurred on his first visit to Corinth, the images before the "inward eye," would be not merely the general aspect of the houses and temples of Corinth, with the great citadel overtowering them, but the Synagogue and the house of Justus, the incidents which happened in their neighbourhood, and the gestures and faces of those who encountered each other in the street.

If an interest is attached to the places, a still deeper interest is attached to the persons referred to in the history of the planting of the Church. In the case of Corinth, the names both of individuals and families are mentioned in abundance. The name of Epænetus is the first that occurs to us: for he seems to have been the earliest Corinthian convert. St. Paul himself speaks of him, in the Epistle to the Romans (xvi. 5), as "the first-fruits of Achaia."[2] The same expression is used in the First Epistle to

[1] Rom. xi. 11.

[2] Ἀπαρχὴ τῆς Ἀχαΐας. Some MSS. have Ἀσίας. If that reading is correct, all the difficulty of reconciling Rom. xvi. 5 with 1 Cor. xvi. 15 disappears.

the Corinthians (xvi. 15) of the household of Stephanas; from which we may perhaps infer that Epænetus was a member of that household.[1] Another Christian of Corinth, well worthy of the recollection of the Church in after ages, was Caius (1 Cor. i. 14), with whom St. Paul found a home on his next visit (Rom. xvi. 23), as he found one now with Aquila and Priscilla. We may conjecture, with reason, that his present host and hostess had now given their formal adherence to St. Paul, and that they left the Synagogue with him. After the open schism had taken place, we find the Church rapidly increasing. "Many of the Corinthians began to believe, when they heard, and came to receive baptism."[2] (Acts xviii. 8.) We derive some information from St. Paul's own writings concerning the character of those who became believers. Not many of the philosophers,—not many of the noble and powerful (1 Cor. i. 26)—but many of those who had been profligate and degraded (1 Cor. vi. 11) were called. The ignorant of this world were chosen to confound the wise: and the weak to confound the strong. From St. Paul's language we infer that the Gentile converts were more numerous than the Jewish. Yet one signal victory of the Gospel over Judaism must be mentioned here,—the conversion of Crispus (Acts xviii. 8),—who, from his position as "ruler of the Synagogue," may be presumed to have been a man of learning and high character, and who now, with all his family, joined himself to the new community. His conversion was felt to be so important, that the Apostle deviated from his usual practice (1 Cor. i. 14–16), and baptised him, as well as Caius and the household of Stephanas, with his own hand.

Such an event as the baptism of Crispus must have had a great effect in exasperating the Jews against St. Paul. Their opposition grew with his success. As we approach the time when the second letter to the Thessalonians was written, we find the difficulties of his position increasing. In the first Epistle the writer's mind is almost entirely occupied with the thought of what might be happening at Thessalonica: in the second, the remembrance of his own pressing trials seems to mingle more conspicuously with the exhortations and warnings addressed to those who are absent. He particularly asks for the prayers of the Thessalonians, that he may be delivered from the perverse and wicked men around him, who were destitute of faith.[3] It is evident that he was in a condition of fear and anxiety. This is further manifest from the words which were heard by him in a vision vouchsafed at this critical period.[4] We have already had occasion

[1] It is possible that Stephanas and Epænetus (assuming the reading 'Αχαΐας to be correct) were natives of some other place in Achaia; but it is nearly certain they were from Corinth, as St. Paul was writing in one case from, in the other to, that city.

[2] Ακούοντες ἐπίστευον καὶ ἐβαπτίζοντο.

[3] See below, 2 Thess. iii. 2.

[4] Acts xviii. 9, 10.

to observe,[1] that such timely visitations were granted to the Apostle, when he was most in need of supernatural aid. In the present instance, the Lord, who spoke to him in the night, gave him an assurance of His presence,[2] and a promise of safety, along with a prophecy of good success at Corinth, and a command to speak boldly without fear, and not to keep silence. From this we may infer that his faith in Christ's presence was failing,—that fear was beginning to produce hesitation,—and that the work of extending the Gospel was in danger of being arrested. The servant of God received conscious strength in the moment of trial and conflict; and the divine words were fulfilled in the formation of a large and flourishing church at Corinth, and a safe and continued residence in that city, through the space of a year and six months.

Not many months of this period had elapsed when St. Paul found it necessary to write again to the Thessalonians. The excitement which he had endeavoured to allay by his first Epistle had increased, and the fanatical portion of the Church had availed themselves of the impression produced by St. Paul's personal teaching to increase it. It will be remembered that a subject on which he had especially dwelt while he was at Thessalonica,[3] and to which he had also alluded in his first Epistle,[4] was the second advent of Our Lord. We know that our Saviour Himself had warned His disciples that "of that day and that hour knoweth no man, no, not the angels of heaven, but the Father only;" and we find these words remarkably fulfilled by the fact that the early Church, and even the Apostles themselves, expected their Lord to come again in that very generation. St. Paul himself shared in that expectation, but being under the guidance of the Spirit of Truth, he did not deduce any erroneous conclusions from this mistaken premise. Some of his disciples, on the other hand, inferred that if indeed the present world were so soon to come to an end, it was useless to pursue their common earthly employments any longer. They forsook their work, and gave themselves up to dreamy expectations of the future; so that the whole framework of society in the Thessalonian Church was in danger of dissolution. Those who encouraged this delusion, supported it by imaginary revelations of the Spirit;[5] and they even had recourse to forgery, and circulated a letter purporting to be written by St. Paul,[6] in confirmation of their views. To check this evil, St. Paul wrote his second Epistle. In this he endeavours to remove their present erroneous expectations of Christ's immediate coming, by reminding them of certain signs which must precede the second advent.

[1] Above, p. 283.
[2] Compare Matt. xxviii. 20.
[3] As he himself reminds his readers (2 Thess. ii. 5), and as we find in the Acts (xvii. 7). See p. 327.
[4] 1 Thess. v. 1–11.
[5] 2 Thess. ii. 2.
[6] 2 Thess. ii. 2. Compare 2 Thess. iii. 17.

He had already told them of these signs when he was with them; and this explains the extreme obscurity of his description of them in the present Epistle; for he was not giving new information, but alluding to facts which he had already explained to them at an earlier period. It would have been well if this had been remembered by all those who have extracted such numerous and discordant prophecies and anathemas from certain passages in the following Epistle.

SECOND EPISTLE TO THE THESSALONIANS.[1]

I.

Salutation. Paul, and Silvanus, and Timotheus, to the Church of 1
the Thessalonians, in the name of God our Father, and our
Lord Jesus Christ. Grace be to you, and peace, from God 2
our Father and our Lord Jesus Christ.

Encouragement under their persecutions from the hope of Christ's coming. I[2] am bound to give thanks to God continually 3
on your behalf, brethren, as is fitting, because of the
abundant increase of your faith, and the overflowing
love wherewith you are filled, every one of you, towards each
other. So that I myself boast of you among the churches of 4
God, for your stedfast endurance and faith, in all the persecu-
tions and afflictions which you now are bearing. And these 5
things are a token that the righteous judgment of God will
grant you a share in His heavenly kingdom, for whose cause
you are even now suffering. For doubtless God's righteous- 6
ness cannot but render back trouble to those who trouble you,
and give to you, who now are troubled, rest with me,[3] when 7
the Lord Jesus shall be revealed to our sight, and shall descend
from heaven with the angels of His might, in flames of fire, to 8
take vengeance on those who know not God, and will not
hearken to the Glad-tidings of my Lord Jesus Christ. Then 9
shall there go forth against them from[4] the presence of the

[1] It is evident that this Epistle was written at the time here assigned to it, soon after the first, from the following considerations:—

(1) The state of the Thessalonian Church described in both Epistles is almost exactly the same. (A.) The same excitement prevailed concerning the expected advent of Our Lord, only in a greater degree. (B.) The same party continued fanatically to neglect their ordinary employments. Compare 2 Thess. iii. 6–14 with 1 Thess. iv. 10–12 and 1 Thess. ii. 9.

(2) Silas and Timotheus were still with St. Paul. 2 Thess. i. 1.

[2] See note on 1 Thess. i. 3.

[3] See above, note on the use of the plural pronoun, p. 391, n. 1

[4] 'Ἀπὸ, proceeding from.

Lord, and from the brightness of His glorious majesty, their
10 righteous doom, even an everlasting destruction. In that day
of His coming shall the full light of His glory be manifested
in His people, and His wonders beheld in all who had faith[1]
in Him; and you are of that number, for with faith you re-
11 ceived my testimony. To this end I pray continually on your
behalf, that our God may count you worthy of the calling
wherewith He has called you, and may, in His mighty power,
perfect within you the love of goodness and the work of faith.
12 That the name of our Lord Jesus may be glorified in you, and
that you may be glorified[2] in Him, in such wise as may fitly
II. answer to the mercy of our God, and of our Lord Jesus Christ.

Warning against an immediate expectation of Christ's coming.

1 But concerning the appearing of our Lord Jesus
Christ, and our gathering together to meet Him, I
2 beseech you, brethren, not rashly to let yourselves be
shaken from your soberness of mind, nor to be agitated
either by any pretended revelation of the Spirit, or by any rumour,
or by any letter[3] supposed to come from me, saying that the
3 day of Christ is close at hand. Let no one deceive you, by any
means; for before that day, the falling away must first have
come, and the man of sin be revealed, the son of perdition;
4 who opposes himself and exalts himself against all that is
called God, and against all worship; even to seat himself[4] in
the temple of God, and take on himself openly the signs of
5 Godhead. Do you not remember that when I was still with
6 you, I often[5] told you this? You know, therefore, the hin-
drance why he is not yet revealed, as he will be in his own
7 season.[6] For the mystery of lawlessness[7] is already working,

1 The reading πιστεύσασιν rests on the authority of the best MSS.

2 The glory of our Lord at His coming will be "manifested in His people" (see v. 10); that is, they, by virtue of their union with Him, will partake of His glorious likeness. Cf. Rom. viii. 17, 18, 19. And, even in this world, this glorification takes place partially by their moral conformity to His image. See Rom. viii. 30, and 2 Cor. iii. 18.

3 See the preceding remarks upon the occasion of this Epistle.

4 The received text interpolates ὡς θεὸν before καθίσαι, but the MSS. do not confirm this reading.

5 Observe that it is ἔλεγον, not ἔλεξα.

6 Νῦν here is not an adverb of time, but (as often) a conjunction; so "now" is often used in English.

7 The proper meaning of ἄνομος is, *one unrestrained by law:* hence it is often used as *a transgressor*, or, generally, *a wicked man*, as ἀνομία is used often simply for *iniquity;* but in this passage it seems best to keep to the original meaning of the word.

only he, who now hinders, will hinder till he be taken out of
the way; and then the lawless one will be revealed, whom the 8
Lord Jesus shall consume with the breath of His mouth,[1] and
shall destroy with the brightness of His appearing. But the 9
appearing of that lawless one shall be in the strength of Satan's
working, with all the might and signs and wonders of falsehood,
and all the delusions of unrighteousness, taking possession of 10
those who are in the way of perdition; because they would not
receive the love of the truth, whereby they might be saved.
For this cause, God will send upon them an inward working 11
of delusion, making them give their faith to lies, that all should 12
be condemned who have refused their faith to the truth, and
have taken pleasure in unrighteousness.

Exhortation to stedfastness and obedience.

But for you, brethren beloved of the Lord, I am 13
bound to thank God continually, because He chose
you from the first unto salvation, through sanctification of the
Spirit, and faith in the truth. And to this He called you 14
through my Glad-tidings, to the end that you might obtain the
glory of our Lord Jesus Christ. Therefore, brethren, be sted- 15
fast and hold fast the teaching which has been delivered to you,
whether by my words or by my letters. And may our Lord 16
Jesus Christ Himself, and our God and Father, who has loved
us, and has given us in His mercy a consolation which is eter-
nal, and a hope which cannot fail, comfort your hearts, and 17
establish you in all goodness both of word and deed.

He asks their prayers.

Finally, brethren, pray for me, that the word of 1
the Lord Jesus may hold its onward course, and
that its glory may be shown forth towards others as towards
you; and that I may be delivered from the perverse and 2
wicked; for not all men have faith. But our Lord is faithful, 3
and he will keep you steadfast, and guard you from evil. And 4
I rely upon you in the Lord, and feel confident that you are
following and will follow the charges which I give you. And 5
may our Lord guide your hearts to the love of God, and to
the patient endurance which was in Christ.

Exhorts to an orderly and

I charge you, brethren, in the name of our Lord 6

[1] This appears to be an illusion to (although not an exact quotation of) Isaiah xi. 4:—"With the breath of His lips He shall destroy the impious man." (LXX version.) In the Targum Jonathan, this prophecy (which was probably in St. Paul's thoughts) is applied to the Messiah's coming, and "the impious," רשע (ἀσεβῆ, LXX.), is interpreted to mean an individual Antichrist.

diligent life, appealing to his own example.

Jesus Christ, to withdraw yourselves from every
brother whose life is disorderly, and not guided by
7 the rules which I delivered. For you know your-
selves the way to follow my example; you know that my life
8 among you was not disorderly, nor was I fed by any man's
bounty, but earned my bread by my own labour, toiling night
9 and day, that I might not be burdensome to any of you. And
this I did, not because I am without the right[1] of being main-
tained by those to whom I minister, but that I might make
10 my own deeds a pattern for you to imitate. For when I was
among you I gave you this rule: 'If any man will not work,
11 neither let him eat.' I speak thus, because I hear that some
among you are leading a disorderly life, neglecting their own
12 work, and meddling[2] with that of others. Such, therefore, I
charge and exhort, by the authority of my Lord Jesus Christ,
to live in quietness and industry, and earn their own bread by

Mode of dealing with those who refused obedience.

13 their own labour. But you, brethren, notwithstand-
14 ing,[3] be not weary of doing good. If any man re-
fuse to obey the directions which I send by this let-
ter, mark that man, and cease from intercourse with him, that
15 so he may be brought to shame. Yet count him not as an
16 enemy, but admonish him as a brother. Now may the Lord
of peace Himself give you peace in all ways and at all sea-
sons. The Lord be with you all.

An autograph postscript the sign of genuineness. Concluding benediction.

17 I, Paul, add my salutation with my own hand,
which is a token whereby all my letters may be
known. These are the characters in which I write.
18 The grace of our Lord Jesus Christ be with you all.[4]

Such was the second of the two letters which St. Paul wrote to Thessalonica during his residence at Corinth. Such was the Christian correspondence now established, in addition to the political and commer-

[1] See note on 1 Thess. ii. 6.

[2] The characteristic paronomasia here, μηδεν ἐργαζομένους ἀλλὰ περιεργαζομένους, is not exactly translateable into English. "Busy bodies who do no business" would be an imitation.

[3] *I. e.* although your kindness may have been abused by such idle trespassers on your bounty.

[4] Ἀμήν here (as in the end of 1 Thess.) is a subsequent addition.

cial correspondence existing before, between the two capitals of Achaia and Macedonia. Along with the official documents which passed between the governors of the contiguous provinces,[1] and the communications between the merchants of the Northern and Western Ægean, letters were now sent, which related to the establishment of a "kingdom not of this world,"[2] and to "riches" beyond the discovery of human enterprise.[3]

The influence of great cities has always been important on the wide movements of human life. We see St. Paul diligently using this influence during a protracted residence at Corinth, for the spreading and strengthening of the Gospel in Achaia and beyond. As regards the province of Achaia, we have no reason to suppose that he confined his activity to its metropolis. The expression used by St. Luke[4] need only denote that it was his head-quarters, or general place of residence. Communication was easy and frequent, by land or by water,[5] with other parts of the province. Two short days' journey to the south were the Jews of Argos,[6] who might be to those of Corinth what the Jews of Berœa had been to those of Thessalonia.[7] About the same distance to the east was the city of Athens,[8] which had been imperfectly evangelised, and could be visited without danger. Within a walk of a few hours, along a road busy with traffic, was the sea-port of Cenchreæ, known to us as the residence of a Christian community.[9] These were the "Churches of God" (2 Thess. i. 4), among whom the Apostle boasted of the patience and the faith of the Thessalonians,[10]—the homes of "the saints in all Achaia" (2 Cor. i. 1), saluted at a later period, with the Church of Corinth,[11] in a letter written from Macedonia. These churches had alternately the blessings of the presence and the letters—the oral and the written teaching—of St. Paul The former of these blessings is now no longer granted to us; but those long and wearisome journeys, which withdrew the teacher so often from his anxious converts, have resulted in our possession of inspired Epistles, in all their freshness and integrity, and with all their lessons of wisdom and love.

1 Cicero's Cilician Correspondence furnishes many specimens of the letters which passed between the governors of neighbouring provinces.

2 John xviii. 36.

3 Eph. iii. 8.

4 'Εκάθισε. Acts xviii. 11.

5 Much of the intercourse in Greece has always gone on by small coasters. For the Roman roads, see Wesseling. Pouqueville mentions traces of a paved road between Corinth and Argos.

6 See pp. 18 and 385.

7 See above, p. 340.

8 We have not entered into the question of St. Paul's journey from Athens to Corinth. He might either travel by the coast road through Eleusis and Megara, or a sail of a few hours, with a fair wind, would take him from the Piræus to Cenchreæ.

9 Rom. xvi. 1.

10 Compare 1 Thess. i. 7, 8.

11 It is possible that the phrase ἐν παντὶ τόπῳ (1 Cor. i. 2) may have the same meaning.

NOTE.

THERE are some difficulties and differences of opinion, with regard to the movements of Silas and Timotheus, between the time when St. Paul left them in Macedonia, and their rejoining him in Achaia.

The facts which are distinctly stated are as follows. (1) Silas and Timotheus were left at Berœa (Acts xviii. 14) when St. Paul went to Athens. We are not told why they were left there, or what commissions they received; but the Apostle sent a message from Athens (Acts xviii. 15) that they should follow him with all speed, and (Acts xviii. 16) he waited for them there. (2) The Apostle was rejoined by them when at Corinth (Acts xviii. 5). We are not informed how they had been employed in the interval, but they came "from Macedonia." It is not distinctly said that they came together, but the impression at first sight is that they did. (3) St. Paul himself informs us (1 Thess. iii. 1), that he was "left in Athens alone," and that this solitude was in consequence of Timothy having been sent to Thessalonica (1 Thess. iii. 2). Though it is not expressly stated that Timothy was sent from Athens, the first impression is that he was.

Thus there is a seeming discrepancy between the Acts and Epistles; a journey of Timotheus to Athens, previous to his arrival with Silas and Timotheus at Corinth, appearing to be mentioned by St. Paul, and to be quite unnoticed by St. Luke.

Paley, in the Horæ Paulinæ, says that the Epistle "virtually asserts that Timothy came to the Apostle at Athens," and assumes that it is "necessary" to suppose this, in order to reconcile the history with the Epistle. And he points out three intimations in the history, which make the arrival, though not expressly mentioned, extremely probable: first, the message that they should come with all speed; secondly, the fact of his waiting for them; thirdly, the absence of any appearance of haste in his departure from Athens to Corinth. "Paul had ordered Timothy to follow him without delay: he waited at Athens on purpose that Timothy might come up with him, and he stayed there as long as his own choice led him to continue."

This explanation is satisfactory. But two others might be suggested, which would equally remove the difficulty.

It is not expressly said that Timotheus was sent *from Athens* to Thessalonica. St. Paul was anxious, as we have seen, to revisit the Thessalonians; but since he was hindered from doing so, it is highly probable (as Hemsen and Wieseler suppose) that he may have sent Timotheus to them *from Berœa*. Silas might be sent on some similar commission, and this would explain why the two companions were left behind in Macedonia. This would necessarily cause St. Paul to be "left alone in Athens." Such solitude was doubtless painful to him; but the spiritual good of the new converts was at stake. The two companions, after finishing the work entrusted to them, finally rejoined the Apostle at Corinth.[1] That he "waited for them" at Athens need cause us no difficulty: for in those days the arrival of travellers could not confidently be known beforehand. When he left Athens and proceeded to Corinth, he knew that Silas and Timotheus could easily ascertain his movements, and follow his steps, by help of information obtained at the synagogue.

[1] We should observe that the phrase is "from Macedonia," not "from Berœa."

But, again, we may reasonably suppose, that in the course of St. Paul's stay at Corinth, he may have paid a second visit to Athens, after the first arrival of Timotheus and Silas from Macedonia; and that during some such visit he may have sent Timotheus to Thessalonica. This view may be taken without our supposing, with Böttger, that the First Epistle to the Thessalonians was written at Athens. Schrader and others imagine a visit to that city at a later period of his life; but this view cannot be admitted without deranging the arguments for the date of 1 Thess., which was evidently written soon after leaving Macedonia.

Two further remarks may be added. (1) If Timothy did rejoin St. Paul at Athens, we need not infer that Silas was not with him, from the fact that the name of Silas is not mentioned. It is usually taken for granted that the second arrival of Timothy (1 Thess. iii. 6) is identical with the coming of Silas and Timotheus to Corinth (Acts xviii. 5); but here we see that only Timothy is mentioned, doubtless because he was most recently and familiarly known at Thessalonica, and perhaps, also, because the mission of Silas was to some other place. (2) On the other hand, it is not necessary to assume, because Silas and Timotheus are mentioned together (Acts xviii. 5), that they came together. All conditions are satisfied if they came about the same time. If they were sent on missions to two different places, the times of their return would not necessarily coincide.[1] In considering all these journeys, it is very needful to take into account that they would be modified by the settled or unsettled state of the country with regard to banditti, and by the various opportunities of travelling, which depend on the season and the weather, and the sailing of vessels.[2]

COIN OF CORINTH.[3]

[1] Something may be implied in the form δ,τε Σ. καὶ T. (Silas as well as Timotheus)

[2] Hindrances connected with some such considerations may be referred to in Phil iv. 10.

[3] From the British Museum. The emperor is Caligula.

CHAPTER XII

"Corinthus, Achaiæ caput, Græciæ decus, inter duo maria, Ionium et Ægeum, quasi spectaculo exposita."—Florus, ii. 16.

THE ISTHMUS.—EARLY HISTORY OF CORINTH.—ITS TRADE AND WEALTH.—CORINTH UNDER THE ROMANS.—PROVINCE OF ACHAIA.—GALLIO THE GOVERNOR.—TUMULT AT CORINTH.—CENCHREÆ.—VOYAGE BY EPHESUS TO CÆSAREA.—VISIT TO JERUSALEM.—ANTIOCH.

Now that we have entered upon the first part of the long series of St. Paul's letters, we seem to be arrived at a new stage of the Apostle's biography. The materials for a more intimate knowledge are before us. More life is given to the picture. We have advanced from the field of geographical description and general history to the higher interest of personal detail. Even such details as relate to the writing materials employed in the Epistles, and the mode in which they were transmitted from city to city,—all stages in the history of an Apostolic letter, from the hand of the amanuensis who wrote from the author's inspired dictation, to the opening and reading of the document in the public assembly of the Church to which it was addressed, have a sacred claim on the Christian's attention. For the present we must defer the examination of such particulars. We remain with the Apostle himself, instead of following the journey of his letter to Thessalonica, and tracing the effects which the last of them produced. We have before us a protracted residence in Corinth,[1] a voyage by sea to Syria,[2] and a journey by land from Antioch to Ephesus,[3] before we come to the next group of the Apostle's letters.

We must linger first for a time in Corinth, the great city, where he staid a longer time than at any other point on his previous journeys, and from which, or to which, the most important of his Epistles were written.[4] And, according to the plan we have hitherto observed, we proceed to elucidate its geographical position, and the principal stages of its history.[5]

1 Acts xviii. 11–18. 2 Acts xviii. 18–22. 3 Acts xviii. 23. See xix. 1.

4 The Epistles to the Thessalonians, Corinthians, and Romans.

5 Of four German Monographs devoted to this subject we have made use of three: Wilckens' "Rerum Corinthiacarum specimen ad illustrationem utriusque Epistolæ Paulinæ," 1747; Wagner's "Rerum Corinthiacarum specimen;" Darmstadt, 1824; Barth's "Corinthiorum Commercii et Mercaturæ Historiæ particula," Berlin, 1844.

The Isthmus[1] is the most remarkable feature in the geography of Greece; and the peculiar relation which it established between the land and the water—and between the Morea and the Continent—had the utmost effect on the whole course of the history of Greece. When we were considering the topography and aspect of Athens, all the associations which surrounded us were Athenian. Here at the Isthmus, we are, as it were, at the centre of the activity of the Greek race in general. It has the closest connection with all their most important movements, both military and commercial.

In all the periods of Greek history, from the earliest to the latest, we see the military importance of the Isthmus. The phrase of Pindar[2] is, that it was "the bridge of the sea." It formed the only line of march for an invading or retreating army. Xenophon speaks of it as "the gate of the Peloponnesus," the closing of which would make all ingress and egress impossible.[3] And we find that it was closed at various times, by being fortified and refortified by a wall, some traces of which remain to the present day. In the Persian war, when consternation was spread amongst the Greeks by the death of Leonidas, the wall was first built.[4] In the Peloponnesian war, when the Greeks turned fratricidal arms against each other, the Isthmus was often the point of the conflict between the Athenians and their enemies. In the time of the Theban supremacy, the wall again appears as a fortified line from sea to sea.[5] When Greece became Roman, the Provincial arrangements neutralized, for a time, the military importance of the Isthmus. But when the barbarians poured in from the North, like the Persians of old, its wall was repaired by Valerian.[6] Again it was rebuilt by Justinian, who fortified it with a hundred and fifty towers.[7] And we trace its history through the later period of the Venetian power in the Levant, from the vast works of 1463, to the peace of 1699, when it was made the boundary of the territories of the Republic.[8]

[1] It is from this Greek "bridge of the sea" that the name *isthmus* has been given to every similar neck of land in the world. See some remarks on this subject, and on the significance of Greek geography in general, in the Classical Museum, No. I., p. 41.

[2] *Πόντου γεφύρα*, Nem. vi. 44. *Γεφύραν ποντιάδα πρὸ Κορίνθου τείχεων*, Isth. iii. 38.

[3] Agesilaus, when he had taken Corinth, is spoken of as *ἀναπετάσας τῆς Πελοποννήσου τὰς πύλας*. Xen. Ages. 2.

[4] Herod. viii. 71. See Leake's remarks on this early and rude fortification, and on the remains of the later wall. Travels in the Morea, III. 302–304, also 287.

[5] Polyb. ii. 138. See Plutarch's Life of Cleomenes.

[6] *Ἐπὶ Οὐαλεριανοῦ δὲ καὶ Γαλιηνοῦ πάλιν οἱ Σκύθαι διαβάντες τὸν Ἴστρον ποταμὸν τήν τε Θρᾴκην ἐλῄισαν, κ.τ.λ. . . . . Πελοποννήσιοι δὲ ἀπὸ θαλάσσης εἰς θαλάσσαν τὸν Ἴσθμον διετείχισαν.* Syncelli Chronog. p. 715, ed. Bonn. See Zonaras.

[7] See Phrantzes, pp. 96, 107, 108, 117, &c. of the Bonn. edition.

[8] See the notices of the fortress of *Hexamilium* in Ducas, pp. 142, 223, 519 of the Bonn edition: and compare what is said in Dodwell's Travels in Greece, pp. 184–186 The wall was not built in a straight line, but followed the sinuosities of the ground.

Conspicuous, both in connection with the military defences of the Isthmus, and in the prominent features of its scenery, is the *Acrocorinthus*, or citadel of Corinth, which rises in form and abruptness like the rock of Dumbarton. But this comparison is quite inadequate to express the magnitude of the Corinthian citadel. It is elevated two thousand feet[1] above the level of the sea; it throws a vast shadow[2] across the plain at its base; the ascent is a journey involving some fatigue; and the space of ground on the summit is so extensive, that it contained a whole town,[3] which, under the Turkish dominion, had several mosques. Yet, notwithstanding its colossal dimensions, its sides are so precipitous, that a few soldiers are enough to guard it.[4] The possession of this fortress has been the object of repeated struggles in the latest wars between the Turks and the Greeks, and again between the Turks and the Venetians. It was said to Philip, when he wished to acquire possession of the Morea, that the Acrocorinthus was one of the *horns* he must seize, in order to secure the heifer.[5] Thus Corinth might well be called "the eye of Greece" in a military sense, as Athens has often been so called in another sense.[6] If the rock of Minerva was the Acropolis of the Athenian people, the mountain of the Isthmus was truly named "the Acropolis of the Greeks."[7]

It will readily be imagined that the view from the summit is magnificent and extensive.[8] A sea is on either hand. Across that which lies on

The remains of square towers are visible in some places. The eastern portion abutted on the Sanctuary of Neptune, where the Isthmian games are held.

[1] Dodwell. The ascent is by a zigzag road, which Strabo says was thirty stadia in length.

[2] "Qua summas caput Acrocorinthus in auras
Tollit, et alterna geminum mare protegit *umbra*."
Stat. vii. 107.

Compare the expression of Dr. Clarke: "Looking down upon the isthmus, *the shadow of the Acrocorinthus*, of a conical shape, extended exactly half across its length, the point of the cone being central between the two seas."

[3] Dodwell and Clarke. The city, according to Xenophon, was forty stadia in circumference without the Acropolis, and eighty-five with it. Hell. iv. 4, 11.

[4] See Plutarch, who says, in the Life of Aratus, that it was guarded by 400 soldiers, 50 dogs and as many keepers.

[5] Polyb. vii. 505.

[6] Cicero (Off. ii. 22) calls it "Græciæ lumen." For the application of the same phrase to Athens in another sense, see the last chapter but one.

[7] This expression (Ἑλλάνων ἀκρόπολις) is used of it in the Scholiast on Pindar. Ol. xiii. 32.

[8] Strabo had visited Corinth himself, and his description of the view shows that he had seen it. Wheler's description is as follows:—"We mounted to the top of the highest point, and had one of the most agreeable prospects in the world. On the right hand of us the Saronic Gulf, with all its little islands strewed up and down it, to Cape Colonne on the Promontory Sunium. Beyond that the islands of the Archipelago seemed to close up the mouth of the Gulf. On the left hand of us we had the Gulf of Lepanto or Corinth, as far as beyond Sicyon, bounded northward with all these famous

the east, a clear sight is obtained of the Acropolis of Athens, at a distance of forty-five miles.[1] The mountains of Attica and Bœotia, and the islands of the Archipelago, close the prospect in this direction. Beyond the western sea, which flows in from the Adriatic, are the large masses of the mountains of north-eastern Greece, with Parnassus towering above Delphi. Immediately beneath us is the narrow plain which separates the seas. The city itself is on a small table land[2] of no great elevation, connected with the northern base of the Acrocorinthus. At the edge of the lower level are the harbours which made Corinth the emporium of the richest trade of the East and the West.

We are thus brought to that which is really the characteristic both of Corinthian geography and Corinthian history, its close relation to the commerce of the Mediterranean. Plutarch[3] says, that there was a want of good harbours in Achaia; and Strabo speaks of the circumnavigation of the Morea as dangerous.[4] Cape Malea was proverbially formidable, and held the same relation to the voyages of ancient days, which the Cape of Good Hope does to our own.[5] Thus, a narrow and level isthmus,[6] across which smaller vessels could be dragged from gulph to gulph,[7] was of inesti-

mountains of old times, with the Isthmus, even to Athens, lying in a row, and presenting themselves orderly to our view. The plain of Corinth towards Sicyon or Basilico is well watered by two rivulets, well-tilled, well-planted with oliveyards and vineyards, and, having many little villages scattered up and down it, is none of the least of the ornaments of this prospect. The town also that lieth north of the Castle, in little knots of houses, surrounded with orchards and gardens of oranges, lemons, citrons, and cypress-trees, and mixed with corn-fields between, is a sight not less delightful. So that it is hard to judge whether this plain is more beautiful to the beholders or profitable to the inhabitants." This was in 1675, before the last conflicts of the Turks and Venetians. Compare Dr. Clarke's description. He was not allowed, however, by the Turkish authorities, to reach the summit. Wagner alludes in terms of praise to Pouqueville's description. It may be seen in his Travels, ch. vii.

[1] Dodwell (ii. 189), whose view was from an eminence to the S.W., from whence Mohammed II. reduced the Acrocorinth in 1458. Compare Clarke: "As from the Parthenon at Athens we had seen the citadel of Corinth, so now we had a commanding view, across the Saronic Gulf, of Salamis and the Athenian Acropolis." See above, under Athens.

[2] Τὸ *μὲν πρὸς ἄρκτον μὲρος* 'Ακροκορίνθου *ἐστὶ τὸ μάλιστα ὀρθίον· ὑφ' ᾧ κεῖται ἡ πόλις τραπεζώδους επὶ χωρίου πρὸς αὐτῇ τῇ ῥιζῇ τοῦ* 'Ακροκορίνθου. Strabo. Leake's description entirely corresponds with this, p. 251.

[3] Plut. Ar. 9. Barth patriotically compares the relation of Corinth to Greece with that of Hamburg to Germany: "Erat igitur hæc Corinthi ratio similis ei, quæ interest Hamburgho cum reliqua Germania," p. 6, note.

[4] He adds that the Sicilian sea was avoided by mariners as much as possible.

[5] The proverb concerning Malea in its Latin form was "Ubi Maleam flexeris, obliviscere quæ sunt domi."

[6] See above, note on the word "Isthmus."

[7] Hence the narrowest part of the Isthmus was called *δίολκος*, a word which in meaning and in piratic associations corresponds with the *Tarbat* of Scotch geography. The distance across is about three miles; nearer Corinth it is six miles, whence the name of the modern village of *Hexamili.*

COIN OF CORINTH.[1]

mable value to the early traders of the Levant. And the two harbours, which received the ships of a more maturely developed trade,—Cenchreæ[2] on the Eastern Sea, and Lechæum[3] on the Western, with a third and smaller port, called Schœnus,[4] where the isthmus was narrowest,—form an essential part of our idea of Corinth. Its common title in the poets is "the city of the two seas."[5] It is allegorically represented in art as a female figure on a rock, between two other figures, each of whom bears a rudder, the symbol of navigation and trade. It is the same image which appears under another form in the words of the rhetorician, who said that it was "the prow and the stern of Greece."[6]

As we noticed above a continuous fortress which was carried across the Isthmus, in connection with its military history, so here we have to mention another continuous work which was attempted, in connection with its mercantile history. This was the ship-canal;—which, after being often projected, was about to be begun again about the very time of St. Paul's visit.[7] Parallels often suggest themselves between the relation of the parts of the Mediterranean to each other, and those of the Atlantic and Pacific: for the basins of the "Midland Sea" were to the Greek and Roman trade, what the Oceanic spaces are to ours. And it is

1 Millingen. Sylloge of Ancient Unedited Coins, Pl. II. No. 30.

2 For Cenchreæ, see below. It was seventy stadia from the city.

3 Lechæum was united to Corinth by long walls. It was about twelve stadia distant from the city. Strabo, and Xen. Hellen. iv. 4 and Agesel. See Leake, p. 251.

4 Schœnus was at the point where the Isthmus was narrowest, close to the Sanctuary of Neptune and the eastern portion of the Isthmian wall. The ship is described as sailing to this port in the early times when Athens had the presidency of the games.

5 The "*bimaris Corinthus*" of Horace and Ovid. See Hor. Od. I. vii. 2. Ov. Her. xii. 27. So Julius Pollux calls it *ἀμφιθάλασσος*. Compare Eurip. Troad. 1097: *δίπορον κορυφὰν Ἴσθμιον*.

6 The phrase seems to have been proverbial. *Ὑμεῖς ἐστε τὸ δὴ γεγόμενον πρῶρα καὶ πρύμνα τῆς Ἑλλάδος.* Dio Chrys. Orat. xxxvii. 464.

7 Demetrius Poliorcetes, Julius Cæsar, and Caligula had all entertained the notion of cutting through the Isthmus. Nero really began the undertaking in the year 52, but soon desisted. See Leake (pp. 297–302), who quotes all the authorities. The portion of the trench which remains is at the narrowest part, near the shore of the Corinthian Gulf. Dodwell came upon it, after crossing Mount Geraneia from Attica P. 183

difficult, in speaking of a visit to the Isthmus of Corinth in the year 52,[1]—which only preceded by a short interval the work of Nero's engineers,—not to be reminded of the Isthmus of Panama in the year 1852, during which the active progress will be going on of an undertaking often projected, but never yet carried into effect.

There is this difference, however, between the Oceanic and the Mediterranean Isthmus, that one of the great cities of the ancient world always existed at the latter. What some future Darien may be destined to become, we cannot prophesy: but, at a very early date, we find Corinth celebrated by the poets for its wealth.[2] This wealth must inevitably have grown up, from its mercantile relations, even without reference to its two seas,—if we attend to the fact on which Thucydides laid stress that it was the place through which all ingress and egress took place between Northern and Southern Greece, before the development of commerce by water.[3] But it was its conspicuous position on the narrow neck of land between the Ægean and Ionian Seas, which was the main cause of its commercial greatness. The construction of the ship Argo is assigned by mythology to Corinth.[4] The Samians obtained their ship-builders from her. The first Greek triremes,—the first Greek sea-fights,—are connected with her history.[5] Neptune was her god. Her colonies[6] were spread over distant coasts in the East and West; and ships came from every sea to her harbours. Thus she became the common resort and the universal market of the Greeks.[7] Her population and wealth were further augmented by the manufactures[8] in metallurgy, dyeing, and porcelain, which

[1] The arguments for this date may be seen in Wieseler. We shall return to the subject again.

[2] See Hom. Il. ii. 570. Pind. Ol. xiii. 4.

[3] Οἰκοῦντες τὴν πόλιν οἱ Κορίνθιοι ἐπὶ τοῦ Ἰσθμοῦ ἀεὶ δή ποτε ἐμπόριον εἶχον, τῶν Ἑλλήνων τὸ πάλαι κατὰ γῆν τὰ πλείω ἢ κατὰ θάλασσαν, τῶν τε ἐντὸς Πελοποννήσου καὶ τῶν ἔξω, διὰ τῆς ἐκείνων παρ' ἀλλήλους ἐπιμισγόντων, χρήμασί τε δυνατοὶ ἦσαν (ὡς καὶ τοῖς παλαίοις ποιηταῖς δεδήλωται), κ. τ. λ. Thuc. i. 13.

[4] Ναῦν ἐναυπήγησατο αὕτη ἡ πόλις, οὐ τριήρη μόνον, ἀλλὰ καὶ αὐτὴν τὴν Ἀργώ. Aristides, Isthm. p. 24.

[5] Πρῶτοι Κορίνθιοι λέγονται ἐγγύτατα τοῦ νῦν τρόπου μεταχείρισαι τὰ περὶ τὰς ναῦς, καὶ τοιήρεις πρῶτον ἐν Κορίνθῳ τῆς Ἑλλάδος ναυπηγηθῆναι. φαίνεται δὲ καὶ Σαμίοις Ἀμεινοκλῆς Κορίνθιος ναυπηγὸς ναῦς ποιήσας τέσσαρας. ναυμαχία τε παλαιτάτη ὧν ἴσμεν γίγνεται Κορινθίων πρὸς Κερκυραίους. Thuc. i. 37. See Poppo's remark on the word Ἑλλάδος. "Apud alios populos quidem, ut apud Phœnices, triremes jam prius in usu fuisse, sed *e Græcis* Corinthios primos fuisse, qui ejusmodi naves ædificarent, vult dicere." Eusebius attributes the origir of triremes to the Phœnicians and Egyptians. Wilckens, p. 43.

[6] Corcyra, Syracuse, &c.

[7] Κοινὴ πάντων καταφυγή· ὅδος καὶ διέξοδος πάντων ἀνθρώπων, κοινὸν ἄστυ τῶν Ἑλλήνων, μητρόπολίς τε ἀτεχνῶς καὶ μητήρ. Aristides, p. 23. In another place he compares Corinth to a ship loaded with merchandise (p. 24), and says that a perpetual fair was held yearly and daily at the Isthmus.

[8] For some of the details concerning these manufactures, see Wilckens, § xxxix

COIN OF CORINTH.[1]

grew up in connection with the import and export of goods. And at periodical intervals the crowding of her streets and the activity of her trade received a new impulse from the strangers who flocked to the Isthmian games;—a subject to which our attention will be often called hereafter, but which must be passed over here with a simple allusion. If we add all these particulars together, we see ample reason why the wealth, luxury, and profligacy of Corinth were proverbial[2] in the ancient world.

In passing from the fortunes of the earlier, or Greek Corinth, to its history under the Romans, the first scene that meets us is one of disaster and ruin. The destruction of this city by Mummius, about the same time that Carthage[3] was destroyed by Scipio, was so complete, that, like its previous wealth, it passed into a proverb.[4] Its works of skill and luxury were destroyed or carried away. Polybius the historian saw Roman soldiers playing at draughts on the pictures of famous artists;[5] and the exhibition of vases and statues that decorated the triumph of the Capitol, introduced a new era in the habits of the Romans.[6] Meanwhile the very place of the city from which these works were taken remained desolate for many years.[7] The honour of presiding over the Isthmian games was given to Sicyon;[8] and Corinth ceased even to be a resting-place of travellers between the East and the West.[9] But a new Corinth

1 From the British Museum.

2 *Οὐ πάντος ἀνδρος εἰς Κόρινθον ἔσθ' ὁ πλοῦς* (Non cuivis homini contingit adire Corinthum). The word *Κορινθιαζεσθαι* was used proverbially for an immoral life.

3 See Ch. I. p. 11.

4 "Corinthos olim clara opibus, post clade notior." Pompon. Mela, ii. 3.

5 Strabo, viii. 6.

6 Müller's Archäologie, § 165.

7 Strabo, viii. Paus. ii. 2. "The words of Strabo are: *Πολὺν δὲ χρόνον ἐρήμη μείνασα ἡ Κόρινθος ἀνελήφθη πάλιν ὑπὸ Καίσαρος*, &c. Those of Pausanias are not less explicit as to the desolation of Corinth: *Κόρινθον δὲ οἰκοῦσι Κορινθίων οὐδεὶς ἐτι τῶν ἀρχαίων, ἔποικοι δὲ ἀποσταλέντες ὑπὸ 'Ρωμαίων*. Nevertheless, the site, I conceive, cannot have been quite uninhabited, as the Romans neither destroyed the public buildings nor persecuted the religion of the Corinthians. And as many of those buildings were still perfect in the time of Pausanias, there must have been some persons who had the care of them during the century of desolation." Leake, p. 231, note a.

8 Pausan. ii. 2.

9 On Cicero's journey between the East and West, we find him resting, not at Corinth, but at Athens. In the time of Ovid the city was rising again.

rose from the ashes of the old. Julius Cæsar, recognising the importance of the Isthmus as a military and mercantile position, sent thither a colony of Italians, who were chiefly freed men.[1] This new establishment rapidly increased by the mere force of its position. Within a few years it grew, as Sincapore[2] has grown in our days, from nothing to an enormous city. The Greek merchants, who had fled on the Roman conquest to Delos and the neighbouring coasts, returned to their former home. The Jews settled themselves in a place most convenient both for the business of commerce and for communication with Jerusalem.[3] Thus, when St. Paul arrived at Corinth after his sojourn at Athens, he found himself in the midst of a numerous population of Greeks and Jews. They were probably far more numerous than the Romans, though the city had the constitution of a *colony*,[4] and was the metropolis of a *province*.

It is commonly assumed that Greece was constituted as a province under the name of Achaia, when Corinth was destroyed by Mummius. But this appears to be a mistake.[5] There seems to have been an intermediate period, during which the country had a nominal independence, as was the case with the contiguous province of Macedonia.[6] The description which has been given of the political limits of Macedonia (Ch. IX.) defines equally the extent of Achaia. It was bounded on all other sides by the sea, and was nearly co-extensive with the kingdom of modern Greece. The name of *Achaia* was given to it, in consequence of the part played by

1 Ἐποίκους τοῦ ἀπελευθερικοῦ γενοῦς πλεῖστους. Strabo, viii. 6. See Pausan. ii. 1.

2 See the Life of Sir Stamford Raffles, and later notices of the place in Rajah Brooke's journals, &c.

3 See the preceding chapter for the establishment of the Jews at Corinth.

4 See the Latin letters on its coins. Its full name was "Colonia Laus Julia Corinthus."

5 A memoir was read on this subject by Professor K. F. Hermann of Göttingen, at the Philosophical Meeting at Basle in 1847. The substance of the memoir is given, with additional matter, in the Classical Museum, vol. vii. p. 259. "When did Greece become a Roman province?" The drift of the argument is to show that the provincial organisation did not immediately follow the destruction of Corinth by Mummius; but that Achaia was not formed into a province till the civil war between Cæsar and Pompey, or perhaps not until the time of Augustus. The apparent evidence in favour of the common hypothesis, from Pausanias and Strabo, adduced by Sigonius, is shown to be inconclusive; and direct evidence against it is brought from Plutarch, and the list of early proconsuls given by Pighius is proved to be erroneous. To Professor Hermann's arguments the writer in the Classical Museum adds further evidence from Cicero and Zonaras. There is a mistake, however, in the statement (pp. 267, 268) that Athens and Delphi were not in the province of Achaia. See the limits of the province as mentioned above.

6 From 169 to 147. See Liv. xlv. 29. The ten commissioners who, with Mummius, regulated the affairs of Greece, had a similar task with those in Asia (Liv. xxxvii. 55), which was not at that time reduced to a province; and the phrase of Rufus, "provincia obtenta est," is used in the case of Armenia.

the Achæan league in the last independent struggles of ancient Greece; and Corinth, the head of that league, became the metropolis.[2] The province experienced changes of government such as those which have been alluded to in the case of Cyprus.[3] At first it was proconsular.[4] Afterwards it was placed by Tiberius under a procurator of his own.[5] But in the reign of Claudius it was again reckoned among the "unarmed provinces,"[6] and governed by a proconsul.[7]

One of the proconsuls who were sent out to govern the province of Achaia in the course of St. Paul's second missionary journey was Gallio.[8] His original name was Annæus Novatus, and he was the brother of Annæus Seneca the philosopher. The name under which he is known to us in sacred and secular history was due to his adoption into the family of Junius Gallio the rhetorician.[9] The time of his government at Corinth, as indicated by the sacred historian, must be placed between the years 52 and 54, if the dates we have assigned to St. Paul's movements be correct. We have no exact information on this subject from any secular source, nor is he mentioned by any heathen writer as having been proconsul of Achaia. But there are some incidental notices of his life, which give rather a curious confirmation of what is advanced above. We are informed by Tacitus and Dio that he died in the year 65.[10] Pliny says that *after his consulship* he had a serious illness, for the removal of which he tried a sea-voyage:[11] and from Seneca we learn that it was *in Achaia* that his brother went on shipboard for the benefit of his health.[12] If we knew the year of Gallio's consulship, our chronological result would be brought within narrow limits. We do not possess this information; but it has been reasonably conjected[13] that his promotion, if not due to his brother's influence, would be subsequent to the year 49, in which the philosopher returned from his exile in Corsica, and had the youthful Nero

1 Καλοῦσι δὲ οὐκ Ἑλλαδος ἀλλ' Ἀχαΐας ἡγεμόνα οἱ Ῥώμαιοι, διότι ἐχειρώσαντο τοὺς Ἑλληνας, Ἀχαίων τότε τοῦ Ἑλληνικοῦ προεστηκότων. Paus. Ach.

2 See Wilckens, § xiv. Ritter says that this is the meaning of "Corinthus Achaiæ *urbs*," in Tac. Hist. ii. 1.

3 See Ch. V. 4 Dio Cass. lx. 5 Tac. Ann. i. 76.

6 "Inermes provinciæ,"—a phrase applied to those provinces which were proconsular and required the presence of no army. See p. 249, n. 11.

7 Suet. Claud. 25. 8 Acts xviii. 12.

9 Tac. Ann. xv. 73. Senec. Epist. 104. Nat. Qu. 4 Præf. Dio Cass. xl. 35.

10 Tac. as above. Dio, lxii. 25.

11 "Præterea est alius usus multiplex, principalis vero navigandi phthisi affectis . sicut proxime Annæum Gallionem fecisse *post consulatem* meminimus." Plin. N. H. xxxi. 33.

12 "Illud mihi in ore erat domini mei Gallionis, qui, cum *in Achaia* febrem habere cœpisset, protinus navem ascendit, clamitans non corporis esse sed loci morbum." Senec. Ep. 104.

13 See Anger and Wieseler.

placed under his tuition. The interval of time thus marked out between the restoration of Seneca and the death of Gallio, includes the narrower period assigned by St. Luke to the proconsulate in Achaia.

The coming of a new governor to a province was an event of great importance. The whole system of administration, the general prosperity, the state of political parties, the relative position of different sections of the population, were necessarily affected by his personal character. The provincials were miserable or happy, according as a Verres or a Cicero was sent from Rome.[1] As regards the personal character of Gallio, the inference we should naturally draw from the words of St. Luke closely corresponds with what we are told by Seneca. His brother speaks of him with singular affection; not only as a man of integrity and honesty, but as one who won universal regard by his amiable temper and popular manners.[2] His conduct on the occasion of the tumult at Corinth is quite in harmony with a character so described. He did not allow himself, like Pilate, to be led into injustice by the clamour of the Jews;[3] and yet he overlooked, with easy indifference, an outbreak of violence which a sterner and more imperious governor would at once have arrested.[4]

The details of this transaction were as follows:—The Jews, anxious to profit by a change of administration, and perhaps encouraged by the well-known compliance of Gallio's character, took an early opportunity of accusing St. Paul before him. They had already set themselves in battle array[5] against him, and the coming of the new governor was the signal for a general attack.[6] It is quite evident that the act was preconcerted and the occasion chosen. Making use of the privileges they enjoyed as a separate community, and well aware that the exercise of their worship was protected by the Roman state,[7] they accused St. Paul of

[1] For a description of the misery inflicted on a province by a bad governor, see Cic. pro leg. Man. 23.

[2] "*Gallio frater meus, quem nemo non parum amat, etiam qui amare plus non potest.* . . . . Ingenium suspicere cœpisti, omnium maximum et dignissimum. . . . . Frugalitatem laudare cœpisti, qua sic a numis resiliit, ut illos habere nec damnare videatur. . . . Cœpisti mirari comitatem et incompositam suavitatem, quæ illos quoque, quos transit, abducit, gratuitum etiam in obvios meritum. *Nemo enim mortalium uni tam dulcis est, quam hic omnibus. Cum interim tanta naturalis boni vis est, ut artem simulationemque non redoleat.*" Quæst. Nat. iv. Præf. The same character is given of him by the poet Statius. Sylv. ii. 7:

"Hoc plus quam Senecam dedisse mundo,
Aut *dulcem* generasse *Gallionem.*"

[3] Acts xviii. 14. [4] Acts xviii. 17.

[5] See above, note on ἀντιτασσομένων.

[6] Ὁμοθυμαδόν, Acts xviii. 12.

[7] See Walther's Geschichte des Römischen Rechts, p. 320: "Zuweilen war eine Stadt aus mehreren Nationen zusammengesetzt; namentlich bildeten die Juden auch ausserhalb ihres Landes in jeder Stadt ein *anerkanntes* Gemeinwesen für sich, das sich

violating their own religious law. They seem to have thought, if this violation of Jewish law could be proved, that St. Paul would become amenable to the criminal law of the empire; or, perhaps, they hoped, as afterwards at Jerusalem, that he would be given up into their hands for punishment. Had Gallio been like Festus or Felix, this might easily have happened; and then St. Paul's natural resource would have been to appeal to the emperor, on the ground of his citizenship. But the appointed time of his visit to Rome was not yet come, and the continuance of his missionary labours was secured by the character of the governor, who was providentially sent at this time to manage the affairs of Achaia.

The scene is set before us by St. Luke with some details which give us a vivid notion of what took place. Gallio is seated on that proconsular chair [1] from which judicial sentences were pronounced by the Roman magistrates. To this we must doubtless add the other insignia of Roman power, which were suitable to a colony and the metropolis of a province. Before this heathen authority the Jews are preferring their accusation with eager clamour. Their chief speaker is Sosthenes, the successor of Crispus, or (it may be) the ruler of another synagogue.[2] The Greeks [3] are standing round, eager to hear the result, and to learn something of the new governor's character; and, at the same time, hating the Jews, and ready to be the partizans of St. Paul. At the moment when the Apostle is "about to open his mouth,"[4] Gallio will not even hear his defence, but pronounces a decided and peremptory judgment.

His answer was that of a man who knew the limits of his office, and felt that he had no time to waste on the religious technicalities of the Jews.[5] Had it been a case in which the Roman law had been violated

nach seinen vaterländischen Gebräuchen regierte und die Abgaben für den Tempel in Jerusalem einsammelte." Compare Joseph. B. J. ii. 14, 4, on Cæsarea. In Alexandria, there were four distinct classes of population, among which the Jews were citizens under their Ethnarch, like the Romans under their Juridicus. For the later position of the Jews, after Caracalla had made all freemen citizens, see Walther, p. 422.

1 The βῆμα is mentioned three times in the course of this narrative. It was of two kinds; (1) fixed in some open and public place; (2) movable, and taken by the Roman magistrates to be placed wherever they might sit in a judicial character. Probably here and in the case of Pilate (John xix. 13) the former kind of seat is intended. See Smith's Dictionary of Antiquities, under "Sella." See also some remarks on "the tribunal—the indispensable symbol of the Roman judgment-seat," in the Edinburgh Review for Jan. 1847, p. 151.

2 Whether Sosthenes had really been elected to fill the place of Crispus, or was only a co-ordinate officer in the same or some other synagogue, must be left undetermined. On the organisation of the synagogues, see Ch. VI. p. 185. It should be added, that we cannot confidently identify this Sosthenes with the "brother" whose name occurs 1 Cor. i. 1.

3 See below, note on Ἕλληνες.

4 Μέλλοντος δὲ τοῦ Παύλου ἀνοίγειν τὸ στόμα, v. 14.

5 See some good remarks here by Menken, Blicke in das Leben des Apostels Paulus.

by any breach of the peace or any act of dishonesty, then it would have been reasonable and right that the matter should have been fully investigated; but, since it was only a question of the Jewish law, relating to the disputes of Hebrew superstition,[1] and to names of no public interest, he utterly refused to attend to it. They might excommunicate the offender, or inflict on him any of their ecclesiastical punishments; but he would not meddle with trifling quarrels, which were beyond his jurisdiction. And without further delay he drove the Jews away from before his judicial chair.[2]

The effect of this proceeding must have been to produce the utmost rage and disappointment among the Jews. With the Greeks and other bystanders[3] the result was very different. Their dislike of a superstitious and misanthropic nation was gratified. They held the forbearance of Gallio as a proof that their own religious liberties would be respected under the new administration; and, with the disorderly impulse of a mob which has been kept for some time in suspense, they rushed upon the ruler of the synagogue, and beat him in the very presence of the proconsular tribunal.[4] Meanwhile, Gallio took no notice[5] of the injurious punishment thus inflicted on the Jews, and with characteristic indifference left Sosthenes to his fate.

Thus the accusers were themselves involved in disgrace; Gallio obtained a high popularity among the Greeks, and St. Paul was enabled to pursue his labours in safety. Had he been driven away from Corinth, the whole Christian community of the place might have been placed in jeopardy. But the result of the storm was to give shelter to the infant Church, with opportunity of safe and continued growth. As regards the Apostle himself, his credit rose with the disgrace of his opponents. So far as he might afterwards be noticed by the Roman governor or the Greek inhabitants of the city, he would be regarded as an injured man. As his own discretion had given advantage to the holy cause at Philippi, by involving his opponents in blame,[6] so here the most imminent peril was providentially turned into safety and honour.

Thus the assurance communicated in the vision was abundantly fulfilled. Though bitter enemies had "set on" Paul (Acts xviii. 10), no one had "hurt" him. The Lord had been "with him" and "much peo-

[1] *Ζήτημα περὶ ὀνομάτων*, v. 15. We recognise here that much had been made by the Jews of the *name* of "Christ" being given to Jesus.

[2] *Καὶ ἀπήλασεν αὐτοὺς ἀπὸ τοῦ βήματος*, v. 16.

[3] The manuscript evidence tends to show that Ἕλληνες is a gloss. It cannot, however, be well doubted that the persons in question were Greeks. The reading Ἰουδαῖοι, found in some MSS., is evidently wrong.

[4] *Ἔμπροσθεν τοῦ βήματος*, v. 17.

[5] *Οὐδὲν τούτων τῷ Γ. ἔμελεν*, v. 17. See above, on Gallio's character.

[6] See p. 311.

ple" had been gathered into His church. At length the time came when the Apostle deemed it right to leave Achaia and revisit Judæa, induced (as it would appear) by a motive which often guided his journeys, the desire to be present at the great gathering of the Jews at one of their festivals,[1] and possibly also influenced by the movements of Aquila and Priscilla, who were about to proceed from Corinth to Ephesus.[2] Before his departure he took a solemn farewell of the assembled Church.[3] How touching St. Paul's farewells must have been, especially after a protracted residence among his brethren and disciples, we may infer from the affectionate language of his letters; and one specimen is given to us of these parting addresses, in the Acts of the Apostles. From the words spoken at Miletus (Acts xx.), we may learn what was said and felt at Corinth. He could tell his disciples here, as he told them there, that he had taught them "publicly and from house to house;"[4] that he was "pure from the blood of all men;"[5] that by the space of a year and a half he had "not ceased to warn every one night and day with tears."[6] And doubtless he forewarned them of "grievous wolves entering in among them, of men speaking perverse things arising[7] of themselves, to draw away disciples after them." And he could appeal to them, with the emphatic gesture of "*those hands*" which had laboured at Corinth, in proof that he had "coveted no man's gold or silver," and in confirmation of the Lord's words, that "it is more blessed to give than to receive."[8] Thus he departed, with prayers and tears, from those who "accompanied him to the ship" with many misgivings that they might "see his face no more."[9]

The three points on the coast to which our attention is called in the brief notice of this voyage contained in the Acts,[10] are Cenchreæ, the harbour of Corinth; Ephesus, on the western shore of Asia Minor; and Cæsarea Stratonis, in Palestine. More suitable occasions will be found hereafter for descriptions of Cæsarea and Ephesus. The present seems to require a few words to be said concerning Cenchreæ.

After descending from the low table-land on which Corinth was situated, the road which connected the city with its eastern harbour extended a distance of eight or nine miles across the Isthmian plain.[11] Cenchreæ has fallen with Corinth; but the name[12] still remains to mark the place of

[1] See Acts xviii. 21. There is little doubt that the festival was Pentecost. See Wieseler.

[2] Vv. 18, 19. [3] Τοῖς ἀδελφοῖς ἀποταξάμενος, v. 18. [4] V. 20.

[5] V. 26. Compare xviii. 6, and see p. 398.

[6] V. 31. Compare what is said of his tears at Philippi. Philip. iii. 18.

[7] Vv. 29, 30.

[8] Compare vv. 33–35 with xviii. 2 and with 1 Cor. iv. 12.

[9] Vv. 36–38. [10] Acts xviii. 18–22.

[11] See the descriptions in Dodwell and Leake.

[12] The modern name is Kichries. In Walpole's Memoirs, a conjecture is offered by

the port, which once commanded a large trade with Alexandria and Antioch, with Ephesus and Thessalonica, and the other cities of the Ægean. That it was a town of some magnitude may be inferred from the attention which Pausanias devotes to it in the description of the environs of Corinth;[1] and both its mercantile character, and the pains which had been taken in its embellishment, are well symbolised in the coin[2] which represents the port with a temple on each enclosing promontory, and a statue of Neptune on a rock between them.

From this port St. Paul began his yoyage to Syria. But before the vessel sailed, one of his companions performed a religious ceremony which must not be unnoticed, since it is mentioned in Scripture. Aquila[3] had bound himself by one of those vows, which the Jews often voluntarily took, even when in foreign countries, in consequence of some mercy received, or some deliverance from danger, or some other occurrence which had produced a deep religious impression on the mind. The obligations of these vows were similar to those in the case of Nazarites,—as regards abstinence from strong drinks and legal pollutions, and the wearing of the hair uncut till the close of a definite length of time. Aquila could not be literally a Nazarite; for, in the case of that greater vow, the cutting of the hair, which denoted that the legal time was expired, could only take place at the Temple in Jerusalem, or at least in Judæa.[4] In this case the ceremony was performed at Cenchreæ. Here Aquila,—who had been for some time conspicuous, even among the Jews and Christians at Corinth, for the long hair which denoted that he was under a peculiar religious restriction—came to the close of the period of obligation; and before accompanying the Apostle to Ephesus, laid aside the tokens of his vow.

Dr. Sibthorpe, that the name was given from a certain kind of grain which is still cultivated there. Some travellers (for instance, Lord Nugent) make a mistake in identifying Cenchreæ with Kalamaki, which is further to the north.

[1] Pausan. ii. 2.

[2] An engraving of this coin will be given in the second volume.

[3] It may be said that we have here cut what De Wette calls a Gordian knot, in assuming that the vow was taken by Aquila and not by Paul. This view rests partly on the arrangement of the words, the order being *Πρίσκιλλα καὶ Ἀκύλας*, contrary to St. Luke's ordinary practice; partly on the improbability that St. Paul should have taken a vow of this kind. See Meyer on this latter point. The opinion of commentators is divided on the subject. Chrysostom, Hammond, Grotius, &c., advocate the view we have taken. Heinrichs says:—"Præferendum mihi videtur, quia constructio fluit facilior, propiusque fidem est, notitiam hanc, quæ breviter nonnisi et quasi per transennam additur, de homine ignotiore adjunctam esse:" but what follows is merely a conjecture:—"videtur votum fecisse Aquila, see nullam novaculam admissurum, antequam ex fuga, quam Roma in Judæam capessebat, sospes ad ultimum Europæ portum venisset." Niemeyer had, perhaps, the same idea:—"Sie nahmen den Weg über Cenchrea nach Ephesus, weil Aquila ein Gelübde hatte, sein Haupt daselbst zu bescheeren." Char. der Bibel. p. 197 (ed. 1778).

[4] See De Wette and Meyer.

From Corinth to Ephesus, the voyage was among the islands of the Greek Archipelago. The Isles of Greece, and the waters which break on their shores, or rest among them in spaces of calm repose, always present themselves to the mind as the scenes of interesting voyages,—whether we think of the stories of early legend, or the stirring life of classical times, of the Crusades in the middle ages, or of the movements of modern travellers, some of whom seldom reflect that the land and the water round them were hallowed by the presence and labours of St. Paul. One great purpose of this book will be gained, if it tends to associate the Apostle of the Gentiles with the coasts, which are already touched by so many other historical recollections.

No voyage across the Ægean was more frequently made than that between Corinth and Ephesus. They were the capitals of the two flourishing and peaceful provinces of Achaia and Asia,[1] and the two great mercantile towns on the opposite side of the sea. If resemblances may be again suggested between the Ocean and the Mediterranean, and between ancient and modern times, we may say that the relation of these cities of the Eastern and Western Greeks to each other was like that between New York and Liverpool. Even the time taken up by the voyages constitutes a point of resemblance. Cicero says that, on his eastward passage, which was considered a long one, he spent fifteen days, and that his return was accomplished in thirteen.[2]

A fair wind, in much shorter time than either thirteen or fifteen days, would take the Apostle across from Corinth to the city on the other side of the sea. It seems that the vessel was bound for Syria, and staid only a short time in harbour at Ephesus. Aquila and Priscilla remained there while he proceeded.[3] But even during the short interval of his stay, Paul made a visit to his Jewish fellow-countrymen, and (the Sabbath being probably one of the days during which he remained) he held a discussion with them in the synagogue concerning Christianity.[4] Their curiosity was excited by what they heard, as it had been at Antioch in Pisidia; and perhaps that curiosity would have speedily been succeeded by opposition, if their visitor had staid longer among them. But he was not able to grant the request which they urgently made. He was anxious to attend the approaching festival at Jerusalem;[5] and, had he not proceeded with the ship, this might have been impossible. He was so far, however, encouraged by the opening which he saw, that he left the Ephesian Jews with a promise of his return. This promise was limited by an expression of that

[1] See how Achaia and Asia are mentioned by Tacitus, Hist. ii.

[2] Cic. Ep. [3] Κἀκείνους κατέλιπεν αὐτοῦ, v. 19.

[4] Διελέχθη, v. 19. Contrast the aorist with the imperfect διελέγετο (v. 4), used of the continued discussions at Corinth.

[5] V. 21. See above.

dependence on the Divine will which is characteristic of a Christian's life,[1] whether his vocation be to the labours of an Apostle, or to the routine of ordinary toil. We shall see that St. Paul's promise was literally fulfilled, when we come to pursue his progress on his third missionary circuit.

The voyage to Syria lay first by the coasts and islands of the Ægean to Cos and Cnidus, which are mentioned on subsequent voyages,[2] and then across the open sea by Rhodes and Cyprus to Cæsarea.[3] This city has the closest connection with some of the most memorable events of early Christianity. We have already had occasion to mention it, in alluding to St. Peter and the baptism of the first Gentile convert.[4] We shall afterwards be required to make it the subject of a more elaborate notice, when we arrive at the imprisonment which was suffered by St. Paul under two successive Roman governors.[5] The country was now no longer under native kings. Ten years had elapsed since the death of Herod Agrippa, the last event alluded to (Ch. IV.) in connection with Cæsarea. Felix had been for some years already procurator of Judæa.[6] If the aspect of the country had become in any degree more national under the reign of the Herods, it had now resumed all the appearance of a Roman province.[7] Cæsarea was its military capital, as it was the harbour by which it was approached by all travellers from the West. From this city roads[8] had been made to the Egyptian frontier on the south, and northwards along the coast by Ptolemais, Tyre, and Sidon, to Antioch, as well as across the interior by Neapolis or Antipatris to Jerusalem and the Jordan.

The journey from Cæsarea to Jerusalem is related by St. Luke in a single word.[9] No information is given concerning the incidents which occurred there :—no meetings with other Apostles,—no controversies on disputed points of doctrine,—are recorded or inferred. We are not even sure that St. Paul arrived in time for the festival at which he desired to be present.[10] The contrary seems rather to be inferred; for he is said simply to have "saluted the Church,"[11] and then to have proceeded to Antioch. It is useless to attempt to draw aside the veil which conceals the particulars of this visit of Paul of Tarsus to the city of his forefathers.

[1] Τοῦ Θεοῦ θέλοντος. See James iv. 15. Ἐὰν ὁ Κύριος θελήσῃ καὶ ζήσωμεν.

[2] Acts xxi. 1. xxvii. 7.

[3] See Acts xxi. 1–3.

[4] See p. 115. Compare p. 53.

[5] Acts xxi., &c.

[6] Tac. Ann. xiv. 54, and Josephus.

[7] See pp. 28 and 55.

[8] See the map of the Roman roads in Palestine, and the remarks, p. 84.

[9] Ἀναβάς, v. 22. Some commentators think that St. Paul did not go to Jerusalem at all, but that this participle merely denotes his going up from the ship into the town of Cæsarea: but, independently of his intention to visit Jerusalem, it is hardly likely that such a circumstance would have been specified in a narrative so briefly given.

[10] We shall see, in the case of the later voyage (Acts xx. xxi.), that he could not have arrived in time for the festival, had not the weather been peculiarly favourable.

[11] Ἀσπασάμενος τὴν ἐκκλησίαν, v. 22.

As if it were no longer intended that we should view the Church in connection with the centre of Judaism, our thoughts are turned immediately to that other city,[1] where the name "Christian" was first conferred on it.

From Jerusalem to Antioch it is likely that the journey was accomplished by land. It is the last time we shall have occasion to mention a road which was often traversed, at different seasons of the year, by St. Paul and his companions. Two of the journeys along this Phœnician coast have been long ago mentioned. Many years had intervened since the charitable mission which brought relief from Syria to the poor in Judæa (Ch. IV.), and since the meeting of the council at Jerusalem, and the joyful return at a time of anxious controversy (Ch. VII.). When we allude to these previous visits to the Holy City, we feel how widely the Church of Christ had been extended in the space of very few years. The course of our narrative is rapidly carrying us from the East towards the West. We are now for the last time on this part of the Asiatic shore. For a moment the associations which surround us are all of the primeval past. The monuments which still remain along this coast remind us of the ancient Phœnician power, and of Baal and Ashtaroth,[2]—or of the Assyrian conquerors, who came from the Euphrates to the West, and have left forms like those in the palaces of Nineveh sculptured on the rocks of the Mediterranean,[3]—rather than of anything connected with the history of Greece and Rome. The mountains which rise above our heads belong to the characteristic imagery of the Old Testament: the cedars are those of the forests which were hewn by the workmen of Hiram and Solomon; the torrents which cross the road are the waters from "the sides of Lebanon."[4] But we are taking our last view of this scenery: and, as we leave it, we feel that we are passing from the Jewish infancy of the Christian Church to its wider expansion among the Heathen.

Once before we had occasion to remark that the Church had no longer now its central point in Jerusalem, but in Antioch, a city of the Gentiles.[5] The progress of events now carries us still more remotely from the land which was first visited by the tidings of salvation. The world through which our narrative takes us begins to be European rather than Asiatic. So far as we know, the present visit which St. Paul paid to Antioch was his last.[6] We have already seen how new centres of Christian life had

[1] Κατέβη εἰς Ἀντιόχειαν, v. 22.

[2] The ruins of Tortosa and Aradus.

[3] The sculptures of Assyrian figures on the coast road near Beyrout are noticed in the works of many travellers.

[4] These torrents are often flooded, so as to be extremely dangerous; so that St. Paul may have encountered "perils of rivers" in this district. Maundrell says that the traveller Spon lost his life in one of these torrents.

[5] Pp. 108, 109.

[6] Antioch is not mentioned in the Acts after xviii. 22.

been established by him in the Greek cities of the Ægean. The course of the Gospel is further and further towards the West; and the inspired part of the Apostle's biography, after a short period of deep interest in Judæa, finally centres in Rome.

COIN OF CORINTH.[1]

[1] From the British Museum.

CHAPTER XIII.

"We see not yet all things put under Him."—Heb. ii. 8.

THE SPIRITUAL GIFTS, CONSTITUTION, ORDINANCES, DIVISIONS, AND HERESIES OF THE PRIMITIVE CHURCH IN THE LIFETIME OF ST. PAUL.

WE are now arrived at a point in St. Paul's history when it seems needful for the full understanding of the remainder of his career, and especially of his Epistles, to give some description of the internal condition of those churches which looked to him as their father in the faith. Nearly all of these had now been founded, and regarding the early development of several of them, we have considerable information from his letters to them and from other sources. This information we shall now endeavour to bring into one general view ; and in so doing (since the Pauline Churches were only particular portions of the universal Church), we shall necessarily have to consider the distinctive peculiarities and internal condition of the primitive Church generally, as it existed in the time of the Apostles.

The feature which most immediately forces itself upon our notice, as distinctive of the Church in the Apostolic age, is its possession of supernatural gifts. Concerning these, our whole information must be derived from Scripture, because they appear to have vanished with the disappearance of the Apostles themselves, and there is no authentic account of their existence in the Church in any writings of a later date than the books of the New Testament. This fact gives a more remarkable and impressive character to the frequent mention of them in the writings of the Apostles, where the exercise of such gifts is spoken of as a matter of ordinary occurrence. Indeed, this is so much the case, that these miraculous powers are not even mentioned by the Apostolic writers as a class apart (as we should now consider them), but are joined in the same classification with other gifts, which we are wont to term natural endowments or "talents."[1] Thus St. Paul tells us (1 Cor. xii. 11) that all these

[1] The two great classifications of them in St. Paul's writings are as follows :—

I. (1 Cor. xii. 8.)

Class 1. ᾧ μὲν	Class 2. ἑτέρῳ δὲ	Class 3. ἑτέρῳ δὲ
(α¹) λόγος σοφίας.	(β¹) πίστις.	(γ¹) γένη γλωσσῶν.
(α²) λόγος γνώσεως.	(β²) χαρίσματα ἰαμάτων.	(γ²) ἑρμηνεία γλωσσῶν
	(β³) ἐνεργήματα δυνάμεων.	
	(β⁴) προφητεία.	
	(β⁵) διακρίσεις πνευμάτων.	

charisms, or spiritual gifts, were wrought by one and the same spirit, who distributed them to each severally according to His own will; and among these he classes the gift of healing, and the gift of Tongues, as falling under the same category with the talent for administrative usefulness, and the faculty of Government. But though we learn from this to refer the ordinary natural endowments of men, not less than the supernatural powers bestowed in the Apostolic age, to a divine source, yet, since we are treating of that which gave a distinctive character to the Apostolic Church, it is desirable that we should make a division between the two classes of gifts, the extraordinary and the ordinary: although this division was not made by the Apostles at the time when both kinds of gifts were in ordinary exercise.

The most striking manifestation of divine interposition was the power of working what are commonly called Miracles, that is, changes in the usual operation of the laws of nature. This power was exercised by St. Paul himself very frequently (as we know from the narrative in the Acts), as well as by the other Apostles; and in the Epistles we find repeated allusions to its exercise by ordinary Christians.[1] As examples of the operation of this power, we need only refer to St. Paul's raising Eutychus from the dead, his striking Elymas with blindness, his healing the sick at Ephesus,[2] and his curing the father of Publius at Melita.[3]

The last-mentioned examples are instances of the exercise of the *gift*

II. (1 Cor. xii. 28.)

1. *ἀπόστολοι.*
2. *πρoφῆται.* See (β^4).
3. *διδαυκαλοι;* including (a^1) and (a^2) perhaps.
4. *δυνάμεις.* See (β^3).
5. (1) *χαρίσματα ἰαμάτων.* See (β^2).
   (2) *ἀντιλήψεις.*
   (3) *κυβερνήσεις.*
   (4) *γένη γλωσσῶν.* See (γ^1).

It may be remarked, that the following divisions are in I. and not in II.; viz. ρ^1, β^5, and γ^2: a^1 and a^2, though not explicitly in II., yet are probably included in it as necessary gifts for *ἀπόστολοι*, and perhaps also for *διδάσκαλοι*, as Neander supposes.

It is difficult to observe any principle which runs through these classifications; probably I. was not meant as a systematic classification at all; II., however, certainly was in some measure, because St. Paul uses the words *πρῶτον, δεύτερον, τρίτον*, &c.

It is very difficult to arrive at any certain conclusion on the subject, because of our imperfect understanding of the nature of the *χαρίσματα* themselves; they are alluded to only as things well known to the Corinthians, and of course without any precise description of their nature.

In Rom. xii. 6 another unsystematic enumeration of four charisms is given; viz. (1) *προφητεία*, (2) *διακονία*, (3) *διδασκαλία*, (4) *παράκλησις*.

[1] Gal. iii. 5, *ὁ ἐνεργῶν* [observe the present tense] *δυνάμεις ἐν ὑμῖν*, is one of many examples.

[2] Acts xix. 11, 12.

[3] On this latter miracle, see the excellent remarks in "Smith's Voyage and Shipwreck of St. Paul," p. 115.

of healing,[1] which was a peculiar branch of the *gift of miracles*,[2] and sometimes apparently possessed by those who had not the higher gift. The source of all these miraculous powers was the charism of *faith;* namely, that peculiar kind of wonder-working faith spoken of in Matt. xvii. 20. 1 Cor. xii. 9 and xiii. 2, which consisted in an intense belief that all obstacles would vanish before the power given: this must of course be distinguished from that *disposition* of faith which is essential to the Christian life.

We have remarked that the exercise of these miraculous powers is spoken of both in the Acts and Epistles as a matter of ordinary occurrence; and in that tone of quiet (and often incidental) allusion, in which we mention the facts of our daily life. And this is the case, not in a narrative of events long past (where unintentional exaggeration might be supposed to have crept in), but in the narrative of a cotemporary, writing immediately after the occurrence of the events which he records, and of which he was an eye-witness; and yet farther, this phenomenon occurs in letters which speak of those miracles as wrought in the daily sight of the readers addressed. Now the question forced upon every intelligent mind is, whether such a phenomenon can be explained except by the assumption that the miracles did really happen. Is this assumption more difficult than that of Hume (which has been revived with an air of novelty by modern infidels), who cuts the knot by assuming that whenever we meet with an account of a miracle, it is *ipso facto* to be rejected as incredible, no matter by what weight of evidence it may be supported?

Besides the power of working miracles, other supernatural gifts of a less extraordinary character were bestowed upon the early Church; the most important were the *gift of tongues*,[3] and the *gift of prophecy*. With regard to the former there is much difficulty, from the notices of it in Scripture, in fully comprehending its nature. But from the passages where it is mentioned[4] we may gather thus much concerning it: *first*, that it was not a *knowledge* of foreign languages, as is often supposed; we never read of its being exercised for the conversion of foreign nations, nor (except on the day of Pentecost alone) for that of individual foreigners; and even on that occasion the foreigners present were all Jewish proselytes, and most of them understood the Hellenistic[5] dialect. *Secondly*, we learn that this gift was the result of a sudden influx of supernatural inspiration, which came upon the new believer immediately after his baptism, and recurred

[1] Χάρισμα ἰαμάτων. [2] Χάρισμα δυνάμεων. [3] Χάρισμα γλωσσῶν.

[4] viz. Mark xvi. 17. Acts ii. 4, &c. Acts x. 47. Acts xi. 15–17. 1 Cor. xii., and 1 Cor. xiv. We must refer to the notes on these two last-named chapters for some further discussion of the difficulties connected with this gift.

[5] This must probably have been the case with all the foreigners mentioned, except the Parthians, Medes, Elamites, and Arabians, and the Jews from these latter countries would probably understand the Aramaic of Palestine.

afterwards at uncertain intervals. *Thirdly*, we find that while under its influence the exercise of the *understanding* was suspended, while the *spirit* was rapt into a state of ecstacy by the immediate communication of the Spirit of God. In this ecstatic trance the believer was constrained by an irresistible[1] power to pour forth his feelings of thanksgiving and rapture in words; yet the words which issued from his mouth were not his own; he was even (usually) ignorant of their meaning; they were the words of some foreign language, and not intelligible to the bystanders, unless some of these chanced to be natives of the country where the language was spoken. St. Paul desired that those who possessed this gift should not be suffered to exercise it in the congregation, unless some one present possessed another gift (subsidiary to this), called the "*interpretation of tongues*,"[2] by which the ecstatic utterance of the former might be rendered available for general edification. Another gift, also, was needful for the checking of false pretensions to this and some other charisms, viz., the gift of *discerning of spirits*,[3] the recipients of which could distinguish between the real and the imaginary possessors of spiritual gifts.[4]

From the *gift of tongues* we pass, by a natural transition, to the *gift of prophecy*.[5] It is needless to remark that, in the Scriptural sense of the term, a *prophet* does not mean a *foreteller of future events*, but *a revealer of God's will to man;* though the latter sense may (and sometimes does) include the former. So the gift of prophecy was that charism which enabled its possessors to utter, with the authority of inspiration, divine strains of warning, exhortation, encouragement, or rebuke; and to teach and enforce the truths of Christianity with supernatural energy and effect The wide diffusion among the members of the Church of this prophetical inspiration was a circumstance which is mentioned by St. Peter as distinctive of the Gospel dispensation;[6] in fact, we find that in the family of Philip the Evangelist alone,[7] there were four daughters who exercised this gift; and the general possession of it is in like manner implied by the directions of St. Paul to the Corinthians.[8] The latter Apostle describes the marvellous effect of the inspired addresses thus spoken.[9] He looks upon the gift of prophecy as one of the great instruments for the conversion of unbelievers; and far more serviceable in this respect than the gift of tongues, although by some of the new converts it was not so highly esteemed, because it seemed less strange and wonderful.

[1] His spirit was not subject to his will. See 1 Cor. xiv. 32.

[2] Ἑρμηνεία γλωσσῶν.

[3] Διάκρισις πνευμάτων

[4] This latter charism seems to have been requisite for the presbyters. See 1 Thess. v. 21.

[5] Χάρισμα προφητείας. If it be asked why we class this as among the *supernatural* or *extraordinary* gifts, it will be sufficient to refer to such passages as Acts xi. 27, 28.

[6] Acts ii. 17, 18.

[7] Acts xxi. 9.

[8] 1 Cor. xi. 4, and 1 Cor. xiv. 24, 31, 34.

[9] 1 Cor. xiv. 25.

Thus far we have mentioned the *extraordinary* gifts of the Spirit which were vouchsafed to the Church of that age alone ; yet (as we have before said) there was no strong line of division, no "great gulf fixed" between these, and what we now should call the ordinary gifts, or natural endowments of the Christian converts. Thus the *gift of prophecy* cannot easily be separated by any accurate demarcation from another charism often mentioned in Scripture, which we should now consider an ordinary talent, namely, the *gift of teaching*.[1] The distinction between them appears to have been that the latter was more habitually and constantly exercised by its possessors than the former: we are not to suppose, however, that it was necessarily given to different persons ; on the contrary, an access of divine inspiration might at any moment cause the *teacher* to speak as a *prophet ;* and this was constantly exemplified in the case of the Apostles, who exercised the gift of prophecy for the conversion of their unbelieving hearers, and the gift of teaching for the building up of their converts in the faith.

Other gifts specially mentioned as charisms are the *gift of government*[2] and the *gift of ministration*.[3] By the former, certain persons were specially fitted to preside over the Church and regulate its internal order ; by the latter its possessors were enabled to minister to the wants of their brethren, to manage the distribution of relief among the poorer members of the Church, to tend the sick, and carry out other practical works of piety.

The mention of these latter charisms leads us naturally to consider the *offices* which at that time existed in the Church, to which the possessors of these gifts were severally called, according as the endowment which they had received fitted them to discharge the duties of the respective functions. We will endeavour, therefore, to give an outline of the constitution and government of the primitive Christian churches, as it existed in the time of the Apostles, so far as we can ascertain it from the information supplied to us in the New Testament.

Amongst the several classifications which are there given of church officers, the most important (from its relation to subsequent ecclesiastical history) is that by which they are divided into Apostles,[4] Presbyters, and

[1] *Χάρισμα διδασκαλίας.*

[2] *Χάρισμα κυβερνησεως.*

[3] *Χάρισμα διακονίας* or *ἀντιλήψεως.*

[4] *Ἀπόστολοι καὶ πρεσβύτεροι* are mentioned Acts xv. 2 and elsewhere, and the two classes of presbyters and deacons are mentioned Phil. i. 1, *ἐπισκόποις καὶ διακόνοις.* See p. 434, n. 1.

The following are the facts concerning the use of the word *ἀπόστολο* in the New Testament. It occurs—

once in St. Matthew ;—of the Twelve.

once in St. Mark ; of the Twelve.

Deacons. The monarchical, or (as it would be now called) the episcopal element of church government was, in this first period, supplied by the authority of the Apostles. This title was probably at first confined to "the Twelve," who were immediately nominated to their office (with the exception of Matthias) by our Lord himself. To this body the title was limited by the Judaizing section of the Church; but St. Paul vindicated his own claim to the Apostolic name and authority as resting upon the same commission given him by the same Lord; and his companion, St. Luke, applies the name to Barnabas also. In a lower sense, the term was applied to all the more eminent Christian teachers; as, for example, to Andronicus and Junias.[1] And it was also sometimes used in its simple etymological sense of *emissary*, which had not yet been lost in its other and more technical meaning. Still those only were called emphatically *the* Apostles who had received their commission from Christ himself, including the eleven who had been chosen by Him while on earth, with St. Matthias and St. Paul, who had been selected for the office by their Lord (though in different ways) after His ascension.

In saying that the Apostles embodied that element in church government, which has since been represented by episcopacy, we must not, however, be understood to mean that the power of the Apostles was subject to those limitations to which the authority of bishops has always been subjected. The primitive bishop was surrounded by his council of presbyters, and took no important step without their sanction; but this was far from being the case with the Apostles. They were appointed by Christ himself, with absolute power to govern His Church; to them He had given the keys of the kingdom of Heaven, with authority to admit or

6 times in St. Luke;—5 times of the Twelve, once in its general etymological sense.
once in St. John;—in its general etymological sense.
30 times in Acts;—(always in plural) 28 times of the Twelve, and twice of Paul and Barnabas.
3 times in Romans;—twice of St. Paul, once of Andronicus.
16 times in Corinthians;—14 times of St. Paul or the Twelve, twice in etymological sense, viz. 2 Cor. viii. 23, and xi. 13.
3 times in Gal.;—of St. Paul and the Twelve.
4 times in Ephes.;—of St. Paul and the Twelve.
once in Philip.;—etymological sense.
once in Thess.;—of St. Paul.
4 times in Timothy;—of St. Paul.
once in Titus;—of St. Paul.
once in Hebrews (iii. 1);—of Christ himself.
3 times in Peter;—of the Twelve.
once in Jude;—of the Twelve.
3 times in Apocalypse;—either of "false apostles" or of the Twelve.

Besides this, the word ἀποστόλη is used to signify the Apostolic office, once in Acts and three times by St. Paul (who attributes it to himself).

[1] Rom. xvi. 7

to exclude; they were also guided by His perpetual inspiration, so that all their moral and religious teaching was absolutely and infallibly true; they were empowered by their solemn denunciations of evil, and their inspired judgments on all moral questions, to bind and to loose, to remit and to retain the sins of men.[1] This was the essential peculiarity of their office, which can find no parallel in the after history of the Church. But, so far as their function was to govern, they represented the monarchical element in the constitution of the early Church, and their power was a full counterpoise to that democratic tendency which has sometimes been attributed to the ecclesiastical arrangements of the Apostolic period. Another peculiarity which distinguishes them from all subsequent rulers of the Church is, that they were not limited to a sphere of action defined by geographical boundaries; the whole world was their diocese, and they bore the Glad-tidings, east or west, north or south, as the Holy Spirit might direct their course at the time, and governed the churches which they founded wherever they might be placed. Moreover, those charisms which were possessed by other Christians singly and severally, were collectively given to the Apostles, because all were needed for their work. The *gift of miracles* was bestowed upon them in abundant measure, that they might strike terror into the adversaries of the truth, and win, by outward wonders, the attention of thousands, whose minds were closed by ignorance against the inward and the spiritual. They had the *gift of prophecy* as the very characteristic of their office, for it was their especial commission to reveal the truth of God to man; they were consoled in the midst of their labours by heavenly visions, and rapt in supernatural ecstasies, in which they "spake in tongues" "to God and not to man."[2] They had the "*gift of government*," for that which came upon them daily was "the care of all the Churches;" the "*gift of teaching*," for they must build up their converts in the faith; even the "*gift of ministration*" was not unneeded by them, nor did they think it beneath them to undertake the humblest offices of a deacon for the good of the Church. When needful, they could "serve tables" and collect alms, and work with their own hands at mechanical trades, "that so labouring they might support the weak;" inasmuch as they were the servants of Him who came not to be ministered unto, but to minister.

Of the offices concerned with Church government, the next in rank to that of the Apostles was the office of Overseers or Elders, more usually known (by their Greek designations) as Bishops or Presbyters. These

[1] No doubt, *in a certain sense*, this power is shared (according to the teaching of our Ordination Service) by Christian ministers now, but it is in quite a secondary sense; viz. only so far as it is exercised in exact accordance with the inspired teaching of the Apostles.

[2] See note on 1 Cor. xiv. 18.

terms are used in the New Testament as equivalent,[1] the former (*ἐπίσκοπος*) denoting (as its meaning of *overseer* implies) the duties, the latter (*πρεσβύτερος*) the rank, of the office. The history of the Church leaves us no room for doubt that on the death of the Apostles, or perhaps at an earlier period (and, in either case, by their directions), one amongst the presbyters of each church was selected to preside over the rest, and to him was applied emphatically the title of *the* bishop or overseer, which had previously belonged equally to all; thus he became in reality (what he was sometimes called) the successor of the Apostles, as exercising (though in in a lower degree) that function of government which had formerly belonged to them. But in speaking of this change we are anticipating; for at the time of which we are now writing, at the foundation of the Gentile Churches, the Apostles themselves were the chief governors of the Church, and the presbyters of each particular society were co-ordinate with one another. We find that they existed at an early period in Jerusalem, and likewise that they were appointed by the Apostles upon the first formation of a church in every city. The same name, "Elder," was attached to an office of a corresponding nature in the Jewish synagogues, whence both title and office were probably derived. The name of Bishop was afterwards given to this office in the Gentile churches, at a somewhat later period, as expressive of its duties, and as more familar than the other title to Greek ears.[2]

The office of the Presbyters was to watch over the particular church in which they ministered, in all that regarded its external order and internal purity; they were to instruct the ignorant,[3] to exhort the faithful, to confute the gainsayers,[4] to "warn the unruly, to comfort the feeble-minded, to support the weak, to be patient towards all."[5] They were "to take heed to the flock over which the Holy Ghost had made them overseers, to feed the Church of God which He had purchased with His own blood."[6] In one word, it was their duty (as it has been the duty of all who have been called to the same office during the nineteen centuries which have succeeded) to promote to the utmost of their ability, and by every means within their reach, the spiritual good of all those committed to their care.[7]

[1] Thus, in the address at Miletus, the same persons are called *ἐπισκόπους* (Acts xx. 28) who had just before been named *πρεσβυτέρους* (Acts xx. 17). See also the Pastoral Epistles, *passim*.

[2] 'Επισκοπος was the title of the Athenian commissioners to their subject allies. See Scholiast on Aristoph. Aves, 1023.

[3] 1 Tim. iii. 2. [4] Tit. i. 9. [5] 1 Thess. v. 14. [6] Acts xx. 28.

[7] Other titles, denoting their office, are applied to the presbyters in some passages; viz *οἱ προιστάμενοι* (Rom. xii. 8, and 1 Thess. v. 12), *οἱ ἡγούμενοι* (Heb. xiii. 7), *οἱ κατηχοῦντες* (Eph. iv. 11), *διδάσκαλοι* (1 Cor. xii. 28). It is, indeed, possible (as Neander thinks) that the *διδάσκαλοι* may at first have been sometimes different from

The last of the three orders, that of Deacons, did not take its place in the ecclesiastical organisation till towards the close of St. Paul's life; or, at least, this name was not assigned to those who discharged the functions of the Diaconate till a late period; the Epistle to the Philippians being the earliest in which the term occurs[1] in its technical sense. In fact, the word (*διάκονος*) occurs thirty times in the New Testament, and only three times (or at most four) is it used as an official designation; in all the other passages it is used in its simple etymological sense of *a ministering servant.* It is a remarkable fact, too, that it never occurs in the Acts as the title of those seven Hellenistic Christians who are generally (though improperly) called the seven deacons, and who were only elected to supply a temporary emergency.[2] Although the title of the Diaconate, however, does not occur till afterwards, the office seems to have existed from the first in the Church of Jerusalem (see Acts v. 6, 10); those who discharged its duties were then called the *young men*, in contradistinction to to the presbyters or *elders;* and it was their duty to assist the latter by discharging the mechanical services requisite for the well-being of the Christian community. Gradually, however, as the Church increased, the natural division of labour would suggest a subdivision of the ministrations performed by them; those which only required bodily labour would be intrusted to a less educated class of servants, and those which required the work of the head, as well as the hands (such, for example, as the distribution of alms), would form the duties of the deacons; for we may now speak of them by that name, which became appropriated to them before the close of the Apostolic epoch.

There is not much information given us, with regard to their functions, in the New Testament: but, from St. Paul's directions to Timothy, concerning their qualifications, it is evident that their office was one of considerable importance. He requires that they should be men of grave character, and "not greedy of filthy lucre;" the latter qualification relating to their duty in administering the charitable fund of the Church. He desires that they should not exercise the office till after their character had been first subjected to an examination, and had been found free from all

the *πρεσβύτεροι*, as the *χάρισμα διδασκαλίας* was distinct from the *χάρισμα κυβερνήσεως;* but those who possessed both gifts would surely have been chosen presbyters from the first, if they were to be found; and, at all events, in the time of the Pastoral Epistles we find the offices united.

[1] In Romans xvi. 1, it is applied to a woman; and we cannot confidently assert that it is there used technically to denote an office, especially as the word *διάκονος* is so constantly used in its non-technical sense of one who ministers in any way to others.

[2] We observe, also, that when any of the seven are referred to, it is never by the title of deacon; thus Philip is called "the evangelist" (Acts xxi. 8). In fact, the office of the seven was one of much higher importance than that held by the subsequent deacons.

imputation against it. If (as is reasonable) we explain these intimations by what we know of the Diaconate in the succeeding century, we may assume that its duties in the Apostolic Churches (when their organisation was complete), were to assist the presbyters in all that concerned the outward service of the Church, and in executing the details of those measures, the general plan of which was organised by the presbyters. And, doubtless, those only were selected for this office who had received the *gift of ministration* (διακονίας) previously mentioned.

It is a disputed point whether there was an order of Deaconesses to minister among the women in the Apostolic Church; the only proof of their existence is the epithet attached to the name of Phœbe,[1] which may be otherwise understood. At the same time, it must be acknowledged that the almost Oriental seclusion in which the Greek women were kept, would render the institution of such an office not unnatural in the churches of Greece, as well as in those of the East.

Besides the three orders of Apostles, Presbyters, and Deacons, we find another classification of the ministry of the Church in the Epistle to the Ephesians,[2] where they are divided under four heads, viz.,[3] 1st, Apostles; 2ndly, Prophets; 3rdly, Evangelists; 4thly, Pastors and Teachers. By the fourth class we must understand[4] the Presbyters to be denoted, and we then have two other names interpolated between these and the Apostles; viz. *Prophets* and *Evangelists*. By the former we must understand those on whom the gift of prophecy was bestowed in such abundant measure as to constitute their peculiar characteristic; and whose work it was to impart constantly to their brethren the revelations which they received from the Holy Spirit. The term *Evangelist* is applied to those missionaries, who, like Philip the Hellenist,[5] and Timothy,[6] travelled from place to place, to bear the Glad-tidings of Christ to unbelieving nations or individuals. Hence it follows that the Apostles were all Evangelists, although there were also Evangelists who were not Apostles. It is needless to add that our modern use of the word Evangelist (as meaning *writer of a Gospel*) is of later date, and has no place here.

All these classes of Church-officers were maintained (so far as they required it) by the contributions of those in whose service they laboured. St. Paul lays down, in the strongest manner, their right to such maintenance;[7] yet, at the same time, we find that he very rarely accepted the offerings, which, in the exercise of this right, he might himself have claimed. He preferred to labour with his own hands for his own support, that he

[1] Rom. xvi. 1. See p. 435, n. 1.

[2] Eph. iv. 11.

[3] A similar classification occurs 1 Cor. xii. 28; viz., 1st, Apostles; 2dly, Prophets; 3rdly, Teachers.

[4] See above, p. 434, n. 7

[5] Acts xxi. 8.

[6] 2 Tim. iv. 5.

[7] 1 Cor. ix. 7–14.

might put his disinterested motives beyond the possibility of suspicion; and he advises the presbyters of the Ephesian Church to follow his example in this respect, that so they might be able to contribute, by their own exertions, to the support of the helpless.

The mode of appointment to these different offices varied with the nature of the office itself. The Apostles, as we have seen, received their commission directly from Christ himself; the Prophets were appointed by that inspiration which they received from the Holy Spirit, yet their claims would be subjected to the judgment of those who had received the gift of *discernment of spirits.* The Evangelists were sent on particular missions from time to time, by the Christians with whom they lived (but not without a special revelation of the Holy Spirit's will to that effect), as the Church of Antioch sent away Paul and Barnabas to evangelise Cyprus. The presbyters and deacons were appointed by the Apostles themselves (as[1] at Lystra, Iconium, and Antioch in Pisidia), or by their deputies, as in the case of Timothy and Titus; yet, in all such cases, it is not improbable that the concurrence of the whole body of the Church was obtained; and it is possible that in other cases, as well as in the appointment of the seven Hellenists, the officers of the Church may have been elected by the Church which they were to serve.

In all cases, so far as we may infer from the recorded instances in the Acts, those who were selected for the performance of Church offices were solemnly set apart for the duties to which they devoted themselves. This *ordination* they received, whether the office to which they were called was permanent or temporary. The Church, of which they were members, devoted a preparatory season to "fasting and prayer;" and then those who were to be set apart were consecrated to their work by that solemn and touching symbolical act, the laying on of hands, which has been ever since appropriated to the same purpose and meaning. And thus, in answer to the faith and prayers of the Church, the spiritual gifts necessary for the performance of the office were[2] bestowed by Him who is "the Lord and Giver of Life."

Having thus briefly attempted to describe the Offices of the Apostolic Church, we pass to the consideration of its Ordinances. Of these, the chief were, of course, those two sacraments ordained by Christ himself, which have been the heritage of the Universal Church throughout all succeeding ages. The sacrament of Baptism was regarded as the door of entrance into the Christian Church, and was held to be so indispensable that it could not be omitted even in the case of St. Paul. We have seen that although he had been called to the apostleship by the direct interven-

[1] Acts xiv. 21.

[2] Compare 2 Tim i. 6. "The gift of God which is in thee by the putting on of my hands."

tion of Christ himself, yet he was commanded to receive baptism at the hands of a simple disciple. In ordinary cases, the sole condition required for baptism was, that the persons to be baptized should acknowledge Jesus as the Messiah,[1] "declared to be the Son of God with power, by his resurrection from the dead." In this acknowledgment was virtually involved the readiness of the new converts to submit to the guidance of those whom Christ had appointed as the Apostles and teachers of His Church; and we find[2] that they were subsequently instructed in the truths of Christianity, and were taught the true spiritual meaning of those ancient prophecies, which (if Jews) they had hitherto interpreted of a human conqueror and an earthly kingdom. This instruction, however, took place *after* baptism, not before it; and herein we remark a great and striking difference from the subsequent usage of the Church. For, not long after the time of the Apostles, the primitive practice in this respect was completely reversed; in all cases the convert was subjected to a long course of preliminary instruction before he was admitted to baptism, and in some instances the catechumen remained unbaptized till the hour of death; for thus he thought to escape the strictness of a Christian life, and fancied that a death-bed baptism would operate magically upon his spiritual condition, and ensure his salvation. The Apostolic practice of immediate baptism would, had it been retained, have guarded the Church from so baneful a superstition.

It has been questioned whether the Apostles baptized adults only, or whether they admitted infants also into the Church; yet we cannot but think it almost demonstratively proved that infant baptism[3] was their

[1] This condition would (at first sight) appear as if only applicable to Jews or Jewish proselytes, who already were looking for a Messiah; yet, since the acknowledgment of Jesus as the Messiah involves in itself, when rightly understood, the whole of Christianity, it was a sufficient foundation for the faith of Gentiles also. In the case both of Jews and Gentiles, the thing required, in the first instance, was a belief in the testimony of the Apostles, that "this Jesus had God raised up," and thus had "made that same Jesus, whom they had crucified, both Lord and Christ." The most important passages, as bearing on this subject, are the baptism and confirmation of the Samaritan converts (Acts viii.), the account of the baptism of the Ethiopian eunuch (Acts viii.), of Cornelius (Acts x.), of the Philippian gaoler (Acts xvi.) (the only case where the baptism of a non-proselyted heathen is recorded), of John's disciples at Ephesus (Acts xix.), and the statement in Rom. x. 9, 10.

[2] This appears from such passages as Gal. vi. 6, 1 Thess. v. 12, Acts xx. 20, 28, and many others.

[3] It is at first startling to find Neander, with his great learning and candor, taking an opposite view. Yet the arguments on which he grounds his opinion, both in the *Planting and Leading* and in the *Church History*, seem plainly inconclusive. He himself acknowledges that the principles laid down by St. Paul (1 Cor. vii. 14) contain a justification of infant baptism, and he admits that it was practised in the time of Irenæus. His chief reason against thinking it an Apostolical practice (Church History, sect. 3) is, that Tertullian opposed it; but Tertullian does not pretend to call it an innovation. Surely if infant baptism had not been sanctioned by the Apostles, we

practice. This seems evident, not merely because (had it been otherwise) we must have found some traces of the first introduction of infant baptism afterwards, but also because the very idea of the Apostolic baptism, as *the entrance into Christ's kingdom*, implies that it could not have been refused to infants without violating the command of Christ: "Suffer little children to come unto me, and forbid them not, for of such is the kingdom of heaven." Again, St. Paul expressly says that the children of a Christian parent were to be looked upon as consecrated to God (ἅγιοι) by virtue of their very birth;[1] and it would have been most inconsistent with this view, as well as with the practice in the case of adults, to delay the reception of infants into the Church till they had been fully instructed in Christian doctrine.

We know from the Gospels[2] that the new converts were baptized "in the name of the Father, and of the Son, and of the Holy Ghost." And after the performance[3] of the sacrament, an outward sign was given that God was indeed present with His Church, through the mediation of The Son, in the person of The Spirit; for the baptized converts, when the Apostles had laid their hands on them, received some spiritual gift, either the power of working miracles, or of speaking in tongues, bestowed upon each of them by Him who "divideth to every man severally as He will." It is needless to add that baptism was (unless in exceptional cases) administered by immersion, the convert being plunged beneath the surface of the water to represent his death to the life of sin, and then raised from this momentary burial to represent his resurrection to the life of righteousness. It must be a subject of regret that the general discontinuance of this original form of baptism (though perhaps necessary in our northern climates) has rendered obscure to popular apprehension some very important passages of Scripture.

With regard to the other sacrament, we know both from the Acts and the Epistles how constantly the Apostolic Church obeyed their Lord's command: "Do this in remembrance of me." Indeed it would seem that originally their common meals were ended, as that memorable feast at Emmaus had been, by its celebration; so that, as at the first to those

should have found some one at least among the many churches of primitive Christendom resisting its introduction.

[1] 1 Cor. vii. 14.

[2] Matt. xxviii. 19. We cannot agree with Neander (Planting and Leading, I. 25 and 188) that the evidence of this positive command is at all impaired by our finding baptism described in the Acts and Epistles as baptism *into the name of Jesus;* the latter seems a condensed expression which would naturally be employed, just as we now speak of *Christian* baptism. The answer of St. Paul to the disciples of John the Baptist at Ephesus (Acts xix. 3), is a strong argument that the name of the Holy Ghost occurred in the baptismal formula then employed.

[3] The case of Cornelius, in which the gifts of the Holy Spirit were bestowed *before* baptism, was an exception to the ordinary rule.

two disciples, their Lord's presence was daily "made known unto them in the breaking of bread."[1] Subsequently the communion was administered at the close of the public feasts of love (ἀγάπαι[2]) at which the Christians met to realise their fellowship one with another, and to partake together, rich and poor, masters and slaves, on equal terms, of the common meal. But this practice led to abuses, as we see in the case of the Corinthian Church, where the very idea of the ordinance was violated by the providing of different food for the rich and poor, and where some of the former were even guilty of intemperance. Consequently a change was made, and the communion administered before instead of after the meal, and finally separated from it altogether.

The *festivals* observed by the Apostolic Church were at first the same with those of the Jews; and the observance of these was continued, especially by the Christians of Jewish birth, for a considerable time. A higher and more spiritual meaning, however, was attached to their celebration; and particularly the Paschal feast was kept, no longer as a shadow of good things to come, but as the commemoration of blessings actually bestowed in the death and resurrection of Christ. Thus we already see the germ of our Easter festival in the exhortation which St. Paul gives to the Corinthians concerning the manner in which they should celebrate the paschal feast. Nor was it only at this annual feast that they kept in memory the resurrection of their Lord; every Sunday likewise was a festival in memory of the same event; the Church never failed to meet for common prayer and praise on that day of the week; and it very soon acquired the name of the "Lord's Day," which it has since retained.

But the meetings of the first converts for public worship were not confined to a single day of the week; they were always frequent, often daily. The Jewish Christians met at first in Jerusalem in some of the courts of the temple, there to join in the prayers and hear the teaching of Peter and John. Afterwards the private houses[3] of the more opulent Christians were thrown open to furnish their brethren with a place of assembly; and they met for prayer and praise in some "upper chamber,"[4] with the "doors shut for fear of the Jews." The outward form and order of their worship differed very materially from our own, as indeed was necessarily the case where so many of the worshippers were under the miraculous influence of the Holy Spirit. Some were filled with prophetic inspiration; some constrained to pour forth their ecstatic feelings in the exercise of the gift of tongues, "as the Spirit gave them utterance." We see, from St. Paul's directions to the Corinthians, that there was danger

[1] Luke xxiv. 35.

[2] Jude xii. This is the custom to which Pliny alludes, when he describes the Christians meeting to partake of *cibus promiscuus et innoxius* (Ep. x. 97).

[3] See Rom. xvi. 5, and 1 Cor. xvi. 19, and Acts xviii. 7.

[4] "The upper chamber where they were gathered together." Acts xx. 8.

even then lest their worship should degenerate into a scene of confusion, from the number who wished to take part in the public ministrations; and he lays down rules which show that even the exercise of supernatural gifts was to be restrained, if it tended to violate the orderly celebration of public worship. He directs that not more than two or three should prophecy in the same assembly; and that those who had the gift of tongues should not exercise it, unless some one present had the gift of interpretation, and could explain their utterances to the congregation. He also forbids women (even though some of them might be prophetesses[1]) to speak in the public assembly; and desires that they should appear veiled, as became the modesty of their sex.

In the midst of so much diversity, however, the essential parts of public worship were the same then as now, for we find that prayer was made, and thanksgiving offered up, by those who officiated, and that the congregation signified their assent by a unanimous Amen.[2] Psalms also were chanted, doubtless to some of those ancient Hebrew melodies which have been handed down, not improbably to our own times, in the simplest form of ecclesiastical music; and addresses of exhortation or instruction were given by those whom the gift of prophecy, or the gift of teaching, had fitted for the task.

But whatever were the other acts of devotion in which these assemblies were employed, it seems probable that the daily worship always concluded with the celebration of the Holy Communion.[3] And as in this the members of the Church expressed and realised the closest fellowship, not only with their risen Lord, but also with each other, so it was customary to symbolise this latter union by the interchange of the kiss of peace before the sacrament, a practice to which St. Paul frequently alludes.[4]

It would have been well if the inward love and harmony of the Church had really corresponded with the outward manifestation of it in this touching ceremony. But this was not the case, even while the Apostles themselves poured out the wine and broke the bread which symbolised the perfect union of the members of Christ's body. The kiss of peace sometimes only veiled the hatred of warring factions. So St. Paul expresses to the

[1] Acts xxi. 9. [2] 1 Cor. xiv. 16.

[3] This seems proved by 1 Cor. xi. 20, where St. Paul appears to assume that the very object of *συνελθεῖν ἐν ἐκκλησιᾷ* was *κυρίακον δεῖπνον φαγεῖν*. As the Lord's Supper was originally the conclusion of the Agape, it was celebrated in the evening; and probably, therefore, evening was the time, on ordinary occasions, for the meeting of the church. This was certainly the case in Acts xx. 8; a passage which Neander must have overlooked when he says (Church History, sect. 3) that the church service in the time of the Apostles was held early in the morning. There are obvious reasons why the evening would have been the most proper time for a service which was to be attended by those whose day was spent in "working with their hands."

[4] See note on 1 Thess. v. 26.

Corinthians his grief at hearing that there were "divisions among them," which showed themselves when they met together for public worship. The earliest division of the Christian Church into opposing parties was caused by the Judaizing teachers, of whose factious efforts in Jerusalem and elsewhere we have already spoken. Their great object was to turn the newly converted Christians into Jewish proselytes, who should differ from other Jews only in the recognition of Jesus as the Messiah. In their view the natural posterity of Abraham were still as much as ever the theocratic nation, entitled to God's exclusive favour, to which the rest of mankind could only be admitted by becoming Jews. Those members of this party who were really sincere believers in Christianity, probably expected that a majority of their countrymen, finding their own national privileges thus acknowledged and maintained by the Christians, would on their part more willingly acknowledge Jesus as their Messiah; and thus they fancied that the Christian Church would gain a larger accession of members than could ever accrue to it from isolated Gentile converts: so that they probably justified their opposition to St. Paul on grounds not only of Jewish but of Christian policy; for they imagined that by his admission of uncircumcised Gentiles into the full membership of the Church, he was repelling far more numerous converts of Israelitish birth, who would otherwise have accepted the doctrine of Jesus. This belief (which in itself, and seen from their point of view, in that age, was not unreasonable) might have enabled them to excuse to their consciences, as Christians, the bitterness of their opposition to the great Christian Apostle. But in considering them as a party, we must bear in mind that they felt themselves more Jews than Christians. They acknowledged Jesus of Nazareth as the promised Messiah, and so far they were distinguished from the rest of their countrymen; but the Messiah himself, they thought, was only a "Saviour of His people Israel;" and they ignored that true meaning of the ancient prophecies, which St. Paul was inspired to reveal to the Universal Church, teaching us that the "excellent things" which are spoken of the people of God, and the city of God, in the Old Testament, are to be by us interpreted of the "household of faith," and "the heavenly Jerusalem."

We have seen that the Judaizers at first insisted upon the observance of the law of Moses, and especially of circumcision, as an absolute requisite for admission into the Church, "saying, Except ye be circumcised after the manner of Moses, ye cannot be saved." But after the decision of the "Council of Jerusalem" it was impossible for them to require this condition; they therefore altered their tactics, and as the decrees of the Council seemed to assume that the Jewish Christians would continue to observe the Mosaic Law, the Judaizers took advantage of this to insist on the necessity of a separation between those who kept the whole law and all others; they taught that the uncircumcised were in a lower condition as to spiritual privileges, and at a greater distance from God; and that only the circumcised converts were in a state of full acceptance with Him: in short, they kept the Gentile converts who would not submit to circumcision on the same footing as the *proselytes of the gate*, and treated the circumcised alone as *proselytes of righteousness.* When we comprehend all that was involved in this, we can easily understand the energetic opposition with which their teaching was met by St. Paul. It was no mere question of outward observance, no matter of indifference (as it might at first sight appear), whether the Gentile converts were circumcised or not; on the contrary, the question at stake was nothing less than this, whether Christians should be merely a Jewish sect under the bondage of a ceremonial law, and only distinguished from other Jews by believing that Jesus was the Messiah, or whether they should be the Catholic Church of Christ, owning no other allegiance but to Him, freed from the bondage of the letter, and bearing the seal of their inheritance no longer in their bodies, but in their hearts. We can understand now the full truth of his indignant remonstrance, "If ye be circumcised, Christ shall profit you nothing." And we can understand also the exasperation which his teaching must have produced in those who held the very antithesis of this, namely, that Christianity without circumcision was utterly worthless. Hence their long and desperate struggle to destroy the influence of St. Paul in every Church which he founded or visited; in Antioch, in Galatia, in Corinth, in Jerusalem, and in Rome. For as he was in truth the great prophet divinely commissioned to reveal the catholicity of the Christian Church, so he appeared to them the great apostate, urged by the worst motives[1] to break down the fence and root up the hedge, which separated the heritage of the Lord from a godless world.

We shall not be surprised at their success in creating divisions in the Churches to which they came, when we remember that the nucleus of all those Churches was a body of converted Jews and proselytes. The Judaizing emissaries were ready to flatter the prejudices of the influential body; nor did they abstain (as we know both from tradition and from his own letters) from insinuating the most scandalous charges against their great opponent.[2] And thus, in every Christian church established by St.

[1] That curious apocryphal book, the Clementine Recognitions, contains, in a modified form, a record of the view taken by the Judaizers of St. Paul, from the pen of the Judaizing party itself, in the pretended epistle of Peter to James. The English reader should consult the interesting remarks of Mr. Stanley on the Clementines (Stanley's Sermons, p. 374, &c.), and also Neander's Church History (American translation, vol. ii. p. 35, &c.).

[2] We learn from Epiphanius that the Ebionites accused St. Paul of renouncing

Paul, there sprang up, as we shall see, a schismatic party, opposed to his teaching and hostile to his person.

This great Judaizing party was of course subdivided into various sections, united in their main object, but distinguished by minor shades of difference. Thus, we find at Corinth, that it comprehended two factions, the one apparently distinguished from the other by a greater degree of violence. The more moderate called themselves the followers of Peter, or rather of Cephas, for they preferred to use his Hebrew name.[1] These dwelt much upon our Lord's special promises to Peter, and the necessary inferiority of St. Paul to him who was divinely ordained to be the rock whereon the Church should be built. They insinuated that St. Paul felt doubts about his own Apostolic authority, and did not dare to claim the right of maintenance,[2] which Christ had expressly given to His true Apostles. They also depreciated him as a maintainer of celibacy, and contrasted him in this respect with the great Pillars of the Church, "the brethren of the Lord and Cephas," who were married.[3] And no doubt they declaimed against the audacity of a converted persecutor, "born into the Church out of due time," in "withstanding to the face" the chief of the Apostles. A still more violent section called themselves, by a strange misnomer, the party of Christ.[4] These appear to have laid great stress upon the fact, that Paul had never seen or known Our Lord while on earth; and they claimed for themselves a peculiar connexion with Christ, as having either been among the number of His disciples, or at least as being in close connexion with the "brethren of the Lord," and especially with James, the head of the Church at Jerusalem. To this subdivision probably belonged the emissaries who professed to come "from James,"[5] and who created a schism in the Church of Antioch.

Connected to a certain extent with the Judaizing party, but yet to be carefully distinguished from it, were those Christians who are known in the New Testament as the "weak brethren."[6] These were not a factious or schismatic party; nay, they were not, properly speaking, a party at all.

Judaism because he was a rejected candidate for the hand of the High Priest's daughter. See p. 97.

1 The MS. reading is *Cephas*, not *Peter*, in those passages where the language of the Judaizers is referred to. See note on Gal. i. 18.

2 1 Cor. ix. 4, 6. 2 Cor. xi. 10.

3 1 Cor. ix. 5.

4 Such appears the most natural explanation of the Χριστοῦ party (1 Cor. i. 12). De Wette's view of it is different, and will be found in the Introduction to his Commentary on the Epistle. Another hypothesis is stated and defended at length by Neander. (Planting and Leading, p. 383, &c.) It appears to us that both De Wette's view and Neander's is inconsistent with 2 Cor. x. 7—*εἴτις πέποιθεν ἑαυτῷ Χριστοῦ εἶναι, τοῦτο λογιζέσθω πάλιν ἀφ' ἑαυτοῦ ὅτι καθὼς αὐτὸς Χριστοῦ οὕτω καὶ ἡμεῖς Χριστοῦ;* for surely St. Paul would never have said, "*As* those who claim some *imaginary communion* with Christ belong to Christ, *so also do I* belong to Christ."

5 Gal. ii. 12.

6 Rom. xiv. 1, 2. Rom. xv. 1. 1 Cor. viii. 7. ix. 22.

They were individual converts of Jewish extraction, whose minds were not as yet sufficiently enlightened to comprehend the fulness of "the liberty with which Christ had made them free." Their conscience was sensitive, and filled with scruples, resulting from early habit and old prejudices; but they did not join in the violence of the Judaizing bigots, and there was even a danger lest they should be led, by the example of their more enlightened brethren, to wound their own conscience, by joining in acts which they, in their secret hearts, thought wrong. Nothing is more beautiful than the tenderness and sympathy which St. Paul shows towards these weak Christians; while he plainly sets before them their mistake, and shows that their prejudices result from ignorance, yet he has no sterner rebuke for them than to express his confidence in their further enlightenment: "If in anything ye be otherwise minded, God shall reveal even this unto you."[1] So great is his anxiety lest the liberty which they witnessed in others should tempt them to blunt the delicacy of their moral feeling, that he warns his more enlightened converts to abstain from lawful indulgences, lest they cause the weak to stumble. "If meat make my brother to offend, I will eat no meat while the world standeth, lest I make my brother to offend."[2] "Brethren, ye have been called unto liberty, only use not liberty for an occasion to the flesh, but by love serve one another."[3] "Destroy not him with thy meat for whom Christ died."[4]

These latter warnings were addressed by St. Paul to a party very different from those of whom we have previously spoken; a party who called themselves (as we see from his epistle to Corinth) by his own name, and professed to follow his teaching, yet were not always animated by his spirit. There was an obvious danger lest the opponents of the Judaizing section of the Church should themselves imitate one of the errors of their antagonists, by combining as partizans rather than as Christians; St. Paul feels himself necessitated to remind them that the very idea of the Catholic Church excludes all party combinations from its pale, and that adverse factions, ranging themselves under human leaders, involve a contradiction to the Christian name. "Is Christ divided? was Paul crucified for you? or were you baptized into the name or Paul?" "Who then is Paul, and who is Apollos, but ministers by whom ye believed?"[5]

The Pauline party (as they called themselves) appear to have ridiculed the scrupulosity of their less enlightened brethren, and to have felt for them a contempt inconsistent with the spirit of Christian love.[6] And in their opposition to the Judaizers, they showed a bitterness of feeling

[1] Phil. iii. 15.
[2] 1 Cor. viii. 13.
[3] Gal. v. 13.
[4] Rom. xiv. 15.
[5] 1 Cor. i. 13, and 1 Cor. iii. 5.
[6] Rom. xiv. 10. "Why dost thou despise (ἐξουθενεῖς) thy brother?" is a question addressed to this party.

and violence of action,[1] too like that of their opponents. Some of them, also, were inclined to exult over the fall of God's ancient people, and to glory in their own position, as though it had been won by superior merit. These are rebuked by St. Paul for their "boasting," and warned against its consequences. "Be not high-minded, but fear; for if God spared not the natural branches, take heed lest He also spare not thee."[2] One section of this party seems to have united these errors with one still more dangerous to the simplicity of the Christian faith; they received Christianity more in an intellectual than a moral aspect; not as a spiritual religion, so much as a new system of philosophy. This was a phase of error most likely to occur among the disputatious[3] reasoners who abounded in the great Greek cities; and, accordingly, we find the first trace of its existence at Corinth. There it took a peculiar form, in consequence of the arrival of Apollos as a Christian teacher, soon after the departure of St. Paul. He was a Jew of Alexandria, and as such had received that Grecian cultivation, and had acquired that familiarity with Greek philosophy, which distinguished the more learned Alexandrian Jews. Thus he was able to adapt his teaching to the taste of his philosophising hearers at Corinth far more than St. Paul could do; and, indeed, the latter had purposely abstained from even attempting this at Corinth.[4] Accordingly, the School which we have mentioned called themselves the followers of Apollos, and extolled his philosophic views, in opposition to the simple and unlearned simplicity which they ascribed to the style of St. Paul. It is easy to perceive in the temper of this portion of the Church the germ of that rationalising tendency which afterwards developed itself into the Greek element of Gnosticism. Already, indeed, although that heresy was not yet invented, some of the worst opinions of the worst Gnostics found advocates among those who called themselves Christians; there was, even now, a party in the Church which defended fornication[5] on theory, and which denied the resurrection of the dead.[6] These heresies probably originated with those who (as we have observed) embraced Christianity as a new philosophy; some of whom attempted, with a perverted ingenuity, to extract from its doctrines a justification of the immoral life to which they were addicted. Thus, St. Paul had taught that the law was dead to true Christians; meaning thereby, that those who were penetrated by the Holy Spirit, and made one with Christ, worked righteousness, not in consequence of a law of precepts and penalties, but through the necessary operation of the spiritual principle within them. For, as the law against

[1] See the admonitions addressed to the *πνευ ματικοί* in Gal. v. 13, 14, 26, and Gal. vi. 1–5.

[2] Rom. xi. 17–22.

[3] The *συζητηταὶ τοῦ αἰῶνος τούτοι*, 1 Cor. i. 20.

[4] 1 Cor. ii. 1.

[5] See 1 Cor. vi. 9–20.

[6] See 1 Cor. xv. 12.

theft might be said to be dead to a rich man (because he would feel no temptation to break it), so the whole moral law would be dead to a perfect Christian;[1] hence, to a real Christian, it might in one sense be truly said that *prohibitions were abolished.*[2] But the heretics of whom we are speaking took this proposition in a sense the very opposite to that which it really conveyed; and whereas St. Paul taught that prohibitions were abolished for the righteous, they maintained that all things were lawful to the wicked. "The law is dead"[3] was their motto, and their practice was what the practice of Antinomians in all ages has been. "Let us continue in sin, that grace may abound" was their horrible perversion of the Evangelical revelation that God is love. "In Christ Jesus, neither circumcision availeth anything, nor uncircumcision."[4] "The letter killeth, but the Spirit giveth life."[5] "Meat commendeth us not to God; for neither if we eat are we the better, nor if we eat not are we the worse;"[6] "the kingdom of God is not meat and drink."[7] Such were the words in which St. Paul expressed the great truth, that religion is not a matter of outward ceremonies, but of inward life. But these heretics caught up the words, and inferred that all outward acts were indifferent, and none could be criminal. They advocated the most unrestrained indulgence of the passions, and took for their maxim the worst precept of Epicurean atheism, "let us eat and drink, for to-morrow we die." It is in the wealthy and vicious cities of Rome and Corinth that we find these errors first manifesting themselves; and in the voluptuous atmosphere of the latter it was not unnatural that there should be some who would seek in a new religion an excuse for their old vices, and others who would easily be led astray by those "evil communications" whose corrupting influence the Apostle himself mentions as the chief source of this mischief.

The Resurrection of the Dead was denied in the same city and by the same[8] party; nor is it strange that as the sensual Felix trembled when Paul preached to him of the judgment to come, so these profligate cavillers shrank from the thought of that tribunal before which account must be given of the things done in the body. Perhaps, also (as some have inferred from St. Paul's refutation of these heretics), they had misunderstood the Christian doctrine, which teaches us to believe in the resurrection of a spiritual body, as though it had asserted the re-animation of "this vile body" of "flesh and blood," which "cannot inherit the kingdom

1 This state would be perfectly realised if the renovation of heart were complete; and it is practically realised in proportion as the Christian's spiritual union with Christ approaches its theoretic standard. We may believe that it was perfectly realised by St. Paul when he wrote Gal. ii. 20.

2 Compare 1 Tim. i. 9.—δικαίῳ νόμος οὐ κεῖται.

3 Πάντα μοι ἔξεστιν, 1 Cor. vi. 12.

4 Gal. v. 6.

5 2 Cor. iii. 6.

6 1 Cor. viii. 8.

7 Rom. xiv. 17.

8 This is proved by 1 Cor. xv. 33, 34.

of God;" or it is possible that a materialistic philosophy[1] led them to maintain that when the body had crumbled away in the grave, or been consumed on the funeral pyre, nothing of the man remained in being. In either case, they probably explained away the doctrine of the Resurrection as a metaphor, similar to that employed by St. Paul when he says that baptism is the resurrection of the new convert;[2] thus they would agree with those later heretics (of whom were Hymenæus and Philetus) who taught "that the Resurrection was past already."

Hitherto we have spoken of those divisions and heresies which appear to have sprung up in the several Churches founded by St. Paul at the earliest period of their history, almost immediately after their conversion. Beyond this period we are not yet arrived in St. Paul's life; and from his conversion even to the time of his imprisonment, his conflict was mainly with the Jews or Judaizers. But there were other forms of error which harassed his declining years; and these we will now endeavour (although anticipating the course of our biography) shortly to describe, so that it may not be necessary afterwards to revert to the subject, and at the same time that particular cases, which will meet us in the Epistles, may be understood in their relation to the general religious aspect of the time.

We have seen that, in the earliest epoch of the Church, there were two elements of error which had already shown themselves; namely, the bigoted, exclusive, and superstitious tendency, which was of Jewish origin; and the pseudo-philosophic, or rationalising tendency, which was of Grecian birth. In the early period of which we have hitherto spoken, and onwards till the time of St. Paul's imprisonment at Rome, the first of these tendencies was the principal source of danger; but after this, as the Church enlarged itself, and the number of Gentile converts more and more exceeded that of the Jewish Christians, the case was altered. The catholicity of the Church became an established fact, and the Judaizers, properly so called, ceased to exist as an influential party anywhere except in Palestine. Yet still, though the Jews were forced to give up their exclusiveness, and to acknowledge the uncircumcised as "fellow heirs and of the same body," their superstition remained, and became a fruitful source of mischief. On the other hand, those who sought for nothing more in Christianity than a new philosophy, were naturally increased in number, in proportion as the Church gained converts from the educated classes; the lecturers in the schools of Athens, the "wisdom seekers" of Corinth, the Antinomian perverters of St. Paul's teaching, and the Platonising rabbis of Alexandria, all would share in this tendency. The latter, indeed, as rep-

[1] If this were the case, we must suppose them to have been of Epicurean tendencies, and, so far, different from the later Platonising Gnostics, who denied the Resurrection.

[2] Col. ii. 12. Compare Rom. vi. 4.

resented by the learned Philo, had already attempted to construct a system of Judaic Platonism, which explained away almost all the peculiarities of the Mosaic theology into accordance with the doctrines of the Academy. And thus the way was already paved for the introduction of that most curious amalgam of Hellenic and Oriental speculation with Jewish superstition, which was afterwards called the Gnostic heresy. It is a disputed point at what time this heresy made its first appearance in the Church; some[1] think that it had already commenced in the Church of Corinth when St. Paul warned them to beware of the knowledge (*Gnosis*) which puffeth up; others maintain that it did not originate till the time of Basilides, long after the last Apostle had fallen asleep in Jesus. Perhaps, however, we may consider this as a difference rather about the definition of a term than the history of a sect. If we define Gnosticism to be that combination of Orientalism and Platonism held by the followers of Basilides or Valentinus, and refuse the title of Gnostic to any but those who adopted their system in its full-grown absurdity, no doubt we must not place the Gnostics among the heretics of the Apostolic age. But if, on the other hand (as seems most natural), we define a Gnostic to be one who claims the possession of a peculiar "Gnosis" (*i. e.* a deep and philosophic insight into the mysteries of theology, unattainable by the vulgar), then it is indisputable that Gnosticism had begun when St. Paul warned Timothy against those who laid claim to a "knowledge falsely so called" (ψευδώνυμος γνῶσις).[2] And, moreover, we find that, even in the Apostolic age, these arrogant speculators had begun to blend with their Hellenic philosophy certain fragments of Jewish superstition, which afterwards were incorporated into the Cabbala.[3] In spite, however, of the occurrence of such Jewish elements, those heresies which troubled the later years of St. Paul, and afterwards of St. John, were essentially rather of Gentile[4] than of Jewish origin. So far as they agreed with the later Gnosticism, this

1 This is the opinion of Dr. Burton, the great English authority on the Gnostic heresy. (Lectures, pp. 84, 85.) We cannot refer to this eminent theologian without expressing our obligation to his writings, and our admiration for that union of profound learning with clear good sense and candour which distinguishes him. His premature death robbed the Church of England of a writer who, had his life been spared, would have been inferior to none of its brightest ornaments.

2 Neander well observes, that the essential feature in Gnosticism is its re-establishing an *aristocracy of knowledge* in religion, and rejecting the Christian principle which recognises no religious distinctions between rich and poor, learned and ignorant. Church History, sect. 4.

3 Thus the "genealogies" mentioned in the Pastoral Epistles were probably those speculations about the emanations of spiritual beings found in the Cabbala; at least, such is Burton's opinion. (Pp. 114 and 413.) And the angel worship at Colossæ belonged to the same class of superstitions. Dr. Burton has shown (pp. 304-306) that the later Gnostic theories of æons and emanations were derived, in some measure, from Jewish sources, although the essential character of Gnosticism is entirely Anti-Judaical

4 See the note at the end of this Chapter.

must certainly have been the case, for we know that it was a characteristic of all the Gnostic sects to despise the Jewish Scriptures.[1] Moreover, those who laid claims to "Gnosis" at Corinth (as we have seen) were a Gentile party, who professed to adopt St. Paul's doctrine of the abolition of the law, and perverted it into Antinomianism: in short, they were the opposite extreme to the Judaizing party. Nor need we be surprised to find that some of these philosophising heretics adopted some of the wildest superstitions of the Jews; for these very superstitions were not so much the natural growth of Judaism as ingrafted upon it by its Rabbinical corrupters and derived from Oriental sources. And there was a strong affinity between the neo-Platonic philosophy of Alexandria and the Oriental theosophy which sprang from Buddhism and other kindred systems, and which degenerated into the practice of magic and incantations.

It is not necessary, however, that we should enter into any discussion of the subsequent development of these errors; our subject only requires that we give an outline of the forms which they assumed during the lifetime of St. Paul; and this we can only do very imperfectly, because the allusions in St. Paul's writings are so few and so brief, that they give us but little information. Still, they suffice to show the main features of the heresies which he condemns, especially when we compare them with notices in other parts of the New Testament, and with the history of the Church in the succeeding century.

We may consider these heresies, first, in their doctrinal, and, secondly, in their practical, aspect. With regard to the former, we find that their general characteristic was the claim to a deep philosophical insight into the mysteries of religion. Thus the Colossians are warned against the false teachers who would deceive them by a vain affectation of "Philosophy," and who were "puffed up by a fleshly mind." (Col. ii. 8, 18[2]) So, in the Epistle to Timothy, St. Paul speaks of these heretics as falsely claiming "knowledge" (gnosis). And in the Epistle to the Ephesians (so called) he seems to allude to the same boastful assumption, when he speaks of the love of Christ as surpassing "knowledge," in a passage which contains other apparent allusions[3] to Gnostic doctrine. Connected with this claim to a deeper insight into truth than that possessed by the uninitiated, was the manner in which some of these heretics explained away the facts of revelation by an allegorical interpretation. Thus we find that Hymenæus and Philetus maintained that "the Resurrection was past already." We have seen that a heresy apparently identical with this existed at a very early period in the Church of Corinth, among the

[1] Dr. Burton says:—"We find all the Gnostics agreed in rejecting the Jewish Scriptures, or at least in treating them with contempt." P. 39.

[2] Compare ἡ γνῶσις φυσιοῖ, 1 Cor. viii. 1.

[3] Eph. iii. 19. See Dr. Burton's remarks, Lectures, pp. 83 and 125.

free-thinking, or pseudo-philosophical, party there; and all the Gnostic sects of the second century were united in denying the resurrection of the dead.[1] Again, we find the Colossian heretics introducing a worship of angels, "intruding into those things which they have not seen:" and so, in the Pastoral Epistles, the "self-styled Gnostics" (ψευδων. γνωσ.) are occupied with "endless genealogies," which were probably fanciful myths, concerning the origin and emanation of spiritual beings.[2] This latter is one of the points in which Jewish superstition was blended with Gentile speculation; for we find in the Cabbala,[3] or collection of Jewish traditional theology, many fabulous statements concerning such emanations. It seems to be a similar superstition which is stigmatised in the Pastoral Epistles as consisting of "profane and old wives' fables;"[4] and, again, of "Jewish fables and commandments of men."[5] The Gnostics of the second century adopted and systematised this theory of emanations, and it became one of the most peculiar and distinctive features of their heresy. But this was not the only Jewish element in the teaching of these Colossian heretics; we find also that they made a point of conscience of observing the Jewish Sabbaths[6] and festivals, and they are charged with clinging to outward rites (στοιχεῖα τοῦ κόσμου), and making distinctions between the lawfulness of different kinds of food.

In their practical results, these heresies which we are considering had a twofold direction. On one side was an ascetic tendency, such as we find at Colossæ, showing itself by an arbitrarily invented worship of God,[7] an affectation of self-humiliation and mortification of the flesh. So, in the

[1] Burton, p. 131. So Tertullian says: "Resurrectionem quoque mortuorum manifeste annuntiatam in imaginariam significationem distorquent, asseverantes ipsam etiam mortem spiritaliter intelligendam . . . et resurrectionem eam vindicandam quâ quis aditâ veritate redanimatus . . . ignorantiæ morte discussâ, velut de sepulcro veteris hominis eruperit." Tertul. de Resurrect. Carnis, xix.

[2] See p. 449, n. 3. According to the Cabbala, there were ten *Sephiroth*, or emanations proceeding from God, which appear to have suggested the Gnostic æons. Upon this theory was grafted a system of magic, consisting mainly of the use of Scriptural words to produce supernatural effects.

[3] St. Paul denounces "the tradition of men" (Col. ii. 8) as the source of these errors; and the word Cabbala (קבלה) means tradition. Dr. Burton says, "the Cabbala had certainly grown into a system at the time of the destruction of Jerusalem; and there is also evidence that it had been cultivated by the Jewish doctors long before." P. 298.

[4] 1 Tim. iv. 7. [5] Tit. i. 14.

[6] This does not prove them, however, to have been Jews, for the superstitious heathen were also in the habit of adopting some of the rites of Judaism, under the idea of their producing some magical effect upon them; as we find from the Roman satirists. Compare Horace, Sat. I. 9, 71. ("Hodie tricesima sabbata," &c.), and Juv. VI. 542–547. See also some remarks on the Colossian heretics in our introductory remarks on the Epistle to the Colossians.

[7] Ἐθελοθρησκεία.

Pastoral Epistles, we find the prohibition of marriage,[1] the enforced abstinence from food, and other bodily mortifications, mentioned as characteristics of heresy.[2] If this asceticism originated from the Jewish element which has been mentioned above, it may be compared with the practice of the Essenes, whose existence shows that such ascetism was not inconsistent with Judaism, although it was contrary to the views of the Judaizing party properly so called. On the other hand, it may have arisen from that abhorrence of matter, and anxiety to free the soul from the dominion of the body, which distinguished the Alexandrian Platonists, and which (derived from them) became a characteristic of some of the Gnostic sects.

But this asceticism was a weak and comparatively innocent form, in which the practical results of this incipient Gnosticism exhibited themselves. Its really dangerous manifestation was derived, not from its Jewish, but from its Heathen element. We have seen how this showed itself from the first at Corinth; how men sheltered their immoralities under the name of Christianity, and even justified them by a perversion of its doctrines. Such teaching could not fail to find a ready audience wherever there were found vicious lives and hardened consciences. Accordingly, it was in the luxurious and corrupt population of Asia Minor,[3] that this early Gnosticism assumed its worst form of immoral practice defended by Antinomian doctrine. Thus, in the Epistle to the Ephesians, St. Paul warns his readers against the sophistical arguments by which certain false teachers strove to justify the sins of impurity, and to persuade them that the acts of the body could not contaminate the soul,—"Let no man deceive you with vain words; for because of these things cometh the wrath of God upon the children of disobedience."[4] Hymenæus and Philetus are the first leaders of this party mentioned by name: we have seen that they agreed with the Corinthian Antinomians in denying the resurrection, and they agreed with them no less in practice than in theory. Of the

[1] Which certainly was the reverse of the Judaizing exaltation of marriage.

[2] St. Paul declares that these errors shall come "in the last days;" but St. John says "the last days" were come in his time; and it is implied by St. Paul's words that the evils he denounces were already in action; just as he had said before to the Thessalonians, *τὸ μυστήριον ἤδη ἐνεργεῖται τῆς ἀνομίας* (2 Thess. ii. 7), where the peculiar expressions *ἀνομία* and *ὁ ἄνομος* seem to point to the Antinomian character of these heresies.

[3] Both at Colossæ and in Crete it seems to have been the Jewish form of these heresies which predominated; at Colossæ they took an ascetic direction; in Crete, among a simpler and more provincial population, the false teachers seem to have been hypocrites, who encouraged the vices to which their followers were addicted, and inoculated them with foolish superstitions (*Ἰουδαϊκοὶ μύθοι-μώρας ζητήσεις καὶ γενεαλογίας*); but we do not find in these Epistles any mention of the theoretic Antinomianism which existed in some of the great cities.

[4] Eph. v. 6. See also the whole of the warnings in Eph. v. The Epistle, though not addressed (at any rate not exclusively) to the Ephesians, was probably sent to several other cities in Asia Minor.

first of them it is expressly said that he[1] had "cast away a good conscience," and of both we are told that they showed themselves not to belong to Christ, because they had not His seal; this seal being described as twofold—"The Lord knoweth them that are His," and "Let every one who nameth the name of Christ depart from iniquity."[2] St. Paul appears to imply that though they boasted their "knowledge of God," yet that the Lord had no knowledge of them; as our Saviour had himself declared that to the claims of such false disciples He would reply, "I never *knew* you; depart from me, ye *workers of iniquity*." But in the same Epistle where these heresiarchs are condemned, St. Paul intimates that their principles were not yet fully developed; he warns Timothy[3] that an outburst of immorality and lawlessness must be shortly expected within the Church beyond anything which had yet been experienced. The same anticipation appears in his farewell address to the Ephesian presbyters, and even at the early period of his Epistles to the Thessalonians; and we see from the Epistles of St. Peter and St. Jude, and from the Apocalypse of St. John, all addressed (it should be remembered) to the Churches of Asia Minor, that this prophetic warning was soon fulfilled. We find that many Christians used their liberty as a cloak of maliciousness;[4] "promising their hearers liberty, yet themselves the slaves of corruption;"[5] "turning the grace of God into lasciviousness;"[6] that they were justly condemned by the surrounding Heathen for their crimes, and even suffered punishment as robbers and murderers.[7] They were also infamous for the practice of the pretended arts of magic and witchcraft,[8] which they may have borrowed either from the Jewish soothsayers[9] and exorcisers,[10] or from the Heathen professors of magical arts who so much abounded at the same epoch. Some of them, who are called the followers of Balaam in the Epistles of Peter and Jude, and the Nicolaitans (an equivalent name) in the Apocalypse, taught their followers to indulge in the sensual impurities, and even in the idol-feasts of the Heathen.[11] We find moreover, that

[1] 1 Tim. i. 19.
[2] 2 Tim. iii. 19. [3] 2 Tim. iii. [4] 1 Pet. ii. 16.
[5] 2 Pet. ii. 19. [6] Jude iv. [7] 1 Pet. iv. 15.
[8] Rev. ii. 20. Compare Rev. ix. 21, Rev. xxi. 8, and Rev. xxii. 15.
[9] Compare Juv. VI. 546: "Qualiacunque voles Judæi somnia vendunt."
[10] See Acts xix. 13.
[11] Such, at least, seems the natural explanation of εἰδωλόθυτα φαγεῖν (Rev. ii. 20), for we can scarcely suppose so strong a condemnation if the offence had been only eating meat which had once formed part of a sacrifice. It is remarkable how completely the Gnostics of the second century resembled these earlier heretics in all the points here mentioned. Their immorality is the subject of constant animadversion in the writings of the Fathers, who tell us that the calumnies which were cast upon the Christians by the heathen were caused by the vices of the Gnostics. Irenæus asserts that they said, "as gold deposited in the mud does not lose its beauty, so they themselves, whatever may be their outward immorality, cannot be injured by it, nor lose their

these false disciples, with their licentiousness in morals, united anarchy in politics, and resistance to law and government. They "walked after the flesh in the lust of uncleanness, and despised governments." And thus they gave rise to those charges against Christianity itself, which were made by the Heathen writers at the time, whose knowledge of the new religion was naturally taken from those amongst its professors who rendered themselves notorious by falling under the judgment of the Law.

When thus we contemplate the true character of these divisions and heresies which beset the Apostolic Church, we cannot but acknowledge that it needed all those miraculous gifts with which it was endowed, and all that inspired wisdom which presided over its organisation, to ward off dangers which threatened to blight its growth and destroy its very existence. In its earliest infancy, two powerful and venomous foes twined themselves round its very cradle; but its strength was according to its day; with a supernatural vigour it rent off the coils of Jewish bigotry and stifled the poisonous breath of Heathen licentiousness; but the peril was mortal, and the struggle was for life or death. Had the Church's fate been subjected to the ordinary laws which regulate the history of earthly commonwealths, it could scarcely have escaped one of the two opposite destinies, either of which must have equally defeated (if we may so speak) the world's salvation. Either it must have been cramped into a Jewish sect, according to the wish of the majority of its earliest members, or (having escaped this immediate extinction) it must have added one more to the innumerable schools of Heathen philosophy, subdividing into a hundred branches, whose votaries would some of them have sunk into Oriental superstitions, others into Pagan voluptuousness. If we need any proof how narrowly the Church escaped this latter peril, we have only to look at the fearful power of Gnosticism in the succeeding century. And, indeed, the more we consider the elements of which every Christian community was originally composed, the more must we wonder how little the flock of the wise and good[1] could have successfully resisted the overwhelming contagion of folly and wickedness. In every city the nucleus of the Church consisted of Jews and Jewish proselytes; on this foundation was superadded a miscellaneous mass of heathen converts, almost exclusively from the lowest classes, baptized, indeed, into the name

spiritual substance." Iren. vi. 2, quoted by Burton. And so Justin Martyr speaks of heretics, who said "that though they lived sinful lives, yet, *if they know God*, the Lord will not impute to them sin." Tryph. 141. And Epiphanius gives the most horrible details of the enormities which they practiced. Again, their addiction to magical arts was notorious. See Burton, p. 179, &c. And their leaders, Basilides and Valentinus, are accused of eating εἰδωλόθυτα (like the Nicolaitans of the Apocalypse) to avoid persecution. Burton, pp. 148 and 453.

[1] Whom St. Paul calls τέλειοι (Phil. iii. 15), *i. e.* mature in the knowledge of Christian truth.

of Jesus, but still with all the habits of a life of idolatry and vice clinging to them. How was it, then, that such a society could escape the two temptations which assailed it just at the time when they were most likely to be fatal? While as yet the Jewish element preponderated, a fanatical party, commanding almost necessarily the sympathies of the Jewish portion of the society, made a zealous and combined effort to reduce Christianity to Judaism, and subordinate the Church to the Synagogue. Over their great opponent, the one Apostle of the Gentiles, they won a temporary triumph, and saw him consigned to prison and to death. How was it that the very hour of their victory was the epoch from which we date their failure? Again,—this stage is passed,—the Church is thrown open to the Gentiles, and crowds flock in, some attracted by wonder at the miracles they see, some by hatred of the government under which they live, and by hopes that they may turn the Church into an organised conspiracy against law and order; and even the best, as yet unsettled in their faith, and ready to exchange their new belief for a newer, "carried about with every wind of doctrine." At such an epoch, a systematic theory is devised, reconciling the profession of Christianity with the practice of immorality; its teachers proclaim that Christ has freed them from the law, and that the man who has attained true spiritual enlightenment is above the obligations of outward morality; and with this seducing philosophy for the Gentile they readily combine the Cabbalistic superstitions of Rabbinical tradition to captivate the Jew. Who could wonder if, when such incendiaries applied their torch to such materials, a flame burst forth which well nigh consumed the fabric. Surely that day of trial was "revealed in fire," and the building which was able to abide the flame was nothing less than the Temple of God.

It is painful to be compelled to acknowledge among the Christians of the Apostolic Age the existence of so many forms of error and sin. It was a pleasing dream which represented the primitive church as a society of angels; and it is not without a struggle that we bring ourselves to open our eyes and behold the reality. But yet it is a higher feeling which bids us thankfully to recognise the truth that "there is no partiality with God;" that he has never supernaturally coerced any generation of mankind into virtue, nor rendered schism and heresy impossible in any age of the Church. So St. Paul tells his converts[2] that there must needs be heresies among them, that the good may be tried and distinguished from the bad; implying that, without the possibility of a choice, there would be no test of faith or holiness. And so Our Lord himself compared His Church to a net cast into the sea, which gathered fish of all kinds, both good and bad; nor was its purity to be attained by the exclusion of evil, till the end

[1] Οὐκ ἔστί προσωπολήπτης ὁ Θεός, Acts x. 34.

[2] 1 Cor. xi. 19.

should come. Therefore, if we sigh, as well we may, for the realisation of an ideal which Scripture paints to us and imagination embodies, but which our eyes seek for and cannot find; if we look vainly and with earnest longings for the appearance of that glorious Church, "without spot or wrinkle or any such thing," the fitting bride of a heavenly spouse;—it may calm our impatience to recollect that no such Church has ever existed upon earth, while yet we do not forget that it has existed and does exist in heaven. In the very lifetime of the Apostles, no less than now, "the earnest expectation of the creature waited for the manifestation of the sons of God;" miracles did not convert; inspiration did not sanctify; then, as now, imperfection and evil clung to the members, and clogged the energies, of the kingdom of God; now, as then, Christians are fellow heirs, and of the same body with the spirits of just men made perfect; now, as then, the communion of saints unites into one family the Church militant with the Church triumphant.

NOTE.

Upon the Origin of the Heresies of the later Apostolic Age.

In the above sketch we have taken a somewhat different view of these heresies from that advocated with great ability by Mr. Stanley. He considers all the heretics opposed by St. Paul in the Epistles to the Colossians and Ephesians, and in those to Timothy and Titus, and even those denounced by St. Peter, St. Jude, and St. John, to have been *Judaizers:* and he speaks of St. Paul's opposition to them as "the second act of the conflict with Judaism."[1] In deference to a writer who has done much to give clearness and vividness to our knowledge of the Apostolic age, we feel bound to justify our dissent from his view by a few additional remarks.

First, we think that even if the Jewish element had been the chief ingredient in the teaching of these heretics, still they ought not to be called *Judaizers*. The characteristic of the original Judaizers was a determination to confine Christendom within the walls of the Synagogue, and to put Christianity on the same footing with Pharisaism or Sadduceeism, as a tolerated Jewish sect. The rapid increase and gradual preponderance of the Gentile portion of the Church, soon rendered the existence of this Judaizing party impossible, except in Palestine. Hence it seems to introduce unnecessary confusion, if we apply the distinctive name of Judaizers to heretics whose opinions were so very different from those advocated by the party originally called by that name.

But farther; we cannot think that the Jewish element had that preponderat-

[1] P. 210.

ing influence in the heresies of the later Apostolic period which Mr. Stanley assigns to it. On the contrary, the accounts of them in the Epistles incline us to believe that the Jewish element was only the accidental, and the Gentile element the essential, constituent of these heresies. Mr. Stanley's reasons for the opposite opinion are mainly as follows :—

(1) That the party claiming ψευδώνυμος γνῶσις [1] is the same party who are called νομοδιδάσκαλοι.[2] But the former are mentioned in quite a different part of the Epistle from the latter, and there is no proof that the same persons are meant in the two passages: and even if they are, the expression νομοδιδάσκαλοι might very well be applied to learned Platonising Jews like Philo, who taught what they considered the true and deep view of the Mosaic Law, by which it was allegorised away into a mystic philosophy. And, in the teaching of such Jews, Judaism was quite subordinated to Hellenism.

(2) Mr. Stanley argues that the anarchical policy of the heretics denounced by St. Peter and St. Jude, is to be attributed to the Jewish national aspiration after earthly empire, and impatience of the Roman yoke. It may be conceded that some Jewish Christians may have joined these agitators from such feelings; but is it not equally probable that, as Arnold supposes, this lawless party consisted mainly of nominal converts from heathenism, who "took part with Christianity for its negative side, not for its positive;" outlawed by their vices or their crimes from the existing order of society, and anxious to revolutionise it, and hoping to find in the Church an instrument for promoting their sinister ends?

(3) Mr. Stanley assumes that "those who say they are Jews and are not," [3] are to be identified with the Nicolaitans or Balaamites, mentioned in the same chapter. But this is not quite clear; and even if they be the same party, there is no proof that they were Judaizing Christians; on the contrary, the practices attributed to them are in direct opposition to Judaism.[4] And we should therefore be inclined to agree with Dr. Burton,[5] that their profession of Judaism was only adopted to shield them from heathen persecution, at a time when it was directed against *Christians*, Judaism being a *religio licita*, which Christianity was not.

(4) Mr. Stanley argues that as Cerinthus is (traditionally) connected with the Ebionites, and as St. John is represented (traditionally) as opposing Cerinthus, therefore St. John wrote against the Ebionites, and consequently against a Judaizing sect of heretics. But we do not think it would be safe to rely upon such inferences, founded upon conditions of a vague and somewhat inconsistent kind. It is true that Cerinthus is sometimes classed with the Ebionites by the early writers against heretics; but this appears only to be because some of their less important doctrinal tenets were the same; [6] for in the most essential points they

[1] 1 Tim. vi. 20. [2] 1 Tim. i. 7. [3] Rev. ii. 9.

[4] Neander (Church History, sect. 4) thinks that the Nicolaitans of the Apocalypse were not properly a *sect*, but only a class of people who were in the practice of seducing Christians to partake in the heathen sacrificial feasts, and, therefore, clearly Anti-Judaistic. But see "Planting and Leading," vol. ii. p. 533.

[5] P. 237, &c.

[6] The chief point of agreement seems to have been, that Cerinthus (as well as the later Gnostics) traced back all divine attributes in Christ to the descent of the Holy Spirit on Him at His baptism.

seem to have been the very antipodes of one another. The Cerinthians are represented as advocates of gross sensuality and unbridled licence, like the Antinomians of Corinth; whereas the Ebionites were a sect of ascetics, who practised the most austere temperance, and resembled the Essenes in the strictness of their morality. Again, we are told by Epiphanius[1] that Cerinthus considered the Law as the work of an evil spirit, like the later Gnostics; whereas the Ebionites were strict Judaizers, the true representatives of the original party so called. Moreover, St. John is universally believed to have written against heresies which manifested themselves at Ephesus; whereas the Ebionites were confined to Palestine. And though Cerinthus adhered to some of the observances of the Law, yet he is recorded[2] to have derived his theology, not from Palestine, but from Alexandria.

Having thus mentioned Mr. Stanley's principal reasons for thinking the heresies in question to be Jewish, we will state the arguments which have led us to think them of Gentile origin.

(1) Their strong resemblance to the Corinthian Antinomianism; shown by Hymenæus and Philetus denying the Resurrection; and by the Sophists of the Epistle to the Ephesians (κενοὶ λόγοι[3]), who justified fornication; and by their name of "followers of Balaam," as explained to arise from their persuading their followers to commit fornication.[4]

(2) Their eating εἰδωλόθυτα,[5] which we cannot easily conceive any Jewish sect doing.

(3) The whole tone in which they are spoken of by St. Peter and St. Jude, whose denunciations are directed against a system of open and avowed profligacy, such as might be supposed with greater ease to spring from Heathen laxity than from Jewish formalism. Surely, had they been a Judaizing sect, some notice of the fact must have been found in these Epistles; whereas it seems implied that they were perverters of St. Paul's doctrines.[6]

(4) The fact that the Epistles of St. John are directed against heretics who claimed a peculiar "knowledge of God," and maintained their right to sin; still reminding us of the Corinthian Antinomians, and with no trace of Judaism.

(5) The close connection between the opinions of all these heretics and those of the later Gnostics; which leads us to infer that Judaism could not be a predominant feature in their heresies, since later Gnosticism was so especially opposed to Judaism. For though the Gnostics borrowed some Jewish notions which they blended with their own system,[7] yet they all agreed in referring the

[1] See Burton, p. 478. It is true that in the representation of the doctrine of Cerinthus given by others, and adopted by Neander in his Church History (sect. 4), Cerinthus only taught that the Law was given by an angelic Demiurge, who unconsciously did the work of God. But even on this view, he taught that the Jews as a nation worshipped this Demiurge by mistake as the supreme "God," and that beyond this inferior standing point the Law could not raise them. Surely this is enough to show how completely the Alexandrian element preponderated over the Jewish in Cerinthus's doctrine.

[2] By Theodoret, whose statement is believed by Neander.

[3] Eph. v. 6. [4] Rev. ii. 14. [5] Rev. ii. 20. [6] 2 Pet. iii. 15.

[7] It is remarkable that the three earliest leaders of the Gnostics, viz. Cerinthus, Basilides, and Valentinus, were all Alexandrians; and the pagan name of the son of

origin of the Mosaic Law either to an evil spirit, or to an inferior and unenlightened Demiurge.

Basilides (Isidorus) seems to show that Basilides could not have even been of Jewish race. It is true that Neander divides the Gnostic sects into two classes, one connected with, and the other opposed to, Judaism. But the *connection* with Judaism of which he speaks in the former, only consisted in their transferring to their own systems some elements derived from Judaism, which, as a whole, they all considered a religion suited only to the unenlightened and "psychical" mass. In all of them the speculative and philosophising element, whether derived from Hellenic or Oriental sources, predominated over the Judaical.

CPSIA information can be obtained
at www.ICGtesting.com
Printed in the USA
LVHW100509130422
716029LV00002B/41

9 783752 591538